Forever in Your Embrace

Also by Kathleen Woodiwiss

Ashes in the Wind
Come Love a Stranger
The Elusive Flame
The Flame and the Flower
A Rose in Winter
Shanna
So Worthy My Love
The Wolf and the Dove
Petals on the River

KATHLEEN E. WOODIWISS

*Forever in
Your Embrace*

AUTHOR'S PREFERRED EDITION

AVON BOOKS ◆ NEW YORK

AVON BOOKS, INC.
1350 Avenue of the Americas
New York, New York 10019

Copyright © 1992, 1999 by Kathleen E. Woodiwiss
Interior design by Kellan Peck
ISBN: 0-380-97831-8

Library of Congress Cataloging in Publication Data:
Woodiwiss, Kathleen E.
Forever in your embrace / Kathleen Woodiwiss.—Author's preferred ed., 1st ed.
p. cm.
1. Russia—History—1613–1689 Fiction. I. Title.
PS3573.0625F66   1999   99-38101
813'.54—dc21   CIP

First Avon Books Hardcover Printing: November 1999

AVON TRADEMARK REG. U.S. PAT. OFF. AND IN OTHER COUNTRIES, MARCA REGISTRADA,
HECHO EN U.S.A.

Printed in the U.S.A.

FIRST EDITION

QPM   10   9   8   7   6   5   4   3   2   1

www.avonromance.com

To my granddaughter,
Amber Erin,
who makes everyone in the family
feel special.

*Forever in
Your Embrace*

1

Russia, somewhere east of Moscow
August 8, 1620

The lowering sun shimmered through the dusty haze looming in languid stillness above the treetops, tinting the tiny grains of sand with vibrant shades of crimson until the very air seemed aflame. An ominous portent, the reddish aura offered no promise of rain or respite for a parched and thirsty land. Excessive heat and a lengthy drought had scorched the plains and barren steppes, wilting endless areas of grass down to densely matted roots. But here in the mixed wooded region of Russia, bordered on the north and east by the Volga River and on the south by the Oka, the thick forests appeared relatively unscathed by the lack of rain. Even so, amid the voluminous clouds of choking dust stirred aloft by the horses' hooves, the occupants of the coach and its escort of soldiers still suffered the same as they traversed the vast wilderness.

In her full score years of life, the Countess Synnovea Zenkovna had seen a wide variety of faces her homeland could present. They were as unique as the changing seasons. The long, brutal winters could be a test of endurance for even the most hearty. In spring, the thawing ice and snow created deceptively treacherous bogs, which in times past had proven formidable enough to dissuade hordes of marauding Tatars and other invading armies. Summer was a temperamental vixen. Warm, lulling breezes and the gentle patter of rain could placate the soul, but when imbued with dry, scorching temperatures such as those that were presently hampering the land, the season served vengeance on anyone foolish enough to travel beneath its broiling sun, a fact which the Countess Synnovea had morosely considered prior to leaving her home.

The conditions were intolerable for a lengthy trek through Russia, especially one that had been embarked upon with equal amounts of urgency and reluctance. If not for His Imperial Highness, Tsar Mikhail Romanov, requesting her presence in Moscow ere the week was out and a full dozen mounted guards sent under the direction of Captain Nikolai Nekrasov to serve as her escort, Synnovea would never have ventured upon such an arduous journey until the heat had adequately abated. Given a choice, she would have remained in Nizhni Novgorod, where she'd have continued mourning the recent death of her father. It was useless, of course, for a mere countess to belabor her lack of options when the Tsar of all the Russias had issued a command. Immediate compliance was the only prudent choice for any loyal subject, but leaving her home had not been the worst of it. His Majesty's announcement that she would become the ward of his cousin upon her arrival in Moscow had dragged her grieving spirit into a darker gloom.

She was, after all, the only offspring of the late Count Aleksandr Zenkov, and now, much to her chagrin, the recipient of royal attention. The tsar hadn't elaborated on his purpose for assigning her a guardian. Yet when one took into account her sire's notable performance as an emissary and the many honors that had been heaped upon him, the favor she was presently receiving was understandable. Still, Synnovea found it difficult to think of herself as a helpless waif in need of protection. She had passed an age when most maidens marry, and now with her parents both dead, she had begun to assume the responsibilities of a mistress of vast holdings. Why in heaven's name did she need a guardian?

Neither a youngling nor a pauper, yet treated like one, Synnovea mused morosely. Against her will, a more viable reason for Tsar Mikhail's dictate came to mind, causing her to cringe inwardly. Her elongated spinsterhood had in all probability influenced his decision, especially if he had become convinced that her father had failed to address that issue satisfactorily before his death. Despite the demands of protocol, Aleksandr Zenkov had refrained from forcing his daughter into marriage, having nurtured a hope that she would someday discover a love the likes of which he had shared with her mother, Eleanora. Though others might have been convinced that he had dragged his heels in procuring a spouse for Synnovea, Aleksandr had nevertheless made provisions for her far beyond the standard for female descendants, securing lands and wealth in her name while gaining guarantees from the tsar that, upon the demise of her sire, none of these assets would be stripped from her.

Much earlier, Aleksandr had confounded tradition by arranging for Synnovea to be tutored by some of the most respected mentors in Russia as well as abroad. Those who had once wagged their heads while lamenting the count's lack of a male heir had been taken aback by his zeal to elevate his daughter to a status equal to any son. Then, after the death of her mother some five years ago, Aleksandr had enlisted Synnovea's assistance in the realm of diplomatic affairs and foreign dignitaries, entrusting her with significant responsibility in those areas, which had ultimately involved her in his extensive travels abroad. Having had an English mother, Synnovea could speak that language as fluently as she could her native Russian, and with a good grasp of French as well, she had been able to pen letters to officials in all three. No son could have done any better.

Yet here she was, being whisked to Moscow like so much chattel belonging to the tsar. And she was loathing every moment of it.

Wearily Synnovea braced an elbow upon the corner armrest and, with a trembling hand, clasped a dampened handkerchief to her brow as she sought to quell another attack of nausea, elicited no doubt by the writhing instrument of torture in which she rode. The wild gyrations of the coach remained unyielding as it swept around curves and jounced over deeply rutted roads. To some degree, the tinkling of harness bells and the jangling of horses' necklets mellowed the din of drumming hooves and a rumbling conveyance, yet Synnovea was convinced that nothing short of the end of the journey would ease the pain throbbing in her temples. Even the late-afternoon sun seemed puckishly bent on punishing her as it cast its blinding rays into the windows, forcing her to squeeze her eyes tightly shut until the coach passed into the cooler, mottled shade of the lofty trees that flanked the road. When she finally dared open them again, a spotted red haze obscured the interior and the other two occupants of the coach.

"Can it be that you're distressed, Countess?" Ivan Voronsky inquired with a sardonic smile.

Synnovea blinked several times in an attempt to focus her gaze upon the man who, through no design of her own, had become her traveling companion and temporary protector of sorts. For all of her schooling and travels, it seemed unthinkable that she was destined to be placed under the tutelage of strangers and, toward that end, was being escorted by an individual who she strongly suspected was a Polish sympathizer and a leftover fanatic of Sigismund's Jesuits. Comments that the self-proclaimed cleric and scholar had made during their enforced proximity had progressively abetted such notions, and although his leanings were nothing that she could positively affirm, Synnovea was nevertheless leery.

"I'm hot, and I'm dirty," she complained with an exasperated sigh. "This unrelenting pace has left me weary beyond belief. At every station along the way we've had to exchange horses because of their exhaustion. When we haven't been allowed a comparable time to rest throughout the whole of these three days, have I not cause to be distressed?"

On the seat beside her, Ali McCabe shifted restlessly, offering mute testimony to her own fatigue. At the moment, the aging maidservant seemed far more fragile than her three-score two years might normally have indicated, but then, Synnovea was sure her own face evidenced a similar tension.

"Princess Anna urged me to hasten back lest her plans be set awry," their dour-faced chaperon haughtily informed Synnovea. "Out of respect for her bidding and the behest of His Imperial Highness, we've no choice but to obey."

Annoyed by the man's Spartan logic, Synnovea whisked slender fingers over a puffed sleeve and promptly wrinkled her fine, straight nose as dust billowed up from the fabric. She had acquired the dark green and black-striped traveling gown in France at the cost of no small sum, and even if she were to find Anna Taraslovna more tolerant of her foreign fashions than Ivan Voronsky had thus far proven himself to be, Synnovea could only conclude that after such a grueling jaunt, the garment's continued usefulness had been seriously hindered.

Lifting her gaze, Synnovea found herself the recipient of another derisive smirk. She could hardly mistake its import, but then, the man's contempt was hardly surprising. Soon after establishing his darkly austere presence in the opposite seat, Ivan Voronsky had relentlessly subjected her and her aging Irish maid to rudely critical inspections. Even now, he seemed to wear piety like some accolade of well-deserved honor, and when he looked down his long, thin nose at them, Synnovea had the distinct impression that he had judged them and found them seriously wanting.

"Perhaps you might enlighten us as to your reasons for insisting upon our manner of travel, sir," she prodded. "Had we journeyed by night as Captain Nekrasov suggested, we might have been able to escape the worst of this heat and perhaps even some of the grime."

Ivan's dark eyes chilled significantly. "The night belongs to the devil, Countess, and the tender soul should be wary of treading where demons are wont to wander."

Synnovea rolled her gaze upward, pleading for heavenly support to enable her to extend some kindly forbearance toward the highly opinionated individual. The fact that they had already suffered through many hellish torments apparently hadn't even entered into the man's consideration. "Since you were the one who insisted upon this pattern of flight, sir, I'm sure you understand the benefits far better than we've been able to."

Her thinly veiled barb evoked a slightly more caustic tone as the cleric offered a more reasonable excuse than he had hitherto been inclined to do. "Before I left Moscow, I heard rumors of a band of renegades roaming this territory. Since it's usually the practice of murderers and thieves to pounce upon their victims in the stealth of darkness, it seemed prudent for us to travel during the daylight hours to escape the possibility of being waylaid."

"A wise decision indeed, *if* we manage to endure this sweltering heat," Synnovea rejoined dryly.

Ivan lifted his chin in pompous arrogance and considered her with frosty aloofness. "If you're uncomfortable, Countess, may I suggest that your extravagant attire is fully at fault. A simple *sarafan* would've better served your needs while modestly adhering to the customs of a Russian maid."

"I suppose you're right." Synnovea sighed, bridling the

urge to argue. The conventional *sarafan*, with its loose lines flaring slightly from shoulder to floor, would have definitely disguised her form better, but the traditional layers worn beneath and over the sometimes costly, heavily ornamented gowns would have literally stifled her. "After sailing abroad so many times, I've become accustomed to the styles of the French and English courts and have ceased to consider that anyone would find them offensive."

"Then you do indeed err, Countess," Ivan Voronsky asserted with vigor. "Indeed, had I not the discipline of a saint, I would have detached myself posthaste from the duties to which the Princess Anna has assigned me and sought other means of travel. Truly, I've never seen a Russian-born maid so partial to wearing such lewd foreign trappings."

The man's unbridled faultfinding chafed Synnovea's patience no less now than when he had first voiced his aversion to her garments shortly after his arrival at her stoop. No doubt, had she matched his own stoic black garb, she'd have fallen into better favor with the man.

"Oh, sirrr . . ." Ali McCabe's voice trembled with barely suppressed ire as she dared to enter the conversation. "I can understand that ye've no ken o' what's acceptable 'cross the seas, seein' as how ye've ne'er ventured beyond these climes. Ta be sure, sir, there's a whole different world o'er there. Why, ye'd be appalled at the license some highborn ladies take ta walk an' talk right out in the open wit' men what be neither monk nor close kin. Take, for instance, Queen Elizabeth, God rest her soul. Nary a soul e'er entertained thoughts o' her bein' locked away in a *terem* or secluded in a castle wit' only women an' a few holy men in attendance. Can ye imagine all o' them fine, high-ranking lords flockin' 'round the late queen, an' nary a Brit thinkin' her depraved?"

"Disgusting behavior!" Ivan rose to the bait with eager outrage. "Indeed, I have to wonder why I'm even here after the many visits your mistress made to that realm. I fear my protection has come too late to be of benefit."

Whatever humor Synnovea had felt over Ali's bantering discourse vanished abruptly at the man's slur. Bristling with indignation, she was considering how best to air her objection when Ali McCabe drew herself up sharply in a highly offended snit.

"As if me own sweet lamb is anythin' less than the innocent she's always been!" The old woman twitched on the seat, growing more irate with each passing moment. Having closely attended her charge from infancy, the maid was greatly incensed by the cleric's insinuations. "Whether it be here or there, sir, I can assure ye that no man has e'er laid a wayward hand ta me mistress."

"That remains to be seen, does it not?" Ivan challenged, a thin eyebrow elevated loftily. "When your mistress wears such close-fitting attire, I can only think that her main purpose is to attract male attention."

"How dare you suggest such a thing, sir!" Synnovea gasped, taking umbrage at his slander.

Ali's rancor deepened. "Seein' as how ye're ridin' in me mistress's coach an' eatin' meals an' stayin' in rooms what she's been payin' for, sir, ye might consider showin' her the proper respect due a lady just ta show how grateful ye ought ta be."

Ivan fixed the tenacious little maid with a disdaining sneer. "You've been ill-tutored in the treatment of saints, old woman, else you'd know that charity is expected, especially from those who can afford it. Apparently you haven't been in this country long enough to understand our customs."

The old woman cocked her head at a curious angle. It was fresh in her mind that Ivan Voronsky had claimed poverty soon after presenting himself to the countess, declaring himself without wealth or possession beyond the clothes on his back and those few he carried within his black valise. Thereafter he had left the full burden of his subsistence upon her mistress, as if he had every right to expect her benevolence. Only the day before, he had voiced the belief that few were worthy of such charity, which had obviously been his way of trying to dissuade the countess from giving a generous purse to a young mother who had been left stranded with an infant at a coach station after the sudden death of her husband. Ivan's efforts to halt her mistress's largesse had seemed onerous enough, but when he had suggested the contribution be given to him instead so he could carry the gift to the mother church, Ali had felt rankling spurs dig deeply into the flanks of her Irish temper. His solicitations had solidified her belief that he was far less concerned with the needs of the poor and the destitute than with his own wealth and circumstance.

"Yer pardon, Yer Eminence." The address was greatly exaggerated as Ali yielded to her unmeasured distrust of the man. " 'Tis a simple fact that I've not laid me poor eyes on a real saint in some years now, though there be some what seek ta convince folks o' their piety. Wolves in sheep's clothin', I'll warrant, but that's neither here nor there, seein' as how ye're so fine and saintly yerself."

The veins in Ivan's temples became darkly distended as his beady eyes pierced the servant. His stare was so menacing that he seemed on the verge of concocting some strange incantation to make the maidservant vanish into thin air. If he meant to frighten Ali, then in that quest he failed miserably. The fact that Ali had come to Russia with Count Zenkov's bride some twenty-odd years ago and, since that time, had been treated with kindly deference, which a lord might bestow upon a favored servant, had instilled within the old woman an unshakable confidence in herself and in those whom she loyally served.

"You dare question my authority?" Ivan demanded sharply. "I am of the church!"

"O' the church?" Ali repeated in an inquisitive tone.

"There be churches far an' wide, sir. Which be the one what sanctioned ye?"

His thin lips twisted in a repugnant sneer. "You wouldn't know the order, old woman. It was founded a great distance from here."

It wasn't the first time that Ivan Voronsky had skirted around his affiliations and ordination, but his evasive answers only heightened Ali's curiosity. "An' the direction, sir? Which way would it be? Up or down?"

For a moment Ivan seemed ready to explode. "Were I to hold out some hope that you'd have knowledge of the province from whence I came, old woman, I might deem an answer worthy of being uttered, but I see no reason to discuss such matters with an old dullard of a servant."

Ali squawked and flapped her thin arms in high-flying indignation as she twitched on the seat. Indeed, she seemed ready to catapult herself with claws bared upon the man.

Synnovea laid a lightly restraining hand upon her servant's arm to forestall such a possibility. Nevertheless, the two combatants glared at each other as if tempted to duel to the death, leaving her bereft of any hope that a truce could be established between them. On the outside chance that their ire could be diminished by some slight degree, Synnovea turned a plaintive appeal to the pinch-faced man. "When our tempers have been sorely tested by the horrible conditions that we've had to endure these past days, 'tis understandable that we are wont to quarrel among ourselves, but I plead with you both to desist of this bickering. 'Twill only extend the ordeal."

Had Ivan been of a gentler, more kindly or manly bent, he might have given pause to Synnovea's plea, for her softly cajoling expression was most engaging. He may have admired the translucent radiance of the large, thickly fringed eyes that slanted slightly upward beneath delicately winged brows. Those mesmerizing orbs were a curious blend of shades: variegated shards of jade flaring outward from pupils and darkening to a warm, clear brown. As a man, he might also have appreciated the fair skin presently glowing with a moist, reddish sheen or even savored her delicate features. Most assuredly, had he been cast from the same mold as others of his gender, he might have been held much in awe by her stunning beauty, but Ivan Voronsky was not like most men. He was more of a mind to think that feminine pulchritude was a finely devised tool of a darker realm, primarily invented for the purpose of diverting extraordinary men like himself from a path toward exalted greatness.

"You err if you think your benefactress won't hear of this, Countess. You've allowed your maid to insult me, and I shall be most specific in telling Princess Anna of your toleration for your hireling's impertinence."

Synnovea made her own conjectures as to Ivan's origins as his hissing whisper filled the confines of the coach. "Tell her what you will, sir," she invited stiltedly, refusing to be intimidated. "And should I be of such a mind, I might also caution His Majesty about those who yet hold out some hope of a Polish pretender or another false Dmitri gracing the throne. I'm sure such a hero as the Patriarch Filaret Nikitich would find your sympathies misplaced, considering his recent release from a Polish prison."

Ivan's small, dark eyes shot sparks as he recognized the havoc she could create in his life. "Misplaced sympathies? Why, Countess, I've never heard of anything so absurd. However did you manage to concoct such a ludicrous notion?"

"Was I mistaken?" Surprised by her own trembling disquiet, Synnovea struggled to convey an aplomb that was, at best, strained. "Forgive me, sir, but with all of your chatter about the possibility of a direct descendant of the late Tsar Ivan Vasilievich being alive, I couldn't help but recall two previous occasions when the Poles tried to place a man upon the throne by claiming he was the late Tsar Ivan's own son come back to life. How many times must a false Dmitri be revived to vie for the tsardom when everyone knows his father killed him in a fit of temper?"

Ivan detested being challenged by a woman, particularly one who had acquired just enough knowledge of history and the events of the world to be dangerous. It was even more galling to be forced to assuage her suspicions. "You do me a grave disservice, Countess. What I spoke of was no more than speculations derived from reports that I had heard some months ago. Believe me, my lady, I hold Tsar Mikhail in the highest esteem. Why, I wouldn't be here if the Princess Anna didn't trust me implicitly." He managed a stiff smile for Synnovea's benefit. "Despite your doubts, Countess, I hope to prove myself a worthy escort, certainly one of higher merit than His Majesty's guards. They are, after all, no more than common men incapable of entertaining any aspirations beyond their own selfish desires."

"And what of you, sir?" Synnovea inquired with a touch of skepticism. In her mind the cleric fell far short of the gentlemanly standards to which the officer who led the entourage adhered. Throughout his career, Captain Nekrasov had been praised for his unswerving valor and gallant manners. Tsar Mikhail couldn't have sent a more dedicated soldier to serve as her protector. "Have you truly vaulted well beyond that moat which poses a hindrance to mortal man and founded your feet upon the lofty elements of sainthood? Forgive me, sir, but I remember as a child being cautioned by a kindly priest not to think of myself as some magisterial gift to mankind, but, with humbleness of mind, to consider my frail form to be temporal and with a fervent zeal to look toward a higher source for the wisdom and perfection which I am obviously lacking."

"What have we here? A learned scholar?" Ivan chortled, failing badly in his attempt at humor. If anything, his tone communicated an underlying hint of malice. He was a man who had set himself to the task of influencing the misguided and had little patience with anyone who overlooked his potential or questioned his importance or ideas. "Imagine such wisdom ascribed to so fair a maid. What is to become of those ancient scribes who, for their enlightenment, have cleaved to the weighty tomes of bygone eras?"

Synnovea sensed the man was chiding her for voicing a logic he considered worthless. Apparently he had his own schemes for the universe, and far be it that any should try to dissuade him from his purpose. Yet she was not above trying. "When a person has a fault deeply rooted within his reasoning, if he continues to nurture that defect, though he may study the works of a thousand philosophers, he shall remain no wiser than before."

Ivan's thin lips twitched with growing irritation as he accepted her reasoning as a personal affront to himself. "And, of course, you know such a man."

Synnovea stiltedly directed her gaze out of the window, knowing full well what he thought. Considering the cleric's irascibility, it seemed advisable for her to retreat into silence and endure his company without further comment on *any* subject. She only wasted her breath trying to reason with the man.

The four-in-hand swept past a thick stand of lofty firs edging the road and, in its wake, left widely spreading boughs swaying vigorously. The sweating, foam-flecked steeds strained to pull the weighty coach up yet another incline, and though the animals were nearly spent from the harsh extremes and the unrelenting pace, the driver's whip gave them no reprieve. It continued to flick out with fiery urgency, forcing them to expend whatever strength they still possessed in a quest to reach the next station before nightfall.

The soldiers valiantly kept pace, yet even those well-seasoned stalwarts, with their faces and tunics darkened by the grime of the road, were beginning to show signs of deep fatigue. No doubt each of them anticipated a respite offered by a night's lodging in the village up ahead. The seemingly endless trek, the miserable conditions, the countless hours spent in the saddle or enduring the spine-jarring jolts of the carriage, had all coalesced into a diabolical torment, one which seemed particularly bent on sapping the last shred of spirit and vitality from each of them. It was disheartening to think that there was still another grueling day of travel left before they would come in sight of Moscow.

The coach lurched heavily as the team raced around another sharp bend, and once again Synnovea braced back into the plush cushions to keep from being launched into the lap of her maid. Heavy fir branches snapped back suddenly against the conveyance, momentarily startling the passengers, but in the very next instant a more terrifying sound intruded. The exploding bark of gunfire muffled the din of loudly crashing branches and thundering hooves, wrenching frightened gasps from the three and bringing them upright in their seats.

"We're being attacked!" Ivan exclaimed in high-pitched panic.

Synnovea went cold with dread as another deafening volley reverberated in diminishing waves through the forest. The barrage ebbed to a more tolerable level. Then a shot cracked from the rear of the coach and was promptly answered by a more distant report that ended abruptly in the footman's shriek of pain. As his scream faded, the driver sawed on the reins, bringing the steeds to a jolting halt. A heartbeat later, the door was snatched open and the occupants found themselves gaping at the unwavering bore of a huge flintlock pistol.

"Out!"

The rumbling command wrenched surprised starts from the three as a giant of a man leaned inward, enhancing the threat of his massive weapon. His slanted gray eyes flicked from one to the other until they came to rest upon Synnovea.

14

Half masked by a long, drooping mustache, the brigand's mouth slowly twisted into a leer.

"Eh, now, what a pretty pigeon we caught for ourselves."

Synnovea could imagine what the presence of this miscreant meant and she was absolutely terrified. It was difficult to determine the origin of the brigand, for his countenance was as fierce as any she had ever seen. His head was bald except for a long thatch of tan hair tied with a thin leather cord near the scalp and left to hang free over one ear. His faded, sky-blue military coat might have once graced a Polish officer of wide girth, but it now hung open to accommodate the broad chest of its present owner. Perhaps for the same purpose, the sleeves had been stripped away, leaving the bulging arms bare. A dingy yellow sash encircled the brigand's thick waist, securing a pair of boldly striped, wide-legged pantaloons, the bottoms of which had been stuffed into the slouched tops of a pair of boots frivolously adorned with silver buckles.

Synnovea lifted her chin in an attempt to subdue its trembling and, with more spirit than she had deemed herself capable of, inquired sharply, "What's the meaning of this outrage? What do you want from us?"

"Treasures," the rogue answered with a deep chortle. Lifting his powerful shoulders briefly, he enlarged upon his reply as he ogled her. "One kind or another. It make no difference."

Ivan craned his neck from his dour little collar as he eyed the weapon that threatened them. Anxious about his prospects for survival, he settled on the premise that if he informed this brash intruder of his close association with people of power, the fellow would be reluctant to do him harm. Perhaps the oaf would even see some advantage in ransoming him unharmed. Surely the Princess Anna would be willing to pay a sizable sum for his safe return. Or perhaps her cousin Tsar Mikhail could be persuaded to offer a minute part of his wealth to guarantee the outlaws' good comportment.

"I urge you, sir, to take heed that you do not set awry the

disposition of the tsar by doing harm to those he favors." Ivan clasped a stubby-fingered hand to his own bony chest, managing to achieve a more dignified mien than he had been able to demonstrate since their forced halt. "I am Ivan Voronsky, and I'm here for the purpose of escorting the Countess Zenkovna to Moscow. . . ." The hulking giant's cocky grin never wavered, and Ivan's apprehensions intensified as he realized he had failed to impress the brute. In rising panic, he screeched the last words out in a frantic rush. *"By order of the tsar!"*

The thief began to guffaw in deepening mirth, utterly destroying the cleric's expectations. When the miscreant finally sobered enough to speak, he poked a long finger into the darkly garbed chest of the other, making that one wince sharply. "What you mean, you come as escort? You too skinny to fight Petrov. You make a jest, eh? You grow some, then maybe you fight."

Ivan's pinched features quivered with ill-suppressed emotions. A confused blend of fear, fury, and humiliation rendered him momentarily incapable of speech and action. Yet when the pistol beckoned him out, he hastily complied amid the sporadic chuckles of the oaf, who stepped back several paces to allow him room to alight. Upon stumbling to the ground, the cleric froze in sudden awe. Everywhere his gaze flitted he could see mounted men, dressed in all manner of array, surrounding the coach and its escort of soldiers. Each bore an assortment of weapons clutched in hand, tucked in sashes, or crisscrossed over their chests. They looked to be a murderous lot, and he could only wonder how he'd fare as their captive.

At the rear of the conveyance, the footman clasped a bloodstained handkerchief over his ear as he, too, cautiously eyed the villains. His still-smoking musket lay in the dust some distance behind the rear wheel where it had fallen after his wounding. Another armed bandit sat on the scrawny back of a mottled gray steed, from whence he covetously eyed the servant's red livery over the sights of a cocked pistol. A similar threat was carried home to Captain Nekrasov and his men by a vast number of highwaymen. It was widely presumed by the hostages that any attempt to resist would be tantamount to inviting complete annihilation.

In freshening apprehension, Ivan Voronsky began to quake as Petrov sauntered near, for it seemed the towering hulk would commit mayhem upon his person, but in passing him, the brigand only smirked in amusement and leaned into the coach. Seizing the black valise the cleric had guarded so zealously during the journey, Petrov turned with a chortle and emptied the contents into the dust at his feet.

Ivan came alive with a cry of alarm and bolted forward, sweeping his arms about in anxious haste as he sought to catch his belongings before his money pouch could be discovered. He was promptly brushed aside by Petrov, whose well-practiced ear had detected an all-too-familiar clink of coins. Plucking the purse from the tangled mound of clothes, the thief tossed it into the air and guffawed in glee over its significant weight.

"Give me that!" Ivan demanded, jostling the larger man in his quest to seize the small pouch. "It belongs to the church!" His voice rose to a piercing shriek. "I was only carrying tithes to the Moscow church! You mustn't steal from the church!"

"Aha! The crow now flap his wings like big hawk, eh!" Petrov glanced toward the two women, who were watching from the doorway, and grinned at Synnovea. "Little man protect his gold more than you, pretty lady."

Petrov hunkered down on his haunches in search of more wealth, shredding the dark vestments that lay in the dust to glean whatever they might hold. His hunt proved futile, and with a roar of rage he soared to his feet, extracting a frightened yelp from Ivan as he seized him. "You tell Petrov where you hide more gold, little bird. Maybe then he won't squash you."

Though the sight of Ivan's hoarded wealth had repulsed Synnovea, it went against her grain to sit calmly by and allow him to be abused without offering some defense, as frail as it promised to be. "Let him go," she enjoined from the coach. "The satchel is all that belongs to him. Everything else you see is mine. Now let him go, I beg you!"

Petrov complied, and Ivan sagged to his knees in enormous relief as the huge man stalked back to the coach. Lending the countess his full attention, he grinned broadly while he stretched forth a hand to her. Reluctantly Synnovea settled trembling fingers within the enormous paw and alighted as courageously as her shaking limbs would allow. When she came into view of the outlaws, wild hoots and exaggerated cries of admiration rose to a deafening intensity as the thieves expressed their delight with her uncommon beauty. The thunderous din heightened Synnovea's trepidation, and she glanced around in deepening dismay as a dozen or more stalwarts rushed forward, shouldering each other roughly aside in their quest to be among the first to reach her, already anticipating the succulent sweetmeat they would soon devour. Everywhere her frantic gaze darted she saw a deepening wall of the lecherous leers and assaulting perusals. Their lusting eyes left no curve untouched, no piece of garment intact. Eagerly they pressed in close around her, suffocating her with their hot, panting breaths and rudely pawing hands.

Synnovea clamped her jaw tightly in an effort to subdue her rising panic. Though a virgin still, she could imagine the degradation that would be forthcoming, and her mind raced in a frenzied search for escape or at least some reasonable argument that would convince the thieves to leave her and her companions unscathed.

Ali McCabe was no idealistic fool to hold out any hope that these lawless brutes would honor the gallant creed of highborn gentlemen, and certainly not when they held such a winsome captive within their grasp. The servant scrambled down from the coach and snatched up a stout stick from the ground as she hastened forward. Thrusting herself between her charge and those who sought to test the pliant curves, she raised her weapon threateningly. Though it might well mean her own death, she was totally dedicated to the defense of her mistress. "I'll warn the lot o' ye vile vermin!" she railed in frail, strident tones. "The next beastie ta lay a filthy hand on the Countess Synnovea will deal wit' me. An' I swear ta do ye ill aforc I die!"

Uproarious laughter came from the slavering beasts. They readily dismissed her threats as feeble and stretched forth grubby hands to capture the prize, but Ali proved as cantankerous as an old Tatar warrior. Setting her bony jaw with unquenchable tenacity, she swung the cudgel with swift and wicked intent, cracking a fair share of knuckles and noggins. Teeth were bared in irate snarls as tempers flared beneath the vicious swat of her club. Intent now upon showing her just how easily they could trample hcr underfoot, the rabble began to close in around the old woman.

Captain Nekrasov surmised that he had been virtually forgotten as he observed the events from beyond the confines of the fray. Rising to the occasion, he leaned forward in his saddle and clobbered a nearby raider with a driving fist. Even as the thief tumbled to the ground, the deafening roar of an exploding pistol cracked through the air, heralding a shot that tore with splintering pain through the captain's arm and wrenched a cry of anguish from grimacing lips. He clapped a hand to his reddening sleeve and then, in sudden wariness, glanced around, detecting the metallic clicking of several weapons close around him. At least a half-dozen flintlocks were now aimed at him, and by the fixed snarls on the faces of the brigands who held them, they were more than willing to dispense with him.

A dastardly scamp squinted up at him. "Ye'll die, Kapitan! Ye move one eyeball, an' 'twill be yer death." He snapped grimy fingers to demonstrate just how quickly they could deal with him. "Just like that!"

The captain lifted his gaze as several bandits began shuffling back to open a path for another giant, this one flaxen-haired, clean-shaven, and riding on a horse. The thieves' dispatch in giving ground to this newcomer clearly attested to their obeisance. Scars marked the newcomer's face, giving rise to the supposition that he had fought many battles in the past. His very presence proved his success, perhaps to the extent that he had dispatched many to their death.

The man leisurely reined his black stallion to a place where he could easily assess the proceedings and settled a confident grin upon Nikolai as he shoved a still-smoking flint-lock into his sash. "Your efforts to defend the ladies against such odds gives me cause to wonder if you're daft, Captain. I'd advise you to be more careful of your life in the future. Next time I shall have to kill you."

The thieves eyed their commander in a cautious gauging of his mood, but they found nothing unduly disquieting in the contemplative smile he swept over them. Accepting his silence as mute consent, they chortled once again in boisterous merriment and eagerly returned their attention to the countess, roughly buffeting the Irish maid about as she sought to safeguard her mistress.

Outraged gasps were wrenched from Synnovea as she twisted this way and that in a desperate attempt to escape the hands that reached out to seize her. The bandits' eyes gleamed in avid lust, instilling within her an undermining horror of what she would soon suffer. Though she strained away from this one and that, the rending of cloth affirmed their eagerness to unmask whatever delights remained hidden from view. Her hat was knocked askew, and a sleeve was ripped from her shoulder. The stiffly pleated ruff adorning her throat was no more safe from their greedy divestment than the heavy silk ruching that trimmed the stomacher of her gown. A scream was finally torn from Synnovea as they pulled open her bodice in ravenous greed, revealing the creamy fullness swelling above a lacy chemise. One glimpse of her womanly curves seemed to incite them more, and in frenetic haste they reached out to rip away whatever else they could grasp.

"Rutting louts!" the pale-haired chieftain bellowed without warning, startling the lechers who immediately stumbled back from their prey. Passions cooled in rapid degrees beneath the icy gaze that swept them. "Would you maul the wench to death before we leave this place?" he barked. "Is that how you would treat a rare prize? Hell and damnation! Can you not see that she's worth a pretty coin to us alive? Now loose her and stand aside, the lot of you! Henceforth, I shall claim the wench for my own, for 'tis evident you rogues are unappreciative of what has fallen into your hands!"

Daring any to defy him, the lord-of-thieves urged his steed forward. The brigands stumbled back, readily yielding ground before him until the two women stood alone. Synnovea and Ali were hardly exempt from the awe that had been elicited. The suspicion that this ruffian was to be feared more than his followers filled their hearts with burgeoning trepidation.

The lawless chieftain braced a muscular arm across the elaborate horn of his saddle and subjected Synnovea to a careful scrutiny that ranged slowly downward over the entire length of her. Though she clasped the torn bodice over her bosom, she held herself proudly aloof, seeming far more regal and refined than any woman he had ever known. Her uncommon beauty was equally unmatched.

"Forgive my delay in coming to your rescue, Countess." His smile conveyed a leisured confidence. "My men are wont to seek diversions wherever they find them and demand recompense when heretofore they've found naught but injustice."

"Injustice, do ye say!" Ali squawked, taking exception to

his statement. "As if we weren't within our proper rights ta defend ourselves against yer murdering riffraff!"

The rogue commander chose to ignore the maid. "What you see around you, my lady, are men whose every possession was stolen by those boyars who wield their power as if directed by demons and who saw fit to reduce them to serfs. Had we been of such a mind, Countess, we might've added to your misery by killing your escort. Your footman and the captain were foolish to challenge us. Be grateful they're still alive and my aim true, for I might have taken exception to their faulty attempts." He swept a hand about to indicate the soldiers, who were being ordered to dismount. "Anyone who intends to do us ill is in peril of his life."

Synnovea realized her chin had sagged as she endured a moment of monumental dread of this man. Though he had spoken with a well-tutored tongue, she was nevertheless riveted by the disquieting realization that here indeed was a fierce barbarian the likes of whom might have ridden with Genghis Khan and his army of Mongols, except that his sky-blue eyes and flaxen hair were products of a different breed. His square jaw was devoid of whiskers, and his hair was clipped so short that it looked more like a scruffy, close-fitting skullcap. Despite the countless tiny scars that crisscrossed his face, he was still handsome in a rugged way. That fact did little to ease her qualms, for she found his demeanor absolutely terrifying.

Synnovea managed to reclaim some fragment of her composure. "And what exactly do you and your companions intend?"

"To share a portion of your wealth. . . ." He smiled down at her with unrestrained confidence as his eyes caressed her again. "And perhaps for a time the richness of your company." He threw back his head and laughed uproariously, raising the hairs on the backs of his captives' necks. When he sobered, he clapped a brawny arm across his wide chest in a crisp salute. "Permit me to introduce myself, Countess. I am Ladis-laus, misbegotten son of a Polish prince and a Cossack wench, and these worthy hearties"—he swept a hand in a wide arc to encompass his roughly garbed compatriots—"are my royal courtiers. They serve me well, do they not?"

The ruffians guffawed at their leader's wit, but Ali snorted in derision. "A bastard barbarian, and a thief ta boot!"

Ladislaus was amused by the audacity of the gnat-sized woman and nudged his stallion forward, deliberately separat-ing maid from mistress. "Aye, old woman! That I am," he acknowledged, peering down at her. "My father sought to pay his due by hiring tutors to teach me a gentleman's manners and language, but he felt no inclination to gift me with the use of his name or his title. Thus, I am what I am."

Ali's eyes fairly snapped as she swung her makeshift weapon toward the stallion, but in swift reaction Ladislaus kicked the piece from her hands, spinning the elder about. Struggling to keep her balance, Ali staggered back several steps, but she was fully alert a moment later and unwilling to relent when the man threw a leg over the horn of the saddle and slid to the ground. She skittered toward him and launched a fresh assault with her cudgel. His arm swept out almost gently to knock the club away, but Ali caught the muscular limb and clung to it with as much pertinacity as an outraged bee who had just been swished by the tail of a horse. Before he could shake her off, she sank her teeth into his bronzed skin. A low growl issued forth from the thick throat as Ladis-laus jerked free. In the next instant, his fist shot forward, striking the small, wrinkled chin. It was no contest. Ali's eyes rolled upward, and she slowly slithered to the ground in a senseless void.

"Yooouuu monster!" Synnovea railed, incensed by his heavy-handed treatment of her maid. Flying at him with fin-gers curled into claws, she raked her nails across his face, drawing blood, but with a backward swipe of his arm Ladislaus

sent her stumbling away. She fared better than Ali and, though shaken, managed to retain her senses. Her fury remained undiminished, and she berated him in scathing tones. "You cowardly oaf, is this the best your brawn can display? Have you no courage to face one of your own size? Or does the dainty form serve your inflated valor better?"

Ivan Voronsky carefully kept his distance through this fray, justifying his lack of assistance by blandly dismissing the countess's predicament as something she rightfully deserved. If she had garbed herself appropriately and given credence to his warnings, she might have escaped the rogue's attention. He wasn't about to draw notice to himself and court certain disaster because of her foolishness.

Synnovea tried to scurry past the thieving lordling in an effort to reach her maid, but she promptly found her way blocked. Her head snapped up in rising ire, and with lips curling in sneering distaste, she raked her gaze down his long form. Above hide breeches, a leather jerkin hung open to reveal a broad, muscular chest. His arms were bare and bulging with rippling sinews, evidencing a strength that could easily immobilize her. In all, he was a fine specimen of mighty brawn, but at the moment, she saw the epitome of a cruel beast.

Ladislaus stared into the most enraged green-brown eyes he had ever chanced to view. The flaring orbs fairly seared him in her hot displeasure. "You needn't fret, Countess," he consoled almost pleasantly. "Your servant will live through this with nothing more to boast about than a small bruise and an aching head."

"Should I, then, be grateful for your gentle care of us, milord Ladislaus?" Synnovea sneered, offended by the fact that she and all who were with her were completely vulnerable to the frivolous whims of these black-hearted plunderers. "You halted my coach on this lonely road and gave your foul consent to your murderous band of cutthroats to do whatever mischief they might construe. You abused the captain of my guard and, by your twisted reasoning, cast him as the villain! You wounded my footman and now my maid. Would you, *beastly tyrant,* have me fall to my knees before you in humble apology for daring to travel where your bloodthirsty vipers lurk? *Ha!*" With a toss of her head, Synnovea demonstrated her belief that such an idea was preposterous. "Were I armed, knave, you'd be breathing your last this very moment! That's as much as I sympathize with your claims of ill-treatment from the hands of boyars! Whoever your father is, I've no doubt he fervently regrets the creature he spawned during a passing night's whimsy."

Ladislaus braced his massive fists against his hips and grinned in hearty amusement at her insults and logic. "I'm sure the old rascal has had much cause to repent that deed, for I give him no more homage than he has given me. 'Twas only his pride at finally siring a son after a brood of daughters that led him to have me tutored at all. He even tried to take me into his home after his wife died, but my pious little sisters couldn't abide the idea of having a nameless whelp under the same roof. They chided him continually for bringing shame upon the family until he was forced to send me away. Aye, he saw me tutored with the best of them, but he gave me nothing else, not even a father's affection."

"I'm sure you've taken great delight in withholding your regard in return and bringing him a like amount of humiliation by becoming a thieving scoundrel," Synnovea rejoined bitingly. " 'Twould even seem you've extended your revenge by entrapping others in your devious exploits."

"Your imagination is most vivid, Countess. I'm sure you'll prove entertaining through the long winter nights ahead. But to say that I revel in retribution when I seize treasures as rare as you lends far too much credit to my vindictiveness. I assure you, my lady, I'm not a man to spite myself to gain recompense from an aging cur."

Synnovea clenched her fists in the folds of her skirts, refusing to yield this brigand any show of hysteria. "I believe you're nothing but a coward," she sneered. "Even with nigh forty men under your command, you made your appearance well after the danger had passed, like some sly weasel fearful of coming out of his hole. Now you make brave noises while your men hold us at gunpoint."

Ladislaus shrugged, unaffected by her criticism. "I keep my wits while others lose theirs. I watch until all things are made secure."

"You're nothing but a nameless cur who lurks in obscurity while your pack of wolves strip away the wealth of honest men!"

"Think what you will, my lady," he invited, sauntering leisurely around her. "Your opinions are of little concern to me. They'll change nothing."

The lady was indeed one of exceptional beauty, he concluded. Readily visible were the regal looks of the highborn in her delicate features and lofty bearing. The green-lined brim of her hat was pinned to the crown on one side by an emerald-studded clasp and was reminiscent of those worn by foreign cavaliers. Upon her departure from the coach, it had lent her a jaunty appearance, but it now sat ridiculously askew atop her head. Her silky black tresses, once woven into a sedate chignon beneath the hat, had been disturbed by her recent mauling. Feathery wisps now flared outward from her temples, as if set on ends by her rage.

"Fate has surely been kind to me this eventide, bringing such a beautiful *boyarina* within my keeping," he mused aloud. Reaching out a hand, he lightly rubbed his knuckles against a hotly flushed cheek. "I'm indeed honored by your presence, Countess."

Synnovea flung off his hand and glared at him with all the defiance she could muster. "I'm sure you'll understand if

I fail to appreciate your sentiments, Rogue, for I *most desperately* abhor being your captive."

"In time you'll come to appreciate me, my lady. Most women do."

"The stars will fall from the heavens before the event of such an occurrence!"

Ladislaus grinned back at her. Her fiery spirit had whisked away any lingering impression that she was a cold and haughty wench. *Not even remotely so,* he reflected in growing admiration. "My predictions will come true, Countess. They always do."

"You boast absurdities," Synnovea jeered in disdain. "I'll *never* cease to abhor you and your kind! I can only pray that some miracle may spare me and my escort from the evil you and your foul followers plan."

"Nothing short of a miracle will save you from what I intend, my lady," he promised, his voice imbued with a huskiness that evidenced his deepening interest. "As for me, I'm sure I'll enjoy this night with you as I have no other."

Synnovea served quick death to the notion that her ravishment would be some tender interlude that he might leisurely savor. "Let me assure you that I'll fight you with everything I'm capable of delivering."

Ladislaus recognized the loathing distaste flaring in her eyes and lifted his shoulders in bland dismissal of her threat. "Be assured, Countess, your reluctance will be a welcome diversion from the women who squabble over me."

Reaching up, he swept the hat from her head and plucked the brooch from its brim. He held up the bejeweled piece in a dimming shaft of light and then, turning aside to search out Petrov, tossed it to him. "A reward for you, my friend, for spying out the lady's coach."

The hulking brigand caught the gift between the palms of his hands and roared in glee as he considered it. "What say you, Ladislaus? This bauble be worthy of your attention."

The lord-of-thieves caught Synnovea snugly against his side and held her in a steely vise. "Aye, Petrov, but the countess is a far more enticing piece, definitely a wench to warm me through the long winter to come."

Petrov's brow jutted sharply upward. "What you think Alyona will do when she learn you replace her with another captive?"

Ladislaus shrugged, unconcerned. "She'll have to learn to share me."

Petrov hooted in disbelief. "You take countess to bed, and Alyona will divide you into enough pieces to share with at least a dozen different women."

Ignoring the other's warning, Ladislaus sought to extract a sampling kiss from Synnovea, but in shivering aversion she turned her face away. "Let me go, you swine!"

"Not until I've pleasured myself with you," he breathed, momentarily contenting himself with nuzzling her ear. "And maybe . . . just maybe . . . not even then."

He swept an arm downward to encompass her voluminous skirts and, lifting her with an easy strength, dropped her over his shoulder, nearly jolting the breath from her. He glanced around in some wonder, detecting a sudden scuffling around Captain Nekrasov, who had kicked his mount forward in an attempt to rush to the defense of the maiden, but the officer's steed was swiftly caught and firmly held by several ruffians who proceeded to drag the struggling man from the saddle.

"Come, now, Captain, you cannot expect to keep the countess for yourself. You're only a servant of the tsar," Ladislaus chided, jostling Synnovea as he repositioned her on his shoulder. At her frantic struggles, he whacked her across the buttocks with a broad hand, eliciting an enraged shriek.

"Let me go, you braying ass!" Reaching around, she clawed at his neck, only to have her hand swatted away like a pesky gnat. His stinging blow nettled her, and she railed in a temper. *"You . . . You filthy, baseborn beast!"*

Unconcerned with her epithets, Ladislaus returned to his stallion and, from there, barked a series of orders. When his men gaped back at him, he snapped, "Why do you gawk at me like dumbstruck fools? Must I repeat myself? Take whatever you can lay a hand to. Then ride back to camp and await me there. The men I sent to Moscow will be returning soon with our new compatriots, who'll be famished for want of food after being shackled on the city streets. They'll want to feast and rejoice in their newfound freedom, so make them welcome. I'll return to the camp after I've sported with this wench a while, but don't expect me too soon. If she proves worthy, the tsar may have to find himself another doxy."

A surge of hope blossomed within Synnovea's breast as she was lowered to the back of the black stallion. The reins had been left dangling across the steed's neck, and a short, many-tongued lash hung from the saddle horn, very near at hand. Without pause, she seized the bridle in one hand, the whip in the other, and swept the latter across her captor's face and arms, slashing at him again and again until she drew a curse from Ladislaus who reached up to snatch the lash from her grasp. Eluding his long fingers, she leaned back, bracing a slippered foot against the brigand's hardened chest, and shoved with all of her might.

Ladislaus stumbled backward in keen surprise at the forcefulness of the lady's thrusting kick. He was a man well-seasoned in contests of brawn, but he had marked this winsome maid too delicate to make such a determined onslaught. Even so, she was no serious match for a man.

Another backward swipe of Ladislaus's hand knocked the whip aside, leaving the slender arm bruised and momentarily useless as it dropped limply into Synnovea's lap. Clenching her jaw against the pain that throbbed through it, she jerked the reins with her other hand. Alas, the long fingers were there in an instant, snatching the lines from her. A frustrated cry threaded through her gnashing teeth as she kicked at him again and again, knowing all the while she didn't have the stamina to oppose him beyond the length of a few moments, yet in spite of the odds against her, she was desperately, stubbornly committed to the struggle.

In the next breadth of a heartbeat, Synnovea became aware of just how frail her efforts were against such a man. Ladislaus thrust a broad hand beneath her skirts and squeezed her knee, drawing a shocked gasp from her. When she shoved at his chest, his grip tightened until she could feel his fingers digging cruelly into her flesh. The pressure swiftly intensified to an excruciating degree brutally intended to force her to yield, and yield she finally did.

Having won the skirmish, if not the war of wills, Ladislaus loosened his grip and stroked his hand admiringly over her naked thigh. Synnovea's shocked reaction was hardly subdued. Her eyes flashed with fiery indignation, and with a low, rising shriek of rage, she hauled back an arm and delivered a blow to his cheek with enough force to make his ears ring. It certainly left her arm stinging.

"Take your filthy hands off me, you vulgar viper!" she snarled. "The tsar will have your head for this!"

Ladislaus glared up at her as he withdrew his hand from her skirts and wiped the backs of his knuckles across a reddened cheek. "Before that day arrives, Countess," he rumbled, "your precious tsar will have to find more capable men to catch me. And though rumors are in the wind that he has hired foreign cavaliers to instruct his Russian soldiers in the art of war, they shan't defeat me. There is none in his army whom I haven't already bested. Look you yonder if you doubt my words." Sweeping his arm about, he indicated her escort of soldiers, who were being crowded together at gunpoint. Bestowing his attention upon her once more, Ladislaus clasped her wrists, holding her fast as his eyes bore into hers. "If you're foolish enough to hope that some brave champion will save you, Countess, then consider now your wayward reasoning." He thrust out his chin to indicate Captain Nekrasov, who had been trussed up tightly. He then swept a hand toward Ivan Voronsky, whose outrage had reached its zenith now that he was being forced to shed his clothes. "You see? No one will come to your rescue. It is useless for you to struggle."

Synnovea curled her fingers, trying to claw the brigand's face again, but she could do little more than vow through gnashing teeth, "You'll pay for this offense, Ladislaus. You'll be caught, tried, and hanged. And I'll be there to see it! I promise you that!"

He laughed at her pitiful threats. "On the contrary, Countess, you'll be the one taken and used. You'll be my prisoner as long as I choose to keep you . . . ."

His words were suddenly lost in a deafening roar of exploding pistols as a sudden din filled the forest glade. Ladislaus jerked around with a surprise start just as three of his men crumpled to the ground. Momentarily aghast, he watched a fourth fall forward in the saddle and slowly tumble to the ground, where he lay in grotesque oblivion with eyes staring sightless toward an ever-darkening sky.

In the next instant the narrow pass echoed with another loud volley that fused with the thunder of clattering hooves as a large detachment of mounted soldiers raced into view. Leading the charge was a dust-covered, helmeted officer who brandished a sword high above his head while his stallion surged far ahead of his troop, deep into the midst of the startled highwaymen. In roweling fear the miscreants scattered, stumbling over each other in their haste to flee from this avenging demon.

It was a full moment before the realization dawned on them that this particular officer dared far more than those who followed him. At Petrov's rallying shout, the thieves turned and, with savage eagerness, swarmed around the foolish mortal, intending to drag him from his saddle and deal him a death blow. Alas, they were fools to think that they could kill him so easily. Like a ruthless warrior, the man filled the air with screams of dying men as he swept his blade about in a vicious, venging quest. One after another fell beneath the deadly stroke of his sword until fear again pierced the hearts of the bandits, prompting many to flee.

If Ladislaus had recently boasted that none could defeat him, then it soon became evident that this officer would be equally difficult to overcome. He seemed impervious to the paltry attempts of his attackers as he struck left and right. It was not until a huge, barrel-chested Goliath, standing at the outer limits of the fray, took up a lance and threw it toward the valiant intruder that the hearts of his foes were encouraged. The spear caught the cavalier's helmet and sent it flying, leaving the man reeling unsteadily in the saddle. Hearty cheers arose from his enemies. Much heartened, they began to scramble toward him again.

The rush of elation that Synnovea had briefly experienced when she first espied the officer was rapidly transformed into a deepening anxiety as she saw her would-be deliverer brace an arm across his stallion's withers and shake his head in what seemed a feeble effort to clear his muddled senses. His life hung in precarious balance as the rabble surged back toward him, and though Synnovea prayed fervently that he would recover his wits before they hacked him asunder, that dire fate seemed imminent.

Their zeal renewed, the thieves scrambled forward to finish their prey, confident now that he would soon feel the full thrust of their revenge. Perhaps none anticipated that event more than Ladislaus, who watched from the outer limits of the conflict where he held Synnovea captive. A full dozen of his men gave vent to deafening bellows of triumph, already celebrating their victory as they launched their attack, but just as before, their expectations were soon daunted. Though stunned, the officer reacted with well-versed skill, fully aware of the danger he was in. Spinning his horse about in a tight circle to keep his foes at bay, he swung the heavy sword outward in a broad sweep, nearly beheading those who dared the most. When he finally fought clear of his daze, the reddened blade flashed again with more clever aim, flailing its victims and leaving them moaning or reeling lifeless to the ground.

Synnovea saw the officer's searching gaze reach beyond the melee surrounding him and ferret her out. In that moment he seemed much more than a man to her, though his hair was matted close to his head with sweat and his dirt-smudged face was hardly more than an indistinct blur in the rapidly deepening twilight. His breast of armor was tarnished, dented, and now liberally smeared with blood. Still, if she had ever formed a vision of a knight in resplendent trappings, he was all of that and more to her in that brief moment of time.

Seeing his enemy capable of giving chase, Ladislaus shouted a command for his cohorts to depart and swung up behind his captive, slamming his hard body against her back. He cared not a speck for the bruises she suffered. He was far more concerned with making good his own escape. Jerking the reins, he wheeled the steed about and kicked the gleaming flanks, sending the animal racing away in full retreat.

Synnovea soon found some comfort in the fact that the arm that was clasped about her was strong and fully capable of holding her secure. Otherwise she might have found herself dashed upon the ground, for the stallion fairly flew along the trail. He was of mixed Frisian breeding: strong, long of limb, and swift of pace. He could easily outdistance the short-legged breeds common to Russia. Yet when Ladislaus yanked the animal about to survey the path behind him, Synnovea saw to her relief that the officer had given chase and was actually gaining on them. The warrior-thief was equally surprised, for his breath caught in a sharp gasp of astonishment.

Reining his mount abruptly about again, Ladislaus cursed savagely and kicked the animal into a frightening race through the trees. The solid trunks were merely swiftly passing shadows in the darkening copse, and though Synnovea held her breath in paralyzed apprehension of that moment when disaster would halt them with a crushing collision, in a corner of her mind she found herself amazed by the agility of the steed. Without a doubt, the stallion was swift and nimble-footed, the man who rode him of equal merit. Still, the pair who gave chase followed like baying hounds led eagerly onward by the scent of their prey.

Synnovea winced as the lower branches snatched at them with ferocious greed, cruelly tearing at her bound tresses and opening long rents in her sleeves. She lifted a hand to shield her face from the spiny claws that slashed at her, but reddened weals were raised repeatedly across her arms. She prayed desperately that the punishing ride would soon come to a swift and safe conclusion, yet when she glimpsed an opening up ahead, her fear intensified into a sudden concern that they would actually escape. In rising panic she glanced over her shoulder, but her captor's bulk prevented any glimpse of the trail behind them. Nor could she hear anything beyond the fury of their own passing. The stallion's thudding hooves, the whipping branches, and the harsh breathing of the man who held her seemed to coalesce into a numbing roar in her ears.

Finally they broke into the clearing, and Ladislaus once again turned his mount to apprise himself of the whereabouts of the officer. Heretofore no steed had equaled the speed of his own beast. After the wild plunge through the trackless forest, Ladislaus fully expected to find himself far ahead of the other. It was indeed a shock to see just how little distance actually remained between himself and the one who gave chase.

It was no more than the pause of a breath before the ominous shape of the dark chestnut stallion and its rider charged out of the trees nearly on top of them. Synnovea smothered a startled scream, certain the forceful advance would kill them all. She glimpsed piercing steel-blue eyes beneath sharply scowling brows and, with a sickening dread, awaited the collision, feeling much akin to a helpless sparrow about to be broken by the swift assault of this fierce, hunting hawk.

Ladislaus jerked his arm free and fumbled for his knife, but in the next instant the one who pursued launched himself from his steed. He slammed into Ladislaus and, by some strange miracle, left Synnovea still mounted as he swept the thief out of the saddle. She heard an audible thud as the two men hit the ground. She glanced down over the horse's flank and caught the flash of Ladislaus's dagger as it was lifted high. Another hand shot upward to clasp the sturdy wrist and gradually forced the blade backward, away from its mark. A second later, the rustling of dry leaves and the thud of hard-clenched fists meeting solid flesh attested to the fierce struggle of the two men.

While they grappled beneath him, the now-skittish stallion pranced nervously and stirred up small clouds of dust. Faced with the imminent threat of the animal panicking and racing away with her, Synnovea tried to subdue not only her own deepening dread but the steed as well. Slowly she stroked the black's neck and spoke to him in soft, cajoling tones, all the while cautiously searching for the dangling reins.

Of a sudden, Ladislaus's head was launched backward from the force of a well-delivered blow. It thumped into the underbelly of the steed, and in the next instant Synnovea found herself fighting to keep her seat as the horse, shrieking in fright, reared on his hind legs and pawed at the air with his forelegs. Twisting her hands in the flying mane, she clung to it in desperation, fully aware of the danger of being swept off the black's back as the two men fought beneath her with a knife.

The front hooves of the crazed horse struck earth briefly, hardly enough time for Synnovea to resettle herself before he took a bounding leap forward. Her heart matched the long, vaulting stride as she was nearly catapulted from the saddle. It was a terrifying, zigzagging flight through the same trees they had passed moments earlier. Though her pulse kept pace with startling jolts and frantic skips, Synnovea tried not to yield to the foolishness of panic. She knew she had to gain control of the stallion before she found herself the victim of her own unbridled hysteria, but it was nigh impossible to barricade herself against the cold, prickling fear that assailed her.

Leaning forward over the animal's neck, Synnovea flowed with his movements in a concerted effort to allay his fright. She spoke in a forcefully subdued voice as she tried again to capture a flying rein, but the threat of falling inhibited her reach. Again and again she was forced to retreat to the security of the flying mane. Then, as she stretched out a hand once more in the same fearful quest, a low branch flipped the rein upward, projecting it within easy reach. Anxiously Synnovea swooped her hand around to catch it and, in sobbing relief, clutched the leather strap in her trembling grasp. Good fortune was with her, for hardly a moment later, she managed to capture the second rein in a similar fashion.

Success rallied Synnovea's spirits. Grasping the lines securely, she claimed a small measure of control over the beast, at least enough to turn him onto the path that would lead them back to where the carriage had been halted. Even so, the stallion was reluctant to slow his stride, and though she could see the dark shadow of the conveyance through the ever-deepening gloom, Synnovea could not establish enough restraint on the headstrong animal to lend her assurance that she'd be able to halt him once they reached the area.

Captain Nikolai Nekrasov was sitting near the coach, having submitted himself to the well-practiced care of his sergeant, who was presently bandaging his arm. When the sound of thudding hoofbeats drew his attention toward the lane, he glanced around with a start, fully expecting to see one or more of the thieves returning for their plunder. Espying his charge approaching at an alarming speed, the officer jumped to his feet and shouted orders for his men to form a barrier across the road as he rushed forward to await the charging animal with arms spread wide.

The stallion proved to have a mind of his own. He came to a stiff-legged, jolting halt a short distance from the human trap and then, rearing, thrashed the air with his front hooves. It seemed his intent to continue his flight when he came down again, for his eyes flicked about in search of an avenue of escape, but as the sergeant jumped forward and seized the bridle, Captain Nekrasov whisked Synnovea from the saddle, ignoring the pain that shot through his injured arm as he swept her to safety. The stallion danced sideways in wild-eyed alarm, but the sergeant's soothing voice and reassuring strokes soon quieted the animal until he finally acquiesced to the gentle hand.

Synnovea leaned in trembling relief against Captain Nekrasov as the strength ebbed from her shaking limbs. For a moment she yielded herself to the comforting embrace of the officer's arm, hardly realizing the full extent of his admiration as his gaze dipped briefly into her torn bodice. Gradually the Russian officer released his constricted breath and regained control of his racing senses. The faint brush of his lips against her hair seemed accidental as he continued to lend her support, but when she caught the sound of Ali's weak, plaintive plea, Synnovea gave him no further heed.

"Me lamb," the servant mewled as the driver stopped bathing her brow long enough to lift her upright. "Come here an' let me see for meself that no harm has come ta ye."

Synnovea ran to her maid and submitted herself to the woman's inspection while she made her own assessments of the elder's condition. A massive black bruise now marred the wrinkled chin, and even in the meager light, Ali's pallor was easily discernible.

The exertion proved too much for the tiny maid. Mewling a fretful moan, she collapsed into the supporting arms of the coachman, concluding the worst as she considered her mistress's tattered condition. "Oh, me lamb! Me lamb! What did that foul beastie do ta ye?"

Synnovea soothed the elder's fears as she sank to her knees beside her. "I've suffered a few minor scratches and bruises, Ali, nothing more, thanks to the tsar's officer who came to my rescue."

Ali softly sobbed in relief. "Thank the blessed heavens ye've been spared. An' thank Cap'n Nekrasov for comin' ta yer aid."

Synnovea squeezed the small hand reassuringly. "It was another officer who saved me, Ali. He led his men in an attack against the brigands. We're safe now."

"If only I could've seen the event meself," the maid murmured weakly. "I'd have enjoyed seein' that big lummox gettin' his comeuppance." Barely had she said that than the aging eyelids sagged closed. Heaving a weary sigh, Ali drifted off.

Synnovea met the gaze of her gray-haired driver as she pushed herself to her feet. "You'd better carry Ali to the coach now, Stenka. She can rest there until we're under way again." In caring concern Synnovea continued to fret as she walked beside them. "Gently, now. Ali has had the worst of the fray."

"Jozef and I will take care of her, mistress. Have no fear," Stenka replied kindly and then coaxed, "You'd better see to yourself now, mistress, considering the bad fright you've had."

"I will, Stenka," Synnovea murmured and then noticed the bandage that had been wrapped around the footman's head. Laying a hand upon his sleeve, she claimed his attention. "Your wound, Jozef—is it serious?"

Jozef shook his head and grinned. "No, my lady, but there's a hole in my ear large enough to put a cork through."

"Some lady will find that convenient," Stenka remarked

with a teasing twinkle in his eyes. "She'll lead him about by the ear instead of the nose."

Synnovea patted the footman's arm in a conciliatory manner and managed a smile. "You'd better be wary, Jozef. In Moscow there are plenty of pretty maids who'll take advantage and lead you astray."

"I shall watch for them with great eagerness, my lady," Jozef promised her with a chortle.

Satisfied that Ali was in capable hands, Synnovea lent her attention to their immediate departure. Nikolai's men had suffered only minor wounds and were hurriedly repacking the carriage. The detachment of soldiers who had come to their rescue had given chase to the band of thieves, and no member of either force could now be seen. A short distance from the coach, the ground was littered with the dead, and from what she could ascertain in the swiftly gathering darkness, the highwaymen were the only ones who had suffered loss, for she could see no Russian uniform among the dead. Anxious to be gone before the raiders returned to reclaim their booty, Synnovea faced Captain Nekrasov with a query. "Shouldn't we leave here before we're attacked again?"

Nikolai Nekrasov was in full agreement and urged his men to double their efforts. "We must make haste to take the countess to a place of safety. Finish loading whatever is left and let us be off before we find ourselves once again beset by the brigands."

Synnovea realized she hadn't seen the cleric since her return and glanced around in some bewilderment. "But where is Ivan Voronsky?"

Captain Nekrasov raised his able arm to point toward a shadowed area beyond a clump of tall trees in the distance. Frowning in bemusement, Synnovea stared in the direction he indicated until a vague, pale blur became distinguishable as the leaf-shrouded form of a small, naked man. "They stole away his clothes, Countess, and every spare piece of clothing we had with us as well. We've nothing to share with him."

Synnovea debated the alternatives. Ivan had been so critical of her European gowns, she didn't think he'd accept such frivolous finery even out of necessity. Ruefully she advised, " 'Twould seem there's no choice but to search for clothing among the fallen."

"I've already assigned that task to one of my men, my lady," Nikolai informed her. "Though the selection may not meet with the cleric's approval, there should be enough to clothe him."

Synnovea silently demurred at the idea of undressing the dead and quickly excused herself. "I'll wait in the coach with Ali."

Though night quickly overtook them, Synnovea and her small party of attendants were soon on the road again. The pace was more cautious now as the moon cast ominous shadows far ahead of them. Each bend in the road was carefully approached. Still, the air was cooler and far better tolerated than the oppressive heat of the day.

Once again, Synnovea had to endure the presence of Ivan Voronsky, but this time he wasn't at all inclined to argue after being so thoroughly humiliated. When he talked at all, he mumbled angry insinuations against Captain Nekrasov and his men, convinced that they had been motivated by spite to find the most obnoxious, most malodorous garments available. The outlandishly large breeches and leather doublet reeked of old sweat and garlic, a combination which made it imperative for the diligent application of a scented handkerchief.

Synnovea refrained from placating Ivan's complaints, preferring instead to keep the filtering cloth in place so she wouldn't have to tolerate the stench. She was also appreciative of the darkness that hid whatever gory stains bedecked the garb, for she preferred complete ignorance of the type of death wound the previous owner had suffered.

They were well on their way again before the realization dawned on Synnovea that she had made no effort to send out her escort in search of the officer who had ridden after her. The possibility that he was lying wounded or dead in the forest made her own lack of concern seem shamefully devoid of compassion, especially since he had risked his life to save her. In seeking her own security, she had dismissed any consideration for the safety and comfort of the officer. Utterly scandalized by her disregard for such a valiant soldier, she knew she'd find little relief from the fretting anxiety that now gnawed at her.

2

The golden moon nestled like a newborn babe within the cradling arms of towering pines, firs, and larches. Gradually the orb weaned itself from its earthly breast and began to climb upward in a wide arc across the night sky. Humbling a myriad of stars with its brilliance, the lustrous sphere condescendingly cast its light upon the earth, setting aglow the rustling leaves of the oaks and birches that lined the road through the village, creating scintillating flashes of light as soft breezes bestirred their branches.

Grayed wooden cottages, adorned with painted carvings and fretworked gables, were nestled close behind the trees. Small sheds, gathered like ragged skirts behind the humble dwellings, were joined together with board fences, providing a windbreak against the fierce winds which could savage the land in winter months.

The stately carriage, with its complement of unkempt

guards, rumbled past the houses, drawing young and old alike to the windows. The grandeur of the coach and the frazzled appearance of its escort were noticeable even in the gloom. The small company of soldiers, some of whom were bruised and bloody, aroused speculations as to the likely cause, but no one was more aware of their shabby condition than Captain Nekrasov. At his command, the detachment rode through the town with a practiced cadence that lent some semblance of dignity otherwise lacking in the procession. The entourage passed a single-domed wooden church in stoic silence, yet when Stenka halted the conveyance in front of a sizable inn and a bathhouse was espied nearby, deep sighs of relief were heard from the grime-coated guards as they swung down from their mounts.

Captain Nekrasov entered the inn to make the necessary arrangements for his charge. His bandaged arm and bloody tunic drew curious stares, yet one did not casually delay an officer of the tsar single-mindedly intent upon his duties. Synnovea awaited the captain's return in the privacy of her coach, unwilling to extend the innkeeper's bemusement by the presence of two bruised and badly disheveled women.

Ivan Voronsky hastened off to beg for more appropriate garb from those in the church. As he skittered along the thoroughfare, he kept to the shadows and shielded his face against recognition, however remote the possibility of that occurrence.

The innkeeper was proud of his new bathhouse and boasted of its clever features as he directed his male guests around the facilities. The guided tour allowed Synnovea the privacy she needed to help Ali upstairs to their room. By now, the servant's head was throbbing so painfully that even the slightest movement made her queasy. She had taken on a pallor that was sharply accentuated by the purplish swelling on her pointed chin. Synnovea gratefully accepted the tray of food that the innkeeper's wife brought up to them, but Ali could endure only a few morsels. Solicitously Synnovea filled a basin for the tiny maid, helped her bathe and don a fresh nightgown. Finally, with an agonized groan, Ali sank onto the bed and drifted off to sleep, thoroughly spent.

Synnovea desired more than a mere token washing for herself and settled her mind on having nothing less than a thorough cleansing and a soothing soak for her own sorely bruised body. It became evident, however, that the soldiers had much the same notion in mind after depositing their gear upstairs. In passing her door they made as much noise as a stampeding herd of young colts, jostling and elbowing each other aside in a light-hearted endeavor to be among the first to reach the bathhouse. Listening to their cavorting descent, Synnovea had to wonder how they had managed to find so much energy after such a grueling day.

The delay was hardly objectionable to Synnovea. Eventually it would allow her as much leisured time in the facility as she desired, a privilege reserved expressly for the last in line. As she waited for the soldiers' return, she collected toiletries and nightclothes in a small satchel. Painstakingly she brushed out the debris that had become entangled in her long hair and left the black, silky length unbound as she stripped away her torn clothes. After treating the scratches on her arms, she gathered a voluminous robe around her slender body in preparation of her descent.

The officer who had rushed to her defense came to mind, and she began to pace restlessly about, stricken by her conscience. His face was nothing more than a dark void in her memory, yet she recalled her own blended feelings of awe when, at every turn of the hand, he had seemed to hover behind them like a relentless bird of prey watching for an opportunity to bring down his quarry. She hoped fervently that he was alive and that news of his safety would soon reach her. Only then could she forgive herself.

The soldiers began to drift back to their rooms in varying numbers. Much subdued by their baths, they meandered slowly past her door with only an occasional murmur exchanged between them. Their muted, cheerless voices now clearly bespoke of their weariness.

Synnovea was anxious for them to retire, yet in her growing impatience, it seemed that three times as many came back than those who had left. Her frustration deepened when Ivan sharply commanded a way to be made for him as he passed the soldiers in his descent of the stairs. Answering their exaggerated revulsion to his foul-smelling clothing, he snidely announced that he intended to wash away any residue of filth that remained from their putrid offerings.

Synnovea was inclined to think that this new delay was caused by nothing more than Ivan's unwillingness to associate with men of low rank, especially common soldiers. Obviously he considered them far removed from his self-exalted personage, for in her presence he had openly disdained them as crude, ignorant men. Had he been able to dictate the priority of events, he might have insisted on being allowed to finish his bath before they were permitted on the premises. Of course, if he had tried such a thing, the soldiers would have laughed him to scorn.

The inn grew still and hushed after Ivan's return to the small, private cubicle that he had elected to take, allowing Synnovea to finally consider it safe to go down. Outside the inn, a cool breeze rustled through the tall firs that formed a protective fortress beyond the bathhouse, bringing to her nostrils the fresh, pungent fragrance of their swaying boughs. The burbling of a swiftly flowing stream melded with other soothing night sounds, while high above the treetops, the brilliant moon shone down from its lofty realm, holding back the darkness with a wondrous glow that clearly defined the path to the low-roofed structure.

The door creaked in the hushed stillness as Synnovea pushed it slowly open and stepped within. At the far end of the room, a fire flickered in a large hearth, illumining the shadowed interior with a shifting amber glow. A dim lantern offered a wan light from the rafter where it hung suspended by a pulley rope. Its glow lent eerie life to the swirling mists rolling upward from the stygian surface of the pool. The vapors twined aimlessly through the massive beams buttressing the ceiling as if probing for a way of escape and, in their failure, merged into a thickening, swelling haze that shrouded the interior.

Water, shunted through tin flumes from the stream outside, flowed into a huge cauldron, which hunkered like some enormous beast on squat legs over a hearth of its own. A steady fire licked upward around its swollen belly, lending a blush to the curling vapors and the tenebrous gloom. Steaming water trickled cheerily over its funnelled lip into the main bathing pool, on the opposite side of which the overflow dribbled into a shaft that returned the water to the rivulet.

Synnovea paused at the portal and carefully scanned the interior lest she find herself in error about being alone. The shifting flames cast dancing shadows into the mists. Beyond that, nothing stirred. The only sounds came from the crackling fire and the trickling water. In the spacious hearth, smaller kettles of water hung over a fire, and upon a nearby table, pitchers and basins of water were readily available for an initial scrubbing with soap. Wooden tubs had also been provided for a more leisurely soak in a warm bath.

On a bench near the pool, a man's robe had been left, and Synnovea made a mental note to inform Captain Nekrasov on the morningtide that the garment was there, on the chance that he or one of his men had left it behind. Since Ivan's garments had been stolen by the thieves, it seemed highly unlikely that it belonged to him.

Synnovea dropped the satchel onto a nearby stool, too tired and bruised to think of anything beyond a bath and a refreshing dip in the pool. She prepared the former herself until a wooden tub brimmed with steaming liquid. From a small vial she had brought, she sprinkled droplets of scented oils over the surface and laid out a bar of fragrant soap and a large towel. She ran slender fingers through her hair to remove any lingering snarls, coiled the length into a heavy rope, and wound it on top of her head, where she secured the bulk with ornate combs. The topknot loosened a bit, allowing softly curling tendrils to plummet downward onto her brow and neck, but for the most part, the dark mass was held ensnared.

Freeing the ties at her waist, she sent the robe slithering downward with a shrug of her shoulders until she caught it with a swirling motion of her arm and flung it aside. As the garment settled in a billowing cloud on a nearby bench, she paused in sudden incertitude and tilted her head aslant, wondering at the soft, breathless sighing sound the silk had made, much like the slow expelling of a deep breath.

Nothing more was heard beyond the melding murmurs of a crackling fire and trickling water, allowing Synnovea to banish her doubts. Her nerves had been tested far beyond acceptable limits for her to give credence this evening to her own lurid imagination.

Lifting a foot upon the rim of the wooden tub, Synnovea inspected the dark bruises above her knee where Ladislaus had cruelly clasped her thigh. Another bluish mark at her waist caught her eye, and she cupped a breast within her palm, pressing the fullness upward to examine the dark bruise more carefully. During their frantic flight through the woods, she had suffered much pain and trauma, for the rogue's arm had clutched her so tightly she had feared her ribs would crack.

She dearly hoped the officer had delivered a suitable recompense for the brigand's crimes, especially after Ladislaus had boasted that none of the tsar's soldiers could best him. She was exceedingly glad he had been proven wrong. Indeed, it suited her mood to envision that crude highwayman trussed up like a goose, but an intruding worry soon furrowed her brow, motivating her to repeat a silent petition for the safety of the officer.

A long, pleasurable sigh wafted from Synnovea's lips as she lowered herself into the scented bath. A delightful interlude passed in which she allowed the steaming water to relax and soothe her aching muscles. After a time she began to wash and lathered soap over her shoulders and bosom before progressing to her limbs. Lifting first one and then the other, she worked the suds up along their sleek lengths until she was nigh covered with a whitish foam. Dallying at the task allowed her tensions to fade to near oblivion.

Once her hair was washed, Synnovea leaned her head over the edge of the tub and arched her back as she rinsed away the soap with fresh water from a bucket. When she relaxed again in the tub, she leisurely dribbled the contents of a dripping sponge over her shoulders. The dispersing runnels cascaded in eager channels through the white frosting until the rounded orbs glistened wetly in the rosy firelight.

Synnovea indulged herself in the luxury of the bath until she realized the hour was growing late. But she refused to leave until she had sampled the relaxing pleasure to be found in the pool. Bracing her hands on the rim of the tub, she pushed herself to her feet with an energetic heave, momentarily setting her breasts a-bounce. An odd sound, much like a watery gulp, came from the direction of the pool, and in deepening trepidation Synnovea carefully probed the swirling vapors hovering above the water. A movement near the steps caught her eye, and she jerked her head around with a startled gasp, only to laugh in relief as she espied a frog that squatted there.

"You intrude, my little friend," she laughingly scolded and tossed the contents of a bucket his way, sending him leaping away.

Reassured that her privacy was secure, she finished rinsing herself, pouring warm water over her body and sending the lather flowing back into the tub. By now, the heat of the room was enough to have drawn a fine mist of sweat from her pores, and she left the tub, eargerly anticipating the cooler water of the pool.

Descending the stone steps at its edge, Synnovea nearly crooned with pleasure, feeling immediately refreshed by the cool liquid into which she sank. She deemed the innkeeper especially clever to incorporate a pool of such depth inside a bathhouse, when it was most often the practice of bathers, after steaming up in heavy humidity, to scamper outside and cool themselves in a nearby stream or banks of snow, whatever the weather and location permitted. In the coldest months some would even dare the chill for such an experience. Her English mother, however, had instilled within her father the need for a private bath in their home, and throughout the years Synnovea had clung to the modesty of that custom. Whenever the occasion had warranted her making use of a public facility, Ali had always made the necessary arrangements and paid out coins to secure her solitude, while Jozef and Stenka had stood guard outside. Under the circumstances, Synnovea had been reluctant to disturb her servants, nor had she felt a need to do so, for Captain Nekrasov kept himself and his men well in line.

Leisurely Synnovea stroked through the water, letting the thickening haze envelop her as she swam toward the far side. Her long hair flowed behind her on the surface, much like an opening fan of ebony hue, the ends becoming lost in the shadows behind her.

Of a sudden, Synnovea gasped and recoiled in astonishment and dread as her hand made contact with something human and very manly. A wide, furry chest, to be exact! She sank abruptly in surprise until her thigh brushed against the fellow's loins and then, in rising panic, she struggled to propel herself away from the offending nakedness. Lurching backward with as much grace as a floundering cow, she plunged below the surface and promptly came up choking and coughing. Strong hands reached out to lift her up by the arms, but she fought them off, certain she was in impending danger of being ravished.

Having successfully escaped the helping hands, Synnovea began to sink again, this time against the man. She hardly noticed the muscular torso as her head went under the surface again, for in sudden alarm she realized she was taking in more water than even a competent fish should. This time when the man clamped an arm around her waist and drew her up, she flung both of her own about his neck and gasped for air between strangling, wrenching coughs. So great was her dismay that she gave no heed to the fact that her breasts were pressed tightly against the stalwart chest of the man or that her thighs rested intimately against his maleness. The fleshly heat he displayed failed to impact her consciousness, for she was far too anxious about drawing a normal breath.

Her anxiety ebbed to some degree when she managed to clear the water from her nose and throat. Carefully she inhaled, sucking in deep drafts to fill her lungs. Finally it dawned on her that the man was watching her with an amused yet dubious frown. Highly indignant that he should find some humor in her predicament, she leaned back to consider him with a haughty stare, disregarding the fact that she was completely naked in his encompassing arms. Water dribbled from her hair and trickled downward across her brow into the wetly spiked lashes, leaving her vision somewhat impaired. The thick vapors lent a strange bewitchment to the moment, yet she was sure the distortion she saw in the man's face hadn't been conjured through her own faulty perception or hindered sight. A seer would have been needed to accurately determine if the man was even human.

Lacking such perception, Synnovea briefly perused his badly lacerated visage. A large bump grossly elaborated the curve of his brow where the skin had been split open. The swelling extended downward into his eye, nearly closing it. His upper lip was also distended, and above this protrusion another ugly bruise darkened his cheek. Providing some evidence that his face wasn't totally misshapen, his jaw appeared carefully hewn of granite, while his nose was shaped with a noble, aquiline leanness. Short, wetly spiked strands of hair shaded eyes that seemed of a steel-gray hue rimmed with a deeper blue. Even in the shadowed room, softer lights twinkled within the shining depths as a lopsided grin lifted the smaller corner of his lips.

"Forgive me, Countess, I didn't mean to frighten you," he murmured. "Nor was it my intent to cause you embarrassment. Indeed, my lady, I never in my wildest yearnings ever imagined that my bath would be interrupted by such flawless beauty. I was no less than bedazzled by the sight and reluctant to see it come to an end."

Synnovea scarcely noted that he had spoken to her in English, but in a heated rush, she replied in kind. "You spied upon me without making me aware of your presence," she accused. "Simple truth, sir! Why are you here? Should I assume that your intentions are to accost me for your own evil purposes?"

"Banish the thought, my lady. I merely came here when my duties permitted it. Several of my men needed attention. By the time I had dressed their wounds, most of the soldiers had left the bathhouse, and after the departure of the cleric, I was certain I'd be alone and was much amazed when you joined me. I fear I was momentarily confounded and struck dumb by your entrance. Then it became clear to me. Though I could see you, you were unable to see me." He lifted wide, sleekly bulging shoulders in a casual shrug. "I fear the sight of you proved too much of a temptation for an officer in need of feminine companionship."

"Indeed, sir!" Synnovea fairly flung the words at him. "I

can understand why you're in want! Have you no ken that a gentleman would have informed a lady of his presence ere her disrobing?"

His bruised lips twitched with amusement as his eyes glimmered back at her through the shadowed gloom. "Alas, Countess, I do not claim to be a saint. I greatly enjoyed the interlude and the perfection you displayed and, for the life of me, couldn't bring myself to interrupt. Were I any less a gentleman, I'd surely take advantage of this most provocative embrace . . . ." He settled her a bit closer as she, in some irritation, tried to push herself free again. Her thighs brushed hard against him, snatching the man's breath and flicking a fiery brand across the fibers of his senses until he dared not move lest he lose control of his hard-won poise. With some difficulty, he drew rein on his hotly flaming passions and continued in a warm, mellow voice, stilling her struggles as his words struck home. "Since I've already saved you from one ravishment this evening, 'twould seem I'm honor-bound to carry you to safety again."

"Saved me?" Synnovea's lips pursed in a silent *Oh!* as it came to her just who the man was. "You mean . . ."

"You left ere we could be properly introduced, my lady," he reproved, distracted by the slick, wet feel of her soft breasts against his chest. He doubted that there had ever been such a moment in his life when he had been assaulted by such exquisite torture or when the need to maintain a ruse of imperturbable calm was absolutely crucial to his aspirations. He was certain she'd have flown his embrace posthaste had he foolishly revealed the full extent of his admiration. But then, she had to be an innocent not to be aware of his awakened passion. If not, then she was a woman well-versed in the art of tempting men and was merely being coy. "And though you are a delicious sight to behold and even more delectable to enfold, I must admonish you for your bad manners."

"Sir, this is hardly the time to discuss bad manners, either mine or yours! Now let me go!" Synnovea struggled briefly in the circle of his arms and was surprised when he spread his arms wide. The imminent threat of going under once again made her throw her arms about his neck and tighten her grasp. She reddened profusely beneath his deepening grin, and with a stifled groan, she dove away from him. Swimming back to the edge of the pool, she tossed a glance over her shoulder to find him stroking leisurely through the water behind her. In urgent haste, she leapt up the steps and made a flying dash across the room to fetch her robe. Shaking it out, she quickly sought its protective covering.

Thus armored, Synnovea faced the officer as he climbed those same stone stairs. Wondering what the next moments would bring, she watched him cautiously lest she be taken by surprise. Though obviously far from handsome, the man was exceptionally well-formed. He was as tall as Ladislaus but not nearly as thick or bulky. Even so, he had a hard-muscled look about him. Recalling the agility and easy strength he had displayed battling the outlaws, she could only guess at the discipline he practiced to maintain a good fighting form. His ribs were tautly fleshed, his chest firmly muscled beneath a matting of crisp hair, his waist lean and hips narrow—

A gasp escaped Synnovea as his loins came fully into view, and she whirled with burning cheeks, shocked to the depths of her virginal innocence. Though well traveled, she had been carefully sheltered throughout the span of her life. Even with a score of years behind her, this was her first glimpse of a completely naked man. Yet he didn't seem the least bit abashed by the boldness that he exhibited in her presence.

Synnovea heard his soft, chuckling laughter coming near and faced him in sudden apprehension, fearing that she'd have to fight him off. But he only fetched the robe which had been left on the bench. Careful to keep her glance brief and well-elevated, she gave him a seething glower before she jerked around again. For several moments she stood in mute silence, fuming over the fact that he hadn't made his presence known before she had disrobed.

"You can turn around now," he informed her, mirth liberally imbuing his voice.

"Then I shall make haste to leave!" she declared irately, incensed by his obvious enjoyment of a situation that, for her, had been a horrendously embarrassing experience. Tossing him another glare to convey her outrage, she began to gather up her possessions. "The very idea! Spying upon me like some sneak thief! You're the most despicable knave I've met in some time!"

"Not since this afternoon, at least," he responded with a lopsided grin. An indolent shrug lifted his wide shoulders as he queried, "Or did you appreciate that thief's company more than mine?"

"Ha! I'd venture to say, sir, that Ladislaus has much to learn from you about boorish manners!" Her curiosity got the better of her, and Synnovea paused to peer up at him with narrowed eyes. "What happened to the blackguard anyway?"

The officer emphasized his supreme displeasure with an angry snort. "The cowardly wretch fled when you raced off. And he took *my* horse! A most worthy steed it is, too. Believe me, I haven't a ken which vexes me more, letting that rogue escape or losing my horse! Had I not tried to help you when his stallion reared, I might've been able to capture the brigand. But were you grateful? No, indeed! You gave no slightest thought to my welfare and obviously made no effort to send out any of your escort in search of me. If not for my men beating the woods for me, I'd still be out there! Believe me, Countess, I'm here with no special thanks to you!"

Synnovea raised a dainty chin, pricked by his admonishing tone and her own condemning conscience. "You seem dreadfully rankled by your loss."

"And well I should be! I'll not likely find another steed half as gifted in the field as that one!"

"On the morrow I shall instruct Captain Nekrasov to leave you Ladislaus's stallion," she stated loftily. "Perhaps that will mollify you."

The man scoffed sharply. "Hardly! It cost me a goodly sum to have my own stallions shipped here from England. . . ."

"From England?" she repeated in surprise, and then realized she had overlooked the obvious. His subtly clipped speech clearly betrayed his place of origin. "You're an Englishman?"

"I thought it might have been apparent to one who also speaks the language!" he quipped with rampant sarcasm.

"But you led a Russian troop . . ." Synnovea began, clearly bemused. Then she recalled Ladislaus's comment about foreign cavaliers being hired to teach their fighting skills to the tsar's troops. "You're an English officer in His Majesty's service?"

Though he wore nothing more dashing than a long robe, the man gave her a debonair bow, a gesture which might have been accompanied by the clicking of heels had he worn something more substantial. "Colonel Sir Tyrone Bosworth Rycroft at your service, Countess. Knighted in England and now Commander of the Third Regiment of the Tsar's Imperial Hussars. And you are . . ."

"This is hardly the place for introductions, Colonel," Synnovea replied hurriedly, reluctant to provide him with a name. She could imagine him spreading lurid tales of their watery meeting among his troops and friends, leaving her reputation hopelessly besmirched.

A grin slanted across his swollen lips. "And you are the Countess Synnovea Altynai Zenkovna," he continued smoothly, "en route to Moscow, where you'll be under the tutelage of Princess Taraslovna, the tsar's cousin."

Synnovea felt her chin sagging in surprise and made haste

to close her mouth. Breathlessly she whispered, "You know a great deal about me, sir."

"I wanted to know," Tyrone replied with an air of confidence that shattered her own. "When we arrived here this evening and I found that you had also taken shelter in the inn, I made inquiries among your escort. Captain Nekrasov refused to accommodate me, but his sergeant proved far more generous with the facts. I was relieved to hear that you're unmarried, especially to that pompous little upstart who serves as your companion and who had the audacity to ask me to leave the bathhouse to him! He obliged me by his own departure. From his obvious contempt, I gathered he thinks much of himself or his station in life. Or perhaps he sees some hope of elevating himself through his association with you." The colonel arched an unmarred brow as he looked at her pointedly, awaiting some declaration as to her relationship to the man.

Though desirous of denying any attachment to Ivan Voronsky, Synnovea refused to appease the officer's curiosity. It seemed prudent to keep the man from gaining further knowledge of her lest he prove bothersome or an embarrassment in the future.

Gathering her satchel, Synnovea moved toward the door but found her progress promptly thwarted by the colonel, who stepped in front of her. His uneven lips eased into a gentle smile. "Will you allow me to see you again, Countess?"

"That's impossible, Colonel," she declined coolly. "I shall be traveling on to Moscow on the morrow."

"But so will I," Tyrone assured her softly. "I'm here in this area only because I led my men on an exercise in the field. We're scheduled to return by the morrow's evening."

Synnovea refused to give way to his arguments. "Princess Anna would hardly approve."

"You're not . . . betrothed?" Tyrone held his breath in anticipation of her answer. He couldn't understand why he should suddenly forget the ache of his shattered life and once again allow a woman to strike sparks in his mind, yet he could keenly perceive the depth of his disappointment if he had to give her up to some other swain.

"Nay, Colonel Rycroft, of course not."

"Then, with your permission, Countess, I'd consider it an honor to pay court to you." Tyrone was crushingly aware of his own impatience to settle the matter. In spite of his score, ten and two years of life, he had been caught in a rutting heat over this beauty and was comporting himself like some eager young whelp. True, it had been some time since he had made love to a woman, yet he couldn't remember another, even that fair and comely Angelina, who had looked as ravishing either clothed or completely devoid of raiment.

"Your proposal overwhelms me, Colonel." Synnovea was more than a little astounded by his petition, yet she was grateful for the shadows that masked the heat flooding into her cheeks as she recalled how his warm, well-defined body had pressed against her own in the pool. His entreaty was out of the question for a variety of reasons, perhaps the most pronounced being her guardian's sharp aversion to foreigners, yet for the sake of caution, Synnovea deemed it fitting to soften her rejection. "I shall have to consider your request, Colonel Rycroft. And then, of course, I must seek Princess Anna's permission."

"Then I shall await your pleasure, my lady. Until then, I bid you adieu." Tyrone swept her another courtly bow and slowly straightened as she moved past him and hurried across the room. Her silken robe was now quite damp and clung to her gently swaying hips divinely, reminding him of that moment in the pool when his hand had brushed her buttocks and she had clung to him in an anxious frenzy. His long-starved passions had not yet cooled from that delicious encounter. Indeed, he could easily foresee having to endure a long, restless night tormented by his desires and a relentless onslaught of lustful imaginings.

The portal opened with the same soft creak that had announced the lady's entrance into the bathhouse and closed again to leave him staring musefully at its oaken planks. As he listened to her hastening footsteps, another vision came to mind, one that was dark and dismally devoid of warmth. It was a painful memory of the graveside where he had muttered his last ragged, bitter farewell to his dead wife.

Colonel Sir Tyrone Rycroft turned with a muttered curse. What fool's folly had set him on this path toward his own destruction? How could he dare entertain any hope that he could trust another woman when he hadn't yet gathered the tattered shreds of his emotions and resumed a life unhampered by haunting recollections? The scars he had banished to the dark recesses of his mind burst forth in renewed agony, and with a low growl, he too left the bathhouse.

The dawning sun had not yet touched the land with its torturous glow when Synnovea roused the commander of her escort and bade him to make haste to depart. At Captain Nekrasov's bemused inquiries, she laid the cause of her dispatch to a desire to have the journey behind her. She dared not reveal the fact that she was afraid that she had attracted the attention of an unwanted suitor and that it was expedient for her to leave ere the Englishman arose and sought her out again.

"Leave the stallion for Colonel Rycroft," she told the captain as he escorted her to her waiting coach. " 'Tis the least I can do to repay him for saving me from Ladislaus."

Ali was still sensitive to movement and had to be carried to the conveyance by Stenka. At the gentle urgings of her mistress, the maidservant leaned back against the pillows that had been solicitously tucked into a corner of the seat and once again allowed sleep to overtake her.

Synnovea braced herself at the opposite end of the seat and closed her eyes, refusing to be drawn into conversation with Ivan. She had bade her driver to waste no moment on this, their final day of travel, and if it so pleased him, to take an unfrequented path that, although somewhat more challenging, would get them to Moscow sooner.

Once they were on the road again, Synnovea breathed a sigh of relief, confident that she had seen the last of that English rake. Although he had already failed the standard by which a lady measures a proper gentleman, she fervently hoped he'd prove his merit as an officer of the tsar and refrain from spilling gossip to every person who lent an attentive ear. It was disconcerting enough that her own memory was wont to dwell on the happenings in the bathhouse without having such tales spread abroad throughout all of Moscow.

It was half an hour later when the Commander of the 3rd Regiment of the Tsar's Imperial Hussars rose from his cot and wincingly stretched his aching muscles. He staggered naked across the tiny cubicle that had sufficed as a room for the night and nudged the foot of his second-in-command in passing. Muttering an order, he left that one yawning as he searched out a candle to light.

Another half-turn of the hour saw the first hint of dawn lightening the sky to a dull blue. Colonel Rycroft tucked the battered helm beneath his arm and descended the stairs to make an inspection of his men, who were already awaiting him outside. As he left the open door, his eyes flitted to the right of the porch where he had last seen the lady's coach. Alas, there was nothing there but Ladislaus's black stallion tethered to a post. A muttered curse escaped his lips as he turned to scan the road, already aware that he'd find no evidence of the countess's entourage.

She's flown! The realization sorely tested Tyrone's mood, and he ground out another expletive beneath his breath. He should've known he'd frighten her off with his confounded hot blooded fervor! He had moved on her like a hound sniffing a bitch in heat. In truth, he couldn't blame her much for having flitted off in an anxious quest to put some distance between them.

Letting his breath out in long, slow drafts, Tyrone sought to curb his annoyance with himself and the lady. His men awaited him, and after he had driven them with an iron will the whole week long, they deserved better from him today, especially since they had put the outlaw band to rout. What did the girl matter anyway? He could buy the services of a wench easily enough. Indeed, he found himself ever pressed to reject the advances of those brazen trollops who followed the soldiers' camps or traversed that area in Moscow reserved for foreigners. Still, the idea of accepting the leavings of nearly every male in the tsar's army left him totally uninspired. He was after something more than a sordid, feverish fondling of a passing harlot. Despite the fact that he was reluctant to be ensnared by marriage again, he yearned to ease his passion with an exceptional kind of woman with whom he could exchange a mutual affinity and perhaps even come to cherish. What he truly desired was a mistress who'd be content to stay with him and not be inclined to test the strength of her persuasiveness on some other swain.

"Countess Zenkovna left you a horse, Colonel," Captain Grigori Tverskoy announced, jerking his thumb over his shoulder to indicate the steed. "Will it not serve you as well as your own?"

"I fear Ladislaus has benefited from the trade," Tyrone replied. "But he hasn't seen the last of me yet."

"Will you go after him again?"

"When it's convenient for me to do so," Tyrone assured his second-in-command. "But I have more pressing affairs to attend in Moscow before I can lend Ladislaus my full attention."

"Is it not gratifying to be able to report what none other

has thus far been able to claim in the division, Colonel? We've slain ten and three of Ladislaus's followers with no losses in our ranks. As much as I would like to carry the details of our fight directly to the tsar, I suppose it's too much for me to expect when General Vanderhout is so dedicated about meeting us upon our return from each and every maneuver." A laconic smile traced the captain's lips. "The general delights himself in your many conquests, Colonel, but I've noticed that it is *his* reputation that grows apace."

"The Dutchman is concerned about his future here," Tyrone mused aloud, squinting off toward the horizon. " 'Tis the best pay Vanderhout has yet received, and he doesn't want to lose it ere his contract runs out. Thus he must make his efforts look good."

"At your expense, Colonel," Grigori reminded him.

Tyrone reached out a hand to clasp the younger officer's shoulder consolingly. "A general is always responsible for whatever happens in his division, whether good or bad, Grigori. General Vanderhout realizes his command of foreign officers is under the close attention of the tsar and that our exploits reflect on him." Tyrone shrugged and then immediately winced as his swollen lip cracked open from his attempt to smile. " 'Tis the way of it! For us to protest his practice of claiming fame where he hasn't earned it would make us seem small and petty. Ergo, *tovarish,* we must take the general's conduct in stride, for we've no other choice."

Grigori heaved a laborious sigh. "The general's ineptitude wears on me, Colonel. In making a comparison, I believe you have much more to offer. General Vanderhout takes the ideas you freely supply and incorporates them as his own, and from what I've been able to ascertain, it seems you deliberately advise the man in subtle ways just to keep him from making costly mistakes."

Tyrone held a thoughtful silence for a long moment before he offered a reply. "I've had more experience in the field, my friend, but I'm certain General Vanderhout would not be where he is today without some ability of his own."

Having gained a different impression of the general, Grigori grunted in derision. "I wonder."

3

*S*tenka maneuvered the coach along a narrow street in Moscow, passing vaulted alleyways where a labyrinth of galleries existed. The marketplace of Kitaigorod still bustled with activity even though twilight was swiftly approaching. Bazaars displayed a collection of wares organized in rows for the benefit of patrons. Flax, hemp, icons, silks, and melons had their own particular *ryady,* or section, from whence each was sold. Other articles, ranging from simple foods to more costly treasures of pearls, icons, amber, and furs, were also available in the markets.

Captain Nekrasov's detachment followed the countess's coach as it wended its way toward the heart of Moscow, but the ragtag soldiers were largely ignored in the noisy bedlam surrounding them. Merchants loudly hawked their wares while bands of *skomorokhi* put on their masked mimes, musicals, or puppet shows. Prisoners, with their ankles fastened in stocks, had been incarcerated alongside the road and, in desperation, pleaded for bread and nourishment, a necessity the city did not provide. Blind or crippled beggars diligently shook cups, blending their chants for alms with the low grunts and rumblings of bears that did clever tricks for their handlers.

Rich boyars, those Russian men of nobility, sumptuously garbed in kaftans and high-peaked or rounded hats, rubbed shoulders with the poor as well as with the more prosperously dressed peasants. It was a common sight in the marketplace to see all manner of men. What distinguished the destitute from the affluent was often merely the size of one's purse.

The large, traveling coach continued its painstaking progress over the heavily timbered road as Stenka cried *"Padi! Padi!"* to urge meandering crowds to make way for them, or *"Beregis! Beregis!"* to warn others to take care of the approaching vehicle. The small, swift, elegant open *drozhki* were drawn by a single horse and skirted around them with incredible ease. The summer sledges moved at a slower pace, forcing Stenka to haul the four-in-hand to the far side of the road whenever the conveyances converged from the opposite direction. In winter the troikas would have halted their progress altogether, for the brisk sleighs raced down a lane with three horses abreast, throwing plumes of snow that blanketed everything they passed.

Synnovea had visited Moscow on numerous occasions, and though no less sensitive to the beauty and excitement of the city, she was unable to disregard the fact that only a few moments remained of the freedom she had long cherished under her father's protection. For most of the day she had been inundated by embarrassing details of her recent encounter with Colonel Rycroft. In spite of his misshapen features, she found something strangely fascinating about the man, at least enough to make her blush whenever she remembered his all-too-manly form pressing against her own nakedness. The lurid details she had disregarded in a time of panic, she now privately relished like some dream-bound chit with a penchant for salacious musings. The recurring, often graphic recollection of those moments when her bosom had been crushed against his stalwart chest and her thighs had all but embraced the fullness he had exhibited was so provocative in recall that her nerves were often a-jangle with a concern that her companions would somehow detect her wanton thoughts. Whenever her cheeks darkened to a profuse shade, she found good cause to be thankful for the sweltering heat. For once, she was glad that Ali hid her aching head beneath the folds of a cool, wet cloth and Ivan thought only of Ivan.

At present, the cleric was all but preening in the rosy aura cast by the lowering sun, as if he imagined the radiance as some well-deserved halo or, more far-fetched, held aspirations of presenting a sublime visage to his audience. If that was truly his quest, then he failed to realize just how clearly the ugly pockmarks scarring his bony cheeks were highlighted. Though shabbily garbed in the only robe the priests of the village church had been able to spare, he seemed in much better spirits and perhaps a bit puffed up on his own importance, as if delivering his charge to the custody of her guardians were some great feat that he and no other had accomplished.

The coach left the narrow passageway and entered the open area of *Krasnaya Ploscha* or, as the English were wont to call it, the Red, or Beautiful, Square. The red brick wall of the Kremlin rose like a vast, many-turreted crown above the city, encircling among other structures, several multidomed cathedrals, the bell tower of Ivan the Great, the Palace of Facets, and the nearby Terem Palace, where the future tsarina would be housed. Beneath the brilliance of the late-afternoon sun, the white facades and golden domes adorning many of the buildings gleamed like a sultan's treasure, while other bejeweled edifices, courtyards, and gardens clustered close about them, well protected behind the enveloping wall.

The Frolovskaia Tower was heralded as the main approach to this mighty fortress, and near it, another bauble of architectural brilliance glimmered. The exotic grandeur of the *Pokrovsky Sobor* or, as it was more frequently called of late, the Cathedral of St. Basil, had already bedazzled many a viewer with its many towers and bulging, uniquely shaped domes and spires that glistened beneath the sun like the multihued scales of a fish.

Stenka clucked to the horses as they crossed the open promenade in front of St. Basil's and the squat platform of the *Lobnoe Mesto,* or the Place of the Brow, from whence the patriarchs bestowed their blessings on the people or, on a spot beside it, where rebels and felons were beheaded or tortured for their crimes. Stenka soon turned the team away from the Kremlin into another lane where wealthy boyars lived in large wooden mansions. Synnovea came to alert attention when she espied the stately residence of the Countess Natasha Catharina Andreyevna off in the distance. The woman had once been her mother's dearest companion and was now the only confidante whom Synnovea could truly trust for help and counsel should things go awry with the Taraslovs.

Finally the four-in-hand swept off the main street into a circular drive, and Stenka drew the animals to a halt before an impressive mansion. The event Synnovea had been dreading had finally arrived, and she took a deep breath, bracing herself for the meeting to come.

Captain Nekrasov dismounted and, hastily dusting himself, came around the carriage to open the door for his charge. A smile curved his lips as he raised a hand to assist in the descent of the young woman with whom he had become enamored.

Synnovea heaved a sigh, dismayed by the fact that she'd be placing herself under the authority of people who were hardly more than strangers. As she approached the mansion on the able arm of her escort, a flickering glow of candles drew her gaze upward to glass-paned doors which stood open beyond a balcony that jutted outward above the front portal. There a slender woman stood framed by silken draperies, and with a tentative smile Synnovea lifted a hand in a gesture of greeting, recognizing her new benefactress. Neither smile nor nod came before the woman retreated from view. Behind her, the translucent panels fell forbiddingly into place.

Any assuagement Synnovea might have derived from a warm greeting was abruptly replaced with a morbid sense of gloom. She didn't want to be here, away from her home, away from all the things that her father had cherished and carefully nurtured. It took great resolve for her not to retreat to her coach. If she hadn't feared that her departure would enrage the tsar, she would've gladly endured all the hardships of the long trek home.

Sensing that things were not entirely as they should be, Nikolai conveyed his deepening concern in a query. "Will all be well with you here, Countess?" He had no idea what he might do if circumstances went awry for her, but he felt strongly committed to offer his assistance just the same. "If there should ever come a need . . . ."

Synnovea laid a hand upon the officer's sleeve and sought to reassure him—and perhaps even herself. "Princess Anna and I have met only briefly on three different occasions, Captain. I'm sure she's just as anxious about this meeting as I am."

The officer wasn't necessarily heartened by her claims, but he thought it best not to upset the maid by lingering on the matter. Yet he was motivated to restate his offer and did so cautiously lest he betray the full measure of his heart. "I'd consider it an honor if you'd allow me to serve you in whatever capacity you should either desire or require, my lady. I'll be receiving a promotion next month and shall be in the service of the tsar henceforth as an officer of the castle guard. Should you find that you have need of me, you can send your maid to summon me to your side." Almost emphatically, he declared, "And I shall come, my lady, or I will send no one less than His Majesty to give you my excuse."

Synnovea was overwhelmed by his chivalrous, if somewhat unrealistic, declaration. "I'm truly honored by your pledge, Captain Nekrasov."

"It has been a privilege escorting you here, my lady," he assured her warmly, meaning far more than he actually voiced.

Resolving to persevere through the forthcoming meeting with Anna, Synnovea murmured encouragingly, "My name is Synnovea. I deem the familiarity appropriate for a friend."

"Lady Synnovea," the captain breathed as he gently squeezed the slender hand resting upon his arm. "And if you'd honor me in like measure, my lady. My name is Nikolai."

"Nikolai." Issuing his name with a soft sigh, Synnovea allowed herself to be drawn to the massive entrance by the courtly gentleman.

A brisk rap of knuckles on the portal announced their arrival. Soon the door swung open to reveal a steward garbed in a plain white kaftan. Nikolai faced the man with an undaunted manner of one well acquainted with giving orders. "You may inform the Princess Taraslovna that her ward, Countess Zenkovna, is here requesting admittance."

The butler eyed the captain's bandaged arm curiously before he stepped aside and bade them enter. "The princess is expecting you, Countess."

Synnovea was shown into the parlor where she was politely informed that she would be joined by the mistress of the house. Reassured of her comfort, Nikolai hastened outside to direct the unloading of her baggage, but upon passing Ivan, he found himself the recipient of a haughty glare.

"What ails the cleric?" the officer asked in bemusement as he joined his men.

The sergeant snorted. "Maybe he took offense 'cause you didn't show him the same respect you gave the countess."

Nikolai cocked a brow in dubious wonder. "I wasn't aware that he was deserving any. If you ask me, he's probably an embarrassment to his order, though I still haven't determined what that may be."

Musefully the sergeant stroked the light stubble bristling his chin. "I'd say the man is naught but a weed sprung up from a wayward seed. He's bound to cause trouble for some unwary soul one day. I pray it may not be the countess, though I sense the man will try."

"For her sake, Sergeant, I hope you're wrong."

Ivan entered the front door without knocking and stalked into the front parlor where he bestowed a chilling glower upon Synnovea. "Captain Nekrasov seems quite taken with you, Countess. Your pride must be greatly bolstered by your triumph in acquiring another male conquest."

"*Another* male conquest?" she repeated cautiously. "Are you referring to someone in particular?"

"The way that beast Ladislaus claimed you, it's a miracle you're even here."

Synnovea almost breathed a sigh of relief. For a fearful moment she had thought the cleric had been talking about Colonel Rycroft. "Ladislaus saw me as nothing more than a helpless captive at his mercy. By now he has probably found another coach to strip and another woman to ravish. 'Tis indeed a pity he wasn't captured."

Ivan tossed his head jeeringly. "We can fault the Englishman for his escape."

Synnovea cast him a cautious glance. "Of whom do you speak?"

"I'm referring to the officer who rode after you and Ladislaus," Ivan explained testily. "From what I could gather from his appearance last night, Ladislaus clearly won the fray."

Synnovea yearned to correct the cleric, but she rejected such a notion, aware that her knowledge would only arouse his curiosity. "A dreadful shame, to be sure."

They glanced around in unison as Princess Anna Taraslovna floated across the threshold with willowy grace. An elegant, pearl-encrusted *kokoshniki,* adorned with gold stitchery that matched the design decorating her satin brocade *sarafan,* covered her head. Flowing from it in waves of shimmering gold was a gossamer veil hemmed with the same metallic threads. It dutifully covered the long braids of pale hair.

Anna Taraslovna was of an age about twoscore and bore herself with a dignified yet pragmatic confidence that brooked no interference or refusal. She was as tall as Synnovea, and her good looks, though slightly worn with the passage of years, were marked with a lean, squarish jaw and aristocratic features. Her eyes of silver-gray were bright and alert behind dark lashes. Above them finely plucked eyebrows were thinly drawn as if by a single sweep of a quill. Small, telltale wrinkles between her brows and around her lips bespoke of the heavy weight of concern and its consequence. The lightest evidence of a dewlap trembled at her throat, which was otherwise long and elegant. In spite of these tiny flaws brought on by aging, she was still a very attractive woman.

"My dear Synnovea," Anna murmured, extending slender hands to the younger woman, who rose to her feet in response. "You haven't changed at all since we last met. You're just as lovely as ever."

Synnovea dared make no reference to that particular event, but sank into a deep curtsy, acknowledging the loftier status of the other. In Russia there was certainly no dearth of princely boyars and their ladies even after Tsar Ivan the Terrible had indiscriminately laid waste to so many during his reign of terror years ago. "Thank you, Princess. I'm grateful to have the journey behind me."

"I trust everything went well and that Ivan proved to be of great comfort and assistance to you. I was sure he would be."

Synnovea managed a fleeting smile. "We were waylaid by thieves, but I shall allow Ivan Voronsky to relate the details of the attack. He was offended nearly as deeply as Captain Nekrasov was wounded."

Startled by the news, Anna faced Ivan, expecting an explanation, but his ragged appearance obviously caused her greater shock, for she was quick to suggest, "You'll of course want to refresh yourself before we talk."

Several soldiers entered the hall, making Anna's brows gather in annoyance as she noted the abundance of trunks being carried in, but she promptly faced the steward, who had entered the parlor bearing wine-filled goblets on a tray. "Boris, be good enough to escort the soldiers upstairs to the countess's chambers and direct the good Voronsky to the quarters I've reserved for him. Clean garments are awaiting him in the blue chest."

The servant left his burden on the table and bade the soldiers to follow. Trailing far behind them, the sergeant carried a small bag in his hand and another huge chest balanced on his shoulder. Upon espying Ivan, he set the dusty valise at the cleric's feet before making his way to the stairs.

"Oh, but I see you've brought clothes with you," Anna surmised as she recognized the satchel.

Ivan shook his head, drawing a perplexed frown from his benefactress. "On the contrary, Your Highness, I've been stripped of every possession I took with me, even the clothes off my back. Indeed, I'm grateful to have escaped with my life." He laid a hand limply into the palm of the other and raised a brow, lending dramatic emphasis to his claim. "It was most severely threatened, Princess, but I've accomplished your bidding, as you can see, and, despite the great losses I've suffered, have escorted the countess here as you instructed me to do."

Synnovea had the greatest urge to roll her eyes heavenward at his exaggeration. She noticed, however, that he readily elicited the princess's dismay.

"Anything you've been deprived of during your mission

of aid will certainly be replaced, good Voronsky," Anna assured him. "You must tell me of this dreadful event soon or I shall be overwhelmed by curiosity and worry. Come to my chambers after you've attended to your needs. You can explain what has transpired then."

"Though I suffered unduly, my lady, I'm alive to tell of my hardships, for which I'm indeed thankful," Ivan valiantly avouched and, with a brief bow, took his leave.

Anna faced her young charge and made no attempt to hide her disdain as she perused the plain but fashionable gown the younger woman wore. It was apparent the girl didn't regard herself a Russian *boyarina,* but rather, a lady of English blood.

Remembering the edict her cousin had issued, Anna seethed inwardly, resenting the arrangement, yet she forced a smile that was at best stiff. "Would you care for some refreshments, Synnovea? Boris has brought glasses of chilled *Malieno* for us to savor on this warm day. My cook, Elisaveta, keeps the flasks stored near the ice the servants haul into the cellar during the winter. I find the wine quite refreshing myself."

Synnovea accepted the libation and tentatively sipped the dark red liquid. She had sensed her new guardian's displeasure over her attire and waited tensely as that one slowly sipped the brew.

"First let me express my deep remorse over your father's untimely death, my dear," Anna continued. "I understand that he took a fever and died quite suddenly."

Tears still had a tendency to blur Synnovea's vision when she reflected on her recent loss. "Yes, I'm afraid so. My father appeared so hale and hearty before his illness, we were truly astounded by how quickly he was taken from us."

Anna latched onto the single word *we* with keen interest, hoping it held some significance. She would've snatched at dust motes if they'd have given her an alternative to what the tsar had forced upon her. "Did you have other relatives visiting you at the time, my dear? Your aunt from England, perhaps? It was my understanding that you have no kinsmen here in Russia with whom you could've gone to live. Is that indeed the case? I'm sure, since we're hardly more than strangers, that you'd likely feel more comfortable living with relatives or a close acquaintance."

Synnovea felt a sudden surge of empathy for the princess, for it was apparent that Anna felt as trapped by the tsar's decree as she did. His Majesty might have supposed that he was bestowing great compassion upon each of them by bringing them together, Anna as a childless wife, and she, a young woman without parents, but he had failed to consider that as two entirely different individuals who had never been intimate friends and who were totally bereft of bonding by blood ties, a definite threat existed that they'd eventually become enemies caged in the same house together, one forced to extend her hospitality and the other compelled to accept it. Synnovea could only wonder if the day would ever come when one of them would gather enough courage to approach Mikhail with a plea to be released from this uncomfortable arrangement he had concocted for them.

"Did you have someone visiting you at the time of your father's death?" Anna repeated, making no effort to curb her exasperation at the girl's delay in answering.

Synnovea vividly recalled the venom the princess had displayed toward their friend at the last diplomatic function to which her father had escorted them. Anna's hostility had seemed to surprise everyone but the recipient of her disfavor. Indeed, it had been so apparent that Synnovea had grave doubts that it had diminished since then. "Countess Andreyevna was visiting us at the time."

Anna drew herself up in cool reticence, unable to squelch the animosity that rose within her at the mention of that woman's name. "I wasn't aware you had befriended Natasha. What with her stealing your father's affections from your mother and trying to take her place in your life, I had imagined that you hated her."

Feeling her cheeks warm with rising ire, Synnovea stared into the swirling dark liquid as she twirled her goblet. "I'm afraid you misunderstood the relationship my father enjoyed with Natasha. It wasn't one esteemed by lovers, but a friendship based on mutual respect. The countess was my mother's friend long before she became ours. And as far as I know, my father and Natasha were never lovers and never discussed plans to marry each other. They were simply good friends, that is all."

Anna's lips twisted grimly as the girl defended a woman whom gossips had labeled immoral. A widow after three husbands and a whole host of other men chasing her, eager to be the fourth! Why, the very idea of a *boyarina* inviting men to her socials like some unscrupulous harlot was absolutely unheard of! "As far as you know," Anna goaded. Her tight smile barely disguised the malice churning within her. "But then, you may not have been aware of what was really going on behind your back."

"There is that possibility, of course, but only a minute one," Synnovea responded and considered her wine in an effort to hide her irritation. The princess was dragging up stale slander, talk which she had probably been instrumental in starting in the first place. To hear it again reawakened Synnovea's resentment.

"How long did you say your mother has been dead?"

"Five years," Synnovea replied in a strained whisper.

"Speak up, please," Anna snapped, ignoring how trite and petulant it might seem for one of her standing to act in such an acrimonious manner, but she had never asked for the girl to come and live in her home. And she most certainly didn't want her here. "I can barely hear what you're saying. And I don't like being kept waiting for a reply either. You're not backward, so stop acting as if you were. In the future I must insist that you pay heed to whatever is being said and be more punctual with your response. Is that too much to ask?"

"No, Princess." Synnovea's reply came readily enough and was spoken in a clear tone, but the task of suppressing a freshening ire was a hard-won victory. Still, she knew the folly of being drawn into a quarrel with the princess.

"That's better!" Anna set her goblet aside and rose to her feet as Boris led the soldiers downstairs again. Synnovea followed her example, and Anna made haste to dismiss her. "I'm sure you'll want to refresh yourself before the dinner hour. Boris can show you to your chambers."

Though the woman turned to leave, Synnovea saw the necessity in delaying her. "I pray a moment more of your time, Princess, if you wouldn't mind."

Anna faced her again with brows sharply elevated over cool gray eyes. "Yes, Synnovea? What is it?"

"I brought some of my servants with me to attend my needs while I'm here, and I must arrange a place for them to stay. If you have room to house them here, that would serve my purposes well. My coach and horses should also be stabled if there is enough space."

Anna's thin lips twisted in vexation. "You've taken much upon yourself if you think to keep them here. There's little enough room for your maid in your chambers without expecting us to house your coachmen and equipage as well. You'd better send them back to Nizhni Novgorod. You won't be needing them while you're living here with us."

"Then if you'd allow my coachmen to rest here for the night," Synnovea replied with far more cordiality, "I shall make other arrangements on the morrow. I shouldn't like to be without my coach while I'm here and thereby impose an inconvenience upon you whenever I have need of it."

Synnovea fervently desired to live in peace with the Taraslovs, at least until she could disentangle herself from their protection and become her own mistress, but if it meant being imprisoned within the confines of their home and permitted to venture out only at their whim, she knew she wouldn't be able to endure such restrictions for very long. She wasn't a child, and she didn't believe it was Tsar Mikhail's intent for his cousin to treat her like one.

"And just where do you think you'll keep them?" Anna challenged acidly.

Though Synnovea knew her suggestion would prick the woman to the core, it was a far more acceptable alternative than what Anna had in mind. "I'm sure Natasha will permit me to use her carriage house while I'm here. She lives only a short distance away."

"I know where she lives!" Anna snapped, offended by the girl's efforts to instruct her. Her inability to present a plausible excuse by which she could fortify an outright denial of the girl's petition only deepened her resentment, yet Anna knew the foolishness of testing her cousin's sense of fairness.

It was a rare event indeed when Anna acceded to anyone but Tsar Mikhail's dictates. Even then, she had a strong aversion to accepting his will over her own, a fact which she kept prudently to herself. By disguising her reversal now as submission to her husband's authority, she hoped to save face. Fairly soon she'd take her revenge by demanding enormous remunerations for the added expense of housing servants and stabling horses. If the girl wanted them near her so badly, then by heavens, Anna would see that she paid dearly for the privilege.

"Prince Aleksei will have to decide if you can keep your coachmen and use our facilities while you're here." Having issued that statement, Anna excused herself with a curt nod and left the room, throwing back over her shoulder, "Boris will see you to your chambers."

Synnovea heaved a sigh of relief, feeling as if she had just won a horrendous battle, but only by the skin of her teeth.

Obviously Princess Anna was going to be a lot more difficult than she had first surmised.

Returning outside, Synnovea gave instructions to her coachmen and left them to find their own way to the carriage house. Then she paused to bid farewell to the captain. "Thank you for your care and kindly consideration, Nikolai. I hope we shall meet again in the future."

Gallantly Nikolai bestowed a kiss upon her slender fingers. "Adieu, my fair lady, but I pray that it may not be for long."

Synnovea had no way of knowing what the morrow would bring and could find no adequate response. "Take care, Nikolai . . . *druga,* my friend."

"I'm honored by your friendship, Lady Synnovea. Perhaps we shall meet again . . . and soon. It would give me great pleasure to see you . . . now and then."

Lightly touching two fingers to her lips, Synnovea reached up and pressed those same digits against his lean cheek. "Even if we're destined never to cross paths again, Nikolai, remember that I shall value you as a man worthy of my trust. His Majesty did me a great service by sending you to serve as captain of my escort. I'm truly indebted."

Synnovea moved away before Nikolai could offer further comment and waved to the rest of the soldiers, who grinned and responded in kind. Then she slipped an arm around Ali's thin waist and gently guided her to their suite of rooms in the manse.

In the flickering glow of nearly a score of candles that burned atop a trio of candelabra, it became immediately evident that their new accommodations could not be faulted. A tiny cubicle just off the main bedchamber was furnished with a narrow bed and basic essentials to meet Ali's requirements for comfort and cleanliness. Within that tiny niche, Synnovea pushed open the windows to let in the cooling evening breezes and then folded down the linens on the cot. Intent upon the maid's comfort and full recovery, she bade the maid to rest until it was time for the servants to eat. After blowing out the tapers, she withdrew and closed the door quietly behind her.

The main bedchamber was spacious and comfortably furnished with a chaise, several large chests, and a canopied bed draped with gold silk panels. A heavily decorated porcelain stove stood in a favorable spot where it would provide heat for both rooms during the winter. In all, the room was fit for royalty, yet at the moment, Synnovea felt much like an impoverished orphan within its opulence. Simple truth, she'd have been much happier at home, living well away from the Taraslovs.

Privately ensconced at last behind closed doors, Synnovea washed thoroughly and then wrapped a long robe about her naked body before snuffing out the candles. The chaise was inviting, and she collapsed in pure exhaustion upon its cushions. Though she needed solace and rest from the ordeal of her meeting with Anna, sleep seemed as evasive as the legendary firebird that Tsar Ivan had purportedly searched for in a Russian fable. Her mind wandered far afield, lingering for a time on the servants whom she had left to tend her home and the myriad questions they had presented about her expected return, which, sadly, had been beyond her ability to answer.

In greater detail Synnovea mulled over the qualms she had battled after receiving the tsar's message. Anna was his cousin and touted to be his favorite, though some close to the monarch had offered the theory that the princess had been the one to exaggerate their fondness for each other since their contact in past years had been, at best, distant. Anna had just recently moved to Moscow from the small province wherein she had grown up. Mikhail, on the other hand, had been sequestered for most of his life in a monastery where, as a child, he had been taken by his mother. Throughout his youth it had been a safe haven from the dark plots, schemes, and intrigue of ambitious boyars. Considering the fact that they hadn't spent much time together over the years, the deep regard the cousins supposedly shared for one another didn't seem likely.

No, their relationship really didn't bother Synnovea as much as Anna's aversion to Natasha. With the princess's most recent insinuations roiling in retrospect through her mind, Synnovea was hard-pressed to think kindly of her hostess. Indeed, if Anna continued to express her animosity toward Natasha, a sharp wedge would likely be driven between them, and they'd be ever at odds.

Curling up on her side, Synnovea stuffed the pillows beneath her head as she probed the possible causes for Anna's intense dislike. Natasha had socialized with affluent boyars for many years now, having gained a substantial number of friends over the course of three marriages, but Anna stubbornly refused to recognize her as a person of any import. Earlier in the year Natasha had reproved Ivan Voronsky for his gauche manners in insulting one of her guests and had kindly advised him to be more considerate in the future. Having witnessed his overt contempt for anyone who wasn't immediately appreciative of his every thought and deed, Synnovea could imagine the scope of his complaints to anyone who would lend him a sympathetic ear. The princess certainly seemed a gullible candidate.

As for Prince Aleksei, it was widely rumored that he had a roaming eye that was wont to wander to maidens much younger than his wife. For years, the blame of a barren womb had been laid upon Anna, but of late, gossips were more apt to surmise the judgment against the princess had been unfair, since it was believed that Prince Aleksei was scattering his seed among a whole battery of young women whose reputations had never been publicly compromised. When the tsar had issued his decree, Synnovea had found such hearsay disturbing, for she had had no way of knowing what she'd encounter under the Taraslov roof. It was one thing to vie with

Anna, but quite another to be ravished by the woman's lecherous husband.

Sleep finally lent peace to Synnovea's troubled mind, but alas, it was only a brief respite. She came awake in slow degrees, her mind roaming in a detached search for the cause of her disturbance. She couldn't remember hearing anything, yet she was inundated with a feeling that something wasn't quite right in her universe.

From beneath sluggish lids, the jade-brown eyes wandered in a drowsy inspection of the ceiling. A shaft of light stretched across it, reaching to the far wall to her right. Languidly Synnovea lifted a hand to the luminous ray and thought it strange that only the tips of her fingers caught the glow, and they, in turn, were cast in similar shape against the wall above a dark configuration that looked very much like the head and shoulders of a man.

The shadow moved, and with a gasp Synnovea sat upright in sudden alarm, realizing this was no figment of her imagination. She swung about to face the door from whence the light was flowing and saw to her surprise that it had been pushed open. A tall man stood silhouetted against the candlelight filling the hallway, but as her gaze fell on him, the intruder moved beyond the doorway to the left and, with muffled tread, disappeared from sight.

Synnovea glanced down at herself and realized that her silken robe had fallen open to reveal a goodly length of thigh and the upper curves of her bosom. Her cheeks fairly flamed with indignation as she snatched the silken robe closed and leapt from the chaise. By the time she reached the door, not even the shuffle of footfalls could be detected. Squat tapers burned in several sconces located along the corridor, dispelling any shadows that might have invited one to lurk there. Across the hallway, a door stood ajar, opening into a room that was as dark as the night outside.

A wary prickling crawled upward along Synnovea's nape.

If the man was waiting there, expecting her to follow, it seemed advisable for her to stay behind a locked door where she'd be safe. Retreating, she pushed the heavy portal closed and slid the bar home noisily, forbidding any further intrusion by Prince Aleksei Taraslov, a most notorious debaucher of women!

4

*S*ynnovea carefully debated her alternatives. As much as she considered prostrating herself before Tsar Mikhail and begging him to release her from this prison he had inadvertently created for her, it wouldn't be wise to do so. She'd only expose herself to harsh criticisms, if not from him, then surely from the Taraslovs, who'd be outraged by her suppositions. They'd naturally resent any grievances that would make them seem less than worthy of the tsar's trust. And who could predict what they might say or do to save face? They could twist her petitions to their liking, possibly causing severe judgments to be leveled against her. Very simply, she could be maligned as ungrateful and hopelessly self-willed. It was therefore crucial that she hold her peace and endure whatever hardships might arise until she could think of a more judicious way of gaining her freedom.

The traditional garments of a Russian maiden would defi-

nitely be the best choice to wear on her first evening at the
Taraslovs, Synnovea decided. Not only did she hope to guard
against Aleksei's rudely prying eyes by wearing such garb, but
she deemed it wise not to test Anna's tolerance. Over a ribbon-
trimmed underskirt and a shirtwaist fashioned with full, bil-
lowy sleeves, she donned a *sarafan* of rich ruby satin elabo-
rately stitched with threads of silk. Upon this embroidery, an
ornate overlay of gilded threads had been sewn to enrich the
artistry of the piece, copying the pattern of tiny flowers that
embellished the blouse. Low-heeled slippers of ruby-red, bedecked with the same needlework, were also adorned with
soles that formed wedges of gold. Her long, lustrous black
hair had been intertwined with ribbons and woven into the
customary single braid for unwed maids. Upon her head, she
settled a rounded *kokoshniki,* formed in the shape of a cres-
cent. Tiny jewels and beads of gold and red shimmered amid
the elaborate needlework. Lastly she fastened on earrings of
finely worked gold filigree adorned with delicate clusters of
rubies.

When the last bow was tied, the final clasp fastened, Synnovea assessed the results in a long, silvered looking-glass, a
luxury she also enjoyed while at home and was grateful to
find here. At least, in furnishing the guest chambers, Anna
had been keenly aware of what would please her guests, even
if she hadn't had the present one in mind at the time. Boyars
never knew when they would be entertaining or housing
important visitors. In short, it was far better to be prepared
than embarrassed.

It had been far from Synnovea's intent to achieve such a
stunning radiance that she'd actually complicate her dilemma.
Yet when she joined the Taraslovs and Ivan in the parlor
downstairs, the sly, seductive narrowing of Aleksei's eyes and
the ebullient smile curving his generous lips readily summoned forth an impression of a snake slyly perusing a bird,
clearly for the purpose of devouring it. Synnovea's quick

glance toward Anna caught a sharp frown being subdued behind a stiffly fixed visage and a forced smile of greeting. No words parted the princess's grimacing lips. The prince, however, proved more vocal.

"My dear Countess Synnovea," he murmured warmly, stepping forward to cradle her hand within the slender length of his. Garbed in a royal blue kaftan bedecked with elaborate embroidery, Aleksei looked like some bronze-skinned sheik from the deserts of Arabia. His warm brown eyes glowed with provocative fervor as they held her gaze in a commanding vise. Beneath a carefully groomed mustache, his red lips widened into a sultry smile. "I had nigh forgotten how lovely you are, my dear. You're as enchanting as an elegant swan."

A barrage of accusations tempted Synnovea's tongue, and though her eyes chilled briefly to indicate her displeasure with his unabashed invasion of her privacy, she held her silence. Still, she was not above purloining some subtle revenge. Deftly she slipped her hand from his, forbidding him the opportunity to kiss the pale fingers, and opened a bejeweled fan between them. Cleverly she denied his compliments as well, aware that Anna was regarding them with icy shards of enmity glittering in her eyes. As the recipient of that chilling glower, Synnovea understood clearly what it felt like to be loathed by another woman.

"I'm humbled by such words of charity, Prince Aleksei." She feigned a doleful look of regret. "Though sweet succor to my ears, I fear your kindness is exceeded only by your pity for me."

Her gentle scolding brought a smile of amiable humor to Aleksei's sensual lips. While he recognized the vexation in her distant manner, it served to whet his appetite all the more. He was intrigued by her spirit, for he had often derived ecstatic pleasure in making conquests among the most reluctant virgins and noting their subsequent compliance to his every whim. Because of the accessibility of her tremendous beauty, this particular maiden promised to be exceptionally sweet provender upon whom his ravenous lusts could be indulged. Her grace and charm would lend great satisfaction to the tryst, at least more than any in which he had recently indulged.

The prince met Synnovea's aloof stare while his own smoldering gaze promised a fervent seduction. He was confident of achieving his goal. What woman could long resist his amorous attentions and hawkish good looks? His black hair, streaked with gray at the temples, and his warm, swarthy complexion enhanced his handsome features and accentuated his appeal despite a total of twoscore and three years behind him. As he leaned toward Synnovea, his husky whisper conveyed an unfaltering boldness. "Are you really so innocent of your marvelous beauty and its effect on men, my dear?"

"Kind sir, pity me and desist of such flattery before you turn my head," Synnovea begged coolly, recognizing the challenge twinkling in his darkly shining eyes.

"Flattery?" He laughed in warm amusement. "Oh, nay! I fear it's infatuation, pure and simple, that makes me speak as I do."

Feeling decidedly threatened by his temerity, Synnovea lifted the fan higher to flick it in irritation before her hotly burning cheeks. She could understand more accurately now why Aleksei's reputation had preceded him. He applied his beguiling enticements with the crafty art of a true philanderer and boldly advanced his exploits with unmitigated verve. He didn't seem the least bit inhibited by his wife's presence. Indeed, he was brazenly forward, showing little regard for her feelings, while he forced their guest to strike down his overtures and parry his comments in such a way as to hopefully deflect the sharp blade of Anna's resentment.

Synnovea was adamant in her resolve not to fall victim to his lascivious gambits. Nor would she, for even a moment, allow him to entertain the idea that she would become another willing plaything. Circumventing his ploy, she deliberately drew Anna into the contest. "No need to extend your mercy to the extreme, my lord. I can see quite clearly the high degree of beauty by which I must be judged and am quite resolved to endure the shortcomings of this poor flask that you see before you, knowing it's far beyond my ability to hold a candle to Princess Anna who would shame the very sun with her radiance."

Aleksei drew back to stare at his glowering wife with a jaundiced eye and managed a brief twitch of a smile. "Why, of course," he replied with a dearth of enthusiasm and then allowed himself to be more magnanimous. "I suppose it's like the gem that's too close at hand."

"Sometimes," Anna interjected in glacial tones, barely moving her tensed lips, "the rare jewel is overlooked when a more colorful yet far less worthy bauble attracts the eye."

Ivan came forward from the windows, where he had been all but obscured by shadows, and gave Synnovea a lengthy scrutiny which by no means was intended as a compliment. "I'm greatly heartened, Countess, that you've finally regarded the garments of your homeland suitable to don. I was sure you were averse to wearing them."

"On the contrary," Synnovea replied, forcing a smile. "I simply had no desire to see such treasures ruined by the journey."

"But surely you have less extravagant *sarafans* that you could've worn while traveling," Ivan argued, reveling in the disapproval that Anna had already demonstrated toward the girl. To exact revenge at every turn of the hand while remaining a saint in the eyes of the princess was a temptation he couldn't resist. "Now tell us true, my lady, was your goal to look your prettiest for your escort?"

His question awakened a nettling irritation within her. "You imagine too much, Ivan."

Aleksei interceded on her behalf, fully aware of the hostility to which she had fallen prey. He disregarded as irrelevant the fact that his wayward propensities were primarily to blame for his wife's animosity. For the most part, he ignored Anna's temper tantrums and visited her bed only when no other distractions were conveniently at hand or when he wanted to maneuver her opinions on certain matters. Like most women, she found it hard to resist his lustful bent, but her penchant for nagging usually drove him off in frantic pursuit of unexplored territories. "Synnovea is fortunate to be so well traveled, and as she has clearly demonstrated, she has become well versed in both cultures and is just as comfortable in our *sarafans* as in those horrible, stiff English ruffs." He turned to Synnovea. "I do applaud your diversity, my dear. You're clearly young enough to be pliable to a variety of changes."

Anna gritted her teeth in a badly feigned smile as her husband met her glare with a purposefully dull gaze. His dark brow lifted tauntingly, deepening her resentment until she promised herself that if he didn't escape the manse, as was his habit at late hours, she'd take him to task for blatantly flaunting the youth of their ward in her face.

Boris entered the room to announce that a *zakuski* had been laid out in the dining room in honor of the guests. As the servant withdrew, Anna faced Ivan and Synnovea. "You both must be thoroughly exhausted after your recent encounter with that band of thieves." She ignored Aleksei's start of surprise and continued with her carefully delivered ruse of concern. She was anxious to air her displeasure with her husband in the privacy of her chambers and made the necessary excuses for their guests' speedy withdrawal. "I shall endeavor to remember your great weariness and not delay you overlong with my chattering. But for now, a little wine and a few delicious morsels will help assuage your hunger."

Anna led the way into the dining hall, but not without directing a warning glower over her shoulder as Aleksei fell in behind Synnovea. The princess was aware that from that angle he could appease himself with a closely attentive perusal of their young ward, a practice he had long employed with every beautiful young woman who had come into their home.

The Taraslovs and their guests came together around the food-laden buffet to partake of the caviar, sardines, *balyk,* ham, and other delectable selections often served prior to the main meal whenever visitors were present. In making his own way to the sideboard, Aleksei deliberately passed near the girl to sample the elusive fragrance of English violets that drifted from her before he deigned to join his wife. Boris laid out an intricately woven bread basket filled with slices of freshly baked *khlebny* and poured a lemon-flavored vodka for the men and a milder, wild-black-cherry *Chereunikyna* for the ladies.

Aleksei accepted the piece of bread that Anna had spread with a generous portion of caviar before stepping back with his libation and directing a question to their new charge. "What is this that I hear about thieves, Synnovea? Am I to believe you were accosted by renegades on your journey here?"

Synnovea had actually opened her mouth to explain when Anna interrupted with her own version. In good manner the younger woman could do naught but close her mouth and listen.

"A ghastly tale of murder and mayhem." The princess shook her head almost sorrowfully as a long, dismal sigh slipped from her. "Poor Ivan was fortunate to escape with his life. And dear Synnovea—why, it's inappropriate for me to say what that wretched man claimed from her after he seized her and rode off into the forest. . . ."

Synnovea gaped at the woman, feeling thoroughly victimized by her suggestive remark. The coy smile that came upon Anna's lips and the hard flint in the gray eyes openly conveyed the injury she had meant to reap with her insinuations. Her motives seemed simple enough to her young guest. Beyond a mere ruse to cause her undue shame, the woman obviously meant to frustrate her husband's hopes of adding yet another virgin to his collection. Synnovea didn't mind that at all, but she certainly resented her honor being besmirched.

Aleksei was clearly taken aback. "What's this? Synnovea, dear child, were you offended by those ruffians?"

Synnovea tossed a covert glower toward Ivan who was no doubt to blame for spawning this latest infraction. "I fear the tale has been much enlivened by hearsay, my lord. There's no need for alarm. I was saved from ravishment by the timely appearance of an officer of Tsar Mikhail's Hussars. Were Colonel Rycroft here, I'm sure he'd attest to my claims, which he'll likely have to do in a report to his superior."

Aleksei relaxed enough to smile. Though a self-proclaimed gallant, he had always prided himself in the care he took to avoid those grim maladies associated with indiscriminately lewd activities. His own father had suffered many ills and woes stemming from the disease until finally, amid excruciating agony and frenzied hallucinations, the man had ended his own life. Even to this day, Aleksei was haunted by the memory of that wild-eyed, slavering being slicing his own throat. Nearly overwhelmed as a young man by the horror of that ghastly sight, he had vowed that he would never let himself fall prey to that kind of dark pestilence. It was exceedingly more gratifying to mount the tender, pristine thighs of a virgin and, for a time, dally with her until he grew bored enough to seek entertainment elsewhere.

"And this colonel?" Aleksei directed his attention to his beautiful guest. "He was perhaps the one who escorted you here?"

"Captain Nekrasov was appointed that particular duty by His Majesty. The one who actually came to my deliverance is an Englishman in service to the tsar. He was on practice maneuvers in the area when he and his men happened upon my halted carriage and put the thieves to rout."

"How can a foreigner claim the rank of colonel in Russia?" Anna asked caustically.

Synnovea felt her neck prickle as she took umbrage at the princess's obvious disdain. "I would assume that Colonel Rycroft had already acquired that rank before entering the tsar's service."

"But he's an Englishman!" the woman exclaimed, unwilling to dismiss that fact. "What is my cousin thinking of to incorporate an Englishman in his troops? Or is this more of his father's doings? Patriarch Filaret will have us all killed in our beds by bringing foreign mercenaries into the city!"

"My dear, how can you speak of the good patriarch like that?" Aleksei mocked with a slanted smile.

"Ivan can tell you! Filaret has assumed the powers of the tsar through his son. His ambitions have asserted themselves beyond the duties of patriarch. Indeed! He'd be sitting on the throne today in place of his son if not for the fact that Boris Godunov forced him to become a monk to save his own tsardom."

Aleksei scowled darkly at the cleric, who conveniently addressed his attention to the food. "Such talk is dangerous, Anna, and you know as well as I do that His Majesty has no real interest in ruling Russia without his father's counsel. His negotiations for peace with Poland not only gained an armistice but obtained the release of Filaret. True, the treaty cost us a number of Russian towns and cities, yet it has gained us a far more valuable asset. Patriarch Filaret Nikitich has the wisdom to make the right decision for our country. If he has brought foreigners here to secure our peace and train our troops, I can find no fault against the man for wanting to strengthen our capabilities and defense. They need to be!"

"What are you saying, Aleksei?" Anna asked, amazed that her husband could lightly accept such a notion. "Colonel Rycroft is an Englishman!"

Synnovea rallied to the colonel's defense, not entirely sure why she should feel so offended in his behalf, except that she was half English herself and felt a deep loyalty to the memory of her mother, who had been far more gracious than Anna Taraslovna could ever hope to be. "That rogue Ladislaus made light of the abilities of the tsar's men until Colonel Rycroft confronted his pack of wolves. Then the thief had to lament the loss of those brought down by the Englishman's sword. I, for one, am most appreciative of the colonel and his skill as a soldier. I wouldn't be here this very moment enjoying the safety of your house if not for him."

Anna mentally sneered at her guest's input. "I can understand why you'd be grateful for such a one. After all, your mother was English, but other *boyarinas* are more discriminating than to value the presence of a foreigner." Her mouth curved in a derisive smile as she offered a conjecture. "No doubt you found the colonel attractive."

"Not particularly," Synnovea replied stiltedly, somewhat miffed that Anna could suggest that her feelings of gratitude had been inspired merely by the looks of a man. But then, such an idea had likely been spawned by Ivan's claim that she had garbed herself for the sole purpose of attracting male attention. "In truth, Captain Nckrasov is much more pleasing in appearance, though not quite as daring with a sword. I certainly valued the captain's attendance, but after his wounding, he was allowed no opportunity to save me."

"Such a rescue must be construed as fortuitous unless by chance there was a weightier hand guiding events," Anna rejoined in haughty aloofness. "It was indeed fortunate that Colonel Rycroft happened to be near enough to come to your aid. Perhaps he was only waiting there to advance your appreciation of his exploits."

"Considering the danger the Englishman was in, I find no evidence to support your insinuation that he might have arranged the attack for his own gain," Synnovea countered with uncompromising fervor. " 'Tis simply inconceivable. He very nearly laid down the highest price a man could pay for my deliverance and, in the process, killed many of Ladislaus's men. I, for one, am deeply grateful for having escaped the brigands and am equally relieved that Colonel Rycroft came through it alive as well."

Anna bestowed her regard upon Ivan, who was cramming a caviar-stuffed pancake into his mouth with such greed that one had to wonder if he intended to embark upon a long fast on the morrow. "Was that the way you perceived it, good Voronsky?"

The beady eyes flicked upward in surprise and momentarily fastened on the princess. Realizing an answer was expected, Ivan worked his lean jaw vigorously to dispense with the food. He swallowed hard and promptly washed the mass down with an ample swig of vodka before he cast a glance toward Synnovea and found himself the object of her curiosity. Wiping the back of his hand across his mouth, he cleared his throat and spoke for once in agreement with her, knowing she could name him a liar if he dared dispute her words. " 'Tis much as the countess has said." He noticed a spark of irritation in the silver eyes and hastened to mollify his hostess. "Though it's impossible for me to clearly discern what was in the heart of the Englishman at the time. He was rather brutal in his assault on the thieves."

Synnovea was incredulous. "Sir, are you suggesting that Colonel Rycroft should have treated them like errant children and slapped their wrists or perhaps waited to launch his attack until they had actually killed one of us? Thieving bands rarely show compassion for their victims. They seize and slay, whether a man be noble or common born. I say that we're lucky to have escaped alive! And as for that, I'm sure you have cause to remember Petrov threatening you with dire consequences unless you gave him more coins to appease his greed."

Seeing his chance to extract a greater measure of concern

from his benefactress, Ivan validated her claim. "And quite violently so. The oaf would have thought nothing of taking my life."

Aleksei considered the scholar with a slyly malevolent smile. "I see no scars from your encounter, Ivan. Indeed, you seem in rare good health and of superior appetite. I daresay we shall be enjoying your company for many a meal yet."

A deep blush stained Ivan's pockmarked face as he felt the sting of the man's sarcasm. The prince was immensely fond of casting aspersions upon his poor frame, perhaps because they were both cognizant of the one from whom he garnered protection. Being favored by the princess certainly had its reward. Her presence guaranteed Ivan impunity from physical aggression, which allowed him to enjoy a prideful arrogance. He was not above flaunting his position over the prince or even needling him about it now and then. Actually, the idea seemed quite appealing at the moment. "As it stands now, my lord, you'll be seeing more of me for some time to come."

"Oh?" Aleksei's dark brows jutted sharply upward as he awaited the cleric's explanation.

"The princess has wisely prescribed a daily tutoring of your new charge."

"What?" The single word came unbidden from Synnovea's lips, and she turned to stare aghast at Anna, unnerved by Ivan's announcement. "You don't mean to say that you've engaged this . . . this . . ."

"Synnovea!" Anna snapped sharply, halting the insults that threatened to rush forth from the astonished woman. "Remember your place!"

Synnovea drew herself up in rigid silence, daring no further utterance while she bristled in outrage, but her mind ranged far afield, already searching for some avenue of escape. Coping with Ivan on a diurnal basis was not a situation she was capable of enduring. Their journey to Moscow had convinced her of that!

Anna smiled at the younger woman, demonstrating a cool reserve that bordered on frigidity. "The fact that you've been sent to me for instruction will eventually lead to your advantage, Synnovea. You were indubitably coddled by your father and allowed to nurture unpleasant tendencies. That will cease, of course. I'll not tolerate boorish manners . . . or an argumentative disposition. If you're wise, my dear, you'll learn to curb those inclinations. Do you understand?"

It was readily apparent to Synnovea that any objections she offered would be considered of a quarrelsome nature. Being thus warned against speaking her mind, she held her tongue, yet inwardly she still stewed.

Ivan's pleased smirk evidenced his own satisfaction with what he considered a well-deserved subjugation of the countess. He was not above heaping burning coals upon the hapless victim. "You may trust that my directions will be thorough, Princess. I'll address myself with careful diligence to polishing your ward's manners."

Aleksei seemed immensely pained by such a prospect. "Surely this is some kind of jest, Anna. Synnovea has no need of more tutoring. She has been enlightened by some of the best scholars in the country. You can't possibly mean to prolong this arduous climb to knowledge."

"The girl needs instruction in the rigors of life and conventional decorums," Anna stated obstinately, daring anyone to challenge her decision.

"Damned nuisance, if you ask me!" her husband retorted. Slamming down his glass, he turned with a harsh scowl and, offering no excuse or explanation, stalked to the pair of doors leading into the hall and threw them open.

"Where are you going?" Anna demanded, sensing that she was about to be denied his company for yet another evening.

"OUT!" Prince Aleksei flung back over his shoulder. Halt-

ing in the hall, he braced his arms akimbo and bellowed at the top of his lungs. *"BORIS!"*

Rushing footsteps were heard in the hush that followed the master's summons. A moment later, the white-haired steward breathlessly made an appearance. "Here I am, Your Highness."

Facing the man, Aleksei continued in a lower commanding tone. "Hie yourself out to the stable and tell Orlov to ready my *drozhki* with my fastest horses. I'll be going out this evening."

"Immediately, sir?"

"Would I urge you to make haste if I had the patience to wait for our guests to dine?" Aleksei barked sharply. "Of course I mean immediately!"

"As you wish, sir."

Synnovea lifted her gaze to find Anna staring rigidly toward the place where, only a moment ago, her husband had stood. The typically pale cheeks were now imbued with a vibrant shade of red, and except for a small tick at the corner of her mouth, she appeared to have taken on the quality of stone.

Ivan dared no further comment, and the meal was soon entered into and stoically endured. Synnovea was completely distraught over the idea of Ivan becoming her tutor, and though under normal circumstances she would have savored each course, the roasted grouse with its cranberry sauce seemed as tasteless to her as the flaky pastry stuffed with steamed vegetables and dressed with a light sauce. Ivan was profuse with his compliments to the cook and devoured every morsel with gusto, totally amazing Synnovea. His slight frame seemed much too frail to handle the amount he consumed, and she could only wonder how he accomplished such a feat without bursting open.

When the meal came thankfully to an end, the two guests retreated to their respective chambers. Anna was left to make her own way to a suite of rooms she shared far too infrequently with Aleksei. Even their arguments were more tolerable than the loneliness that greeted her and the wild imaginings of her mind that placed her husband in the arms of another woman.

The night proved as wearisome for Synnovea as the journey she had just endured. She found nothing within the stuffy shadows of her bedchamber to assuage her apprehensions, for she could foresee only doom descending upon her in the days and weeks ahead. How in the world would she be able to maintain a quiet, gentle manner under such conditions? She'd be defeated before she even began, for if there was one thing that Ivan seemed proficient at, it was provoking her temper.

Synnovea tossed restlessly upon her bed, unable to sleep while her mind raged on in a state of turmoil. It was only when her thoughts drifted unbidden to Colonel Rycroft and the moment wherein he had held her close against his sleek, manly body that she was strangely lulled into a peaceful slumber.

The heat of the night was oppressive, holding the land in a stagnant vise until the morning sun lifted its burning face above the horizon and unleashed its sweltering rays far beyond the vales and hillocks that surrounded the city. Even at an early hour, the dusty roads seemed to shimmer in undulating waves beneath the full light of the heavenly fireball. Those who could, took shelter where they could find it, whether in grand houses or beneath lackluster trees that struggled for survival.

Oblivious to the insidious warmth creeping through the house, Ali arose from her tiny cot, much refreshed after a lengthy night's sleep. She busied herself in the narrow room, bathing, dressing, and unpacking her belongings until sounds of movement finally came from the larger chamber. With a quick knock and a cheery smile, she bustled into the adjoining room, but halted in sharp surprise as she espied her mistress sitting in bed with an elbow braced upon a knee, staring listlessly across the room. Her mistress's solemn countenance hinted of a troubled spirit, and Ali gently laid a consoling hand upon the slender arm, thinking she understood the reason for the countess's dismay. "Ah, me lamb, be ye mournin' again for yer pa?"

Though Synnovea braved a smile, the sparkle of tears in her eyes readily evidenced her pensive mood. Wistfully she sighed. "If I had been wise, Ali, I would've eagerly sought marriage while Papa was still alive. Then I wouldn't be here now, contending with the dictates of strangers."

Ali hadn't been with her mistress all these many years without learning to keenly perceive the young woman's moods. Something dire had happened. "Me lamb, have the Taraslovs been unkind ta ye?"

Synnovea dared not reveal the full extent of her concerns. The maid was too loyal to keep still about a lecher spying on her. Nor would Ali take kindly to Ivan being engaged as her tutor, but that fact couldn't be hidden like the other, for it was about to become part of her daily routine.

"I was in error, Ali, when I thought we'd soon be parted from Ivan." Synnovea saw the servant's brows lift sharply in suspicion, and with a small shrug, she added, "He's to instruct me while I'm here. Anna has declared it so."

"Ye don't say!" The diminutive woman settled her fists firmly on her narrow hips and snorted in contempt. "An' what would the li'l weasel be teachin' ye, pray tell? How ta hide from yer left hand what yer right one be doin'? Aaarrgghh!" She shook her head in acute disgust. "I've had a bad feelin' in me bones 'bout that warty li'l toad since he first hopped onta yer stoop."

"Nevertheless, Ali, we must keep silent about his faults lest we antagonize the princess. I fear she dotes upon the man." A darkly winged brow was raised in question as Synnovea met the tiny woman's gaze. "Do you understand?"

"Aye, that I do, me lovely. Still, if the Princess Anna is imposin' his teachin' on ye, what must she be thinkin' herself? He's not so hard ta see through if'n a body be carin' ta take a close look. Ta be sure, if *he's* a man o' God, then *I'm* the butcher's uncle. Makes me wonder if the princess has all her wits 'bout her."

"Perhaps we'll understand in time what Anna sees in him. Until then, give her no cause to take us to task. I've a feeling she's well acquainted with devising punishments for actions she considers offensive. As for me, I must keep my own wits about me and refrain from angering Ivan overmuch." A long moment passed before the corners of Synnovea's lips lifted puckishly and a mischievous gleam brightened her eyes. She arched a meaningful brow toward the servant. "Still, I might plead a few days' rest before my studies begin."

Catching her intent, Ali responded with a gleeful cackle. "Ta be sure, me lovely! Ye're deservin' o' that much, what wit' travelin' from Nizhni Novgorod in such a dither an' bein' attacked by thieves ta boot! Why, 'tis a wonder ye've lasted this long wit'out faintin' clean away."

And so the two plotted to confound the schemes of Princess Anna, at least for the day. When assured that the household was up and moving about, Synnovea sent the Irish maid down to convey the message that she was temporarily indisposed with a painful headache and would be unable to address her attention to Ivan's instructions. It was certainly no lie Synnovea had concocted, for every time she thought of being forced to study the scholar's views, she suffered a deep revulsion and her head began to throb.

Anna had to accept the excuse or confront Synnovea openly and accuse her of falsehood. Though tempted to march up to her new charge's chambers and express her suspicions, upon further consideration Anna decided to bide her time to see what the girl's manner would be on the morrow. It would indeed be a miracle if the girl managed to tolerate her chambers the whole day long.

Ensconced upstairs, Synnovea remained oblivious to just how narrowly she had escaped Anna's interrogation. By midafternoon, however, she had started questioning her own wisdom in avoiding Ivan's lectures. She couldn't be entirely certain if someone with a vicious bent had deliberately planned her torture or if the location of her rooms had never been considered, but Synnovea soon became convinced that there wasn't another chamber in the whole manse as unbearable as her own. Situated on the west side of the house, the rooms became a sweltering oven soon after the daystar reached its zenith.

In determining her alternatives, Synnovea realized there was none she cared to exercise. She couldn't escape from her chambers without drawing some inquiry or challenging remark from Anna, and she refused to give the woman that satisfaction. Thus, in an effort to cope with the heat, she lounged about in a thin shift that soon became a transparent film over her perspiring skin.

Ali closed the heavy draperies on the west side to shade the chambers and pushed the windows wide on the front of the house, allowing the sultry breezes to flow through the room. Still, the cruel flaming tongues of the summer sun proved unrelenting, and Synnovea sweltered in the heat. Seeking a way to combat her mistress's distress, the maid went down to the kitchen and asked Elisaveta's permission to fetch ice from the supply stored in the cellar. She brought back a large chunk to the upper rooms and, after breaking it into smaller pieces, wrapped them in a linen towel.

Synnovea heaved a grateful sigh as she rubbed the cooling towel over her bare skin, leaving refreshing wet trails in its wake, but as the afternoon wore on, she found herself unable to bear the stuffiness of her compartment and went to perch cross-legged on a windowsill shaded and protected from the street by a large tree growing at the front of the house. There she lazily stroked the ice-filled cloth along her arms as she observed the comings and goings of passersby who seemed urgently intent upon completing their errands and finding shade. Too disturbed by their own discomfort to concern themselves with another's obscure presence, those who ventured forth quickly retreated from sight, leaving the broiling thoroughfare virtually empty.

Synnovea draped the ice-laden towel around her neck and leaned her head back against the window frame. Closing her eyes, she allowed her thoughts to roam homeward. Her musings helped to assuage her loneliness and seemed so real at times she could almost smell the breezes that wafted from the rivers near Nizhni Novgorod. She recalled the numerous times her father had ridden up the lane to their home, and even fancied that she could hear the slow clip-clop of his horse's hooves and the familiar creak of a leather saddle which, during the summer months, had always accompanied his dismounting at the front of their house. Although her recollections were stirringly detailed, they were flawed to some extent. It was the custom of Russian gentlemen to bedeck their mounts with silver bells, necklets, and wealthy trappings, which allowed their approach to be heard from some distance away. Yet in spite of her desire to vividly recall her memories, Synnovea couldn't quite convince herself that she could hear the soft tinkling of tiny bells.

The muted click of booted heels on a stone walk caused Synnovea some perplexity as she continued to reminisce. It was clearly not the stride she had come to recognize as her father's. Opening her eyes and tilting her head aslant, she scanned both ends of the thoroughfare. The street was devoid of travelers, but when she shifted her gaze nearer the Taraslov manse, she saw a tall man striding up the path toward the front portal. His footfalls were unmistakably the ones that had confounded her.

The visitor's wide-brimmed hat prevented a clear view of the stranger's face, but she immediately recognized the proud bearing and crisp, purposeful stride of a military officer. This particular fellow was outfitted in the mode of a foreign cavalryman, though that fact puzzled her, for she couldn't feature Anna allowing a European to visit her domain unless by royal decree. Neither could Synnovea imagine Captain Nekrasov or anyone of similar reserve wearing anything but Russian garb. A sword had been strapped over the visitor's trunk hose of deepest brown. Beneath them he wore lighter-hued canions, over which long boots had been pulled up to his thighs. Compared to the skirted kaftans boyars wore and the long tunics and wide-legged pantaloons of Russian soldiers, such close-fitting hosiery and breeches seemed almost shameless. Yet the man had the length of leg and narrowness of hip to complement the garments as perhaps few could. His shirt gleamed dazzling white beneath the sun. A wide collar lay open over his leather doublet, and was trimmed with lace as were the turn-backed cuffs. In all, the man's manner of dress was more reminiscent of an English cavalier . . . .

Synnovea smothered a gasp of dismay as it came to her just who the man might be. Cautiously she leaned outward to peer through the lower branches of the tree and almost gasped when her worst suspicions were confirmed. There, tethered to a hitching post near the entrance to the drive, was an animal that had been forever forged in her memory. Her wild ride through the forest on the back of the headstrong stallion had left such a lasting impression that she had no doubt that she'd be fearful of approaching another steed for some time to come. Once the pride of Ladislaus, the black horse now glistened from the care and attention of his present owner.

Worrisome doubts cast the darkest veil of mistrust upon Colonel Rycroft's reasons for paying a visit to the Taraslovs. In rising panic Synnovea could imagine him deliberating seeking revenge because she had left him without granting him permission to court her. If he meant to cause her shame, then he'd surely tell all to Anna, who would then hasten to her cousin with the complaint. No predicting what would follow.

Or was she being too skeptical of Colonel Rycroft's motives and not giving him a chance to prove himself a gentleman? After all, he had been in a position to take her by force and had held himself in restraint. It seemed rather silly to fly into a state of hysteria or to burrow down into a hole like a fearful mole just because the Englishman had been bold enough to come to the manse.

Her pummeling fears eased to a more tolerable level as Synnovea made an earnest effort to subdue them. Deliberately turning aside her doubts, she had to admit, if only to herself, that when she had been all but wallowing in the tedium and despair of her predicament, the officer's presence offered a more promising diversion from the boredom of her confinement than she had hitherto hoped to find.

Though proper decorum demanded that a young maid squelch any show of pleasure over a strange man's visit and to regard such a one with stilted aloofness, Synnovea leaned back with a smile, luxuriating in her freedom to enjoy a few delights in the secrecy of her mind. She found it especially stimulating to peruse the colonel at her leisure. Having admired the memory of him in the altogether, she now let her gaze glide over him with meticulous care, unaware that her eyes gradually took on a warming glow. It truly seemed a waste of his extraordinary physique that the man wasn't more handsome. His long, muscular thighs accepted the sleek, glovelike fit of the boots with ease, but then, having gained firsthand knowledge of the perfection of their length, she was hardly surprised. The short trunk hose were narrow enough to be suggestive and no less arresting to an innocent maid. An abashed giggle escaped Synnovea as she became aware of the source of her curiosity, but she quickly squelched her amusement when she realized that Ali might be near. With a dismayed grimace, she cast a wary glance askance to see if the maid had been there to witness her response. Much to her relief, she found that the chambers were empty save for herself.

The front door was pulled open, and Synnovea leaned outward as much as she safely dared, anxious to learn what matter had brought the Englishman to the Taraslov manse. She dearly hoped he wouldn't disappoint her by proving himself a cad.

"Dohbriy dyehn," he greeted, tucking his hat beneath his arm. *"Pazhahlusta."* After the polite plea, he carefully pronounced the syllables "Goh-voh-reet-yeh lee vwee poh-ahn-GLEE-skee?"

Synnovea cringed at his effort to question the steward's ability to understand English. As was to be expected, there followed a long pause. Boris, who spoke no English, had no doubt gone to fetch his mistress, who could.

"May I be of assistance to you, sir?" Anna inquired upon her arrival at the front portal.

Colonel Rycroft swept his hat off in a gracious bow. "Princess Taraslovna, I presume?"

"I am she. What is it that you want?"

"A favor, if you would be so kind," the colonel answered and then, with a soft chuckle, offered an apology. "I haven't been in your country very long, and my Russian is poor and laborious to the point that I fear I confused your butler. Forgive my intrusion, but I am Colonel Rycroft, Commander of the Third Regiment of His Majesty's Imperial Hussars. I was fortunate enough to be of service to the Countess Zenkovna on her way to Moscow, and I was wondering if I might be permitted to speak with her for a few moments."

"I'm afraid that will be impossible, Colonel," Anna replied stiffly. "You see, the Countess Zenkovna isn't feeling well enough to receive visitors today. She has retired to her chambers, and only her maid has been allowed to see her."

"Then perhaps I might be granted permission to return on the morrow."

"Have you a reason to bother her?" Anna's tone was definitely stale and unenthusiastic.

"One of my men found a brooch that we believe belongs to the countess. I'd like to question her about it, if I may."

"If you'd care to give me the brooch, Colonel, I shall see that it's taken up to her straightaway." Anna stretched forth a slender hand expectantly to receive the mentioned item.

Tyrone handed over the piece, and then, as the princess made to close the door, he stepped nearer, placing a booted toe upon the threshold to prevent her from shutting the barrier. Anna gaped down at the formidable wedge before she glanced up at the man in surprise, wondering if she should scream. Her eyes narrowed suspiciously.

Tyrone smiled pleasantly as he clarified his position. "If you don't mind, Princess. I shall await an answer. You see, if the brooch doesn't belong to the Countess Zenkovna, then by all means it must be returned to the man who found it."

"If you insist," Anna replied icily.

"I must," he answered simply.

"Then wait here," she snapped. "I shall fetch her maid for you. I'm sure the woman will be able to recognize the piece if it truly belongs to her mistress." Anna lowered her gaze pointedly to his foot and then raised a meaningful brow as she looked with steely coldness into the man's eyes. "Boris will attend the door while I'm gone."

With a casual nod to the woman, Tyrone retreated several paces. As he waited, he clamped his hat on his head again and, strolling away from the door, leisurely moved into the shade of the tree, the very same that hid the upper windows of the countess's bedchamber.

Smothering a gasp, Synnovea pressed back against the

window frame and held her breath as the colonel paused in the outer boundaries of the shade. She chanced no movement lest he discover her, but her heart seemed wont to race frantically as she imagined the deep chagrin she'd suffer if he should glance up. Her chemise was far from adequate as a covering, and though she dared not look downward for fear of attracting his attention, she could feel the delicate batiste clinging cloyingly to her wet skin.

Even as Synnovea stared at the man in roweling apprehension of detection, it seemed as if some sharp instinct warned Tyrone that he was being watched. Abruptly he raised his head, and Synnovea gasped sharply when she found herself caught. Frozen by the shock of her discovery, she could only gape back at him, while he, in so brief a moment, drank in every detail of her beauty, the mass of dark hair piled casually high upon her head, the soft tendrils curling wetly against her throat, the bare arms and the gossamer cloth that clung like a hazy film over her delicately hued breasts. The slow grin that came to his lopsided lips evidenced his deep appreciation of her beauty. Her appearance gratified his sharply honed curiosity and completely appeased his reason for coming. In truth, this vision of incomparable beauty assured Colonel Tyrone Rycroft once and for all that he hadn't conjured the Countess Synnovea in some wanton dream.

Synnovea leapt from her perch with a muffled groan of despair and flung herself far from the window to stand panting for breath in the middle of the room. Her cheeks flamed more from the scorching heat of his perusal than from the sultry confines of her prison. Now her heart kept time with her racing mind. What must he think of her? What tales would he spread of her brazen exhibition? Had she not given him enough to stare at in the bathhouse without embarrassing herself a second time? Oh, if he'd just go away! Back to England where he belonged! Without humiliating her further!

The front door creaked as it was pulled open, and Tyrone

snatched his mind free of its entanglement and, sweeping off his hat, concentrated on presenting a coolheaded aplomb as he turned his gaze from the window. Whatever else came of the day, his brief glimpse of the countess had been well worth the long, blistering ride from his quarters.

Ali stepped out into the light and squinted up at the stranger, who stood head and shoulders above her. With some curiosity, she considered his badly bruised visage before she cautiously asked, "Ye be the one what saved me mistress?"

" 'Tis my honor to claim that fame," Tyrone replied amiably and winced as he tried to grin at the old woman.

Peering down at the emerald brooch now nestled in the palm of her hand, Ali tapped it lightly with a gnarled forefinger. "This be the Countess Synnovea's, all right. What be yer reward for findin' it?"

"The reward is not mine to claim. The piece was found on the ground by one of my men. If your mistress so desires, she may lay such a favor upon him, but you need not trouble her now for a reply. I shall return on the morrow. Perhaps by then I may be allowed the privilege of addressing the countess personally."

"I see no need for you to trouble yourself," Anna interjected crisply over the small woman's shoulder. "We shall have the reward sent to your regiment."

"It's no trouble at all," Tyrone assured her in good spirits. "I'd take great comfort in seeing the countess again—to assure myself of her good health, of course." He met the chilling stare of the princess and deliberately ignored what it implied, having adroitly claimed an excuse to return.

Tyrone glanced down to see the sparkling blue eyes of the Irish maid resting on him with smiling approval and realized he had gained an ally. Despite the discomfort he embraced whenever he stretched his bruised, swollen lips, he gave the tiny servant his best attempt, displaying gleaming white teeth behind a crooked smile.

"Would ye be needin' yer hurts tended, sir?" Ali offered and then glanced around in disappointment as Anna cleared her throat impatiently.

"I'm sure there are physicians to whom he can go," the princess stated, not even bothering to hide her annoyance with the pair.

"I fear such attention is limited by the reluctance of your benefactress," Tyrone responded with another painful grin. "I must be on my way, but if you will, you may carry my solicitations for a quick recovery to your mistress. I hope she'll be feeling better on the morrow when I return."

"Oh, she will be," Ali assured him. "I'll see to it!"

Tyrone swept the women a brief bow and, settling his hat on his head, chuckled softly as he retreated down the walk. Even if he hadn't won the consideration of the countess, at least he had gained the support of someone very close to her who might prove of great benefit in persuading the younger woman to think more kindly of him.

5

*S*ynnovea's slender feet fairly flitted down the stairs the next morning. She had given up all pretense of being indisposed for another day, having come to the decision that she wasn't particularly fond of being roasted alive. She doubted that even the cleric's stodgy instructions could be as punishing as the hellish discomfort she had endured in the solitude of her chambers. Thus, with a lighthearted ambiance and a new-found tolerance for Ivan Voronsky, Synnovea swept into the dining hall and smiled cheerily as she extended a morning greeting to the man.

Ivan had entered only a few moments earlier, but it seemed as if he had devised his strategy well in advance of her appearance, for he nearly stumbled over himself skittering around to a place where he could bar her departure from the room, no doubt fearing she'd be tempted to escape like an errant child once he confronted her. When she picked up a plate and went to the sideboard, he followed with his own platter and heaped the morning fare upon it.

"This morning, Countess, we shall address the value of humility and self-denial," he announced, licking sauce from his thumb.

Slanting a glance toward his overflowing plate, Synnovea couldn't resist a smiling query. "Self-denial in what respect, sir?"

Ivan sniffed arrogantly. "Well, to begin with, in your manner of dress."

Synnovea thought he looked very dour and supercilious in his dark vestment, which he obviously considered appropriate for the seriousness of his duties. But then, he probably would have conveyed an identical demeanor if he wore nothing at all, *not* that she was *at all* interested in having her suspicions confirmed. If fate decreed that she should again be shocked by the sight of a naked man, then she'd just as soon he be a far more worthy specimen, someone with a physique as notable as Colonel Rycroft's but with handsomer features.

Synnovea lifted her own dish aside and looked down at her *sarafan* of turquoise silk, wondering what Ivan had found to fault her for this time. Considering the fact that she was adequately covered from neck to toe to wrist and clad in the traditional manner of her homeland, she had difficulty understanding the cleric's objection. "Is there something wrong with what I'm wearing?" she inquired, her curiosity piqued. She was beginning to suspect that he'd be averse to anything she wore. "Is this not the proper attire of a Russian *boyarina?*"

"Somewhat reminiscent of a peacock, I would imagine. Indeed, a bit too colorful to be considered demure. No modest maiden should strut about like some pretty hen in her finery."

Synnovea played the innocent, disinclined to accept his assessments with the same appreciation that Anna might have displayed, though she seriously doubted the man would have offered such criticisms to the princess. One did not wisely bite the hand that nourished him. "I thought peacocks were male birds. Or do you mean peahens? They, of course, don't have much finery, not like peacocks."

"That's strictly beside the point!" Ivan snapped in an indignant huff. "And as a young maid and now a student of mine, you'll have to learn to show proper respect to your savants and be humble of both spirit and mode. After all, the tsar is looking for a bride, and who is to say what maid he will finally select."

Synnovea promptly rejected such a notion. "With all due respect to His Majesty, sir, I have no wish to be subjected to the intrigue and jealousies associated with that particular position. I'm quite content living my life outside the confines and stricture of a *terem* and avoiding the fear of what potion might be added to my food. His Majesty has suffered much in trying to find a bride, but not as much as his wife will have to once he marries."

Ivan eyed her narrowly, trying to plumb her logic. "What do you mean?"

Casually Synnovea settled herself in a chair at the table. "Maria Khlopova was once Tsar Mikhail's prospective bride, and look what happened to her."

Ivan took a seat nearby, placing his heavily laden plate before him. In his opinion, his student needed to be given an example of what might befall a woman full of wiles and deceit. "Maria was undone because, in her eagerness to become tsarina, she sought to conceal her illness from Tsar Mikhail. If not for her untimely collapse into violent and convulsive frothing in front of His Majesty and his guests, she might have accomplished her deception. Sending the Khlopovs to Siberia was hardly punishment enough for the trickery they planned."

Synnovea stared at the man, rather amazed by his lack of knowledge. Apparently the more recent occurrences at court had escaped his attention. "Oh, but didn't you hear? Shortly after his return from Poland, Patriarch Filaret uncovered a plot by the Saltykovs to discredit Maria Khlopova and her family. It seems that several members of the Saltykov family had doused Maria's food with an emetic and then bribed the attending physicians to spread the lie that she had an incurable illness. Patriarch Filaret learned of their subterfuge and told his son. That's why His Majesty has recently banished the Saltykovs from court and confiscated some of their lands." Synnovea heaved a sigh. "Though it's done poor Maria little good now."

"But the Saltykovs are relatives of Tsar Mikhail's mother," Ivan argued. "Marfa would never abide such an edict against her kin, even from her son. You must be mistaken."

Synnovea allowed him the benefit of a kindly smile. "That's exactly why Marfa now staunchly refuses to give her consent to her son's marriage to Maria Khlopova. She was positively in an uproar over his treatment of her kin." Briefly Synnovea addressed her attention to her plate before lifting her gaze to the dumbfounded man. Though wisdom pleaded caution, the opportunity to subtly suggest that her knowledge equaled or even surpassed his was far too tempting to resist. It would only be a gentle gibe. "Do you suppose you've had enough instruction for the day, Ivan? I do so wish to visit the Countess Andreyevna this morning ere it gets too warm. Perhaps we could continue our discussion on the morrow."

Ivan's pockmarked cheeks reddened profusely as he lowered his gaze to his food. He resented being mocked and made to appear the simpleton, especially by the Countess Synnovea, whose sire had been rich enough to hire the best sages and master tutors to instruct his daughter, while he, Ivan, had found it necessary to grovel and abase himself with menial tasks in order to acquire every bit of learning he could, all in an effort to crush those reviling jeers that still haunted him from his youth. After his mother's death, he had attached himself to the *starets* and the priests of the church, shared their paltry meals and tattered robes, merely for the purpose of learning the written word and delving into their weighty tomes and ancient archives. Now, having obtained a rich patroness of influential standing, he wasn't about to be generous to those who had known only a life of ease. He wouldn't allow this fine feathered bird to flit about in carefree abandon after making sport of him. Either she'd learn to be respectful of his importance and mastery . . . or else.

"On the contrary, Countess, you may *not* be excused today or any other day unless it is by *my* recommendation."

Ivan turned from her as if in stern rebuke, but it was a ruse to protect himself from the curiosity of those green-brown eyes, which had widened in stunned surprise. Once again he became a helpless victim of a nervously twitching eyelid and of hands that trembled violently enough to spill liquid from any glass he dared hold while in the midst of those damnable afflictions. From the deepest, darkest recesses of his boyhood memories came haunting visions of his mother standing over him with lips turned sharply downward in contempt as she shouted hateful insults at the little bastard she had whelped. Though he had tried countless times to scour those distressing apparitions from his heart and brain, he was nevertheless tormented by the seizure they evoked.

The demoralizing spasm finally passed, and Ivan drew a steadying breath before facing the maiden. She had congenially addressed her attention to the meal, seeming completely undisturbed by his denial. Her lack of concern was hardly gratifying. Indeed, it was like sharp fangs gnawing at him. He yearned to taste the sweet succor of revenge and devised a plan to make her pay twofold.

Ivan's thin lips stretched stiffly into a sneer. "It has come to my attention, Countess, that there are duties in the kitchen to which you can devote yourself instead of wasting your time associating with such questionable creatures as the Countess Andreyevna."

Aghast at his slight of her friend, Synnovea leaned back

in her chair and stared at him with eyes that now flashed fire. It seemed there was no sentiment that Ivan and the princess didn't share. "Countess Andreyevna is a woman of sterling character, sir. Knowing her as I do, I can offer you hearty assurances to that fact."

Ivan scoffed. "I've been to one of those receptions she gives. Rich boyars and high-ranking officers. Her reasons are obvious to everyone. A widow after three husbands, she's just searching for one rich enough to keep her wallowing in luxuries from now until she dies."

Synnovea recognized the slander to which Anna had given voice two days past. Yet she also sensed Ivan's spitefulness, no doubt elicited by her own foolishness in taunting him. He was perhaps hoping to provoke her wrath by maligning Natasha, but Synnovea vowed not to give him the satisfaction of seeing her defeated by his little ploys. "The kitchen, you say? Well, of course. What would you have me do there that I should consider part of my studies?"

"You need to learn the humbleness of a servant before you'll ever be considered suitable for the institute of marriage by any Russian gentleman. Princess Anna has given me leave to instruct you as I see fit, and my first order of the day will be to teach you about the ignoble concept of servitude and the hardships of serfs and peasants." His small eyes flicked over her costly garb, losing none of their dullness. "I'm sure you'll want to change into something less ostentatious now that you'll be working in the kitchen."

"Then, if you'll excuse me," Synnovea begged graciously, "I must return to my chambers to prepare myself, as you suggest." Smiling all the while, she rose and removed her plate from the table. What the cleric evidently didn't understand was that she had not only served as mistress of her father's house after the death of her mother, but she had often worked alongside some of the servants, especially when close attention to detail had been needed in preparing the house for guests or cooking special dishes for visitors or her father. She had taken personal delight in helping the gardeners. She had loved nurturing the flowers, herbs, and vegetables and seeing their labors manifested into food for the table and large, riotously colored blooms that she had often arranged in vases and brought inside. If Ivan thought he had gained some leverage by ordering her to work, then once again he had displayed his ignorance.

Ivan grew suspicious of her obliging mien. "If you think to barricade yourself in your chambers again today, Countess, I beg you to reconsider. Princess Anna will never allow you to dawdle when I've assigned you specific duties."

"Why, I wouldn't dream of such a thing." Synnovea tossed a chiding chuckle over her shoulder as she went to the door. "Really, Ivan," she said, deliberately using the familiarity to impart her own lack of veneration for him, "there's no need for you to sulk or fret yourself about my intentions. I'm only taking your advice."

The winds of glee, which had momentarily filled Ivan's sails, collapsed into dully hanging shrouds of disappointment. The very least he had been expecting was the angry outburst of a thoroughly irate female.

Synnovea returned to her chambers and doffed her attire. In its stead she donned the peasant garb she normally wore when she lent herself to household duties. Her abrupt return had ignited Ali's suspicions, but the change of garments solidified them. Synnovea soon found herself confronted by the servant, and though she carefully explained that her assignment now included a short stint in the kitchen and that it was a more enjoyable task than suffering through Ivan's lectures, Ali was simply outraged at the audacity of the cleric.

"What! Does that toad take it upon himself ta order ye 'bout as if'n ye be some common drudge? Well, I say a pox on the man!"

"I'll be doing nothing more than what I did at home,"

Synnovea reasoned, trying to calm the maid, who, despite her bantam size, was given to exhibitions of temper and temerity befitting a mother bear whose cub had just been set upon. "It won't hurt me in the least, I assure you."

"Aye, me dearie, but 'twas yerself decidin' the chores ye'd be doin', not another givin' ye commands like some high-an'-mighty lordlin'." Ali flounced about the chambers in a high dander. "That toad'll rue the day he set his mind ta doin' ye ill, that he will!"

"Ali McCabe! I forbid you to give Ivan or Princess Anna the satisfaction of seeing us put out by his peevish bent! We'll abide by Ivan's dictate as graciously as we can, do you understand?" Receiving no response, Synnovea stamped her foot, demanding to be answered by the cantankerous little woman. "Ali! Do you understand?"

Petulantly the maid folded her arms across her flat chest and pouted, not in total agreement with her mistress. "He's a beggarly scamp, that he is."

Synnovea had difficulty maintaining a disapproving frown when the temptation to laugh was all but overwhelming, but she raised a warning finger in front of the woman's nose. "I want you to promise me, Ali McCabe, that you'll do all that you can to keep the peace while we're here."

Ali glared at the threatening digit and assumed her best martyred demeanor. Briefly she cast her eyes heavenward as if appealing to the saints and sucked air through her teeth to indicate her deep distress. Finally, with a wry shake of her head, she grudgingly relented. "Aye, I'll be doin' it 'cause ye told me ta, but 'twill not sit well, ye know that!"

Synnovea chuckled softly as she laid a comforting arm about the woman's narrow shoulders and copied her brogue. "Aye, I know that, Ali, me dearest, but 'twill be better this way. Mayhap by a bit o' kindness, we'll be turnin' aside their resentment."

"That'll be the day, for sure! Aye! Though the priests assured me miracles have a way o' happenin' e'en today, I still have me doubts that ye can gather wool searchin' through a wolf's lair."

Her eyes sparkling with amusement, Synnovea dared to point out the error in the tiny woman's thinking. "Perhaps you might if that's all that's left of the carcass the wolf has dragged in."

Ali paused with mouth aslack, considering the truth of her mistress's reasoning. Finally she heaved a sigh of lament. "But that bodes ill for ye, me lamb."

"Help me finish dressing," Synnovea sweetly urged. "Then you can put away my clothes while I go downstairs and confront the cook." She paused to consider the wisdom of Ivan's decree. "Poor Elisaveta, she may be in for a bit of a shock. She'll be so nervous with a *boyarina* working in the kitchen, she might well burn the food."

" 'Twouldn't hurt none if she did," Ali rejoined tartly. "The way that crow Ivan's been fillin' his craw since he come ta Nizhni Novgorod, it'll serve him right ta have ta choke down burnt vittles for a while."

As predicted, Elisaveta, the sad-eyed cook, gawked in open astonishment when Synnovea entered her domain dressed not entirely like a servant, but not quite like a noble lady either. Her apparel might have put even Ivan's morose convictions on servitude to rout, for her white, lace-trimmed blouse, bodice of forest green, and wide white apron decorated with variegated rows of trim and worn over a dark skirt lavishly embroidered with a colorful profusion of flowers, created a very fetching costume. Layers of lacy petticoats gave the skirt volume. Beneath the ankle-length hem could be spied slender, slippered feet and darkly stockinged ankles as trim and shapely as a man could hope to view. A large, lace-edged kerchief covered her dark head, and the single braid was left to hang unadorned to her hips.

"Countess!" Elisaveta cried, clearly flustered. "What be ye doin' here?"

"I've come to help, Elisaveta," Synnovea announced cheerily. "Is there something I can do?"

"Nyet! Nyet, spaséeba!" the plump woman squawked and waved her hands wildly above her head, as if sorely beset by worry. She had never heard of anything so preposterous! "The princess will never allow such a thing! You're a guest!"

"But I would very much like to learn how to create those wonderful dishes you're so gifted at making, Elisaveta, so I might instruct my own servants once I return home." Giving the woman a pleading look, she coaxed, "Will you not teach me?"

The cook waggled her graying head as a tentative smile touched her lips. It finally deepened into a grin that dimpled her round cheeks. Tucking her massive arms under the folds of her apron, Elisaveta snuggled them up close beneath her large bosom, pleased with the lady's compliments. "I can show ye what little I know, Countess."

"Then I'll surely learn all there is to be taught about cooking," Synnovea smilingly surmised. "What will you show me first?"

"Well, this be what I'm doin' now," Elisaveta announced as she waddled over to a long wooden table where she had been cleaning and heaping up separate mounds of carrots, onions, truffles, and wild mushrooms. "When I finish chopping these, I'll be making *pirozhki*. The master likes the little stuffed patties very much."

Synnovea glanced up at the woman. "Will Prince Aleksei be here this evening?"

"Oh, he's usually not gone more'n a day or two." Elisaveta sighed heavily. "If not for him, there'd be no need for me to cook. The mistress eats less than a sparrow when the master's here and almost nothing at all when he's gone. It's a pity to see all this food go to waste."

"Surely there are enough servants in the household to eat whatever isn't served at your master's table," Synnovea ventured as she perused the various boiling pots and the large bowl of dough that waited to be rolled out.

The gray head moved sorrowfully. *"Nyet,* it's forbidden."

"Forbidden? How so?"

"The mistress won't allow the servants to eat what's been prepared for her and those what sit at her table," Elisaveta explained. "It would spoil their taste for simple food, she says. There're so many others who could benefit, if only . . . ."

The jade-brown eyes chased to the glum-faced woman. Elisaveta hastily brushed a hand across her cheek, wiping away a tear that trickled slowly downward.

Synnovea felt her own heart wrenched by the sadness of so much food going to waste when, without extra cost to the Taraslovs, a goodly number could be helped by it. Sharing in the woman's misery, she laid a gentle hand upon the stout arm. "Do you know of someone in particular who's in need, Elisaveta?"

The cook's chin trembled despite her efforts to keep it firm. "It's my sister, Countess. Her husband died this past winter, and she's poor in health. She has a young daughter of three at her side, but she cannot work to make ends meet. They're wasting away to nothing, and here I be, in this fine house, cooking all this fine food, but I'm forbidden to take anything to her. I cannot even leave to help her."

"Well!" Synnovea settled her hands on a waist that was narrow enough to be envied. If this was the state of affairs in the Taraslov manse, then she wouldn't sit quietly by and do nothing. "I have a maid I can send to buy food and whatever else is needed, and a coachman to take her to your sister. Though I may not be allowed to leave without special permission"—Synnovea gave a small shrug as Elisaveta glanced up in surprise—"they won't trouble themselves overmuch about the absence of my maid."

"You mean you can't leave here without me mistress giving you the say?" the cook questioned in amazement.

"I'm sure 'tis only for my protection," Synnovea responded with a comforting pat on the servant's arm.

"Hmph!" Elisaveta drew her own conclusions as she cast a glare toward the kitchen door, intending it for the woman who roamed well beyond it. She had once been employed by the family who had given birth to the Princess Anna and long ago had formed definite opinions about the woman who had sent her own aging parents to live in a monastery because she preferred to live alone with her husband in the house in which she had grown up. Even when the princess had moved to Moscow, she had not allowed her parents to return home lest they disturb the order of the home place.

By late afternoon Synnovea had finished her chores in the kitchen, whereupon Ivan, eager to demonstrate his authority over her, gave her a weighty tome to read. The garden behind the house offered a seat in the dappled shade of a tree, from which she could watch the return of Ali and Stenka, who had left some time ago on their mission of goodwill. Elisaveta came to the back door often to peer out, but Synnovea could only shake her head, having viewed nothing more than a few small carriages and a handful of mounted riders passing in front of the manse. Dismissing these, she returned her attention begrudgingly to the boring passages Ivan had lauded. The work seemed so full of absurdities she had trouble believing the cleric had actually been serious about his praise.

Dusk had tainted the sky with gloom before Synnovea finally espied the familiar coach. When she rushed into the kitchen to tell Elisaveta that Ali was returning, the cook chafed in frustration, unable to leave her duties. Hardly pausing, Synnovea swept through the dining hall and was hurrying across the hall when Anna turned from the front portal with a harsh frown gathering her thinly drawn brows.

"You should've discouraged that pompous Englishman

from coming here when you first met him," the princess rebuked, incensed that she had been called to the door again to
answer his inquiries. The man apparently lacked the sense to
know when he wasn't welcome or was just too pigheaded to
accept that fact. "Colonel Rycroft was quite adamant about
seeing you this time and had the audacity to inform me that
he'll return on the morrow, as if another visit will do him
any good!"

Synnovea's eyes flew to the portal. Earlier that morning,
her spirits had been strangely buoyed by the fact that Colonel
Rycroft had expressed his intentions to call upon her during
the day. In setting her servants upon her benevolent quest to
help Elisaveta's sister and young niece, however, she had allowed his planned visit to slip from the forefront of her mind.
Regrettably Anna's haughty outrage left no doubt that he had
been treated rudely. Almost cautiously Synnovea asked, "Is
Colonel Rycroft still here?"

"He was a moment ago, but he has gone now," Anna
informed her caustically. She flung up a hand in the same
angry manner with which she had banished the officer from
her stoop. "I informed him that you didn't wish to be disturbed ever again by him! I gave him some coins for a reward
to carry back to his man when he tried to use that again as
an excuse for his return. Personally, I have grave doubts he'll
be giving them to another. A simple trick for gain, if you
ask me."

Synnovea struggled to curb her irritation, resenting the
fact that the woman had taken it upon herself to dismiss the
man without first informing her. Even if Colonel Rycroft was
an Englishman bent on courting her, Synnovea considered it
entirely her prerogative to grant him permission to see her or
send him on his way. Taking into account that the man had
risked his life to save her from ravishment or worse, he certainly deserved better treatment than Anna had obviously

given him. "You say Colonel Rycroft will be returning on the morrow?"

"He may if he dares to ignore what I said, but 'twill do him little good," Anna declared emphatically. "I won't let you see him!"

"I can't imagine the harm in showing Colonel Rycroft a few common courtesies," Synnovea replied frostily, ignoring the fact that she hadn't yet forgiven the man for not informing her of his presence prior to her bath. Even so, she reserved the right to berate him for those offenses in a manner she deemed appropriate. "I owe the colonel a debt of gratitude."

"That doesn't mean he'll be accepted in this house," the princess snapped. "I detest the man, and you'd better honor my wishes or, by heaven, you'll wish you had."

"And so I shall," Synnovea assured her with a tight smile. The subject of Colonel Rycroft's visitations was hardly worth getting into a fracas over. Still, she resented the woman making dire threats to ensure that her dictates were carried out to the letter.

Anna reclaimed her imperious demeanor. "I shall expect to be paid back for the coins I gave the man on your behalf . . . which brings us to another matter. You have enough wealth to compensate us for the cost of your existence here, as well as for the servants whom you've brought with you. It's only fair that you pay accordingly. I'll attach to your debt the rents I feel are due me and write you out a notice of your weekly obligation. You'll be expected to pay such funds at the beginning of each week."

"If you so desire," Synnovea replied, wondering if the woman's decision to charge her rents sprang from greed or from a growing resentment of her presence in the manse.

"I'm pleased that you're so agreeable, Countess."

Declining comment to the converse, Synnovea begged, "I should like to go and dress for dinner now."

Rigidly Anna inclined her head, granting permission, and

watched as the younger woman crossed the hall. But when Synnovea passed the stairs and continued toward the back of the house, Anna hastened to follow her. "Where are you going?" she questioned with sudden suspicion and stated the obvious. "Your chambers are upstairs!"

Synnovea never paused in her stride, but tossed back an answer as she gained the doorway. "I'm going out to fetch Ali to help me dress. She's in the carriage house with Stenka."

Anna shot a worried glance toward the front door as Synnovea departed through the rear. She had no way of accounting for the time that had elapsed since she had sent the colonel on his way, but she refused to take any chances that he was still dawdling nearby.

Lips tightly set in an angry grimace, Anna stalked to the front portal and snatched it open, more than primed to chastise the man for his delay. Finding no one upon whom to vent her rage, she casually sauntered out onto the stoop and, from there, glanced up and down the thoroughfare. The horse was gone from the tethering post and the street was empty save for a lone carriage wending its way past the manse. Smiling smugly, Anna closed the door again, assured that the Englishman had taken his leave. Perhaps she *had* managed to impress him with the fact that he wouldn't be received in her house. If not, then she'd find a more effective way of crushing his aspirations for winning the attentions of a rich Russian countess.

Synnovea dashed along the narrow pathway that led from the house to the stables and was in the process of rounding a hedge when she caught sight of the familiar black stallion tied to a hitching rail near the rear gate. She stumbled to a halt as her eyes flew in search of the indomitable colonel. He was standing near the coach with his leather helm tucked beneath one arm, his other hand casually resting on the hilt of the sword that hung at his side. He seemed quite affable as he conversed with Ali, whose eager giggles were mingled with sly looks and animated flourishes of her pale hands. Far-fetched as the idea seemed, the old woman gave every indication that she was flirting with the officer.

Colonel Rycroft was garbed more in the mode of a working soldier than he had been the previous day. Somewhat rough, worn but equally slender boots had been pulled up over tan canions. Trunk hose of a taupe leather, discolored from much use, covered his hips, while a thick leather cuirass swathed his chest. Beneath the armored vest, he wore a full-sleeved blouse absent of any adornment. Dark bruises were still visible around his eye and cheek, but the swelling, which had once distended his brow and lip, had dwindled in size, lending him more of a human, if not handsome, appearance. His hair had recently been clipped close against his nape and was now smoothly combed, allowing sun-bleached strands to show amid the tawny brown.

Ali glanced around and, espying her mistress, eagerly beckoned her forward. "Mistress! Here be the officer what saved ye from the highwaymen!"

Colonel Rycroft turned abruptly to face Synnovea, and though his eyes were shaded by the approaching dusk, they seemed to linger on everything they touched. Synnovea had no way of discerning the workings of the man's mind, but perhaps that was just as well for her own peace of mind, for she had never felt so completely devoured in all of her life as when this Englishman looked at her.

Tyrone Rycroft was momentarily of the conviction that he admired the countess garbed in clothes almost as much as he had when he had seen her wearing nothing at all, but then he wasn't being quite truthful with himself. Though they were strangers at best, vivid memories of her entrance and departure from the wooden tub swept with recurring frequency through his mind and had the ability to snatch him awake from the deepest sleep.

Synnovea wasn't sure how to react when a suitor made

no effort to disguise the intense hunger in his eyes. She felt the heat of a blush suffuse her cheeks as he considered every detail of her, from shapely ankles and the slender feet that brought her slowly forward to the wisps of hair that had escaped the kerchief and now curled softly against her face. "Colonel Rycroft, this is a surprise," she stated, astonished by the slight tremor in her voice. "Princess Anna just now advised me of your visit, but she also told me that you had left."

"I delayed my departure when I saw Ali arriving by coach, and I came back to chat with her." Tyrone set aside his helmet and closed the remaining distance between them, giving Synnovea a grin that she was just beginning to suspect was naturally lopsided. "I'm greatly favored by your appearance and your apparent good health, Countess. I was afraid I'd again be forced to leave here bereft of an opportunity to see you. Now that I have, my heart has come alive again. The merest glimpse of you nourishes my very soul."

His eyes glowed with such warmth beyond the thick length of his dark lashes Synnovea was of a mind to think that no other smile bestowed upon her by a man had ever turned so quickly into a leer. The burning heat in her cheeks refused to abate when he fed his senses upon every minute detail of her and plied her with such silken words. The sudden suspicion that he had practiced the same cajolery on other maids abruptly accomplished a cooling. "I regrct that you've had to come all this distance to fetch the rcward, Colonel. I should've sent Stenka to take it to you."

Tyrone thrust a pair of fingers into a small purse hanging from his belt and drew forth a pouch of coins. Taking her slender hand, he turned it over and pressed the soft leather bag upon her palm before closing her fingers around it. For a moment he encompassed her small fist within the warmth of his hand. "I shall gladly pay the man myself as evidence of the delight that I glean from your company, my lady," he avouched with warmly persuasive boldness. "I only used the reward as an excuse to see you again. If I hadn't wanted to come, I could've sent my man to fetch it."

Synnovea cautiously withdrew her hand from his, fearing he'd detect her frantically leaping pulse and mistake it for something more than a growing uneasiness. How could she not feel a restive disquiet at his touch when his mere presence set her at odds with herself? "I cannot allow you to suffer the payment of the reward, Colonel." She earnestly sought to return the purse and was frustrated by his refusal to accept it. "I fear you can ill afford the loss of these coins."

"The cost is of little consequence, my lady," Tyrone replied chivalrously, his tone subtle as silk. "The prize I seek is of far greater worth to me."

One glance at Ali was enough to convince Synnovea that the petite woman was secretly applauding the man as a challenger for her heart. As much as she disliked disillusioning the old servant, the Englishman was definitely not in her plans, in the near or the distant future. Even if she had thought him handsome, which didn't seem quite so farfetched now, he was still a roaming adventurer who apparently called no country his home, not even England. She wanted something more, at the very least a husband who'd be close at hand for most of their marriage. "Your sacrifice is pointless, Colonel. Princess Anna would prefer that you not return at all." Synnovea felt a prickling of her conscience as she laid the full weight of rejection upon Anna, but she ignored the prodding as she stated what was near to being the truth. "I'm under her guardianship and must respect her wishes. You must also."

Raising a querying brow, Tyrone searched the variegated orbs until they fell in nervous confusion. After a long pause, he released a pensive sigh as he contemplated her blushing cheeks and downcast lashes. He peered briefly askance at Ali and saw the servant's troubled frown and the disappointment clouding her eyes. Had he been of such a mind, he might have offered the tiny woman some hope to rally her spirits. He knew himself well enough to be confident of one important fact, and that was when he wanted something badly enough, he wasn't inclined to give up until absolutely certain no chance remained for him. After their meeting in the bathhouse, he had come to the realization that Synnovea was a woman he could not easily forget. Princess Anna had made her aversion to him apparent, and he wanted to believe that Synnovea's answer had been forced upon her by the dictates of the older woman, but even if she agreed with her guardian, her rebuff was but a small hindrance to his ultimate goal, and that was simply to win the maid for himself.

"I can only hope Princess Anna will change her mind about me in time," Tyrone rejoined. Knowing he'd likely frighten the girl with what he was about to say, he kept his voice smooth and pliant, though the fires of his enthrallment were ignited anew by the nearness of her. "But I must confess, Countess, that I'm more concerned with your desires and wishes than I am with the feelings of others. You offer the brightest hope for companionship that I've seen here, and I'm reluctant to ignore the fact that you exist merely because I've been ordered not to return. The very sight of you kindles an unquenchable joy within my heart. In truth, Countess, I find myself hopelessly enamored." He paused for a moment to allow her time to absorb his words, and then continued with a lazy shrug. " 'Tis a fact I've learned in my life that when great toil and effort have gone into winning a prize, 'twill be esteemed far more than if it had been easily gained." He managed a twisted grin without a wince of pain. "My lady, I can only avouch that I've not yet begun to do battle for the honor of your company."

Synnovea was aghast at his unswerving persistence. If she had given him special leave to court her as he pleased, he could not have been more brazen or confident of himself. Still, there was something about his declaration that left her fairly breathless with excitement. Yet knowing the trouble that Anna could cause both of them, she made another effort to dissuade him. "Colonel, I beg you to consider the authority under which I now reside. I'm not free to do as I please. I must adhere to the wishes of those who now decide matters for me."

"Would it help if I petitioned the tsar for his favor?" Tyrone queried with a hint of humor shining in his eyes. He closely observed her reaction. If truly cold and haughty, then he'd have his answer soon.

The lovely mouth dropped open in astonishment, and Synnovea stared at him, astounded that he could suggest such a thing. The initial shock of his question eased only slightly as she hurried to deny the possibility. "Indeed no, sir! Gracious, no! I mean, the whole of Moscow would be aflutter with the news! You mustn't! I forbid it!"

Ali coughed behind her hand as she fought a private battle not to cackle in glee. She had been an eager witness to the colonel's pleas and had found it hard to contain herself in her desire to give encouragement to her mistress. She was absolutely ecstatic with the Englishman's determination to fight for what he wanted. As evidenced by his deeds and words, this was no weak-willed swain who could be tossed about with every conflicting wind. This man knew his own mind and zealously sought to gain what he desired to have. And with a name like Tyrone, he had to have a fair amount of Irish blood in him somewhere. It certainly would account for his unfaltering fortitude.

"No need to worry, my lady," Tyrone assured Synnovea with a grin. Her response had not cooled his ardor in the least. "I'll win his favor first, and then make my petition."

Synnovea pressed a hand to her throat in horrified dread that he'd actually take his suit all the way to the throne. Surely he was jesting! Surely she had nothing to fear! Surely he would not!

"As much as I am loath to leave you, my lady, I must return to duty now," Tyrone informed her in a warm murmur. "I have a late drill and, on the morrow, a full day on the training field. Even if Princess Anna hadn't warned me away, I rather doubt that I'd be able to break away long enough to visit you, but never fear," he added with a wink and a promise, "you'll be seeing me again fairly soon."

He gave her a brief bow and then, retrieving his leather helm and settling it on his head, strode back to the stallion. After swinging up into the saddle, he reined the steed about to face the two women and casually touched two fingers to the brim in a salute of farewell before turning from them and nudging the stallion with his heel.

"He's a bold man," Ali declared happily as she watched him ride away. A grin teased the corners of her wrinkled mouth, and in the silence that followed she cast a brief glance toward her dumbstruck mistress and smugly folded her arms across her chest. "Ye know, he reminds me o' yer pa when he came courtin' yer ma. He wouldn't take no for an answer either. He persisted till he finally persuaded yer ma's kin ta give her ta him in marriage. But then, me dearest Eleanora, God rest her soul, she thought the sun an' moon rose an' set especially for Count Zenkov!"

"Well, I don't think the sun and moon rise and set for Colonel Sir Rycroft!" Synnovea declared in a huff, regaining a fair measure of her tenacity. "But I can imagine that he may try and tell them what to do!"

"What can ye expect, me dearie?" Ali tossed her head in rampant delight. "He's a commander o' His Majesty's Hussars! An' an Irishman ta boot, I'll wager!"

Synnovea fixed the scrawny woman with an accusing glare. "Ali McCabe, you're supposed to be on my side, not his.

The way you were eyeing him, a body would think you were measuring him up for an appointment as my husband!"

"Now, now, me lamb, there's no reason ta get yerself in such a snit," Ali soothed. "I be likin' the man, that's all."

A vexed sigh, definitely related to a snort, accompanied a glower of genuine distrust. "I know you only too well, Ali McCabe, and I've no doubt that you'll be discovered as an accomplice to the colonel should he persist in this foolhardy endeavor. You're not to be trusted around such a man!"

"Can I help it if I've a keen eye for pickin' a prime man?"

Synnovea settled her hands on her waist and groaned in mute frustration. The occurrence was rare indeed when she could out-argue Ali McCabe. "I don't suppose, after your delight over the colonel's visit, that you remember what I sent you out for."

Ali squawked at the idea that she was growing addlepated. "Ye know I do!" Her temper mellowed as her mood changed to one of compassion. "An' a poor sight I saw, too! Elisaveta wasn't far wrong. Her sister is in a bad way. I cooked an' tended her an' the little girl, Sophia. Then I gave them a few coins an' promised some more ta a neighbor woman so she'd look after them till I come back. Wit' a little care, they'll be fine, but Danika will be needin' ta find work ta support herself an' her child once she's up an' about."

"I doubt that Princess Anna will allow her to come to work here, not with a child hanging onto her skirts."

"But surely, there be somethin' we can do," Ali fretted in concern.

At the moment, Synnovea could think of no better plan than sending the pair to her home in Nizhni Novgorod, but as difficult as the journey had been for them, a woman in a weakened state of health would be unable to endure it. A new idea promptly came to her, and immediately her hopes brightened. "Perhaps the Countess Natasha would be willing to hire her on."

"An' do ye think Princess Anna will be lettin' ye visit Countess Natasha long enough ta ask her?" Ali queried, doubting the possibility. "Ye know she has no likin' for the countess."

"Anna will never restrict me from going to church," Synnovea said resolutely. "I shall be able to speak with Natasha about the matter there."

"An' once the princess finds out ye've talked wit' the countess, 'tis in me mind she won't be lettin' ye go back."

"She can't be as forbidding as all that," Synnovea replied. Still, her words lacked conviction.

Ali responded with a genuine snort of derision. "Ye might as well be locked in a tsarina's *terem* as much freedom as ye've got here. Ta be sure, the princess won't be takin' it kindly, ye seein' the Countess Natasha behind her back."

"Let's not fret about that now," Synnovea urged, taking Ali's arm. "Elisaveta is waiting to hear about her sister, and I must get dressed for dinner before Princess Anna comes out in search of us!"

A short time later, Synnovea joined Ivan and Princess Anna in the great hall. Promptly thereafter the woman presented her with a bill, but it was not until Synnovea had returned to her chambers that she noticed Anna's accounting for the reward did not match the total coins that Tyrone had given her in the pouch. Either he had taken some out or the princess had greatly enlarged upon the amount she had supposedly given him. Yet there had been no need for the colonel to give her the purse. He could've kept the whole of it for himself, and she would never have known the difference. His fervent declaration that he had used the reward merely for the purpose of visiting her made Synnovea wonder about the greed of the princess. Anna had more than enough wealth of her own; why should she lie to gain more?

In the morning Synnovea returned to the dining hall to find Ivan already filling his plate. He seemed rather smug about his performance as disciplinarian and closely watched for further infractions upon which he could pounce. Synnovea was almost relieved when the front door was thrown open and Aleksei came striding into the room, looking as formidable as the burly Petrov. He was unshaven, his red eyes bespoke of many hours quenched with copious libations and riotous living. He was also as irascible as his appearance indicated.

"You there!" he bellowed at Ivan, giving the smaller man a violent start. The plate slipped from the cleric's bony hands and crashed to the floor, where it flung food helter-skelter as it gyrated in undulating circles. Aleksei seemed almost mesmerized by the whirling dish until it finally ceased its motion. Then he raised glowering eyes and fixed them on Ivan. "You seem brave enough when my wife is present," he taunted with a contemptuous sneer. "Why do you quake with fear now?"

Ivan swallowed convulsively and tried to ignore the vindictive prodding of the other man. Little evidence remained of the brashness he had displayed in the presence of his patroness. When he finally spoke, his voice cracked with trepidation, "Princess Anna hasn't awakened yet, Your Highness. Do you wish me to fetch her for you?"

"When I want my wife, I'll fetch her myself!" the prince bellowed, setting the other man back upon his heels. It was only when he glanced toward the disquieted Synnovea that Aleksei made an attempt to control his temper. Though his nostrils still flared with rage, he released his breath in low, irritated snorts until he was able to speak to Ivan in a fairly reasonable tone. "I've just been informed by a messenger that Anna's father has fallen ill in the monastery. Her mother would like her to come as soon as possible. It's in my mind that the princess will deem you a worthy escort whenever she decides to go. She usually takes her time making up her mind about when to leave, but at least you've been warned of the possibility."

Ivan seemed stunned by the prospect of yet another long,

arduous journey ahead of him, especially when they could be waylaid again by renegades. "But I just returned—"

"You'll have more than enough time to ready yourself," Aleksei cut in with weary indifference. "She isn't inclined to rush off at *anyone's* behest." Having thoroughly detached himself from any smallest concern for Ivan's discomforts, he raised his head in silent eloquence and stared at some distant point until the cleric quietly departed the room.

Aleksei took up a plate and began selecting tidbits from the platters that Elisaveta had laid out upon the sideboard. He cast a glance askance to note the countess's reaction and caught the worried frown that drew her brows together. "Do I detect a hint of sadness in your sweet visage, my dear Synnovea?" He smiled slyly, knowing full well what troubled her. "Or perhaps a concern that after my wife leaves the two of us will be ensconced entirely alone here in the house with only the servants in attendance."

Synnovea answered him unflinchingly. "I'm sure when the time comes, Anna will be willing to give me permission to stay with Natasha during her absence. 'Twould be unseemly for you and me to remain in this house together without a proper chaperon. You know how tongues are wont to wag, and I wouldn't want to see your sterling character besmirched by my presence here."

Aleksei threw his head back and laughed in uproarious amusement at the absurdity of her suggestion. "You're a woman of clever wit, Synnovea. I find myself much refreshed by your presence." His brown eyes gleamed warmly as he stroked a forefinger beneath his mustache, sweeping up the ends. "I shall enjoy getting to know you better."

"When we're properly attended by others, of course," Synnovea agreed with a crisply challenging smile.

Settling briefly into a pert curtsy, she left him to dine alone and made her way to her own chambers. She was not at all anxious to be within close proximity to the man when the princess gave vent to her tirade. Perhaps she was merely speculating on Anna's displeasure, but she had sensed that the woman was anxious to take him to task for his recent absence.

6

*S*ynnovea awoke with a start, her heart thumping nigh out of her chest. Anxiously she searched the shadows of her bed-chamber, hoping fervently that she had been dreaming, that she wasn't really locked in a dungeon somewhere and that the strange rattling sounds she had heard hadn't been the tip of Aleksei's sword tapping tauntingly against the iron bars of her cell. Frightening images of the prince standing before the locked door of her dungeon cubicle still hovered before her like some dreadful ghost left over from her dreams. His swarthy face gleamed back at her from the gloom as his voice, blandly laying out the conditions for her release, came winging back to her. Haughtily he had assured her that unless she yielded him everything he desired from her, she'd never leave her dark, dank prison until they carried out her bones.

The faint, clattering noise came again, wrenching a fright-ened gasp from Synnovea as she came upright in bed. Her heart hammered in her throat, sounding so loud in her ears that it was useless for her to listen for some evidence of her tormentor's presence. Anxiously she probed the deeply shadowed gloom in a desperate search for the one who lurked just beyond her reach and sight. By slow degrees, the moonlit chambers began to take on a comforting familiarity, and with overwhelming relief, Synnovea realized she was ensconced in her bed at the Taraslovs' manse.

The lightest rattle against a glass pane drew another start from her, and her eyes flew to the front window from whence the sound had come. Like the other three windows in the room, it stood wide to catch whatever evening breezes were stirring. Silvery shafts of moonlight illumined the silken draperies fluttering inward on gentle currents, but she saw nothing that resembled human form.

Leaving her bed on trembling limbs, she crept stealthily across the bedchamber and pushed aside an opaque panel to peer out, fully expecting to find Aleksei standing beneath the tree in front of the window. The night sky twinkled with myriad stars, while a bright moon cast its radiance through the leaves of the tree, allowing her to see the one who waited beneath it. A strange blend of relief and surprise flooded through her when she saw that it wasn't Aleksei at all, but Tyrone Rycroft. Feeling no hesitancy now about brushing aside the draperies, she leaned out to confront him, aghast at his boldness in seeking her out in such a manner.

"What are you doing here?" she queried in a carefully subdued whisper. She conveyed a fair measure of irritation at his foolishness as she demanded, "Don't you realize you could be shot for coming here this time of night?"

Tyrone swept off his hat in a flamboyant manner and grinned up at her as his eyes flicked over her, savoring the sights that were there for the taking. Bathed by a silvery aura, she was the very replica of the dream from which he had awakened in a lusting fever. The soft, gossamer gown molded the wanton fullness of her breasts divinely, seeming eager to reveal what they barely concealed. Such a vision of loveliness made his dreams appear almost lackluster. "My lady," he called in a hushed tone. "How wondrously fair you look."

Suddenly abashed by her lack of modesty, Synnovea crossed an arm in front of her, allowing the long, billowing sleeve to mask her scantily garbed bosom. "Prince Aleksei's chambers are on the opposite side of the house," she hissed, frustrated by the Englishman's lack of discretion. "If he wakes and sees you down there, he'll shoot you for an intruder without even asking why you're here."

"Thinking of you thwarted my sleep," Tyrone declared, dismissing her warnings. "I had to come and assure myself once again that you're indeed real and not a figment of my imagination."

"If you won't take heed of the danger you're in, then I urge you, Colonel Rycroft, to consider what my punishment may be if you're caught here! Princess Anna will likely think I encouraged you and will order my windows nailed shut. These rooms will become my prison, but she won't stop there. She'll see you arrested, and you'll spend the rest of your life in a dungeon, never seeing the light of day again."

Ignoring her admonition, Tyrone caught hold of a stout vine twining over the facade of the house and climbed it as easily as he would a ladder. Upon reaching the window, he grasped the frame above his head and swung inward feet-first. Synnovea's astonished gasp evoked a wayward grin from him as he lowered his booted feet to the floor and sat back upon the sill.

Though she had grave doubts that any garment would protect her against the colonel's aggression, Synnovea quickly sought the covering of a dressing gown and then, with fingers trembling uncontrollably, managed to light a candle. The tiny flame danced beneath her fluttering breath, and she lifted the taper high above her head as she warily approached her visitor. His translucent eyes reflected the flickering light, and the hungry yearning visible in those luminous depths was so intense it seemed almost tangible.

Tyrone released his constricted breath in halting degrees. Even the simple act of taking air into his lungs became difficult when he was near Synnovea. Indeed, he felt much as he had that night in the bathhouse when he had watched her padding barefoot and stark naked alongside the pool. "No need to fear, my lady," he assured her in a husky whisper. "I mean you no harm."

"I believe you said that in the bathhouse right after I caught you spying on me like some unprincipled libertine," Synnovea whispered chidingly. She couldn't meet those flaming orbs without sensing the depth of his hunger. Never before had she been looked at with such tangible longing.

"Did I not make my presence known to you tonight?" Tyrone asked her softly, avoiding the subject of his past guilt. "Had you been of such a mind, you could have closed the window and kept me out."

"I was too astonished by your nerve!" Synnovea protested with a blush. Even so, she suffered no uncertainty that she would've barred Aleksei's entrance by whatever means proved necessary. Halting the Englishman, however, had never even entered into her consideration. Was she fooling herself into believing that she was safe in his presence merely because he had let her leave the bathhouse unscathed? Or was she so bedazzled by the strange, stirring excitement that started pulsing within her at every conjured image of his naked beauty that she could allow herself to be reduced to the level of some mindless twit who irrationally sought the company of the one who awakened those delectable feelings?

Synnovea tried once again to make him aware of what he chanced. "Whether you intend mayhem or not, Colonel, you'll likely ruin my good name if you're found here in my room. I must insist that you leave. You're taking liberties which will likely have serious repercussions. At the very least, the Taras-lovs will see you imprisoned for trying to accost me and will send me to a monastery."

The smiling blue eyes delved into hers as he cajoled in a hushed tone, "I'll leave if you truly insist, my lady, but I'd go more readily if you'd give me a token to remember you by."

Synnovea was immediately suspicious and managed a faint question. "Such as?"

Tyrone's eyes wandered leisurely over her, taking in as much detail as the meager light afforded him. A single braid fell over one shoulder, leading his eyes downward to where the robe softly molded her round breasts. The memory of their unconfined perfection and her lithe, shapely form lingered in his mind, haunting him through the days and making his nights a blissful torment. After a man had glimpsed such a rare, perfect vision, how could he find ease for his body and rest for his mind until he had made such a goddess his own?

Synnovea could hardly ignore where his gaze wandered, and though her breasts tingled beneath the languid caress of his gaze, she thought it prudent to warn him. "Your eyes give away the direction of your thoughts, Colonel, so I'd advise you to leave here ere I start screaming, because I don't intend to keep still while you force yourself upon me."

" 'Twould be a dreadful shame if any man ever took you against your will, my lady," Tyrone murmured, imagining the passion that would be sacrificed by such brutishness. "I ask nothing more from you than a scented handkerchief or a lock of your hair," he murmured huskily. "If you're in a mood to be generous, a painted miniature would serve as a sweet reminder of your beauty. A kiss would even send me away in rapture."

His suggestion sent a strange thrill coursing through her veins and a brighter hue flooding into her cheeks, but Synnovea hastened to act the outraged maid, no matter how inappropriate it had been for her to let him into her bedroom.

"You're impertinent to suggest such a thing, sir. Why, I don't even know you."

Tyrone lifted his wide shoulders, casually rejecting such logic. "How can you say that, my lady, when we've shared pleasures few others would dare indulge in outside the bonds of marriage?"

"*You* may have indulged in them, Colonel, but I certainly did not," Synnovea declared, trying to subdue the blushing heat that nearly stifled her. No matter how many times she had allowed herself to bask in the giddy detail of their bathhouse meeting, she now sought to issue quick death to the notion that she had relished such an occasion. "Believe me, sir, I cringe every time I think of you lurking in the pool like some wily sea serpent waiting to consume his victim."

Though Tyrone had in recent hours indulged his imagination by devouring her in a variety of lascivious ways, it was definitely a fantasy too lewd to confess to an untried maid. With a soft chuckle, he folded his arms across his chest and assumed an air of unyielding tenacity. "If you won't give me a kiss, then I shall sit here until I gain a more permanent reminder. A lock of hair, a handkerchief . . . a tiny portrait . . ."

Synnovea had no doubt that the contumacious colonel would carry through with his threat and enjoy every moment of his stay in her room. He had already proven his dedication to visiting her in spite of Anna's attempts to dissuade him. If she didn't give him the gift he sought, she'd never get any peace . . . or sleep.

Synnovea approached him cautiously as she searched his features in the shifting light. "If I give you something of that nature, Colonel Rycroft, will you promise to leave posthaste? I fear someone will overhear us if you stay much longer."

Recognizing the plaintive appeal in her soft tone, Tyrone smiled into those darkly translucent orbs. "A portrait would almost be as nice as a kiss."

"You . . . you wouldn't boast to others if I were to give you one, would you?"

"I would keep it close against my breast to hasten the beat of my heart," he promised warmly. "No one would see it but me, that much I swear as a knight and an officer."

Synnovea dipped her head, accepting his word. "Then I shall grant your request, but only because you saved me from Ladislaus."

Tyrone's eyes caressed her softly lit face. He was no less amazed now by the regal beauty of her delicate features than he had been that night in the tenebrous gloom of the bath-house. No maid had ever ensnared his mind as firmly as she had, and though he sought to pass his infatuation off as simply a fleeting fancy awakened by his lengthy celibacy, she was the only one with whom he yearned to appease himself in the months and years to come. "I'd treasure the gift far better if you'd give it with some tender sentiment, Synnovea."

"I dare not encourage you," she demurred. "You've evinced your gall by entering my bedroom in the dead of night without concern for the danger you might be in."

"The few moments I spend with you are worth whatever dangers I invite," he breathed warmly.

"You mustn't come back like this again," she insisted. "Your persistence in visiting me will see your life forfeited ere you're aware of the jeopardy. If you have no care for the danger you're in, then I must discourage you in taking similar chances by assuring you that in the future I will ignore your clandestine summons though you throw large rocks through my windows. Do you understand me?"

"Aye, I do."

"Good!" Heaving a sigh of relief, Synnovea set the candle on a nearby table and went to rummage through the upper compartment of her largest trunk. Upon finding the miniature that had once belonged to her father, she clutched it near her heart, remembering that her parent had always taken it with him wherever he had gone away. In a way, it seemed a betrayal of his affection to give it to a man who was hardly more than a stranger, yet when the Englishman had saved her honor and possibly her life by risking his own, was he not deserving of such a gift?

Synnovea could feel the blue eyes feeding upon her every movement as she returned to the window. Those shining orbs gave her cause to wonder if the man could see through her dressing gown, for they appeared to dwell overlong on her soft curves. Handing him the portrait, she watched for a long moment as he admired the image.

Finally he raised his head and smiled at her. "I shall treasure it always, my lady."

"Please be careful that you don't awaken anyone making your departure," she urged cautiously. "Most boyars are suspicious of foreigners, and with your English garb, they'll likely shoot you for the sheer pleasure of it."

Slipping her gift inside his doublet, Tyrone tucked it into the pocket resting over his heart. "I'm encouraged by your concern for me, Synnovea," he replied in a husky whisper. "It gives me hope that you like me well enough to at least consider my courtship once I've gained proper approval. Perhaps you'll even come willingly into my arms one day."

"Princess Anna will never allow it," Synnovea stated emphatically. "She hates foreigners, and your audacity has only intensified her dislike for you."

"My heart bleeds with remorse." Tyrone heaved a sigh of regret, but his lopsided grin completely nullified his claim.

A smile stretched across Synnovea's lips. "Aye, I can see that you're terribly grieved by her lack of veneration for you, so much so that you seem to be having trouble controlling your mirth."

His eyebrows flicked upward briefly. "In truth, I care not a whit what she thinks about me and would be much heartened if she'd take a long voyage across the ocean so I can court you without her interference."

Synnovea dared not tell him that a similar occurrence might well be in the offing. If he had ignored Anna's efforts to get rid of him before, then Synnovea could imagine how bold he'd become once the path was clear. "No more of that now," she admonished and, with an outward flick of her fingers, urged him to take his leave. "Hold to your promise and go before I lose patience with you."

"Only a moment more of your time," he murmured, settling his hands lightly on her narrow waist and drawing her between the spread of his legs. He felt her stiffen in sudden apprehension, but with another whispered promise that he wouldn't harm her, he leaned forward and pressed his softly parted mouth upon hers. Synnovea was too astonished to even think of resisting and endured his kiss with growing awe, hardly aware that her lips slackened beneath his, allowing his tongue to flick briefly inward.

Long after Tyrone had made his departure, Synnovea wondered at the gift that he had given her as she stood with trembling fingers pressed to her smiling mouth. For some reason the night seemed sweeter, the moon brighter, the air cooler . . . and her heart warmer.

7

An early-morning breeze wafted over the city as Tsar Mikhail Fyodorovich Romanov strolled leisurely along the walk stretching atop the Kremlin's high wall. His dark eyes closely followed the mounted regiment that practiced its riding skills down below in the vast, open area of Red Square. The horsemanship of the commander of the elite cavalry unit easily claimed his attention. Except for perhaps the Cossacks, who could mesmerize the casual observer with their daring equestrian skills, Mikhail had seen few riders that equaled the talent of this Englishman, but then, it was not the first time the colonel had been brought to his attention.

In speaking to several Russian generals, General Vanderhout had boasted of his own successful accomplishments in devising the tactics that had supposedly directed a detachment from his foreign-led division in a foray against a large band of thieves a day's distance from the city, but Mikhail had been much enlightened when he had asked the newly promoted Major Nekrasov to report on Countess Zenkovna's journey to Moscow. He had heard a tale of highwaymen, led by a bastard of Polish and Cossack descent, attacking the young *boyarina's* entourage and then, without prior design, being put to flight by a certain English colonel and the Russian Hussars he had trained, part of the same regiment which, unbeknownst to them, performed for the tsar now.

The crisp performance and pulsing cadence of the mounted horsemen struck Mikhail's heart with fervor as he watched from his elevated position. The helmeted heads turned in unison at the sharp count of their commander, and beneath the gilded rays of the morning sun, their swords flashed in dazzling brilliance as the men lifted those weapons high for a moment and then snapped them blunt-side against their shoulders. It was a presentation Mikhail had not previously witnessed, but an exercise he was just beginning to realize he greatly enjoyed. He'd have to make a point of meeting this Englishman in the near future, he decided. Obviously the officer had a flair for organizing flamboyant exhibitions in an open field as well as effectively proving his military prowess in actual combat.

Mikhail cocked his head thoughtfully and peered askance at his officer of the guard, who stood just beyond the field marshal. "Major Nekrasov?"

At the summons, the officer approached forthwith and, with a briskly executed salute, paid a soldier's obeisance to his sovereign. "Yours to command, Great Tsar of all the Russias."

Mikhail clasped his hands behind him as his eyes lightly skimmed the neatly uniformed officer. "Major Nekrasov, do you speak English?"

Nikolai was somewhat taken aback by the question, but answered without hesitation. "Yes, Your Exalted Worship."

"Good! Then you may kindly inform the commander of the regiment which we're now viewing that I would like an opportunity to address him within the next several days. Tell him to make a request for an audience in the petitioner's box. He'll be informed some days hence of my reply. Do you have any questions?"

"None, Your Excellency."

"The man is a foreigner," Mikhail stated thoughtfully. "Instruct him on the diplomacy of the court so he may not embarrass himself or cause me to see him unduly punished because another has been offended."

"Yes, Your Excellency."

"That is all."

Nikolai abruptly clasped an arm across his breast and went down on a knee before the tsar, who, with a casual gesture, granted him dismissal. The major took his leave with great dispatch and descended to the ground level through the closest tower. Hastening across the field toward the tightly maneuvering riders, he hailed the commander of the Hussars.

"Colonel Rycroft!" he called and, after failing to gain a response a second time, advanced another lengthy space before trying once more to be heard above the clattering hooves and sharply barked commands. "Colonel Rycroft!"

Finally the summons penetrated the din, and Tyrone reined his mount around to face the one who approached. Recognizing the major, he gave a nod to Captain Tverskoy, temporarily yielding the drilling of the cavalry unit to his second-in-command. As he awaited the rapidly approaching officer, Tyrone pushed back the leather helm and wiped a knuckle across his sweat-dappled brow.

"Colonel Rycroft!" Nikolai cried again with great excitement as he halted beside the Englishman's steed. "His Majesty, the tsar, would like to see you!" He raised an arm and, half turning, pointed toward the high wall, directing the colonel's gaze upward to the men who stood there. "He has been watching you for some time now!"

Tyrone raised a hand to shield his eyes from the sun and

squinted up at the small cluster of high-ranking officers who had gathered there. "What do you suppose he wants with me?"

"You've impressed him!" Nikolai answered in amazement, almost in awe of anyone who could perform such a feat. "You're to arrange an audience with him in the next several days!"

Tyrone dragged the reins loosely through his fingers and, gathering them close, rested his hand upon the pommel of the saddle as he cocked a brow at the major. The tsar's recognition was what he had been striving for, but he was rather astonished at how quickly he had gained his objective. "And how should I go about accomplishing that visit?"

"I've been enlisted to instruct you on what will be expected, Colonel. If you're free this evening, we can meet at my quarters. The sooner you respond, the better you'll be showing respect for his majesty."

"Of course," Tyrone agreed, giving up his plans to ride out to the Taraslov house later on in the evening. In the past fortnight he had drilled his men with unswerving diligence, allowing himself no time to appease his desire to see Synnovea again and plead his cause through Ali. That was not to say that the dark-haired beauty hadn't occupied his mind with singular persistence since he had last seen her. If anything, his moonlit visit to her bedroom had intensified his dilemma. Now more than ever, he'd wake from a fitful sleep with her face before him, a sense of her naked softness lingering hauntingly against his skin. The difficulty in banishing those persistent yet delectable memories robbed him of sleep, and though he'd pace the length and breadth of his bedchamber in an effort to settle his mind on something less disturbing, his failure left him painfully tormented by his growing desire for her. Staring at her miniature only increased his longings. Though he had once teased her about claiming an audience with the tsar, he had been far more serious about his quest than he would have admitted to anyone. Finding favor with His Majesty was essential in getting what he really wanted, and only in that respect did he deem the meeting with Major Nekrasov more important than a visit to the Taraslov manse. Without a doubt, Tsar Mikhail could open any door in Russia that had been slammed in his face.

More than a fortnight had fled since Synnovea's arrival in Moscow, and in that time she had been forced to endure Ivan's phlegmatic instructions, Anna's harsh criticisms, and Aleksei's zealous pursuits, the latter always well out of earshot and eyesight of his wife. Synnovea was beginning to feel as jittery as a tiny bird beneath the sharp, watchful eye of a raven. It seemed in every shadowed area she passed there lurked a danger of being surprised by the prince and, even more disturbing, a threat of being fondled in either a feigned or a more deliberate manner. It was maddening to find herself the prey in his game of chase, but Aleksei seemed intent on taking advantage of every opportunity that presented itself while Anna devoted most of her time and attention aiding Ivan Voronsky in his ambitious climb to fame.

Anna had postponed her visit to her father's bedside, having decided her plans to honor Ivan at a reception were of greater importance. The princess and the cleric had become all but inseparable. While Aleksei roamed elsewhere, they visited boyars of great power and wealth in an effort to abet kindred spirits. If the atmosphere and temperaments were right, they carefully encouraged the airing of whatever adverse sentiments existed against the Patriarch Filaret Nikitich. Synnovea had gleaned at least this much from her bedchamber where she had been cautioned to stay during a meeting of boyars whom Anna had invited to the manse. It had certainly not been Synnovea's intent to eavesdrop, but the outraged shouts, which Ivan seemed to liberally provoke with his suggestions, were impossible to ignore even upstairs. In light of the bizarre views the cleric had expressed during their journey to Moscow, she could only wonder if he held aspirations of uprooting Tsar Mikhail from his throne. It seemed doubtful that Anna would be party to such a goal, being Mikhail's cousin. Even so, Synnovea couldn't banish her own strengthening suspicions.

It was early on a Wednesday morning when Aleksei informed his wife that he'd be attending business affairs in a neighboring city and that she shouldn't expect him back until late the following day. His announcement and departure bolstered Anna's confidence that she could leave her charge behind at the manse and nothing untoward would transpire while she ventured out with Ivan. Shortly after the two left, Synnovea sent Ali off with Stenka to attend the needs of Elisaveta's sister. As she awaited her servants' return, she retreated to the Taraslov garden, where she began reviewing a book which Ivan had given her earlier in the day, no doubt to keep her aware of his power even in his absence.

It was midafternoon when a somewhat surprised Boris opened the door for his master. "We weren't expecting you to return until the morrow, my lord."

"A change of plans, Boris." Aleksei glanced casually about. "Is my wife here?"

"No, my lord. Princess Anna left more than an hour ago with . . ."

"The good Ivan Voronsky," Aleksei concluded for the elder, allowing some irritation to show for the steward's benefit.

Boris hurried to allay any husbandly jealousy. "They went to visit Prince Dimitrievich at his home, my lord. I'm sure Princess Anna would be delighted if you joined them there."

"What? And suffer through another boring discussion of that old boyar's prospects for producing another brood of children in his dwindling years?" Aleksei laughed with a negative shake of his head. "I think not, Boris. At his advanced age, Vladimir should be thinking of dividing his wealth between the sons he has already rather than looking for a new wife upon whom he can spawn new ones."

Boris chuckled, having overheard for himself the old boyar's expectations. "I've no doubt that it's the wish of every man facing advancing years to be equally as capable as Prince Vladimir when they reach his age."

Cocking a curious brow, Aleksei peered at the steward, wondering if he was voicing aspirations of his own. "Perhaps the old prince isn't nearly as *capable* as he'd like everyone to believe."

"That may be true, sir," Boris agreed, and then heaved a sigh. "But it's nice for a man to believe there's some hope."

Aleksei grinned in agreement. "Absolutely."

Only a few moments passed before the prince entered the garden and found Synnovea sitting with her chin propped in her hands. Intent upon her studies, she failed to notice him until he spoke.

"My dear child, what are you so engrossed in?"

The softly coiffed head snapped up in surprise, and Aleksei found himself staring into startled green-brown eyes. He smiled as he plumbed the depths of her sudden disquiet. She was as skittish as a young hare that had just been cornered by a wily fox.

"Prince Aleksei!" Synnovea rose nervously to her feet. "We weren't expecting you until the morrow. My goodness, won't Anna be surprised!" Her breathless tone readily conveyed her rampant distrust. "I think she should be back any moment now. . . ."

Her words dwindled to an uneasy silence as his dark eyes gleamed back at her in dubious amusement. "Come now, Synnovea," he gently reproached. "We both know that Anna dallies overlong whenever she accompanies Ivan on one of his jaunts to fame. She has ambitions not unlike his, you know."

Almost in mesmerized distraction, his gaze dipped to the higher curves of her bosom, which her square, lace-edged neckline coyly revealed. Even so minute a glimpse was more than he had been afforded since he had opened her bedchamber door and found her sleeping on her chaise. Since then, the girl had discreetly garbed herself in *sarafans* . . . until today. A crisp, lacy ruff now adorned the slender column of her throat and was daintily fastened with a lavender ribbon, a color found in the flowery lawn of her gown. Below the charming neckpiece, the close-fitting bodice accentuated the narrowness of her waist, while the neckline left him appreciative of the youthful luster of her creamy skin.

"May I join you?" he inquired, presenting his best manners.

"O-of course," Synnovea replied. How could she deny him? If she had taken the initiative to tell him nay, he probably would have seized her outright.

Aleksei closed the space between them, and in swift reaction, Synnovea skirted around the marble table, where she poured herself a chilled glass of watered wine. Managing a tremulous smile beneath his ever-warming regard, she gulped a sip before she recalled her manners. Reluctantly she swept a hand to indicate the pitcher of wine and a small plate of cakes that Elisaveta had brought out to her. "Would you care for some refreshments?"

Aleksei smiled at her guise of gracious hostess, well acquainted with the ploys of a reluctant maid. She had been most eager to place a barrier between them, as if the tiny table could offer her protection against the encroachment of a passionate swain. "Perhaps a glass of watered wine."

Aleksei accepted the goblet from her and, lifting his head, gazed out over the carefully tended garden. He wasn't a man who normally gave himself over to the enjoyment of such simple pleasures, but with Synnovea near at hand he could feel himself relaxing in the peaceful tranquility of the glade. Perhaps if he had wed a woman who would have been content with his wealth and princely possessions instead of being driven with an insatiable ambition to have the best of every-

thing, he might have been satisfied to devote more of his attention to nurturing a love for her. With increasing frequency
now, he felt compelled to flaunt his many conquests before
Anna. Perhaps unconsciously it was his way of seeking revenge for the disquiet she awakened within him.

"Will you walk with me through the garden, Synnovea?"
he invited, continuing around the table. He took her arm and
swept his free hand toward the paths that were bordered with
flowers. "It has been more than a season of years since I've
taken time to admire such riotous blooms."

Hesitantly Synnovea moved along the lane beside him,
cautiously giving an excuse for a timely escape. "Elisaveta is
expecting me back in the kitchen any moment now. I promised to help her make bread, so I mustn't be away too long.
She'll come looking for me."

"A simple walk through the garden doesn't require too
much time," Aleksei assured her. "I have to leave again
shortly anyway. I left some important documents behind
when I left this morning, and I had to come back to fetch
them. I thought everyone had gone, and then I noticed you
out here." He raised his head and slowly inhaled the sweet,
heady fragrance that wafted from several large blossoms
adorning a nearby bush. "I had almost forgotten such pleasures exist."

Glancing over her shoulder, Synnovea noticed that they
were no longer in sight of the house, for the draping limbs
of a tree now obscured the trail behind them. "I should go
back now."

"Not yet, Synnovea." His hand slipped downward to clasp
hers, and when she gasped in surprise and tried to draw away,
he laughed and indicated the path ahead. "Did you ever see
the dovecote? It's just up ahead."

Hearing a soft cooing beyond them, Synnovea conceded
him a cautious victory and allowed him to draw her with him.
He released her hand as they approached a white, circular

structure where a dozen or more pigeons calmly roosted. Others flitted to and fro overhead. The fluttering of wings warned them of another approaching bird, and Synnovea turned to observe a dove's flight to a slender perch jutting from an empty cubbyhole.

"This could be dangerous," Aleksei observed drolly as other birds flew overhead. "Let's get away before we find your pretty gown spoiled." Seizing her hand again, he pulled her along behind him down a footpath that turned sharply away from the cote.

Synnovea sought diligently to disentangle her fingers from his grasp, knowing they roamed farther and farther away from the manse. "Please, I should go back now."

Aleksei held fast as he bade over his shoulder, "Don't be afraid, Synnovea. Come, I've something else to show you."

He brought her within sight of a small hut nestled against a high wooden fence which served as a barrier around the estate. Drawing her with him onto the wooden planks of the porch, he pushed open the door and would have ventured in, but Synnovea balked at the idea of being hauled into a dark cottage with a lecher. Stiffening her limbs much like a stubborn calf, she braced her feet wide and refused to be dragged forward another step.

"No!" she cried. "Let me go! I must return to the house!"

Aleksei chortled as he stepped back to her with dark eyes glowing brightly. "Come inside, Synnovea," he coaxed, tilting his head slightly toward the open portal. "Let me make you the woman you deserve to be. No one will know we've spent this time together." His red lips parted in a cajoling smile. "The servants are loyal to me. None of them will tell Anna that I returned home today, so we needn't make excuses to her." With a brief nod, he indicated the door again. "No one comes here. The old woodcutter who lives here during the winter won't be back until fall. We'll have the cabin entirely to ourselves. You needn't be embarrassed or afraid."

"Never!" Synnovea shook her head in passionate fervor. "This thing you ask of me isn't proper, Aleksei! You have no right to even suggest it."

"Right? Wrong?" Aleksei tossed his head from side to side like a small boy chanting a rhyme. "Who can argue this is wrong, Synnovea, when we are meant for each other?"

"I can!" she declared hotly. "I want no part of this!"

His shoulders lifted in a languid shrug, evidencing his lack of concern for her reluctance. "I'll take you as I will, Synnovea. It's of little consequence to me if you struggle. I know in time you'll come to enjoy my caresses."

Aleksei slipped an arm around her waist, but Synnovea snatched away and glared back at him with eyes flashing with feral intensity. "If you force me against my will, Aleksei," she warned in a low, ragged tone, "I swear you'll reap my revenge. I'm *not* one of your little trollops whom you can seize and take at your whim! If Anna won't listen to my complaints, then I'll take them to Tsar Mikhail. But know this, Aleksei: I'll have retribution for any offense you commit against me!"

An abortive laugh displayed his contempt for her threats. Still holding her wrist, he smirked with unswerving confidence. "Do you actually think you can threaten me and dance away to your delight, my girl? Nay, let it never be said. Your words will fall on deaf ears, for I shall make of them a lie and pledge my troth that you speak falsely. Anna will hear no slander from you. So you see how shallow your threats are? Truly, Synnovea, there's no advantage in fighting me."

Smiling in haughty arrogance, he seized the front of her bodice and, with a downward jerk that startled a scream from her, ripped the stomacher free, leaving naught but a chemise to hide her bosom between the rent. Aleksei stretched forth a hand to test the delectable fullness, but with an infuriated shriek, Synnovea whirled away. Alas, her attempt to flee gained her nothing, for he caught his fingers in the cluster of curls on top of her head and, hauling her back, lifted her struggling form into his arms.

Shouldering the door aside, Aleksei pushed his way into the cottage and kicked the portal closed behind him. With nary a pause, he crossed to a narrow cot in the corner and dropped her upon it. As she lit, wolf pelts seemed to enfold her and threatened to smother her as they flew over her face. Fighting her way free, Synnovea scrambled to her knees and quickly apprised herself of her surroundings. She glimpsed an opening between Aleksei and a small table standing near the head of the cot and lunged for it, intent upon slipping through the breach. Promptly he stepped to block her path, but she eluded his reaching hands and sprang to the opposite end of the bed, from whence she crawled hastily toward an open niche. He was there to meet her and thwarted her attempts again and again. Finally she sat back upon her heels, gasping air into her lungs, and glared up at him.

Casually Aleksei began slipping out of his kaftan. "You see? There's no escape for you, my beauty."

Tossing aside the garment, he faced Synnovea, garbed in nothing more than a thin shirt and leggings that clung closely to his scrawny legs. His wide shoulders and the roomy kaftans had made him seem heavier and more muscular than he actually was, for he bordered on thinness and was rather straight from his chest downward. Hardly the sort of physique she had been admiring lately.

Aleksei watched his captive carefully as her eyes flew about the cabin in an anxious quest for escape. She darted toward another opening, but again he caught her and, this time, shoved her back upon the pelts. She gnashed her teeth in frustration and tried to claw him, but he chortled in amusement at her attempts and batted her arms away. Holding her thus, he jerked the cot away from the wall and settled astride the narrow bed, pinning her beneath him and stilling her wildly thrashing limbs.

Synnovea was hardly subdued. When he lifted himself to tug up her skirts, she was bent on wiggling out from under him. Aleksei expected as much and immediately resettled himself across her legs.

In his eagerness to drag her petticoats out from under him, he failed to notice the slender hand closing around a honing stone that had been left on the table beside the bed. Nor did he see her fist swinging upward in an arc away from the nightstand. Synnovea forced every bit of the strength she possessed behind the blow, catching her would-be debaucher squarely against the side of his nose with the edge of the stone, setting it abruptly askew.

Aleksei's pained yowl seemed to shake the hut right down to its foundation as he reeled backward from the blow. He clasped his hands to his face, a vivid array of colors bedazzling him as an unbearable agony blinded him to everything else. Several red droplets splattered onto his white shirt, and as his sight cleared and he spread his hands, he gaped down in slack-jawed awe at the splotches. He could hardly believe his blood had been spilled by so slender a maid, yet the anguish was too intense for him to doubt the fact. Emitting a groan, he pressed a finger beneath his nose and tried to curb the dribbling flow, but alas, it could not be stemmed. The slightest touch sent sharp, splintering shards of excruciating pain shooting upward from his nose into his brow. From there, his torment expanded and seemed to reach to the very ends of his nerves. The anguish was too great to bear, and losing all desire to fulfill his lustful cravings, he lifted himself from the bed and stumbled in an agonized stupor to the washstand, where he snatched a towel and pressed it tightly beneath his nose.

Synnovea dared not pause. Amid a flurry of flying skirts, she leapt from the bed and raced through the door. No one witnessed her frantic entrance into the manse, but it wasn't until she had locked the door of her bedchamber firmly behind her that she felt safe from Aleksei and whatever revenge he might seek. Oblivious to the heat, she waited with bated breath until at long last she heard his carriage rumble away. Then she went to the window to watch and saw his stallion trailing behind at the end of a tether. That fact lent her some hope that he wouldn't be back for several days.

It was the third Sunday after Synnovea's arrival when cooling breezes finally brought a welcome respite from the hot, sweltering days of summer. Scudding gray clouds chased across the early-morning sky and gave some hope to hearts yearning for rain. In only a few weeks the weather would begin to take on a chill and the intense heat would be but a memory.

Aleksei had returned two days earlier, giving the lame excuse that he had broken his nose after a fall from his stallion. For the sake of his handsome profile, he had endured the torment of his nose being righted by a physician, but by now, it could be determined that a definite lump would mar the previous sleekness of it and no doubt serve to remind him by whose hand he had acquired the wound. A dark purplish swelling around his nose and beneath his eyes tarnished his handsome visage, evidencing the depth of his injuries, and he was wont to liberally indulge in strong intoxicants to ease the pain that still plagued him. He was no longer doubtful of Synnovea's ability to do him ill and, for the time being, was reluctant to challenge her stilted reserve, fearful that another such blow would see him completely undone.

On this particular Sunday, Aleksei had announced that he would remain at home, for his vanity prevented him from pursuing other light-o'-loves until his swollen nose dwindled in size and the bruises faded. Earlier, Anna had made arrangements to go with Ivan to a private chapel belonging to the immensely wealthy boyar, Prince Vladimir Dimitrievich. The ancient widower had his heart set on another marriage, and since neither Ivan nor Anna wished him to be distracted from their discourse by the presence of a comely young maid, the possibility of Synnovea accompanying them to the *chasovnyas* was simply out of the question. Yet, while her husband remained abed, Anna didn't trust Synnovea to stay behind either. Thus, she was left with no other choice but to allow the girl to arrange her own sabbatical, as long as it was well away from the Taraslov manse and the invalid, Aleksei.

Whatever reasons Anna had for letting her go, Synnovea was relieved to have finally been granted some freedom. Even the woman's dire warnings to return before dusk couldn't diminish her enthusiasm. She even went out early to wait for Stenka to pull the coach around into the drive and wasn't at all unnerved by the fact that Aleksei came to stand near the windows of his upper-story bedroom. He couldn't do much harm to her today.

For the outing, Synnovea had outfitted herself in a *sarafan* of ice-blue satin liberally adorned with seed pearls and delicate appliqués of white lace. A similarly embellished *kokoshniki* had been settled upon her head, and a blue ribbon, sewn with the same dainty pearls, had been woven through the single dark braid. A matching cloak accompanied her, but after reaching her destination, Synnovea decided to leave the garment behind as she prepared to alight from the coach. The temperature was still warm and the sun had begun to peek intermittently through the clouds, lending her some assurance that the weather would remain clear throughout the day.

Stenka halted the conveyance a short distance from a church on Red Square, close to where the Countess Natasha Andreyevna had paused outside her own carriage. As Jozef swung open the door for his mistress, the older woman hurried across to greet her friend. Catching sight of her, Synnovea descended the steps in a lighthearted rush as Natasha laughed in glee and spread her arms wide. In a thrice of steps, the younger was enfolded within the elder's embrace.

"I should scold you for not coming to see me," Natasha

fussed and drew back amid a profusion of tears. "Or have you forgotten that I'm not welcome at the Taraslovs?"

"Oh, Natasha, you know I haven't," Synnovea replied as her own gaze blurred. "But until today, Anna hasn't allowed me to venture beyond the limits of their estate."

Natasha searched the teary green-brown eyes. "It must be difficult for you to live under such strictures when you've been able to enjoy the same freedom granted to women all over England and France. Your mother laid a good foundation for you by instructing Aleksandr in the genteel deportment of an English gentleman. For a Russian, your father was surprisingly receptive to her persuasions. But then, Eleanora had a most endearing way about her."

"A change may be coming fairly soon."

"How so, my dear?"

Synnovea lifted a hand to caution the elder. "Mind you, there's been no indication as yet that Anna will actually go see her ailing father. Nor should I dare suggest that she'll grant me permission to visit you, but I rather suspect that she won't feel too confident leaving me alone in the house with Aleksei."

"I can hardly blame her there. The man is a rake of the first merit." Natasha raised her brows briefly to lend emphasis to her insinuations and gently patted her young friend's hand as she urged, "Take warning, my child."

Synnovea's own brows flicked upward in agreement. "Oh, I've learned by experience what a horrible lecher he is. I'm afraid to leave my bedchamber while that greedy crow waits to pick my bones. Once his nose is mended, he'll likely seek revenge."

Natasha's elegant brows gathered in bemusement. "What happened to his nose?"

"I broke it when he accosted me."

For a moment the older countess stared at the younger, completely flabbergasted. Then, as the humor of it settled in, she began to laugh in rampant delight. "Poor Aleksei, he's never been abused by a woman before. 'Tis a rare one who doesn't adore him. Hopefully, you've thwarted his attempts sufficiently, and he'll be careful about approaching you in the future."

"I really don't think he'll let my affront slip past without demanding some sort of restitution. The uncertainty of how and when it will come leaves me positively skittish."

Natasha heaved a sigh, extending her sympathy toward the girl. " 'Twould ease your situation if you could leave their house fairly soon. Do you have any idea when Anna might depart?"

"If she goes at all, it certainly won't be until after Saturday next. That's when she intends to honor Ivan Voronsky with a grand celebration."

"Ivan Voronsky?" Natasha repeated the name incredulously and looked at the younger woman with growing sympathy. "Oh, my dear Synnovea, I do pity your plight. I only wish His Majesty had seen fit to send you into my care, but I'm sure he had no idea we were close friends, especially if Anna told him that I was only interested in your father. There's no question that Tsar Mikhail thought he was doing you a favor by sending you to Anna. After all, she is his kin, and under normal circumstances it would be deemed an honor to be the ward of the tsar's cousin. He greatly admired your father, and now that Aleksandr has been taken from us, I know His Majesty would like to be assured of your welfare, so please, try not to judge him too harshly, my dear."

"I shan't, of course. He proved the depth of his concern by sending Major Nekrasov to escort me to Moscow. But tell me, Natasha, if Anna does go to visit her father, will you allow me to stay with you during her absence?"

"Oh, my child, need you ask?" Natasha laughed gaily. "Of course you may! Indeed! I won't tolerate the idea of your staying with anyone else!"

The bells in the belfry began to clang, and as the last grew silent, a lilting hymn drifted from the church. The two women turned their attention to the sweet, melodious voices that beckoned and walked arm in arm into the magnificently embellished interior. A rosy aura, softly cast from the mica windows, seemed to infuse the very air around them as they stood together in a section reserved for women and children. There, they murmured prayers, sang songs, and listened to the oration of the priest and the angelic hymns of young boys dressed in white vestments. It was a peaceful time, like so many others they had shared in the same church, except that now there would be only the two of them after the services. The memory of Aleksandr Zenkov remained sweet to each, and with tears misting their eyes, they clasped hands, silently mourning his passing.

Three hours later, the two women emerged from the church to find dark clouds looming over the city. Lightly splattering raindrops brought sweet respite and stirred forth a refreshing essence, but Synnovea was averse to seeing another gown ruined and stood in the shelter of the portico, worriedly viewing the seemingly endless breach that lay between the church and her coach. Conveyances had already become ensnared in a tangled maze created by drivers intent upon picking up their passengers without delay. Whatever open spaces remained were quickly filling with people hurrying from other churches located in the same area.

"I never expected this," Synnovea said forlornly. It seemed like a century had passed since she had felt such freedom, and after so many weeks without rain, she couldn't believe that it had started this very moment.

"Stenka is nearer," Natasha declared. "We won't have to wait as long for him to get through."

Synnovea cast a dubious glance upward at the dark clouds. "Yes, but it may be another hour before the path clears enough for him to get through. But then, the way the sky looks, we'll get soaked in any case."

"I guess our only option is to run for it." Natasha lifted her cloak and spread it wide as a shelter for them. "We'd better leave now, before we're caught in a downpour."

Synnovea huddled beside Natasha under the costly tent as they left the protection of the portico. They had barely ventured forth when a heavy torrent was unleashed upon them, dispersing the crowd ahead of them. Synnovea caught sight of Jozef scampering down from the footman's seat in his eagerness to be at the door when they arrived. Presently Stenka was leaning down from his lofty bench, talking with another man, who had halted beside the coach. As the driver lifted an arm to point, the one to whom he spoke twisted about to search the crowd for her. Though garbed in an enveloping cloak and a wide-brimmed hat, the man was unmistakable. It took no more than a glimpse of that male visage to bring Synnovea to a sudden, disconcerted halt. The dauntless Colonel Rycroft had ventured forth in search of her again.

Synnovea had no opportunity to retreat as he came at a run toward her, nor even a chance to react. Without warning, a force from behind struck her solidly against her back and sent her sprawling forward onto her hands and knees. The culprit, a huge, simple-minded lummox who had panicked after finding himself separated from those who led him, glanced down briefly as he plowed past her. In spite of the blinding torrent that washed down upon them, a group of strapping youths raced for their mounts, all but treading on the heels of the oaf. By the time they saw Synnovea, it was too late for an orderly evasion. They leapt over, around, and finally upon as one fell short of his goal and came down on her foot, startling a cry of pain from her lips.

Frantically Natasha pushed against those who came dangerously near, but her strength was far too flimsy against such stalwart forms. "Begone with you!" she railed from beneath her cloak. "Can't you see where you're going?"

In the next moment, a dark shape loomed over Synnovea, abruptly discouraging the progress of the youths, at the same time causing Natasha to stumble back in some awe. The cloaked form momentarily provided a protective screen around the girl before the man bent and gently lifted her to her feet.

Synnovea was keenly aware of Colonel Rycroft's arm slipping around her waist and of his hard body pressing near, lending her both shelter and support as she took a limping step forward. A piercing pain shot through her ankle, causing her to wobble and smother a cry. In the next instant, she was being whisked off her feet by arms that were iron-thewed and completely capable, the very essence of a fantasy a maid might create for herself. Her pulse leapt rather strangely as he clasped her to him, and she slipped her arms around his stalwart neck with the same intensity that she had once employed when faced with the threat of drowning. His hat offered some protection from the pelting bombardment of rain, and she pressed her brow against his cheek, giving no regard for the impropriety of her actions. Tyrone lifted a shoulder to cradle her more securely against him and ran with long, sprinting strides toward her carriage, bearing her as easily as he would a child.

Utterly amazed by the boldness of the chivalrous man and, in no smaller degree, by Synnovea's willingness to accept his aid, Natasha Andreyevna gaped after them for one short, astounded moment before she, too, scurried toward the coach, albeit at a much slower pace than that of the one who had spirited away her friend. Her cloak and slippers were now completely soaked, proving more of a hindrance than a benefit, thwarting her efforts to be on hand when the two reached the conveyance.

Jozef swung open the door, allowing the colonel to mount

the step unrestricted by anything more than his winsome burden. After springing onto the step, Tyrone leaned inward to deposit Synnovea safely upon the seat. For the briefest time, his lips caressed her dampened cheek before wandering around to taste the soft mouth that parted in surprise. A quick intake of breath evidenced the lady's astonishment as his tongue passed over her lips in a gently provocative manner and flicked ever so briefly into the moist cavern. For barely an instant, Synnovea bent toward him, yielding him access as she savored the taste of his mouth, but she remembered herself abruptly and pushed back against the cushion. Excruciatingly aware of the unseemliness of her actions, she turned her burning face aside.

"You shouldn't kiss me in public!" she scolded in a whisper. "What if someone were to see us?" Though the downpour served as a protective shield around her coach, it was still daylight, and there was no accounting for what Jozef could see through the gaps between the window frames and the shades that had been lowered to keep out the rain.

"If you won't let me visit you in private, my sweet, how else can I kiss you?" Tyrone reasoned with a teasing grin, drawing her furtive gaze. The dripping brim of his hat shaded his eyes and part of his face, but she could hardly ignore the fact that his gaze was riveted upon her mouth. Tyrone leaned toward her again, wanting more. "What man, after tasting your lips, can easily turn aside from such intoxicating nectar?"

With a gasp Synnovea pressed a hand to his chest to halt his advance. She didn't need to be told what he intended; she could see it in his eyes. The inexplicable tumult he evoked within her was reason enough to be cautious. For the sake of her own emotions and the situation in which she had been cast, she'd be far better off avoiding the man, for she seemed wont to dismiss every rational thought and traditionally accepted behavior in his presence, as if she had no will of her own. "Nevertheless, Colonel, I must insist that you control your ardor ere you see me disgraced."

"Halting the sun in the sky might prove an easier task, my lady," he murmured warmly as his fingers stroked along the inside of her arm, quickening the rhythm of her heart as his lean knuckles brushed the sodden cloth adhering to her breast.

Synnovea was amazed at her own breathlessness and struggled to convey an indignation appropriate for an offended *boyarina.* "You're too familiar in the way you handle me, sir, and if you do not desist, I shall be forced to scream."

"Before you alert others to your cause, my lady, feel how swiftly my heart races." He captured her hand and pressed it to his breast. "Is this the heartbeat of a frivolous suitor?"

Touching him was like being near a lightning bolt when it plunged into the ground. Synnovea could feel the force sizzling through her and every nerve standing at attention. Thoroughly unsettled by what she was experiencing, she sought to disentangle her trembling fingers from his warm grasp. "Please unhand me, Colonel," she whispered. "You'll have my coachmen wondering what we're doing."

Sensing her rising panic, Tyrone complied, yet he watched her yearningly until she had to turn her face aside from the heat his eyes conveyed. She made every effort to slide across the velvet seat, but her sodden clothes hindered her, and as she braced cautiously upon the edge of the cushion and tried to rise, he saw her wince. In growing curiosity he lifted the muddied hem, revealing an ankle that was now swollen and darkly bruised. "Why, you've been hurt."

"Truly, Colonel, it's nothing!" Synnovea insisted, blushing at his forwardness. When he sought to take her ankle within his grasp, she quickly dragged her foot away and once again saw a need to advance her escape to the far corner of the seat. " 'Tis but a small bruise, nothing more. 'Twill heal quickly enough."

Tyrone was thoroughly perplexed. After seeing and holding far more of her than just a shapely ankle, he couldn't understand why she should be so abashed by his inspection. But Jozef still stood near the door, and it seemed advisable not to question the lady lest the man hear them over the deluge beating down upon the roof.

"A cold compress may help reduce the swelling," Tyrone suggested, having dressed a variety of wounds in his years as an officer, including many of his own. "You should stay off the foot for at least a day or two, just to give it time to heal."

" 'Twould seem I'm indebted to you once again, Colonel." Synnovea blinked the raindrops from her lashes and reluctantly met his unwavering regard. She could feel water trickling into the crevice between her breasts and yearned to pluck the clinging *sarafan* from her bosom, but that would hardly be seemly. She waited wide-eyed as his gaze delved into hers, having no idea what he searched for.

"Is something the matter?" Self-consciously she dragged her headdress off and wiped the dribbling moisture from her brow. "I know I must look a sight."

"Aye, that you do, my lady," he breathed huskily, admiring everything his eyes touched. "A sight I've rarely seen."

"Do I look as horrible as that?" Synnovea asked in some chagrin, mistaking his words.

Tyrone chuckled softly. "As beautiful as that, you should ask, my lady."

"You tease me, sir," she chided, unable to subdue the subtle curving of her lips.

His grin was warmly cajoling. "The beating of my heart would surely affirm the truth of my words if you'd but give me your hand again."

"I think not," she whispered, finding little strength in her voice.

"Then accept my devotion for what it is."

Synnovea felt a suffusing warmth eroding the barrier that

she was striving hard to erect. Shoring it up proved far more difficult than she might have supposed, and she hurriedly changed the subject lest she find herself consenting to his courtship. "May we take you somewhere, Colonel?"

"There's no need," Tyrone declined, distracted by her beauty. "My horse is nearby." Yet he made no effort to leave as he continued to stare at her. He was curious to know how many more aspects of her character were waiting to be glimpsed and treasured, like a collection of precious pearls on a strand. He had first seen the outraged countess clutched in the arms of her captor, then the wanton seductress taking a bath and, later, perched upon her windowsill. He had admired the winsome sprite in peasant garb, the gossamer-garbed maid in her bedchamber, and now the vulnerable young girl in need of a champion to defend her.

Though she seemed abashed by this most recent occurrence, he was crushingly aware of the strongly protective instincts that had surged within him when he had seen her in danger of being trodden upon. His reaction had been far more complex than he could rationally explain even to himself. Not so long ago he had been absolutely certain that all those softer, more vulnerable emotions a man could feel for a woman had been utterly destroyed by betrayal and deceit, and though he greatly desired to claim Synnovea as his mistress, he was not at all sure he wanted his heart entangled in a relationship that he had hitherto considered merely a rutting fever.

Tyrone mentally detached himself from his musings and chuckled as he glanced down at his own wet garb. "Neither of us is in any condition to offer comfort to the other, my lady, at least not in a way that would be proper." If he hadn't been thoroughly convinced that she'd turn him down flat, he would have invited her to his quarters, but he knew the foolishness of rushing her. It was far better to cool his heels and his hot blood until he could be assured of her willingness to yield him everything he desired.

Lightly touching the brim of his hat, Tyrone met the troubled eyes that watched him so intently. "Another time . . . Synnovea."

Whirling, he stepped down from the footrest and immediately had to dance aside to avoid colliding with Natasha, who, beneath the shelter of her cloak, had been forging head-downward through the driving rain. His encroaching form caused her head to snap up in surprise. Just as swiftly, her jaw plummeted. Once again Natasha found herself confronting a looming height and shoulders that looked no less than immense beneath sodden rain gear. Taken aback with a fair amount of awe, she gaped up into lean features and shadowed eyes, unable to voice an intelligible greeting.

A stiff twitch of a smile accompanied Tyrone's muttered apology. Then, tugging his hat down lower over his brow, he hunched his shoulders against the pummeling droplets and swung up onto the back of his steed. After a brief backward glance toward the coach, he rode away.

Synnovea felt as if the glow had just been taken from the day. The memory of her name being breathed in a soft caressing sigh from Tyrone's lips filled her with a secret pleasure that made her smile, but she promptly squelched it as Jozef handed her companion into the interior.

Natasha felt definitely akin to a drowned rat as she dragged her rain-soaked skirts through the door and fell back into the seat beside her young friend. Considering her difficulty in reaching the shelter, she might have paused at least to catch her breath, but she was much more interested in learning the identity of the stranger who had rushed to the assistance of her beautiful companion. "My goodness, dear, you certainly attracted the attention of a most capable protector. He seemed quite willing to move heaven and earth to keep you from harm."

The woman paused, noting Synnovea's sudden and decidedly nervous preoccupation with her ankle. It wasn't at all difficult to imagine the girl's reluctance to discuss the incident, and Natasha deftly turned the conversation to another matter. "I'll be most upset with you, Synnovea, if you haven't made plans to come home with me today for a visit. You left some clothes there the last time you visited with your father, and since you don't have to be back until later, I'd be immensely pleased if you'd stay and chat with me for as long as you dare."

Synnovea laughed, feeling her discomfiture easing. "I'd be delighted to stay for the rest of the afternoon if you'd have me," she assured the woman. "I loathe the idea of returning to the Taraslovs, especially while Aleksei lurks in wait for me there. Spending time with you will serve as a healing balm, for which I'm in dire need. Still, I mustn't be late or Anna will find some way to discipline me."

Natasha's heart went out to the young woman. It seemed a visit would do them both good, of that she had no doubt. Directing her attention to the soggy footman, she gave him a smiling nod. "Your mistress will be joining me at my home, Jozef, so we can be off now if you're inclined to leave this deluge."

"That I am, my lady," he replied with a chuckle and closed the door. The coach swayed slightly as he climbed to his rear seat, and a brief moment later, Stenka set the horses into motion.

Synnovea dragged off the sodden headdress and heaved a wistful sigh in distraction. "He always catches me at my worst."

In spite of the pelting rain, the softly whispered complaint reached Natasha's ears, kindling her curiosity to a roaring flame. "Who, dear?"

Realizing she had been caught thinking aloud, Synnovea tossed Natasha a glance askance and lifted her shoulders in an evasive shrug. "No one, Natasha. No one at all."

"Oh," the elder muttered glumly, slumping back against

the seat in disappointment. She knew the girl would never tell when it was a matter she held dear, and evidently the topic of the stranger was a subject Synnovea preferred keeping to herself. If the maid's reaction served as an indication, then Natasha was inclined to believe that whoever the tall man was, he had already made quite an impression on her young friend. Natasha sighed forlornly. "I suppose I must remain ignorant of the identity of the gallant gentleman who carried you to the coach, for it's clear you have no intention of confiding in me."

In restive unease, Synnovea dismissed the matter. " 'Twas no one of any import, Natasha. Really."

The elder countess responded with a sublime smile. "Nevertheless, I can see that you've been thoroughly unsettled by the man."

A deep blush stained Synnovea's cheeks, and in an attempt to turn aside the other woman's curiosity, she feigned distress over her sodden gown. "Ruined! Absolutely ruined! And it was one of my favorite gowns!"

"You did look exquisite in it," Natasha reflected aloud. "But then, my dear, you look exquisite in anything you wear. I'm sure that's why you attracted your friend in the first place. He seems quite taken with you."

"He's not my friend," Synnovea insisted.

Natasha smiled smugly. "Well, my dear, from what I could see of the two of you through the rain, he certainly wasn't your enemy. Tell me, what does Anna think about him?"

"He's an Englishman. Need I say more?"

Some understanding dawned as Natasha considered the other's flushed cheeks. "Then Anna has forbidden him to visit you."

Synnovea nodded mutely and desperately scoured her thoughts in search of another subject upon which they could comfortably converse. She almost relaxed as she recalled the reason she had wanted to see her friend in the first place.

"Dear Natasha, please forgive me for being so bold, but Anna's cook has a sister who, though ailing now, will be needing work when she improves. Do you have some kind of position she can fill?"

Natasha wasted no moment in asking, "Can she cook?"

A vague shrug accompanied Synnovea's reply. "I fear I know very little about Danika's capabilities, other than the fact that she's in need, but I can certainly ask Elisaveta what her experiences have been."

"If she can cook, send her around when she's well," Natasha suggested. "My old cook died since you last visited me, and I need to find a replacement ere I lose my wits trying to teach the scullery maid how to boil water. You know, with all the guests I have, the meals can be something of a disaster without a proper cook on hand."

"The woman has a child at her side," Synnovea cautioned her friend. "A daughter of three."

Natasha smiled at the idea. " 'Twould be delightful to hear the laughter of a young child around the house. Sometimes I get so lonesome in that huge place, in spite of all the company I have. The house needs a little sparkle to brighten its dark mood. And if you're kept from my side, dear Synnovea, then I must find another little girl to cherish." Her lengthy sigh hinted of a nostalgic mood. "I wish I could've had children of my own. As you know, I outlived three husbands, but none of them could get me with a child, as much as I wanted one. I've long despaired of my barren state."

Synnovea reached out a hand to rest it with genuine affection upon the elder's. "I shall always think of you as a woman I've loved nearly as dearly as my own mother, Natasha."

Bright tears blurred the woman's dark eyes as she looked upon the other with great fondness. "And you, my dear, beautiful Synnovea, are the daughter I never had, but desperately wanted so very much."

*　　*　　*

Several days elapsed after Synnovea's initial meeting with Natasha before she was again allowed to venture beyond the boundaries of the Taraslov manse. Having heeded the colonel's advice for her ankle, she had suffered no longer than a pair of days. At present, the house was in the process of being prepared for Ivan's reception, and it was in this endeavor that Anna sent her out to purchase food in the marketplace of Kitaigorod. She had given Synnovea strict orders on what to get, where to buy it, and how much to pay. Anything above that cost would have to come from her own pocket. The princess seemed to stress that fact and advised Synnovea to be prudent. In addition, she warned Synnovea not to dawdle or there would be penalties.

Stenka halted the coach in Red Square near the markets of Kitaigorod, and Synnovea walked with Ali and Jozef the rest of the way to search out the requested items. For the outing, Synnovea wore her peasant attire, not wishing to lend the impression that she had wealth. If her affluence was doubted, the merchants would be more inclined to settle for less.

Synnovea marked the time when she began, taking Anna's threat seriously. She shopped efficiently, accepting the suggestions and wisdom that both Ali and Jozef offered. Each time their baskets were filled, the footman rushed back to the carriage to unload them while the two women continued browsing through the *ryady,* searching for the best vegetables and fowl.

At last the purchases were concluded, and Synnovea and Ali were returning to the coach amid the squawking and honking of the outraged hens and geese, which Jozef had confined in a pair of crates. Upon rounding a corner, they came in sight of a company of mounted soldiers, dressed out in resplendent regalia, who were approaching from the opposite end of the thoroughfare. Synnovea's heart began thumping nigh out of her chest as she espied Colonel Rycroft at the fore of the troop. The stallion he rode was a dark liver chestnut, more beautiful than any she had previously seen. She distinctly recalled that he had said he had paid for his mounts to be shipped from England, and could only assume that this steed had accompanied his arrival in Russia. The sight of the man spiffed and polished in a handsome uniform was so stirring that she felt inclined to pause and stare in admiration, except that Ali, intent upon catching his eye, did a sprightly scamper around an approaching coach and began to wave her arm and shout his name in an eager quest to gain his attention.

"Colonel Rycroft! Yoo-hoo! Colonel Rycroft!"

"Ali! Stop that!" Synnovea gasped, abashed at the undignified conduct of her servant.

Ali promptly obeyed, but realized to her great delight that she had already gained the officer's attention. An amused grin twitched at the corners of Tyrone's lips as he honored the servant with a casual salute. Then he lifted his head and swept his gaze over the crowd beyond her, searching for the one whose face and form now filled many of his waking moments and all of his lusting dreams. Though shaded by a polished helm, his blue eyes glinted with a light of their own as he located amid several crates the profusely blushing and thoroughly mortified countess.

Synnovea desperately yearned for a large crevice to open up in the earth beneath her feet and swallow her up. The hole failed to appear, and she was forced to stand and submit to the colonel's sweeping inspection as he rode near. Stiltedly she responded in kind when he gave her a nod of greeting. It was absolutely impossible for her to ignore the fact that the wayward grin was decidedly more pronounced and that people all around her had turned to stare. Heads came together like melons rolling into a steeply sloped ravine, and had it not been for the loud honking and cackling of fowl, she might have heard a kindred noise from a cluster of women who stood nearby.

Unbeknownst to Synnovea, the serenely smiling Natasha Andreyevna stood at the outer perimeter of the commotion, digesting the event and the comments of her princely companion with great relish. Her escort just happened to be an administrator in the tsar's courts and was keenly knowledgeable about the current happenings within the palace. The fact that the Englishman was at the heart of the rumors circulating throughout the Kremlin certainly intrigued her, and she was not above suggesting that Prince Zherkof introduce her to the one who had so completely captured the tsar's attention.

"Ali McCabe!" Synnovea moaned in misery when she realized they had attracted the curiosity of a vast number of shoppers in the marketplace. "You have made me rue the day my mother hired you!"

Stenka and Jozef choked back their laughter and deliberately devoted themselves to loading the purchases into the coach as the Irish woman wiped away a giggle behind the back of a scrawny hand. Feigning the innocence of a saint, Ali met the accusing stare of her mistress and shrugged her thin shoulders in confusion. "But what did I do?"

"Everything worthy of damnation!" Synnovea groaned and lifted a hand in plaintive appeal to the sky. "Oh, for a plain, simple maidservant who knows when to keep her *silence!*" Lowering a sinister glare upon the woman, she addressed Ali with a chiding finger once more in evidence. "You have caused me tremendous distress this day, Ali! Do you not ken how imperative it is that I avoid the attentions of Colonel Rycroft? But what do you do but hail him from afar at the top of your lungs like some tavern wench! And to the glee of every long-winded gossip within range of hearing! Do you understand what you've done to me? This is sure to get back to Anna's ears ere we even arrive home. Believe me, I'll never hear the last of it!"

"Hmph!" Ali folded her thin arms petulantly. "As if me own dear self ne'er swaddled yer backside from the day ye were born an' I've no wits in me poor noggin ta know what ye be needin'! Ye carp 'bout me manners when it's yerself ye should be lookin' ta! Tyrone is a right fine gentleman, e'en if I say so meself! An' if ye had eyes in yer fine head, me pretty darlin', ye'd be a-thinkin' so, too!"

"Tyrone, is it? And, pray tell, who lent ye permission ta be usin' his Christian name?" Synnovea mimicked sassily. "Are ye so in league wit' the man that ye're now his copemate? Tyrone, indeed!"

" 'Tis a right fine Irish name, it is!" Ali argued. "A proud name, ta be sure!"

"Colonel Rycroft is an Englishman!" Synnovea stated obstinately. "Knighted on English soil! He is *not* an Irishman!"

"Oh, 'tis the good Sir Tyrone, is it? Well, I'll wager me skirts his ma were a proper colleen ta win a man's heart."

Synnovea threw up her hands in disgust. "I've neither the patience nor the time to argue with a woman of your temerity, Ali McCabe. We must return to the Taraslovs before their servants are sent out to bring us back."

"Aren't ye a wee bit curious 'bout where the colonel might be takin' his men bedecked in all o' their finery?" Ali asked, hoping to incite some interest. "Couldn't we follow a ways just ta see?"

"Never!" Synnovea served quick death to the notion. She wasn't about to allow the colonel the privilege of thinking she was chasing after him. Why, the very idea of lending him encouragement made her quake. He had proven himself quite tenacious as it was. She could only wonder how assertive he'd become with a little encouragement.

8

$\mathcal{P}$rince Vladimir Dimitrievitch was a barrel-chested, white-haired, mustached boyar with a total of seventy-plus years to his claim. He had been married and widowered twice and, in those unions, had sired a total of seven sons. It was well known that he was keeping a discerning eye out for a third possibility upon whom he could spawn a new crop, and though many a father was willing to present his daughter as a potential bride in hopes of somehow gaining access to the prince's wealth, the old man was as cautious and discriminating as an ancient dowager afraid of losing her titles and assets to some unscrupulous rake. Despite his white hair, Vladimir was as virile as many men half his age and decidedly more adamant about proving himself capable of exercising his manly functions. He was evidently proud of his unfaltering prowess and, when met with encouragement, waxed gleeful and openly suggestive on the subject of his abilities, especially when a young, winsome maid caught his eye and he gave himself over to his boastful tendencies.

Vladimir's offspring were all strapping young men with a penchant for excessive carousing and heavy brawling. Their tempers were short even with one another. From the simplest source, they could usually glean some excuse for competing against other rowdies. In contests of brawn, they derived no greater pleasure than to defeat a whole army of foes, friends, and family alike. To say that they were an unruly rabble might have been putting it mildly. Still, they were a likable lot in many ways. It only took a person of sharp perception to figure out what those particular qualities were.

Anna Taraslovna knew she was tempting fate by requesting the presence of Prince Vladimir and his sons at her reception honoring Ivan Voronsky. If provoked, the contrary family was aggressive enough to reduce the whole affair to shambles, but she could think of no viable way to separate kith from kin, or, more pertinently, father from offspring. Indeed, it would be an enormous miracle if the pugnacious family managed to get through the entire evening without resorting to fisticuffs, which in the main comprised her greatest worry. The only reason she considered inviting them at all was out of regard for Ivan and his desire to replace the priest whom Vladimir had hired for his private chapel and then dismissed a pair of months later. Ivan had shrewdly lent a sympathetic ear to the old man's complaints about the narrow-mindedness of the monk, who had had the gall to chide Vladimir for his intemperate propensities, not the least of which was his fondness for vodka. In light of the ancient's vast wealth, Ivan was totally dedicated to the idea of Anna inviting the whole family lest their sire be offended by the exclusion of his sons.

As much as Anna chafed over the hazards of inviting the rambunctious clan, she was even more concerned about the risk of allowing her ward to attend. Had she been able to ban Synnovea from the festivities without arousing the curiosity of the guests, who either knew the girl personally or were aware of her through an association with her late father, Anna would've done so without hesitation, just to avoid the havoc that her ward could cause. Many who were acquainted with Synnovea would have considered her an unlikely source for trouble, but Anna was contemptuous of such logic. She could foresee her aspirations being sundered before her very eyes and her rival unwittingly becoming the victor in this evening's affair. Not only could Synnovea's beauty attract the ardent attentions of Aleksei but the unwavering admiration of the ancient Vladimir as well.

Extremely reluctant to allow the girl any leeway in either area, Anna made a point of seeking Synnovea out in her chambers before the guests began arriving. Her intent was to prescribe the proper decorum that would be required of the girl throughout the evening, but upon barging into Synnovea's chambers without knocking, Anna was momentarily taken aback by the vision that greeted her. In that brief moment all of her apprehensions congealed into a cold lump of dread. Arrayed in winter white, Synnovea looked as dazzling as any fabled snow queen of Russian lore.

If it were at all possible, Anna's resentment of the girl increased tenfold as she stalked across the room to confront her. "If I see you cavorting like some mindless little twit among my guests or hear one whisper of complaint about your actions, I swear you won't be allowed to leave this house until you've realized the full import of your folly in provoking me. Though you may have enjoyed your freedom under your father's lax authority, I'll expect you to conduct yourself with acceptable humility and be as demure as any proper Russian maid. Do I make myself clear?"

Synnovea took exception to the woman's intimidation. "As always, Anna, you take special pains to make me cognizant of your demands."

A spark of irritation ignited the gray eyes. "Do I detect some sarcasm in your reply?"

A stiff smile curved Synnovea's lips. "My mode of behavior is normally rather reserved, so it seems rather pointless for you to advise me how a lady should conduct herself. I *have* managed to attend such functions without causing my family or other acquaintances undue embarrassment."

"I'm not referring to your comportment while attending French or English courts, but what it must be here in *my* house!" Anna retorted. "I won't tolerate any of your sly cavorting while you're with my guests!"

"If you're so afraid I'll humiliate you, Anna, why don't you just lock the door and be done with it?" Synnovea struggled to curb her own fermenting indignation as the princess glared back at her. "I'll be quite content staying here in my chambers."

Anna straightened her thin form imperiously. "Unfortunately, I found it needful to invite several of your acquaintances who've gained recognition as attendants to my cousin. Your presence would be missed." Anna sniffed in imposing arrogance. "I understand you're a close friend of Princess Zelda Pavlovna. Since her husband was unable to separate himself from the duties assigned to him by the field marshal, she'll be attending tonight's social with her parents. I'm sure you know them better than I do."

At the heartening prospect of being able to converse with her young friend, Synnovea relaxed and graciously accepted the woman's directives. "Be at ease, Anna. I shall comply with your desires."

"I'm glad you've decided to be reasonable," the princess retorted haughtily.

Synnovea was tempted to tell the woman that it was *her* conduct in serious need of refining, but knowing only too well that her accusations would involve them in another altercation, she refrained from voicing her opinion.

Anna heaved a tedious sigh. "Against my better judgment,

I've extended an invitation to Countess Natasha." She ignored her ward's sudden smile of delight and deliberately avoided any mention of her reasons, which mainly centered on her hope that Natasha would be able to occupy the major portion of the girl's attention and thereby reduce the chances of her associating with other guests and creating disaster in sensitive areas. "I see that you're pleased, and well you should be. The two of you generally seem to be of one mind."

Synnovea knew the princess meant her comment as a slur, but that certainly wasn't the way she chose to accept it. Smiling, she dipped into a curtsy. "You do me great honor, Anna."

An unladylike snort clearly defined the princess's contempt as that one stalked to the door. There she paused to look back at Synnovea. The rich, pearl-encrusted *sarafan* and *kokoshniki* were beautiful beyond anything Anna had ever seen, and though she had expended the contents of an enormous purse on her own gold-and-yellow creation, she was struck by her failure to even come close to matching the other's radiance. Yet, as much as she wanted to, she couldn't order Synnovea to change her attire. Such a directive would reveal the full extent of her jealousy. The best she could do was delay the girl and hope she wouldn't be noticed overmuch when she finally joined the soiree.

"You needn't hurry down, Synnovea. The guests are just now beginning to arrive, and it will be some moments before they're all here. Natasha said she wouldn't be coming until later anyway."

Anna took her departure before further comment could be made. She dreaded Natasha's arrival and wondered if she'd be able to find it in herself to set aside her hatred long enough to offer some semblance of a gracious greeting to the woman.

Synnovea stayed closeted upstairs for another hour, having clearly perceived that her tardiness was what Anna desired. When she finally departed her room, she approached the stairs, intending to make her descent but halted abruptly when Aleksei stepped out of the shadows near the bottom and smiled smugly up at her. It was apparent he had been waiting for her to appear. He bounded up the flight, leaving her no recourse but to retreat. He sauntered forward, his red lips parting in a slow, sensual smile that brazenly hinted of his warming lust as his smoldering gaze glided upward from the bejeweled toes of her satin slippers to the pearl-adorned crest of her headdress.

"I've been meaning to talk with you, Synnovea," he murmured, gently testing his still-tender nose with a lean knuckle, as if to remind her of her folly in doing him harm. "Though some men might have been offended by your determination to preserve your virtue, my dear, I must allow that your nature is perhaps different from that of most women. In the situation you're in here, you have suitable cause to be concerned. Suppose we were to be found out and you were then subjected to the contempt of your friends and the hatred of Anna. Terrifying prospects, I must agree. Still, the pain of discovery seems far more remote than the consequences you'll definitely suffer if you continue to deny me . . ."

Synnovea was resolved to hear no more threats. She had already heard enough from Anna to set her temper on edge. In angry reticence, she brushed past him, but her flight was halted when he caught her arm and yanked her around to face him. Though her heart quickened with trepidation, she lifted her gaze with all the dignity that she could muster and, with a brittle gaze, met his silently taunting smile. Her cool poise seemed to incense him, and with an angry jerk that nearly snapped her head from her shoulders, he sent her reeling to the far wall, where she crashed with a mind-jarring jolt. Momentarily stunned by the force of her collision, Synnovea staggered unsteadily, holding a hand to her head as she tried to halt her spinning world. Aleksei followed and, with a smirk, caught her almost gently by the throat, only to shove her back brutally against the wall.

"You needn't hurry away, my lovely swan," he mocked and lowered his face toward hers until she could feel his hot breath searing her cheek. "You won't be missed downstairs for some moments yet. You see, Anna is completely engrossed in making Ivan known to her guests, which leaves us freedom to enjoy ourselves."

Synnovea clawed at the long fingers that gradually tightened around the bejeweled band of her collar, seriously restricting her ability to breathe. In rising alarm, she tried to free herself. Her efforts only encouraged him to tighten his grip. The hall darkened progressively around them, and she heard his soft, ridiculing laughter as if it came from a great distance away.

"You see, Synnovea? I've reserved this little demonstration to show you just how futile it is for you to continue to deny me. Until you yield to my demands, my beauty, I shall be forced to instruct you in the hazards that you'll invite by resisting me."

Of a sudden, Aleksei loosened his grip and stepped back, allowing Synnovea to crumple in weak-kneed relief against the wall. Gulping for air, she clutched a shaking hand to her bruised throat and found no strength to draw away as her tormentor braced a hand against the wall behind her head and leaned near.

"I would've been gentle with you in the woodcutter's cottage, Synnovea, but I've grown impatient and yearn to settle the matter quickly." Lifting her upright by the arms, he captured her wrists and pinned them to the wall on either side of her head as he slowly perused her face. "You glow with the radiance of a silver moon, Synnovea, but you remain as aloof as a virgin queen . . . a snow maiden who has seized my heart. That's what they call you, isn't it? I've heard them say as much. The Countess Synnovea Zenkovna, the snow queen. The ice maiden! Are you as cold as they say you are, Synnovea? Or will you melt in my arms and become the fire-bird I've roamed this whole world to find?"

"I warn you, Aleksei!" she rasped through her constricted throat. She closed her eyes as her head swam dizzily, and it was a long moment before she again reclaimed some clarity of sense and purpose. Then, with a fiery glare, she vowed, "You'll have to kill me right here and now, for I'll never yield to you. If you intend to persist with your foul deeds, be mindful of this. With my last breath, I'll scream and bring this house down upon your head. I swear I will!"

"Oh, Synnovea, when will you learn?" Aleksei chided, shaking his head sorrowfully. "You have no other recourse but to give in to my demands." Once again he found it needful to demonstrate his greater strength. Slipping a hand behind her neck, he clasped it cruelly, forcing her to rise to the tips of her toes. His dark eyes pierced her pain-filled orbs. "Continue to deny me, my sweet, and *I* swear I will see you betrothed to the first doddering ancient who is old enough to vindicate me. Perhaps thus bound in wedlock, you'll be willing to welcome the manly thrusts of a more competent suitor." He lent emphasis to his words by slamming her back forcefully against the wall and crushing his hips against hers.

"Get away from me!" she choked as her hands came up to push feebly against his unyielding chest. "Just leave me alone and let me be!"

"I'll leave you alone!" he snarled, throwing off her hands and snatching her to him. His mouth came down to seize hers with unbridled greed as his arms crushed her in a cruel vise.

Swept with a seething rage, Synnovea reached back an arm to search for the heavy sconce that she knew was hanging on the wall behind her. In the flickering descent of sputtering candles, she brought the weighty piece down with a vengeance upon the man's thick skull.

Aleksei staggered back in a stunned daze and clutched a

hand to his brow while a red aura blurred his vision. Synnovea gave the lecher no further chance to check her flight. Tearing free, she flung herself down the stairs, nearly stumbling in her haste until she came in sight of Boris, who, becoming mindful of her undignified flight, paused in the lower foyer and half turned to look up at her in surprise.

Though her whole being trembled from Aleksei's recent assault, Synnovea steeled herself against an overt display. Deliberately slowing her breath, she assumed a guise of serenity in spite of the quaking tremors that beset her. She continued her descent with more leisured grace and smiled serenely at the steward even as she listened intently for the warning descent of thundering footfalls behind her.

Upon gaining the lower level, Synnovea went to the kitchen, where she knew she'd be reasonably safe from Aleksei and far removed from the curious stares of Anna and her guests. There, with her back to Elisaveta, she brushed at the tears that continued to well forth and blew her nose in the handkerchief the woman had kindly supplied. The cook dared no questions but pressed a glass of wine into her shaky grasp. Gratefully Synnovea sipped the brew, needing its soothing qualities to quell her violent quaking.

Finally her trembling disquiet ebbed, and Synnovea lent her attention to repairing her appearance. She found that feat much easier than mending the damage done by the stranglehold Aleksei had placed upon her neck, for she now suffered a burning rawness in her throat and a rasping hoarseness in her speech.

Much later than she had ever supposed, Synnovea made her entrance into the great hall, where Ivan, bedecked in a black silk kaftan, seemed to preen in the admiration heaped upon him by Anna and those who were not above indulging the tsar's cousin with ingratiating adoration no matter her particular bent. Others who were more reserved and reticent about offering the man praise watched and listened stoically from a distance.

Synnovea paused at the outer circle of guests and, from there, cast her gaze about for Princess Zelda. She espied the young woman standing with her parents near the far end of the room. By the studied formality of the three, it was evident that they weren't at all enchanted with what they were hearing. Synnovea realized the reason when she, too, gave heed to Ivan's statements. Prince Bazhenov had served as one of the envoys for the tsar in the negotiations that had taken place between Russia and the realm that Ivan currently spoke out against.

"I tell you, my friends, our country is at an impasse," he declared with unusual passion. "We've lost our access to the Baltic by way of a treaty with Sweden, and even now they're usurping our trade in Novgorod and other important cities. Mysteriously they've been granted fishing rights on White Lake, and I'll wager we'll soon be outnumbered by Lutheran extremists here in our own country. If we don't resist fairly soon, they'll likely be fathering your grandchildren! Mark my words!"

A confused blend of voices arose from several of the guests, but none dared voice any disapproval of the authority which had allowed the Swedes to infiltrate their country so insidiously. Prince Bazhenov, however, was bold enough to speak out in valiant defense of it.

"With Sweden's aid, Tsar Mikhail has managed to bring us the first peace we've known with Poland after many years of conflict. What would you suggest we do now?" he queried caustically. "Take up arms against Sweden?"

Ivan was cautious about answering, having perceived the loyalty the old prince felt for the tsar. "Above all, we must *never* alienate anyone against the tsardom, for there beats the heart of our very lifeblood." He paused briefly for effect as he pressed the tips of his stubby fingers together in a contemplative pose. "Perhaps if we seek the advice of another accomplished strategist who is knowledgeable about such affairs, we can gain some insight as to the diplomacy and tactics we should employ against the Swedes."

"Besides the Patriarch Filaret, you mean?" Prince Bazhenov jeered.

Ivan spread his hands in sublime innocence. "Are not two heads better than one?"

The elder was immediately suspicious. "Are you suggesting, sir, that you would be a worthy candidate for that position?"

"I am only a loyal subject of the tsar, my lord," the cleric replied with suitable humbleness. "Still, if I were pressed into service, I think I'd be able to offer satisfactory solutions to ease the plight of our countrymen."

"No doubt," Prince Bazhenov retorted tersely. "You seem to have all the answers, but I wonder where your suggestions would lead us as a nation."

"Who doesn't wonder what the outcome will be?" Ivan countered. "Even now we're being led as a nation by one man's wisdom. Does that give you confidence? Can you offer solid guarantees of the Patriarch Filaret's goals for this country and our future?"

The prince harrumphed loudly, displaying his displeasure over the discussion. Begging Anna's pardon a moment later, he excused himself and his family from the reception, giving the excuse that he had to attend an early-morning inspection with the tsar and needed his rest.

Trailing behind her parents as they prepared for their departure, Princess Zelda glanced around in search of Synnovea and smiled in sudden pleasure when that one finally emerged from the press of people.

"I thought we'd have time to talk, darling," Zelda whispered regretfully in her friend's ear as they hugged each other. "My husband has been telling me things that I was sure you'd be eager to hear. Vassili was wondering if you knew about the rumors making their way around the Kremlin and wanted me to find out. I wish we could talk about this, but as you can see, we must leave. Papa is nearly beside himself. Whoever this Ivan Voronsky is, he hasn't endeared himself to Papa!"

"I'll see you as soon as I'm able," Synnovea promised in a softly rasping murmur. "We can talk then."

"Take care," Zelda bade, brushing her lips against the other's cheek.

Watching from the doorway, Synnovea waited until Prince Bazhenov had handed his family into their carriage and the conveyance had pulled away before she retreated into the house, allowing Boris to close the door behind her. She paused at the entrance of the great hall, listening to Ivan's voice drone on incessantly, but his views were disconcerting and she withdrew to the dining room, where she hoped she'd be able to find something soft to eat that wouldn't irritate her throat.

No sooner had Synnovea entered than several boyars gathered close around her. They numbered seven in all and resembled one another in height, brawn, and visage, with three of them having light brown hair and the youngest four black. Even their quickly widening grins hinted of their kinship.

"Enchanting!" one of them murmured and then, heaving an exaggerated sigh, fell back in a mock swoon into the arms of a companion.

"Captivating! Completely dazzling!" another one avowed exuberantly, closely eyeing her.

"Permit me to introduce myself, *Boyarina,*" the tallest one bade. "I'm Prince Feodor Vladimirovich, eldest son of Prince Vladimir Dimitrievich, and these"—he swept a hand around to indicate his cohorts—"are my brothers, second-born Igor, then Petr, Stefan, Vasilii, Nikita, and Sergei, the youngest."

As he introduced them, each man responded with a broad grin and clicked his heels in a brief, clipped bow. As the eldest, Feodor assumed the part of spokesman while his brothers crowded close around him. Together they awaited her response to his inquiry. "And your name, *Boyarina?*"

Smiling graciously, Synnovea sank into a deep curtsy as she strained to keep the hoarse rasp in her voice softly subdued. "The Countess Synnovea Altynai Zenkovna, recently arrived from Nizhni Novgorod."

Sergei swaggered around his older siblings to eagerly ask, "Do you have any sisters?" Then, with a shrug, he complained, "There are so many of us, but only one of you."

For the first time that evening, Synnovea was able to smile with lighthearted gaiety, and she gave them a pretty shrug. "I fear not, Prince Sergei. As fate would have it, I was an only child."

"And your husband?" Curious, he cocked a dark brow and asked with bated breath, "Where is he?"

Soft, husky laughter preceded her answer. "Your pardon, most gracious Prince, but I have none."

"A pity!" he lamented with a happy chortle.

Smoothing his kaftan in a confident manner, he stepped before her and executed a flamboyant bow. Upon straightening, he begged, "Permit me, Countess, to express an avid appreciation of your beauty. In all my score of years I've never seen a maid so wondrously fair. You'd bestow upon me a great honor if you'd allow me to court you—"

Immediately he was shoved aside by the dark-eyed Stefan, who offered a warm smile as he took the place formerly occupied by his brother. "Sergei is but a boy, Countess, a youth of no experience. I, on the other hand, have a score and ten years to my claim, and though 'tis also true that I've seen none to equal your radiance, I'm sure you'll agree that I'm better-looking than Sergei."

"Ha!" the hulking Igor scoffed and swung an arm backward to send Stefan stumbling in retreat. Stroking his handsome beard, Igor settled in a bold stance before her as his blue eyes twinkled back at her. "None of my brothers can equal my experience . . ." With a challenging brow raised, he cast glances from side to side at his siblings as he boasted, "Or my good looks."

Hearty guffaws accompanied his statement, attesting to the skepticism of his brothers, who commenced to argue among themselves. Amid all of their squabbling, an excessive amount of rough jostling and painful nudging ensued.

"Not so! I'm the best-looking!"

"Come, now! Would you have the countess believe such lies when I'm here for her to see?"

"It's a shame you haven't taken a good look at yourself lately. I'll warrant I've seen better faces on the hind end of a bear!"

Synnovea was about to giggle, but gasped instead as the offended one doubled his fist and bashed the nose of the one who had insulted him. The brothers promptly set themselves to determining the matter by force, at least until a throaty harrumph came from close behind them. The sound had an effect on the brothers that Synnovea found no less than astounding. It cooled their tempers like a pail of icy water. In sudden haste they stumbled backward to open a path for an older man who ambled forward with a rolling gait, as if he had spent his lifetime on the deck of a ship. Not even Colonel Rycroft or Ladislaus matched this one's height, for the new-comer was at least half a head taller than either of those two stalwarts. Synnovea had some difficulty hiding her own amazement as the white-haired ancient approached her. Upon halting beside Sergei, the old man laid a huge hand upon the lad's shoulder.

"What is this bickering about now?" he rumbled in a deep voice, closely perusing the young maiden.

"The Countess Zenkovna has no sisters, Papa," the youth answered. "We were trying to decide which of us would court her."

"Indeed?" The comely maid had already aroused the old

man's interest, and he was much encouraged by his son's comment. Though a bit slender for his taste, she was nevertheless rounded in all the right places and had enough height to accommodate his enormous frame. The idea of such an event appealed to him, and with a brightening gleam in his eyes, he swept a forefinger beneath his heavy mustache, flickering up the curving ends. He offered his most ardent smile, displaying a full set of white teeth. "If you'll allow me to introduce myself, Countess. I'm Prince Vladimir Dimitrievitch, and these, as I'm sure you've already ascertained, are my sons. Have they introduced themselves?"

"Most capably, my lord prince," Synnovea responded, dipping again into a polite curtsy. In the next moment she braced herself for the worst when she happened to glance past his arm and espied Anna forging a channel through a collection of guests who had meandered to the doorway to watch the antics of the princely brood.

"What's going on here?" the princess demanded, trying to sound gracious, but failing badly. Whatever disturbance was transpiring, she marked Synnovea as the source of the trouble. A sidelong glare clearly conveyed that fact to her ward, giving that one cause to wonder what punishment would be forthcoming.

"My sons and I were making the acquaintance of this fair maid," Vladimir explained. "Might I ask why we were not informed of the Countess Zenkovna's presence sooner?"

Anna opened her mouth several times while she struggled to find some viable reason and finally, with a feeble smile, replied, "I wasn't aware that you wanted to meet her."

"Nonsense! Any man would be interested in making the acquaintance of a beautiful woman. At least, she doesn't bore me to tears!"

His comment carried the full weight of his rejection of Ivan's discourse as well as a firm rebuff for Anna's attempts to sway his considerations in favor of the cleric. Though he might have been deemed an ancient by the standards of some, Vladimir hadn't yet lost his wits. What he had heard tonight led him to wonder just where Ivan's loyalties were rooted.

In spite of her temporary defeat, Anna fixed a smile on her lips and, with as much graciousness as she could convey, faced Synnovea. "I believe I saw Natasha's carriage coming up the lane in front of the house. Would you care to greet her, my dear?"

"Yes, of course." Once again Synnovea sank in gracious obeisance before the elderly prince. "If you'll excuse me, Prince Vladimir, my friend has arrived, and I'd like very much to see her."

Bestowing a smile upon her, the old man inclined his head, granting his permission. Synnovea slipped quickly through the guests, greeting friends and acquaintances as she went. When she entered the main hall, Aleksei was just making his way down the stairs. Though she saw no immediate evidence of a wound, he was descending very carefully, as if fearful that his head would tumble from its perch. At her hesitant glance, he gave her a menacing glower, leaving no doubt that he wouldn't rest until he had either his revenge *or* his way with her.

"Synnovea, my dear child!" Natasha cried with a cheery laugh from the doorway, claiming her attention. "Come here and let me look at you!"

Coolly rejecting Aleksei's silent threat, Synnovea turned and eagerly extended her hands in welcome as she hastened forward. "Natasha, you look absolutely ravishing!"

The elder laughed and sashayed around in a circle for the benefit of the younger woman. Her black and silver-trimmed *sarafan* not only complimented her porcelain skin but also lent dramatic emphasis to her darkly lashed, ebony eyes. When left undraped, her black hair seemed touched with a hoary frost, but at the moment, the mass was covered by a shimmering, silver-hued veil and a *kokoshniki* adorned with finely wrought silver filigree and precious stones.

"Lovely!" Synnovea exclaimed, perusing the woman. It came to her suddenly that whatever enmity Anna bore Natasha might have sprouted from a simple seed of jealousy. Though the princess was younger by three years, her pale-haired good looks had declined far more rapidly than those of the countess, whose skin still glowed with a soft, youthful luster. Few wrinkles could be noted in the elegant widow's face. Indeed, she was every bit as ravishing in her maturing years as any woman could hope to be.

"This has been a most enlightening week," Natasha avouched with a warm chuckle. "I've been fortunate enough to hear the most delectable gossip."

"If it's about Princc Alcksci, please spare me," Synnovea begged with a genuine lack of interest. "I've come to detest the man!"

"Oh, I wouldn't bore you with that rubbish, my dear. What I've been hearing is much more thrilling than anything he has ever done."

"Zelda wanted to share some news with me, too, but she had to leave before she could tell me what it was." Synnovea looped an arm through the woman's elbow and led her to a padded bench in a quiet corner of the great room. "Now here you are, seeming enormously elated. Has Tsar Mikhail chosen a wife perchance?"

"Oh, no, my dear." Natasha leaned forward eagerly, but when Boris stepped near to offer them a variety of libations from a silver tray she was forced to bide her time. Accepting a glass of fruited wine, Natasha thanked the servant and waited until he had moved away to other guests before she faced her young friend again. "You wouldn't believe the furor that has been caused in the Kremlin within the last weeks. Why, the very air is abuzz with rumors of a certain Englishman. . . ."

Synnovea's lovely mouth parted in surprise, and in spite of the quickening pace of her heart, she managed to quell the nervous trembling in her voice as she asked, "Do you mean Colonel Rycroft?"

Gathering her brows into a semblance of perplexity, Natasha inquired, "Isn't he the same officer who rescued you from that Polish renegade . . . oh, what was his name . . . ?"

"Ladislaus?" A delicately winged brow arched in sharp suspicion as Synnovea studied the woman. Natasha looked very pleased with herself, as if waiting for the right moment to spring a surprise. "Where did you hear about Ladislaus? I don't recall mentioning anything about his attack on my carriage."

The silver veil glimmered in the candlelight as Natasha shook her head woefully and heaved a dejected sigh. "To think that I was the last to be told. I'm crushed to think how little regard you have for me."

Synnovea was growing increasingly apprehensive. "I only spoke of that brigand when I had to."

"Oh, I've been hearing rumors about him, too," Natasha assured her. "It seems he has been seen a time or two in Moscow since his attack on your coach, but he always manages to elude the tsar's soldiers. There has even been some rumblings about Ladislaus wanting to repay the Englishman for the losses that he and his men suffered at his hands."

Synnovea might as well have been sitting on a powder keg. The best she could offer the woman was a noncommittal conjecture. "Colonel Rycroft would likely welcome a confrontation if it meant the return of the horse that Ladislaus stole from him, but I rather doubt that their encounter would be a contest of arms the fainthearted could easily watch."

"I really don't think the colonel is concerning himself overmuch with Ladislaus at the present time, my dear," Natasha dared to speculate. "I believe he has other things he considers of greater importance on his mind."

Synnovea peered at Natasha obliquely, not knowing if

she'd be able to bear the news which the woman was obviously just brimming to tell. Perhaps it was wiser by far to find a place to hide before she heard what was being bandied about. Still, she couldn't resist a shaky inquiry. "What could be more important to him than catching Ladislaus?"

"Why, his petition to the tsar, for one thing," the older woman replied with an effervescent smile.

Synnovea gulped and repeated in a tentative tone, "Petition to the tsar?"

Natasha curbed a smile of amusement, taking unusual delight in prolonging her friend's discomfiture. "I'm utterly amazed, Synnovea, that you of all people haven't heard about Colonel Rycroft's request." She shrugged blithely. "But then, I must remember that Anna has been keeping you prisoner, hasn't she? A pity."

"Why should the colonel's entreaty be of interest to me?"

The older countess flicked her fine eyebrows upward as she looked at Synnovea in feigned amazement. "Why, because he has been making petitions to the tsar to court you."

Synnovea clutched a trembling hand to her throat, feeling the heat of a blush suffuse her cheeks. "He didn't actually dare?"

It was rare to see the cool poise of the younger woman so thoroughly disrupted, especially by reports of a suitor's bold intentions, but such an occurrence awakened some hope within Natasha's heart that there was indeed a man who could thaw the blood of this beautiful ice maiden. "Oh, but he did!" she eagerly assured her young friend. "Most persuasively, too, from what I hear! He explained about having had the opportunity to meet you after saving you from the band of thieves, and then asked if there were any Russian laws that forbade him from paying court to you."

The rapid racing of her pulse prompted Synnovea to fan herself. Breathlessly she concluded, "I am ruined!"

"On the contrary, my dear. Mikhail told Colonel Rycroft

that he would seriously consider his petition after reviewing the facts. But, of course, since then there has been no evidence to indicate His Majesty's decision, for it seems that shortly after Colonel Rycroft made his plea, Major Nikolai Nekrasov also entreated the tsar for the same favor. If I dare venture a guess, I'd say that Nikolai heard about the Englishman's plea and decided to establish his own claim on you. Indeed, it seemed the two men were on their way to becoming fast friends until they found themselves at odds over you."

Synnovea groaned in abject misery as she thought of the two appealing to the tsar for permission to woo her, as if he didn't have better things to ponder. "How dare they drag my name before the tsar without asking my consent!"

Natasha contemplated her young friend in dubious wonder. "Have you become so accustomed to the mores of other countries, Synnovea, that you've forgotten how such affairs are handled here? You should know that asking a maid first for permission isn't the way an arrangement of courtship is accomplished here in Russia. Besides, if either Colonel Rycroft or Major Nekrasov had been confident of Prince Aleksei granting them approval, they'd have gone to him, but Anna made it apparent, especially to the Englishman, that he wasn't welcome in this house, so he went to a higher authority." Her brows shot up briefly as she chuckled. "The tsar himself, no less. Major Nekrasov only followed his lead."

"I've given Colonel Rycroft no encouragement!" Synnovea declared in swift defense of her own actions, but as soon as the words were uttered, she knew they weren't necessarily the truth. Hadn't she cast the full blame on Anna when she had told Tyrone that he shouldn't come back to the Taraslov manse? Hadn't she allowed him entry into her room without alerting others of his midnight visit? And hadn't she given him a miniature of herself and yielded her lips to his kiss before his departure? If she had casually dismissed the probability of his beseeching the tsar's favor when he had declared that he'd do that very thing, why was she so upset now? Why was she all aflutter? Was she angry at him . . . or with herself for being less than fully dedicated to the task of discouraging him?

Natasha had noticed that Synnovea hadn't offered similar assurances of her conduct with the major. Either the girl had encouraged Nikolai and didn't care to reveal that fact, *or* she had never considered the major a serious contender for her affections. Natasha was curious to know the full extent of the truth. "And did you encourage Major Nekrasov?"

Synnovea was scandalized by the idea. "Of course not! He's a friend, nothing more."

Natasha smiled smugly. "A man like Colonel Rycroft needs no encouragement, does he? He simply seeks out what he desires to have and now has made it evident that he desires to have you, my dear."

"I don't even know the man!" Synnovea insisted in a frail attempt to banish any blame for his efforts to win her.

"Now what are you saying, child? Wasn't he the one who saved you from that rogue Ladislaus? Wasn't he the one who carried you to your coach in the rainstorm?" Natasha's lips curved into a sublime smile as her friend's cheeks took on a bright glow. "You certainly seemed to know him then, for you made no protest when he lifted you in his arms. Would you have willingly allowed a stranger to pick you up?"

"No, of course, not," Synnovea admitted lamely.

"Then the two of you have obviously met."

"Only briefly!" Synnovea emphasized her words, struggling to convince her friend. "Never formally!"

The older countess slowly nodded in smiling serenity. "Apparently it was enough to spark the colonel's interest."

"I intend to discourage the man," Synnovea announced emphatically as she sought to convince herself that that was exactly what she should do.

"What a shame." Natasha's carefully devised dejection was accompanied by a soft, wistful sigh. "I must admit that I'm among the ladies who are simply agog over the officer. There hasn't been this much excitement over a man since the first false Dmitri tried to claim the tsardom a good twenty years ago and his remains were blown out of a cannon. I tell you, Synnovea, Colonel Rycroft excites me!" Almost dreamily, she drummed her slender fingers lightly upon her goblet. "Have you seen the way he sits the back of a horse, my dear?" She already knew the answer, but hurried on with her boasting. "Ramrod-straight he rides, yet with fluid movements that make him seem an integral part of the horse. Can you imagine such a man in your bed?"

Synnovea felt a scalding heat rising in her cheeks as she recalled his hard, naked body pressing against her own. "Certainly not!"

Natasha ignored her breathless answer. Though Synnovea denied the possibility that she had *ever* entertained such thoughts, Natasha was of a mind to think differently. Surely the progressing tide of color sweeping into her cheeks was enough to confirm the vividness of the girl's imagination. She was simply protesting too much to be believed. "So! You *have* thought about him?"

For a moment Synnovea's lovely mouth hung aslack as she met the older woman's smiling regard. Then, ever so slightly, the pearl-encrusted headdress dipped forward in acknowledgment. "Briefly."

"Oh, Synnovea." Natasha sighed in a gently chiding tone. "Were I a score of years younger, I'd certainly see that such a man was adequately distracted by my attentions."

Synnovea looked at the woman in some wonder. Natasha was barely ten years older than the Englishman and attractive enough to be able to ensnare his attention if she so desired it. A younger, less experienced maid would have cause to worry if she found herself hopelessly smitten with the colonel and he had eyes only for Natasha. There would likely be no contest.

"If ever I should relent and admit the colonel into my presence, I shall make haste to introduce him to you," Synnovea gallantly proposed.

"No need for that, my dear," Natasha assured her with an amused chortle. "That event has already taken place. Prince Zherkof introduced us after Colonel Rycroft put on an exhibition in the Kremlin the other day. It was magnificent, my dear. You should have seen it. I was completely enthralled with the horsemanship of the colonel and his troop. I think the tsar was pleased, too. At least, he appeared to be."

"When was that?" Synnovea queried carefully, wondering if she had seen him that day.

Natasha's lips twitched faintly as she fought a small battle with her composure. "Well, I'm not exactly sure, my dear, but it also seems that I saw you near Red Square that day, too. Did you go to Kitaigorod to shop for something, perhaps? And were you perchance wearing your peasant attire?"

Synnovea wanted to groan, fearing the woman had witnessed the event which had caused nearly the whole market-place to halt and stare. "I was there, but I didn't see you."

"Oh, it really doesn't matter," Natasha told her, noting her friend's distress. "What does count is the fact that I've had the opportunity to invite the colonel to my home next week, along with some of his officers and a few of my most intimate friends. Prince Zherkof will be there, and, of course, my dear, you're also invited. I do hope that you can persuade Anna to allow you to attend. I've heard rumors that she has finally decided to hasten to her father's bedside. If that's true, then perhaps you'll be staying with me when the colonel comes to visit. Your presence at the affair would no doubt encourage a windfall of handsome men."

Synnovea's brow peaked as she regarded the elder. "Is it *my* company you seek or that of the colonel?"

"Both!" Natasha answered with unabashed enthusiasm and laid a hand upon the younger woman's arm as she smilingly coaxed, "And this time, my dear, please don't be so formidable and aloof. I'm sure if I hear the name 'ice maiden' bestowed upon you one more time, I shall give up trying to find you a proper husband. I once told your father, 'Aleksandr,' I said, 'that girl should marry ere she's too old to have babies!' And he said to me, 'Natasha, stop your nagging. I'm waiting for her to fall in love.' Bah!" The woman threw up her hands in a gesture of frustration and leaned near Synnovea to share a bit of womanly wisdom. "The way you fall in love, my dear, is to make babies with a man like Colonel Rycroft. I'll wager you wouldn't be so cool and distant with him sharing your bed."

Blushing at the idea, Synnovea answered breathlessly, "Natasha, you're absolutely scandalous."

The older countess heaved a wistful sigh. "That was what my last husband said, and we were married the longest." Her eyes glowed softly in warm remembrance as she confided, "But then, Count Emelian Andreyev"—her tongue rolled his name off with loving ease—"never, to my knowledge, seriously looked at another woman all the time we were married."

Synnovea had often sensed that Natasha had loved her last husband more than her first two. Her own heart warmed with the idea of such devotion. "Should I ever marry, Natasha, I shall come to you for advice. I'm sure you hold all the secrets for keeping a husband happy and content."

Natasha laughed at the notion. "I can probably tell you a thing or two." She paused to more fully contemplate the matter, and then nodded with conviction. "In fact, I can probably tell you a great deal about holding a husband's attention. And should you marry a man of whom I approve, I'll try to be most diligent in instructing you."

Synnovea was immediately suspicious. "And, of course, you would direct me concerning your choice?"

"Naturally, my dear." The corners of Natasha's lips lifted slyly. "I should like to begin the formalities by inviting Colonel Rycroft to talk with you while you're staying at my home."

She held up a hand to halt any protests that might be forth-coming. "Is it so much to ask? After all, Colonel Rycroft did save you from being violated by that renegade thief. Can you not be gracious to the man?"

"You'll nag me until I agree," Synnovea accused with an exaggerated sigh, giving in far more willingly than her earlier protestations seemed to bear out. "And so I shall, but 'twill not be to my liking. I warn you of that!"

Natasha folded her hands in genteel contentment. "We shall see how adamantly you disdain the man, my dear."

"Though I perceive you're a true *svakhi* at heart, Natasha, your matchmaking efforts will do you no good," Synnovea warned. "Anna will never allow the colonel to court me. She simply detests foreigners."

Natasha's smile deepened. "As I've told you, my dear, the man has attracted the attention of the tsar. 'Tis rumored that His Majesty has been so intrigued and entertained by all the mock battles, forays, and drills the colonel and his men have put on that every weekday morning now he goes out and stands on the wall of the Kremlin to watch them. In view of that fact, my dear, do you think that Tsar Mikhail will be so ill-disposed toward the colonel that he'll long deny him his heart's desire? My dearest Synnovea, I wouldn't put odds on Anna's power to dissuade her cousin if he happens to grant the colonel's request."

"You truly are infatuated with the man, aren't you?" Syn-novea accused, amazed that the woman could bring herself to express such delight in one of the opposite gender. Synnovea would have thought that at Natasha's age, the woman would've ceased to be so easily smitten.

Natasha pondered the other's supposition for the briefest moment before changing it slightly. "*Taken* with the man would be a better description of my feelings, my dear. 'Tis my opinion that men like Colonel Rycroft are a rare breed." She nodded. "A rare breed, indeed."

9

A fierce storm swept over the city in the wee morning hours, whipping trees into a frenzy and setting shutters to flapping noisily at nearly every window. In the peaceful lull that followed, relieved sighs were slowly expelled, and it seemed for a time at least that the tempest had passed beyond them. Yet in a trio of hours the hushed stillness was again shattered by another vicious assault that slashed the area with savage winds and pelting rains.

The changing conditions seemed but a mild portent of what was about to occur in Synnovea's life, for she had barely begun to relax in the serenity that had finally settled over the land when her tranquility was once more rudely disrupted, this time by Anna. It wasn't enough that her guardian stood outside her locked door, demanding entrance in outraged tones as she rapped insistently upon the wood. Such simple deeds were effective in forewarning the occupant of the seriousness of her mood, but when Synnovea hastened to open the portal, Anna's entrance could have been likened to another violent squall blowing in.

No dreaded harbinger of doom could have derived as much satisfaction from the delivery of an ominous omen as the princess clearly did when she announced her reasons for intruding. "Since you've managed to lure Prince Vladimir from more noble interests, I can only agree with what Aleksei has suggested. It seems the old lecher and his sons are quite taken with you, so much so that Vladimir begged Aleksei to consider his proposal before leaving the house last night."

"But I barely spoke to him," Synnovea insisted, wary of what would follow.

"Nevertheless, he has been enamored," Anna pointed out venomously. Touching a lace handkerchief briefly to a thin nostril, she continued in a peremptory vein. "Of course, there's no help for it now with the situation facing us. We must act before Colonel Rycroft manages to disgrace us all. Our guests were simply abuzz over the effrontery of that callous Englishman. The very idea of that lowborn knave appealing to the tsar for permission to court you, as if he merited such favor! Why, it's unforgivable! Believe me, my dear, when this matter is finally put to rest, you may be assured of one thing. The colonel's ambitions will not be allowed to come to fruition. I'll see to that. This very hour I've sent Vladimir a missive confirming our approval of your marriage to him. Such a contract will forestall *any* interference, whether it comes from your English admirer or from another who may hope to win you, including Major Nekrasov."

Synnovea clutched a trembling hand to her throat, knowing only too well that it was Aleksei's trap closing in around her. He had warned her what he'd do, but she had hoped to escape the Taraslovs' authority before he could reap his revenge.

By slow degrees, Synnovea became aware of Ali standing

in the doorway of her narrow cubicle. The old servant looked positively horror-stricken, reflecting the spiraling apprehensions that now besieged her mistress. In daunted silence both mistress and maid listened to the plans the princess was presently laying forth.

"Prince Vladimir is anxious to wed, and in view of Colonel Rycroft's zeal to court you, we've decided to indulge the elder's impetuousness by allowing him to arrange the nuptials during my absence. Ivan and I shall be departing in the morning to visit my father, but the cleric has commitments in Moscow which he must attend ere the month is out. I've made arrangements for our return a fortnight hence. You'll be married the following week."

Synnovea was stunned by the dispatch with which the matter would be concluded. Faintly she queried, "So soon?"

Anna settled a cold, unsympathetic gaze upon her charge. "I see no reason for suffering through a lengthy delay before the wedding. Do you?"

Synnovea could think of several. "Given a few more days, I might be able to prepare for the occasion better. I could even have a new gown made and sew handkerchiefs for the *boyarinas* who'll serve as my attendants. Considering our custom, they'll think it strange if I have none to give them."

"Vladimir is too old to endure a prolonged wait," Anna responded, rejecting her ward's arguments with a casual wave of a thin hand. "You'll have to be satisfied with the time you've been granted, Synnovea. Besides, if that Englishman's plans are to be thwarted, we must proceed with all possible haste."

Even as Synnovea sought to blink gathering tears from her eyes, they seemed to well up within her spirit. The Taraslovs had spitefully laid out her future, and she had no recourse but to accept their dictates. She wouldn't even be allowed enough time to enjoy the usual celebrations and festivities associated with a betrothal or a forthcoming marriage.

Stoically Anna strolled to the front windows and gazed out upon the thoroughfare. Mulling over the previous night's events, she watched coaches pass at a brisk pace and boyars riding steeds still frisky from the early-morning chill. Even after the departure of their guests, she had still been hopeful of Ivan's ability to recoup the ground he had lost among the more influential boyars. His ambition to become ensconced in Vladimir's chapel wasn't nearly as important to Ivan as gaining support for his recommendation that a second advisor be appointed to assist in counseling the tsar, a position for which he intended to offer his own qualifications. Certainly in the days and weeks ahead, she had thought, the boyars would come to understand the wisdom of what Ivan was suggesting.

Her heart had even quickened with optimism when Aleksei had entered her bedchambers and, with his usual persuasiveness, demonstrated a husbandly passion. In the glowing aftermath of her bliss, she had lain in his arms, feeling thoroughly content with the world, but those softer emotions were completely sundered by a raging need to seek retribution when Aleksei voiced complaints about Synnovea accosting him before the soiree. Suddenly his suggestion that they consider Vladimir's proposal of marriage had seemed acceptable. Not only would Synnovea be out of their house and away from Aleksei, but she'd likely be utterly miserable married to the old prince. However, in agreeing to the nuptials, Anna had also realized that she would be destroying any hope of Vladimir funding Ivan's rise to power, thereby frustrating her own aspirations to share in the benefits of that authority.

"Natasha begged me to let you stay with her while I'm away," Anna announced blandly over her shoulder. "I was certain you'd agree and have given my consent. I'm sure Natasha will be delighted to help you prepare for your wedding."

"There's not enough time to consider even a few frivolities, much less see anything actually accomplished," Synnovea rejoined dismally.

Outwardly Anna ignored her charge's lackluster statement, but inwardly she smiled in contentment. By dictating the events in Synnovea's life, she had clearly demonstrated the power she wielded over the young countess. The forthcoming evening would serve to intensify the girl's awareness of that fact. "Prince Vladimir has invited us to dine with him this evening to discuss preparations for your betrothal and forthcoming marriage. I've assured him that you'll be joining us."

"How kind of you."

Detecting a break in the other's voice, Anna smirked, feeling totally gratified by the girl's distress. "You may be relieved to know that Ivan is busy preparing for our departure and won't have time for your lessons today, Synnovea. He's convinced that you deliberately set out to thwart his plans to become Vladimir's priestly mentor and is extremely annoyed with you. If I were you, I'd avail myself of the opportunity to make amends with him ere we meet with your intended tonight. 'Twill help the evening pass more congenially inasmuch as I've granted the cleric permission to accompany us. It may be his last chance to redirect the old boyar's attention toward a more admirable goal instead of appeasing his rutting instincts with you."

"I wish Ivan good fortune in his endeavors," Synnovea responded with morose sincerity. "I wouldn't fret in the least if he managed to turn Vladimir's attention away from me."

Anna turned in a guise of surprise. "Why, Synnovea! Can it be that you're upset by the idea of your betrothal . . . ?"

"You said I'd be allowed to stay with Natasha during your absence," Synnovea interrupted, fully cognizant of the woman's smug satisfaction. "When may I anticipate my departure?"

Anna offered a blasé shrug. "In the morning . . . *if* you really desire to leave."

Synnovea wondered what tedious insinuation the princess

was alluding to now. "Why should I not? If I'd been sent to a monastery, I doubt that my freedom could have been curtailed any more than it has been here."

Anna's lips drew up in a disdaining sneer. "No doubt, under your father's authority, you had many admirers visiting your home in Nizhni Novgorod and indulged in liberties that would shock most *boyarinas*. Your conduct here has certainly demonstrated your license with men. I've no doubt that if you had received some kind of encouragement from Aleksei, you'd have found cause to stay here during my absence."

Synnovea grew visibly incensed by the woman's suggestion. "Forgive me, Anna, but I wouldn't *dream* of compromising my reputation by staying here with that . . ." The word *debaucher* was on the tip of her tongue, but upon recalling that Ali was listening to everything that was being said, she refrained from calling the wily fox what he definitely was simply to save herself the ordeal of having to later explain her choice of appellations to the old servant. She smiled crisply as she corrected herself. "I mean, with Aleksei."

The gray eyes were hostile above a sneering turn of thin lips. "No, of course not. You wouldn't do *anything* unseemly behind my back."

Synnovea canted her head as she tried to understand the rationale behind the other woman's disdain. "Have I offended you so much by attracting Vladimir's attention, Anna? Or is there another reason for your resentment?"

Anna strolled away, deeming it wise to avoid a discussion that would lead them into an ugly fray. Already she yearned to claw those green-brown eyes from their sockets. If she *really* unleashed her hostility upon the girl, no telling what she'd be tempted to do. A violent confrontation would only detract from her elevated authority, through which she had intended to seek retribution.

"Just think of it, Synnovea. In a thrice of weeks you'll be Vladimir's bride," Anna prodded shrewishly. "It should please you to know that you'll be marrying such a wealthy boyar. You'll probably be able to wheedle whatever you desire from the old wolfhound." Her lips curved briefly in a dull smile as she considered the girl. "But then, I haven't really noticed any inclination on your part to limit your self-indulgence. Your gowns and jewels readily demonstrate your enormous greed. Still, as Vladimir's wife, you'll be far richer than you are now. That fact should lend you some comfort when it comes time for you to endure his awkward attempts in bed. Though I've heard rumors that he's still capable of mounting a maid, it doesn't promise to be the most enjoyable experience for you, not like it would be if you were to wed a younger man, especially someone as accomplished with women as Colonel Rycroft."

A darkly winged brow arched sharply as Synnovea watched the princess saunter across the room. "I wasn't aware that you knew Colonel Rycroft well enough to offer *any* opinion about him, Anna. You haven't given him more than ten minutes of your time. Yet now it seems you know his most intimate secrets."

"Oh, I hear things now and then." Anna turned her face aside with an attitude of haughty indifference. "The Englishman seems to be the darling of every addlepated *boyarina* who has ever seen him. The fact that he lives in the German district with all of the other outcasts who come into this country increases his opportunity to gratify his manly appetites in the most sordid ways. 'Tis widely rumored among those who know that there's at least a half-dozen strumpets for every foreigner who's housed there. To even suggest that the colonel would deny himself of their availability while vying for your hand seems rather farfetched, don't you agree, Synnovea? Or did you actually think you were the only pigeon in whom that wily English hawk yearns to sink his talons?"

If Synnovea had been asked to explain her rising vexation with the woman at that precise moment, she'd have been unable to provide a viable reason, except that the slander had come from one who knew the Englishman not at all. "Your conjectures are only that, Anna. Unless you spy upon him, you couldn't possibly know what Colonel Rycroft does in his private life."

Anna tossed her head with a contemptuous laugh. "You're a fool, Synnovea, if you think a man like that hasn't tasted his share of trollops. Mark my words, he'll scatter his seed throughout the countryside ere he returns to England. But if you're so naive as to believe that he'll remain chaste while petitioning His Majesty for permission to court you, then I've better things to do with my time than to argue with you over the depth of his coarseness."

Upon reaching the door, Anna paused briefly to consider her charge, feeling rather elated over what she had managed to accomplish. Synnovea's dejection was unmistakable. The intended betrothal had shattered whatever expectations the girl had dreamed of for her future. Indeed, Anna could almost feel sorry for her ward . . . *if* she didn't hate her so much.

The almost imperceptible squeak of door hinges sounded like a death knell in the gloomy silence that followed Anna's departure. Stricken by the news of her forthcoming marriage, Synnovea slumped listlessly upon the bed and stared in utter gloom at nothing in particular. Had her life been declared forfeit, she'd have felt the same. Her despair was too burdensome a weight to bear in mute misery, and with a harsh sob, she flung herself across the mattress. Listlessly pummeling a fist against the bedclothes, she wept and bemoaned the day that she had ever entered the Taraslov manse.

"Oh, me lamb! Me lamb! Do not weep so!" Ali pleaded pityingly as she scurried forward to soothe her mistress.

Synnovea shook her head, refusing to be consoled. Her woeful heart seemed a ponderous burden within her chest; no gentle cajoling could ease the dark gloom that constricted it. "Pack up everything that belongs to us," she choked in a ragged voice. "If I fall under heaven's mercy, I'll never darken the door of this house after my departure on the morrow!"

"Can ye not stop this thing that they're doin' ta ye?" Ali asked fretfully. "Could ye not go ta His Majesty an' beg for his mercy? Or escape ta England an' stay wit' yer widowed aunt?"

"I can go to no one," Synnovea muttered bleakly. "Least of all to England. If I sought passage on a ship, Anna would likely find a way to arouse His Majesty's ire against me, and I'd never be allowed to return. The arrangement of marriage has been agreed upon, Ali, and with naught but the necessary signatures verifying the legality of the contract, I'll be the promised bride of Prince Vladimir."

Anna's elaborate script acknowledging Vladimir as her betrothed would seal her doom, and once the agreement was drawn up, not even Aleksei would be able to undo what he had set into motion. Only Tsar Mikhail or Prince Vladimir could break the pact, His Majesty by whatever reason he might ordain, the ancient by giving evidence of her unworthiness. But the likelihood of that occurrence seemed remote if Vladimir had asked for her hand so soon after their meeting. No doubt Aleksei had relished magnifying her merit as his potential bride.

Synnovea's thoughts lamely sought some avenue of escape. A half-dozen options came to mind, but such notions as insulting Vladimir or telling him how vehemently she disdained the idea of becoming his wife were rejected as quickly as they came. Even if it meant giving up her freedom, she wouldn't cause the old man such grievous hurt just to gain her own end. To do so might lead him to the grave, and she refused to have his death on her conscience. Nay, if *ever* he refused to speak the vows with her, it would be because he had been the one to find fault with her.

Closing her eyes, Synnovea rested a cheek against the counterpane, letting her tensions ease as she forced her mind along a path that had become quite familiar of late, the vision of her English champion in scratched and dented helm. Although she was still incensed by the comments that Anna had made about him, she couldn't help but wonder if they were true. His casual disregard for his nudity in the bathhouse certainly verified the fact that he suffered no unease being unclothed in front of a woman. But then, when a man had a physique as exceptional as his, why should he be embarrassed about it? Indeed, if his face had been equally sublime, Tyrone Rycroft would have gained the unswerving admiration of ladies everywhere, herself included.

It seemed futile to torment herself with wanton memories of her encounters with the Englishman, yet, as the wife of an ancient boyar, she might well have to use her recollections to suffice as conciliation for what she'd likely be missing in her marriage, for she'd never be able to enjoy the excitement and delight of being joined by wedlock to a man of noteworthy face *or* frame. Such reverie was perhaps more than some women were gifted with in a lifetime. Still, Synnovea was inclined to wonder if her brief view of such a magnificent specimen had spoiled her for the mundane and ordinary and made her less than tolerant of what she was about to receive.

A plaintive sigh escaped Synnovea as she made a concerted effort to commit herself to her betrothal. At least Vladimir wasn't as repugnant as some doddering ancients, but when her own sire had been so much younger, she feared it would be tantamount to going to bed with a grandfather. Still, it was highly unlikely that she'd ever become bored while his sons resided with them. In light of the brothers' bent for mischief and mayhem, an enormous probability existed that she'd be wont on occasion to beg for a little peace and privacy.

Steeling herself against the unrelenting disquiet that threatened to dissolve her fragile forbearance, Synnovea wiped away her tears and left the bed. She helped Ali pack and took comfort in the prospect that she'd soon be leaving the Taraslovs for good. Though marrying Vladimir wasn't much of a reprieve, it was nevertheless an improvement.

Synnovea made a point of seeking Ivan out in his chambers and returning the books he had told her to read. The fact that she wouldn't have to contend with the man's bigoted views anymore allowed her some relief.

"I hope you're happy now, Countess."

A weary sigh slipped from Synnovea as she met his glare. "I'll try to be."

"How can you not with all that wealth at your disposal?" he derided caustically.

"Happiness doesn't depend on a person's wealth, Ivan," she stated dully. "A man could acquire all the riches in the world and still be utterly miserable. Possessions are a poor substitute for loving friends and family."

Ivan scoffed at the idea of such platitudes. "My family never meant anything to me. I despised my mother. My father? Well, I was told he was killed shortly before my birth, but I was given my mother's name like any misbegotten offspring. I never saw any evidence that he ever cared a whit about what he was leaving behind. I'd have been much fonder of his memory had he left some inheritance to see me nurtured and clothed until I could fend for myself."

"I'm truly sorry, Ivan," Synnovea murmured in genuine empathy, understanding now why the man was so tormented. "It must have been very hard for you growing up."

"It was hard," he acknowledged with a prideful smirk. "But I overcame it all and made something of myself. I'm here by no one else's will but my own."

"Are you not lonely at times?"

"Lonely for what?" he asked sharply, taken aback by her question.

"People? Friends? Someone perhaps like Anna, who appreciates you for yourself or for what you are or may have done . . ."

"No one appreciates what I am and what I've accomplished more than I."

Synnovea could see no benefit in continuing the discussion when it was apparent that Ivan Voronsky had long ago rejected the notion that friends and a loving family were important to one's well-being. She found it difficult to imagine such a solitary existence even worth living.

The time came for Synnovea to prepare herself for her first visit to the vast estates of Prince Vladimir. She spent a leisurely hour doing so, not caring how she might anger Anna by her delay in joining them. When she presented herself in the lower hall ten minutes past the hour designated for their departure, the princess was absolutely livid.

"Well! You certainly kept us waiting long enough!" Anna barked. "But then, you awful girl, I'm certain 'twas your intent!"

Synnovea dismissed Anna's heated glower and Ivan's scowl with no more than a mental shrug. Aleksei's rude appraisal of her curves, however, thoroughly outraged her. Even after wreaking havoc in her life, he seemed unable to keep his eyes from sliding down her iridescent green silk *sarafan,* as if he still considered her a potential paramour. Curbing an urge to slap his swarthy face, Synnovea displayed a stilted decorum as she faced Anna. "You *had* wanted me to look my best for Vladimir, did you not?"

Weeks ago Anna had discovered that Synnovea complimented her garments far beyond the ability of most women. Her sleekly curving figure, lustrous fair skin, and eyes that seemed more green now than brown were excellent assets. They would've made the dowdiest garment look unique, but her present attire was beautiful by itself. The delicate artistry of the gilded stitchery liberally adorning the stiff collar, lower sleeves, and hem of the *sarafan* as well as her bejeweled *kokoshniki* was so rich and fine that it could only have been created by a gifted artisan. Still, Anna was not above soliciting some criticism from the two men, who seemed, for once, of a kindred spirit in their desire to seize some redress from the girl.

"I really can't see that our lengthy wait was worth the results. What do you think, Aleksei?"

The prince managed a tolerant smile, knowing well what his wife wanted to hear. Although Synnovea's beauty was nearly without equal, he was convinced that she needed subjugation to bring her to heel. He was committed to seeing her wed Vladimir and equally resolved to take his pleasure of her when the time was ripe. To serve his wife's whim now, no matter how trite her ridicule, would bolster Anna's confidence for an early departure, for he was reluctant to see his plans thwarted by her presence not only in the manse but in the city. "Perhaps we should consider delaying a bit longer to allow the girl more time to improve her appearance."

"We've endured too much as it is," Ivan complained tersely. "I beg you, let us be off."

Aleksei bowed stiffly for his wife's benefit. "At your pleasure, my dear."

Anna brushed past Synnovea and accepted the arm Ivan offered her. As they led the way through the front portal, Aleksei waited to claim his usual place at the rear of the procession, where he could freely ogle Synnovea. While the cleric helped Anna into the carriage, Aleksei pressed against the girl's back to feed a prurient fetish of his own. He remained unfazed by her smoldering glare, but her small heel bearing down painfully upon the toe of his soft leather boot convinced him of the wisdom of retreating to a more respectable distance.

Vladimir came out to greet their carriage upon their arrival at his mansion and eagerly pressed an exuberant kiss upon Synnovea's slender fingers as he handed her down. Liberally expounding upon her beauty, he drew her into the great hall, where his sons stood arrayed in rich kaftans and their best manners on display. Ivan and the Taraslovs were left to follow in the couple's wake, and as the ancient proudly escorted Synnovea to a cushioned chair beside his own, the three were left to find their own seats nearby.

Ivan's blood nigh boiled. Before he had been arbitrarily demoted by the girl, he had tasted the rare sweetmeat of success as Vladimir's guest of honor. Now his attempts to draw the man's attention were, at best, randomly given heed to, and only then with a modicum of interest. In sharp contrast, the old boyar doted on every word that issued forth from the gently smiling lips of his intended.

Synnovea chose to make the best of her unfortunate fate and deliberately ignored Ivan's irate glowers and Anna's sharpening frowns as she laughed and chatted with her future family. For a time, the Taraslovs retired with the elder to discuss the nuptials, the dowry Alexandr had set aside for his daughter, and to sign their names to the betrothal agreement. While the three were absent, Vladimir's brood of sons entertained her with hilarious accounts of their many kindred; upon their return, Ivan's ire reached its zenith, for it was then that the old man presented Synnovea with a necklace set with large diamonds and emeralds, earrings to match, and a betrothal ring impressive enough to stagger the wits of the three, who looked on with a strange blend of rancor and awe.

"My dearest Synnovea, please allow me to present these meager offerings as tokens of my affection," Vladimir exclaimed with a buoyant smile. "Once you've become my bride, I'll dress you in robes of gold and precious jewels of every color. You'll want for nothing."

"Tut-tut, Prince Vladimir," Anna chided through a stiff smile, knowing her revenge would be better served if she could believe the old boyar meant to abuse the girl. "You'll spoil Synnovea with such extravagant gifts. I'd advise you to pamper her less and keep her more submissive if you wish a well-ordered marriage."

Her comments caused Aleksei to lower his libation and

stare at her in amazement, but Anna ignored the implication of his dubious regard, which silently challenged her own compliance to his husbandly authority. Admittedly she had always been more ambitious than he. Even as a child she had learned to be assertive to get what she desired. Now she yearned to see her rival vexed by hardships, not elaborate gifts.

"Nonsense," Vladimir rejoined, blustering a bit at the notion that he was being counseled by a woman whose husband, according to frequent hearsay, roamed far afield. "If I've gleaned anything from my earlier marriages, it has been the fact that women can learn to be content with an old rascal like myself much more easily if they're coddled and pampered. In showing their gratitude, my wives nurtured me with their affection, keeping me quite content to stay at home."

Anna's pale cheeks took on a reddish hue as Synnovea turned an enigmatic smile upon her. If it was possible to read anything into the slight turning of those soft lips, then Anna could believe the girl was genuinely relishing Vladimir's rebuke. That suspicion nettled her severely when she thought of such sumptuous treasures being indiscriminately wasted on the one she abhorred. She loathed acceding anything to her rival, especially when Ivan had been so close to winning the old man's support. The bountiful largesse that Vladimir was capable of giving could've swiftly advanced Ivan's efforts.

It was Synnovea's pleading request that the jewels be kept in Vladimir's care for safekeeping that amazed both Anna and Ivan. They stared agog as she sweetly added, "Just until the day I come here to live with you, for I couldn't bear the loss if they were somehow mislaid."

Cognizant of the cleric's dark glower, Synnovea lowered her gaze demurely. Though his profession embodied all the honorable attributes one should possess in dedicated service to a higher order, she was wont to suspect that Ivan used his robe as a sham to bilk whatever lucre could be gained from those generously disposed toward accepting all clergymen as humble and honorable men.

Vladimir gladly deferred to Synnovea's wishes when she laid a gentle hand upon his sleeve and looked up at him beseechingly. After bestowing an ardent kiss upon her slender fingers, he gave the treasures over to Igor, who took them away to a secure place.

"My own mother was uncommonly fetching," Sergei stated as he presented Synnovea a glass of *Visnoua*. "But I think my father has outdone himself this time in selecting you as his future bride."

"Oh, Sergei, what a beautiful sentiment," she replied graciously. "And may I suppose, since you look nothing like your father, that you inherited your handsomeness from your mother?"

With an amiable laugh he kissed her fingertips. "Even my father has said as much, Countess. But if your beauty is an indication of the offspring you'll bear my father, then I shall be put to shame by your children."

Synnovea dipped her head briefly in gratitude for such a compliment, pleased that Vladimir's sons were so willing to accept her into the family. As Sergei looked on, she sipped from the silver goblet. The libation reminded her of a red wine she had always enjoyed in France and was definitely pleasing enough for her to savor another taste.

"Delicious?" Sergei queried.

"Indeed!"

As the youngest of the brood stepped back with a chuckle, Feodor came forth and, after a sweeping bow, delivered a large bouquet of flowers to her. "Like these cherished blooms, my lady, you grace us with your beauty and fragrance."

Feeling at odds with herself because she was unable to summon anything more than a hollow display of pleasure, Synnovea gathered his gift within her arms and lowered her face to the blossoms, inhaling their sweet essence. When she lifted her head again, she offered him a gentle smile. "You do me great honor, Prince Feodor, to compare my unworthy looks to such glorious marvels of nature."

Her eyes grew misty with tears as he, too, took her hand and bestowed a light kiss upon it. It was the deepening anguish of feeling totally undeserving of their esteem that made Synnovea long to escape through the nearest door. She was painfully aware that, in comparison with her own reluctance and foreboding, their gifts of words and tender treasures came forth with sterling sincerity.

As the eldest moved back, Stefan came near to lay a garland of green around her neck. "Your company is cherished far above rubies and gold, Synnovea. Be assured that as a whole, the sons of Prince Vladimir Dimitrievich are enamored with your charm. We're just as excited about having you in the family as our father is."

Synnovea laughed through a fresh gathering of guilty tears. Against her will, she had been charmed by the brothers' gallant display of manners, but their praise did little to ease the burden of regret weighing down her heart. "Dear, kind sirs, you woo me with such sweet tidings and eloquent speeches that I fear my tongue staggers lamely in search of prose equal to their beauty."

Vladimir reached out again to claim her fingers and bring them to his own lips. "In truth, Synnovea, were your tongue forever silenced, we'd still be smitten by your sweet presence in this, our boorish surroundings. We're but churlish clods in need of your gentle, transforming touch."

Despite her rich enjoyment of their company and their chivalrous attempts to show her how much her presence pleased them, Synnovea was unable to accept her betrothal as anything more than an incarceration of Aleksei's making. When it finally came time to take their leave, she experienced a moment of panic when she realized her intended meant to kiss her on the lips. She subdued the urge to flee, and though the blush that swept into her cheeks was well in line with a chaste maid's reaction, Synnovea had no doubt that Vladimir would've been shocked out of his senses if he had had any inkling that she had conjured Tyrone Rycroft's shadowed face before her own just to be able to stand her ground during the old man's kiss.

Synnovea was distraught at the idea of carrying such a farce all the way to her marriage bed, but she knew it would be the only way she'd ever submit to Vladimir with any kind of forbearance. Truly, had the old prince begged her to be his daughter, she'd have gladly yielded him that honor as a living replacement for the father she had once loved and recently lost. Yet to think of Vladimir as her husband and to consider everything that that particular position would entail, she was no less desirous of being liberated from their betrothal than she was to escape the Taraslovs' manse.

Tears spilled unheeded upon Synnovea's pillow long into the night. Staring at the moonlit canopy above her head, she begged wearily for some sweet spirit from heaven to bring peace to her frazzled brain and to somehow impart a way she could be set free without wounding the old man. It was a troubling dilemma in which she found herself, for in spite of their cantankerous reputation, she valued the friendship of Vladimir and his sons, though regretfully not enough to rouse her eagerness to be bound by an oath of wedlock to the elder and certainly not until that time when widowhood finally came to release her. She didn't covet Vladimir's death. Nor did she ever want to yearn for such a fate for him in a marriage in which she'd be unable to find solace for her dreams of love and contentment.

The first rays of the dawning sun were just stretching out across the land when Ali came to her mistress's bedside and awakened her. Not long after that, Synnovea left the chambers and made her final descent. Anna had remained upstairs to attend to some last-minute details which affected her own departure. In her absence, Aleksei had taken up a waiting stance just beyond the front portal. He was there when Synnovea emerged and was bold enough to halt her with a hand on her arm, but he frowned wincingly at the sun that shimmered brilliantly in the eastern sky, definitely pained by the presence of that particular sphere.

To see Aleksei suffering after a long night of copious imbibing that had begun at Vladimir's manse was small recompense for the animosity Synnovea was presently feeling toward him. Tempted to give him a fair piece of her mind, she grudgingly allowed him a moment of her time. At least no further acts of aggression could be made against her person while they stood in clear sight of Ali, Jozef, and Stenka.

"Allowing you to leave here was Anna's idea, not mine," Aleksei informed her bluntly.

"I recognized your intent to keep me in your lecherous lair the day you announced that Anna would be leaving," Synnovea acknowledged coolly. It was only for the sake of her servants that she made an attempt to appear civil in his presence. "Still, I don't know how you might've hoped otherwise. Anna is no fool, you know. That's why she's so anxious to see me married off to Vladimir. She wants me out of the house and well away from you." A slight upward movement of her shoulders prefaced her next comment. "Of course, she has just cause with you as her husband."

"Anna has even more reason to hate you now," Aleksei taunted. "After I told her how you solicited my favors the other night, she was most eager to see you wed."

A lovely brow lifted. "Well, I see you're not above making up ludicrous stories to suit your purposes, Aleksei, but your little ploy to discredit me will have no bearing on my actions, so be warned."

"*You'd* best be warned, my girl," he snarled, gnashing clenched teeth. "I've no intention of letting you escape what has already been decreed, despite the fact that Natasha has a nasty habit of confounding proprieties to meet her own whims . . ."

The peak of Synnovea's eyebrow sharpened challengingly. "And what of you, sir? Have you not done the same?"

Aleksei ignored her intrusion as he continued cynically. "I'm sure Natasha will try to undermine your betrothal by inviting men who can tarnish your reputation . . ."

Synnovea stared at him in growing amazement, never having considered the ruination of her honor as a means by which she could avoid marriage with Vladimir. Such a ploy would be a serious price to pay for her freedom and a sacrifice she was not entirely sure she wanted to make. The very idea went against everything she had been taught about sterling principles, but she was desperate. All she had to do was determine just *how* desperate.

"I can see that you might be worried about my honor, since Vladimir would be reluctant to attach himself to a maid whose virtue has been besmirched," she answered disparagingly. "But for the life of me, Aleksei, I cannot imagine that you'll be content to see me married off to another without trying to extract some further penance from me, which leaves me wondering how you intend to claim me as your conquered victim. It has been widely rumored that you have a preference for virgins, but then, so has Vladimir. Are you willing to allow him first taste of the unblemished fruit?"

"I'll make an exception in your case," Aleksei promised with a hint of a sneer.

"So good of you," Synnovea derided. She glanced away as she sought to regain control of her quickly flaring temper, then turned on him again with renewed vigor, wanting to shatter his cocksure arrogance if only for the moment. "If it falls within my power to frustrate your purposes, Aleksei, let me assure you that I'll use whatever wile within my capability to see your plans thwarted, even if I have to take Colonel Rycroft into my bed to see the deed done."

The dark eyes flared with ill-suppressed rage. "Do you honestly think I'll allow such a thing to happen while I yet breathe, maid?" he hissed. "You do err in conjuring such deceptive fantasies for yourself, for I'll never let another man have you!"

"Not even Vladimir?"

"Through him I'll claim my revenge for the injury you've done me! You'll come back after you've survived a few of that old bull's straining attempts, begging me to satisfy you."

"You're far too confident of your power over women, Aleksei," she rejoined with a noticeable lack of warmth. "What you don't realize is that I'd rather submit to Vladimir for the next hundred years than be tainted even for a moment by your foul attention."

"You won't escape marriage to him!" Aleksei ground out bitingly, infuriated by her unswerving tenacity. "I'll hire men to watch you and any house you're in until the very moment the vows are spoken. There'll be no help for you, my beauty. None will come to your rescue, not even your precious Englishman."

"That remains to be seen, does it not?" Synnovea gave him an ungracious smile as her lashes hovered over a glare. Reaching out, she tapped a forefinger lightly upon his sleeve, as if chiding a naughty student. "Were I you, Aleksei, I would avoid any mention of this matter to your wife ere her departure, for I intend to protect myself henceforth from your malicious bent. If need be, I'll take my complaints to Tsar Mikhail himself and let him deal with the both of you as you justly deserve. I swear I will!"

With a last irritated rap of her finger, Synnovea turned from him and made her way to the coach. It was only a short distance to the larger Andreyevna mansion, and when the conveyance pulled into the drive, Natasha came hurrying out to greet her with open arms. The morning seemed suddenly brighter for both women. Synnovea's anger diminished to a more tolerable level, and as for the elder, she was anticipating the delight to be found in the sweet promise of companionship with the daughter of a woman whom she had once cherished as her closest friend and confidante.

In the ensuing days, Synnovea realized that she would have to make a choice fairly soon or see her options seriously hindered by Anna's return. Whether to nobly abide by the betrothal contract or to seek freedom at the expense of her own honor, that was the question she'd have to answer for herself. The more dutiful course for a chaste maid would be to comply with Anna's dictates, which would issue her forthwith into a respectable marriage with Vladimir. The alternative was drastic. Should she dare such an escape, damaging slurs would likely be brought to bear upon her name and she'd have to face the threat of being ostracized by her peers. Society was wont to judge a fallen woman harshly, and she'd be no less susceptible than the foulest tart. Still, if she could somehow preserve the secrecy of her actions *or* even feign her defilement (if such a feat were possible), then perhaps her ploy would yield her everything she yearned for.

Despite the clarity of her options, finding an acceptable answer to the riddle that confronted her was far more involved and complicated than Synnovea had thought it would be. The difficulty lay in her burgeoning apprehensions about the role of conniving seductress that she'd have to play with Tyrone, the only man she deemed suitable for the deed. Not only was he more acceptable to her than anyone she presently knew, his reputation as a rake, however false that might have been, solidified his credentials. Despite the best-contrived plans, however, events had a way of going awry. At the very least, she could suffer the rending of her virginity, but more disastrously, she could even bear a bastard child nine months later. Was her freedom to choose a husband worth the risks she'd be taking?

Synnovea's fears far outweighed her dedication to gaining her own end, and she solemnly approached the idea that she just had to do what was proper. Her parents would have expected her to keep herself pure until her wedding night, and even if she had to marry Vladimir, she'd likely outlive him. Then she'd have the freedom to wed whomever she wished. All it would take would be waiting weeks, months, or even years for an old man to die. . . .

Synnovea recoiled at such a diabolical notion as yearning for a human being to die, and she promptly found herself back at the crux of her dilemma, whether to ignobly pine for her husband to succumb to some malady or, by devious means, to seek the liberty to marry for love.

It was not until Synnovea ventured out with Natasha and Ali to a small, rough-hewn chapel located beyond the outskirts of the city that she actually became cognizant of just how persistent Aleksei was to see her wed and, in that endeavor, how closely he—and others—observed her comings and goings. The three women had set aside other duties to help a kindly old monk who devoted himself to acts of charity. Whether old, blind, wretched, decrepit, or lame, those in want were never turned away from the humble, tumbledown sanctuary where the kindly Friar Philip labored to serve their needs. His main concern was tending *his flock,* which included anyone who came to him lacking sufficient food, clothing, or peace for the soul. The afflictions of the poor were often decreased to a more tolerable level by his compassion or by those who assisted him in his selfless struggle. To his following, he was known as Saint Philip, though he wore shabby robes and denounced the acquisition of wealth for the church, which many of the Josephites had insisted upon. A number of the more powerful members of that particular sect had demeaned his attempts as self-serving and claimed that his real motive was to destroy a higher order of ordained servants to appease his own vindictive bent. They continually sought evidence to convict the man of his crimes.

Natasha was just as adamant to rally her friends to his cause and found Synnovea to be a willing participant. Upon their arrival early that morning, the women addressed themselves to the task of preparing a meal in the kitchen, located in a lean-to behind the chapel. Even though their coach evidenced their wealth, they wore plain garments made from a common cloth to ease the apprehensions of the poor, who had reason to be wary of the nobility. Soon after the food had been cooked, Synnovea busied herself handing out loaves of bread and ladling a hearty stew into wooden bowls held forth by ragged peasants who shuffled past. Natasha sorted apparel from several bundles that she had either sewn or collected from friends, while Ali entertained the younger children with mimes and craggy-voiced songs, allowing their mothers to search through the donated clothing in an effort to fortify their families for the approaching winter.

Into this gathering of destitute humanity, Aleksei came swaggering arrogantly in, bearing himself like the mighty prince he obviously envisioned himself to be. Forcing the more unsightly commoners to scurry out of his way, he strode up to the two countesses and, with flamboyant mockery, bowed before them. Upon straightening, he glanced around in lofty disdain. "How generous you ladies are to devote your time to serving these paltry beings. Ivan Voronsky would be impressed."

If Aleksei had declared that only one sun existed in the sky, Synnovea would've found some argument to refute his claim. "I doubt that Ivan has any real perception of charity other than what goes into his own pockets."

Synnovea realized the peasants who had been waiting in line for food were now hanging back, fearful of moving past the elegantly garbed prince. "Begone with you, Aleksei!" She swept a hand about to indicate the ones who were shuffling away. "Can't you see what you're doing? They're afraid of you!"

"Afraid of me? Why so?" His astonishment was badly concocted. "I've only come to witness your compassion toward these foul-smelling oafs. What has set you on this path of benevolence anyway? Are you seeking to pay penance for your sins?"

Synnovea's eyes narrowed menacingly. "My greatest sin has yet to be committed, Aleksei. That's when I'll hire henchmen to string you up. Just why are you here, may I ask?"

"I've come as you have, as a benevolent lord to give ease to the poor." He turned and addressed the friar. "See here, Philip, or whatever your name is! I've come to give my dues to your cause." He drew forth a few coins of meager worth and scattered them at the elder's sandaled feet.

"I will thank God for your kindness, my son," the white-haired monk murmured graciously as he knelt to pick them up. Though he sensed the boyar wanted to see him groveling at his feet, he couldn't ignore the insufficiencies plaguing his small ministry.

"You'd do better to thank *me,* old man," Aleksei sneered, staring down his less-than-perfect nose at the elder. "I've power here on earth to see you imprisoned for consorting with thieves." He indicated the tattered folk who huddled in growing apprehension of the boyar's intentions. "Have I not seen the likes of these rogues stealing bread?"

"Oh, but surely, if they have, it was only a morsel or two, and you would forgive them for such meager offenses," the monk hurriedly entreated as he struggled to his feet. "Many would starve without the bit of food they're given here."

"Have I not also seen you feeding those foul prisoners locked in stocks in Kitaigorod? Perhaps you're also in league with the rogues who come to stealthily seek their release. I heard it said that the felons who escape flee the city to take up with bands of raiders and highwaymen. Perhaps they even stop here for sustenance to aid them on their way."

The holy man spread his hands in appeal as he begged for understanding. "It's true that you may have seen me helping the convicts fettered there, but the law makes no provisions for their needs. Whether guilty of pitiful deeds or those declared unworthy of reprieve among more worldly judges, they grow equally famished for a piece of bread or a cup of water. I don't question them about their crimes when I distribute food. I only try to assure them that there is love and forgiveness for whatever they've done. But your pardon, my son, are you so perfect and pure that you're able to cast the first stone at these poor wretches?"

Aleksei's face took on a ruddy hue as he lifted his head in haughty arrogance. "I'm a prince! An aristocrat by birth!"

A kindly smile curved the wrinkled lips of the elder. "Do you seek to impress God with your aristocracy when all are equal in His sight, my son? None are perfect, whether prince or pauper."

Tossing his head in contempt, Aleksei confronted the holy man with a sneer. "Is God blind to the faults of thieves and murderers?"

"God sees all, my son, but He also forgives. We need only ask with a contrite heart."

Aleksei scoffed. "If there *is* a God!"

"Each man must decide that for himself, my son."

The prince's brows lowered darkly. "It's foolishness to believe in something you cannot see!"

The kindly priest spoke gently. "I'm sorry, my son, but I don't understand why you've come here if that is your belief. Do you seek counsel from a fool?"

"Oh, I've heard of your kind," Aleksei derided. "You can be certain of that! *Bozhie liudi!* Men of God! Holy fools! That's what they call you! *Skitalets!* Holy wanderers! You set up your *skity* in areas like this in compliance with that so-called order of Nilus Sorsky, that most foolish of fools! But you know as well as I do that Nilus died after his arguments against the wealth of the church were overridden by Joseph Sanin, and thereafter his followers have been persecuted by the Josephites and the grand dukes of Muscovy—as *you* will be!"

"Your knowledge of history seems well intact, my son, but you haven't yet answered my question. Do you seek counsel from me?"

Aleksei laughed caustically. "You couldn't possibly instruct me with your fool's wisdom, holy man. I came only to guarantee the safety of my ward while she is among these filthy peasants."

The monk shifted his gaze toward the young countess, who earlier that morning had arrived with her maid and the Countess Andreyevna. In recent years the latter had proven herself a most gracious and generous benefactress. Though he tended a garden and a small flock of sheep to enable him to serve the needs of the poor, he was grateful when such kindly and charitable workers as these offered their assistance. They had even sent their coachman to purchase more food when it had become evident that there wouldn't be enough victuals to feed everyone who came. Now, because of them, all who ventured in today would be fed.

"None here would harm her," the priest declared. "These people are appreciative of what the *boyarina* is doing for them."

Aleksei responded with a snort of derision. "It's beneath the countess's station to consort with these vile vermin."

"What kind do you suggest she consort with?" the holy man asked, beginning to understand the prince's motives. "Do you mean to persuade her to go back with you, perhaps?"

Synnovea cast a pointed glare toward Aleksei, gaining his attention. Without a word she strode to the front door, luring him away from the old man. There she turned on him with fire in her eyes. "If you're capable of any decency at all, Aleksei, then I beg you leave here and let us be," she ground out in muted tones. " 'Tis obvious what your real concerns are. Even Saint Philip now sees through your ploys."

"You must heed my words, Synnovea," the prince insisted. "I won't let you thwart my plans."

"And I warn you, Aleksei! You'd better heed mine! I've had enough of your lies and your filthy attempts to bed me! Now get out of here ere I take a lash to you! And don't *ever* come back!"

Overhearing Synnovea's threat, Natasha approached them with an amused smile. "Beware, Aleksei. I do believe the girl means it."

His sharply penetrating scowl bore into the younger countess. "I've hired men to follow you wherever you go, Synnovea. You'll not escape! They'll hound you until you beg me to set you free of them."

"Shall I complain to Vladimir about your close attention?" Synnovea needled. "He has wealth enough to send guards of his own to protect me from your spite."

"Aye! Send for him!" Aleksei challenged. "He'll insist upon speaking the vows posthaste just to save you from the ruffians I've hired. Then I'll have my revenge that much sooner." Saying nothing more, he swept into a shallow bow and stalked out.

Synnovea glared after his departing form and was somewhat surprised when he strode beyond his mount and made his way to an open field where a large party of mounted riders awaited him. From a distance the men appeared to be nothing more than unruly rabble garbed in a variety of outlandish apparel. Synnovea could only question Aleksei's wisdom in hiring such questionable guards, for they looked more like cutthroats and renegades.

Despite the rather questionable attributes of her newly acquired guards, Synnovea soon realized that they were, at the very least, proficient at provoking her ire. After Aleksei left, they set up their surveillance closer to the church, built up a huge fire, and liberally guzzled large quantities of *kvass* and vodka while they involved themselves in lewd cavorting and riotous dancing with several strumpets who had joined them.

Thoroughly abashed by the group's unrestrained revelry, Synnovea begged forgiveness from Friar Philip. "I had no idea that I would be inviting this shameful exhibition by coming here."

"You're not to blame, my child," the old man assured her kindly. "Today you've done a good service. The coins you've given will go a long way toward buying food for these poor people." His eyes briefly flitted toward the rapscallions who taunted those who had taken shelter within the church. "Don't let their presence demean the good deeds you've done here this day."

Synnovea took his rough, work-hardened hand and pressed a kiss upon it. "I'll come back when I'm free of them. Until then, my servant will bring a regular stipend to enable you to feed those who come to you."

"Bless you for your kindness, my child."

Kneeling before him, Synnovea accepted his prayers for her safety and well-being. Then she and her companions returned to Natasha's coach. As it rumbled off down the road, the rowdies climbed into their saddles and followed, deserting the harlots, who shook their fists in disappointment and screamed profanities after them.

The coachman recognized the need for haste and cracked his whip often, urging the steeds to their fastest gait, but the band of ruffians only grew bolder and came alongside to hoot and chortle in glee as they performed dangerous stunts in and out of their saddles. Once the coach reached the safety of the Andreyevna manse, the rabble gathered in front, sending servants scurrying to bolt portals and windows against the possibility of a forced entrance, while the houseman took up arms and stood guard to ensure the miscreants kept their distance.

The occupants of the mansion faced another quandary when the steward heralded the approach of Vladimir and his sons. Natasha quickly instructed her servants to arm themselves with whatever tool, weapon, or implement they could find to lend support to the princes if they were attacked. Considering the willingness of the princes to brawl, it promised to be a serious altercation.

Mere moments passed before a maid called her mistress's attention to the fact that the riffraff had left. When Natasha and Synnovea flew to the windows to see for themselves, relief rallied their spirits when they found the announcement to be true. The doors were promptly flung open to welcome the boyars. Still, no one made mention of the callous oafs who had escorted the ladies home, lest the princes give chase.

In the next several days, the disorderly band made its presence known the few times that Synnovea ventured out in her carriage. The men followed along behind, forcing her to return without even leaving the conveyance. Had she dared visit friends, she feared the scalawags would create a scene similar to the one in which they had been involved outside Friar Philip's chapel. No telling what the results would be.

When at the conclusion of the third day Aleksei stood outside the mansion with a pleased smirk on his face, Synnovea felt as if he had just laughed in her face. That was all it took for her to finally settle her mind on her final course of action. She'd be hanged and quartered before allowing him the ultimate triumph.

Even so tenuous a solution to her problem was enough to calm the brooding indecision that had beset Synnovea since Anna's announcement of her betrothal. She resigned herself to the controversial means of escape, lending her attention to the task of devising a plan by which she could entice the worldly Colonel Rycroft to serve as her seducer. That feat presented no great challenge. It was the withholding of her virtue that promised to be the formidable part, for she had no doubt that the man would have his mind set on claiming that very thing she wished to preserve. If his cavalier boldness in the bathhouse sufficed as an indication, then she could believe the man was quite adept at a game she knew little about, and if she couldn't control his ardor to her liking, where would she be left but in his bed?

"I shall need your assistance if you're inclined to give it," she begged Natasha after gingerly explaining her proposal. "It could well mean danger for us both if my plans go awry, so if you've no heart for it, I'll surely understand. Aleksei is adamant about halting any intervention that would see me rejected as a fit bride by Vladimir, yet he has boasted that he'll see the old man cuckolded before he relents. If you help me in this, you may not be safe from his revenge."

"I'm not afraid of that pompous crow, but I do have a concern for what may happen to you in this scheme of yours." Natasha chose her words carefully, not wanting to strip away the last shred of hope to which her young friend now clung. Yet she'd be doing the girl a grave disservice if she didn't caution her. "I'd not be a true friend, my dear, if I only encouraged you to continue and did not warn you of the danger you'll be courting. Frankly, I think you have more to fear from the Englishman than you do from Aleksei. Aleksei is certainly acting out of character by trying to preserve your virtue for Vladimir, and to me, that indicates he's sincere about having you after you're wed. But take heed. Colonel Rycroft has no cause to play such waiting games. Once you encourage him, you may be hard-pressed to dissuade him from carrying out your initiation forthwith. You're but a girl, innocent of the passions that can goad a man. If you tempt him overmuch, I'm afraid you'll see just how hard the colonel is driven."

"Surely he is besieged with strumpets where he lives. I've heard it rumored that the harlots zealously seek out the foreigners who come here without kith and kin. Colonel Rycroft should be exhausted by now from all their attention."

"Who spills such gossip about the man?" Natasha queried indignantly.

Synnovea was amazed by her friend's outrage. "Anna was positive that Colonel Rycroft liberally availed himself of their services."

"As if *she* would know!" Natasha scoffed in derision. Beckoning Synnovea near, she spoke in a hushed tone as if revealing an intimate secret in a crowded room. "I've heard it said that Colonel Rycroft has dumbfounded many of his fellow officers by turning down invitations put forth by several young *boyarinas* who've recently been widowed and yearn to have him as their lover. In view of the fact that he has refused to accept what has been freely offered by women who are attractive as well as wealthy, do you suppose that he'd be wont to lay out coins to appease himself with harlots? He seems intent upon his work and winning you, so if it's your plan to trick him, you should be warned. He won't consider it kindly if you tempt him unduly and then torment him with a refusal."

Synnovea felt strangely placated by Natasha's news, yet she searched the woman's face wonderingly. "Are you suggesting that I choose another to serve as my so-called debaucher?"

"Are you really so bent on going through with this farce?" Natasha countered in amazement, but she waved away any answer when she searched the translucent orbs and recognized the depth of the girl's mettle. "Never mind. I can see for myself that you mean to have your way in this matter, and although I'm reluctant to see you sacrifice the affections of the Englishman in your wild scheme, I cannot imagine anyone who'd serve your purpose as well as Colonel Rycroft. At least, if you cannot hold him off, you'll likely be gifted with a beautiful child to remind you of him long years after he's gone."

Synnovea frowned petulantly. "You're not being at all encouraging."

"No, but I am being truthful," Natasha pointed out. "If the thought of bearing a child outside of marriage frightens you, my dear, then you should at least consider the difficulty you'll have holding off the colonel's advances. He has made it clear that he wants you enough to petition the tsar for an opportunity to court you. He hasn't done that for any other woman. How can you even dare believe that he'll keep his breeches in place once you've lured him to his quarters? If you ask me, you haven't taken into consideration the harsh consequences you'll suffer if things go awry."

"I *have!* Night and day! I've also imagined the horror I'll likely feel once I'm ensconced in Vladimir's bed. That's exactly the kind of reaction that Aleksei is counting on to drive me to him, but if he thinks Colonel Rycroft has had his way with me, Aleksei will be leery of what vermin a man with his reputation may have left behind."

Natasha heaved a laborious sigh, yielding to her arguments. "What do you intend?"

Synnovea thoughtfully set forth the requirements needed for the success of her plan. " 'Twill be necessary for Aleksei and his paid cohorts to discover their mistake about an hour and a half after you leave here. That will give the colonel and me time to reach his quarters and have a glass or two of wine, but little else. It's a fair distance to the German district. I dared to time it the other day while those hooligans followed my coach. Still, if you tell Stenka to halt the coach too late, or if something else goes awry, there'll be no help for me. You're the only one I can trust to see this thing through according to my directions. I won't be able to hold the colonel at bay forever. Once Aleksei arrives with his rabble, hopefully circumstances will appear far worse than they actually are and Aleksei will be convinced that he has little choice but to tell my betrothed of my indiscretion. Vladimir's rejection of me will accomplish the rest."

Feeling a niggling apprehension about the whole ruse, Natasha sought again to offer her young friend counsel. "What do you expect will happen when Colonel Rycroft and Aleksei confront each other? Do you honestly think the colonel will give you up without a fight?"

"Hopefully he will be wise enough to know that quarreling with Aleksei will be futile, and will make good his escape as I will urge him to do."

"I doubt the colonel will be in a logical frame of mind after being interrupted on the very threshold of having his way with you."

"He'll have no choice but to flee once he sees the band of men that Aleksei will bring with him."

"Dear child, this whole plan of yours is dangerous," Natasha replied fretfully. "In time you may be sorry you've scandalized your reputation, but after the deed is done, there'll be little you can say or do to make it all right again. And don't imagine that it will go as smoothly as you hope. Even in the best of plans, something usually goes wrong, and if you're not the one who'll pay, then have some regard for Colonel Rycroft. He's a foreigner in this country. Who will go to his aid or defense if he's taken? The tsar may consider the divestment of your virginity an affront to your father's memory and seek serious retribution from the colonel."

"Then I shall speak in his behalf," Synnovea stated stubbornly and, at the elder's incredulous stare, lifted her shoulders in a dismal shrug. "If need be, I'll plead my cause to Tsar Mikhail and admit that it was I who deliberately enticed the Englishman for the purpose of escaping marriage to Vladimir."

"Now *that* should be a tale to raise a few brows," Natasha remarked, flicking her own eyebrows briefly upward to display her skepticism.

Synnovea went down on her knees before the woman and gazed up at her pleadingly. "Oh, Natasha, if I don't try this, there'll be no escape for me. Aleksei will never give me peace until I yield myself to him, and once I'm married, I'll be forever bound to Vladimir until one of us is laid in the grave."

Natasha heaved a gloomy sigh. "I can certainly understand your reluctance to wed an ancient. When I was much younger, I abhorred the idea of submitting myself to my first husband. Though he was kind, he was great in years, actually younger than Vladimir by five years, and I found no joy in our bed."

Synnovea laid her cheek upon the woman's knee. "I don't hate Vladimir, Natasha. He's a far better man than Aleksei might have chosen had he been given more time. It's just that—"

"I know, Synnovea. There's no need for you to explain. Your head has been filled with glorious visions of love and marriage similar to what your parents shared together. If anyone is to blame for the hopes you cling to, then it's Aleksandr and Eleanora. They wanted you to know the same joy and devotion they shared."

"Perhaps Anna was right," Synnovea murmured dejectedly. "Perhaps I've been pampered too much in my life."

"If that be true, my dear, then I'm inclined to believe that all children should be coddled in the same manner, for you have all the qualities I would desire to see in a daughter." Natasha stroked the dark head affectionately. "Don't concern yourself about Anna and the insults she would lay upon you. She lives in her own private hell, and she seeks to share her fate with others. We must forget her and set our minds now to more important matters, such as refining this ingenious plan of yours. The less left to chance, the better it will be for you—*and* Colonel Rycroft. Of course, you know there'll be a definite chance that he'll hate you after this. A man's pride is most tender when his affections and emotions are carelessly used by a woman."

Synnovea was discomforted by the idea that Tyrone would come to hate her, but she had already laid out the path that she must take, and she wasn't about to veer from it now. "The colonel will live through this blow to his confidence far better than Vladimir would if I were to reveal my aversion to him. Should I tell the truth and lay the old man low, even so much as in the grave?"

Natasha shook her head in doleful denial. "No, no, child! I would not see you harm the old prince in such a way. Still, I'm reluctant to see you waste the affections of such a man as the colonel."

Synnovea lifted her head and searched the saddened eyes of the elder. "Would you have me give myself to him so his pride might be spared?"

A glum frown puckered Natasha's brows. "If only we could find another way to accomplish what you have in mind. I had such high hopes for Colonel Rycroft. I was sure that of all the men who've admired you, he'd be the one to win you."

Synnovea averted her face, not willing to admit that she had seen more in him than she had ever cared to divulge to anyone. It was some moments before she tore her mind free from her own misgivings and glanced up to see that the dark eyes had grown misty with tears. Though the woman's despondency brought home to her the gravity of her plot, Synnovea couldn't find it in herself to halt the plummeting grains of time that would see her own ends accomplished in this affair.

10

$\mathcal{T}$he pendulum swung through the long hours as night followed day and day followed night until the evening of the planned seduction finally arrived. Synnovea was as jittery as a young bride on her wedding night with the realization that Tyrone would be in attendance and that she'd actually be making an attempt to beguile him by whatever means proved effective. Lacking the finesse and skill of a more experienced temptress, she had no real knowledge of how to go about preparing herself for such an event. In matters of feminine persuasion, she knew she'd have to rely on her own instincts, but in selecting a gown, she sought Natasha's guidance. A deep blue creation of European design was chosen to compliment her fair skin and to reveal just enough cleavage to be subtly alluring.

"If Colonel Rycroft wasn't able to resist an overflowing bosom, my dear," the older countess counseled, "I'm sure he'd be content to coddle strumpets. Instead, he has set his eye on you and with good cause, but I doubt that you've given him much more than a glimpse or two of a dainty ear or a creamy nape. Therefore I'm inclined to think his tastes are more refined in the area of women and their attire."

Synnovea lifted a hand in the guise of brushing aside a rebellious curl from off her brow as she sought to hide the vibrant color that flooded into her cheeks. She would never have verbally disputed her friend's theory, but she was wont to wonder if Tyrone Rycroft would have been so anxious to court her at all if he hadn't already seen as much of her as there was to see.

"Have you told Ali what you're planning?" Natasha queried, settling back upon a chaise as Synnovea rose from the tub and slipped into the large pool fed by an underground spring. The Irish woman had left some moments ago, having forgotten the violet balm to rub into her mistress's skin. Since Synnovea's bedchambers were located at the far and uppermost end of the house from the bathing chamber, it was highly unlikely the maid would return within the next few moments. "Ali's simply beside herself over the idea that Colonel Rycroft will be coming tonight. In light of her infatuation, I've been wondering if she has any idea what you're going to do to the man."

"What? And have her lay me low with her scolding, too? Why, I'd never hear the end of it!" Synnovea shook her head, denying the possibility, and then promptly voiced objections to the woman's choice of words. "It isn't what *I'm* going to do to the colonel, Natasha, but what I'll be letting *him* do to me! You seem to imagine that I'll be forcing myself upon his flanks. Believe me, if Colonel Rycroft's hands move as fast and freely as his eyes do, I'll be facing hazards just being alone with him."

Natasha held up a hand to halt the other's testy remarks.

"I'll say no more, for 'tis plain you're easily riled by my lament."

"Aye!" Synnovea agreed with a pert nod. "In your eagerness to plead the colonel's cause, you've shown no similar compassion for me."

Natasha leaned forward on an elbow and braced her small, pointed chin upon a slender knuckle as she peered intently into the brooding eyes of the other. "You may rant in outrage against my charity toward him all you want, Synnovea, but I've seen the weapons at your disposal and do tremble in fear at the havoc you may cause in that man's life."

Synnovea reddened profusely when she felt the meaningful flick of the other's perusal, and with an indignant groan she sank beneath the surface of the water until the ripples lapped beneath her chin. "You're not being at all fair to take his side over mine."

"On the contrary, my dear. When you deliberately set out to entice a man solely for the purpose of using him as a pawn for your own gain, then I have no difficulty comparing your actions to the deeds of a well-versed courtesan, but I fear your ruse will be far more damaging. At least a courtesan would stay and pay her due, but what of you? The moment he seeks to take you, you fly."

"Natasha, have pity!" Synnovea begged fretfully. "You wound me to the quick!"

"Good!" the older woman retorted and fixed a condemning finger upon the girl. "Because that's exactly what you'll be doing *to* him."

A sullen frown troubled Synnovea's brow as she peered up at Natasha. "Do you like the man so much?"

"Aye! I do!"

Synnovea lifted a dainty nose to indicate the injury she felt at the woman's continual harping. "And do you loathe me so much for this thing I plan?"

Feeling defeated, Natasha lifted her arms in a lame gesture of appeal. "My dearest Synnovea, I understand why you're intent upon doing this." Overwhelmed by her own frustration, she shook her head. "I'm just reluctant to see you waste what had every potential of being a cherished love."

"I may never know what I could've had with Colonel Rycroft," Synnovea admitted dismally. "But I know I'll be sorely grieved if I'm forced to wed an ancient or if I must continue to wage my wits against Aleksei to keep myself safe from his wayward bent. If I cannot gain my freedom, that's exactly what lies ahead of me. Will you not give me your understanding and blessings as I try to avoid that end?"

Again the frosted head moved negatively. "Nay, Synnovea, I cannot do that, but I will give you my prayers, for I think you'll be needing them—you *and* Colonel Rycroft. Aleksei may be tempted to kill you both."

"Do you have to be so morbid about it all?" the younger countess grumbled.

Natasha stared at the radiant beauty for a long, thoughtful moment before heaving a laborious sigh. "Synnovea, my child, I don't think you have any idea what you're letting yourself in for."

The door opened behind them, and the two women glanced around as Ali skittered in. "Here I be at last," the maid gasped, clearly out of breath. "An' meself hurryin' all the while. Why, if this house be any grander, ye could set the Taraslovs' manse right square dab in the middle o' it an' still have room for a banquet! Poor Danika's ne'er seen such a large pantry, not ta mention the livin' quarters what she an' li'l Sophia's been given. They're a happy pair, ta be sure."

Natasha chuckled. "I'm delighted that Danika has proven herself such an excellent cook. She's definitely a talented addition to the staff. Our guests will soon be raving over her capabilities."

"Elisaveta is no less talented, but she fears her labors are mainly wasted at the Taraslovs'," Synnovea interjected as she tried to set her mind on something less troubling than her planned gambit with Tyrone Rycroft. The old servant came to the edge of the pool, prompting Synnovea to suggest, "Why don't you visit Elisaveta this evening, Ali? She'd enjoy hearing about Danika's good fortune. Stenka can drive you over to the Taraslovs' and return for you later."

"A right fine idea, me dearie, but if'n ye wouldn't mind, I'd like ta take a peek or two o' Colonel Rycroft afore I go, just ta see himself decked out in his finery. Why, he's nearly the handsomest man I've seen since yer pa came courtin' yer ma."

Having already suffered much admonition because of the Englishman, Synnovea was in a mood to demur the woman's boast. "I fear you're exaggerating beyond your usual bent, Ali. The man has a nice enough form, I'll grant you, but hardly a face to turn a lady's head."

Natasha's brows jutted upward in some wonderment as she contemplated her house guest. She could only wonder if the girl would find any man exceptional if she dismissed the colonel's looks so easily.

The appointed time for the guests' arrival rapidly approached, until only a few moments remained. Natasha went downstairs to the long entrance hall, where she would greet them. When Synnovea joined her there and extended the voluminous skirts of her gown, the elder nodded in smiling approval.

"Do I pass inspection?" the maiden queried with a charming smile, turning about in a slow circle.

"Admirably!" Natasha fervently avouched. "You cannot believe how much your mother's necklace enhances the luster of your skin. And the gown? Why, it's simply magnificent, my dear!"

The scalloped lace of the stiff ivory collar was a smaller version of the rabato that Queen Elizabeth of England had been fond of wearing during her reign. Lightly seeded with tiny pearls, it fanned outward from the neckline much like the ornate petals of a flower, complimenting the dark blue hue of the gown and the girl's elegantly upswept coiffure. The lace insert covering her bosom seemed quite demure at first, but upon closer inspection, the piece proved most provocative, allowing minute glimpses of the round bosom swelling above the shallow blue bodice. The necklace was a massive creation, studded with large sapphires interspersed with diamonds and adorned around the lower edge with a collection of pearl teardrops. From the elaborate setting, a much larger pearl pendant dangled coyly above the fleshly crevice.

"I fear the poor colonel will have difficulty recovering his wits after he sees you, my dear," Natasha commented ruefully. "He'll be as vulnerable as a bleating lamb being led to slaughter."

"Natasha, please," Synnovea implored. "Have done with your nagging ere I'm rent asunder." From beneath gathered brows she peered up at the woman, sulking like a beautiful child. "The way you harp at me, a body would have reason to think you're my mother."

Natasha flung back her head and laughed in hearty amusement. When her mirth finally ebbed, she met the solemn green-brown eyes with a warm radiance shining within her own. "If it's so apparent that I have a mother's concern for you, Synnovea, can you not understand that I value your happiness above all else? Thus I must beg you to have a care for the pride of the man whom you lead into your trap tonight."

The tinkling of tiny bells announced the arrival of a carriage before the stoop, and soon the mingled voices of several men could be heard. Synnovea managed a tremulous smile as she searched the other's dark eyes. "I shall do whatever I can to soften the blow to Colonel Rycroft."

Natasha inclined her regal head in acknowledgment of the other's assurance and moved toward the entrance to greet her first guests. For the time being, the pledge would be enough to appease her apprehensions.

It was nearly a quarter turn past the hour when Tyrone Rycroft entered the foyer with his second-in-command, Captain Grigori Tverskoy. The Russian officer was dressed in a red silk kaftan and looked quite dashing. The Englishman had garbed himself according to the fashion of his homeland and wore a rich velvet doublet, knee breeches, and stockings, all of the blackest hue. The only relief from the somber color came from the white, lace-edged cuffs and wide, flat collar that had been similarly adorned. In contrast to the colorful robes of the boyars, the elegant simplicity of his clothes seemed quite sober. Even so, his appearance was no less than magnificent.

The ornately adorned vaulted ceiling looming above the staircase was well lit with chandeliers, allowing visitors to view the beauty of it as they approached Natasha, who awaited them near the arched colonnade bordering the entrance to the manse's great room, which was itself a work of art with its intricately painted tiles, motifs, and richly paneled walls. Ali kept vigil from the second flight of stairs, and it was there that Tyrone espied her soon after his entrance. Much to the maid's delight, he swept her a courtly bow. "You've made this evening brighter by your cheery smile, Ali McCabe. So far, I've seen none to bless my heart more."

"Ah, but ye will, Colonel, mark me words," she warbled cheerily and scampered up the stairs to fetch her wrap. Now that she had seen the gentleman handsomely outfitted in his best, she'd be content to leave and visit with Elisaveta in the Taraslov kitchen.

"No wonder Ali is taken with you, Colonel," Natasha observed with a gracious smile. "With a name like Tyrone and enough charm to crumble Lord Blarney's castle, you've managed to endear yourself to the woman. She's convinced you come from Irish stock."

"Actually, my grandmother is Irish," Tyrone admitted with a grin. "But then, she all but raised me, for my own mother often sailed the seas with my father."

"And what is his profession?"

"Once he plied his trade as a merchant seaman and sailed to foreign climes, but now he owns a small fleet of ships, which are used in the same commerce."

"Not a soldier?" Natasha queried. "I would've thought him to be a proud cavalier like yourself, Colonel. Wherever did you gain such equestrian skills if not from your father?"

"My grandmother Meghan is very fond of horses, my lady." A brief flash of white teeth accompanied his answer. "Shortly after I was weaned, she put me in a saddle. Even at an age of threescore, ten, and three years, she still rides for an hour or so every morning."

"Doesn't your grandmother object to your being in a foreign land? Wouldn't she prefer to have you closer at hand in her advancing years?"

"Aye, but I fear there's no help for it. At least not yet."

Natasha's brows lifted curiously. "The cause sounds most dire, Colonel."

Tyrone saw no reason to deny the seriousness of the deed. "I killed a man in a duel, and since his family had both rank and power, whereas mine had only wealth, I was advised to leave the country until their tempers cooled or they could see the light of it."

"The light of it being?" She held her breath in dread of his answer.

" 'Twas a quarrel over a woman," he murmured candidly.

"Oh." Natasha paled considerably and managed a shaky smile to hide her concern for the innocent who was about to lead this man into a trap. "Are you prone to quarreling over women, Colonel?"

"Not usually, Countess."

"And the lady? Is she content now to have you gone?"

"It matters no more to her, I fear. She died shortly before I left England."

"How sad for you, Colonel. You must have loved her very much to have fought over her."

"At one time I was thoroughly convinced that my fondness for her would endure every trial." His lips twitched briefly in a bleak smile. "I was mistaken."

Natasha dared no more questions, for she sensed by the brevity of his reply that the colonel wished to speak no more of the matter. A timorous smile sketched her lips as she shifted her attention to his companion. "How good of you to come this evening, Captain Tverskoy. I believe you're acquainted with at least two other guests of mine. Naturally, when I heard you'd be here, I made certain that Prince Adolphe and his daughter, Tania, were also planning to attend. If I'm not mistaken, you and the Zherkofs come from the same province, do you not?"

The Russian brightened considerably. "Why, yes, we do, Countess. In fact, I've been acquainted with that particular family for a number of years, certainly well before I accepted my commission into His Majesty's services. But please, my lady, I'd be especially honored if you'd call me by my given name, Grigori."

"Thank you, Grigori," she replied graciously and beseeched both men, "and, of course, you are both welcome to call me Natasha."

"Only if you'll address me by Tyrone, my lady," the colonel suggested with a cajoling smile.

The countess dipped her adorned head in a consenting nod. "Of course, Tyrone." She laid a fine-boned hand lightly upon his arm. "Would you wait here until I return? The Zherkofs are anxious to renew their acquaintance with their friend, and I promised I'd bring him over as soon as he arrived. As for you, Colonel, I'd like to formally introduce you to a young guest of mine."

Tyrone grinned in anticipation. "I shall eagerly await your return, my lady."

Drawing on her close friendship with Prince Adolphe Zherkof and his beautiful daughter, Natasha engaged them in conversation with the captain before making her way back to the Englishman. Accepting his proffered arm, she drew him to the food-laden tables, where Synnovea was presently assisting a pair of ancient dowagers with the service of *zakuski* and glasses of *Amarodina*.

"A moment of your time, Synnovea," Natasha murmured and glanced aside at the officer as the younger countess excused herself from the elders. "I know the two of you have met, Colonel, but as I've been advised, not with proper decorum."

Pasting a smile on her lips, Synnovea tightened her grip on her wine goblet to hide the fact that her hands were trembling as she faced the Englishman. Inwardly she could feel herself quaking in apprehension of that moment when their eyes would actually meet, and she delayed it as long as possible, sweeping her gaze upward from buckled shoes to the braid-trimmed doublet that defined the taut, lean waist and broad shoulders. Her inspection rose higher still to lips that were now totally devoid of distortion. Dazzling white teeth sparkled behind a roguish grin, and Synnovea held her breath as she forced herself to meet the startlingly beautiful blue eyes that glowed back at her. Against her will, her jaw slowly sagged.

Natasha raised a hand to introduce her guest. "Synnovea, this is Colonel Sir Tyrone Rycroft, of His Majesty's Imperial Hussars. . . ."

Tyrone stepped into a chivalrous bow. "It gives me sublime pleasure to formally make your acquaintance, Countess Zenkovna."

Synnovea closed her mouth abruptly and nervously plied the fan to hide her confusion. "Why, Colonel Rycroft, I would never have recognized you," she replied breathlessly, a bit flustered by his crisply chiseled good looks. He straightened to a towering height above her, or so it seemed to her. She hadn't remembered him being so tall. Her heart began to race, and in an unsteady, disconnected rush, she enlarged upon her statement. "You were still quite bruised the last time we met . . . but then, I really didn't see you that well . . . I mean, with the rain and all. I was so thoroughly soaked, I didn't give much heed to anything else."

The glittering twinkle in the blue eyes rapidly evolved into a rakish gleam. "The last time we met, Countess, I fear we were both rather sodden, though perhaps not quite as wet as I've had the pleasure of seeing you."

"Oh!" Though the syllable was barely audible, Synnovea wielded the fan with disconcerted haste, heedless of the chill in the air. Indeed, she was nigh suffocating from the hot blush sweeping over her. She chanced a sidelong glance at Natasha to see what the woman might have garnered from his comment, but even after being reassured that nothing untoward had been noted by her friend, the nervous rhythm of her heart refused to slow. "Well, no matter," she hurried to add in disarray, filling the empty space of their exchange with shaky comments. "That seems so long ago now! Weeks have flown."

"Have they?" Tyrone's voice was warmly hushed as his eyes plumbed the depths of hers. "I was sure it was only yesterday, but then, I relive the experience daily . . . nightly . . . and every hour of my waking."

Synnovea would have fled in whatever direction had allowed for an easy escape, but when she looked in frantic appeal to Natasha and found the woman smiling in smug satisfaction, it required no mean mental feat for her to realize their hostess was absolutely delighted by the colonel's ability to scatter her wits and dismantle her defenses.

Gathering her sundered poise by the grit of her teeth, Synnovea tapped her fan lightly upon Tyrone's forearm to rebuke him for his brazen reminder. "Perhaps you should give your imagination a rest, Colonel. It seems to be caught in a definite rut."

Tyrone's lips twitched with humor as his eyes lightly caressed her. "I assure you, Countess, my imagination ranges far afield, but usually well within the confines of the same subject."

Synnovea struggled to subdue the fiery heat that continued to surge upward into her cheeks. She could perceive the particular quintessence of the man's dreams if he allowed his mind to dwell on what he had already seen. No doubt she had been mauled and ravished a score or more times in his fantasies.

Whipping up her flagging will, Synnovea won a small battle with her composure and lightly stroked the fan back and forth along his arm. Had she given vent to her true feelings, she might have used the delicate apparatus in a more vengeful quest and wiped that maddening grin from his lips. A slap across the cheek was definitely what the blackguard deserved for being so forward, but it would hardly serve her purpose. "You've come to my rescue so often, Colonel, I fear I've lost count. I can only hope that you're as kind to me in your musings. I wouldn't want to admonish you for being coarse."

Tyrone chuckled softly at her reproof, allowing that she had just cause to blush, for his fantasies were indeed sensual and not meant for sharing with a young innocent. "I sometimes find myself a victim of my dreams, Countess, but may I assuage your worries with a pledge of my devotion?"

"A pledge will hardly suffice," Synnovea responded, managing to tease him with a bewitchingly winsome pout. She didn't feel the least bit vindicated by his feeble excuse and was tempted to extract some further revenge. "I'll need proof of your claim, Colonel, and since I haven't seen you of late, you can probably understand how I might think you're only toying with my affections."

Natasha restrained the urge to roll her eyes in disbelief as she witnessed the sassy flirtation. She was now reasonably confident that the Englishman could take care of himself, but when the cannons of Synnovea's warfare were loaded to the hilt and primed to blow the man's heart right out of his chest, she found it difficult to remain distantly detached. Doubting her ability to curb her interference, she begged leave of the couple, fervently hoping the girl's scheme wouldn't result in another deadly duel.

"You'll watch after Synnovea, won't you, Tyrone? I promised Princess Anna that I'd keep her well guarded." Natasha smiled as she gave a little shrug. "I just never committed myself to doing so entirely alone."

A lopsided grin once again made an appearance, nearly bedazzling Natasha, who had seen a goodly share of handsome men in her lifetime. She just hoped that when the fray ended, this prime specimen of the male gender wouldn't be so outdone with her young friend that he'd sail back to England on the first ship available.

" 'Twill be my greatest delight to devote myself entirely to the task, Lady Natasha," he declared magnanimously.

The woman patted his arm almost in sympathy. "Take care of yourself, Tyrone."

He gave her a clipped nod that sufficed as a bow. "I can assure you, Lady Natasha, that I've tried my best to do that for most of my life."

"Please continue," she said encouragingly and tossed a meaningful glance toward Synnovea. Turning from the couple, she joined the pair of elderly ladies who were now giggling like adolescents as they sipped wine and reminisced on days of old.

Tyrone was fully conscious of the long-coveted gift he had just been granted. Having been restricted from Synnovea's

company until now, he found himself feasting upon her stirring beauty. " 'Tis true enough that you've held my thoughts
and dreams entangled, Synnovea," he breathed softly. "Any
man would be hard-pressed to forget what I have seen."

Synnovea groaned inwardly at his audacious reminder.
"I'm not accustomed to flaunting myself in front of men, Colonel, and I would take it much amiss if you were to speak to
anyone about the incident in the bathhouse or anything else
that would cause me shame, including your visit to my
chambers."

"No need to fear, Synnovea. I shall continue to guard our
secrets with utmost diligence," he averred softly.

Synnovea's qualms were eased by his gentle pledge,
allowing her to sip her wine. "I fear I've been much beset by
worry, Colonel," she admitted. "My mother was English, you
see, and she instilled within me an aversion to bathing in
public. You were my first encounter to the converse."

The blue eyes kindled brightly. "I'm glad no other man
has seen the treasures I've beheld."

In all of her trips abroad and those taken within the borders of Russia, Synnovea couldn't remember a time when she
had beheld more beautiful eyes. They were definitely not the
gray she had first supposed when she had glimpsed them in
the forest and then later probed in the shadowed bathhouse.
In the glow of the nearby candles they seemed almost an
azure hue rimmed by deeper sapphire. In contrast to his
warmly bronzed face, they were all the more vivid, but the
same sun which had darkened his skin had also bleached his
neatly clipped hair. Lighter strands capped the top of his head
and streaked the darker tawny brown at his temples. The
bruises and swelling were no longer in evidence, and what
Synnovea now saw before her made her realize that Ali's declaration could no longer be challenged. Tyrone Rycroft was
an exceptionally handsome man.

Synnovea offered him a beguiling smile. "I was certain Anna had been successful in frightening you off."

The blue eyes twinkled back at her. "She only made me more determined to impress His Majesty."

"Pray tell me, sir, how have you fared in that endeavor?" Synnovea asked, deliberately positioning her battery of arms as she leaned forward to set her half-filled goblet upon a nearby table. A candelabra sitting atop the gleaming wooden surface cast forth the radiance of a dozen tapers, the warmly flickering flow of which pierced the scalloped white lace that lay like a hazy veil over her bosom.

"I'm not exactly sure," Tyrone replied huskily as his gaze probed the translucent cloth. Her young breasts seemed to glow with a luster of their own and were just as tempting as he had recalled. "His Majesty has yet to grant my request."

Though Synnovea had been admired by men in the past, this was like some potent nectar she had never sipped before, a full, heady draught that made her breasts tingle and her senses come alive. Basking in this new, indescribable awakening, she traced a slender finger around the rim of her glass, averse to curbing the titillating excitement he had awakened within her. "And what request was that, Colonel?"

"The very same that I declared to you when Princess Anna turned me away from her door—to pay court to you." Tyrone replenished his memory with a more rewarding view into her décolletage as he bent forward to claim the goblet she caressed. When he lifted the glass and his gaze, his warmly glowing eyes delved into hers as he sipped the brew. "In truth, my lady, you've become my heart's desire."

Synnovea smoothed his lace cuff, allowing her fingers to lightly caress the back of his lean hand. "Do I dare ask how many maids you've sworn the same to, Colonel?"

"Ask on," Tyrone whispered, advancing a step closer, "and I will answer 'None.'"

"How is it that you've escaped the banns of marriage so long, then? I'd guess you to be of an age. . . ."

"A score, ten, and two, my lady," he murmured, sampling her fragrance.

"Old enough to be properly wed, then . . . *if* you've lent as much heed to other maids as you've recently bestowed upon me. Or mayhap you've been the one pursued and have denied any the chance to catch you."

"I must admit that I enjoy initiating the chase, my lady."

"Ah, then there *have* been other ladies whom you've fancied," Synnovea gently prodded. Under his close attention, she felt as flighty as a bird in hand.

"Are there other maids as worthy of a man's attention as you are?" Tyrone breathed warmly. "I haven't noticed any, if they do indeed exist."

"Are you really so intent upon courting me?"

"Aye," he whispered without hesitation, moving forward until his thighs pressed into the fullness of her wide skirts. The smoldering blue embers touched her lips, and unwittingly Synnovea yielded their softness to his visual caress, parting them as she drew a shaky breath. She had no idea what sorcerer's enchantment he used upon her. Beneath his lingering stare, she could almost feel his mouth moving upon hers. Much entranced, she watched again as he tasted the edge of the goblet where she had sipped.

"Ah, a most delectable brew." He sighed above the rim. "It seems as if years have passed since I tasted its equal in your coach."

Synnovea mentally shook herself free from the fascination of his unswerving gaze and flicked a glance about the room in an effort to subdue the delicious tumult within her. Had she quaffed several glasses of wine, she would have felt no less giddy.

All around them, guests were involved in animated conversations. It didn't seem to matter that some were no more

251

than a score in age, while others were three times as old; each seemed imbued with a zeal and a passion for life. Those who were more mature had certainly made the most of their lives, as well as of their fortunes, and had no need to draw succor from the adventures, accomplishments, or affairs of others. The younger ones were on their way to making their own lives noteworthy and were eager to learn from the experiences of the elders. Comfortably absent from the affair were the gossipmongers who were ravenous for any delectable tidbit.

Her companion reached past her to set the goblet on the table, causing Synnovea to catch her breath and stumble back in surprise as she felt his velvet-clad arm brush boldly across her breast. Though it might have been a chance encounter, every instinct within her denied the possibility. More disturbing was the delicious thrill that catapulted through her, searing holes in her carefully contrived facade of cool restraint.

Synnovea's widened eyes chased upward to meet the colonel's closely attentive regard. As she searched his visage, a tawny brow rose in challenging amusement, as if he dared her to accuse him of some dastardly crime when both of them were aware that she had intentionally teased him. For Synnovea, it was like coming up against a cold, hard reality. The Englishman was no untried youth whom she could blithely lead along with engaging words and flirtatious smiles. He knew the game far better than she and had accepted her ploy as an invitation. That realization made her question her own wisdom in selecting such a man for her gambit. When Tyrone Rycroft was able to see clearly through her subterfuge, how could she hope to successfully maneuver him into a compromising situation and still expect to remain unscathed when it was obvious he had every intention of ushering her to a fate she fervently wished to avoid?

In contrast to his audacity, her strategy seemed suddenly seriously flawed, for he was progressing with greater dispatch than she, in her naiveté, could safely handle. The alacrity with which he was advancing would see her tossed upon her back and divested of her virginity before she even had a chance to reach his quarters.

"I must be excused for a moment," she begged unsteadily, knowing she had to think this matter through once again, just to make sure she wanted to subject herself to perils that appeared much more real now. Of a surety, her courage needed bolstering if she meant to carry through with her ruse. In truth, she felt as if she had just been bombarded by a volley of cannonballs.

"May I be of some assistance, my lady?" Tyrone asked with exaggerated politeness. She seemed so distraught by his touch, he wondered if he might have mistaken her enticement. "You appear . . . disturbed."

Recognizing the esprit in his wayward smile, Synnovea lifted a hand to halt his advance. She had to keep her wits well aligned or all would be lost. She didn't need him touching or wooing her at the present moment, not when she had to escape to some haven where she could recapture some semblance of intrepidity. She shook her head and sought to step past him. "I must go."

"Perhaps a glass of wine will help soothe you," Tyrone suggested, deftly catching her fingers within his and bestowing a gentle kiss upon them. He was reluctant to see her leave, for he was not at all sure she'd return, and if she fled now, it appeared unlikely she'd ever allow him to see her again.

"I must go!" Synnovea gasped again, astonished by the way her fingers trembled beneath his lips. Disentangling them from his grasp, she pressed her palm against his broad chest, growing increasingly wary of being detained. "Please stand aside, Colonel."

"Will you come back?" The tawny brow jutted upward again. "Or should I forget that we ever met?"

Though the inquiry was quietly spoken, the vulnerable

disappointment in his tone pierced her heart. Pausing, she stared up at him in amazement. As she probed the depths of those translucent orbs which observed her with a shadowed reserve in return, she realized that this was no casual game for Tyrone Rycroft. He was serious about having her for his own.

Synnovea's panic began to ebb as she recognized his dedication to winning her. How could a man force a woman to yield to his ardent bent when he seemed so sensitive to the possibility of losing her? A tentative smile curved her lips as she traced a trembling finger along the silk cording that trimmed his doublet. "I need a few moments to myself, Colonel, that is all, but I'll be back. That much I promise you," she vowed in a hushed voice. "Will you wait for me?"

"As long as it takes," Tyrone replied, gathering her slender fingers within his again and bending over them.

His kisses lingered warmly upon her skin, evoking feelings that she could not fully explain, an incredibly stirring experience that flooded her heart with tenderness and a strange sense of joy. She felt as if she were melting inside and leaned toward him, brushing her fingers almost lovingly over his closely cropped hair. When he straightened to search her face, she drew back, a blush suffusing her cheeks. Synnovea dared not test the strength of her voice, and with an inarticulate murmur, she left him staring after her in some bemusement as she fled across the hall.

Ali's absence allowed Synnovea the solitude she desperately needed to find in her bedchambers. Though she sought to bring some clarity to her thoughts, she paced about like a caged animal, finding no rational solution for what she was experiencing. If by his mere presence the colonel could suffuse her being with feelings that closely resembled a gentle regard and then, in the next moment, send her senses reeling giddily out of control, a definite chasm existed between what he had awakened within her and the apathy she had felt toward her betrothed. It only affirmed what she had known all along: she'd never be content with Vladimir as her husband.

Pushing open a window, Synnovea leaned back against the frame and gazed out upon the starlit sky. She needed the bracing chill of the night air to clear her mind and to cool her skin after the heat of Tyrone's kisses. Yet, as the moon came out from behind a cloud, a movement across the thoroughfare drew her attention. Shading her eyes against the flickering radiance of the candles burning in her room, she peered intently through the lantern-lit darkness until two shadowy figures standing side by side became discernible. It was a moment before she recognized the shorter one as Prince Aleksei. She could only assume his hulking companion was one of the rogues he had hired to watch her, but she found that one's appearance oddly troubling. Though the man's head was covered with a *karakul* similar to those worn by Mongolians in bygone years, his powerful frame seemed hauntingly familiar.

Aleksei swaggered forward with unmeasured confidence and settled his hands on his narrow hips. Assured of her undivided attention, he threw back his head and roared his mirth to the night sky. Synnovea stiffened, feeling scalded by the mocking sound. He was laughing at her, scorning whatever hopes she had of escaping him.

Of a sudden, Synnovea regained her fortitude with an intensity that would have shocked the prince had he known he had been instrumental in perfecting it. Like a full-blown temptress, she addressed her attention to her appearance, preparing it for a more thorough siege. Resolved to show no clemency lest she find herself wedded and bedded forthwith, she readjusted her laces, cinching her slender waist tighter while loosening her bodice to a more tempting degree. No matter the extent of Tyrone's experience with the fairer gender, she was now committed to setting him back upon his heels with a more impassioned courtship. And if Natasha's warnings about the hazards of pushing a man beyond his limits were correct, then Synnovea silently vowed to make him fairly quake with frustration until he felt compelled to fly to his apartments with her.

Synnovea examined the results of her revamping both fore and aft in the tall looking glass and pronounced herself fit and trim. Surely no seaworthy galleon had ever been outfitted for battle with the same equipage and weapons she possessed within her cache, but this fine vessel of womanly softness was rigged for a most unusual contest, the entrapment and studied rebuff of no pompous youth, but a man well versed in the art of seduction.

Synnovea descended the stairs with measured tread as her gaze slipped past the colonnades into the great hall. The candles had been snuffed around the outer perimeter of the room, lending emphasis to a flaming wreath of tapers that encircled a blind balladeer recounting a tale of a princely warrior and a beautiful maiden. The guests were enthralled by the poetic lilt of his voice and seemed to hang on every word as the man wove his magic.

Tyrone Rycroft proved the singular exception. He had joined several men in the great hall, but by the swiftness with which his eyes reached her, Synnovea could believe he had been watching eagerly for her return. He promptly excused himself from his companions and seemed to move through the guests with only one purpose in mind, for his eyes never strayed from her. When he entered the vaulted alcove enclosing the stairs, those deeply hued orbs measured every detail of her, much like an avid collector of art might assess a treasured piece. Synnovea had no difficulty recalling that he had seen and perhaps even understood things about her that no one else ever would. When his eyes touched her hair, she knew he had seen the glory of it tumbling down her naked back. When his gaze dipped to her bosom, it was as if he but brought to mind the sight of those pale spheres glistening wetly in the warm glow of the lanterns. Even when his perusal swept down the length of her skirts, he seemed to probe the fullness for some hint of the sleek limbs that he had once viewed.

Synnovea shivered at the wealth of emotions his slow, meticulous inspection elicited. Upon halting on the last step, she tried to snatch her mind free from the slavery of her thoughts, yet the impressions remained, merging with memories of their first encounter, when he had lifted her from the murky depths of the dark waters and she had clung to his manly form. Her breasts almost ached with a vivid reminder of that moment when she had been caught against his steely hard chest. In her mind's eye she could see the fascinating play of muscles across his wide shoulders, the rippling sinews along his ribs, and the taut, flat belly, so briefly glimpsed and yet keenly defined in her mind, with its tracing of hair that mentally led her eye downward to the pure manly heat of him.

Synnovea took a deep breath and released it in a long, shuddering sigh, strangely excited by the wantonness she was experiencing and would have to surreptitiously convey, yet fearful of tempting this man beyond the threshold through which she'd find no easy retreat. Dragging her mettle up the full length of her spine, she sought to demonstrate a serenity that one might expect of a maiden sheathed in ice, yet inwardly she trembled with the danger of being caught in the vortex of her own growing involvement in this game of enticement.

As he halted before her, Synnovea could do naught but submit to the flame burning in those darkly translucent orbs. He slipped a hand behind her waist, and her breath nigh halted. Delicious shivers rippled up her spine as his lean fingers lightly strummed the laces at the back of her bodice.

"You're even more beautiful than when you left a century ago," Tyrone breathed, leaning provocatively near to indulge himself in her heady fragrance. "Or is it that I've forgotten the details in so long a time?"

Synnovea flicked a glance upward through silken lashes. Even with the added height of the step, she still had to look up to meet his gaze. "I've never met a man so perceptive in the mores of a woman that he can readily detect the repairs she has made to her appearance," she murmured silkily. "Am I to be faulted for wanting to look my best for you?"

Her heart quickened as his long fingers paused on the laces, as if he toyed with the idea of testing the security of the knot that held the cords in place. Had they been in a private place, he might well have tried.

"Can any man fault perfection?" Tyrone's smile was engaging, commanding her stare. "Truly, Synnovea, you have my undivided attention. I only wish we were alone so I could prove how genuinely I covet your companionship."

Sensing the effectiveness of her subterfuge but recognizing her own vulnerability to his charm, Synnovea struggled to slow the crazy, staccato beat of her heart. "Should I imagine that you wish to take me to your quarters, Colonel?"

He brushed his lips against her hair as his hand ascended to a place between her shoulder blades and pressed her forward until her breasts were lightly thrust against his chest. "Though I dare not hope that you'd bestow such favor upon me, I must confess 'tis my most fervent desire, my beauty. The merest thought of being alone with you takes my breath away, for I cannot forget the bliss of our encounter in the pool and do fervently wish that such a meeting may be repeated."

In spite of the queer knots in her stomach, Synnovea struggled to feel some victory, but the hand she braced against the solid rampart of his chest trembled noticeably. Even the subtle hint of his cologne caused a curious headiness, not unlike some strong intoxicant capable of sapping the strength from her limbs and stripping away the last vestiges of her womanly will. It would have been so easy to lean into him and appease a quickening desire. Yet Synnovea pushed away from that stalwart physique, deeming the distance between them safer for her own racing heart. "I think I should be cautious of such an event, sir," she murmured with more truth than coyness. "You allowed me to escape unscathed once, but I shouldn't think you'd be as generous a second time."

" 'Tis extremely doubtful that I'd be able to display such control again." He grinned with an allure that was becoming familiar to her. "Still, if such an occasion were repeated, I would hope that you'd at least consider calling me by my given name. After all we've been through together, Synnovea, wouldn't it seem appropriate? Is it so difficult for you to call me Tyrone? Or, if you'd prefer, Ty or Tyre. The latter is the name my grandmother calls me."

"Ty . . . Tyre . . . Tyrone." Synnovea tested the names as if sampling a luscious fruit. "Until I know you better, I think Tyrone must suffice. In truth, we're barely acquainted."

"The name sounds as delectable as honeyed mead when your lips sweeten it." His eyes tarried hungrily on her mouth, making her breath waver. "When I remember the sweet tidbits I've stolen from them, I'm beset with an unquenchable longing to kiss you in a way that would convince you of my desire for you, yet I would also enjoy teaching you how to respond."

A deeper color flooded into Synnovea's cheeks, evidencing her chagrin. Though it wasn't considered proper for a young maid to be conversant in the art of kissing, she was reluctant to have him think her an awkward chit when he compared her to all the other women he had kissed. "Do I need instruction?"

Tyrone's lips curved with amusement. "I'd be jealous if you didn't."

Synnovea met his smiling regard with wide, searching eyes. "Should I be jealous of all the women who've taught you?"

"You needn't be, my sweet," he assured her. "Since our first meeting, I've been your absolute slave."

"I wonder whose slave you truly are, Tyrone," she countered, arching a winged brow dubiously, not at all convinced of his sincerity. "If mine, as you claim, then I've not seen you much of late."

In an attitude of sincere regret, Tyrone pressed a hand to his breast. "A complaint you must take up with the tsar, since it has been his pleasure I've been serving. Yet, even while gratifying his desires, you've been on my mind."

"I've heard rumors, and I have no real assurance of your claims," she needled winsomely.

Sagaciously Tyrone turned the subject elsewhere, sensing her growing curiosity about the other women he had courted in his life. "Though I'd prefer to keep your beauty well hidden from every male eye but mine, sweetest Synnovea, I must introduce you to a close friend."

He took her elbow, lending her assistance from the last step, and drew her arm through his before escorting her into the great hall. Once there, he motioned to the young Russian whom Synnovea had seen enter with him. That one stood near the far wall with Natasha's frequent escort, Prince Adolphe, and his daughter, but at Tyrone's summons, he promptly excused himself from his companions. He joined them as they returned to the vaulted alcove.

"May I present my second-in-command, Captain Grigori Tverskoy," Tyrone said in a quietly subdued voice so as not to intrude upon the balladeer's verse. "Grigori, this is the Countess Synnovea Zenkovna."

The handsome Russian stepped into a decorous bow. " 'Tis indeed an honor to finally make your acquaintance, Countess," he replied graciously in English for the benefit of his superior. "You probably don't recognize me, since you were occupied with Ladislaus at the time, but I was fortunate enough to be among those who came to the assistance of your entourage after your coach was halted by outlaws. Of course, the tribute belongs solely to Colonel Rycroft, who ordered our detachment to search out the cause for the gunshots we heard."

"I'm grateful for your participation, Captain," Synnovea replied graciously, "and, of course, to your commander for his attention to duty."

Grigori tossed a grin toward his superior. "If you're not aware of it, my lady, Colonel Rycroft has derived enormous delight in having been the one to accomplish your rescue. Although he performed nearly the same service for several *boyarinas* when they were accosted by ruffians at a coach station only a few days before your attack, the colonel fervently denied his availability when they invited him to meet their father upon our return to Moscow."

Tyrone lifted a challenging brow toward the man and, with a wayward grin of his own, applied some good-natured needling in reverse as he directed his comments aside to Synnovea. "Among the sisters, there was one in particular who found it difficult to get through doorways, yet she was eager to win Grigori for her spouse. To save himself, he hid in the smokehouse until she finally gave up her search and departed with her kin."

"Much to my relief," the captain admitted with an amiable chortle.

Tyrone noticed Princess Tania timidly eyeing them from the great room. "I perceive there's yet another lady wistfully pining for your attention, my friend. You *do* seem to have a flair for enchanting sweet, young damsels."

Grigori cast a glance askance, and his smile broadened when his gaze lit on the one who stared back at him with more than a hint of longing in her eyes. He promptly faced his commander. "Since we'll be at liberty on the morrow, Colonel, I've agreed to accept Prince Adolphe's invitation to spend the evening at his home. I'll be journeying with them in their coach, so you'll have the hired livery to yourself this evening."

Tyrone stared after his friend, considering his haste to return to the girl. "It seems the princess has endeared herself to Grigori far better than most," he said, glancing down at Synnovea. "Otherwise he'd be running to the stable to hide."

"Should I take heart that you're here with me and not hiding out somewhere, Colonel?"

Tyrone faced her with eyes gleaming above a tantalizing smile. "Were I you, Synnovea, I'd consider myself the one being pursued. If I must make it any plainer . . . I'm quite ravenous to claim you for my lady."

Synnovea felt his lean fingers entwining hers and was amazed at how swiftly her senses began racing. Still, she teasingly demurred his assertion. "Simple words are hardly enough to validate your claims, sir."

Tyrone laid a hand possessively upon the small of her back and pressed her forward again, making her breath halt as he leaned near her ear. "Must you still be given proof after all my efforts to see you, my lady?" he queried warmly. "That would indeed demand a more private place than I've seen here. If you'd be willing to accompany me, I shall address that issue without delay."

Tyrone drew her along with him as he crossed the great hall and entered an enclosed veranda where several doors stood open to the garden. The fragrance of late-blooming shrubs wafted inward on cooling breezes, but the chill that went through Synnovea had nothing to do with the zephyrs. A sudden nervous fluttering in the pit of her stomach had made her recall Natasha's dire warnings about the man. Tyrone was no milksopping suitor who could be led along with teasing smiles and coy glances toward an unspoken promise of carnal fulfillment and then be held at bay with feeble excuses. So why was she ignoring all the warning signs and blindly taking her virtue and possibly her life in her hands by deluding a man who truly, deeply wanted her?

Tyrone gathered her shaking fingers within his and, pulling her near, brushed his lips across her brow in a caress as light as the brush of a butterfly's wings. His gentleness was unexpected, and whatever threat Synnovea had momentarily imagined he might pose in this gambit of hers faded from conscious thought as she enjoyed the moment. A sigh wafted from her as she relaxed in his arms, and she felt no need to be wary of what would follow.

Tyrone glanced around when another couple came to stand near the door through which they had just escaped. The pair's presence hindered the privacy he fervently coveted with Synnovea, and in some frustration he caught her fingers within his and drew her into the shadowy depths of the porch. When he faced her, his gaze caressed her dimly lit face and paused almost hungrily upon her soft mouth before venturing downward into her bodice.

"Are you so starved for companionship that you must consume me for your sup, Tyrone?" she queried in a faint, tremulous whisper.

" 'Twas my hope that we could be alone," he murmured huskily. "Until we find such a place, I must feast upon your comeliness the only way I can."

Rising to her toes, Synnovea pressed her lips near his ear, hoping he wouldn't detect the quaver in her voice as she breathed, "Have you seen the garden? 'Tis a rare sight even at night."

She smiled up at him invitingly as she stepped back, and like a gracefully floating wraith, she turned and glided as if on silken wings into the enclosed garden. A bright moon cast its silvery light through the lofty canopy of a huge tree, and it was there she waited, seeming as cool and serene as a high priestess of Roman hierarchy. It was merely a guise, for under that tranquil facade, Synnovea felt as anxious as a new bride awaiting the approach of her groom. Unable to predict what the next moments would bring, she felt as if she were opening a door to an unknown world.

Tyrone paused long enough to assure himself that Natasha

hadn't seen the girl leave. Their hostess was standing beside Adolphe and several others who had drawn near the storyteller. They stood with their backs to the door, listening intently to his tale, lending Tyrone some hope that he and Synnovea would remain undisturbed, at least until it ended.

He followed slowly, searching for some hint of the area in which Synnovea had hidden herself, peering into shadows, probing for the moonlit path that she might have taken. Then he glimpsed a bejeweled necklace twinkling in the mottled light filtering downward through the rustling leaves of a tall tree and advanced with more purposeful strides. When he halted before Synnovea, a shaky smile curved her lips. For a split moment he perused the beautiful, uplifted face and the dark eyes that seemed to mirror his own yearnings. Then he caught her hard against him until her breasts ached from the sheer pleasure of his unrelenting embrace. In the next phase of a heartbeat, his parting lips plummeted downward, seizing hers with a wild, frenzied passion.

Synnovea was too surprised by his ferocity and the bold intrusion of his tongue to know how to set aright her spinning world. Her feeble grasp on reality seemed to slip through her fingers as artfully devised tactics were sundered beneath the sweet, brutal onslaught of his kiss.

They came apart with a gasp, panting as if they had raced with abandon across the steppes. Synnovea turned her face aside, struggling to halt the careening flight of the earthbound sphere wherein she had been caught, but her suitor was intent upon savoring every minute detail of her. His mouth traveled downward, pressing warm, sultry kisses along her silken throat. Caught up in the bliss that he evoked, she yielded the ivory column to his fancy, unable to find any strength within her limbs. In her reeling world, he had become the only stable core to which she could cling.

Tyrone was hardly content with a mere sip, not when he was nigh famished for the full draught. Tiny specks of moonlight illumined the silken skin beneath the costly white lace, and the strengthening temptation to test the true depth of the lady's involvement goaded him onward. The weighty necklace proved but a meager obstacle to be bridged, for in the next instant he was pressing parted lips against the swelling ripeness above her gown.

Synnovea caught her breath, jolted by the swiftness of his daring advance. His boldness vividly expressed his manly cravings, yet her trembling disquiet was not entirely due to the abashed modesty of an innocent maid. Rather, it was the flaring flash of ecstasy catapulting through her that left her feeling closely akin to a ship that had just been bombarded. No well-aimed broadside could have blown apart her composure quite so effortlessly.

Steeling herself against a strong inner urge to abscond with her virtue intact, Synnovea persevered through another deliciously titillating experience as his warm mouth traced to the edge of her gown. After all, she reasoned with a growing reluctance to interfere, it was nothing more than a light caress, hardly harmful to anything but her reserve. Even so, she laid a cautious hand upon his chest, availing herself of the opportunity to claim her escape should the need arise.

Tyrone had traversed the road of conquest long enough to know by heart the rules of the game. It was basically the same whether he was in a bed with a woman or on a field of battle facing an enemy. When no resistance was in evidence, he could assume with some degree of confidence that his opponent was acceptable to the idea of surrender. He was just as eager now to regard his companion's reticence as submission. Still, he was one to move with caution until reasonably assured of his position. As a soldier, he clearly understood the wisdom of applying the strategy of retreat to confound the opponent.

His open mouth returned to ensnare her lips in an insatiable quest to win her eager response. He mentally sighed over his success as her slender fingers threaded through the short hair at his nape. Their lips were forged with fiery intensity, and Tyrone drank his fill, slanting his open mouth across hers and plumbing the honeyed depths with a flaming brand. A soft, fluttering sigh of pleasure wafted from Synnovea's lips when his mouth slipped downward again, leaving hers throbbing for want of more. He tasted again the fragrant dew of her silken throat and ventured slowly past the hollow in her throat, on toward softer, more tantalizing ground.

Synnovea's head tipped backward as she gave herself over entirely to the bliss of his sultry kisses, but she was hardly prepared for the devastating salvo he was about to launch as he swept her bodice downward beneath a creamy breast, baring its soft peak to the night air and to the branding heat of his tongue.

"No, you mustn't!" Her shocked gasp was a desperate whisper as her daunted propriety rallied in full strength. "What you're doing isn't proper!" The heat of a blush suffused her, warming her almost as much as the jolting fires that leapt through her senses when he took her nipple into his mouth. Feeling consumed by the moist, fiery torch that swept over the sensitive pinnacle, she strained away.

"Lovely Synnovea, do you not ken how much I want you?" he rasped hoarsely, holding her easily with an arm clamped around her narrow waist. "I'm a man sorely beset by a goading desire to make you my own. Yield to me, sweet love."

Synnovea caught her breath at the intensifying jolts of pleasure that shot through her senses as he greedily devoured the silken orb. Until now, she had never imagined that such wildly wanton sensations were possible. She was just as much a stranger to the liquid fire spreading upward from her loins, awakening a strange, burning hunger within her that seemed to set her whole being ablaze with desire. The persuasive titillation of his mouth and tongue blunted her will to resist, and though she relished each blissful stroke that strummed across the gutstrings of her being, she strove desperately to gather the scattered fragments of her wits.

Tyrone bent and swept Synnovea up into his arms. Though he had been reluctant to take his ease of her without first securing some private haven for the patient nurturing of her pleasure, his passions were soaring well beyond the point of caution. It didn't matter so much now that he couldn't hold her naked in his arms. A shadowed spot would serve his mounting lusts, and if it had to be done while they were both still fully clothed, it wouldn't be the first time he had fought the voluminous skirts of some rich creation to take his ease.

Some shred of reason awakened Synnovea. His aim was all too obvious; he intended to claim her virginity, and as yet, she was doing nothing to deter him from his goal. A bit overwhelmed by her own vulnerability, she slipped her arms around his neck and gently pressed her brow against his temple. "Please, Tyrone," she whispered pleadingly, "give me a moment to catch my breath."

"I need you, Synnovea," he rasped in a hoarse whisper.

"These gardens aren't private enough to protect us from being caught. Natasha would quickly come to rue the day she asked you here. If you would have it so, Tyrone, I'll go with you to your quarters."

He drew back to search her face in the dimly speckled light. The hungering ache in his loins had now manifested itself into a throbbing density, and he felt driven to assuage his cravings ere the tormenting agony rent him asunder. When he considered the delay and the chances of her abandoning him, he knew he didn't have the patience to endure another lengthy wait.

"My quarters are so far away, Synnovea." His softly rasped appeal could hardly convey the turmoil roiling within him, for she was ignorant of the goading desires that could wreak havoc with a man. Only when she yearned for the same release would she understand. His mouth parted as it swept downward again over the ivory fullness, and with a greed he hoped she could not long withstand, he caressed the sweet ambrosia of her sweet flesh, nearly splintering her reserve.

For one long, delicious moment, Synnovea forgot everything but the ecstasy of being devoured by his hotly consuming hunger, but the sudden reminder of Aleksei's ridiculing laughter served to strengthen her resolve. "Would you instruct a virgin in so open a place?" she breathed shakily near his ear. "Where we could be discovered by anyone who happened upon us?"

Disinclined though he was to delay the moment of their union, Tyrone struggled to curb his hard-pressing needs. She was right, of course. This garden was no treasured place where lovers could leisurely feast upon their passion. She deserved much more than this, if only because he desired her more than any woman he had ever known, including Angelina. He had displayed care and patience with his virgin bride years ago. The very least he could do with this maid was to pamper her with the same consideration.

"Waiting will test me sorely, Synnovea, but if that is your wish, then I can only acquiesce." He kissed her passionately and then removed his arm from beneath her knees, letting her feet slide between his to the ground. In pained forbearance he watched as she straightened her clothing. "Will you come with me now?" he queried. "My hired coach is waiting in front."

"Only a few moments more I would beg, Tyrone," Synnovea whispered unsteadily, unable to ignore the hotly flaming craving he had kindled deep within her. "If you wait here, I'll return to you as soon as I've changed my gown and fetched a cloak."

"Surely there's no need for that, Synnovea," Tyrone argued, anxious to accomplish the union and ease his lusts. "I'll keep you warm, and your gown will be of little consequence once we reach my quarters."

Synnovea pinkened at the full import of his insinuation. The idea of her garments being stripped away brought back bold reminders of their meeting in the bathhouse. The possibility of being confronted by his male nudity almost made her demur the coach ride to his quarters, for she knew the sight of such manly magnificence would likely lead to her doom. It was her own weakening will that concerned her. Yet if she fled from him now, she'd be throwing away her only chance to thwart Aleksei's plans. Her whisper waned in strength as she feebly offered an excuse. "I would prefer to prepare myself for you."

Tyrone understood all too well her womanly petition. It was her right to come to him when she was ready to receive him. "Another kiss before you go." He slipped his arms around her. "It must last me."

Synnovea met his parting lips with her own and, gleaning from her meager experience, slid her tongue provocatively into his mouth. Somewhat abashed by her forwardness, she braced her hands upon his chest and sought to leave him, but the gentle enticement had been enough to awaken a desire within Tyrone to prolong the kiss. A long moment passed before he released her, but this time Synnovea was averse to leaving his embrace.

"Another," she pleaded breathlessly.

Tyrone lifted her up hard against him, allowing her to feel the thunderous beating of his heart. "We must go ere I take you here and now," he whispered raggedly while his hand wandered down to clasp her buttock and press her to him. " 'Tis difficult for a man to wait so long."

Synnovea searched his features in the mottled light, and though the layers of her skirts prevented intimate contact, the tense frown creasing his brow clearly conveyed his urgency. "I won't be long."

Tyrone lowered her to her feet and almost groaned in frustration as he watched her depart. In her absence he paced to and fro, seeking to divert his thoughts and ease his plight, but he knew if she didn't come back, it would be nigh impossible for him to endure the long ride home alone. He had never forced a woman before, but the way Synnovea held his mind entrapped, he'd be tempted to seek her out in her chambers upstairs and have his way with her upon her own bed.

11

Synnovea paused just outside the veranda doors to collect herself. It would have been a mild assessment of her over-whelmed sensibilities to say that she felt much like a crippled frigate listing back into port. Her womanly weapons had been spiked and plundered. The sails of her self-assurance, which not so long ago had billowed wide with the winds of her fanci-ful ideas, now hung slack, deflated by the full import of her own naiveté.

Still atremble from the lustful intensity of Tyrone's ad-vances, she did what she could to smooth her hair and repair her appearance, for the moment in which she would have to subject herself to the perusal of others was upon her. Con-fronted by the need to present a calm exterior, she struggled to subdue the turmoil roiling within her body and, upon her failure, wondered if anyone would be able to discern how deeply she had been affected by merely peering into her face.

If her entrance wasn't challenging enough, having to face Natasha in her chambers upstairs would be tantamount to inviting defeat. It was crucial that she trade gowns with her friend, but she feared her breasts were still rosy from Tyrone's caresses. If Natasha so much as suspected that his advances had progressed as far as they had, then Synnovea knew the game would likely be over before it even began. And where would she be but married to Vladimir?

Lifting her chin with a hard-won guise of serenity, Synnovea entered the house and cast a glance about in search of Natasha. She met the dark, radiant eyes across the width of the room and inclined her head in a slow nod before making her way to the hall. Her pace quickened on the stairs, and almost in a frantic rush, she burst into her chambers, her heart hammering from the stress of having to maintain such a farce.

Weakly Synnovea leaned against the closed door until, by slow degrees, her trembling eased to a more tolerable level. At long last she regained enough poise to approach the front windows and part the draperies. She stood before them with arms spread wide until Aleksei strode from the shadows. Then, at his mocking salute, she snatched the silken hangings closed again and indulged in a languid smile of victory.

By the time Natasha joined her, Synnovea had managed to doff her gown and clothe herself within the rich velvet folds of another creation, this one of a deep green hue which, by its simple elegance, complemented her beauty. Not being entirely of the same conviction as the older countess, she had modified the garment for the occasion, stripping away a demure inset of lined lace which once had modestly covered her bosom. The décolletage was now tempting enough to ensure that she would hold Tyrone's attention completely ensnared until well after the two of them had reached his residence. If she had any regrets about her alterations, they were caused by a growing awareness that he needed no encouragement. In light of his unswerving ardor and her own declining reserve, a definite threat now existed that she'd no longer be a virgin by the time Aleksei arrived at the colonel's quarters.

Having foreseen a need to preserve a reasonable facade of decorum in Natasha's presence, Synnovea had wrapped a shawl around her shoulders to hide from view any telltale blush that might have remained on her bosom. As prudently as she had guarded the secret of her first encounter with Tyrone, so she deemed it necessary to maintain her reticence about everything that had transpired between them in the garden. Otherwise the woman would refuse to help her.

Synnovea allowed Natasha to tighten the laces of her bodice and then she helped the woman out of her *sarafan*. As she did so, she recognized the soft tinkling of tiny bells that heralded the approach of her coach.

"That must be Stenka returning from the Taraslovs'. I've given him instructions to wait in front until he sees me come down."

Natasha expressed her own apprehension in a worried question. "Do you actually think he can be fooled into believing that I am you?"

To blandly say that Natasha was nervous about this ruse would clearly have been an understatement, especially after she had heard from the colonel's own lips that he had been involved in a deadly duel. He hadn't explained how the woman he had fought over had died and that uncertainty clearly worried her for Synnovea's sake, but Natasha knew the girl was dedicated to having this travesty accomplished. Indeed, it might do more harm than good to frighten her now with such revelations.

"There's no reason for Stenka to suspect that you've come in my stead. Since we're the same height, I rather doubt he'll notice the difference. I've already told him that I wish to see the city by moonlight, so there's no need for you to say anything. The game will certainly be lost if he recognizes your voice while Aleksei is at hand."

"Adolphe has promised to serve as host in my absence," Natasha informed her. "I gave him the excuse that you're indisposed and need my attention, so he won't be surprised by my delay in returning to the hall. As long as no one sees us depart, we should be reasonably safe. Where did you leave Tyrone?"

"He's waiting for me in the garden. He hired a coach for this evening, so there'll be no need for me to use yours."

Natasha held up her arms expectantly as Synnovea lowered her own deep blue gown over the woman's head. "Naturally he was terribly agreeable to all of this, taking you to his quarters and all the rest, I mean."

"Reasonably so." Synnovea refused to elaborate and began tightening the laces at the back of the woman's bodice.

A moment later, Natasha perused her newly revised appearance in the tall looking glass. "From a distance, even Aleksei may not be able to tell us apart." She swept her fingers across the sapphire necklace admiringly, but when her eyes lifted to her hair, she frowned testily as she plucked at a strand. "I fear this graying thatch will give me away. Have you a veil to cover my head?"

"This one will serve that purpose." Having already considered the matter, Synnovea lifted a white lace mantle which she had worn in Aleksei's presence and draped it loosely over her friend's head to cover the silver-streaked tresses.

Turning with a smile, Natasha submitted herself to Synnovea's inspection. "How do I look?"

"As beautiful as always," Synnovea avowed with an eager nod. "Now stand in front of the window as if you're searching for the coach and wait there until Aleksei makes himself known to you. Once you're outside, don't let him get close enough to recognize you. He may try, but as long as he thinks that I'm the one climbing into the coach, he'll probably be curious enough about my destination to follow along behind with that rabble he has hired. By the time Stenka halts the coach, I should be at Tyrone's quarters."

"Does Aleksei know where the colonel lives?"

"If he doesn't, I'm sure he'll make a point of finding out ere long," Synnovea replied ruefully.

Natasha heaved a pensive sigh and reached out to pat the younger's cheek. "The way Tyrone doted on you this evening, he'll not likely want to delay having his pleasure too long. You may have difficulty holding him off until Aleksei arrives."

"If I can't, then I'll have no one to blame but myself," Synnovea murmured, averting her face. She was rather amazed by her own dwindling resolve to hold herself aloof from the man. Somehow she'd have to renew her waning dedication or there'd be no hope of producing the results she had earlier aspired to attain.

"I must go." Natasha sighed and tried to console herself as she mused on her lonely carriage ride. The corners of her mouth lifted puckishly as she proposed a more attractive arrangement than Synnovea had planned for her. "Perhaps I could trade places with you and go with Tyrone while you tour the city alone."

Synnovea laughed at the impossible suggestion. "I doubt that such a change of plans would bring about the same results."

Feigning a pout of disappointment, Natasha protested her solitary task. "But 'twill be so dreadfully boring riding alone, and the colonel is *so* handsome."

No reprieve came, and with a dramatically heaved sigh of resignation, Natasha readjusted the mantle over her head. Bracing herself for carrying out the deception, she lifted her chin in an elegant manner and stepped in front of the window to look out. Synnovea pressed close against the wall, keeping well out of sight until the silken panels were again closed to the outside world. Natasha brushed a kiss upon Synnovea's cheek, bade farewell while staring intently into the green-brown eyes. Then swept from the chambers with a desperate plea. "Be extremely careful, my dear."

Synnovea waited in the silence of the room until she heard the carriage departing. Several moments passed before she considered it safe to peer through the draperies. Her heart leapt in a triumphant rush when she espied Aleksei and his hirelings leisurely following the coach down the thoroughfare.

"No doubt the lecher thinks to catch me unawares and unattended." Synnovea vented the supposition smugly. " 'Twill serve his pride well to be made the fool."

Sweeping a black velvet cloak around her shoulders and lifting the hood carefully over her head, Synnovea readied herself for her own departure. She made her descent by way of the private stairs near Natasha's rooms and, gaining the garden, flew into Tyrone's welcoming arms.

"I was beginning to wonder if you were going to return," he gasped in relief as he snatched her hard against him.

Synnovea tilted her head back to meet his searching lips and returned his kiss with matching zeal, clinging to him for support as her limbs weakened apace. Finally Tyrone drew back and, catching her hand, pulled her along with him to his waiting coach. He addressed the driver in Russian, having learned enough of the language to get him to and from his quarters. Then he handed his beautiful companion into the interior.

"You're progressing very well, Colonel," Synnovea commented with a smile. "It doesn't take nearly as much imagination to understand you now."

Tyrone chuckled before he addressed himself the task of lowering the shades over the windows and lighting the tallow lantern afixed on the wall near the door. "Had I foreseen the likelihood of my coming here to this country, I would've started learning Russian three years ago. If I had, I might have been fluent in it now, but it's not the easiest language I've ever tried to learn. I can speak French fairly well, but my attempts to understand the language here have failed for the most part." Leaning back in the seat beside her, he searched the shining luster of her eyes. "But as long as you and the tsar can understand me, it really doesn't matter how crude my efforts are. Discovering you here, fairest Synnovea, has been worth it all."

"Oh, but didn't Natasha tell you that I'd be at her home tonight?"

Tyrone realized she had mistaken his meaning. "Meeting you was worth my tour in Russia," he corrected. "As for to-night, I was informed in advance that you'd be at Natasha's soiree. I was most eager to attend and even considered mutiny when General Vanderhout tried to find duties elsewhere for Grigori and me. The general seemed quite taken aback when I refused his directive, but he didn't dare order me out on maneuvers as punishment, fearing my influence with the tsar." A grin flashed briefly across Tyrone's lips. "Of course, I didn't dare explain that I'm no more able to sway the tsar's opinion than I can demand the moon to change course."

"Why didn't the general want you to come?"

"He seems to be suspicious of any underling who might seize a bit of fame and honor from his grasp. When he heard that we'd be associating with Russian nobility, he was sure we'd do just that. I could've eased his qualms by telling him that my only reason for attending was to pay court to a certain *boyarina* with whom I've become enamored. Had I done so, he might have felt more at ease letting me go, but by then, he had sorely tested my temper, and I refused to assuage his concerns."

"Should I assume this general is your immediate superior?"

"Aye, a position he jealously guards."

Curiously Synnovea searched his face. "Should I also assume that he has good cause to be wary of you?"

Tyrone canted his head thoughtfully. "I believe the man

imagines me a serious threat to his ambitions, but as yet, I've done nothing to undermine his authority."

"Perhaps he's aware of his own shortcomings and is afraid that he'll be found wanting if people begin to discern a difference between the two of you."

Tyrone was hardly desirous of discussing General Vanderhout when he was cozily ensconced with such a beautiful companion. Sweeping an arm behind her shoulders, he drew her near. "I nearly despaired of your return to the garden," he murmured huskily. "I even considered how successful I'd be if I went in search of you. I had no idea how long a century could be until I found myself waiting for you."

Reaching up a hand, Synnovea swept a finger down the bridge of his lean, aquiline nose, following its noble descent before tracing the lines of laughter at the corners of his mouth and then brushing her fingers caressingly across his lips. "How goes the time now, sir?"

"Much too swiftly, I fear."

Her thumb smoothed a tawny brow before the tips of her fingers stroked down a lean cheek once more. "What must we do to keep it still?"

"Stay with me forever."

Her hand paused in flight as she searched the unrelenting blue eyes that watched her closely in return. "I have only a pair of hours to spend with you, Tyrone. I must return before midnight."

"Then each moment that flies past is forever lost to me," he breathed, turning his face into her palm and pressing an ardent kiss into it. He lifted his head and, leaning near, caressed the beautiful visage with the soft, gentle brush of his lips. "I must make haste to make you mine."

"I pray you nay," Synnovea said with a sigh as his mouth came to play upon hers. "Rather, I would urge you to relish the time we spend together and make of it a lasting memory that we can both treasure. Is it not better to savor love slowly to glean every measure of delight from its offering?"

Tyrone moved his mouth to where he could feel the pulse quickening in her temple. "Your wisdom astounds me, Synnovea. If not by experience, where do you attribute its source?"

"My mother," she murmured, fingering the silken closures on his doublet.

"An intelligent woman. She must have loved your father dearly to have given up her homeland and all that she had ever known to come and live here with him."

" 'Twas no great sacrifice for her, considering what they had together. They were very much in love." Another plaintive sigh slipped from Synnovea's lips. "I wish I would've had them with me a while longer. Princess Anna was a poor replacement, and Prince Aleksei proved himself a ravenous rake. I tell you truly, any woman is better off fleeing from him ere they're introduced. I lived in constant dread of him catching me unawares. Though I was hampered by his threats, I consider it something of a miracle that I have thus far escaped his prurient bent."

Tyrone peered into her lovely visage. "Prurient bent?"

Beneath his searching gaze, Synnovea was unable to hold back a blush. "Prince Aleksei made it obvious that he wanted me in his bed and threatened me with dire consequences if I denied him."

"Though I can't blame him for wanting you, his methods are to be abhorred."

"Truly, I've come to loathe the man."

Tyrone's open mouth hovered closely above her soft lips. "I'd rather have you come to me willingly, my sweet. If a man coerced you against your will, he'd lose the joy and pleasure of your willing participation."

Synnovea's lashes trembled downward as she yielded her lips to the fiery heat of his kiss. His mouth was warm and gentle, bestirring her eager response. A long moment passed before Tyrone straightened, leaving her sighing with bliss. In a shaky whisper she acknowledged, "Your kisses make me willing."

"Do you find them satisfying?"

"Nay, not satisfying," she complained, leaning toward him again with eagerly parting lips. "They only make me want more."

He indulged her growing enthrallment with his kisses, allowing his mouth to slowly feed upon the sweet nectar of her response. Even while their lips played, his lean fingers searched out the ties of her cloak and plucked the silken cords free. Sweeping the deep hood from her head, he aided its descent as he slipped the enveloping velvet from her shoulders. The garment fell unheeded to the seat behind her, and for a moment he leaned back to relish her beauty with eyes that glinted with hotly smoldering desire. The swelling mounds of her bosom came nigh to overflowing the shallow bodice and, in the flickering candlelight, glowed with a luster of their own. He now considered the long wait in the garden well worth the results.

Evoking a riotous rhythm from her swiftly beating heart, Tyrone traced a lone finger downward from her shoulder and then along the edge of her bodice, sketching across the fullness of a breast before moving into the crevice and rising again to the far peak barely hidden by the cloth. Once again Synnovea was confronted with her own dwindling reserve as her nipple grew taut beneath the playful strokes of his thumb. Luxuriating in the delectable pleasure awakening within her, she sat in quiescent stillness until a sultry heat began to quicken in her loins, and she realized she was becoming much too involved in his game of seduction. In an earnest effort to halt his exploration of her bosom and to bestir some small fiber of her determination, she leaned toward him with lips eagerly seeking to ensnare his, but it was like fighting fire with kindling. His arm came around her like a band of steel, catching her close against the solid bulwark of his chest. His mouth slanted across hers as his tongue greedily plumbed the dewy sweetness, flicking awake her senses and arousing an ever-heightening hunger in the depths of her being.

Tyrone slipped a hand beneath her and lifted her effortlessly across his lap, but it wasn't until Synnovea drew back for a trembling breath that she realized her skirts and petticoats no longer separated them. Her bare buttocks were resting atop his velvet-clad thighs, making her aware of a bulging hardness pressing snugly against her thigh.

Fully comprehending the precariousness of her situation, Synnovea sought to leave his lap, but Tyrone gently detained her within an encircling embrace. Nothing was quite as arousing to his senses as having her bare backside against him, except perhaps having his own equally naked beneath hers.

"I like the way you feel against me," he breathed near her ear. "You're soft and womanly. Even with all your clothes on, you're as beautiful as you are in all of your naked glory."

He kissed her again, holding nothing back as his open mouth ravished hers in frenzied greed, devouring her intoxicating sweetness while demanding that she answer him in kind. By slow degrees, Synnovea dismissed the danger of sitting on his lap and gave him what he sought, tentatively at first as she allowed her tongue to be drawn into his mouth and then with passion as she met his daring thrusts with quickening fervor.

When Tyrone lifted his head a century later, the flaming blue orbs burned into hers. Once more his hand moved across her bosom, roaming the hills and vales, but this time his thumb slipped beneath the seam that joined the top of the bodice to a sleeve and gently tugged it down, baring a shoulder. His eyes flicked downward, delving into the gown that now gapped away from her.

Synnovea had become passionately intrigued with his kisses and leaned forward to caress his softly yielding mouth with timid strokes of her tongue. Much to her dismay, however, he seemed to hold back, meeting her playful kisses with pondered care. Experiencing some confusion at his lack of zeal, she locked her fingers behind his neck and, resting her forearms upon his chest, peered up at him in the meager light.

"Are you bored with my novice kisses?" she questioned in a tiny whisper, confounded by his lagging participation.

Tyrone chuckled at such an absurd notion. Shaking his head, he lowered his gaze to the rich fare swelling above the shallow bodice. "I'm entranced by every part of you, Synnovea, though at the moment, I find your bosom especially captivating."

His eyes smoldered like brightly burning coals as they rose to meet hers, and just as Synnovea had wanted, his open mouth came upon hers with the same urgency that only moments earlier had worn away the outer perimeters of her will. Tyrone was eager to progress far beyond impassioned kisses and, with a subtle tug, encouraged the descent of her second sleeve. Slipping a finger beneath the neckline, he lowered the shallow bodice and chemise beneath her bosom, allowing him to clasp the fullness of a creamy breast within his hand. Synnovea caught her breath at the thrill that catapulted through her as he gently fondled her. When he drew back to appease himself with a lingering perusal, she watched him with bated breath, her heart thudding a new, chaotic rhythm.

Tyrone was nigh famished for want of such soft, delectable sweets. Her breasts gleamed like satin in the faint light and were as enticing as a lavish feast after a lengthy famine. Since their meeting in the bathhouse, he had been unable to forget the perfection he had seen there. More than a few times he had been snatched from lusting dreams with his body tense and filmed with sweat, his breathing harsh and ragged as he suffered through recurring pangs of unrequited passion. Now his arm tightened around the small of her back, arching her spine until her bosom was thrust forward into the luminous glow of the lantern.

Synnovea struggled to draw breath as he lowered his head and devoured the soft mounds with rapacious greed. The fires pulsing within her loins were now flaming upward, growing ever hotter, drawing soft mewling sighs from her as his tongue licked across the soft pink pinnacles. With each flicking stroke, she was being swept closer to the steep precipice which would eventually lead to her doom . . . and yet, strangely, that singular fear had dimmed.

Caught up in the thrilling excitement elicited by his mouth and swirling tongue, Synnovea gave no notice to his hand leaving her breast and slipping beneath her skirts, until the shock of his intrusion wrenched a startled gasp from her. She caught his wrist and struggled to rise, only to find his mouth covering hers again. The fiery heat of his kiss bespoke of his lusting need, but when she was being shaken by jolts of fire that leapt upward with ever-increasing intensity through her being, she couldn't think of anything beyond the need to stop his caresses before she melted in pure bliss. Tearing her mouth free, she begged in a trembling whisper, "Please! You mustn't! Not here!"

The dewy softness was too delectable, too tempting for Tyrone to resist. Every manly instinct he was capable of feeling had coalesced into a lusting eagerness, urging him to press on until, hopefully, she would acquiesce and allow him to advance. Yet when she began to writhe and turn aside in an attempt to get away from his encroaching hand, he could only foresee the possibility of hurting her if he persisted. He was no fool to think he could force her and still give her pleasure. He'd have to bide his time, at least for a little while longer.

It took every fragment of restraint that Tyrone could ransom from his floundering will to retreat from her softness. The idea was paramount in his mind that with a little patience, Synnovea could become a mistress he could cherish as much as any wife. He yearned to bring her to such heights of rapture that she would find it hard to withhold herself from him, but as he now knew, she was a virgin and no doubt fearful of the bridge between pain and pleasure.

"Come, Synnovea," he coaxed as she clutched an arm across her naked breasts to shield the rounded curves from his gaze. He lifted her cloak and spread it protectively around her shoulders, allowing her the covering she apparently sought. "Calm yourself, love. I didn't mean to frighten you."

Synnovea still quaked from the shock of his invasion and was unwilling to yield to his pleas while he encouraged her to relax against him. Refusing to look at him, she pulled her bodice up over her breasts and shoulders, fearing he would glimpse a different kind of fear than what he might have expected. When his hand had made its claim on her, she had felt as if she had just been flung face-to-face with the stark reality of his single-minded goal to make her his. The proud hawk, whom she had chosen to carry her through her soaring quest, was becoming increasingly difficult to handle. Unless she could find a way to escape the sharp descent of his plunging flight, she'd be devoured for a succulent morsel ere the hour was out.

Tyrone freed a softly curling strand of hair that had become entrapped beneath her cloak and laid it within the velvet cowl. "The way I touched you, Synnovea, is no different than what every husband and lover does with the one he adores," he murmured soothingly. " 'Tis common in marriage."

"We're not married!" Synnovea groaned, suddenly haunted by an image of her mother's deeply distraught visage.

"Would you feel any differently if we were?" he queried and, after a moment of silence, continued with disarming candor. "You seem to want this union as badly as I do, and yet you apparently have no idea what to expect. Dearest Synnovea, were you to return the caress in like fashion, it would be a delicious sweetmeat I've yearned to savor ever since we came together in the pool."

Synnovea's eyes chased upward, and she stared at him in astonishment, drawing a smile from Tyrone.

"Do you think me untouchable, Synnovea? Nay, love, I'm a man and I want you as much as any husband wants his wife. I want to touch you, love you, and do yearn that you do the same. The giving of pleasure is only natural during a time of intimacy." He laughed as she relented and allowed him to pull her close against him. "I thought you knew what to expect."

"I've never been with a man before," she replied in a small voice.

"I know that with a certainty now," he breathed. Though he had guessed as much from their first meeting, the past few hours had made him wonder if she was truly chaste. The fact that she was both pleased and excited him, for it was an honor he hadn't been entirely expecting. "I was too hasty in my zeal to claim you. I didn't mean to shock you."

"My mother told me what to anticipate in marriage, but her instructions were rather general and definitely lacking in detail," Synnovea whispered. "But this is hardly the kind of situation she desired for me. An honorable marriage was what she assumed I'd have someday and no doubt thought my husband would fill in the particulars."

"I'll be as careful as any husband," Tyrone promised with compelling warmth. "You needn't be afraid that I'll misuse you, Synnovea. 'Tis much more enjoyable for a man when a woman responds with matching ardor."

Tyrone leaned back in the seat, and tentatively she relaxed against him. In the stillness of the evening, the soft tinkling of silver bells accompanying the leisurely clip-clop of horses' hooves helped to soothe the senses to some degree. He made no further effort to advance his cause in the carriage, though it was difficult for him to ignore the tantalizing softness within his arms and to thrust from memory the silkiness of her woman's flesh. Still, his patience seemed to assuage her fears, for it was she who snuggled against his chest with a soft sigh. He smiled with pleasure, pressing his cheek against her brow, and was satisfied for the present moment to nurture her affection.

The coach swayed to a halt before the two-story, narrow-framed structure which Tyrone rented within the German district of Moscow. Had there not been such a shortage of available housing in the community at the time of his arrival, he would have secured smaller quarters for himself, thereby saving on rents and perhaps even a few of the coins that went toward cleaning the house. The rooms were sparsely furnished yet neat enough for his tastes, thanks to the efforts of a bovine widow who came on a regular basis to keep them so. Yet having to continually deal with the city's segregation of foreigners had proven a tiresome inconvenience. It was a lengthy jaunt to where his Russian recruits were quartered and an even longer one to the mansion where Synnovea was ensconced.

Tyrone alighted from the conveyance and handed Synnovea down before he stepped around to pay the coachman. With her assistance in translation, he promised the driver a goodly sum for his time if he'd consent to wait at the end of the thoroughfare for the space of two hours. As the carriage rumbled off, Tyrone swept Synnovea within his arms and kissed her with all the passion he had been holding in check. Nuzzling her cheek, he staggered haphazardly toward the door, provoking her giggles.

"You make me drunk," he crooned near her ear.

"Then I pray you sober quickly lest you stray too far from the path," she urged, casting a glance over her shoulder to see what risks lay ahead. He tottered precariously along the edge of the walk, and with a disconcerted groan, she locked her arms around his neck, bracing herself for a fall.

Tyrone's laughter rang out suddenly, and Synnovea gasped in surprise as he whirled her about, affirming the fact that he was in full command of his faculties and had only been teasing her. Even as he came to a halt, Synnovea's only reality seemed to be his hotly flaming lips searing hers as the world careened crazily around her.

At the front door, Tyrone bent slightly aside to unlock the latch while he complained about its temperamental tendency to come apart if not carefully worked. Issuing a grateful sigh at his success, he disengaged the bar and then nudged the stout plank open with a shoulder. Spinning inward with a chuckle, he kicked the door closed behind him and swept Synnovea around into the dark room. His mood grew serious as he braced back against the front wall and withdrew his arm from beneath her knees. Her voluminous skirts were snared upon his velvet-clad thigh as her feet settled between his on the floor, but she hardly noticed as she searched the shadowy face above her own.

The uneasiness that had plagued Synnovea since she had launched her peculiar campaign came back to haunt her now that she was in the hawk's nest. Though the threat of becoming his prey would have unsettled a prim and proper virgin, she was becoming increasingly wary of the pleasure she derived from his manly pursuits. Even as he lowered his lips to hers, she had to brace herself against the delicious assault of her senses. His kisses were truly succulent morsels that could lure her into his bed with unmeasured haste. His gently stroking tongue moved provocatively inward and around her mouth, creating a sensual lushness within her that no artist's brush could have produced. With incredible care he applied a profusion of warm pigments to the canvas of sensual pleasure, lulling her until he could feel her leaning into him with growing eagerness.

Suddenly their bodies were straining together as their mouths melded in a crushing, devouring search. Vaguely Synnovea was aware of her intentions being turned topsy-turvy as he dragged up her skirts and lifted her astraddle his loins. In truth, keeping her wits well aligned to her goals was becoming more difficult with each passing second, for she was growing increasingly conscious of a hungry void that yearned to be sated as her soft flesh rested vulnerably upon a steely hardness. If she had any hope of coming through this evening unscathed, she needed desperately to cool the hot blood flowing upward from that area or she'd find her objective completely cindered by her own passionate fervor.

"Give me a moment to catch my breath," she pleaded faintly, withdrawing from his lustful embrace. Her rumpled skirts fell into place, allowing her to reclaim some degree of composure. She patted his chest as if cajoling an impatient stallion to ignore a mare in season, but there was now no satisfying the ravenous throbbing at the root of her being. If anything, she wanted to do more than just feel that hard bulge nestling against her womanly softness.

By dent of will, Tyrone curbed his rutting instincts and, capturing her hand, bestowed a gentle token of his admiration in the form of a kiss upon her slender knuckles. Upon leaving her, he moved about the parlor, lighting several tapers and bringing into view a room that was rather stark and bare.

Synnovea's eyes swept around the furnishings, seeing nothing more grand and comfortable than several straight chairs, a small table, a desk, and a pair of tall cabinets . . . as well as the man who had risked his life to save her from an unprincipled rogue.

Tyrone swept a hand about to indicate the interior. "These quarters are clean enough, but rather dreary for a woman's taste."

"It looks the way I imagined it would," Synnovea replied softly, far more intrigued with the man than with his surroundings. The candle he carried accentuated the handsomeness of his noble profile as well as the beauty of his eyes as they reflected the dancing flame. It came to her with a suddenness that surprised her that she could recall no other man whose appearance pleased her more than the one who moved before her now. Nor had any ever caused such delectable sensations within her. She could not lightly dismiss the fact that her heart had skittered rather strangely while she had been caught up in his embrace only moments ago, and she had to wonder what power this Englishman held over her.

Turning her face aside, she sought to shrug away any significance she might be inclined to attach to these realizations. "You're a soldier in His Majesty's service, here for only a few years before you're gone again. You keep the place amazingly well, despite that fact."

"I pay a woman to clean and cook for me," Tyrone said, setting aside the taper. He came back to her and, lifting the cloak from her shoulders, draped it over the back of a nearby chair. Bedazzled by the flawless beauty of her ivory skin, he reached out and swept his palm over her shoulder, marveling at the silkiness of her skin. His gaze dipped into her gown, yearning to peruse her bosom unhindered by clothing or covering of any kind, much as he had done weeks ago in the bathing chamber. "She comes for an hour or two every day, but leaves before I return. If not for the fact that she probably outweighs me by several stone, I'd be inclined to think she's afraid of me."

"Perhaps I, too, should be afraid of you," Synnovea breathed, trembling beneath his soft caresses. Cognizant of the warming glow in his eyes, she struggled to set her own thoughts aright by reminding herself of what she might suffer nine months from now if she let him have his way with her. "I hardly know you, and yet here I am alone with you."

Tyrone kissed her brow. "Were you afraid of me in the bathhouse?"

Synnovea shook her head. "No, just outraged because you had made no effort to inform me that you were there."

Tyrone peered down at her with smiling skepticism. "Would you have allowed me to watch if I had made my presence known to you?"

"Of course not."

"Then perhaps you can understand why I didn't enlighten you. The temptation to watch you far exceeded my ability to resist. Even now, I'd like to see you as you appeared then and hold you as I did in the pool. Has anyone ever told you how absolutely beautiful you are when your skin is wet and glistening with droplets?"

Synnovea recognized the disquiet within her and turned aside cautiously. His kisses could render her pliable to his every whim, and she knew she had to barricade her wits against their potency. Yet denying herself the fulfillment that she now found herself craving was swiftly becoming a thing she didn't want to do.

Stepping near, Tyrone pressed his long, muscular form close against her back and slipped his arms around her, close beneath her bosom, causing Synnovea's knees to weaken apace with the thudding of her pulse. Her head fell back upon his shoulder as his lips traced upward along her throat, and her breath nigh halted in bliss at the sultriness of his kisses.

Afforded a liberal view, Tyrone slowly basked in the sight of her ripe breasts flowing into the shallow bodice. Though the pliant peaks remained hidden beneath the cloth, he could see past the deep crevice separating the swelling mounds. Her pale, lustrous skin glowed enticingly in the warm glow of the candles, whetting his manly lusts until it seemed as if molten lead flowed into the root of his manly being. Gazing down upon such lush fare, he spoke from present observation. "Your breasts are as sweet as dew upon the honeycomb and so soft and tempting, it staggers my wits to think of caressing them . . . and making love to you."

Synnovea allowed her imagination the freedom to conjure such an occurrence. If the event itself was as heady as his amorous attentions had been thus far, she wondered how she'd be able to endure the exhilaration of their union without becoming a wanton. But then, she reminded herself once again, she wasn't here to be ravenously consumed by his desires. She shivered in anticipation as his hands slid slowly around to the sides of her breasts, and she waited expectantly for them to make their claim upon her.

Detecting the slight tremor, Tyrone tilted his head aslant as he queried, "Are you afraid of me, Synnovea?"

"I didn't think so until tonight." Her breath stilled in wonder as those lean hands cupped her breasts and teased their peaks, and for a moment her eyelids drooped in sultry pleasure as she luxuriated in the delectable sensations he elicited within her, but when his thumbs slipped beneath her gown to tease her nipples, she seized tentative rein on her weakening resistance, knowing the folly of indulging beyond her ability to resist. With a shaky laugh, she moved away from him and tossed a glance over her shoulder. "Now I'm sure I am."

"Perhaps a glass of wine will soothe your fears," Tyrone suggested, plucking open his doublet as he went to search through a small cupboard. Upon doffing the garment, he hung it over the back of a chair and then casually loosened the front of his shirt to his waist as he examined several flagons. He selected a bottle, poured a small draught into a cup, and then, realizing that neither of them had eaten, set out a plate of *yarpakh dolmasy*, which the housekeeper had made for him. He was especially fond of the lamb- and rice-stuffed grape leaves, and if not for the fact that he was hungrier for Synnovea than he was for food, he'd have laid out a small supper for them.

When Tyrone returned with a small cup of wine, Synnovea realized it was not within her power to ignore his altered appearance. Unbidden, her gaze ventured into the opening of his shirt, finding his muscular chest just as she had remembered it. Bronzed and lightly swathed with crisply curling hair, it was a sight that had become increasingly familiar to her after the many fantasies in which she had indulged. No longer a dream, that view brought to mind an actual occurrence wherein she had clung to him and been distantly aware of the muscular hardness of his whole body. Now that memory seemed as clear and corrosive to her tranquility as the man himself.

In his every action and deed, no matter how great or insignificant the feat or movement, she was sure that Tyrone Rycroft exhibited an uncompromising masculinity that made other men seem somehow lacking in comparison. She had, with a maidenly curiosity, contemplated many of his gender throughout her adult years and travels—all respectfully clothed, of course. She was now of a mind to think that, from a physical sense, the colonel was several notches above those she had viewed. Aleksei would've come across as tired and a bit worn in the younger man's presence, and certainly the white-haired Prince Vladimir would have fared badly in comparison. Since the announcement of her betrothal, she had become greatly appreciative of the memory of the Englishman's unadorned form, especially when an image of the bandy-legged elder garbed only in tight-fitting chausses interrupted her musings. To view the colonel now in reality was even more disturbing to her senses.

Tyrone poured the wine and came to her bearing a mug from which he invited her to sample an offering of *Chereunikyna*. "We'll share," he whispered close above her mouth. "The taste of you makes it sweeter for me."

With trembling fingers, Synnovea raised the drinking vessel and, beneath his warm perusal, took a sip from its edge. When she returned the cup, Tyrone tipped the cup and then leaned forward and, with a somewhat wicked smile, slowly caressed her soft mouth with his own as he shared the brew with her, evoking her giggles. Staggering back amid his chuckling amusement, she wiped her chin to catch the escaping dribbles and promptly decided he wasn't the only one who could play at such games. Cutting off part of a stuffed grape leaf with a fork, she deposited it in her mouth, chewed for a moment while he watched her with warmly glowing eyes, and then, pulling his head down to hers, shared the food with him. He proved eager to devour far more than the *dolmasy* and was soon probing the depth of her mouth in a totally titillating attack on her senses.

It was a very long moment later when he drew back and stared down into those limpid pools. Her lips still glistened from his kiss, drawing him back for more. A saner moment followed in which he inclined his head toward the narrow flight of stairs that led up a dark passageway. "I'll go upstairs and light some candles for us."

Synnovea lifted her gaze toward the blackened void above the steps. "What's up there?"

"My bedchamber," Tyrone answered and cocked a curious brow as he saw her tremble. "The room is far more comfortable than it is down here, Synnovea." He swept a hand about to indicate the furnishings. "As you can plainly see for yourself."

"Of course," she said, accepting his statement. Now that the moment wherein he planned to rend her virginity upon his pallet swiftly approached, Synnovea was challenged by the fact that little time remained for her to make good her escape. And yet, here she remained. Even as she sought to quell the qualms that had suddenly begun to assail her, she felt as if another woman stood in her stead, doing everything she would've condemned a month or two ago. It was bold in her mind that in a scant few moments everything she had encouraged with her flirtations would likely end in a culmination of his desires, not her own. When faced with the truth of what she had instigated, she found it impossible to meet his gaze.

Tyrone was too sensitive to the mood of the woman with whom he had become enamored not to notice a subtle change.

Though bewildered by her sudden shyness and cooling ardor, it soon dawned on him that Synnovea was not altogether committed to the idea of letting him make love to her. He now doubted that even his kisses could appease whatever fears she was battling, and it seemed prudent to allow the lady some time to herself to consider her choices.

Resigning himself to the bleak and disappointing possibility of being left without the sweet solace of her company as well as her body, Tyrone approached the stairs as he announced over his shoulder, "I'll be back in a moment."

The sound of his footsteps lightly scraping against the bare wood planks seemed to resonate in diminishing waves throughout the house as Synnovea faced the last stronghold of opposition to her quest. With the game nearly at its end, her own conscience rallied in objection to her devious schemes and sought to beat them down with bludgeoning blows that seemed too painful to resist. Honesty! Honor! Integrity! Modesty! Scruples! Virtue! Kindness! Everything that her mother and father had both cherished and honored was being reduced to an ashen heap with her deceitful, scandalous behavior. She had brazenly strode the path upon which milder, more timid maids were disinclined to venture, all because she wanted a man whom she could love as a husband.

The course she had chosen was hardly moral, Synnovea reflected morosely. She had deliberately tempted a man who she knew desired her and, by allowing him to maul her, would be leading him into a trap that would deftly sunder the hopes of another who had aspired to have her as his wife. Why could she not endure the hardships thrust upon her for the sake of honor? Other women had. Long years ago Natasha had taken an older man as husband and had later reaped a love which she had greatly treasured. *Why can't I do the same?* Synnovea's mind screamed. What made her so obstinate that she had felt driven to flaunt the rules of society just to gain her own end?

Had she no regard for the ones she would hurt or the shattered spirits she would leave in her wake?

Of a sudden, Synnovea saw herself from afar, and she realized with some chagrin that she didn't necessarily like the image which came to mind, that of a spoiled, unscrupulous *boyarina* intent upon gaining her own end. What she was doing was callously using the affections of an eager suitor and leading him into a trap from which he might not escape unscathed, all because she had been reluctant to wed an ancient. The growing awareness of her own diabolical deceit rose up like bitter bile in her throat, and suddenly it was all she could do not to turn tail and run.

Synnovea mentally shook herself as if awakening from a trance. What in the world was she doing here? What had ever possessed her to forget the values of her parents and flaunt some imagined right to be wed to a man of her own choosing, to the extent that she could lightly entertain the possibility of becoming a harlot to gain her own end?

As the weight of her own condemnation came upon her, Synnovea almost cringed. She thought of Tyrone standing at the forefront of those injured by her deception and could no longer blandly dismiss his involvement as one of no consequence. He was a human being! He had feelings! He was susceptible to being wounded by her antics!

What was she to do? How could she escape from all that she had planned?

Just go!

Synnovea winced in pain as the guilt-driven command lashed across her mind, and she took several stumbling steps toward the door as unspent sobs solidified into a painful lump in her chest. Then she halted abruptly, sick at heart, knowing what her departure would cost her. There was that element within her that urged her to go, but there was another conflicting voice which bade her to hold fast lest she suffer the consequences.

A sense of panic began to build within Synnovea as she found herself caught in a vortex betwixt the two. Broodingly her eyes wandered back to the black velvet doublet dressing the chair, and inwardly she groaned, realizing that she couldn't go through with her ploy. Colonel Rycroft was everything Natasha had said he was; he didn't deserve to be entrapped by a conniving woman. She must fly before Aleksei arrived!

Choking back the sobs as she heard him coming down the stairs, Synnovea snatched up her cloak and fled to the door. In her panic, she seized the latch, ready to fly, but the handle broke off in her hand in her haste, frustrating her efforts to leave before she had to face her suitor.

"Synnovea . . ."

She whirled at the sound of her name and stared at him with tears blurring her vision. He stood on the bottom step with a hand braced on the low beam above his head, just watching her. She could see the pain in his face, feel it in her heart. She ached for him and for herself, but there was no help for it. She must flee!

"Don't go," he rasped. "Don't leave me. . . ."

Synnovea tried to find the strength of a denial within her, but her voice was gone. She could only open and close her mouth as she struggled in mute agony to deliver the words that would bring about her escape.

"Stay with me . . . please. . . ."

His appeal tore through her, and her heart crumpled within her. The cloak slid from her fingers as she took several faltering steps toward him. "We must hurry! 'Tis urgent that I leave—"

Suddenly Synnovea found him standing before her, sweeping her up into his arms. It seemed in no more than a thrice of steps he was up the stairs, following the beacon of light that came from the open doorway at the far end of a dark, narrow hallway. Her eyes swept the bedchamber as they entered. A large, rough-hewn four-poster stood in the middle of the room, its bedding turned down to reveal sheets that were clean but rather coarse. Skimpy draperies, effective enough in providing privacy, had been drawn over a pair of windows on the far side of the bed. A rather stark armoire, a chair, and a shaving stand with a simple pitcher and basin completed the furnishings.

Synnovea's feet had barely touched the floor beside the bed when Tyrone's lips came crushing down upon hers in a fiercely possessive kiss that shattered any lingering notion that she might have had of absconding with her virtue intact. As their mouths and tongues merged in a wildly frantic search, his fingers tore the lacings loose at the back of her gown, and then he was tugging down the bodice, following its descent with hotly flaming kisses.

Synnovea's breath hissed inward through her teeth as his tongue licked greedily over the mounds and valley of her bosom. A soft moan readily evidenced her heightening involvement, as she arched her back, willingly offering him the lush fruit. Tyrone eagerly devoured the fare, clasping the fullness of one ripe orb within his hand while drawing the other into the sultry heat of his mouth. A flicking flame torched a sensitive pinnacle, fanning the hotly glowing coals burning within her womanly loins. It was a scintillating attack on her senses, a sweet undermining of her goals, and a succulent plum she could no longer resist.

Tyrone left the blushing pinnacles throbbing for want of more as he freed her arms from her sleeves and, with ravenous kisses, followed the descent of her clothes. The gown and chemise caught on her hips, where they lay bunched in a confused tangle, and he went down on a knee, working feverishly to free the snag. By now Synnovea had caught the heat of his zeal and leaned over him to drag the shirt from his shoulders, bringing her lustrous bosom temptingly close to his face.

Yanking his arms free of the garment, Tyrone tossed it aside and, with a muted groan, seized the womanly fullness and plied the pale peaks with the greedy warmth of his tongue. The ecstasy that shot through Synnovea was like a blazing arrow, with vanes ignited, coursing through her senses, setting her whole being aflame with a heightening desire. There was no halting the flight of the invisible shaft now, for it soared swiftly to its mark, sinking deeply within her heart and awakening a hungering need to savor the delights to be found with a lover.

Of a sudden, Synnovea knew not where to put her hands, and in an anxious frenzy she rubbed them over the sinews rippling across Tyrone's back and shoulders. She could feel the muscles knotting beneath her palms and swept a hand to the back of his corded neck, pressing his head forward until his face was resting within the cleavage between her breasts. With a subtle twisting of her shoulders and upper torso, the soft, ripe melons caressed the manly visage, drawing a muted moan of pleasure from Tyrone. Greedily he caught a nipple, nearly devouring the whole of it within his mouth as he suckled her. Synnovea felt as if she were being drawn inside out and could only stand transfixed at the delectable sensations that pulsed with quickening fervor through her womanly being.

His hand wandered past the small of her back and slid downward beneath her clothes to clasp a round buttock. Lifting her with him, he rose to his feet and began to drag the garments from her hips. He whisked her free of the restricting clothes, leaving them to fall in a puffy mound upon the floor. When he resettled her to her stockinged feet, he began ridding himself of his own garments as his eyes feasted upon the perfection that had held his mind solidly entrapped for some weeks now.

Synnovea perched timidly upon the edge of the bed, where she stripped off her stockings and surreptitiously witnessed his disrobing. The broad shoulders, tautly muscled ribs, and flat, hard belly were just as she had remembered them, but it was the proud fullness evidencing his manly desires that brought a heated blush to her cheeks.

Becoming aware of her flitting glances, Tyrone stepped near, forcing her to meet his smiling gaze. The flush of color imbuing her creamy skin was unmistakable. "No need to feel embarrassed, my sweet," he whispered cajolingly. "I give you leave to look at me as much as you desire. In truth, it pleasures me to have you do so. You may even touch me if you'd like."

Synnovea stared up at him in painful chagrin, unable to understand his cavalier attitude. She certainly couldn't imagine herself accepting his invitation.

His hungering eyes swept over the length of her as he sought to put her at ease. "I'm not ashamed that I'm a man and that I want you, Synnovea. I yield you everything, my body, my mind, my regard. . . ."

Even as he reached out and captured her fingers, she remained motionless. Holding both her gaze and her hand firmly entrapped, he slid her palm down the length of him, over the muscular bulges and taut ridges, past a furred chest and hardened ribs, along a line of hair traversing his flat belly, on downward to the bold, manly heat of him.

A shocked gasp escaped Synnovea as he closed her fingers around the steely shaft and held them in an unrelenting grasp. She could hardly draw breath for the heat infusing her, extending upward from the hot, fleshly hardness throbbing within her grasp. Though she averted her face, she could not banish the realization of what she held.

"Look at me," he commanded gently.

"I can't," Synnovea whispered, unwilling to obey, yet every instinct she was capable of acknowledging rallied in curiosity.

Capturing her chin within the palm of his free hand, Tyrone lifted it until he could meet her gaze. "Do you hate touching me so much, my sweet?"

Synnovea bit her lip in discomfiture, but honesty prevailed as she shook her head. Never had she experienced anything that thrilled *or* embarrassed her more.

"If we're to be lovers, my sweet, you must know how to please me," he reasoned softly. "Will you not lend yourself to my instructions?"

Reluctantly Synnovea yielded a cautious peek and then squeezed her eyes tightly shut. Yet the impression of his maleness was now forever branded upon her memory; there was no banishing it to the four corners of the universe. If she lived a thousand years, she'd never forget his bold display.

It took a full moment before Synnovea calmed herself enough to open her eyes again. She stared fixedly at him, and gradually Tyrone loosened his tenacious hold, sensing her growing willingness to yield herself to his guidance. He began to move her fingers in a tutorial tour, halting his own breath more than once by the secret places he encouraged her to titillate.

"Enough of this," he rasped hoarsely, aware of the hazards of submitting himself too long to such rousing stimulation.

His mouth descended, greedily devouring her breasts and snatching her breath with each voluptuous stroke of his tongue. The rapturous delights intensified rapidly until Synnovea forgot everything but the need to satisfy the fermenting hunger in the pit of her being. Seeking some relief for that indescribable void which now craved to be sated, she pressed close against him. Tyrone readily accommodated her, lifting her up against him until the moist inner haven of her womanly softness was snuggled against the warmth of him. The pulsing heat of his manhood inflamed the greedy fires burning within her, and she sought instinctively to quench them, moving against the forging iron in a quest as old as time itself. She was unprepared for the sizzling pleasure that began to surge upward through her, though she knew that there was more to come than just this teasing enticement, for they had not yet merged together.

"Hurry," she begged in an urgent whisper, snatching Tyrone's breath as her fingers closed around the hard shaft again. What propelled her now had nothing to do with a fear that Aleksei would discover them. It was a desire for appeasement, pure and simple.

"Have a care, Synnovea," Tyrone cautioned, knowing he was being dragged too close to the brink of expulsion as she drew him back with her to the bed. "The pleasure is too sweet."

Synnovea couldn't think of anything but the bedlam that had been created within her loins. Relinquishing her claim on him, she sank back upon the bed and wriggled across the freshly scented sheet until she reached the pillows near the headboard. Tyrone followed and, bracing on a knee beside her, slipped an arm beneath her waist and lifted her across the feather ticking to the middle of the bed. Caressing her cheek and lips with wanton kisses, he lowered his loins between her eagerly parting thighs and reached down a hand to gently part the silken folds. Synnovea turned her face aside and bit her lip as the unyielding hardness intruded, gently testing the delicate shield. Her breath was snatched from her as the long saber surged forward, piercing her with a pain that made her pitch upward. Tyrone lost whatever ground he had gained, and though it took every speck of willpower he was capable of gathering to maintain a gentlemanly forbearance, he drew back, allowing Synnovea a moment to calm herself as he kissed and caressed her.

"I'm sorry," she whispered tearfully beneath his lingering kisses. "I didn't think I was such a coward."

"Shhh, love," Tyrone soothed, stroking her womanly softness.

This time Synnovea surrendered herself completely to

him, totally abashed that she had acted like a spineless chit when she had desired the consummation as feverishly as he. Her hand came up to rest tentatively upon his chest. "May I touch you again?"

"Not yet, love," Tyrone answered, too shaken by the pain of his mounting desires to accept such sweet, excruciating enticements. "Let me pleasure you; then I'll seek mine."

It seemed only a passing of a moment before Synnovea found her embarrassment eclipsed by new, rapidly expanding sensations. Overwhelmed by the waves of effervescent bliss that began washing over her in crescendoing rapture, she began to twist and writhe beneath his persuasive fondling. Arching her hips upward against him in an invitation he could not resist, she was soon leading the stirring hardness to the tender breach.

Tyrone was shaking nearly as much as she as his hands clasped her buttocks for the final thrust. The hardened shaft plunged inward, drawing a sharp gasp from her as the membrane split. Just as quickly, Synnovea was searching out his mouth, seeking the sultry kisses that would sweep her beyond the pain. He indulged her with tantalizing exchanges of lips and tongues, yet he was now sheathed in her warmth, and a spiraling ecstasy began to goad him. His thrusts were long and sure, stirring her ardor until she began to rise up to meet him. Beneath his kisses, soft mewls were transformed into astonished gasps as she soared ever higher toward that delectable culmination of their union. Tyrone was not far behind. His breath rasped harshly in her ear when the first, thrilling fruits of ecstasy began to wash over him. Then suddenly a rapidly approaching sound intruded, wrenching his mind clear with a brutal abruptness.

"What is it?" Synnovea whispered as he lifted his head to listen. Her eyes widened when she heard the clattering hooves of many riders thundering toward the house.

"Someone's coming!" Tyrone muttered.

Synnovea moaned in despair as he snatched away and rolled to the edge of the bed. Grabbing up his clothes, he thrust his feet through a pair of chausses and, jerking the close-fitting hosiery up over his narrow hips, hurriedly knotted them at his waist.

"Get your clothes on, Synnovea!" he bade anxiously as the hoofbeats came to a halt before his quarters. "Hurry!"

She just stared at him, frozen by the realization of what she had done. Despite her change of heart, everything was occurring just as she had planned. In another moment Aleksei would be ordering his men to break down the door, and Tyrone would be caught in the middle, exactly where she had contrived to place him.

Seeing her horrified stare, Tyrone seized her by the arms and gave her a shake. "Good Lord, woman, what ails you? Do you not ken? There are men outside the house, and in all likelihood they'll be coming in here! I cannot defend the two of us with you stark naked! They'll likely kill me to get to you."

Sweeping her off the bed, he set her on her feet and then gathered up her clothes. He dumped them on the bed near at hand and shook out her chemise just as a heavy fist pounded on the front portal and a mumbled voice called through the barrier.

"Colonel Rycroft! I must speak with you."

"Lift your arms!" Tyrone commanded in an anxious whisper, for the moment ignoring the summons. As Synnovea complied, he yanked the chemise down over her head and settled it into place around her slender waist.

"I can dress myself!" she declared, coming to her senses as she felt his lean fingers fastening the tiny buttons between her breasts. "You'd better get your own clothes on and get out of here!"

"What! And leave you here by yourself to confront those

men alone?" Tyrone laughed harshly, denying the possibility. "If I leave at all, Synnovea, I'll be taking you with me."

From down below came the rattle of the broken latch accompanied by a garbled question. "Colonel Rycroft, are you there?"

It was obvious after another testing of the lock that the portal would not yield to the intruders' attempts to open it. Heavy fists began to pound the planks, demanding entry.

"Colonel Rycroft, we know you're in there!"

Tyrone stepped to the door of his bedchamber and yelled down the stairs, "I'll be down in a moment. I'm getting dressed."

"You must come now, Colonel!" came a reply. "I know the Countess Synnovea is with you. If you don't open this door immediately, my men will break it down."

"Aleksei!" Synnovea whispered. Meeting Tyrone's questioning glance, she blushed and lifted her slender shoulders in a disconcerted shrug. "He hired men to watch Natasha's house."

"Good Lord, Synnovea! Why didn't you tell me earlier? We could've gone elsewhere." Tyrone gave her a gentle shove toward the bed. "Put your gown and shoes on. We've got to get out of here! And fast!"

His statement was promptly underscored by the sudden contact of several stout thuds against the front door. Another crashing blow soon followed, testing the sturdiness of the formidable barrier.

Seeing now a chance to escape the consequences of her ploy, Synnovea quickly obeyed as Tyrone yanked on a pair of hide breeches, boots, and a shirt. Belting on his sword, he seized her hand and led her in a brisk descent of the stairs. He paused briefly in the lower room to judge the strength of another assault against the front portal and roughly estimated the time they had remaining before the sturdy planks would give way. Scooping up her cloak from the floor, he wrapped it around her shoulders and pulled her along with him to the back door.

Tyrone drew forth his sword and laid a silencing finger across his lips before he motioned her to stay where she was. Receiving her nod of compliance, he slid the bolt back carefully, quietly from the lock and then pulled the door open. His cautious tread was just as noiseless as he slipped through the portal. Pausing just outside with his sword held ready, he scanned the shadows, slowly turning until he glanced up suddenly to his right, where a burly fellow squatted atop a wooden barrel residing in the corner of the house, only a couple of steps away from the back door. Like a flash of quicksilver in the night, Tyrone's blade whipped upward to block the descent of the other's ax. A shout from the man brought the sound of running feet around the end of the house as Tyrone parried the next blow, but any hope for his escape with Synnovea dwindled rapidly when a dozen more stalwarts came charging toward them with swords and weapons drawn. Tyrone swiftly retreated, slamming and bolting the door behind him.

"Get upstairs!" He jerked his head in the direction of his bedchamber as he faced Synnovea. "I'll try to hold them off down here!"

"You must leave me and escape!" she cried frantically.

"Woman, do as I say!" Tyrone barked. "I'll not leave you to your own defense!"

Frustrated by his commanding tone, Synnovea clenched her fists at her sides and tried again, this time in a louder tone so she could be heard above the jarring jolts that were now bombarding both doors. "Will you please listen to me, Tyrone Rycroft! I know what I'm saying!"

"What? And allow Aleksei a chance to rape you before he takes you to safety? Go, I said!"

Groaning in despair, Synnovea whirled toward the stairs just as the front portal crashed inward, sending several stout

hearties stumbling in on top of it. Their entry hastened Synnovea's flight even as she heard Aleksei bellow her name from
a safe distance behind the first battery of men. Tyrone leapt
to cover her retreat with the long blade boldly in evidence.

"Seize him!" Aleksei railed out the command, thrusting a
long finger toward the colonel.

Tyrone chortled as he mocked the prince. "Have you no
heart to do it yourself, my lord?"

A half-dozen men plowed forward to accomplish the
prince's bidding and promptly yelped and stumbled back, suffering the pain of newly inflicted wounds.

"A weighty purse to the one responsible for that rascal's
capture," Aleksei promised, incensed by the colonel's tenacity.
"You wanted him! Now here he is! Do with him what he did
to you and those who rode with you! Seize him!"

Tyrone had no chance to answer as a full dozen toughs
raced toward him, forcing him to retreat up the stairs. Upon
gaining the upper level, he dashed into the bedchamber and
slammed the portal closed behind him. He tossed the sword
onto the bed and then pulled the tall, weighty armoire in front
of the door to bolster the strength of the heavy planks. Synnovea watched in helpless bewilderment while he grabbed a
small chair and raced across the room to throw it through a
window. He returned to the bed and, whipping the top sheet
away, tied a knot in the end before he stepped back to the
window. A small ledge, wide enough to comfortably accommodate a man's boots, jutted out from beneath it. Then his gaze
flicked outward and carefully searched the shadows enclosing
the house.

Turning, Tyrone beckoned for Synnovea to draw near. "I'll
lower you to the ground with the sheet and then climb down
behind you." He glanced toward the door as the ponderous
blows strengthened against it and was forced to speak over
the din. "If I don't make it, run to the carriage and have the
driver take you back to Natasha's! Do you understand?"

"Clearly, Tyrone, but I plead with you. Flee before you're taken."

Sweeping her into his arms, Tyrone thrust her through the window and clasped her hand tightly as she balanced on the ledge. Loud, booming laughter came from below, prompting Tyrone to lean out through the opening. A huge fellow with a long, shaggy mustache and a lock of hair sprouting from a bald pate strode forward with arms widely outstretched.

"Oh-ho! Colonel Rycroft! We meet again, eh? So good of you, my friend, to toss the wench down to me." The huge man chortled in uproarious mirth as he held out his arms expectantly. "The little pigeon is tasty sweetmeat, eh? Now I taste for myself what you have feasted upon."

"Petrov!" Synnovea gasped in shock and glanced back at Tyrone. "That means Ladislaus is here!"

Tyrone cursed beneath his breath, then muttered derisively, "I must question the sort of friends Prince Aleksei consorts with!" He helped Synnovea back through the window and swept her to her feet. "I fear the prince has made the place secure against our escape if he's hired those thieving miscreants to seek me out. You can be certain they're hungry for revenge, a fact which I'm sure Aleksei was cognizant of ere he went searching for them."

"How would he have known where to find them?" Synnovea asked in confusion.

"That is a question I'd like to ask Aleksei if I'm given the opportunity."

"You'll have a greater chance of escaping without me," she replied, laying a hand upon his furred chest. "Will you not try? I promise you, Aleksei won't let these men take me, not when there's a chance the tsar will find out."

Tyrone scoffed at the idea. "Aleksei may not even have a choice with Ladislaus and his men breathing down his neck.

That brigand wanted you before. This time he may not stop until he takes you."

"Please listen, Tyrone," she pleaded desperately. "I've no liking for Aleksei *or* Ladislaus, but if you leave me and seek your freedom, then you may be able to arrange an assault on those brigands and take me back. You all but snatched me out of Ladislaus's hands before. Can you not do so again?"

Tyrone musingly lifted a brow as he considered her suggestion. If they were both captured, he'd be confronting an overwhelming force anxious to kill him. The thieves would probably keep him shackled or so busy trying to protect the two of them that he wouldn't be able to carry out her rescue. "I might be able to arrange such an event within the hour," he replied thoughtfully. "I have friends living nearby. English officers. If I can get through Ladislaus's men, I know they'll help me."

Beneath the ramming bombardment of the door, the wood facing around the bolt began to splinter away, motivating Tyrone to take up his sword again. As he sheathed the weapon, the splotches of red marring the whiteness of the bottom sheet caught his attention. He paused briefly to consider the stains and then, facing Synnovea, pressed a hurried kiss upon her lips.

"I'll finish what I started ere long," he promised in a warm whisper. "Save yourself for me."

Fighting back a rush of tears, Synnovea braved a smile. "Just be careful!"

"Tell Aleksei *and* Ladislaus that I'll kill them if they harm you in any way," Tyrone said before he strode to the window. With a casual salute, he ducked through the opening, bringing her forward on flying feet.

Synnovea watched, fear throbbing in her throat, as Tyrone climbed out onto the ledge. There he braced his feet wide to balance himself and, tucking two fingers into his mouth, whistled loudly, drawing an astonished gasp from her. At the shrill summons, Petrov came racing back to serve as the colonel's audience of one. The brawny giant leaned his head far back and gaped upward with jaw aslack as Tyrone swept him a jaunty bow.

"So good of you to come when I call, Petrov. Now catch me if you can," he taunted with a chuckle and, springing lightly from the ledge, somersaulted once through the air and then dove directly toward the burly one, who staggered backward in rapidly expanding amazement. Synnovea clapped a hand over her mouth to squelch a frightened scream, but any sound that might have escaped was quickly overshadowed by the loud, wavering warble that issued forth from Petrov's thick throat. His scream strengthened to a deafening roar until it was abruptly squelched beneath the falling weight of the colonel.

As Tyrone had hoped, his daring dive had been sufficiently broken by the thief's bulk, and, no worse for wear, he drew back a clenched fist and delivered a powerful blow to the stout jaw of the dazed man, knocking that one completely senseless. The large head lolled limply as Tyrone tested the brigand's lack of response. Satisfied, he jumped to his feet and dusted off his clothes as if on a casual errand. Turning with a lopsided grin, he swept into another debonair bow, this time for his lady love, who still stood at the window with her hands clasped tightly over her mouth. It was a full second before the shock faded, and Synnovea clapped her palms to her cheeks, laughing in relief.

Briefly she acknowledged his daring feat with applause and blew him a kiss before he whirled and raced toward a nearby house. She observed his flight, peering after him intently as far as she could see until the darkness consumed his tall form, leaving her strangely disquieted yet relieved by his escape.

The cabinet began to slide inward, and a brief moment later, Synnovea whirled to face the men who burst through.

Ladislaus led the brigands with a drawn sword. He halted just inside the door as his pale eyes scanned the length and breadth of the bedchamber for the Englishman. Dragging the furry cap from his flaxen head, he strode across the room, but paused briefly beside the bed to consider the bloodied sheet. His ice-blue eyes chased to her and then swept beyond her, narrowing to angry slits when he noticed the curtains fluttering at the window. Racing forward to the opening, he leaned out and scanned the area, finding his hulking companion sprawled limply upon the ground.

Synnovea lifted her chin, giving Ladislaus her best attempt at a haughty demeanor as he came back to her. "You're too late," she announced. "The Englishman has gone."

"I can see that for myself, Countess. I'm also aware of the pretty bauble he left behind." His eyes raked her cloaked form before he reached out a hand and thoughtfully rubbed a soft, dark curl between his fingers. "You've allowed my enemy to feed upon your rich treasures, my beauty. I'll forgive you for that, for there's clearly enough for me to savor, but I would know where he has gone."

"Do you think I would tell you?" she scoffed in amazement. "You must be as addlepated as your unconscious friend."

Aleksei pushed his way through the door, safely behind an escort of four stout-chested men. "Don't waste time trying to get any answers from her," he snapped, glowering at her. "She'll never tell you where her lover has fled. You'll have to find him yourself." Turning imperiously, he snapped his fingers at the bandits, sending them running out again. "Remember!" he shouted after them. "A weighty purse to the one who captures him!"

Aleksei listened to their thudding footfalls on the stairs before he turned a challenging sneer upon Ladislaus, who had made no effort to follow. "Well? Are you going to help your men scour the area for that English rogue, or do you intend to hunt him down yourself?" He arched a taunting brow at the hulking man. "Don't tell me you're afraid of him."

Ladislaus jeered at the man's gibe. "There's only one coward here, and I'm looking at him."

The insult ignited Aleksei's dark eyes, leaving them flaring with fiery rage. "From what I hear of your attack on the countess's entourage, you ran when the Englishman appeared on the scene."

"Be careful," the giant warned him ominously. "One less boyar in this city won't be noticed, I assure you."

Synnovea glanced between the two men, her hopes rising. Though in league with each other, they apparently shared a mutual dislike. If prodded into a violent quarrel, they might even forget about searching for the Englishman long enough to ensure his escape. "Your hired henchman doesn't seem to appreciate your elevated status, Aleksei. But then, I must remember, he's also a prince, albeit of questionable descent. Has he been in your employ very long?"

The lord-of-thieves snorted loudly. "No man employs Ladislaus," he rumbled. "Your precious boyar came to search me out in Kitaigorod when I let it be known that I was seeking the whereabouts of a certain Englishman. Otherwise, Countess, you wouldn't be seeing us together."

Warily Synnovea queried, "Is it your intent to kill Colonel Rycroft?"

"I'll allow the prince to have his due ere I take mine," Ladislaus replied and smiled at her mockingly. "In any case, my lady, there'll be little left for you to enjoy after we're finished with your precious colonel."

"*If* you manage to take him," Aleksei interjected with rancor. "I'm sure this delay will cost you his capture."

Ladislaus smirked at the other man. "I promised you that we'd take him, and so we shall."

With that, the lordling thief strode across the room and took his leave. Several moments later, his booming voice was heard outside the bedroom window as he bade Petrov to rouse from his stupor.

Contemptuously Aleksei glanced around the room, disdaining the plain, barren look of it. Then his eyes blazed with sudden fury when he espied the dark splotches that marred the whiteness of the bed linen. With a savage curse he whirled upon Synnovea and lashed out with swiftly spiraling vengeance, laying the back of his hand viciously across her cheek and sending her reeling in a daze across the room. She slammed into the far wall, emitting a muffled groan as her head hit the barrier. Then she staggered back in a stunned stupor and gingerly touched the growing knot on her forehead.

"So, you bitch!" Aleksei snarled in seething rage. "You've done what you threatened! You've given yourself to that filthy blackguard!"

Synnovea blinked in an earnest attempt to focus her gaze upon her adversary. Considering that the whole side of her head felt as if it had just been slammed against a stone wall, she didn't think it unusual that her vision and senses were beclouded. Lamely she jeered at the prince, conveying her contempt as she wiped a trickle of blood from a corner of her bruised mouth. "Not long ago I would've given myself to Tyrone Rycroft for no other purpose than to thwart your plans, Aleksei, but henceforth, I shall seek his favor with eager diligence, for without a doubt he's more of a man than you'll ever hope to be."

"You will watch him pay!" Aleksei railed, incensed by her disparagement. His much-inflated pride was sorely pricked by the realization that she had taken a foreigner to her breast after steadfastly denying him that same privilege the whole of her stay in his mansion. As if that insult wasn't enough to rile his temper, he had to endure the added indignity of being told that she'd now willingly share her company with the other man. "Because of you, Synnovea, the Englishman will suffer well beyond his feeble endurance."

A sudden, niggling apprehension encompassed Synnovea's heart. She didn't doubt in the least that Aleksei would resort to torture to have his revenge upon his rival. Yet, when she remembered Tyrone's skill at fighting, it seemed unlikely that any common man could best him. Confidence in his abilities eased her qualms significantly, allowing her to boast, "You'll have to catch him first, Aleksei, and I really don't think you or your hired lackeys are skilled enough for that task."

Aleksei smirked. "I'm of a different opinion, my dear, for you see, Ladislaus and his men have grown to hate the Englishman almost as much as I do. 'Twill be only a matter of time before the colonel falls into their hands. They'll lie in wait until he appears, and then pounce on him as they would a ravenous dog that has been freed from his cage." Bending toward her, he sneered into her face. "Once I have your lover within my grasp, my dear, I'll make sure he remembers this night forever. Before I'm done with him, I'll see the hide stripped from his back and then assure myself that he'll never bed you or another woman as long as he lives."

Some distance from the house, the dense darkness was held secure within a cluster of trees growing near the narrow dirt lane. It was here that Tyrone tarried to canvass the open, rutted stretch. After peering carefully up and down the thoroughfare, he scanned the area bordering it. No dark specter moved beyond the copse, not even the coachman who snoozed atop his conveyance a short distance away. Tyrone silently unsheathed his sword and crept to the outer edge of the trees, warily pausing there for a long moment as he again surveyed the terrain. He was unable to put aside the feeling of uneasiness that had settled down upon him after his entry into the grove. He sensed that all was not as it should be despite the openness of the place beyond where he stood. Still, he was unable to detect any movement or even a shadow which might have alerted him to another's presence. He was, however, a man who had learned to take heed when his instincts warned him of danger. For the sake of caution, he eased back a step and was about to turn in stealthful retreat when a sudden pain exploded against his head. He sagged to his knees as a billion piercing lights burst in a sea of radiant colors before his eyes and then slowly dimmed to a dull shade of gray. Through the tenebrous gloom, he became vaguely aware of a dark shape stepping close and an arm lifting high above him. His hampered faculties were sluggish and slow to react as a stout club came crashing down upon his skull once again, darkening the murky shadows into the deepest shade of night until all that remained of his world was total oblivion.

12

In the silence of the still night, a growing din reached the upstairs bedroom, and Aleksei raised his head to listen as the sounds of rumbling wheels and thundering hooves heralded the approach of a coach and a large party of riders. Loudly shouted orders accompanied the arrival of the conveyance and its escort in front of the colonel's quarters. A moment later, Ladislaus called up the stairs from the room below.

"You can come down now, Your Most Gracious Highness." The disdain in his tone could not have gone undetected. "We've caught the Englishman."

Synnovea gasped as the renegade's words struck fear into her heart. Though Tyrone's abilities had seemed to extend well beyond that of normal men, she now had to face the full import of Aleksei's threats and could only tremble in deepening apprehension as she thought of the vengeance the prince and the band of highwaymen intended to exact from her lover.

"Now you'll see!" Aleksei flaunted his triumph with a victorious chortle. Catching Synnovea's arm in a cruel vise, he hauled her along with him as he hurried down the stairs. When she stumbled to her knees after leaving the last step, he dragged her to her feet and shoved her toward the door. "Get out there, bitch!"

The rented livery had been halted in front of the house where Ladislaus now waited with Petrov and several of his men. Another score or more miscreants were still mounted beyond the coach. Confronted by their vast number, Synnovea began to understand the reason for Tyrone's lack of success in gaining his freedom. There were enough rogues to have formed a human web around a wide area, greatly reducing his chances for escape. It was just as apparent that Aleksei had been willing to promise Ladislaus and his men a generous stipend to see his orders carried out, one way or another.

Aleksei's long fingers gripped Synnovea's arm, and with a savage curse he thrust her roughly against the side of the carriage, drawing a sharp wince of pain from her. Having been completely thwarted in his efforts to claim the girl as his mistress, he was hardly in a mood to relent. He stalked toward her and, bracing a hand against the conveyance, took a finely boned wrist within his grasp. He smirked in smug satisfaction as he squeezed it nigh to the point of breaking and then chortled vindictively when she writhed in silent agony. "I know you'll never bow to me for your own comfort, but listen well, my girl. If you try anything, I can assure you that it will go far worse for the Englishman."

Having observed the intimidation, Ladislaus stepped beside them and, with a satirical glint in his pale eyes, fixed the boyar with a chiding stare. Then, as if amused by the prince's baffled regard, the thief grinned broadly and swung open the carriage door. "Your quarry is inside, Great Prince Aleksei," he announced, jerking a thumb inwardly. "Your rival is trussed up like a goose awaiting a roasting, just the way you wanted him. He shouldn't do you any harm now."

"Excellent!" Aleksei exclaimed buoyantly.

Feeling a mixture of terror and revulsion roiling within her, Synnovea wrenched free of Aleksei's grasp and pushed with all of her might against his chest, managing to catch him unawares. He stumbled back at the impetus of her assault. Synnovea didn't waste a moment, but scrambled up into the carriage's dark interior just as Aleksei recovered his balance. He thrust out an arm toward the brigands on the far side of the coach and barked out a strident order for them to secure the door. Then he scurried into the conveyance after Synnovea and seized her arm to halt her flight, but he soon realized there was no need to restrain her, for with a moan of despair she sank to her knees beside the seat where the colonel lay as still as death.

The ominously inert form cauterized Synnovea's mind with burgeoning fear. She wasn't even sure that Tyrone was breathing. He lay on his side with his wrists and ankles tightly bound. A woven leather rope had been tightly looped several times among the weighty hemp cords that secured his hands and feet, nullifying any possibility of him launching an attack once he roused from his senseless state. The thieves' precautions had at least one benefit. They reassured Synnovea that Tyrone was still alive.

Fearing the gravity of his injuries, Synnovea searched beneath his shirt and along his long torso for an open wound. Her hopes rallied briefly when she found no evidence of an injury, but her worry intensified sharply into panic when she slipped her fingers through his tousled hair to cradle his head and immediately discovered a large, swollen lump, the ridge of which was marred by a bloody gash. She lifted her hand before her face and, in paralyzed horror, stared through the tenebrous gloom at the dark splotches of glistening wetness now staining her fingers.

"That's only the beginning," Aleksei needled, recognizing her rapidly expanding trepidations. His cocky arrogance was greatly inflated by the power he presently held in his grasp. Now that the Englishman was his hostage, he could make the girl plead for mercy, and he promised himself that he'd see her groveling at his feet before he finished with the man. Piece by bloody piece, he intended to exact his revenge upon the colonel until the girl was reduced to a quivering mass of daunted humanity. "Take comfort, my dear. Your cherished colonel is still alive, but he'll soon beg us to kill him."

"You can't blame him for what I did!" Synnovea cried harshly, jerking around to glare through welling tears at her adversary.

"Oh, but I can, Synnovea," Aleksei assured her almost pleasantly and lifted his broad shoulders in an indolent shrug as the conveyance lurched into motion. The moon was bright enough to illumine the interior, which had been darkened, and in its silver-hued glow he could see tears glistening in her dark eyes and streaming in shining rivulets down her pale cheeks. It incensed him that she could display so much concern for the colonel when, in sharp contrast, she hadn't shown the slightest bit of remorse for the wounds she had inflicted upon him. Even now, his nose was still sensitive to the touch, not to mention the lump that had formed after the fracture, marring its aristocratic lines. "Colonel Rycroft has stolen from me a very special pleasure I had reserved entirely for myself, my dear, and for that I intend to make him pay dearly." Smiling in self-complacency, Aleksei bent toward her. "And you will watch it all, my beautiful Synnovea, as part of your punishment."

Her eyes grew cold with hatred. "Reserved for yourself, Aleksei? I thought it was your intention to deliver me unsullied to Vladimir."

Aleksei swept a knuckle across his mustache as he sniffed

in stilted arrogance. "I might have allowed your husband first taste, but then again, I might not have."

Synnovea bit her tongue to keep from venting several appellations that would have done the cocky boyar justice. If she dared, in all probability he'd spite her by heaping more violence upon Tyrone's frame. Yet maintaining her silence hardly diminished the hatred she felt toward him. Even the idea of sitting within close proximity to the man sickened her, but she could do something to remedy that situation.

Pushing herself up from the floor, Synnovea ignored Aleksei's sudden wariness and, gently lifting Tyrone's head, slid into the seat beneath it, giving no thought to the blood that would stain her gown as she laid his head in her lap.

"How loving and kind you are to him!" Aleksei derided with a caustic laugh. "I'm sure the colonel will feel greatly indebted to you once I explain that he was nothing more than a petty pawn in your frivolous little game. After the jewels of his manhood have been stripped from his loins, I'm sure he'll want to heap accolades of honor upon your winsome head."

Synnovea clutched a trembling hand to her throat and averted her face, tormented by his threat and the role she had played in bringing Tyrone into his hands. She knew she wouldn't be able to live at peace with herself if Aleksei accomplished everything he vowed to do. It would be far better if the overflowing draught of his dark vengeance fell upon her head alone.

Curling his handsome lips scornfully, the prince leaned forward to antagonize her further, seeking additional retribution to ease his rage and jealousy. "Do you know what that means to a man, Synnovea?" He became vulgarly explicit in his explanation and was spurred on to further crudeness by the sharp intake of her breath and her horrified stare. Perhaps he might have only imagined the deepening stain that seemed to darken her cheeks, but seeing the look of stark terror on her face was almost enough to satisfy him. "You're no longer an innocent, Synnovea, so you know I'm telling you the whole dirty truth of it. He'll never again have the ability to make love to you. He'll be a eunuch when I get through with him, and you'll have no one to blame but yourself. I warned you, but you were too stubborn to listen. Now you'll both pay."

If Synnovea had been able to summon some minute hope that Aleksei would listen to her pleas for clemency, she would've gladly gone down on her knees before him and begged for Tyrone's release, but the prince was clearly in a vengeful mood and wouldn't be content until his deeds were carried out. He made no idle threat. She could believe he would do exactly what he had threatened.

In spite of her frantic search for a way to bring about Tyrone's escape from this predicament in which she had entangled him, Synnovea was frighteningly aware that with each whirling turn of the wheels, she and her valiant but senseless suitor were being taken ever closer to a moment of reckoning. And she could do nothing whatsoever to stop it from happening.

The conveyance turned into a lane near the Taraslov manse and came to a halt in front of the carriage house. As the steeds jaunced to a halt and the coach finally ceased its motion, Synnovea realized she was neither mentally nor physically prepared to face the frightening ordeal that Aleksei had planned for them. She was overwhelmed with feelings of regret for having devised the diabolical scheme that had led them to this end. Indeed, had some reprieve been extended toward them with payment being her marriage to Prince Vladimir, she'd have gladly gone that very same hour to see the nuptials performed. She couldn't abide the thought of Tyrone suffering because of her offenses.

Ladislaus and his men dismounted and crowded around the coach as if fully expecting the Englishman to be awake and dangerous. They seemed relieved when they found him insensible to his surroundings and incapable of even the smallest struggle.

Aleksei bade four of the burly outlaws to carry their prisoner into the carriage house and hang him by his wrists from the rafters. For good measure, Ladislaus instructed several more to stand guard with pistols held at the ready, just in case the good colonel revived before they had made him sufficiently secure.

Aleksei barely considered the idea of Synnovea trying an escape now. She seemed far more intent upon following the procession, which he pompously led. His attention was occupied with giving orders to his recruited culprits, and so delighted was he with that particular task that he failed to notice a diminutive form quickly scurrying behind a shrub as he and Ladislaus's men passed with their burden. He was equally unobservant when the tiny, shadowy shade reached out to grasp Synnovea's arm and yank her behind that same bush.

"Ali!" Though the cry was no more than a startled whisper, Synnovea could have shouted out the servant's name in sheer joy. Her relief to see someone who could help was nearly overwhelming. "Why are you still here?"

"As ye can probably guess for yerself, me lamb, Stenka is takin' his own sweet time comin' back for me." The Irishwoman cocked a curious eye after the departing men. "What's that thievin' beastie Ladislaus doin' here anyway? An' Prince Aleksei, is he in cahoots wit' the brigand?"

Synnovea had no time to answer the woman's questions. "Ali, you must help me! Colonel Rycroft is in great danger."

"Well, I figgered as much meself as soon as I seen him bein' toted an' guarded by so many," the servant commented dryly. Ali peered around the bush, closely eyeing the four who hauled their captive through the door of the stable. "But I haven't a ken what I can do ta save his handsome self from all 'em foul brutes. They'd only knock me senseless again if'n I interfere, an' what help would I be then?"

"Listen carefully, and I'll gladly tell you!" Synnovea whispered urgently. "You must leave here posthaste and halt the carriage on the street before any of Ladislaus's men have a chance to see you. Once you find Stenka, have him take you immediately to the tsar's palace. There you must urge a guard to fetch Major Nekrasov for you. Tell the major that Ladislaus is here in the city and that Colonel Rycroft is in imminent peril. It is imperative that a force of men come at once to his rescue. Do you understand?"

"Aye, that I do, lamb," Ali replied with a nod. "But I gotta go now 'cause I hear Stenka comin' down the lane." With a leaping skitter, she raced off to meet the coach as it rumbled up the thoroughfare toward the manse.

Now, with some hope for Tyrone's rescue flourishing within her breast, Synnovea caught up her skirts and raced after the men who were crowding inside the carriage house. Several tallow lanterns had been lit here and there throughout the barn, but for the most part, the light seemed concentrated upon an open area which they were now surrounding. Synnovea grew cold with dread as the brigands chortled and loudly boasted of their own participation in the capture of the Englishman, but she slipped through narrow breaches in their broad-shouldered ranks until she gained the inner circle. Aleksei stood near the core of that area, and she suffered a moment of panic as she sensed his heightened exhilaration. Facing her, he smirked with malevolent glee and raised a hand to beckon her forward.

"You're just in time, my dear." He casually indicated the long, manly form dangling from the rafters. "We were about to awaken your handsome lover with a cold bath. Would you care to admire him for one last moment ere he's forever scarred and mutilated?"

The strength ebbed from Synnovea's limbs when her eyes found Tyrone. He now wore only the chausses he had donned beneath his breeches, but they drooped around his narrow hips, barely preserving his modesty as he hung by his wrists. His head dangled forward limply between upstretched arms. His ankles had been shackled to a pair of huge, weighty anvils, which had been separated to keep his legs widespread and at an uncomfortable angle. She could imagine the reason.

Synnovea stifled an anguished moan as Ladislaus reached up a hand and seized a short thatch of pale-streaked hair, jerking his captive's head upright. Then, with a snort of derision, he let it fall again and signaled a comrade to awaken their prisoner. In the next instant a bucketful of water was flung into Tyrone's face, bringing him around to a half-muddled state. His head only lolled listlessly between his shoulders while the trickling water cascaded down his body, weighing down the stockings until they sagged against him wetly. Once more the pail was filled from the watering trough and heaved into his face, this time startling Tyrone awake with a gasp of surprise. Tiny droplets of water sprayed outward as he jerked up his head and glared about him. His gaze softened briefly when it paused on Synnovea, but his eyes hardened just as quickly when he took note of the dark bruises on her brow and cheek and the split and swollen bottom lip.

Aleksei stepped forward almost jauntily and held a tallow lantern high to see the Englishman's face better. "So, Colonel Rycroft, we meet at last."

"Forbear the introductions," Tyrone growled, and squinted against the light to fix the man with a piercing scowl. "I know who you are. You're the toad who tried to force Synnovca into serving your pleasure. It must gall you considerably to think that she prefers me over you."

Aleksei laughed harshly in loathing disdain. "About as much as it might provoke you to be told that she only used you for her own devices. Only a few days ago my ward became formally betrothed to Prince Vladimir Dimitrievich. She swore to see herself disgraced by the likes of you rather than submit to the marriage. So you see, my friend, you've been foolishly duped into believing the wench cared for you. 'Twas but a ruse she invented to save herself from an arrangement of marriage which she abhorred."

Tyrone shifted his gaze to Synnovea, feeling her treachery pierce his heart as deeply as any steel-tipped pike. Though she stepped awkwardly forward and struggled in vain to speak the words that came to her lips, he knew of a sudden that everything Aleksei had said was true. He had been used! Deceived! Played the fool! And now he would pay for it!

The blue eyes turned coldly away from her to peruse the leering faces of the men who watched him; he recognized several from his first encounter with Ladislaus's pack. He had heard their sniggering laughter when someone made the translation into Russian. It was just as obvious that they were gloating over their good fortune at having seized him at last.

"So now you have me in your trap." He faced Aleksei with the declaration. "What do you plan to do with me?"

"Oh, I've reserved a special punishment for you, Colonel, one that I'm sure you'll forever revile. 'Twill serve to remind you of your folly in sullying a Russian *boyarina*. Indeed, my friend, after tonight you'll never be able to make love to another woman as long as you live. After you're given a proper lashing, you'll be gelded while the girl is forced to watch."

Aleksei strode around Synnovea, reveling in the revenge he would take, but Tyrone gnashed his teeth against the effort of propelling his body forward against the ponderous weights ensnaring his ankles. Relaxing as he swung backward, he recouped his strength and strained forward again. Over and over he tried until he was swaying to and fro, with each subsequent movement gaining momentum to pull the anvils with him. He saw his goal near and stretched his legs outward to lock the prince in the steely vise of his thighs, but a warning shout from one of the men alerted Aleksei, who, upon espying the imminent threat, gasped in sudden alarm and stumbled back from the dangerously encroaching limbs. From a place of safety, he looked at the colonel with eyes that momentarily portrayed evidence of fear.

When the prince finally regained his aplomb, he gave a crisp nod to the tall, brawny fellow who had stripped himself to his waist, baring a massive chest that was covered with a thick thatch of curling black hair. It was the Goliath who had once sent the colonel's helmet sailing off his head. Now it seemed that he would have the personal pleasure of dealing out what the thieves deemed a befitting punishment upon their adversary.

The Goliath hefted a many-tongued lash as he strode to a spot slightly behind and to the right of Tyrone. "Brace yourself, Englishman," he rumbled deeply. "The weapons I wield are more often spikes and cutlasses, but I can assure you that you'll wish for a quick end ere I'm finished."

Aleksei smiled in eager anticipation. Bracing his feet apart, he folded his arms across his chest like some dark-skinned sultan as he awaited the first scourging stroke. The titan drew back his arm, shaking out the lash in preparation.

"*NOOOooo!* You mustn't!" Synnovea railed and threw herself at Aleksei's feet, where she sobbed out a desperate plea. "Oh, please spare him! I beg you, Aleksei, don't do this thing! I yield you whatever you want from me if you would only have pity on him. I'll give myself to you gladly! Just don't hurt him!"

"Do you think I'll sully myself by taking his leavings?" Aleksei sneered as he glared down at her. "You were merely one of the colonel's fleeting fancies, my dear. Don't you know that? Bedding every wench who strikes his fancy is what a soldier does best when he's not chasing the enemy. There's no accounting for how many others your precious colonel had before bedding you! But no! You had to give yourself to him! Well, I don't want you now! After this, as far as I'm concerned, you can serve Ladislaus's pleasure. 'Twill be a fitting punishment for ignoring my warnings." Lifting his head, Aleksei looked inquiringly at the leader of the thieves. "What say you, Ladislaus? Will she be payment enough for you?"

Synnovea's head snapped around, and she stared in horror at the flaxen-haired thief whose ice-blue eyes gleamed back at her above a broad grin.

"Oh, Great Exalted Prince," the lordling thief casually mocked. "With the colonel rendered his just due, she'll be more than payment enough for me. My men, however, will have to be paid in gold, as you have promised."

Whirling back to face Aleksei, Synnovea glared at him. "You wouldn't dare attempt this outrage! The tsar—"

Aleksei intruded curtly. "Natasha was responsible for you during the absence of my wife," he informed her loftily. "If she allowed you to wander off with the Englishman, and you and he were never seen again . . . then the fault will lie with her. You can be sure that is as much as the tsar will ever know about this matter."

Dismissing her with a wave of his hand, Aleksei faced the bare-chested brute and gave him a nod, urging the man to continue. That one hauled back the whip, and an instant later it fell, bringing a pained grimace from Tyrone and a sobbing scream from Synnovea as she threw herself between him and the one who had delivered the stroke. Clasping her slender arms around her lover's thighs, she braced herself to be his shield and glowered back at the men in defiance.

Tyrone's rage was supreme. He saw the taunting grins of his foes through a furious red haze. He had no need for them to call him a fool for having played into the countess's hands. The throbbing in his back served to remind him of that fact, but the pain was not as unbearable as the one that throbbed near his heart and in his brain. Gnashing his teeth in a savage snarl, he tossed Synnovea away with a sideways heave of his body, curtly rejecting her protection. "You conniving little bitch! Get away from me! Even if these louts mean to skin me alive, I'll take nothing from you, least of all your pity or your shelter! As far as I'm concerned, Ladislaus can have you! With my most earnest blessings!"

Aleksei chortled in uproarious glee as he contemplated her completely astounded visage. " 'Twould seem neither of us wants you anymore, Synnovea," he mocked. "That must be a new revelation for a woman as winsome as you. To have not one but two men reject your attentions. Why, you must be devastated." Wary of drawing near the colonel, he picked up a barn rake and, holding it like a sword, nudged her away from that one. "Now get back and let the fellow be dealt his due. Learn from his example and grit your teeth against the pain of our rejection. Be content that Ladislaus still wants you."

With another imperious nod, Aleksei bade the Goliath to continue, but retreated hastily to a safe distance before the second stroke fell. Blinded by a deluge of tears, Synnovea stumbled away to a dark corner and cringed in silent, agoniz-ing anguish each time the cat-o'-nine-tails made its venging descent. She heard no mumbled plea for mercy issue forth from Tyrone's lips, not even a muffled groan as he hung help-less before the master whip. Yet every blow laid to the stal-wart back ripped through her with equal savagery.

Covering her head with her arms as the scourging contin-ued, Synnovea couldn't still her violent quaking or her re-morseful weeping. Though she had lost count through her own unending torment, she was crushingly aware of the omi-nous repetition of the punishing whip. Each time the lash fell, she cringed in horror, and then shuddered in agonizing dread when the whip was dragged back for yet another blow. The strain seemed beyond her endurance, and her spirit whim-pered beneath the terrible punishment exacted upon her.

Though Tyrone now sagged limply in his fetters and had no strength to lift his head, his valor and spirit hadn't yet been daunted. His display of unyielding tenacity captured the reluctant admiration of those who had sought to deliver their own form of justice upon his frame. Ladislaus and his followers were a band of outlaws who had lived and fought with the smell of death all around them for a good many years. They had taken the worst of what the colonel had given them. Some had died by his sword, but it had been an honorable fate, with weapons in hand. It was in their minds that this stalwart enemy deserved the same consideration. A flogging was what they reserved for whimpering, cowardly dogs, and as they all knew, Colonel Rycroft was a warrior of superior skill and courage. Thus, as a whole, the brigands ceased to enjoy the whipping. Instead, they began to mutter among themselves, growing increasingly agitated as Aleksei pressed for at least a hundred or more lashes. A score and ten strokes from the lash crisscrossed Tyrone's back before the flogging finally ceased, but it was only because the Goliath threw down his whip in disgust and refused to pick it up again.

"Are you mad?" Aleksei railed in outraged astonishment. He was unique among their number in that he suffered no similar convictions of honor and respect but insisted that his revenge be sated to the utmost. "I give the orders here! And **I** say you must carry out the discipline as **I** see fit—or, I swear, you'll not be paid!"

"We've done your service!" Ladislaus roared as he strode forward to confront the prince. "You'll pay us or you'll die!"

Petrov smirked as he drew forth a gleaming blade and twirled the shining tip between his thumb and forefinger. "We take payment from your hide, maybe, just like you mean for the Englishman."

"I'll pay you *after* he's gelded and not one damn minute sooner!" Aleksei declared, too incensed by their lack of commitment to consider the threats they made against him.

"Do it yourself, then!" Ladislaus snarled in derision. "We'll not hurt him anymore for the likes of you! As far as we're concerned, he has paid his due. We're fighting men and give him honor as a swordsman. If you had wanted us to duel with him, then we'd have seen him killed by our blades, but not your way." Contemptuously the brigand jerked his chin outward to indicate the bloodied, lacerated back. "Your way is the penalty for gutless cowards. Outnumbered by scores, the English colonel was taken and abused by your decree, but I tell you this, Boyar, he's more of a man than you'll ever hope to be!"

It was the second time that evening that Aleksei had heard the likes of such a statement. The insult infuriated him all the more. His reddened lips drew back from gnashing teeth for barely a moment. Then, with a savage snarl, he glared around him and cursed them viciously for their refusal to help him. His ire heightened progressively until he whirled and, snatching up a sharp blade, plowed forward to seize the top of the colonel's leggings. Tyrone struggled to protect himself against the mutilation and struck out in defense of himself, but in his much-weakened state, his efforts proved far too feeble.

It was Synnovea who threw herself against Aleksei in a desperate bid to stop him from doing his evil. Even if she must accept the thrust of the blade herself and sacrifice her own life, she was determined to halt his assault. Viciously she clawed at his face and sank her teeth into the hand that held the knife as he tried to yank free of her. A pained yowl curdled upward from Aleksei's throat, but she gave him no heed as she gnashed her teeth tighter against his flesh, drawing blood and forcing his grip to slacken until the blade finally plummeted from his grasp. Snatching herself free, Synnovea stooped to retrieve the weapon, but the dark eyes of her antagonist flared with highly inflamed fury. With a horrendous curse, Aleksei caught her by the wide-spreading cloak and whirled her around with all the strength at his command, in a furious temper flinging her deliberately into a sturdy post.

Jolted nearly senseless by the sudden impact, Synnovea tottered unsteadily away.

Dismissing her with a satisfied smirk, Aleksei caught up the knife again and plunged toward the object of his jealousy, but the carriage house rang with a loud bellow of rage as Ladislaus leapt to Tyrone's rescue and knocked the blade from the prince's hand, sending it skittering across the rough planking of the floorboards.

"No more!" he bellowed. "You've had your bloodletting! Now be content, or I'll see you unmanned myself!"

All reason was sundered beneath the unrestrained fury of Aleksei's indignation, and he gave no thought to backing down in the face of the other's challenge. "You filthy barbarian! How dare you threaten me! Why, I've had better men than you slashed and split in twain for daring to oppose me!"

"You frighten me unduly, my friend," Ladislaus taunted with a smirk and gestured casually over his shoulder as his men gathered close around them. "Perhaps you should consider the error of your ways, since we have no liking for boyars."

Suddenly the stable door burst open, and Ladislaus and his men jerked around in sharp surprise to see Major Nekrasov charge inward, quickly followed by the first thrust of a dozen armed soldiers. Ladislaus immediately recognized the man who led them and the rather resplendent uniforms of the new arrivals and promptly decided the time was critical for him and his men to make their escape. It was one thing to accost a small detachment of soldiers in the wilds, but quite another matter entirely to set themselves against the tsar's imperial guards inside the limits of Moscow, where any number of troops could be waiting to pounce on them. He had no clear opportunity to seize the wench, for he knew from experience that taking her would see him involved in another fray with the major, the likes of which he wished to avoid at the moment. With swift, leaping strides, he raced across the carriage house as he shouted warnings to his compatriots, sending them fleeing in every direction and through any available opening or door. Once outside, they fought their way to their mounts and, after swinging astride, never looked back in their haste to put the gates of the city behind them.

Aleksei was not so astute. He stepped forward to protest this intrusion into his private affairs. Then he stumbled back in stunned awe when he recognized the one who strode through the widening barrier of soldiers. Struck speechless, he fell to his knees before his sovereign lord.

"Your Majesty!" His voice squeaked as it reached a high octave. "What brings you here to my humble house at this late hour?"

"Mischief!" Tsar Mikhail thundered as his dark eyes ranged around the interior. He acknowledged Synnovea's clumsily executed curtsy and briefly noted her bruised face and disheveled appearance before he stepped over to the colonel. Tyrone had lost his tenuous grip on reality and dangled pendulously from the ropes that secured him to the rafters. He was oblivious to the tsar, who winced visibly as he considered the officer's striped and bloody back.

"Cut Colonel Rycroft down from there at once!" Mikhail commanded, gesturing to Major Nekrasov, who ran forward with several other men to lift and loosen the Englishman from his bonds. "Take him to my carriage. He will be tended by my own physicians tonight."

Nikolai glanced yearningly toward Synnovea as his men took up their burden, but she paid him no heed while she gathered up the colonel's clothing. She wept over the bundle for only a moment before handing it to a guard.

"Please be careful with Colonel Rycroft," she pleaded through her tears as they carried him to the door.

Mikhail cocked a curious brow when he noted her concern, and then faced Aleksei with a sharp question. "Did you have some reason for whipping this man?"

"Your pardon, Your Most Sovereign Lordship and Majesty," Aleksei mumbled as he bowed contritely. He spoke discreetly so as not to encourage more of the tsar's disfavor. "We caught Colonel Rycroft at his quarters with our ward, the Countess Zenkovna, and he did indeed defile her in his bed. We could hardly allow his affront to a Russian *boyarina* to go unpunished and were in the process of administering a suitable chastisement."

Mikhail's tone was incredulous. "You consorted with thieves to carry out his punishment?"

"Thieves, Your Majesty? How so?" Aleksei seemed greatly perplexed.

"Didn't you know with whom you were dealing?"

The prince sought to play the innocent. " 'Twas the first time I laid eyes on the men. They said they were for hire, and I engaged them to instruct the colonel on the folly of insulting a Russian maid."

Mikhail scowled in sharp displeasure and turned to peer at the countess, who stood across the breadth of an aisle. She was no longer weeping, but her demeanor indicated that she had been mentally vanquished after witnessing the whipping. "Do you have anything to say in this matter, Synnovea?"

"Your Majesty . . ." She spoke pleadingly from a distance, as if wary of tarnishing his presence with her guilt. "May I be allowed to come forward and speak in the colonel's defense?"

The tsar beckoned her near. "Come, Synnovea. I'm interested in hearing what you have to say."

Going before him, she humbly knelt and refused to lift her eyes as she struggled to cope with the shame of what she had contrived to do and what her deceit had actually brought about. "I beg your most humble pardon, Your Majesty. I'm the one completely at fault for what happened here tonight. I couldn't find it within myself to accept the circumstances of my betrothal to Prince Vladimir Dimitrievich and did intentionally entice Colonel Rycroft to take me into his bed. I preferred to forfeit my virtue rather than be bound to the contract of marriage that had been arranged for me. Do with me as you may, Your Majesty, for I am surely guilty of this havoc which has befallen the colonel. I didn't mean for him to be caught and chastised. It would have been better if I had been whipped."

"I'm sure Colonel Rycroft would have found it hard to resist you, considering your beauty and his great desire to court you, Synnovea." As Mikhail voiced his observations, he lifted his consideration to the prince. That one offered no explanation for the betrothal, though Mikhail was sure that everyone within his court knew he was seriously pondering the Englishman's request to court the countess. Either his cousin and her husband had been totally deaf to the winds of gossip or they had chosen to dismiss his consideration of a foreigner.

Mikhail looked down upon the bowed head of his subject and gently laid a hand upon the disarrayed curls. "I will talk more of this with you and the colonel, Synnovea. You may arrange a time to see me two days hence, but for now, I would have you find safety beyond this house. Is there someone to whom you can go?"

"Countess Andreyevna is a very close friend of mine, Your Majesty. My coach may be waiting even now to take me back to her home."

"Excellent! Then go! And mind you, speak no word of this matter to anyone. I'd be averse to having the anger of the boyars aroused against the colonel. Nor would I see you harmed by wagging tongues. Do you understand?"

"Your kindness is beyond measure, Your Majesty."

When Synnovea had gone, Mikhail faced Aleksei with a stiff smile. "Where is my cousin anyway? I would have a word with her."

"Anna is not here, Most Sovereign Lord. Her father was ailing and asked her to come and stay with him for a time."

"Should I, then, believe that this matter rests solely upon your shoulders?"

Aleksei gulped and tried to recoup his scattered wits as he carefully asked, "What matter do you mean, Your Worship?"

"Did you not make arrangements for the betrothal between Countess Synnovea and Prince Vladimir Dimitrievich while you had full knowledge of the colonel's interest in courting her? Or should the blame be laid solely upon Anna?"

Aleksei spread his hands in a helpless quandary. "Of course we heard of the colonel's interest, but we weren't aware that we had to give a foreigner serious heed. At the time, it seemed prudent to arrange a marriage between the girl and Prince Vladimir, considering the old man's wealth and the fact that he would treat Synnovea kindly. At least, Anna thought so."

"I see." Mikhail pursed his lips as he pondered the prince's answer. "And did Anna not hear of my considerations toward the colonel?"

"What considerations are those, Your Majesty?" The dark brows came together as Aleksei feigned bemusement. "Have we erred in some way and offended Our Supreme Highness?"

"It could be," Mikhail retorted angrily. The other man apparently thought he could be fooled by a guise of innocence, but he wasn't that gullible. " 'Twould seem that I erred in sending Countess Synnovea here to be my cousin's ward. I should have given more consideration to the fact that the girl was raised unfettered by most of the strictures of other *boyarinas*. In view of her upbringing, 'tis understandable that she felt compelled to rebel when you arranged such a betrothal for her. That matter is of no consequence now. You'll discreetly inform Prince Dimitrievich that Countess Synnovea is unable to marry him for the simple reason that I have decreed otherwise. I must warn you that if you spread one word of this affair involving the colonel beyond Vladimir, who hopefully is wise enough to keep silent, I shall personally be in attendance when your tongue is detached from the place where it now resides. Do you have any questions?"

"None, Your Most Gracious Worship. I shall be completely reticent concerning this matter." Extremely anxious to placate the tsar, Aleksei bowed several times to lend emphasis to his ingratiating show of respect.

"Good! Then we understand each other."

"Most affirmatively, Your Majesty."

"Then I shall say good night and farewell, Prince Taraslov. I hope you'll never again be so foolish as to address your venom upon someone to whom I have given favor, nor hire thieves to see such mischief done. I've yet to judge you on the truth of this affair, but I'm patient enough to see justice carefully preserved until I am otherwise persuaded. For your sake, I hope you're innocent of deliberately consorting with thieves, because if you're not, I'll see that you receive a harsher sentence than any of your cohorts."

With that, the tsar stalked out of the carriage house, leaving Aleksei unusually pale and haggard-looking.

13

Synnovea arrived at the Palace of Facets much earlier than the time designated for her appointment with His Majesty Mikhail Romanov, the Tsar of all the Russias. It was exactly twoscore hours after His Royal Highness had first bidden the countess to come and see him, and though her apprehensions hadn't been alleviated by even the slightest degree, she was nevertheless the very essence of serene beauty as she waited outside his private offices. Not only did she appear composed and sweetly demure in a mauve *sarafan* and beribboned *kokoshniki,* but she gave every indication that she was content with her summons. But then, she had little choice after making a decision to set the record straight about what she had done.

It was here that Synnovea became a compassionate witness to the carefully executed entrance of Colonel Rycroft. His movements were slow and painfully stiff, but only the slightest grimace could be noted by the one who watched him move away from the doorway. The antechamber was narrow enough that he couldn't miss seeing her. At first, his only indication at having done so was a brief upward flick of a tawny brow. Then his scowl deepened and his jaw tightened beneath tensely flexing muscles. Disinclined to take a chair, he stood ramrod-straight while he stared stoically toward the entrance to the tsar's chambers. Synnovea had never seen such a tenacious stance, but the message he conveyed was clear. He was loath to even acknowledge her proximity.

Some moments later, Major Nekrasov came out to escort the colonel into the tsar's presence, and in the stark solitude following Tyrone's passage, Synnovea was reminded of the contempt she had heard in his voice shortly before the first stroke of the whip. He had thrust her away in distaste and given his hearty approval for Ladislaus to take her for his own, confirming Natasha's warnings that he would come to hate her for her coyly contrived entrapment. The knowledge of his vehement rejection now evoked within her a gloomy regret for which she could find no assuagement. So bleak were her hopes to reconcile herself to him that it wouldn't have surprised Synnovea at all to hear the objections which the Englishman was presently voicing in response to the tsar's suggestions.

"I plead your pardon, Your Majesty, but I must respectfully decline." Tyrone tried to check his darkly brooding vexation, but it was impossible for him to even consider such a proposal. "I could never take the Countess Zenkovna as my wife after she used me for her own end. If, in the months and years to come, my life's blood is required upon a field of battle, then I hope it will be spilled honorably as a soldier in your service, but your recommendation is too much to ask of me."

"I fear you've mistaken my words, Colonel Rycroft." Mikhail smiled benignly. "I don't request your compliance with my proposition. While you're here in this country, you'll obey my every directive. It's my express wish that you take Synnovea to wife with all possible haste. I promised her father before his death that I would see to the welfare of his daughter. I would be lax in the performance of that pledge if I allowed you to escape your personal participation in this affair without seeking some remuneration for what has been done."

"Was not the scarring of my back enough punishment for my involvement?" Tyrone asked bluntly.

"The whipping was indeed dreadful, but it hardly corrects the problem. Synnovea has confessed her guilt in deliberately seeking you out to be her champion of sorts." Mikhail glanced up briefly as a faintly audible snort came from the colonel. After musing briefly on the disdain visible in the man's visage, he continued with unswerving dedication to his proposal. "Nevertheless, you were the one who accomplished her deflowering and are the only one who can properly amend the situation. After all, you're no young whelp who can plead innocence. You're old enough to accept the consequences of your actions and, may I presume, far more knowledgeable about this matter than the maid. 'Tis obvious she had good reason to believe you were willing to bed her or she would never have considered her defilement by you a viable option . . . which causes me to think that surreptitiously you had already begun courting the maid. Is that not true?"

Tyrone's face darkened to a ruddy hue. "I saw her several times, but for the most part, Princess Anna denied my requests."

"Did you take it upon yourself to see the girl in private?"

Most reluctantly, the colonel admitted that fact. "I did, Your Majesty."

"And were you successful?"

"Aye."

"Where did this tryst take place?"

"In her bedchamber at the Taraslovs'."

337

"And did Synnovea invite you in?"

"No, Your Majesty. I climbed through a window after I had awakened her."

Mikhail was aghast at the man's audacity. "And if you had been caught and been forced to pay penance, would you have claimed that the girl had deliberately enticed you into her chambers?"

"No, Your Majesty. She had cautioned me to leave."

"Well, there you have it!" Mikhail threw up a hand, indicating the matter settled.

Tyrone was not so willing to accept defeat. "Your Majesty, will you not kindly ponder my position?"

Mikhail was losing patience with the persistence of the man. "Was Synnovea not a virgin ere you took her into your bed?"

Tyrone's lean cheeks flexed tensely with the effort of keeping his temper under tight rein. "She was a virgin, but—"

"Then there is no more to be said! I wouldn't have another man mend your wrongs because you were duped by a young chit! Would you roar deception on a field of battle if you were tricked by a general whose face still bore the fuzz of his youth?"

"No, of course not, but—"

Mikhail slammed his open palm down upon the arm of his chair. "Either you'll marry Synnovea or, by heaven, I'll see you discharged without honor from your service here!"

In the face of such a threat, Tyrone could only yield to the monarch's authority. He abruptly clicked his heels as he gave the tsar a crisp salute. "As you so deign, Your Majesty."

Mikhail reached up and jerked on a silken cord, bringing Major Nekrasov quickly back into the chamber. "You may escort the Countess Zenkovna into my presence now."

Tyrone dared to interrupt, bringing the major to a halt as he made another plea. "I beg a moment more of your time, Your Majesty."

Mikhail was immediately skeptical of what the colonel would request. "Yes? What is it?"

"I shall abide by your order as long as I am here, Your Majesty, but once I leave, I'll no longer be under your authority." Tyrone paused as the tsar inclined his head in cautious agreement and then continued in a respectful tone. "If you should determine at that time that I have pleased you in the performance of my duties and have held myself away from Synnovea, which may be confirmed by her inability to produce an heir of mine, will you grant me an annulment from this marriage ere I return to England?"

Major Nekrasov's head snapped around, and he glanced between the two men, feeling horrendously distraught by the fact that Synnovea would be marrying another. Knowing he would have gladly endangered his own life in his quest to have her as his wife, he couldn't even begin to understand the colonel's request.

Mikhail was abruptly taken aback by the Englishman's petition, but he could find no viable way to refuse. If the dissolution wasn't granted here within the boundaries of Russia, the colonel would likely seek it in England. Mikhail would not tolerate a Russian countess being subjected to that kind of humiliation in a foreign land. "If all will be as you say near the time of your departure, and you still wish such a separation, then I shall grant your petition. But I must remind you that you still have three years to serve under my authority."

"Three years, three months, and two days, sire."

"That is an extremely long time to withhold yourself from so enchanting a woman, Colonel. Can you even consider being successful in that endeavor?"

Tyrone faced the question frankly in his own mind. He had no firm assurance that he'd be able to ignore Synnovea as his wife during the full extent of that time or even that he'd be able to curb his desires for her once the pain of her deceit subsided to a more tolerable level, but he had to leave open an option wherein their marriage could be dissolved should he find no further reason to continue with her. At the moment, with so much anger roiling within him, he was hell-bent to go his own way without her, but there was always the possibility that his mood in time would soften toward her. As the tsar had unerringly pointed out, Synnovea was as enchanting as she was beautiful, and when it had obviously been his foolish desire to trust her, he couldn't promise with unswerving finality that he'd never fall victim to her siren's song again. Then, too, his heart might never recover from the wounds she had inflicted upon him.

"My failure or success will be revealed prior to my departure, Your Majesty. You may take full account of the condition of our marriage at such a time. Until then, I'll make no guarantees, for I cannot in truth deny my zeal to have her before she played me for a fool."

"I will hope by that time that your heart will be softened by forgiveness, Colonel." Mikhail sighed. "I cannot imagine such a beautiful woman being ignored by her husband. I once considered taking Synnovea for a bride myself, but I didn't think she'd be able to abide the stricture of a *terem*. I'd be appalled to see her hurt by your rejection of her."

"You may save her both the pain and the humiliation of our annulment by allowing us to go our separate ways now," Tyrone suggested, peering at the tsar from beneath his brows.

"Never!" Mikhail flung himself from his chair in a fitful rage. "By heaven, Colonel, you'll not maneuver your way out of this marriage! Indeed, I'll see you wed before the week is out!"

Tyrone was wise enough to know when he had been defeated and immediate obeisance was advisable. Clasping a hand to his chest, he bowed stiffly before the Russian tsar though the agony of his movement nearly splintered his control. "As you deem fit, sire."

Mikhail gave a crisp nod to Major Nekrasov, who made

an about-face to carry out his order. As Nikolai entered the antechamber, he managed a wan smile as he approached the woman he both admired and cherished.

"Tsar Mikhail will see you now, Lady Synnovea."

A hesitant smile touched her lips as she rose to her feet. "I thought I heard shouting. Is His Majesty very angry?"

"Surely not with you, dearest Synnovea," Nikolai assured her.

"Did he say why he wanted to see me?" she asked uneasily.

"I wasn't permitted to stay in the room while he spoke with Colonel Rycroft. You'll have to ask His Majesty."

"I never thought I'd anger so many people by what I did . . . ." Her words trailed off when she realized that Nikolai was regarding her quizzically.

"And what may that have been, my lady?"

Synnovea lowered her eyes hurriedly to avoid meeting his gaze any longer than she had to. " 'Twas nothing I'm proud of, Nikolai, and if you wouldn't mind, I'd rather not speak of the matter, for the memory of my deeds pains me sorely." Recalling that she had not thanked him for what he had accomplished by coming to the colonel's rescue, she laid a trembling hand upon his and looked up at him. "I shall be eternally grateful for your help in rescuing Colonel Rycroft, Nikolai. I never dreamt that you'd actually bring Tsar Mikhail with you. However did you manage such a feat?"

"I did nothing more than tell His Majesty that the colonel was in danger. After that, he took matters into his own hands. The Englishman had already won the tsar's favor and respect by his own merits. Quite clearly, 'twas that fact alone which prompted his Highness to fly to his side." Nikolai glanced askance toward the chamber wherein the tsar held unofficial court and hastened to advise, "We mustn't delay any longer, my lady. Tsar Mikhail is waiting to speak with you."

Synnovea took a deep breath, hoping to settle her restive

nerves, and entered upon the major's arm. Her gaze flitted about the large room until she found Tyrone standing at attention just to the left of the tsar's chair. He made no attempt to glance around in her direction but maintained his stoic reticence as Mikhail beckoned her forward. Drawing near, she sank into a deep curtsy and waited in trembling silence while Major Nekrasov took his leave.

"Synnovea, I have made several decisions concerning your future," His Majesty announced. "I hope you'll not find them too burdensome."

"Your will is my command, Your Majesty," Synnovea answered, her voice declining in strength until her last words were barely audible. She had no idea what lay in store for her, but she was resolved to find no fault with what was commanded of her. At the very least she expected to be sent to a monastery.

"I have decreed that you and the colonel shall wed. . . ."

Astounded by his revelation, Synnovea jerked her head up to stare at him. Then, just as quickly, she looked around to see Tyrone's response. He stood ramrod-straight and stubbornly refused to meet her shocked gaze, though the muscles in his sun-bronzed cheeks tensed and flexed in his attempt to check any outward show of abhorrence.

". . . Before the week is out," Mikhail continued, allowing her hardly enough time to catch her breath. "You'll be married in my presence day after the morrow. That should give you both time to decide several matters concerning your quarters. 'Tis unthinkable that a Russian *boyarina* should live in the German district. Therefore, Synnovea, you may ask the Countess Andreyevna if she will accommodate your new marital status as a personal favor to me. Assuming that she'll agree, I'll deem the matter already settled. Once the ceremony has been concluded, you and Colonel Rycroft may celebrate as you see fit. I'm sure Natasha would enjoy making much of the occasion, and though the colonel is still indisposed with his back, I would urge you both to participate in such a way as to make it seem a festive occasion to alleviate the possibility of damaging rumors being circulated among my boyars. It isn't often that the Tsar of all the Russias personally initiates the union of two of his favored subjects. You may consider my attention in this affair as a personal compliment to you both. To celebrate, I shall order a midday banquet to be held here in the palace soon after the nuptials are performed. Now, are there any concerns you wish to voice?" He waited as each made a negative reply, and then smiled as he bade, "Then you may go."

Together they paid homage, Synnovea with a sweeping curtsy and the colonel by a painfully executed bow. Tyrone shifted his gaze in her direction, briefly assessing the beauty of his intended, but without word or other form of acknowledgment, he turned crisply to make his exit from the room.

"Colonel Rycroft." Mikhail's voice brought that one to an abrupt halt. "I hope you'll consider how fortunate you are to be gaining such a winsome bride and treat her accordingly. Is it not proper for a gentleman of your country to graciously escort his betrothed upon his arm and make a show of cherishing her, especially while there is an audience in attendance? If there is no such requirement in your country, then I shall deem that circumstances warrant such care here in this land. Do I make myself clear, Colonel?"

"Absolutely, Your Majesty," Tyrone replied succinctly and, stepping beside the countess, stiltedly presented his arm as he faced the door.

Synnovea could sense his roiling displeasure at having to extend any show of chivalry toward her and found it terribly ironic that he had come to loathe her, while she, during either her contrived seduction or her initiation into sensual pleasures, had fallen under the colonel's bewitchment and was now thoroughly infatuated with the very one she had singled out to be her victim.

"Is your coach still outside?" Tyrone inquired as they entered the antechamber.

"Yes," she answered softly, "but you needn't escort me out if you find the task too burdensome."

"I've been ordered by Tsar Mikhail to show you favor," Tyrone jeered icily, "at least while we have an audience. Until we find ourselves alone, I'll try to comply with the directive he has given. 'Twould seem I've little choice if I want to leave here in good graces with His Majesty."

Tyrone came to abrupt attention as the field marshal strolled through the front door. With a crisply executed salute, the colonel greeted the Russian, who passed them with a casual wave. No movement came from Tyrone as the man departed, and Synnovea glanced up to find her escort standing in rigid silence. The color had drained from his face, and the muscles in his lean cheeks had tightened to an intensity that clearly conveyed the fact that he was silently enduring a moment of intense pain.

"Are you all right?" she whispered in concern.

He nodded rigidly and, with a slight twitch of his shoulders, reclaimed tenacious control of his bearing. But now he moved at a much more deliberate pace as they passed through the front portal.

Managing the steps with only a wince or two, Tyrone handed her into the waiting coach and, closing the door, stepped back with an abbreviated gesture to Stenka. As the conveyance rumbled away from the palace, Synnovea leaned back against the seat, biting a quavering lip and squeezing her eyelids tightly shut against the tears that flooded upward within her. Despite her effort to stem the tide, they trickled down her cheeks in widening channels. One could say she had made her bed and now would have to lie in it, but it gave her no pleasure to think that there was so much resentment bound up in the man who was about to become her husband.

When the carriage arrived at the Andreyevna mansion a

short time later, Natasha was at the front portal, anxiously awaiting her return. Synnovea choked out a lame excuse and, with an unchecked torrent of tears, rushed past the woman. Once she gained the safety of her chambers, she found herself confronted by Ali and a barrage of dismayed questions.

"Oh, me lamb! Me lamb! What has broken yer heart so?"

Bidding the maid to leave her, Synnovea fell across the bed and sobbed in bleak misery until she felt totally drained of emotion. The delicate eyelids grew swollen and seemed to scratch her eyes as she sought sleep as an escape from her anguish, but such a respite was not within reach. Thus, for a time she stared listlessly toward the window, dismally taking distant note of the brightly colored leaves fluttering to earth beyond the panes of glass. Sometime later, a light rap came upon the door of the anteroom, and in solemn dejection Synnovea went to let Natasha into the chambers.

"I couldn't wait a moment longer." The woman searched the reddened eyes with grave concern as she begged excusal for the interruption. "Dear child, what has happened to bring you to this end? Have you been banished from court?" A lame shake of the beautiful dark head gave tacit answer. "Denounced by the tsar?" A slash of a slender hand negated such an idea. "Sentenced to a nunnery?"

"Not anything so trivial," Synnovea whispered miserably.

Natasha lost her aplomb. Catching the girl by the shoulders, she shook her as she demanded in desperation, "Good heavens, child! What has His Majesty decreed your sentence to be?"

Synnovea gulped back another torrent of tears and carefully pronounced each word as she gathered them together in a strained reply. "His Majesty, Tsar Mikhail, has ordained that Colonel Rycroft should marry me ere the week is out."

"What?" Natasha almost shrieked the word out in sudden jubilation. "Oh, great sainted mother! How could he have been so clever?"

Synnovea frowned at her friend through a new wealth of tears. "You don't understand, Natasha. Colonel Rycroft hates me, just as you said he would. He wants nothing to do with me, and he's especially loath to take me to wife."

"Oh, my dear child, lay aside your grief and dismay," the older woman cajoled. "Don't you see the way of it? The colonel's anger will surely soften in time. A man can hardly ignore a woman who is his wife."

"He detests me! He loathes me!" Synnovea declared glumly as she returned to her bedchamber. "He didn't even want to escort me from the palace! 'Twas only by the tsar's mandate that he did so."

"He will change," Natasha reassured her enthusiastically, following in her wake. "When are the nuptials?"

"Day after tomorrow. His Majesty also asked if you'd consent to let us both stay here with you."

Natasha chortled as she stroked a finger thoughtfully across her chin. "Never let it be said that Tsar Mikhail isn't shrewd and wise enough to handle Russia's affairs on his own. Why, just by this edict alone he has shown his ability to manage matters wisely." She smiled into Synnovea's teary eyes and tried to encourage her. "For a time your rage and aversion to each other will punish you both, but when your anger has been spent . . ." She lifted her shoulders in a lighthearted shrug. "Only God can foresee the end of all things, my dear. We can only bide our time and hope for the best."

Natasha returned to the anteroom and opened the outer door, where Ali was still anxiously fretting. The elder's sad eyes and deeply wrinkled countenance evidenced the distress she was presently suffering. Natasha smiled down at the servant and, taking the frail hand into hers, drew Ali into the bedchamber, where her mistress sat staring dejectedly out the window.

"You'll never guess, Ali," Natasha said in a cheery tone.

"Colonel Rycroft has been commanded by the tsar to take your mistress to wife."

The wispy brows jutted upward in surprise as Ali glanced toward Synnovea. "Ye don't say!"

"Ah, but I do," Natasha reassured her. "In fact, they're to be wed day after the morrow."

"So soon?" Ali squinted up at her in surprise. "Are ye sure?"

"Your mistress has said as much herself."

"Then why is me lamb so put out?" Ali was genuinely perplexed, for she couldn't understand why any woman would grieve about her forthcoming marriage to such a fine specimen of a man.

"A mystery, to be sure, but her lamentations are bound to turn to joy, do you not agree, Ali?" Natasha paused briefly to receive the tiny woman's eager nod. " 'Twill only be a matter of time. But we must plan a celebration to mark the event! The colonel must encourage his friends to come, while we shall invite our own." Natasha laughed with the sheer excitement of it and clapped her hands together in glee. "I'm almost tempted to ask Aleksei to the nuptials just to see him suffer, but I fear his presence would only provoke the colonel, and we cannot have that." Natasha leaned near the widely grinning servant as she continued to voice an avalanche of conjectures. "Of course, you know Princess Anna will probably be utterly devastated when she returns to find the couple already wed. When last I saw her, she was absolutely in a snit over Colonel Rycroft petitioning the tsar for Synnovea's hand. If not for her, the couple might have already been wed."

"Go away, the two of you!" Synnovea groaned in wretched misery. "You're both making light of all of this, but I'm so distraught I shan't able to sleep for a whole year!"

"Then we'll leave you to mourn in solitude," Natasha replied, completely bereft of sympathy. "Ali and I will be happy to do all the planning while you're indisposed." She paused in the anteroom to glance back at the younger woman. "Where are the vows to be spoken? Did you think about that?"

"His Majesty made the decision for us. They're to be said in his presence at the palace."

Natasha again clapped her hands together in glee, like a small child anticipating a confection. "Then we'll have to find you a rich gown to wear in honor of the occasion. You must look your best for both the tsar and the colonel."

"I don't think either of them will care what I look like, especially the colonel," Synnovea retorted morosely.

"Nevertheless, you must be outfitted in a grand manner if you're to arouse a warm response from your groom."

Ali was eager to report, "Me mistress had settled on a *sarafan* for her wedding to Prince Dimitrievich. 'Tis prettier than anything she can have made or perhaps find in so short a time. 'Twill do her justice, a pink one nearly as comely as she."

"The day will be fair," Natasha proclaimed, heaving a contented sigh, "and the bride shall be absolutely breathtaking. . . ."

Absolutely breathtaking! Major Nekrasov mused after witnessing Synnovea's entrance into the palace's antechamber. She had entered with the two older women fussing attentively over her costume as they followed closely behind. Her *sarafan* of heavy, pale pink satin was beautiful beyond compare. The long, slightly flaring sleeves and lower skirt were embellished with elaborate scrolls of gold-silk stitchery and masses of tiny pearls. Lending immeasurable elegance to her appearance was the elaborate *kokoshniki* which was encrusted with the same lustrous jewels interspersed with tiny loops of delicately corded pink satin. Strings of delicate seed pearls hung in a generous fringe over her forehead to a length that all but brushed the sweeping eyebrows. The dainty tassels swayed gently with her movements, and though no further ornament was needed to emphasize the stirring splendor of her face, pearl teardrops hung from delicate diamond clusters that adorned her earlobes. She was so radiant that Nikolai was wont to believe that the tiny flames dancing atop the tapers bowed in humble awe. Indeed, her beauty was such that even a reluctant bridegroom would be bedazzled, for no man could turn a cold shoulder to such perfection. As for himself, Nikolai knew he'd always be smitten, though his heart pined in remorse at the realization that another man would soon be claiming her for his own.

At the bride's entrance, a sudden hush fell over the guests as they stared in awe of her beauty. Just as quickly, there arose a low drone of murmuring comments attesting to their admiration. Tyrone had been conversing with Grigori and had his back to the door, but even he could not resist a surreptitious perusal over his shoulder. After all the ire he had been contending with since his whipping, he hadn't expected his heart to lurch within his chest or the slow, sinking feeling in the pit of his belly as his eyes fed upon her beauty. Truly, if men had the ability to sense defeat prior to its occurrence, then Tyrone Rycroft had his first inkling of it as he stared at his bride-to-be. He didn't know the day or the hour that it would come upon him, but he'd face it fairly soon, definitely well before the time he was due to leave Russia.

Both Grigori and Nikolai became immediately mindful of Tyrone's close inspection, which was far more exacting than the colonel's mood of angry reticence seemed to support. Their reactions, however, contrasted. Though a smile traced across Grigori's lips, a sharp frown creased the major's brows.

Natasha had bade Synnovea to halt soon after her entrance, and at the time of her bridegroom's inspection, she was standing obediently still as the older countess and Ali straightened her gown and smoothed down the hem, which had been turned up by her departure from the coach. When the women stepped back to search for other flaws, Synnovea found a chance to glance around the room and readily smiled at friends and acquaintances who beckoned to her, but her heart began to thump with a swifter rhythm when her gaze paused on the one whose attention seemed riveted on her. The blue orbs were moving with slow, meticulous deliberation over the length of her, but the flaming heat, which had briefly warmed them, vanished abruptly when their gazes finally met. Of a sudden, Synnovea found herself staring into cool shards of blue. With no more than a brief nod, Tyrone turned aside as if to deny his close perusal. His readily assumed guise of coldly forbidding detachment was enough to drain the rosy hue from Synnovea's cheeks, and though she stood helplessly admiring his handsome profile, she was left with the realization that his anger had abated no tiny degree.

"Your bride is beautiful beyond words, my friend," Grigori observed, feeling a strong sense of loyalty and compassion for his commander but also some empathy for the girl, who had been caught between two men who desired her. He had seen the colonel's lacerated back for himself and knew more than most what the man had suffered at the command of Prince Aleksei, who, Tyrone had grudgingly admitted, had ordered the punishment done because of his own jealous rage. "After your diligent pleas to the tsar, are you not happy to win the countess for yourself?"

"She is indeed beautiful," Tyrone acknowledged distantly, refusing to comment on his emotions. It was true that his pride had been stung by the fiery nettles of her deceit, but when she hadn't felt enough regard for him to care what he might have suffered because of her gambit, then he had forseen no hope of her ever yielding him anything that remotely resembled love.

" 'Tis obvious poor Nikolai is lamenting the tsar's decision," Grigori prodded gently. "You could have been standing in his stead right now if His Majesty had favored his own countryman's request above yours."

Tyrone cast a glance askance toward the major. The Russian stared at Synnovea longingly, his distress clearly evident, his pain acute. But then, it was no less than his own, Tyrone concluded. "Aye, and if not for me, he could have been suffering in my stead."

Grigori looked at his superior sharply. "Do you speak of your wounds, Colonel?"

Tyrone's eyebrows twitched upward briefly in mute response. Even as close a friend as Grigori wouldn't understand his plight if he voiced his complaints about being forced to marry such a beautiful woman.

Princess Zelda Pavlovna made her way hurriedly through the cluster of people and, with a buoyant smile, embraced Synnovea before stepping back and clasping the girl's slender hands within her own. "Oh, I'm so happy for you, my dear. I never dreamed Colonel Rycroft would be successful in winning you for his bride."

"I'm relieved to see you here, Zelda," Synnovea assured her friend, avoiding any comment on the victory which the colonel could supposedly claim. "I was afraid with the suddenness of the affair, that you and your husband wouldn't be able to attend."

"Vassili will join us later, my dear, and begs your forgiveness for not being able to attend the wedding. He had to meet with the field marshal again, but if I may be so bold as to repeat his comments on His Majesty's haste to see you and the colonel wed, Vassili said no other foreigner has endeared himself to the tsar as much as your groom. Tsar Mikhail has definitely bestowed a great honor upon the colonel by giving you to him."

"Vassili is most kind," Synnovea replied graciously, though she seriously doubted that Tyrone would view their marriage as anything but a harsh reprimand for having foolishly become her dupe. She just hoped the Pavlovs wouldn't be too shocked or repulsed by her actions if they ever learned the truth.

As Zelda moved away to talk with other friends, a directive came for the wedding party and its guests to join Tsar Mikhail and the priest in the chapel. In compliance with the summons, Tyrone approached his bride and stiltedly presented his arm.

The weight on Synnovea's heart seemed to drag her spirits down into a darker gloom as she considered her bridegroom's aloofness. Her delay in accepting his offer caused him to lift a challenging brow as he peered at her askance.

"Afraid, Countess?"

"Of you, yes," she admitted in a wavering whisper.

His smile was terse at best. "You needn't be, my dear. At least you can be assured that I intend no similar punishment for what I've had to endure because of you."

His statement was hardly encouraging, and in undiminished dismay Synnovea laid a trembling hand upon the sleeve of his dark blue doublet and moved along beside him as their guests fell in behind them.

Synnovea felt strangely detached from the ceremony, as if she wandered aimlessly through a shadowy fog somewhere beyond the room into which she had been led. She was distantly aware of her groom sometimes standing or at other times kneeling beside her, of his brown hand taking her thin fingers within his grasp and sliding a large signet ring upon her first, of his lips lowering dutifully upon her own as a token of his affection. Feeling rather overwhelmed by his tall, manly presence and then, just as certainly, by his abrupt withdrawal, Synnovea closed her mouth, realizing that it had opened shakily beneath his. Her cheeks flamed at what seemed a blunt rejection of her unconscious response, and as Tyrone stepped back, she cast her eyes away, afraid that she'd see some evidence of ridicule or repugnance in his gaze.

Mikhail came forward with a smile and bestowed his good

wishes upon the couple before he looked pointedly at the colonel. "Your bride's beauty is beyond the measure of most women, Colonel Rycroft. You should be grateful for such a one. Your offspring will naturally be handsome. They cannot help but be. I hope you give careful consideration to that possibility before you commit yourself to the folly of your proposal. In light of your anger, I shan't hold you to anything, except to say that my promise has been solemnly vowed, and I will not retract it. In other words, Colonel, you have my leave to enjoy yourself completely if you so choose. You need no further audience with me to be assured of that."

Tyrone's face took on a ruddy hue, the only hint of the carefully masked emotions roiling within him. He was aware that his bride had become genuinely perplexed by the tsar's comments, but he had no wish to relieve her confusion. He could only utter a muted answer to the monarch. "You are as gracious as always, Your Majesty."

Mikhail turned to face his guests. "Please join us as we toast the joining of this couple with wine and food."

The tsar took the honored seat at the head of the table and, as he bade the bride and groom to take their places, swept his hand to indicate the chairs on either side of him. After their marriage and several tributes to the pair were sanctioned by the lifting of goblets and a hearty chorus of agreements, servants began to offer lavish platters of meats and accompanying dishes to their sovereign lord and his guests. Synnovea found her own appetite sorely lacking and picked at her food while Mikhail questioned Tyrone about his intentions to go after Ladislaus once his back had properly healed. Giving the excuse that the foray was still in the planning stage, the colonel refrained from laying out definite details about his intended raid, but assured his host that whenever he set himself to the mission, he'd bring the thief back or die trying.

It was some time before Mikhail glanced around and noticed the absence of Tyrone's immediate superior. Turning back to the officer with a curious smile, he queried, "But where is General Vanderhout and his wife?"

Tyrone's gaze lowered to his plate as if he contemplated what succulent morsel to sample next. "It didn't seem suitable to invite them, Your Majesty, considering the fact that I am but a lowly colonel and he a general."

"*A lowly colonel?*" For a moment Mikhail chortled and seemed highly amused by the lame excuse the Englishman had offered him. Then he grew progressively suspicious, until he was motivated to ask, "Is that what General Vanderhout called you?"

"If you don't mind, Your Majesty, I'd rather not say," Tyrone answered with careful diplomacy.

The tsar wouldn't let him off so easily. "When did the general call you that?"

Tyrone was growing immensely sorry he had repeated the derogatory slur. "I'm afraid it was when I refused to accept the duties that General Vanderhout tried to assign to me."

"But why did you refuse?"

Tyrone chafed uncomfortably. "Because I wanted to attend Countess Andreyevna's soiree."

"And that soiree was where you visited Synnovea before your confrontation with Prince Taraslov?"

"Yes, Your Majesty," Tyrone rejoined, casting a glance across the table at his bride, who had stopped eating altogether. Her cheeks flamed beneath his brief regard, but the color in his own came close to matching hers when the tsar offered a supposition.

"Considering your years as a dedicated soldier, you must have been anxious to see Synnovea if you refused a direct order from your superior."

The colonel was aware of the monarch's close scrutiny, and though he felt compelled to answer, he did so in a hushed tone. "I was, Your Majesty."

"Adamant to meet Synnovea, you mean?" Mikhail prodded.

"Yes," Tyrone reluctantly acknowledged.

The tsar smiled in pleasure. "You have good taste, Colonel, and in the weeks and years to come, I hope you don't lose sight of what you were willing to sacrifice just to be with Synnovea."

The gentle chiding brought Tyrone the curious regard of his bride, but as yet, he could offer nothing more than a brief glance in response. Meeting those wide green-brown eyes had suddenly become a labor he wished to avoid.

Finally the couple were being escorted to her coach, and with stilted decorum Tyrone handed his bride into the interior and took his place beside her. Natasha had instructed Stenka to take the long way around so the guests could arrive before the bride and groom, and it proved a lengthy ordeal indeed for the two ensconced in the coach. The groom sat on the far side of the seat from his bride, as if she were something tainted he wished to avoid. His eyes were partially masked by heavy lids as he braced his chin on a lean knuckle and glowered out the window. After the need for proper decorum had been dispensed with, his brows gathered and his crisply chiseled jaw flexed with angry tension. Synnovea's tentative glances lent no hope that her husband's mood would improve once they reached their destination. Indeed, his angry reticence allowed her no smallest glimmer of optimism for their life together.

Carriages were still being unloaded in front of the house when Stenka pulled the team to a halt near the approach to the drive and waited for a chance to deliver his mistress and her new husband directly before the stoop. After a pelting rain during the night and the passage of so many conveyances, the lane had become a veritable avenue of endless muck. It didn't take long for the rear wheels of the coach to become firmly mired in the stiff sludge. Despite Stenka's best attempts to rally the horses to such a strenuous feat, the conveyance refused to budge.

Tyrone was hardly in a mood to wait until another team could be brought around to lend their strength to the four-in-hand. Stepping down into the well-churned road, he gestured for Synnovea to move near the door and, when she cautiously complied, lifted her within his arms. Considering the aversion he was wont to display toward her, she was painfully flustered by his assistance and had no idea where to put her arms. A brief moment later she felt his booted feet slip in the sludge, and with a sudden gasp of alarm, she flung them about his neck, fearing he'd drop her into the filth just to vent his rage upon her.

Tyrone read her trepidation only too well and deigned to meet her worried gaze with a sardonic quirk slanting his brow. "Truly tempting, my dear, but hardly chivalrous of a groom, do you not agree?"

"Just put me down," she urged testily, well aware of the distance between herself and safety. "I can make my own way to the house."

"What? In the mud?" he scoffed with a humorless laugh. "Now *that* would be something for our guests to see, truly a fine demonstration of the groom's affection."

"What do you care about them?"

"Unfortunately, I've been ordered to maintain a festive mood," he retorted. "Otherwise I'd dump you here and be done with you."

Synnovea struggled briefly in his arms, but he tightened his grip until she was forced to relent. When his long, steely fingers continued to dig into her ribs, causing her to squirm uncomfortably beneath the pressure, she was forced to complain. "You're hurting me."

"Am I?" Tyrone smiled blandly and loosened his grasp. "You must excuse me, madam. Sometimes I don't know my own strength."

"I think it was deliberate," she accused. "Perhaps part of the retribution you said you wouldn't seek."

His harsh smile clearly conveyed the fact that he didn't give a damn what she thought. "To a tiny degree, perhaps, but certainly nothing to equal what I'm really feeling toward you."

"Why don't you just have me flogged and be done with it!" Synnovea challenged acidly. "Perhaps that would assuage your anger some small whit."

"I'd never tarnish a form as fair and alluring as yours, madam. As your husband, 'twould be the same as spiting myself."

Natasha was awaiting them near the front portal, and as she escorted Synnovea into the great room to join their guests, Tyrone doffed his muddy boots and made his way in stocking feet to the kitchen, where a manservant took the boots away to clean them. While Tyrone waited for their return, a young girl of no more than three peeked at him from behind the cook's apron, gaining his attention. Her wide, beautiful green eyes and softly curling dark hair were very much like Synnovea's, but it was her faltering timidity that clearly reminded him of what he had recently perceived in his bride's manner. In the past few hours he had seen little evidence of that haughty maid whom he had confronted in the bathhouse, and he could believe that Synnovea was now as much afraid of him as this tiny elfin creature who presently shied away.

Tyrone went down on a knee near a spot where wooden blocks had been left scattered over a small area of the floor. The child watched him with growing interest as he began to construct a tiny edifice. Degree by small, cautious degree, she approached to admire his handiwork and, in sudden glee, chortled with him when a more difficult addition collapsed his creation into a disorganized heap.

The cook, Danika, observed the making of their friendship with a warm smile, but when the man began to speak to her daughter in a foreign language, she, too, was completely lost in confusion and unable to ease the girl's perplexed frown. When he sought to translate, Danika's confusion only deepened and she shrugged and spread her hands, conveying the fact that she didn't understand.

Synnovea was sent to fetch her bridegroom for the wedding guests, who were awaiting his presence in the great room. Having been informed of his whereabouts, she approached the open door of the kitchen, but when she espied him chatting with the child, she paused outside the portal, not wishing to intrude. Though the child was unable to catch the drift of his words, she seemed captivated nonetheless, as evidenced by the slowly widening grin that curved her small, angelic mouth. Synnovea found her own heart strangely warmed by his gentle manner with the girl. She could not help but think of those moments when he had carefully nurtured her passion even at the sacrifice of his own pleasure. Were it not for his animosity toward her now, she'd have been content to have such a man as her husband. There was no doubt in her mind that he was far and away more honorable and handsome than either Aleksei or Vladimir.

The manservant brought Tyrone's boots back and presented them not only clean but neatly polished. After slipping them on, Tyrone rose and took the girl's small hand in his. "I must go now," he informed her, "but I'll be living here, and I'd be delighted to visit you here in the kitchen before I go to work each morning. Will that be all right with you?"

The little one looked up at him, bewildered by his questioning tone, but her small face brightened suddenly when Synnovea entered the kitchen. Having grown immensely fond of the *boyarina* in the short span of time they had lived in the same house, she ran to take her hand. Tyrone straightened and, in stilted reticence, watched his bride as she spoke to the girl in Russian. Of a sudden, the child's face grew radiant, and turning to the colonel, she dipped into a curtsy, eagerly babbling an answer.

Synnovea reluctantly lifted her gaze and timidly translated the child's answer as she met the blue eyes that rested upon her. "Sophia would like you to know that she'd be pleased to have you visit her as often as you'd like."

Tyrone noticed his bride's heightened blush and, when she hurriedly dropped her gaze, realized that she had misread his close attention as some fierce displeasure. He didn't feel generously disposed toward explaining that in spite of his hostility toward her, he was nevertheless taken with her soft, beguiling manner.

"I was reluctant to interfere in your discussion with the girl," Synnovea apologized, laying a gentle hand upon Sophia's shoulder as the child, in some awe, lightly fingered the pearls that adorned the *sarafan*. "But I thought you needed a translator."

Tyrone conveyed a cool reserve as he suggested, "Now that we'll be living under the same roof, I suppose you should teach me the language. We'll have to find something to pass the time together since we have so little in common."

Synnovea almost cringed at his blatant derision, but at the sound of footfalls hurrying down the hall, she forced back a start of tears and faced Natasha as that one swept into the kitchen in an anxious dither.

"Synnovea!" the woman gasped breathlessly, clutching a hand to her heaving bosom. "Prince Vladimir and his sons are here! I'm sure they've come to look Tyrone over, and from the mood they're in, he'll likely be needing reinforcements."

Tyrone met his bride's worried glance with smiling mockery. "Your rejected betrothed, I presume?"

Synnovea wrung her hands in dismay, unconsciously voicing a frantic whisper. "What are we to do?"

"Calm yourself, madam," her groom advised. "It won't be the first time I've met one of your suitors. I just hope this particular prince doesn't prove as irascible as the last."

"You'd better be warned," Natasha cautioned him. "Prince

Vladimir's sons have a penchant for brawling. They like nothing better than settling arguments with their fists. In other words, Colonel, they might make Aleksei seem like a blessed saint by comparison."

"Then the next moments may well see the end of our celebration," Tyrone predicted ruefully. Raising a brow, he offered his arm to his bride. "Shall we face them together, my dear? After all, it isn't every day that a rejected swain meets the husband of his betrothed."

Synnovea felt the sting of his sarcasm and lifted her chin loftily. "You've no ken what the brood is capable of when riled, and right now, you're in no condition to make light of the matter."

"Perhaps not, my dear, but the introductions should prove interesting, don't you agree?"

"*If* you survive them!" Synnovea quipped, reluctantly accepting his arm as Natasha hastened away.

Tyrone glanced down at his bride with a sardonic smile curving his handsome lips as he led her into the hallway. "I suppose I should brace myself to face not only these but a whole legion of discarded suitors who've been left in your wake. It might prove more challenging than fighting the enemies of the tsar. Had I been more astute, I might've taken a warning when I espied you with Ladislaus."

Synnovea dared to express what his words seemed to insinuate. "Perhaps you might have reconsidered my rescue."

"Definitely a possibility, madam," Tyrone replied, feeling in no mood to reassure her. Still, when Synnovea tried to withdraw her arm in sudden exasperation, he clamped his own arm against his side, forbidding her escape. "Tut-tut, my dear. We must obey His Majesty and keep up appearances for our guests."

Synnovea bestowed a heated glower upon him, but made no further effort to pull away, sensing that it would be futile to even try. Thus, Tyrone escorted his bride into the great hall in an overtly chivalrous manner, just as one might expect of a newly wedded groom.

Applause and burbling compliments from the guests greeted the couple's entry into the crowded room, but Vladimir wasn't in the mood to be gracious. As Natasha had already ascertained, he was feeling as surly as an old, wounded bear. He swung around with a loud snort of derision when his eldest son advised him that Synnovea was approaching on the arm of her groom. While several of his offspring followed the newly wedded pair, affirming their eagerness to fight, his faded blue eyes pierced the tall man at her side.

Synnovea glanced about in growing dismay, espying familiar faces closing in around them. It unsettled her unduly to think that Tyrone would again be called upon to pay the penalty for her outrageous scheme.

A short distance behind the bellicose clan, several English officers lowered their goblets and cautiously observed the proceedings, sensing the intent of the princes to entrap the groom in a brawl. Considering the colonel's avid quest to have the girl, they hadn't been at all surprised when they had heard that he had gotten into a fray with her guardian, who had hired men to punish him for his audacity. Nor were they astonished by the repercussions they were presently witnessing, no doubt brought about by the tsar's quickly executed directive to negate further intervention. It was no secret that trouble followed one who coveted a forbidden treasure. And it was obvious by the bride's beauty that she was a prize some men would kill for.

Grigori joined the Englishmen and spoke to them in a hushed tone, warning them to be prepared if his commander was attacked. "If they want to brawl about this matter, we'll invite them outside. Understood?"

Eager smiles lit the faces of the colonel's friends, but for the time being, Grigori cautioned them to merely watch until it became evident that Tyrone couldn't defend himself. They had seen their comrade in action before and were confident of his ability to handle most situations, but if a confrontation was in the offing, they were ready to even out the score, since he was definitely outnumbered and not in a condition to fight his way through on his own.

"So! You're the rascally devil who stole the maid from me," Vladimir rumbled caustically. "What are you Englishmen, anyway? Savages that you must steal our brides from beneath our noses and make off with them to do your evil deeds? You intruding rake, you should be horsewhipped!"

The threat seemed imminent as his sons muttered irately and pressed close around the couple. Tyrone cocked a challenging brow at the white-haired boyar when the elder's hand settled on the hilt of his sword. The intimidation was too obvious to ignore.

Synnovea stepped toward Vladimir, hoping to placate him with a softly cajoling plea, but she was prevented from accomplishing her objective when Tyrone caught her elbow in an unrelenting vise. He was no more inclined to hide behind her skirts now than he had been when he had hung from the wooden beams in the carriage house.

"Stay out of this, Synnovea," he growled low. "I'm quite capable of handling this matter on my own without your interference."

"But Vladimir may listen to me," Synnovea implored in a whisper, briefly glancing toward the towering ancient. Daring much, she laid a trembling hand in plaintive appeal upon her husband's chest. "Please let me try, Tyrone. You've been through enough on my account, and I'd rather not see you harmed more than you have been."

Vladimir loudly harrumphed at the girl's marked concern for the foreigner. Goaded by jealousy, he stepped forward and, clasping the colonel's arm, pulled him around to face him. "Would you take counsel from a woman?"

"Aye! If there is wisdom in it!" Tyrone retorted, jerking

free of the man's grasp. "No man tells me to whom I should give heed!"

With an angry growl, the old man voiced his contempt for the stranger. "The tsar may have asked you and other young whelps like you to come here and give our soldiers instruction, but most boyars are offended by the presence of foreigners in this country. You not only intrude into our ways of doing warfare, English knave, but you tamper with our women as well!"

"Who bleats about intrusion?" Tyrone barked. "I gained audience before His Majesty's throne and begged him for petition to court the maid long before you ever knew she existed. You came well after and secretly connived with the Taraslovs to write a betrothal contract without consideration for the tsar's wishes. Now the nuptials have been performed, and you're still seeking to challenge my right to the girl. Do you argue with a royal decree when the vows were spoken in the presence of Tsar Mikhail?"

A low snarl tore free of Vladimir's throat. "I served a gentleman's proper due and followed the formal rite of behavior in asking Prince Aleksei for the Countess Synnovea's hand in marriage. Where were you when the contracts were being signed and sealed?"

Tyrone sneered at the ancient's feeble declaration. "I was forbidden to even see the maid by the very ones who sealed the documents with you. By deed and favor, I had more claim to her than you. If not for me, she'd never have reached Moscow. She'd have been forced to appease the lusting appetites of some bastard thief who thought to seize her for his own!"

"You think because you saved her once from a band of rogues that you own her now?" Vladimir bellowed incredulously.

"Nay!" Tyrone flung back. "Synnovea is mine because we spoke the vows together as witnessed by the tsar! So vex me no longer with your trifling arguments, old man, for I'm not in the least compassionate toward your failed endeavors."

Tyrone stepped back slightly, eyeing the sons, who had begun to move forward in an overt show of aggression. Drawing Synnovea with him, he retreated another step, but only to ensure that none would be at his back if they launched an assault.

He glanced at the ancient and managed a casual shrug without being unfavorably reminded of the discomfort he still suffered in his back. "If you and your sons would care to join us for the festivities, Prince Vladimir, you're welcome to remain. Willy-nilly, go or stay, you can do as you wish, but know this: if it's a fight you want, you'll have to come back another day."

"So good of you, English Colonel, to invite us to share in your celebration!" Sergei derided, making the mistake of clapping Tyrone on the back. That one sucked his breath in sharply, and at very close range, Synnovea saw her husband's wide shoulders tense with the agony of the other's touch. The blue eyes blazed in sudden fury, and in less than a heartbeat he swung around to face the youth, his breath slashing through tightly clenched teeth.

Seizing Sergei by the front of his kaftan, Tyrone yanked him forward until the younger man saw firsthand the seething rage that fairly flamed in the bright eyes. His feigned friendship was completely fragmented beneath the awe-inspiring dimensions of the colonel's rage. It frightened Sergei mightily, and he reacted instinctively, winning his freedom with a frantic jerk. In the next instant he was snatched again by the scruff of his neck as he tried to scramble away. His left arm was caught and twisted painfully behind his back. At his loud yelp, his brothers leapt forward to intervene, but another agonizing wrench brought a desperate appeal from the young prince that they should hold fast to their places.

"Have a care where you touch me, whelp," Tyrone gritted

close behind the youth's ear. "Or I swear you'll leave here with only one arm. Do I make myself clear?"

Vladimir and his sons had full command of the English language and each clearly understood the warning. It was the father who stepped forward and, with a booming voice, demanded Sergei's release. "Let my son go or I'll set the dogs to your foul carcass ere this night is over!"

Tyrone scoffed at the huge man, not even remotely intimidated by the threat. "Then call off your baying hounds or you'll have good reason to hunt me down."

Vladimir raised his bushy white brows in sharp surprise. It was a rare man indeed who stood up to him and his collection of sons. Lifting a wrinkled hand, he gestured lamely for his family to retreat. In response, Tyrone sent Sergei sprawling forward into his brothers.

Claiming their attention with a rather terse chuckle, Tyrone laid a hand to his breast and dipped his head in an abbreviated bow of apology. "I must beg forgiveness for my ill temper, my lords. I was involved in a confrontation with a band of ruffians several nights past, and they did their best to lay open my back. 'Tis tender yet, so as long as you keep your hands to yourselves, perhaps I can respond to your visit with as much grace as a favorable host might extend."

Sullenly Sergei glared at him as he rubbed his bruised wrist. "You rile easily, Englishman."

"Aye, 'tis a fault I suffer when pain is inflicted upon me."

Tyrone glanced around at the family, noticing their gazes were now centered on Synnovea. As a whole, their yearning expressions evidenced deep measures of regret, as if each of them had become enamored not only with her beauty but with the winsome charm of the maid. The elder, in particular, seemed pained as he gazed upon her with undiminished longing.

Tyrone was not above wresting a bit of revenge for their attempts to bully him. Drawing his bride forward, he laid an arm around her slender waist and held her close against his side, clearly establishing his claim upon her for the benefit of the sons and their sire. "Would you now congratulate me on my good fortune in taking so fair a bride?" His invitation was admittedly farfetched, considering their resentment, but after accepting a goblet from a servant's tray, he held it aloft. "My lords, may I propose a toast to the Lady Synnovea Rycroft, wife of my be-knighted self and good woman of my future house?" He sipped the wine and, leaning near his bride's ear, murmured encouragement as he handed the goblet to her. "Drink up, my sweet. Remember, we're to make merry for our guests."

Synnovea had no heart for concurring to the travesty he proposed, but by order of the tsar she had to make the best of the moment. After taking a tiny sip, she gave the goblet back with a noticeable lack of enthusiasm.

"Smile," Tyrone urged, drawing her away from the guests.

She stiffly complied as she gritted through grimacing lips, "Is that better?"

"You're vexed with me," he chided with exaggerated concern as he escorted her into the entrance hall.

"Does it matter?" She lifted a querying brow, awaiting his answer.

Tyrone glanced away in a museful vein and happened to espy Nikolai, who had just entered the foyer. Perhaps he had no cause to be jealous of the younger officer, but he was clearly in a mood to vent his own frustration with the situation in which he found himself. With a forced smile, he faced his bride as he halted and locked his arms about her. Though she stiffened, he leaned over her ear to whisper, "Appearances, madam. They must be maintained even when you think no one is watching."

Duly warned, Synnovea submitted to his kiss, but she was hardly prepared for the thoroughness with which it was executed. His open mouth slanted across hers with almost brutal intensity, devouring hers with an unchecked hunger as he drew her small tongue into the cavity of his mouth and caressed it with his own. Unconsciously she rose up against him, freely offering everything she had as a sacrifice to the flaming heat of his lips. Though she slipped her arms around him, she suddenly remembered the condition of his back and found no place for her hands to rest above his waist. Finally she let them fall to her sides again as she leaned into him.

Boisterous applause and loud whistles came from the English soldiers, who had entered the hall behind them. The men gathered close around the couple, prompting Synnovea to draw back in acute embarrassment. Tyrone allowed her to escape to a circle of women while he accepted the good wishes of his friends, who drew him back to the great hall.

Nikolai was certainly none too pleased about what he had just witnessed. In light of the guarantee that had been coerced from the tsar, the lustful kiss seemed an affront to the girl. Even if Nikolai hadn't been at odds with the colonel before, he was swiftly approaching that frame of mind. Indeed, he promised himself that if he found a chance, he'd warn Synnovea of her husband's duplicity. Above all, he wanted to beg her to hold herself aloof from her husband until he sailed back to England.

Anxious for such an opportunity to present itself, Nikolai closely observed the couple for the rest of the afternoon, but as the hours passed and evening came upon them, his disposition grew decidedly morose. The pair acted as if they were totally taken with each other as they mingled with their guests. Hand in hand, they stood together and decorously bade farewell to Vladimir and his sons.

Later that evening, when the bride and groom were called to another lavish banquet, they shared a place at the head of the table to which Natasha had directed them. The cushioned bench wasn't overly wide, but their hostess maintained that it had become a traditional place of honor for newlyweds in her household. As narrow as it proved to be, there was much hilarity evoked from the onlookers as the couple strove to wedge themselves in. Once they were ensconced, they might as well have been joined at the hip, for Tyrone was forced to wrap his right arm around Synnovea's ribcage and to lean back enough to allow her shoulder to overlap his. Being for the most part right-handed, that left him ruefully considering how he was going to fair feeding himself with his left.

It nearly broke Nikolai's composure to watch the couple from the far end of the table. Beneath his grim stare, the colonel seemed to delight in handling *his* Synnovea, as if the man had *any* right to touch her after the pledge he had gained from the tsar. The long fingers stroked along her ribs, sometimes pausing near a ripe breast or possessively resting upon her hip. What made it even worse was the fact that she seemed to relish not only her bridegroom's touch but lending wifely assistance in feeding him. They seemed to make a game of it, kissing often and even going so far as to steal food from the other's mouth. Finally, when the bench became a hindrance to their comfort, mainly for Synnovea, who suffered the most against her husband's steely flank, she sought to rise, but Tyrone deftly clamped an arm about her slender waist, lifted her, and then resettled her upon his thigh, much to the hearty approval of his men.

Nikolai realized the worst of his worries was yet to come as the time approached for the couple to retire to their bridal chamber. Because he had been visually confronted by the Englishman's inclination to liberally kiss and handle Synnovea, he refused to trust the man with her. And though he wanted to warn Synnovea of what her husband intended in hopes of preventing their union, he was repeatedly frustrated as the evening wore on, for he found no chance to catch her alone. When she finally left the hall, escorted by Natasha and the handful of women who had been invited to attend her, his hazel eyes sadly followed.

In the moments following Synnovea's departure, some of the men had begun to chide Tyrone for stealing the most beautiful maid from beneath their noses. Questions concerning the haste of their marriage also were presented, but he refused to elaborate and brushed the inquiries off with a grin. "You've all heard rumors of my impatience to court the countess." Hoping the fruit-flavored vodka would deaden his senses sufficiently before he arrived upstairs, he took another sip as he braced a shoulder against the molding of a door. "The tsar took pity on my pain and cast down all other plans for her betrothal by arranging the ceremony himself. That's all there is to it."

Natasha returned to the great room and announced that the bride was awaiting her groom. The men chortled in glee and crowded close around Tyrone, who drained his cup in what appeared to be eager anticipation. Only he was cognizant of his ongoing attempt to deaden more than the wounds in his back, for the idea of being privately ensconced with Synnovea had already stirred memories that sorely threatened his efforts to remain distantly detached from the tempting beauty.

As his friends crowded near, Tyrone immediately retreated, fearing they would forget and pound him upon the back. "Have a care or you'll make me useless to my bride. The condition of my back has a way of dismissing everything else from mind. So I beg you, proceed with care in your attempt to cheer me on."

"Lift him on your shoulders, lads!" an English officer named Edward Walsworth encouraged. "He should save his strength for better things. Besides, he's quaffed so much vodka, he may be unable to find his way upstairs to savor other pleasures."

Amid their guffawing laughter, Tyrone was hoisted onto their shoulders and then carted upstairs, their booming, outrageously ribald chants accompanying their ascent. In the anteroom of Synnovea's apartments, they lowered Tyrone to his

feet before the entrance of the adjoining bedchamber and jostled behind him to get a glimpse of the bride outfitted for her
husband's pleasure.

Tyrone would never have denied the fact that he had liberally indulged in strong spirits throughout the celebration.
Even so, when his eyes beheld a sight that he had both feared
and yearned to see, there was no way that he could blame
his swiftly thudding heart on his heavy imbibing. For some
time now, he had been aware of Synnovea's unrivaled beauty,
but when faced with the fact that she was his by right of
wedlock and that he could freely exercise the many preroga-
tives which that particular union allowed him, he felt a sharp
pang of regret that he, in the heat of outraged pride, had
foolishly allowed himself to set such extreme limits on his
manly lusts. It seemed that Mikhail had been far wiser than
he to acknowledge that a change of heart might be in the
offing, and for that, Tyrone had to give the monarch immense
credit for being able to understand how well the shroud of
rage could blind a man. With the subtly demoralizing and relaxing effects of the fruited vodka he had consumed, Tyrone
wasn't at all sure his staunch objectives could withstand one
night with Synnovea, much less three years. If he maintained
his abstinence, he was certain it would mean a far greater
torment for him than even the whip had reaped.

Standing within the circle of her attendants, Synnovea
looked as enticing as any bride had a right to look. Her dark
hair had been separated into a pair of braids to signify her
newly married state and then interwoven with gleaming gold
ribbons. An exquisite robe of shimmering, translucent gold
flowed loosely to the floor from her shoulders, and though the
meager glow of the candles didn't allow access through the
lustrous silk at the moment, Tyrone was keenly aware that
beneath that particular garment and the gown she wore underneath, his bride was just as soft and beautiful as she had always been. Whether in his memories, his dreams, or reality,

the sight of her never failed to set his body to battling with his brain.

The manly guests loudly hooted their approval of the bride's comeliness, and as Synnovea glanced their way, she graced them with a timid smile. Princess Zelda eyed the groom for a moment before leaning near the bride's ear to whisper. Synnovea nodded eagerly as her gaze swept toward Tyrone, but a blush immediately stained her cheeks when she became cognizant of the fact that they had aroused his curiosity with their hushed comments on his anatomy. With that realization, the two women giggled in secret delight.

Tyrone lifted an arm and braced it against the framework of the arched doorway, well aware that he had become the topic of their discussion. From the way their flitting perusals swept over him, he could believe their dialogue had something to do with his physical attributes. On that subject Synnovea possessed firsthand knowledge, yet as he continued to stare, she refrained from giving further comment, deterring the princess from offering other suppositions. It hardly kept his bride from meeting his gaze with more candor than she had hitherto displayed, at least since their marriage vows had been spoken.

Tyrone's entry into the chamber had brought back a memory of a similar event a thrice or so years ago, when he had glimpsed his first wife, Angelina, bedecked in her bridal finery. His mood had been different then, buoyant and cheerful, as was common among bridegrooms who anticipated the taking of virginal fruit. It could be like that again, he told himself, if only he'd relent . . .

Or it might be even better, the thought intruded as he pondered the difference in his courtship of his two wives. In comparing his sudden attraction to Synnovea to his final capitulation to Angelina's pleas, he was forced to admit that the difference was like night and day. Angelina had been the offspring of his parents' neighbors, yet he had all but ignored her during her younger years. She had finally attracted his attention only a pair of years before their wedding. In truth, their marriage had come about mainly by the wearing down of his manly resistance by a sweet young thing.

Other courtships had waned for different reasons, some because of the brevity of time allowed by his profession, many because of his own dwindling interest or a realization that a deeper union with a particular woman wasn't in his best interest. He could hardly commend his coolheaded logic this time. Indeed, considering his zeal to have Synnovea, it seemed incredibly farfetched to suppose that he could successfully ignore her presence in the same room, much less in the same bed.

He had asked Natasha, with all the discretion he had been capable of mustering, to provide him with separate quarters no matter how tiny or cramped. The woman had smiled graciously and given the excuse that she usually had so many guests, it seemed unlikely that she'd be able to grant his request without restricting her gregarious penchant for hospitality. That was precisely the time he decided he was cursed by his own manly lusts.

Glancing back over his shoulder at his cavorting and frolicking guests, Tyrone shushed their loud bantering until the murmuring comments of the women could be heard above the din. He ambled forward to the circle of ladies, his eyes gleaming brightly as he carefully regarded the radiance of his bride. While her attendants observed every glance, every movement the newly married couple made, Synnovea gave him a diffident smile as she watched him warily. A stiff bow to the ladies sent them scurrying and sniggering from the chambers, allowing Tyrone to step before his bride.

"Again, madam, for the benefit of my escort," he whispered, justifying his close attention. Lifting her small chin, he indulged himself in her delicately refined beauty for a passage of a long moment before lowering parting lips to hers. He made no effort to convince himself that he kissed her merely for the sake of his companions; he knew better than to believe that lie.

Synnovea yielded herself completely to his inquiring kiss, daring to meet his tongue when it slipped inward to search the depths of her mouth. He was her husband, after all, and though no one knew of her longing, she now realized that she desired him more than she had ever thought possible. The taste of vodka pervaded her senses as he devoured her offering with leisured deliberation. When he drew back, he left her silently groaning in disappointment.

Slowly wending his way back to the anteroom, Tyrone cooled his blood and brain forthwith by thinking of Aleksei going freely about his business. If he had been able to obtain the tsar's permission, he'd have chased that boyar down as he fully intended to do with Ladislaus. Nothing short of facing that toad in a deadly contest would satisfy him.

Tyrone drank a last toast with the men to the forthcoming night, as if highly anticipating the torment he would soon suffer. He wasn't so much into his cups that he wasn't aware of Nikolai covertly eyeing Synnovea through the doorway. After encountering so many suitors, Tyrone wasn't in the mood to share even a glimpse of his bride's unconfined beauty with another man, especially one who had followed so closely on his heels to plead his cause with His Majesty, as if the major had striven one-tenth as hard as he to gain the tsar's attention just for the privilege of courting the lady.

Deliberately Tyrone reached back a hand and pushed the door closed behind him before lifting a challenging stare to the Russian major. By the coldness in his eyes, he let it be known that Synnovea was his, and he'd fight any worthy who had intentions of intruding. He stared until Nikolai, flushing a dark angry red, turned crisply on a heel and made his exit.

14

The guests finally took their leave of the bridal chambers, and the stout, wooden outer portal was closed, allowing the groom to secure the bolt against the possibility of any prankish deed befalling them. When a few of his fellow officers had lingered to advise him on the schooling of a virgin, Tyrone had nodded with museful care, and though he had appeared to listen to every word, his thoughts had wandered. His judgment was not so sluggish that he couldn't discount most of his companions' suggestions as irrelevant. If he held true to his resolve, then surely their counsel was for naught even if he were of a bent to use it, which was hardly the case. It wasn't that he considered his skills with women significantly better than those of his cohorts; indeed, some were touted to be daring roués and masterful lovers of several or more women at any given month or year, whereas he, as pragmatic about his personal life as he was with his career, had limited himself to one serious liaison at a time. He simply preferred his own way of doing things, at least when it came to nurturing a woman's pleasurable participation in the intimate rites of love. If Angelina's dying confessions could be counted as trustworthy, then by her own vow she had fallen more in love with him after their marriage. It had only been during that long interval of time, when he had been away in service to his country, that she had grown lonely enough to be otherwise beguiled. Or so she had sworn to him on her deathbed, where she had, with her last breath, begged him to forgive her.

As for the temptress he had just married, Synnovea had proven herself excitingly responsive to his lovemaking, if indeed he could believe her fervor genuine rather than part of her ploy. His musings even now strayed, as if beguiled, to alluring recollections of her sliding naked across his bed in her eagerness to make room for him. Even after he had consumed enough vodka to dull the lacerated rawness of his back, he was still unable to cast that memory as well as other similarly haunting visions from his mind.

With careful diligence Tyrone approached the huge bed wherein his second wife awaited him. She had doffed the golden robe, and at present her womanly form was discreetly covered by a sheet which she had dragged up over her bosom. As he loosened his doublet, his smoldering gaze raked over the hills and valleys that formed a provocative terrain beneath the shroud.

"Tsar Mikhail was right," he remarked with languor, and then cursed his tongue for having lost its subtle eloquence. Even with his faculties somewhat encumbered from the effects of the intoxicant, he couldn't dismiss the turmoil he was about to suffer by withholding himself from her. "You're very beautiful, madam, perhaps beyond the degree of any woman I've ever known."

All signs of Synnovea's feigned gaiety had fled shortly after their guests' departure. Now she eyed her husband guardedly, wondering what to expect from him in his present mood and condition. If he intended to vent his wrath upon her and insult her for having tricked him, she would have no recourse but to accept it. It was the very least she deserved. "We've had no moment alone in which we could talk, Tyrone."

"So you wish to talk." Tyrone painstakingly executed a bow and then stumbled back a step before he caught himself and straightened. He grinned, somewhat amused at himself. "You must pardon my present plight, madam. I've progressed out of character tonight. You see, I've liberally partaken of the fruit of the vine . . . or rather, that deadly libation you Russians quaff so copiously. Wicked stuff, that vodka, but it eases my pain. . . ." He laid a hand over his heart as if mutely declaring the area where serious injury had been inflicted. "What matter did you wish to discuss, wife of mine? My aversion to being used?" He rubbed his chest as if sorely chafed by the idea. "Aye, that has caused me severe wounding by your lovely hand. None other could have cut me so deftly to the quick. While I pledged you all I could offer, paltry though it be, you played me for a fool. Now this poor buffoon is caught, bound by chains of wedlock, and he spies such delectable confection upon his bed that his mind is befuddled by the lusts that goad him. Alas, there's no escape for the poor fool." Clasping a bedpost with one hand, Tyrone leered at her and twirled his free hand through the air, as if urging an audience to respond. "What think you of my folly, madam? And of yours, pray tell? In ridding yourself of one proposed husband, you've caught yourself quite another entirely. Are you satisfied with what your mischief has heaped?"

Holding the sheet clasped over her bosom, Synnovea lifted herself cautiously from the pillows and sat upright. "I wasn't willing to marry Prince Vladimir. . . ."

"You made that abundantly clear ere now, madam." The accusation was launched in sharp retort as he doffed his velvet doublet and flung it onto a nearby chair. What vexed him more than anything was the fact that he couldn't ignore the ravishing vision he was presented. A half-dozen slender tapers burned in the pair of candelabra sitting atop the tables nestled against each side of the bed. The tiny flames flickering behind his bride eagerly cast their radiance through the filmy tissue of her pale yellow nightgown, temptingly detailing her shoulders, arms, and enough of her bosom to whet his desire to peruse everything else the covering held from view.

If a man could feel harried by the beauty of his bride on their wedding night, then Tyrone was definitely subject to that particular plight. As he leisurely assessed the sights, it dawned on him that he wanted Synnovea even more now than he ever had, even before their aborted union. No woman had ever held his mind so completely ensnared as she did now. From the first moment of their meeting, his life had been disrupted by his fervor to have her. Now, having won her, he could believe that he was destined to be punished even more.

"What I'm asking, madam, is whether or not you're pleased with what you've accomplished with your game."

Synnovea's cheeks warmed to a vivid hue as she struggled to find an answer that might serve to mollify his resentment.

"You cannot answer me?" Tyrone demanded sharply.

She started slightly at the animosity in his tone and nervously offered a softly spoken supplication. "Can you not see the truth of the matter yourself, Tyrone? Would not any maid prefer a younger husband above an ancient patriarch? But I never meant to entrap you, please believe me . . ."

"Nay!" His tone was derisive. "You only wanted to use me like some worthless plaything and cast me aside when you no longer had need of me! I was nothing more to you than a rutting coxcomb whom you could use for your own purposes. The price you were obviously willing to expend for my services was far too enticing for me to ignore. By sacrificing your virtue, you meant to gain your end no matter the cost to me!"

Turning from her in a manner of angry dismissal, Tyrone careened across the room and entered the dressing chamber, where he promptly found himself confronted by masses of shoes neatly arranged in little satin bags tucked into crannies, tapestry-covered hat boxes and lacquered jewel coffers set in order on shelves near a melange of small, ornate chests that held stockings, handkerchiefs, and other dainties. Much larger armoires and chests were filled nigh to overflowing with gowns, petticoats, and lace-trimmed chemises. Amazed by the abundance of clothes he saw around him, Tyrone bemusedly tested the rich cloth of several and then lifted a delicate chemise against the light to admire its transparency.

His own clothes and possessions had been unpacked and placed in neat order beside hers, but surprisingly more conveniently at hand. He was rather amazed by the consideration that he had been shown in this matter. True, Ali might have wanted to favor him with such an arrangement, but the tiny servant would never have taken the initiative to do so unless her mistress had first directed her.

Wincingly Tyrone stripped the shirt from his back and tossed it aside. Selecting the pitcher that felt the coldest to his hand of the two that were available, he splashed water into a basin and suffered through a chilly washing, hoping it would aid him in his endeavor to remain levelheaded once he had slipped into bed beside his bewitchingly winsome wife. Past that point, he'd have to rely on his slightly inebriated state to lead him into deep slumber from whence he fervently hoped he'd be hard-pressed to wake until morning.

Tyrone donned a pair of chausses to conceal his nakedness, which seemed a crucial necessity for his return to the bedchamber. Even then, the tight-fitting hose could not be relied upon to hide what would no doubt arise once he saw her again. The side of the bed nearest the antechamber seemed designated as his own, since the sheet had been folded down invitingly and his bride was ensconced closer to the windows on the far side. As he negotiated his way there, he avoided meeting his bride's cautious gaze by perusing the room, noting its wealth of space, rich appointments, and softly feminine elegance. It was apparent their hostess treasured the girl's company, reserving for her use what had to be the best apartments in the mansion, the exception being the chambers in which Natasha resided. He hadn't indulged in such luxuries since leaving England, and only then in much less splendor. The Tudor house, which his father had bequeathed him at the event of his marriage to Angelina, was large and comfortably furnished in the same style as its design, but it was much less ornate than this womanly nirvana in which he found himself.

Pausing near the bedside table, Tyrone pinched out the tiny flames burning atop the candelabrum and turned his back upon his bride, avoiding the visual stimulations that were there waiting to be relished. If he had ever wondered what pleasurable torture was like, then he was catching a clear sense of it now. It was pure agony to think that by his own foolishness he could not taste, touch, or savor the rich sensuality of her feminine form. Merely the awareness of her proximity and the memory of her eager response to his passion warmed his blood, making him grateful for the shadows that allowed him some degree of modesty as he released the knot at his waist and let the chausses fall to the floor. Sitting back upon the bed, he dragged the undergarment off his feet and tossed it onto a nearby bench.

Though the only light in the chambers now came from the candles burning behind Synnovea, the ugly weals crisscrossing her husband's back were vividly displayed. Synnovea almost cringed at the sight, knowing that she was solely to blame. The deep slashes extended around to his right side, where the ends of the lash had fallen, and though most of the stripes were healing, a swollen area along a wider gash indicated a corruption of flesh beneath a dark scab, prompting her to slip out of bed.

Tyrone wasn't a man of such ironclad control that he could resist casting a glance over a shoulder as his wife pulled the silken robe over her head. The candlelight penetrated the translucency of her nightgown before it settled into place, making him face away abruptly as he felt a sudden, sharp craving pierce him. She ran into the dressing room and a few moments later emerged carrying a basin of water, a squat jar of balm, and a towel draped over her arm. Her intent soon became evident as she hastened toward him. Immediately Tyrone snatched the leggings into his lap, perhaps for the first time in his life self-conscious about his nakedness and what it would reveal.

"There's a place on your back that has become tainted," Synnovea informed him, placing the bowl on the table beside him. Striking flint against tinder, she lit the candles, which he had snuffed out only moments ago, and turned back to face him. "It needs a good cleansing and a poultice applied to draw out the poison."

It didn't matter that she wore a robe over her nightgown, the flickering flames now burning behind her shone through her diaphanous garments, displaying her womanly form in tempting detail, forcing him to look away while the hammering excitement built to a painful intensity within his loins. "The sore is of little bother to me now, madam."

"If you let it go, Ty, it *will* matter," Synnovea argued sweetly. "I'll need your dagger to open the wound—"

"I said, let it go!" Tyrone barked, foreseeing the disaster he'd invite by allowing her to touch him. He'd likely see his restraints and resolves completely sundered by the gentle brush of her hand. Indeed, he'd be hard-pressed not to bear her down upon the bed and have his way with her. He couldn't forget, even for a moment, that all-too-brief but exquisite interlude wherein they had been joined as lovers.

Synnovea challenged his authoritative tone with a soft inquiry. "Why won't you let me tend it?"

"I can do it myself," he growled.

"Not hardly," she gently scoffed and tilted her head toward the small bench. "Now, would you kindly sit there where I can tend your back." A long moment elapsed as she watched his brows gather in an ominous scowl. He refused to look at her, but glared across the room until his bride leaned toward him with a softly probing question. "Colonel Rycroft, are you afraid of me touching you?"

Tyrone's temper exploded. "Yes, dammit! I told you before! I want nothing from you, least of all your pity!"

At his thunderous blast, Synnovea stumbled backward and stared in painful confusion at his uncompromising visage, Tears springing up within her spirit and welling blindingly within her eyes. A choked sob escaped her, and she caught up the bowl and whirled away, in her haste flinging a widely reaching spray of water across his chest.

Shocked out of his angry reticence by the chill of the water, Tyrone shot to his feet in surprise, losing his prideful modesty as his protective shield tumbled away from his naked loins. Though barely a second passed before he recovered his wits and snatched for the falling garment, Synnovea's teary eyes chased toward him and then, as they lowered, widened in amazement.

Tyrone ground his teeth as her questioning stare flew up to meet his again. A low growl issued forth from his throat and he flung away the fickle chausses, seeing no further need to try to conceal his arousal. What more was there to hide when a mere glance had stripped him of his pride? "What did you expect?" he snapped. "I'm not made of stone! Good Lord, woman, leave me alone!"

With that, he claimed his place in bed and jerked the sheet up to his waist before rolling onto his left side, away from her. He punched the pillow beneath his head and, refusing to look at her, glowered angrily toward the tiny flames dancing atop the candelabra across the bed.

Shaken by his rage, Synnovea blew out the tapers on his table and carried the basin to the dressing room. There she gave vent to her resentment by exchanging her nightgown for one of heavier cloth which covered her sufficiently from toe to wrist to neck. The rivulets streaming down her cheeks refused to be checked as she made her way back to the bed. There she bestowed a teary glare upon her husband before slipping between the sheets and settling herself also on her left side, as far away from him as she could go. After briefly considering the discomfort of her tenuous perch, she bounced twice on the bed, scooting back from the edge. She tossed him a withering glare over her shoulder, yanked the sheet and quilt high over her shoulder, and then huddled beneath the covering where she continued to weep in silent misery.

In the stillness of the room, the bride and her groom lay together less than an arm's length apart, totally aware of each other, but stubbornly refusing to speak or to move. Despite the wrath that seethed within him, Tyrone kept his eyes tightly closed to alleviate his heightening distress. The sight of his bride's curving form only tormented him the more, but he was determined to beat down his fierce cravings by reining in his thoughts. He did so by deliberately setting his mind on devising plans for a foray outside the city limits. It was of paramount importance that he send his scout, Avar, to search out the location of Ladislaus's camp before he led his men out on such an exercise, for it was definitely a fact that one could go unnoticed far better than a whole regiment.

Synnovea was the first to relent to an exhausted sleep, and her soft, shallow breathing finally lured Tyrone along the same path. For slightly more than a thrice of hours the couple dozed, albeit fitfully. Even so, the brief slumber allowed them some respite from the tension of being together and yet painfully separated.

It was well past two in the morning when Tyrone awakened abruptly, aware that Synnovea was slipping carefully out of bed. In some bemusement, he lay without moving as she crept toward the corner of the chamber where a bright shaft of silvery moonlight streamed in through the windows. As he watched, she slid his dagger from its sheath that hung alongside his scabbard from his belt, which Ali or some other servant had earlier draped over the back of a chair. Stealthily Synnovea returned to the bed with the bared blade, and Tyrone braced himself for her attack, well assured that he'd have no difficulty overpowering her should she launch an attack upon him. If she did, he promised himself that he'd see their marriage nullified forthwith, and let the tsar's threats be hanged. To be sure, his own lucidity would have to be questioned if he remained with a woman who was utterly mad!

Tyrone's brows gathered sharply as Synnovea dragged up the sleeve of her gown and laid the edge of the blade to the inside of her forearm. Her objective seemed clear enough now, and with a low growl he threw himself across the narrow space, startling a gasp from Synnovea, whose head snapped up at the first intrusion of sound. He seized her slender wrist in an unrelenting vise, wrenching a pained yelp from her, and plucked the sharp blade from her grasp.

"Would you take your own life because you were forced to wed me?" he demanded sharply.

"That was never my purpose," Synnovea assured him in a quavering voice. His swift assault had left her shaken to the core of her being, and she could not quiet her frantically thumping heart.

Tossing the dagger back into the chair from whence it had been fetched, Tyrone swung his long legs over her side of the bed and rose to his feet. The chamber brightened considerably as he set ablaze several tapers. Returning to her, he clasped her chin in his hand and lifted her face to the light. He held it thus as his eyes probed hers, searching for some evidence of the truth. "Why else would you make an attempt to slice open your arm if you didn't intend to kill yourself?"

"It may have seemed that way, Ty, but truly, it was never my aim."

"I'm listening," he prodded impatiently.

Synnovea swallowed with difficulty, gathering the nerve to explain. "We've been together in bed for several hours . . . and yet you haven't seen fit to lend me your attention." Her voice faltered in painful chagrin as she continued. "On the morrow . . . my attendants will come and help me dress. If there is no blood on the sheet as proof of my virginity, I will be shamed before my friends."

Tyrone arched a tawny brow as he considered his bride. She seemed unduly embarrassed by having to plead her cause and just as troubled by her inability to escape the disgrace that she'd surely suffer because of their lack of intimacy. "If you'll remember, madam, you're no longer a virgin. I stripped you of that distinction before we were so callously interrupted."

Synnovea bowed her head, shamed by his blunt reminder. "I was expecting you to be rather rough with me . . . after what I did to you."

"Brutish enough to sully the sheets with more blood, you mean." He laughed scathingly as she winced and gingerly nodded. "How chivalrous you think me, madam."

"If you were to beat me, you'd have just cause. My actions were deplorable."

"True," Tyrone agreed, "but a gentleman should never follow a poor example." He considered her dispirited chagrin and sighed heavily. "There's no help for it, I suppose."

Synnovea shuddered and squeezed her eyes tightly closed, trying to hold back the tears that welled up within her spirit. What did it matter if she couldn't provide proof of her innocence? She supposed she wouldn't be the first maid in Russian history to be shamed by the lack of such evidence.

She felt the mattress dip beneath Tyrone's weight and peered up at him curiously as he reached toward the chair. Retrieving the blade, he startled a flinch from her as he whisked the point across the inside of his own arm, opening a small gash. Several red droplets immediately welled forth, and after a small pool of blood had collected, he reached out to the middle of the bed and blotted his arm upon the bottom sheet. When he finally glanced back at Synnovea, he found her staring at him in wide-eyed amazement.

"Does that not serve your purpose, madam?"

"Most definitely, sir," she whispered, astounded by his gallantry. When his manly pride had obviously been severely bruised by her careless use of his ardor, it was difficult to imagine him doing such a thing. "I never expected compassion from you after my deceit. Why did you do it?"

Tyrone casually dismissed his actions with an abortive laugh, unwilling to let her think he could be easily maneuvered by her feminine wiles. "Lend no claims of chivalry to this daunted fool, madam. It was not so much for your reputation as it was for mine. Without evidence of our union, my cohorts might think me incapable of performing the deed, so I've yielded myself to yet another one of your ploys, this time to save face before my own friends, for 'tis evident you have all the assets to lure the most reluctant husband into your arms."

Synnovea lifted her chin as her own pride felt the prick of his needling. "If that be so, sir, then how is it that you've refrained from coupling with me tonight?"

Tyrone made a concerted effort to appear cavalier about a matter which concerned him more than any other, and although he spoke from the heart, he deliberately made light of the injury that had been inflicted upon him. "Oh, madam, were it not for my wounded dignity, which flogs me more severely than the brigand's whip ever could, I wouldn't be able to bear the temptation of sharing a bed with you, but with every twitch of pain, I'm ever reminded of my folly in allowing myself to believe you wanted me as much as I wanted you. I fear my own inanity shames me."

"You're no fool, sir," Synnovea replied in a muted tone. "Indeed, you're far more astute than any man I've ever met."

Tyrone jeered. "Have you knowledge of so many men, my girl, that you can be considered a judge of unquestionable merit?"

Synnovea's cheeks warmed beneath his sarcasm. "I've never known anyone but you on an intimate basis."

"Perhaps not, but you certainly have a legion of hungry males sniffing at your skirts, just waiting for the chance to lift them."

She took exception to his statement. "I've given them no encouragement!"

"Should I believe you singled me out, madam?" Tyrone laughed with rampant skepticism. "Or was I the only poor dupe to be caught in your trap?"

"You know I've been with no other man but you."

He lifted his shoulders in a bland shrug. "Which leaves me convinced that I played the fool with an untutored maid."

"I may not have had much experience with men," Synnovea argued, "but I have a good head on my shoulders and the ability to think for myself. You were the only one I would have chosen in any case."

"Now that statement I must challenge, madam. Not that you don't have a fine head, my dear," he rejoined, intentionally misinterpreting her point. "None better, to be sure. Indeed, it was unquestionably your fair looks and form that caused me to fall prey to your whims."

Synnovea glanced away in frustration. She was beginning to think that this particular Englishman could be as infuriating as he was aggressive.

Having won the argument, at least for the moment, Tyrone bent his attention to his latest wound. He dragged the tail of his bride's nightgown out from under her and began wiping away the blood that had once more collected. As much as he yearned to be made of stone at the moment, it was hard for him to ignore the slender limb and winsomely curving hip which he exposed.

He snorted as he failed to stem the flow. "The way I'm now bleeding, our friends will likely lend you sympathy for having endured my savagery."

" 'Twould seem you're far too acquainted with serving a death blow to your enemies to be anything less than brutish with a blade in your hand, sir."

"I keep the weapon keen for such a purpose, madam. I never once considered that I'd be turning it upon myself. But then, my zeal of late seems to be my own worst enemy."

Synnovea watched his attempts for a long moment before she dared to speak. "Whatever it's worth, Ty, I'm grateful you provided the blood. Otherwise your friends and mine might have thought me . . ." she paused, wondering if she should put words to his thoughts, and then managed to strangle out, "a trollop."

Old memories came flooding back to haunt Tyrone, and he looked away with a pensive sigh. "I suppose preserving his wife's honor is the least a husband can do."

Synnovea's eyes gleamed with sudden moisture. "I have trouble believing you're of such a mind to consider me worthy of your protection, especially when it's a matter regarding my virtue."

"You know little about me, Synnovea," he replied, not caring to explain further.

"That's true," she agreed gloomily. "I know you not at all."

Tyrone heaved another pensive sigh. "I once knew a man who, after hearing the gossip that another had spread abroad about his wife, called her lover out in a duel. The swain made light of her affection and let it be known that he had used her merely for a whim and had tossed her aside when she began to bore him. He was one of those casual gallants who plucked fruit from every skirt he could lift with his charming lies. Had the husband been as vindictive as Aleksei, he might have gelded the man and left him to pine in remorse for all the women he had once bedded."

"What happened after the duel?" Synnovea asked hesitantly. "Did the lover apologize?"

"The husband killed him," Tyrone replied with rueful bluntness. "He found the roué and challenged him to a duel nearly a fortnight after the woman had foolishly tried to rid herself of his child. By that time she was in her fifth month and thought to make amends to her husband, though he had pledged to take her to the country and stay with her until the child was born. For some reason, she had imagined that she could make everything right again if she just rid herself of the other man's child. In her quest to dismiss the babe from her life, she threw herself down the stairs while her husband was away, thinking to kill the child she was carrying. She accomplished her goal, but she took a fever and, a week later, died in her husband's arms."

Synnovea lifted her eyes to search his. "You seem greatly troubled by your tale, Ty. Was this woman someone you were fond of?" A long, silent interlude followed as he stared off into space, and she tried again. "Your sister, perhaps?"

Tyrone finally released a sigh. "No matter now, madam. She's gone, buried in the grave."

During another long passage of a moment, Synnovea considered his aimless efforts to stem the bloody flow, until she finally felt led to break the painful silence with a soft query. "Will you not let me tend your arm now, Ty?"

He was set to brush aside her offer, but he realized with some surprise that he was unwilling to injure her with another brusque refusal. Grudgingly he relented. "If you must."

Suddenly a-smile, Synnovea leapt from the bed, incognizant of the view she presented to her husband as her gown swirled away from her body. The sight of her lithe limbs and shapely derrière nearly made him gasp. It certainly gained his full attention.

When she returned with a fresh basin of water, he was seated upon the bench to which she had earlier directed him. He had draped a towel across his naked loins, allowing her to keep her mind on the task of dressing his wound. Gently she did so, aware of his unrelenting stare while she cleansed and wrapped bandages around his arm.

"May I tend your back now?" Synnovea questioned, bracing herself for another tirade. She kept her gaze carefully lowered and her attention focused on tying off the cloth.

"Do what you must, madam. I'm too tired to argue with you." It was a lame excuse for giving in to her beguiling manner, but it served Tyrone well enough for the moment. He *was* tired and had no desire to fight with her any longer.

Much to his relief, she went to fetch his dagger and the jar of ointment, allowing him to ease his breath out in slow drafts. Whenever she was near, he could hardly breathe, wanting her as he did.

Synnovea gently washed his back with a mild soap before she applied the tip of the blade carefully to the pus-filled lesion. Tyrone stiffened slightly as she slit it open, but he was nevertheless amazed by her gentleness. During his years as a soldier, he had become well acquainted with the hurried roughness of military surgeons. In sharp contrast to their abuse, the touch of her hands seemed like a lover's caress.

Working quickly, Synnovea flushed the wound until fresh blood oozed from the newly opened gash. Then, with tender compassion, she smoothed the balm over the area and wrapped strips of clean cloth around his chest, leaning close over his shoulder as she brought the ends together. As he accepted the strips from her hands, the green-brown eyes swept downward from his temple to the crisp lines of his jaw. Though in recent weeks she had enlivened many a deficient daydream with images of her Englishman, she had never examined his features from this particular angle before. She found the view no less intriguing than all the others she had stored in her memory.

Synnovea moved around in front of him and secured the bandage with a double knot over his chest. "I never meant for this to happen, Tyrone," she stated in a cautious tone, wary of bringing up the subject, but feeling a need to speak her mind. "It was never my intention to see you hurt. You seemed so adept as a soldier, I never dreamt that Aleksei would be able to catch you unawares. Nor did I expect that he and Ladislaus had joined forces."

Tyrone laughed with caustic disbelief. "I could almost be convinced of your charity toward me, madam, except that I've been painfully instructed not to trust you. That particular lesson has been seared into my memory as deeply as the scars on my back."

"I was desperate," Synnovea pleaded in a strained whisper, dearly hoping he would understand. "I couldn't bear the thought of marrying Vladimir. I favored the loss of my good name rather than his attentions as a husband. And you were so willing . . . so tenacious in your desire to have me . . ."

"Aye! I was willing!" Tyrone readily acknowledged. "How could I not be? Your beauty tempted me from the very beginning, and in your resolve, you deliberately lured me on with a sweet promise. I saw it in your eyes and on your lips. How could I have known you'd be leading me into a trap, one that nearly cost me dearly! I'm much relieved to find my head still attached and my cod in good working order!"

A hot blush warmed Synnovea's face as her eyes were drawn to his scantily clad loins. "I never dreamt that Aleksei would become so violent—"

"The hell you say!" Tyrone growled. Coming to his feet, he made no further attempt to hide his nakedness as he strode past her to the far end of the room. Then, when she turned to face him in some bewilderment, he came back to stand close in front of her. At least his rage helped to cool the heat in his loins, if not the roiling resentment burning within him. Settling his hands on his narrow hips, he leaned toward her slightly and gave vent to his vexation. "I don't know the exact moment you singled me out as your victim, madam, but no well-tried harlot could have accomplished the task with such winning appeal. You were as alluring as any earthbound goddess ever craved to be. Aye, madam, that you were, and though I've wandered to countries beyond your imagination, I've seen no finer wench, no fairer form, than you. 'Twas the cunning way you employed your charms that saw me entrapped like some foolishly rutting apprentice. You were so sweet and beguiling, I never had a chance against your powers of persuasion. Your eyes were so warm and inviting, your lips so soft and yielding, your breasts so eager to be touched, and like some blind, weanling fool, I thought your silken thighs would welcome me. Even now I yearn to mount you and appease my desire. There's an unrelenting ache in my loins, and although I'm gratified to be able to feel this lusting need, I'm distraught nonetheless because of this damnable yearning that sorely besets me. I know well enough, should this continue, you'll rend my privy parts more thoroughly than Aleksei's blade ever could."

Synnovea stared up into eyes that fairly blazed into her own, not knowing what to say to ease his indignation. He seemed more incensed by the fact that he had let himself be deceived by a woman, and yet she had been carried away as much by his ardor as he had been by her wiles. Her enticement, at best, had been totally unskilled, whereas his manly persuasions had been firmly bolstered by experience. It was true she had set out to accomplish her will, but somewhere in the midst of it all, she had surrendered not only her body to him but her heart as well. She'd never have been so eager to yield him her virginity had he not worked his own enchantment upon her. Yet if she tried to convince him of that simple fact, she'd no doubt be ridiculed for concocting a farfetched fantasy.

"Ty." Synnovea's voice was soft and gentle, much like a silken caress smoothing down the nettles of his pride. "Could we not go to bed and talk for a while . . . I mean, about each other? I really don't know you at all . . . and I would like to . . . very much."

A terse laugh escaped Tyrone as he dropped his head back upon his shoulders and stared at the shadowed ceiling. He tried to collect his thoughts, but he was like a caged beast distracted by his lusts, an animal smelling the scent of a bitch in heat, driven to a raging hunger by her nearness; and yet, because of some hidden barrier that hearkened back to his injured pride, he refused to salve the rutting instincts that drove him to distraction. And all she wanted to do was go to bed with him—and *talk!*

"Synnovea, Synnovea," he groaned as if plagued by a great pain. "You turn my being inside out, my night into an excruciating anguish, my day into a living hell . . . and then cajole so sweetly in my ear. What am I to do, deny you when you pluck the gutstrings of my manly mettle with your silken pleas? I lose heart for diatribes when you ply your fetching ways upon me."

Synnovea waited in silence until he lifted his head and fastened those penetrating blue orbs upon her. Her voice was barely a whisper in the stillness of the chambers. "Truly, Ty, I didn't foresee such hurt to come to you. You were the one I wanted to claim as my lover, whether by truth or a lie. 'Twas never my intent to bind you to me against your will."

Tyrone sighed heavily and gestured lamely toward the bed, knowing what distress it would cause him to lie down beside her and not touch her. Yet for the time being, he was willing to allow the arguments to lie dormant. "We can talk if you wish, Synnovea, or go back to sleep if you're of such a mind."

Purposefully he took a deep, steadying breath, as if about

to plunge beneath a gigantic wave. Following her to the edge of the bed, he watched her crawl to the far side while his eyes longingly stroked the curving hips and the valley between her buttocks, which the gown molded so enticingly. She slipped beneath the covers and, drawing them up beneath her chin, kept her gaze carefully averted as he stretched out beside her. When he drew the sheet up over his lower torso, she turned eagerly on her side to face him, as if expecting a whole flood of revelations to gush forth from his lips.

Tyrone mentally groaned at the idea and, rolling onto his stomach, reached back for the candelabra. Bringing it near, he blew out the tapers and soon became appreciative of the darkness that shadowed their faces. It was a cold, hard fact that he could lose himself in the variegated depths of those beautiful green-brown eyes.

"Can we not just go to sleep?" he sighed wearily. "Of late, I've been unable to get much rest." He didn't care to elaborate by telling her that he had found most of his nights haunted by his lust for her. "I must confess that I'm in desperate need of it now."

"Whatever your pleasure may be, Tyrone," Synnovea answered softly, grateful for his cordial manner. Her eyes followed his movements as he reached down to the foot of the bed and pulled the down-filled comforter over her. Smiling, she wiggled deeper into the warmth he had provided, content to have him near.

The sun had climbed above the treetops and was just spreading its radiance over the city when Tyrone reluctantly drifted up from the depths of rapturous dreams and roused to a vague awareness that he hadn't been basking in just another lustful fantasy. Full reality suddenly penetrated, and he flicked his eyes open, half expecting to find Synnovea awake and deliberately teasing him. She was there, all right, but sleeping soundly with her head on his pillow and a slender thigh resting across his naked loins. He could feel the faint, tickling brush of her breath against his shoulder and, through her gown, every enticing vale and mound of her softly curving form. Bound as he was to the mattress, he felt as if he had been lashed with silken bonds to a rack upon which he was being scourged by sweet, delectable torture.

Indulging in an occasion that he had never before been granted, Tyrone studied his sleeping bride at his leisure. Try as he might, he could find no hint of the wily vixen who had led him into her trap. Rather, he beheld an innocently slumbering maid not even a stoic heart could resist. Softly curling wisps had escaped her braids and now framed her oval face, leading his gaze enticingly to a dainty ear where a spiraling strand curled coyly around it. She had a fresh, natural radiance about her. A soft, rosy blush brightened her cheeks, and below elegantly winged brows, silkily spiked lashes lay in slumbering repose upon fair skin. Her features were delicately refined, her nose straight and her lips soft and beguilingly parted, temptingly ripe for a lover's passionate kiss. When his eyes caressed such winsome beauty, it was difficult for him to remember that she had deceived him at all.

Obviously his bride had been drawn to him in her sleep, for the sheet and coverlet had fallen to the floor, leaving her with only the lace-trimmed nightgown to provide her protection from the chill now present in the room. The garment had ridden up, leaving a gently curving hip and a slender thigh naked to his gaze. Reluctant though he was to leave such sweet torment, Tyrone knew he'd likely suffer defeat if he remained beside her one moment longer. By simply amending his position a few scant degrees, he could penetrate the vulnerable softness and placate his hotly flaming passion in her dewy warmth. As much as it would have relieved his plight, it hardly would have served his purpose.

Carefully easing himself free of those silky limbs, Tyrone slid across the bed and, without pause, came to his feet. Immediately he repented his lack of caution, for a sudden, splintering pain exploded in his head, giving him cause to wonder if he had been caught in the clutches of something abhorrently evil. Clasping the heels of his hands to his throbbing temples, he held his head carefully in place until the anguish abated to a more tolerable level. He stumbled to the dressing room and there splashed cold water over his face and shoulders.

Having been granted leave for the day, he grabbed casual clothing and thrust his long legs into a pair of breeches. Upon returning to the bed, he allowed himself another admiring perusal before he lifted the bedcovers from the floor and tucked them around his sleeping bride. Departing the chambers, he made his way downstairs and asked directions from a passing servant, encountering one who had been taught English by Synnovea's mother years ago. As the manservant led the way to the bathing chamber, he seemed amiably disposed to exercise his command of the language.

"Yur bride begin coming here to visit vhen she vas young child. Beautiful she vas! And her mother, too! Though zhe boys alvays chase Countess Synnovea, she give them no mind. She vas more interested in her studies and traveling vith her family. She has zhe mind of her own."

"Nothing has changed," Tyrone observed dryly, drawing a chuckle from the servant.

"She is much like zhe Countess Andreyevna, I think. Both can make a man's head swim. At least, my lord, yu vill never grow bored living vith yur bride."

"That comprises my greatest worry—just how long I'll be able to live married to the lady."

The elder wasn't at all surprised by the Englishman's comment. Rumors of his confrontation with Prince Vladimir and the old man's sons had spread throughout the manse well before the wedding reception had ended. "I'm sure even a few scant years vill seem like heaven, sir," he predicted with a merry twinkle in his eyes and then swung open a door for him. "Here yu are, Colonel Sir. Enjoy yur bath."

Tyrone discovered many of his friends already enjoying the bathing facilities, having stayed overnight in chambers reserved for guests. They had gained the march on him by at least an hour and welcomed him with hearty bantering, chiding him for his tardy arrival, as if he had discovered worthier diversions to while away his time. Tyrone cringed at their gleeful laughter, but they only crowed the louder when they saw him grimace in pain.

Grigori came forward with a towel wrapped around his lean hips. Solicitously he handed a small vial of vodka to his commander. "This should ease your plight to some degree, Colonel."

"Or put me in the grave," Tyrone quipped. Nevertheless, he tossed the drink down with a shiver of revulsion, promising himself henceforth that he'd limit his consumption of the libation for his own good. To say the brew was deadly was definitely an understatement of the truth.

Lieutenant Colonel Walsworth gestured to the bandages that still bedecked Tyrone's torso and arm. "Tell us, now. Did your lady claw at your back or try to hold you off?"

Tyrone waved away the officer's raucous speculations. " 'Twas nothing more than a tainted wound or two that my wife treated, so spare me your humor, Edward, until I'm better able to handle the abuse, or I'll be wont to seek revenge."

Walsworth's hearty laughter nearly deafened Grigori's chuckling statement. "There's another day of celebration planned, Colonel." Winning Tyrone's dubious regard, the Russian lifted his broad shoulders in a casual shrug. "It's common to make the most of every occasion here in Russia. It saves us from the tedium of our long winters. And, of course, our fruited vodka seems to lighten the spirits even before we're into the festivities."

"Try to keep your wits clear, my friend," Tyrone cautioned. "On the morrow we must return to duty."

Grigori followed him to a secluded corner where a large bathtub was being filled by a manservant. "You sound as if you have something dire on your mind."

Tyrone cast a glance toward the attendant and, for the sake of caution, delayed his answer until that one had left. If Synnovea's mother had spent enough time on the premises to instruct a servant in the language, no doubt others were also versed in it. "As soon as it's practical, I mean to confront Ladislaus in his lair. My goal is to capture him and other leaders of his band before the year is out. On the morrow I plan to introduce some new tactics to the men in anticipation of that event."

"Will you leave your bride so soon?" Grigori asked in amazement. More than anyone, he knew how fervently his commander had sought to win the maid and was surprised that he had decided to go back to duty so early. "You certainly have reason to take a few days off, considering the condition of your back."

"The tsar has informed me that he'd like us to put on a parade for some foreign dignitaries in weeks to come. Between the task of readying men for a parade and others for the campaign I mean to launch against Ladislaus, I can foresee the possibility of being pressed for time between now and then. And you know well enough that I cannot allow my personal life to interfere with my responsibilities as a commanding officer."

"You've been here for almost a year and haven't yet taken any time off for yourself. I thought, under the circumstances, you'd be staying in the city and training the troops here rather than going after Ladislaus."

"Winter is rapidly approaching. If we delay until spring, we may never find his camp. We must act before the first snow. That means we can't waste any time now. We'll have to plan our strategy and condition the men to be ready for anything we might have to face. I want them thoroughly confident of their own capabilities. We can't leave anything to chance if we intend to capture Ladislaus and his cohorts."

"If you're so adamant about going after them, a scout should be sent out to search for the brigands' camp."

"I've already thought of that. Avar will be the likely choice to go. He has no love for Ladislaus after the brigand stole away his sister last year."

"How do you suppose Prince Aleksei found them?"

"Ladislaus let it be known here in the city that he was looking for me. It's not too hard to guess that Prince Aleksei responded to the call when he realized he'd have to get me out of the way. Whatever their connection, I don't think they're the best of friends."

"Considering the whipping they gave you, I'd say you were extremely fortunate that Lady Synnovea sent her maid to the castle to bid Major Nekrasov to come to your rescue."

Tyrone was clearly bemused. He couldn't remember a time when Synnovea had been given any opportunity to send Ali on such a mission, at least not while he had been in full command of his senses. But then, being clobbered on the head had left much of what had happened hopelessly muddled. "What do you mean? When did she do that?"

"Major Nekrasov told me the other day that Ali brought him word that you were in terrible trouble. From what I understand of it, the old woman was visiting the cook at the Taraslovs' when your captors carried you into the carriage house."

"I must express my gratitude to Ali," Tyrone replied, still somewhat confused by the captain's revelation. "Until now, I never knew how I had actually been delivered from their schemes, except that Nikolai and Tsar Mikhail were there when I most needed them."

"Ali told the major that her mistress had sent her."

Thoughtfully Grigori scrubbed a hand over the bristly stubble covering his chin before cocking a querying brow at his commander. "How could Lady Synnovea have been at the Taraslovs' when she was supposed to be sick upstairs? At least, that's what Prince Adolphe had been led to believe." Though his superior seemed suddenly intent upon loosening the knot which held the bandages together over his chest, Grigori pointedly awaited an answer.

Tyrone's eyebrows twitched upward noncommittally. "Perhaps she wasn't upstairs at all. Perhaps she was with Ali at the Taraslovs'."

Cautiously lowering his voice, the Russian boldly offered a conjecture. 'The countess was with you, wasn't she?"

Tyrone frowned sharply as he grasped the bandages with both hands and ripped them in twain. "Even if true, Grigori, do you actually think I'd tell you?"

"Whether you do or not, my friend, your answer will go no further than the two of us. You know that."

In spite of Synnovea's flagrant disregard for him, Tyrone was unwilling to cause her shame. "Would I boast of such an event? The lady is my wife."

"Tsar Mikhail was most anxious to have you and your bride speak the vows in haste." Grigori gently prodded with a smile. "What really happened that night?"

Tyrone growled in exasperation and tried to make light of his vexation. "You may never get promoted to major, my friend, if you don't learn to keep your questions to yourself."

Chuckling, Grigori voiced a few suppositions of his own. "Now, I know you're no liar, Colonel, so I rather suppose that Prince Aleksei and Ladislaus caught you unawares and ordered the whip laid to your back. And if Ali was sent to fetch Major Nekrasov from the Taraslovs, I'm inclined to believe that the Lady Synnovea was taken there with you. If you were forced to marry her, then I can better understand why you were so out of sorts with her yesterday."

Although surprised at the accurateness of the captain's conjectures, Tyrone carefully maintained his silence.

"It all falls into place," Grigori mused aloud as he thoughtfully scraped a hand across his chin again. "You were obviously caught with the girl and, because of that reason, were forced to pay penance by her guardian, Prince Aleksei . . ."

"The devil you say! He wanted her for himself!"

"Then you were whipped for taking the lady from him." Grigori's eyes danced with humor as he heckled his commander. "All this time you've been hot and eager to take her into your bed. You just couldn't wait for the tsar to give her to you. Now you've had to pay for your error and are angry with her—"

"What the blazes!" Tyrone barked, feeling the prick of truth in the man's conclusions. "Do you imagine yourself able to read my mind?"

"I know you, my friend." Grigori briefly lifted his wide shoulders in an indolent shrug. "If you weren't upset with her, you'd stop this feeble pretense."

"So I'm pretending, am I?"

"If things were as they should be between the two of you, you wouldn't care if the whole Russian army came marching into this house to seek you out. You'd still be making love to her upstairs, and you wouldn't come down until you had thoroughly exhausted your cravings."

Tyrone stared at his second-in-command. He couldn't deny Grigori's deductions, for he'd only be lying. Indeed, the man seemed to know him better than he knew himself.

"And what's more, you're not going to be satisfied until you make peace with her and settle this rift between you. Your bride is very beautiful, Colonel, and if you love her as I think you do, you'd hasten to make amends before she loses heart."

In a show of irritation, the colonel tossed aside the bandages. "It's not that simple, Grigori. I mean nothing to her."

The younger man scoffed in disbelief. "I challenge the truth of that statement. If you asked me, I'd say that she's quite taken with you."

Tyrone tossed his head jeeringly. "She's an actress of great merit. I applaud her skill."

"Spare your lady such slander, my friend! It's absurd to think that she doesn't care for you!"

"How can you claim to know the mind of the maid when she bemuses me at every turn?" Tyrone angrily questioned. "I've no idea what she's thinking, though recently I foolishly imagined I did!"

"Colonel, does our friendship mean nothing to you? Do you consider me a loyal compatriot? A *tovarish*? Have I not proven my worth as such? Did I not warn you that Nikolai had followed your lead and had rushed to the tsar to plead for the countess's hand himself? You wanted to challenge the man outright, yet I cautioned you to wait. Can you not allow that another may be able to see the truth more clearly than you may be able to at the present moment? You're too close to the heart of the matter to view it objectively. You're anxious for answers and entertain hasty judgments. Let your wife have a chance to verify her love."

Tyrone heaved a weary sigh. "She'll have plenty enough time to demonstrate her feelings toward me while we're here. I can't very well have the marriage annulled while Tsar Mikhail is breathing down my neck to see that I comply with his edict."

"Your work here in Russia wouldn't be very effective if you were allowed to do such a thing," Grigori pointed out, piqued with his friend for having contemplated such a thing. "We Russians have a way of taking offense when one of our *boyarinas* is cast aside or embarrassed by a foreigner. Aleksandr Zenkov was a diplomat well respected in this country. I'd urge you as a friend to tender favorable treatment of his daughter."

"Great Caesar's ghost! What do you think I'll do to her? Beat her?" Tyrone was incredulous. "Synnovea is my wife! If for no other reason than that, she's deserving of my protection and care!" A bit outraged at Grigori's warnings, he doffed his breeches and settled his long frame into the steaming bath. Immediately, he sucked in his breath as the hot water reminded him of the mangled condition of his back, especially the area that Synnovea had recently tended. Still feeling the weight of the captain's perplexed frown, he cocked a challenging brow at the man. "Was there something else you wished to discuss with me?"

Thoughtfully Grigori perched on a nearby stool. "You've managed to bemuse me more than any man I've ever known, my friend. You speak of distancing yourself from your wife, and yet in the next breath vehemently declare that she's yours to care for. When you first came here, you seemed loath to involve yourself with women, as if you hated them all. During that space of time I never saw a soldier fight as fiercely as you did. Although you held true to the code of honor, once you were instructed to serve vengeance upon the enemy, you did so with a tenacity that no foe could long withstand. You seemed to take no account of the danger your valor incited, as if you really didn't care if you were killed—"

"Of course I cared!"

Grigori wasn't easily put off by the interruption. "In a way, I suppose you did, but you certainly didn't seem to give serious heed to the risks. Indeed, if you thought a task too dangerous for any of your men, you were always the one who took the chance."

"There's something to be said for experience, or haven't you realized that as yet?" Tyrone countered tersely. "I've more skills in fighting than anyone in our regiment and have faced death many times over. If my ability hadn't been well seasoned by actual clashes of arms, I wouldn't be here in

Moscow doing what I'm being paid to do—instructing the rest of you."

"I've often wondered if you'd consider the perils of warfare with more prudence if you were content with your life."

"You probe too deeply, *tovarish*," Tyrone mumbled through his hands as he vigorously soaped his face. "Though I understand that you're trying to find some logic in all of this, I can give you no guarantee that I'll be doing anything differently from now on. God willing, I'll serve out my due and live to tell of it."

"I shall say that prayer for both of us, my friend. 'Tis my hope that we'll have long life and good fortune, and in that quest I offer an earnest plea that you take into account the brevity of our lives even without the threat of conflict and hasten to restore goodwill between you and your bride."

Tyrone rinsed the soap from his face and peered up at the man, who grinned and casually saluted him before sauntering away. Tyrone eyed him for a moment and then leaned back in the tub to consider the man's advice. Though Grigori's words had vexed him, he couldn't discount the fact that they had been spoken with as much truth as good intent. Frowning musefully, he thought back on a few of his rather expeditious advances into the roiling core of several frays, including his attack on Ladislaus's band. In retrospect, he had to admit that his actions might have seemed reckless and daring, but in each event he had seen the necessity for a strong show of force. Had he acted otherwise, innocents might have suffered and Synnovea would have belonged to Ladislaus rather than to him, a situation he would have detested despite the discord that presently existed between them.

Properly groomed and handsomely attired, Tyrone was again accompanied to the bridal chambers by those same cohorts who had carried him upstairs the night before. When they stood outside the anteroom and called for entry, the sounds that emanated forthwith from the rooms were closely reminiscent of a gaggle of geese coming to rest upon a lake. After a brief elapse of time, the portal creaked open just wide enough to allow a young *boyarina* to peer through the narrow space.

"A moment, please . . . my lords." The plea was punctuated with breathless halts and giggles. "Lady Synnovea . . . hasn't yet finished . . . dressing. . . ."

"Bid her to come forth so we may see her beauty," Walsworth urged with a chortle.

"Come now, maid," Tyrone cajoled as he plied his best grin upon her. "Would you also hold the groom at bay when he has ventured forth to fetch his bride? Stand aside, I say, and let me enter."

Synnovea's muffled voice came from within the bedchamber, bidding the *boyarina* to open the doors of the anteroom. In eager response, the groom and his friends entered amid the vivacious laughter of elegantly garbed ladies and a pair of young chambermaids, who skittered about in their haste to remove a tub from the dressing room. While the men had made use of the bathing chamber downstairs, the copper vessel had served Synnovea's needs upstairs, allowing her to bathe and perfume herself in privacy before she and Ali were joined by tittering maids and curious matrons who had craned their necks in an effort to apprise themselves of the condition of the bed and its sheets. Ali was still smoothing down the hem of her mistress's *sarafan* when the men came striding boldly through the portal, intruding too quickly upon the bride. Synnovea whirled away from their searching eyes as she hastened to fasten the last few silken frogs on her *sarafan*, frustrating Zelda's efforts to cover the loosely flowing black hair with a veil. In the next moment the princess stumbled back in surprise as Tyrone halted beside them and lifted the shimmering cloth from his wife's head.

"If it's all the same to you, Princess, I'd rather see my

wife's hair unfettered by braids and veils," he declared with a dashing grin, but at Zelda's horrified stare, his smile turned somewhat dubious. "Apparently it does make a difference."

With dark eyes dancing warmly, Synnovea glanced over her shoulder at Tyrone, pleased that he should lend some husbandly consideration to her while her friends were there. When he leaned near, her eyes swept his features admiringly. She caught a fleeting whiff of a manly fragrance and, underneath it, the scent of soap, hardly anything at all, yet enough to weaken her knees. "Here in Russia a married woman mustn't reveal her hair to anyone but her husband" she informed him shyly. "If you'd like me to leave it unbound when we're alone, you need only tell me."

Tyrone reached out and slowly stroked a hand down the softly waving length, recalling the first time he had fed his gaze upon the long tresses, though at the time, he had been reluctant to waste any opportunity to peruse her sleek, naked form.

"I'd prefer it," he murmured simply and, with a gracious nod of apology to Zelda, returned the veil to her. The princess accepted the filmy cloth with a demure smile and hurried to attach it. In turning, Tyrone found himself meeting the broad grin of his second-in-command, who approached with a chilled glass of watered wine.

"Perhaps Lady Synnovea would enjoy teaching you the customs of our country," Grigori suggested. "I'm sure both of you would glean great benefit from the lessons."

"I see no need for your matchmaking talents, my friend," Tyrone commented with skeptical humor. "As you well know, we're already married."

The captain's grin widened. "A good *svakhi* wouldn't rest until she is confident that both the bride and the groom are content with each other. And if you're unhappy, Colonel, how will I ever get my promotion?"

"What fickle friendship you portray!" Tyrone admonished

drolly. "And here I was certain you were entirely sincere, but I see now that you only seek to advance yourself!"

Grigori shrugged good-naturedly. "I have to do it somehow."

Smiling radiantly, Natasha swept into the chambers and invited their guests to come downstairs and partake of the feast that Danika had laid out for them in the dining room. She bade Tyrone to lead the procession with his bride upon his arm and encouraged the other men to choose their spouses or unwed maidens to whom they could lend the same consideration. Natasha accepted Grigori's gallant invitation and bestowed a smile upon the young Russians as she queried, "What do you think of your commander's choice for a bride?"

"I believe it to be an excellent match, my lady. I admire your taste in friends."

"And I yours," she replied with a gracious nod. "But tell me, what does the colonel have to say about it all?"

"I'm sure nothing but good will come from this union, Countess," the captain offered magnanimously. "In time, the two will be very happy."

Sensing the officer's clear understanding of the situation, Natasha nodded in smiling contentment, quite willing to accept his prediction, which of course was exactly what she had wanted to hear.

The revelry was launched with a great deal of feasting and tippling as the couple sat together at the morning feast. Exhorted by the guests to follow the customs of the land, the newlyweds kissed to sweeten the meal after each crescendoing cry of *"Gorko! Gorko!* Bitter! Bitter!"

A short time later, a small band of hired *skomorokhi* arrived to entertain them and perform colorful mimes. Many of the guests bedecked themselves in outlandish costumes and eagerly participated in the games and dances. Even Tyrone found his mood lifting to some degree as the wine eased the pain of his lacerated back. As bidden by the tsar, he made a show of enjoying the festivities and cavorted with his bride about the house and grounds, sometimes chasing others or being chased, hiding and then seeking.

The jester played his part with enthusiasm, sniffing and snarling, growling and howling as he prowled around with the pelt of a gray wolf draped across his shoulders, searching for any damsel whom he could catch to be the firebird of the tale. He was still roaming far afield when Tyrone caught Synnovea's hand and whisked her out into the garden.

Deliberately matched together in the pairing off of couples, they had been bound together by a ribbon tied about their wrists. Where one went, the other surely had to follow. Tyrone espied an obscure crevice between two stout trees that had merged at the base some years before and, after slipping into it, lifted Synnovea into the niche between his splayed legs. What made the spot fairly secure as a hiding place was a large shrub that encompassed the sturdy trunks on three sides, but Tyrone hadn't reckoned on the nook becoming a place of torture. The trees grew at the same slanting angles, compelling Synnovea to lean into him as he, in turn, braced his buttocks against the sloping trunk. His care in keeping his mangled back away from the rough, irritating bark forced him to subject himself even more to her alluring proximity and the susceptibility of his own manly cravings, for he had to clamp an arm behind her waist to keep her from losing her balance. The space narrowed progressively as he became aware of nearly every rounded curve and sleek limb hidden beneath his wife's softly textured *sarafan*. But that was not all, by any means. The knoll between her slippered feet caused her to twist and shift her weight fairly often as she sought a more comfortable position. The hard brush of her thighs against his loins lit fires that he had wished to avoid, and he soon found himself battling a far different game than merely playing hide-and-seek with a "wolf."

It wasn't long before Synnovea became cognizant of the

heavy thudding of her husband's heart and the noticeable protrusion beneath his breeches. Her surprise was all too apparent when her eyes dropped to his lap and then flew up to peruse his stoic demeanor. Tyrone gazed down his noble nose at her as if to distance himself from the tumult she had awakened within him, yet as much as his overt display chafed against his pride, there was no denying the obvious.

Tyrone remained unyielding in his reticence, yet Synnovea was nevertheless heartened by the fact that he hadn't yet set her from him. A memory of that moment in his quarters when he had lifted her astride his velvet-clad loins came winging back to her, awakening a heightening hunger within her to feel again that succulent pressure against her womanly softness. She had no hope that he'd relent of his hide-bound taciturnity, but she wasn't above offering him the opportunity. Threading slender fingers through the short locks curling at his nape, she rose up against him, pressing every curve and hollow of her body to his manly torso. She heard his breath catch while her own nigh halted with the bliss elicited by her boldness as she snuggled her loins around his tumescence. Lifting eyes that had grown dark and sultry, she rubbed a hand caressingly over his shirt, admiring the muscular firmness she felt beneath it.

"Can we not appease our desires while we're in this private place?" she whispered softly.

Though Tyrone made no effort to respond, his attitude of acquiescent stillness encouraged his wife to continue her seduction. Her softly parted mouth and caressing tongue played languidly upon his lips. The soft nipples peaked beneath her bodice and teased his manly ardor as she rubbed her breasts tantalizingly against his chest, yet he resisted her offerings, making no effort to either claim or reject them.

Synnovea could take heart only in the fact that her husband was a man and not a stone statue as he gave every evidence of being at the moment, but now her own cravings had intensified and she yearned for appeasement. There was only one thing that would snatch him from his affected indolence, and though she dared much by her impertinence, she slipped a hand down between them and clasped the hard shaft through his breeches.

Tyrone tried in vain to curb the pulsing excitement that robbed him of every sane thought but one, and that was the realization that he was no less susceptible now to his wife's wiles than he had been a few nights ago. Except that she had become emboldened by the sensuality he had awakened within her. Her parted lips were temptingly moist and softly yielding, and he knew that beneath her clothes he'd find a place just as alluring, just as easy to reach. He had only to lift her skirts and pull her thighs astride him to take his ease—

"Someone's coming!" Synnovea's whisper was a mixture of panic and disappointment as she pushed herself away from him, at least as much as she was able.

The gray wolf pounced forward in an exaggerated stance, startling a gasp from the bride. Howling in victorious glee, the jester quickly snipped the ribbon that bound the couple together and, seizing her wrist, dragged her off toward the manse while casting a backward glance at the groom, who scowled after him in rampant annoyance. It was no more than what the jester expected from a newlywed, and blithely he continued on his way, giving the husband no reprieve. Once inside the manse, he took special delight in hiding the bride in a place not easily accessible to discovery.

Tyrone's blood cooled forthwith, and by dent of will he managed to adjust his mien to a facade of good humor. Still, visions of Aleksei garbed in wolf pelt and chortling in vindictive glee sorely nettled his mood as he stalked after the culprit. At his entry into the manse, the gray wolf skipped around him and, in strident tones, tauntingly bade him to find the captured firebird in the gilded cage ere the evil brothers were able to kill him and claim her as their prize. The laughter-laden foray found Tyrone dodging the mock ploys and attacks of his friends, mainly to avoid some painful reminder of the condition of his back. Perhaps it was his own warrior's spirit and years of combat training that prevented him from accepting defeat easily, for his fervor for the game intensified as his failure became more promising, and he flitted from room to room well ahead of the others in his quest to be the first to find Synnovea.

It was the tiny Sophia who beckoned to him from the kitchen door and surreptitiously pointed toward the pantry. There he swooped his young wife up into his arms with a triumphant cry, evoking laughter from her. He dashed ahead of his diabolical kin to deliver the firebird before the Tsarina Natasha, who smilingly crowned him with a flower-bedecked garland. It was this prize that Tyrone took back to the kitchen. Kneeling before the child, he placed the coronal upon her small head, winning a radiant smile and a quick, timid brush of her lips upon his cheek. When Tyrone returned to the portal where he had left Synnovea, he found a strange warmth glowing in the green-brown eyes.

"You seem to have a special way with children, Colonel Sir Tyrone Rycroft. Have you ever considered siring any?"

"Several times," he responded, recalling the disappointment he had suffered each of the three times that Angelina had miscarried in the first two years of their marriage. Her fluxes hadn't come with any regularity, and the physician who had treated her had given her a variety of herbs to strengthen her childbearing ability. Later, when Tyrone had knelt beside her grave, he had found it sadly ironic that she had found it necessary to endanger her own life in order to rid herself of another man's child.

"Then you're not averse to having children?" Synnovea queried forthrightly.

"That, madam, is not my difficulty at all," Tyrone responded with equal candor. Taking her elbow, he escorted her away from the kitchen. " 'Tis the deceit I can't abide. How can I know the truth of your heart when you've proven yourself capable of chicanery?"

"How can I know *your* heart, sir, when you look at me with desire one moment and then seemingly disdain me the next?" she countered, disconcerted. "Are you fickle, Colonel? Your lips speak of diatribes, but when I look into your eyes, I see something smoldering there that awakens my senses to a heady degree."

"Aye, madam, I've recently discovered a certain inconsistency within myself that tears me apart," he readily admitted. "With your unparalleled beauty and coquettish smiles veiling your enticing subterfuge, you have the power to reach deep into the heart of a man and wring him inside out. Though he may stand valiant and resolute against the challenges of a thousand other entities, he's helpless to protect himself against your wiles." Halting, Tyrone faced her squarely as he hoarsely avowed, "I cannot deny that you're able to tempt me beyond my ability to resist, Synnovea, but I'd be a fool if I didn't try to build a fortress to shield my heart from the pain that I fear you'll inflict upon it."

Synnovea almost winced at the sting of his gentle reproach, knowing only too well that she deserved his distrust. "I pray you desist from your harsh judgment of me, Ty, because I intend you no hurt, not now nor in the weeks and months to come. I only seek some mutual ground upon which we can meld together and be content in this marriage of ours. I see you struggling to keep your distance from me when we both know you're binding us both up in a tangle of knots by refusing to make love to me. Will you always be reluctant to nurture me with your attentions as well as with your child?"

A tawny brow jutted sharply upward in surprise at her blunt question. "Always, madam? Who knows what even the next moments will bring, but you should know well enough by now that making a child will require further involvement . . ."

411

"Is that what you're objecting to, Ty?" Synnovea asked softly, her heart aching. "Further involvement?"

"I must confess that I fear indulging in the intimacy which would be required in making a child. 'Tis much like a siren's song that a man hears and then is forever held captive in its silken chains. Once fed, 'tis doubtful that I'll be able to resist you, whatever your ploys."

"I weave no siren's song but a wifely plea that you'll not leave me bereft of your attentions," she insisted, her voice fraught with emotion. "If not for you, I'd have no knowledge of what is beyond the mere joining of our bodies. 'Tis you, sir, who has teased and now deny, and like a helpless sparrow, I must wait for the hawk to seize his prey before I can also be fed."

Tyrone stared down at her in some amazement. He knew he had taken her to that lofty pinnacle of ecstasy which he had aspired to reach himself, but he was rather amazed that she could voice her own yearnings with such openness. He found her frankness no less than intriguing, inspiring him to make confessions of his own.

"Aye, madam, I'm most anxious to relieve this gnawing hunger that drives me like some rutting stag in the wilds. You've grown no less beautiful or desirable since you went with me to my quarters. You'd tempt any man, and I'm probably more susceptible than most."

" 'Twould only be a physical thing for you to make love to me. Men are like that, I've been told." Synnovea felt frustrated by the lack of harmony between his words and his actions. If he were as vulnerable to her womanly wiles as he maintained, then how could he remain so aloof in her presence? "Why not me? You said yourself that you've been without feminine companionship for some time now, so I would assume any woman could serve your needs."

"Not necessarily, madam."

A lovely brow rose in wonder. "I've heard there are harlots

aplenty who roam the German district. Have you never considered them in your quest for a companion?"

"Never," he stated brusquely. "You'll learn in time that I'm rather particular about the woman I bed."

"Which really doesn't include me anymore." Synnovea's voice broke slightly though she valiantly fought the tears that welled forth.

"I didn't say that, Synnovea, so don't put words into my mouth," Tyrone retorted.

Keeping her face carefully averted to hide the wetness streaming down her cheeks, she questioned him. "Have you been so wronged that you are loath to make love to me and give me your child?"

Tyrone glanced away, reluctant to give any answer that would commit him to serving her desires, no matter how much he'd have welcomed both the sowing of the seed and the reaping of the harvest. Well aware of the unstable ground upon which he trod, he feigned an impatience to join their friends as he took her elbow. "Come, Synnovea, we'll be missed by our guests."

It was much later in the afternoon when General Vanderhout and his flaxen-haired wife came to the house. Although neither seemed particularly inclined to wish the newly wedded couple well, they were nevertheless obligated to extend a few superficial congratulations while so many other guests were present. Still, a few comments seemed laden with sarcasm.

"I never dreamt Colonel Rycroft vould cede to the pleas of a voman and actually marry her," Aleta Vanderhout warbled to Synnovea in a coyly affected accent. "Especially a Russian *boyarina*. However did yu manage to ensnare him, my dear?"

Synnovea's brow quirked in curiosity, and she shifted her gaze to Tyrone. Hitherto she had established no clear recollection of having suffered a jealous twinge in her life, but when the large brown eyes had devoured him with more than a token amount of lust, Synnovea experienced a sharp, nettling irritation that clearly set her at odds with the woman. She could not help but wonder what this pretty vixen meant to him, and if the two were secret lovers.

Much to her relief, Tyrone didn't seem to have any difficulty meeting her perusal, allowing her to nurture a burgeoning hope that he had nothing to hide in this particular matter. Daring much, she slipped an arm through his and clasped it closely against her breast as she faced the flaxen-haired coquette. "It wasn't hard at all, Madame Vanderhout. I merely stopped running and allowed him to catch me."

"Much to my relief," Tyrone replied, surprising his bride by smiling down at her and laying a hand in an affectionate manner upon the one she had settled upon his arm. Reluctantly he lent his attention to Aleta, a hot-blooded vamp who had tried countless times to break his continence. Though her husband of two-score-eight years was unaware of his young wife's prurient bent, nearly every officer in his command had become well acquainted with the fact that Aleta had an insatiable appetite for handsome, virile lovers. She had made her way through a goodly number of officers, many of whom were more boastful than wise, considering the rank of her husband. For several months now, Tyrone had avoided her like the plague, not wishing to become embroiled in another scene wherein he'd be required to guard his privy parts with as much dedication as a reluctant virgin. It seemed the woman just couldn't understand why he hadn't wanted to follow in the wake of all her other lovers. "I was desperate enough to petition the tsar in my quest to stake my claim on Synnovea."

Vincent Vanderhout loudly harrumphed as he bestowed a glowering stare upon his second-in-command. Making his excuses to the two women, he bade Tyrone to join him in the garden. There he turned on the younger man with fire in his eyes. "Must I remind you, Colonel Rycroft, that it's the right of a commander to be informed well in advance of an officer's intention to marry. I must verbally take you to task for your negligence in asking my permission to wed and for failing to show proper respect to a higher ranking officer. Obviously your clandestine affair with the countess has cost you your freedom and a bad report from me—"

"Your pardon, General," Tyrone interrupted, growing annoyed with the pompous arrogance of the man. When he had made his decision to come to Russia, he had never committed himself to the idea of asking a foreigner for authorization to deal with matters concerning his personal life. It had been hard enough to accept the tsar's recent interference, and though he was tempted to tell the general bluntly that his marriage was none of the man's affair, he used the truth instead as an effective means by which to silence the elder. "It was the expressed wish of his majesty that I marry the Countess Synnovea."

"What in the hell have you done, Rycroft? Get the maid with child ere you spoke the vows?" the Dutchman railed at the top of his lungs. *"Have you no regard for the fact that you're on foreign soil?"*

The muscles tensed in Tyrone's lean cheeks. His own explosive temper had been tested far too much in recent days for him to consider the wisdom of giving the man a placid rejoinder. Instead he came to abrupt attention and looked over the shorter man's head as he snapped out a reply. "No, General, *sir!* I didn't get her with child, *sir—if* it's any of your damned business, *sir!*"

General Vanderhout fixed the colonel with a piercing glare. "Be careful, Colonel, I can arrange for your swift dispatch to England."

"I'd advise against it, *General sir,* unless you first take up the matter with the tsar! He has assigned me certain duties, *sir,* which I don't think you have the ability to perform."

The general's mouth twisted sharply with ill-restrained

fury. The very idea of an underling telling him that he was unsuited for any kind of duties! Why, such a statement bordered on insubordination. "Apparently, Colonel Rycroft, you've become quite taken with the attention you've been able to garner from the tsar, so much so that you're not above disobeying orders and ignoring proper decorum in an effort to claim what you've been rutting after ever since you snatched the countess from that bastard prince, Ladislaus."

Though Tyrone never lowered his gaze to the man, his blue eyes hardened with fermenting fury. "Perhaps I should return to my bride and our guests, General," he suggested tersely. "I can see no profit in discussing my personal affairs with you any longer."

Mentally Vincent Vanderhout searched for an intimidation that would be effective in reducing the colonel to the size of a squealing piglet. So far, rumors had it that Tyrone Rycroft didn't back down to anyone, not even to his fiercest foes, and although the man had been whipped unmercifully, word had gotten back to their command that the colonel hadn't relented even then. Perhaps it was the admiration that he had heard in the voices of the officers relating the story that had aroused a goading desire within Vanderhout to establish himself the exception. The only problem, he just didn't know how to go about gaining that distinction.

With a loud, angry snort, the general gave up his futile attempt and, turning on a heel, stalked back into the house, leaving Tyrone to contend with his own rage. Everyone inside the house had most likely heard their shouts, and though he could take some comfort in the fact that his friends would show discretion and maintain a respectful silence, he wasn't so sure about all the others.

Tyrone knew without a doubt that if he and Vanderhout came together in the same room again before his temper cooled, he wouldn't be able to suffer through the other's caustic comments beyond the breadth of another moment. It seemed prudent for him to seek some privacy in his bride's chambers upstairs until the general left, or otherwise he'd be sorely tempted to resort to fisticuffs. Right now the way things stood, he was just in the mood to tear the old warthog apart. There was definitely something of a serious note to be said about the growing agitation of a husband who denied himself the pleasure of copulating with his bride and easing the tensions that bound him up in an angry knot.

Tyrone's ascent of the stairs was swift and uneventful, his entrance into the upper chambers even less difficult. Closing the door behind him, he breathed a sigh of relief and considered insuring his privacy further by locking the portal, but he was afraid that if Synnovea came looking for him she'd take it much amiss.

A cold dousing promised to soothe the vexing tide of rage that churned within him. Entering the dressing chamber, he stripped away his shirt and poured water into the basin before he noticed a sweet scent wafting from the *sarafan*, which Synnovea had doffed after the band of *skomorokhi* had departed. It now hung on a nearby peg awaiting Ali's attention after the hem had been snagged by the knoll she had been forced to straddle. If not for the wily wolf's haste to claim his victim, the soft fabric might never have been torn.

Thoughtfully Tyrone reached out and drew the garment to him. Remembering how her nipples had puckered beneath the bodice, he stroked his hand over the cloth, feeling a strange sense of regret that, by his own stubborn tenacity, he hadn't accepted her invitation and caressed those tempting orbs. Considering his lusting fervor, he might have wreaked more havoc on it than the wolf if he had been able to forget his bruised pride and yielded to her seduction.

Lifting the garment, he held it beneath his nose and closed his eyes as he savored the delectable scent. It was the same that had haunted him throughout the previous night, the fragrance of English violets on warm, inviting skin.

Enough of this! Tyrone mentally growled and, cursing himself for being a fool, returned the garment to the peg. Even after what she had done to him, he couldn't thrust aside his collection of memories that seemed to be growing by leaps and bounds. Even now in her absence he wanted to feel her soft, naked body yielding to his and her lithe thighs opening to receive his encroaching hips.

Downstairs in the great hall, Natasha drew Zelda and her husband, Vassili, with her as she approached a vividly blushing Synnovea. "That oaf Vanderhout needs to be horsewhipped!" the countess muttered as her eyes followed Aleta to the stairs. "If I weren't afraid he'd resort to spiting your husband in a most vindictive way, I'd ask him to leave."

Prince Vassili was not above voicing his own conjectures and did so, hoping to assuage the bride's chagrin. "Pay the general and his remarks no serious mind, Synnovea. From what I've been able to ascertain from my brief association with the man, he's definitely a hound for glory. The field marshal and I have both become cognizant of several instances wherein General Vanderhout has deliberately claimed your husband's achievements and plans as his own. And if that isn't enough to set our tempers on edge, he seems to begrudge the favor that His Majesty has shown to the colonel. No doubt he'd like nothing better than to undermine that good will any way he could, even if he must goad your husband into a fight over you."

Zelda gently patted her friend's hand. "Don't fret yourself over the general's boorish manners, Synnovea. He isn't worth a smidgen of your concern."

Natasha accepted a goblet of wine from a servant and passed it on to Synnovea, who accepted it tremblingly. "Drink this down, my dear, while I go and have a little chat with the general. He needs to be instructed in some good Russian manners."

"I think I should like to retire to my chambers for a few moments," Synnovea said, offering a wan smile to her friends. "At least until the general leaves."

Laying a towel over his wet head, Tyrone rubbed his hair vigorously as he paused in the entrance of the dressing room. He hadn't heard the antechamber door open, and he suffered some surprise when he felt a small hand sliding purposefully down the front of his breeches. When he had extracted his pledge from the tsar, he had given no moment's heed to the temptations he'd be confronting if Synnovea became resolved in breaking his restraints. Inanely he hadn't considered her growing appreciation for the delights to be found in copulating; he had foolishly thought she'd be content with a staid, superficial marriage. Since the garden, however, he had become acutely aware of his mistake and seriously doubted that he could remain indifferent to her delicious attacks. At the moment the sheer excitement that jolted through his being was enough to snatch his breath as she clasped his rapidly hardening manhood in a tenacious grip. The pleasure was so intense, he couldn't even imagine continuing his continence one moment longer.

His wavering sigh sounded closely akin to acquiescence even to him as he swept the towel down around his neck. Instantly he stepped back in shock. "Aleta!" If he had taken a plunge in an icy stream, his reaction would have been no different. "What the hell are you doing here?"

"Yu naughty man, yu," the woman chided as she rubbed her fingers over a male nipple. "Getting married vithout Vincent's permission. Tsk, tsk! Vincent said yu vex the tsar's good humor by getting his late ambassador's daughter in trouble, and now yu've had to pay yur due. Aren't yu sorry now yu didn't let Aleta satisfy yur manly needs?"

He glared at the woman who stood before him, recognizing his frustration for what it was. She was *not* Synnovea! Testily brushing aside the woman's hand, he stepped back into the dressing room where he fetched a fresh shirt and dragged it over his head. The more clothes he wore around this wanton, the safer he would feel! "Your pardon, Aleta, but I'm not interested in what you have to offer."

"Vell, yu vere a moment ago!"

"I thought you were my wife," he snapped over his shoulder. "I'm interested in *her,* not you."

"I can make yu forget that little twit," the woman boasted. Hurriedly wiggling up against his buttock, she swept her hand around in front of him as she cooed, "I'll do anything to please yu, Tyrone. Anything!"

He grabbed her wrist before she could seize his private parts again and, turning, stalked out of the dressing room. "I'm not interested, Aleta. I never have been. How many times must I tell you?"

Brown eyes warm and limpid with desire, she sauntered toward him, caressing her own breasts to entice him. "Don't yu vant to touch me, Tyrone?"

"As difficult as it seems for you to understand, Aleta, I don't have any desire to touch you, to kiss you, or to make love to you! What I'd really like now is to be left alone." Tyrone turned his back on her and promptly found her hand searching forward between his buttocks. He leapt away as if he had been stung. "Dammit, Aleta! Leave me be!" Somehow he managed to refrain from insulting her as he stalked through the antechamber and snatched open the outer door. "I think you'd better leave. I don't think your husband would appreciate your being here, and I *know* my wife wouldn't!"

"Come now, Tyrone, yu'll never be satisfied with that little ignoramus Russian yu married. Yu need a more experienced voman to take care of yur needs." She strutted toward him with a sultry smile and pressed her body full-length against his before she began searching for the opening to his breeches. "I can make yu forget she even exists."

Tyrone caught her hand and tossed it aside in anger. "Hell

and damnation, Aleta! I'm not in the mood for this! Can't you understand that?"

"I know better, Tyrone!" she argued, coming back just as quickly and rubbing against him eagerly. Seeking a firmer hold she slipped her hands behind him and clasped his buttocks. "Yu were all hot and ready for me just a moment ago!"

"It wasn't *you* I was thinking of!" Tyrone snapped irately. "It was my wife!"

"Don't be so damned noble! Yu have enough for us both. Besides, vhat she doesn't know von't hurt her."

Tyrone seized the woman's chin and forced her to meet his glower. "You appear to have trouble understanding me, Aleta, so I won't mince words any longer. I'm not interested in *anything* you have *ever* offered me. I never have and I never will, so please—just go away and *stay away!*"

"Yu're afraid of my husband!" Aleta accused, clearly astonished at his rejection. No man had ever rebuffed her advances before, and she found it hard to accept that he didn't want her.

"I don't want any trouble from him, that's true!" Tyrone agreed testily. "But I want nothing from you either. Make an effort to understand me! There'll never be anything between us, so *please,* just leave me alone from now on." He recognized the woman's final acceptance of his statement when her lips twisted downward in a disdaining grimace. With a brief dip of his head, he smiled tersely. "I'm immensely relieved to see you've finally caught on."

Straightening her clothes with a jerk, Aleta stalked out of the door in a vivid display of outrage. In the next moment she gasped in astonishment as she came face-to-face with the young woman who stood in mute shock only a short distance from the door.

"Oh! I didn't know yu vere here," Aleta nervously announced.

Tyrone glanced around in sharp surprise, fully expecting to find the general outside his door. It was Synnovea, and from the curious quirk elevating her brow, she was none too happy.

"I hope I'm not interrupting anything." Her meager smile clearly indicated her lack of concern in that area.

"Synnovea . . . I. . . ." Tyrone hoped he didn't look half as guilty as he felt. "I . . . just came up here to get away . . ."

"No explanations needed," she assured him with noticeable rigidity. "I heard you arguing with the general downstairs and found myself unable to endure the stares of our guests." Her gaze returned to Aleta, and the chilling glare in those green-brown eyes seemed to momentarily freeze the blonde. "Had I known this wench would be here trying to get into your breeches, I might have come better prepared to interfere. Perhaps you need a chastity belt to keep you safe from her wiles."

Though innocent of any wrongdoing, Tyrone found himself struggling for a way to placate his wife's suspicions. "I came up here to find some privacy, not to cavort with her."

"Were you escaping from someone in particular?"

"The general."

Synnovea faced the shorter woman and smiled rigidly as she bade, "Would you mind leaving us alone, Aleta? I have matters to discuss with my husband."

Aleta seemed eager to escape and did so, running down the hall. In her haste to descend she almost stumbled on the stairs, evidenced by the sharp intake of her breath and a fearful little squeal.

"Do you suppose she hurt herself?" Synnovea questioned musefully, closing the outer door of their chambers to secure their privacy.

"Do you care?" Tyrone queried. He had never had the opportunity to view the peevishness of an outraged wife before, but at the moment was of the opinion that Synnovea closely resembled one.

"Not really," Synnovea answered truthfully. Turning, she lent her husband her undivided attention. "Tell me, Colonel, is she the reason you're not interested in me?"

"Don't be absurd, Synnovea!" The very idea angered him.

"That woman means nothing to me! She came in here while I was drying my hair. I thought at first it was you."

Synnovea folded her arms petulantly as she responded with liberal sarcasm. "Well, Colonel Rycroft, if you mistook her for me, then I don't suppose you became too amorous with her. Still, she seemed to enjoy handling you . . . as if she might have been encouraged."

"All women are not paragons of virtue as you are, my dear," Tyrone mocked, lifting a challenging brow. Staring into the dark depths of those beautiful eyes, he realized with some astonishment that he was very close to sweeping her up into his arms and carrying her to their bed, where he'd no doubt appease all of his lusting cravings. He approached a step closer, his heart pounding at the idea, and murmured in distraction, "Aleta doesn't need encouragement."

Taking exception to his comment, Synnovea snubbed him with a well-articulated toss of her veiled head and flounced from their rooms. Tyrone's breath left him in a rush, and it came as something of a shock when he realized he had been holding it in something comparable to heightening arousal as visions of his naked wife dragging him back to their bed bombarded him. In roweling frustration he stepped into the hall to observe her flight. The angry twitch of her skirts evidenced her vexation with him, but her ire was no less than what he was presently feeling toward himself.

It was relatively early that evening when Tyrone begged compassion from their friends and shushed their protests with the excuse that the duties of the morrow required him to be fully alert. Laying an arm around Synnovea's shoulders, he waved them off and then followed behind as she led the way to their chambers. Even so, he had difficulty dragging his gaze from her gently swaying hips.

Ali was waiting in the dressing room to help her mistress undress. While the two women carried out his wife's toilet in private, Tyrone readied his equipment and uniform for the next day. When he went in search of his military trappings and weapons, he had his mind on what he had to fetch and gave no thought to what he'd find in the adjoining cubicle until he saw his wife standing with her arms outstretched in readiness to receive the nightgown Ali was holding. The maid faltered in some confusion, forgetting what she was about, leaving Synnovea sublimely naked.

All the conflicts Tyrone had been battling since their meeting in the bathhouse came back to assault him as he found himself confronting a nymph far too beautiful to be ignored for even an hour. Totally captivated by the stirring vision, he swept his gaze helplessly downward in a lengthy descent over pink-nippled breasts that were soft and round, a rib cage and waist that seemed incredibly narrow, and hips that were trim but utterly tempting. A creamy smooth belly led his eyes downward to a dark nest and long, sleek thighs that were more lithe and smooth than any he had ever viewed. Mumbling an inquiry about the location of his gear, he was too absorbed in the sights to notice where Ali pointed until his wife dragged the gown from the maid's hands and slipped it over her own head, sadly hiding from view everything that held his attention imprisoned. He stepped beyond her and, in a calmer vein, located his gear. Upon his return, he found her watching him curiously, and though for pride's sake he wanted to give a plausible reason for having ogled her undraped form, he deemed it far more noble to remain silent rather than spill a farfetched lie.

Tyrone eased his breath out in slow, shallow drafts as he stripped to his breeches in the bedchamber. It took a concerted effort for him to restore some semblance of what had once been an iron will and to turn his thoughts to something less frustrating than the delectable perfection that he had beheld in the adjoining room. In a valiant attempt to thrust from his mind all the heated conflicts he had endured throughout the day, he sat down on his bedside bench and busied himself with the task of organizing the accouterments of a soldier.

Soon after Ali's departure, Synnovea strolled leisurely into the bedchamber. She was in a singular mood herself after discovering Aleta in their private chambers and was nigh famished for the display of passion that Tyrone had demonstrated so ardently as a lover on the night of his whipping. She was definitely unwilling to be ignored for another long night.

Tyrone almost groaned in misery when he saw her. For his pleasure, her dark hair had been left flowing in shimmering waves down her back, but it was her gown that gave him some inkling of his forthcoming defeat, for it molded itself with endearing delight to her shapely form and was translucent enough to be considered worthless for maintaining a woman's modesty. It seemed to flaunt every curve and hollow, every hue and shadow until Tyrone felt as if he had no more fortitude than a bleating lamb.

"How early will you leave in the morning?" she asked in a tone so sweet and soft it caused goose bumps to rise on his flesh. Pausing close beside him, she observed him as he polished his sword, now in some distraction.

"Shortly after dawn," he answered and hurried to find some way to avoid further temptations. "But I'm used to fending for myself, Synnovea, so there's no need for you to get up. Besides, Ali said that Danika would have food ready in the kitchen and a basket packed for me to take when I come down. I won't be back until late, so there again, you needn't wait up for me."

"I don't mind," Synnovea murmured softly.

Tyrone was diligently concentrating on his labors, trying to avoid looking at her any more than he had to. The way she consumed his attention even now, he'd likely forget he had work to do and men to train. "I'd just as soon you stay here."

Though Synnovea sensed that he was trying to ignore her, she hadn't forgotten how he had devoured her body in the dressing room. She wasn't incapable of winning his regard when she wanted it, and she most certainly wanted it now. Feigning a casualness she did not necessarily feel, she slipped her slender fingers through the short hair at the base of his neck, bringing his head up with stunning abruptness. "Your hair is getting long, Ty," she breathed in a caressing sigh. "Would you like me to clip it for you?"

"Not tonight," Tyrone replied, only vaguely aware that he had even spoken as he found himself staring into her soft eyes.

"It wouldn't take much time at all," Synnovea coaxed, lifting the tawny strands. She reached across his shoulder to retrieve his comb from the bedside table, in the process managing to brush a thinly clad breast against his arm, causing him to close his eyes as he luxuriated in the tantalizing caress. Synnovea was fascinated by the way his hair curled against his neck and threaded her fingers through the strands growing there. "Only a snip here or there to neaten the edges."

"It's getting late, and I need my rest," he managed, totally engrossed in the wealth of beauty revealed by the thin lawn of her gown. The candlelight glowed behind her, clearly defining her softly curving form. The gossamer cloth seemed like nothing more than a vaporish veil, bent on playing havoc with his senses.

Synnovea leaned toward him, allowing the voluminous garment to fall away from her body as she combed his hair across his brow. Tyrone found himself unable to resist her offering, and although he was well aware that such delectable sights would lead to his doom, his eyes greedily consumed everything she offered, ogling her delicately hued breasts and searching out the dark nest where her long, sleek limbs were enticingly joined.

A sudden pain shattered the interlude, drawing a surprised start from Tyrone and making him glance down in search of the cause. Blood welled forth from a long gash on his thumb, which in an instant he had sliced open with his well-honed blade.

"Hell and damnation!" he growled, angry at himself. It seemed that he was just as willing now to be led like a sacrificial lamb to the altar of their bed as he had been when he had taken her to his quarters, and, like before, she'd rend his heart with her tempting ways. "I can't even polish my sword without suffering some damage when you're near!" Tossing her a glare, he paid no heed to her look of wounded dismay as he commanded curtly, "Get into bed before I slice off something vital and serve Aleksei's end."

Tears gushed forth, and with a choked sob Synnovea hastily retired to her side of the bed, where she sat and through a blurring wetness launched glowers aplenty toward the ignoring back of her stubborn husband. Petulantly she braided her hair, sniffing and blowing her nose until she finally drove Tyrone to seek refuge in the dressing room. He knew if he stayed one moment longer, he'd give way to her tears and coddle her with much more than an apology.

Fearing defeat, he was in no hurry to join her in their bed and allowed at least a half hour to drift past as he bathed. He donned a robe for his return to their bedchamber and found that Synnovea had taken shelter beneath the covers, having tucked them up close beneath her chin. It was obvious from her stilted silence that she had sorely resented his boorish reproach.

Tyrone slipped into bed beside her, assured by her efforts to hug the edge of the bed that he wouldn't have to worry about being unduly tempted by her flirtatious ploys for the rest of the night. She wanted nothing to do with him, and though he should have been relieved, he felt like cursing himself for getting caught in such a hellish trap.

15

*I*f Tyrone Rycroft had once imagined that he was expending every ounce of energy and skill he possessed in his quest to impress the tsar, he soon realized that ignoring his stirringly beautiful wife and keeping his mind strictly on his goals and duties even while he was away from her demanded much more fortitude and discipline over his thoughts than his first objective had ever required of him. If his preoccupation with Synnovea had seemed intense before his whipping, then it was rapidly becoming an obsession now that they were ensconced not only in the same chamber but in the same bed as well. He was constantly besieged by sights that would have heartened the most indifferent husband, which he definitely was not. Whether fully clothed or scantily garbed, Synnovea was far too fetching for any normal man to resist, and though he still chafed under the spiny barbs of resentment, he felt much akin to an untried youth who drooled in blighted infatu-

ation over an alabaster goddess. Such a lad might have hoped
to discover a warm, tender heart beneath those creamy breasts,
but Tyrone feared there was nothing there but cold, hard
stone.

Not only was his reserve undermined by what he saw in
their bedchamber, but he had never been so baffled by a
woman in all of his life. Since his encounter with Aleksei,
Tyrone had imagined Synnovea an unscrupulous vixen bereft
of a conscience. He was certain she had deliberately entrapped him with a thoroughly ruthless disregard for what
he'd have to suffer because of her deception, yet the more he
was around her, the deeper his perplexity became. As hard as
he searched, he could detect no tiniest hint of the sly coquette
in that sublime mien. To his utter amazement, Synnovea
seemed the paragon of what every man aspired to have for a
wife. She was soft-spoken, sweetly attentive, and mindful of
him in ways that at times put to rout the image of a conniving,
selfish, spoiled *boyarina*. He might as well have been a king
the way she anticipated and fulfilled his every need well before he even thought of it. Though he feared he'd again be
caught unawares by her subterfuge, there were times when
he could actually feel his bruised heart softening to her winsome smiles and the gentle touch of her hand. His breath nigh
halted with the bliss of her slender fingers threading through
his hair, massaging the tension from his neck or tracing
around an ear. Yet he couldn't shake the suspicion that those
knee-weakening caresses were merely part of another ploy. If
she had spoken some witch's incantation to make him her
slave, he couldn't have been more entranced . . . or more
apprehensive about his fate. Much too often of late, he seemed
unable to subdue familiar flutterings in the pit of his hard
belly, momentarily delectable to be sure, yet savagely brutal
when left unappeased. No fiendish torment could have vexed
him quite as severely.

Tyrone couldn't remember a time in his adult years when

he had been in such a rutting heat over a woman. In spite of his efforts to remain coolly detached in his wife's presence, his rebellious body was ever wont to leave him open to the curious stares of those widely innocent green-brown eyes. Angelina had never stirred such erotic cravings within him, at least not to the degree that he was now experiencing with Synnovea, but then, he only had to lift a brow and Angelina would have come wiggling into his lap. He had no doubt that Synnovea would have done the same, but her motives weren't to be trusted.

The pain of abstinence was becoming so horrendous that there were moments when Tyrone actually feared his lust for his raven-haired wife would rend him permanently useless to any woman. Many nights while Synnovea slumbered peacefully in their bed, he'd pace the floor like a caged leopard, prowling the ebony shadows until finally exhaustion would numb him to everything but a yearning to rest. The emotional upheaval he was being subjected to on a nightly basis made him give serious consideration to the idea of moving back to his old quarters, but as much as he needed the separation, he knew if he returned to his quarters, it would be tantamount to publicly distancing himself from Synnovea. Albeit silently, he'd be casting aspersions against her, a deed that would certainly elicit the tsar's ire.

Had his back been properly healed and his fighting agility restored to the degree that he'd have felt confident of his prowess in deadly combat, he'd have ridden out in search of Ladislaus just to avoid the defeat that lurked in wait for him in his bedchamber. He was no fool to think that he could lie in bed next to an incredibly tempting woman night after night and still deny her existence. Had he been hewn of granite, there might have been some hope for him, but he was very much a man, subject to all the weaknesses and propensities of his gender, and Synnovea was the visual epitome of everything he had ever desired in a woman. At times, frustration, resentment, outright anger, and hostility vied in direct opposition to the softer feelings of compassion, gentleness, and ardor, as well as a strengthening desire to nurture and protect her as any adoring husband might. He was ever mindful of the fact that she was his and that all the aspirations he had once sought to bring into fruition could now be his for the simple taking . . . *if only* he'd relent.

It certainly took no mean mental feat for Tyrone to recognize his own heightening agitation. His temper had never been so quick to flare or his patience so thin. For the sake of his men, he knew he'd soon have to repent of his foolish vow. Yet, in an effort to hold his ground no matter how asinine his own obstinacy was beginning to seem even to him, he pushed himself and his regiment relentlessly day after day through long hours of difficult training, crawling on his belly with his face in the dirt or mud, climbing ropes attached to brick walls, and wrestling his way through men equally motivated to keep him and the rest of the troop from reaching their goal. Only by depleting his strength and draining himself of the ability to function normally at night could Tyrone hold out any hope of resisting the tantalizing seduction that awaited him in his bed and perhaps delay the ever-threatening reckoning.

Tyrone's morning rote began before dawn, when he'd rise, shave, and dress. Shortly thereafter, he'd go downstairs to breakfast with Natasha. He was relieved that Synnovea complied with his wishes to stay abed and refrained from joining them. To face defeat so early in the day would've sorely gone against his grain. Mainly his conversation with the older woman centered around his wife, a subject from which he had difficulty straying of late. He'd then leave and be gone until well past supper, at which time he usually came dragging back, thoroughly spent. Before entering the manse, he'd feed and groom the tall black that Ladislaus had left behind and the fine, liver-chestnut steed which he reserved primarily for parades and demonstrating the quality of horsemanship he hoped to encourage in his men.

Upon concluding his tasks in the carriage house, he'd then enter the kitchen, too starved to think of waiting until after he had bathed away the sweat and grime of his day's labors. If Tyrone might have once supposed that his grubby state would repulse his wife, then in that, too, he found himself mistaken. While the cook worked at other tasks, Synnovea served him his meal and, in doing so, touched him often, which now seemed her wont. Without a doubt, he'd have paid less heed to the server and more consideration to the fare if Danika had been the one laying out his meal. Even bone tired, he couldn't ignore the delicious sight, womanly feel, and intoxicating fragrance of his wife as she bent over him or brushed against him in passing.

After supper, Tyrone soaked his aching body in a steaming bath which primarily served to ease his strained muscles. Synnovea's initial attempt to assist him in his bath had provoked him to such a stormy outburst that she had fled in teary haste. It hadn't taken a great deal of mental prowess for him to recognize the difficulty he'd have to face trying to tether his rampant lusts while she washed his naked body. Thereafter he had been attended by a male servant, who spoke not a word of English, but that suited the quiet serenity Tyrone sought there. It was his only reprieve.

Tyrone was grateful for those nights when, after joining Synnovea in their chambers, he could collapse into bed, too tired to even talk. His one concession to her wifely bent was to allow her to rub a soothing balm over his back for the purpose of keeping the scabs and skin pliable and the scarring to a minimum. For this he'd doff his robe and recline facedown upon the bed. Her gentle massaging relaxed him, and even while she continued kneading his work-strained muscles, his breathing would gradually deepen until he was lulled into sleep.

During these times Synnovea found it difficult to decipher her own emotions, but they seemed pleasantly associated with being a wife. No harsh words disturbed their quiet harmony while she served her husband's needs, and even if Tyrone still refused to make love to her, at least by yielding himself into her care he was granting her privileges and familiarities reserved for a spouse.

She was no longer hindered by Anna's strictures or the threat of Aleksei and could now venture out as often as she liked. While her husband was at work, she took several opportunities to visit friends and old acquaintances of her father. One day a week she could be found assisting Father Philip in his efforts to help the poor. At other times she shopped at Kitaigorod, sometimes for necessities, but mostly in search of clothing, gifts, or wines for her handsome husband. More often than not, she was joined on these excursions by either Zelda or Natasha or both women. After making purchases at the marketplace, they would deposit their bundles in the coach, and though Stenka would follow along behind at a leisurely pace with the conveyance, the three women were often motivated to stroll over to Red Square, where most every morning Tyrone could be found drilling his Hussars for a parade. Synnovea never failed to experience the thrill associated with watching the horsemanship of the men and their sharply executed drills, but their commander was the one who primarily claimed her attention.

Occasionally Tyrone would join the *boyarinas* during a well-deserved break from his rigorous training. As much as he resented the fact that he and his wife were closely observed at odd and sundry times by General Vanderhout, the tsar, his own company of men, Aleta in some instances, and a whole host of strangers, Tyrone realized he was becoming increasingly dedicated to the idea that Synnovea was his wife and therefore deserving of some genuine husbandly respect in public. In staking his claim, he often laid a hand upon her back or offered his arm as they strolled with the other two women to either the coach or a more select spot where they'd sometimes share victuals that Danika had packed for them. The difficulty Tyrone found in openly touching his wife or sitting beside her was what he usually had to contend with: the delectation stirred forth by even their most casual contact.

It was toward the end of the fifth week when Tyrone made the mistake of trying to imagine the changes that would occur in his life should he hold to his word and return to England an unmarried man. He would then be free to court other women, and in an effort to create some enthusiasm for the bachelor status he'd have in that event, he sought to form a vision of the women he had courted before his marriage to Angelina. They weren't nearly as comely in recall, not when he had a young wife whose beauty and charm could easily put them to shame. A few of those former light-o'-loves had even been prone to giggle over the most inane things or else talk incessantly about things that mattered not a whit to him. Not so Synnovea. Though he wouldn't have admitted it, he found her subtle wit and softly spoken comments immensely pleasing.

It was while Tyrone was laboriously mulling through this course of thinking that an unexpected dawning came which served his hidebound honor a death blow. With sudden clarity he realized that if he sailed to England and left Synnovea behind in Russia, it would be equivalent to leaving his own heart behind.

One evening, after another week had come and gone, Tyrone was seated on his bedside stool cleaning his gear and military trappings when he became mindful of Synnovea sitting in a chair across the bed from him, diligently sewing tiny cloth frogs on several garments—to be exact, four tunics and a single kaftan, all of which were far too large for her. He was still laboring at his task when she rose, folded the clothes and left them on his side of the bed, along with four pairs of full-legged trousers such as Russian soldiers were wont to wear. Without offering word or explanation, she disappeared into the dressing room.

Quizzically Tyrone eyed what she had left. The long-sleeved tunics were similar to those worn by his men and were made of a soft, weighty material. The cloth frogs served as closures along the slanted openings that stretched from the banded collars downward to beneath the left sleeves of the shirts and the kaftan. In continuing reticence, his wife returned from the adjoining room and, stepping near, placed a pair of calf-length leather boots on the floor beside his bench.

"Are these for me?" Tyrone finally queried, unable to draw any other conclusion. At her nod, he inquired further. "Do you want me to try them on?"

"If you would, Ty," Synnovea murmured, seeming rather apprehensive as she chewed at a bottom lip.

Tyrone wasn't inclined to strip away his robe, not while she was there to spur a reaction. His pride had been daunted much too often of late for him to even think of leaving himself open to the humiliation that would follow. After gathering up the boots, a tunic, and a pair of trousers, he sought shelter in the dressing room, where he garbed himself in the clothes she had made. Among his wife's many other talents, it seemed that she was also an accomplished seamstress, for he soon found himself marveling at the neat handiwork which had gone into making the garments.

Synnovea came to him with a smile as he emerged from the narrow room and, begging his permission, knotted a braided leather cord around his lean waist. When she stepped back to consider the clothes she had created as well as the man who now wore them, her eyes began to mist with tears. He looked so handsome that she could feel only remorse for having once squandered his affection.

Tyrone stepped before the silvered glass to consider his

reflection and was prompted to cock a dubious brow at his altered appearance. "I look like a Russian."

Synnovea surreptitiously brushed at the moisture blurring her vision and cleared her throat hastily before she spoke. "Aye, and a very handsome one at that."

Mystified by the strange thickness in her tone, Tyrone peered at her over a shoulder, but Synnovea turned aside, refusing to let him ponder the emotion written on her face.

"Are you well, madam?"

She nodded jerkily and managed a strangled reply. "Of course."

Unconvinced, Tyrone canted his head in an effort to draw her gaze, curious to know what was troubling her, but she hurriedly busied herself, straightening bric-a-brac on a nearby chest. Tyrone gave up his efforts, refusing to press her for an explanation. Angelina had often baffled him with her moody tears and melancholy, which had usually come with her fluxes and been just as unpredictable. He thought it prudent to re-turn his attention to the trousers without inquiring into Synno-vea's monthly cycles. After all, they were hardly on intimate terms, considering his continuing abstinence. Despite recent revelations that had brought him face-to-face with his growing mental entanglement with her, there was still that part of him that hadn't yielded to the idea that he couldn't do without her.

Facing the mirror again, Tyrone gathered the loose folds in his hand and considered the roominess of the trousers. "No wonder they're so comfortable. They're large enough for two men."

Covertly Synnovea eyed the torpid bulge molded by the tightly clasped pantaloons, and though she yearned to draw near and press him for a more ardent response than he had thus far been willing to offer her, she couldn't bring herself to destroy the congeniality they were presently sharing. A myriad of different things seemed to hinder it, and she was loath to see it shattered once again. Then, too, she hadn't yet recovered from the shock of her entrance into the bathing chamber, when she had only wanted to offer him help with his bath. Nor could she forget his nakedness and the ruddy hue that had swept into his face when he had caught her eyeing the lusty flag that had hauled itself upright at her approach. The memory of his thunderous explosion even now made her tremble in trepidation, making her cautious of provoking similar outbursts.

"I've also made you a suitable cap and coat to wear with your clothes, if you're of a mind to try them on, Ty," she murmured, unwilling to meet his gaze in the mirror.

Tyrone glanced around the room in search of the articles of clothing. "Where are they?"

"I'll fetch them," Synnovea eagerly replied and returned to the dressing room. Hurriedly she fetched his new coat, the lining of which she had made from the same lamb's wool as the handsome astrakhan. The cap was a necessary item of clothing in Russia, no less than the coat, and though she had searched through her husband's clothing, she hadn't found any outer gear warm enough for what he'd need.

"You made these?" Tyrone asked in amazement, after accepting the items from her and examining the detail of each.

Synnovea inclined her head in a single nod of affirmation. "Here in Russia you'll be needing more protection from our winters than your English garments can provide. I'm not sure how you managed to survive the weather last year, but I'd be remiss in my duties as a wife if I didn't see you properly outfitted for the colder months."

"I'm grateful, madam." Tyrone couldn't have been more sincere. "I was greatly hampered last winter by the crispness of the icy winds until Grigori took pity on me and loaned me some of his clothing. I might not have fared well at all if he hadn't."

After shrugging into the coat, Tyrone settled the cap upon his head at a jaunty angle, but Synnovea giggled and, shaking her head in disapproval, reached up to rearrange the latter. Tyrone accommodated her shorter height by bending his knees, and for a moment their eyes melded in warm communications. Synnovea was feeling no less than giddy when she stepped back, and she caught her bottom lip between her teeth, trying to curb a grin. It was amazing to her how quickly he could move her from tears to laughter without uttering a word, but then, perhaps it was all the roiling emotions to which she was now prey that caused such flighty behavior within her. Her whole world now seemed centered on him, and as yet, he hadn't shown any indication that he'd ever forgive her.

Synnovea's eyes glowed warmly in admiration as she perused her husband's tall, broad-shouldered form outfitted in the simple garments. She thought him no less than magnificent.

"I'm delighted to find my wife so talented," Tyrone said, perusing his reflection. "Your gifts are very fine indeed, madam. I'm both awed and pleasured by them."

"I'm pleased to give them, sir," Synnovea replied, her smile deepening. "How do the boots fit?"

"So well that I can almost believe that they were made for me."

"Actually they were. I found an older pair of yours in your armoire and took them to the only bootmaker my father trusted. Are they comfortable?"

"Very," he answered with enthusiasm.

"Would you like to try on the kaftan now?" she invited. "I thought you might enjoy having one to wear after your baths at night."

"I would indeed," Tyrone agreed and disappeared once again into the safety of the dressing room.

When he returned a few moments later wearing the blue robe, Synnovea stepped behind him and ran a hand admiringly across the full breadth of his wide shoulders as she peered past his arm at his image. "It suits you well, Ty."

Her husband grinned at her in the mirror. "I think you're trying to make a Russian of me, madam."

Synnovea threaded her fingers through the short hair curling at his nape. "Your hair isn't long enough for that."

Even her most casual touch bestirred Tyrone's senses, and though he strove to sound normal, he had lost the strength in his voice . . . and in his knees. "It needs cutting."

"Would you like me to trim it tonight?" she asked near his shoulder.

Knowing the havoc which that simple service would create in him, Tyrone yawned and made the excuse "Not tonight, Synnovea. I'm really tired."

"Then I'll put away your new clothes," she offered, gathering the garments she had made. As she faced him, she held out a hand expectantly for the kaftan, but her husband dawdled as he unfastened the frogs. When she remained near at hand, he finally turned aside before he dared sweep the garment over his head.

Even if her view was from a rearward angle, Synnovea was not above perusing all that she saw. She yearned to reach out and run a hand caressingly over the hard vales and ridges of his back and stroke his granite-hard buttocks, but she knew if she roused his ire again what she'd likely invite.

Feeling the weight of his wife's gaze, Tyrone cast a glance askance and found a yearning in those soft orbs that almost snatched his breath away. He was sure it mirrored his own and could sense his doom drawing nigh.

Synnovea was still waiting in silence when he handed back the kaftan. She folded it over her arm, but her eyes were drawn irresistibly to his long, manly form as he lifted a knee upon the bed and leaned forward toward the pillow, where he braced himself on an elbow. What came into view would have made a meek maid blush and turn aside, but she had never considered herself as such.

Tyrone winced slightly and, slowly expelling a pent-up

sigh, lifted himself to make a necessary adjustment to his privy parts. When he realized his wife was still observing him, he looked around and found her smiling in amusement.

"Something wrong, madam?" he asked, arching a curious brow.

"Oh, I was just wondering to what lengths a man will go to spite himself."

"Are you referring to me?"

"Who else, sir?"

Tyrone didn't rightly know how to answer. Mutely he watched the rather jaunty twitch of skirts as his wife went to the dressing room. Her amused giggles floated back from the dressing room, and he almost groaned, knowing full well what she found so humorous. He *was* spiting himself. He was hot, hard, and eager, and she was everything he yearned to have in all of his erotic dreams.

Synnovea returned to the bedchamber gowned in a filmy creation that left nothing to the imagination. Tyrone was certain she was bent on tormenting him, yet his eyes seemed to have a will of their own as they followed her around to the far side of the bed. She lifted the voluminous gown, allowing him an unhindered glimpse of a shapely thigh as she climbed onto the mattress. After crawling near, she sat back upon her heels, seeming completely at ease beneath his perusal, and began to massage his scarred back with a balm that kept his skin pliable. By dint of will, he turned his face aside and lowered his head to the pillow, at length allowing her gentle ministering to soothe his tensions. Never had he known such tender kindness . . . or unyielding torture.

Finally Synnovea put away the salve, wiped off the excess, and snuffed out the candles behind her. Tyrone pulled the feather comforter up over them before leaning across to his bedside table to do the same. Settling back upon the bed, he turned on his side away from her and lay in pensive silence, trying desperately to forget that she was even there.

"I'm cold," Synnovea complained as she snuggled close against his back. Slipping an arm around him, she threaded her fingers through the hair covering his muscular chest and tucked her bare thighs beneath his buttocks. "And you're always so warm."

Her nearness burned holes through Tyrone's restraints, yet for the life of him he couldn't send her fleeing to the far side of the bed with another angry command. With only a thin veil of a nightgown separating them and every swelling curve remarkably designed for the purpose of tormenting him, he was completely deprived of every sane thought except one, and that was the realization that he had been utterly foolish to imagine that he could successfully ignore the treasure he had fervently craved for so long.

Synnovea was upstairs in their bedchambers the next afternoon when she happened to glance out the windows and espied Tyrone riding down the road toward the manse. He was much earlier than usual, and though a sudden surge of excitement washed through her, she was flustered by the lack of time she had to repair her appearance. Earlier that morning she had donned older peasant garments to help Natasha and her gardener harvest flowers that were to be dried for winter arrangements, but her clothes were hardly pretty enough to claim her husband's attention. In frantic haste she stripped, washed, and perfumed herself before donning her prettiest peasant attire. She brushed her hair until it gleamed, leaving it tumbling free beneath a kerchief. Her cheeks were already rosy and required no further pinch to bring forth color when she paused to check her appearance. In her eagerness to be with her husband, she descended the stairs almost in time with her swiftly racing heart.

By the time she arrived at the door of the carriage house, Synnovea was nearly breathless with anticipation. Calming herself, she stepped within, very quietly closed the portal behind her, and laid a bar across the portal, preventing any threat of intrusion. Then she strolled forward leisurely, as if she were there with no real purpose in mind.

Tyrone was absorbed in his work and failed to notice Synnovea's entrance until she came around the end of the grooming stall, where he was shampooing the chestnut's tail. When he caught sight of her, his eyes slid over her in a lengthy caress, much as they were wont to do whenever she came near. Thoroughly distracted now, he continued squeezing suds through the horse's tail beyond his usual penchant. It was a rare day indeed when his wife left the silky black tresses unbound outside the privacy of their chambers. Considering the male servants who normally moved about the grounds and house, he couldn't help but wonder how he had earned such husbandly consideration.

His meticulous regard brought a deepening blush of pleasure to Synnovea's cheeks, and though her smile wavered unsteadily beneath his close regard, it soon strengthened and seemed eager to stay.

"You're home early," she murmured, noticing that he had also changed his clothes since his arrival home, except that he had chosen to garb himself in just about the oldest and most threadbare in his possession. His knee-length breeches were so limp from use, they clung to him in a way that left no uncertainty they were the only thing covering his loins. The closures which had once fastened the breeches at the knees were gone, allowing the garment to hang loosely above his hardened calves. His shoes were equally worn, his shirt frayed and torn open down the front, leaving his lightly furred chest bare. Synnovea struggled against the temptation to reach out and feel the vibrant life beating beneath that broad, muscular expanse and to move her hand downward to other areas she knew would quicken beneath her slightest touch, but she knew she'd have to proceed carefully lest she find her hopes dashed.

"My men and I will be performing in a parade for His Majesty on the morrow, and I had to get my horse and equipment ready," Tyrone explained, drinking in her beauty. Now that he had come to the realization that he could leave her no better than he could stop breathing, he felt as if he had become her captive, which made him all the more leery of what she could do to him. Still, it was impossible for him to ignore her presence in his life. Only the night before, he had struggled against an overwhelming urge to awaken her from her slumber and make love to her. It seemed doubtful that he'd ever again be as successful at resisting the impulse. "His Majesty will be expecting you to attend the affair as my bride, but then, with foreign dignitaries there, he'll probably be expecting you to enhance the view. If you'd like, you can bring Natasha and even Ali, since many of the officers' wives will be bringing nannies and nursemaids to tend their children."

Having already experienced the thrills associated with watching her husband and his troop practice, Synnovea was eager to view the actual event. She could now understand more keenly why the tsar was so intent upon having them perform. No doubt the excitement of the event would be enough to last a lifetime. "Perhaps you can help me choose a suitable *sarafan* to wear for the parade."

Tyrone chuckled softly. "I'm sure you know better than I what is proper for a woman to wear to functions of that nature, madam. Besides, I haven't yet seen you garbed in anything that hasn't taken my breath away."

Synnovea was both surprised and pleased by his compliment. "Your exhibitions on horseback take mine away."

Her husband grinned and cocked his head curiously aslant as his eyes delved into hers, but he was promptly reminded of his tasks when the horse nickered. He had definitely lost the desire to complete his chores alone now that he had a companion who looked so fetching. "Would you do me a favor?"

Synnovea would have eagerly complied with almost anything he had in mind at that moment. "Certainly."

Tyrone inclined his head toward the end of the stall where he had left a wooden bucket he had earlier filled with water. "Can you bring that pail over here and dribble the contents over the horse's tail while I rinse it? It's rather unhandy doing all of this by myself."

Synnovea lifted the ponderous pail and tugged at a bottom lip as she carried it forward. Near the horse's rump, she braced her feet apart and lifted the bucket to comply with her husband's directive. Affected by the nearness of the man and the curious little bubbles of pleasure coursing through her being, she gave no heed to the puddle that was steadily growing beneath her feet.

"Synnovea, look what you're doing. You're getting your slippers wet," Tyrone gently admonished. Reaching out, he took the pail from her. "You'd better go in and get another pair before you catch your death."

"No . . . please . . ." She shook her head, reluctant to leave. The moment was rare indeed when her husband was in a tractable mood, and she didn't want to miss the occasion, no matter how frigid the water seeping into her slippers. "I'll just take these off." Retreating to the far end of the stall, she kicked them off and lifted her skirts and petticoats to doff her stockings.

Tyrone was hardly aware of the puddle he was creating beneath his own shoes as he became enthralled with the sights. Her bare limbs were so lithe and shapely, one glimpse demanded his full attention.

Synnovea pulled the back of her gown and petticoats forward between her thighs and tucked the hems into her waistband before she tiptoed shivering through the icy water. Returning once more to the horse's rump, she reached out to take the bucket from her husband and promptly laughed when she noticed the pool he had created. "You're no handier than I am, sir."

"Aye," Tyrone agreed with a lopsided grin. "But if you come down sick, Natasha will blame me."

The green-brown eyes glowed with a hint of mischief. "Don't tell me a big, stalwart man like you is afraid of a little woman."

His grin broadened as he briefly lifted wide shoulders. "Not afraid, only reluctant to bestir Natasha's displeasure."

Synnovea was surprised at the sudden twinge of jealousy that tweaked her good humor. Since Tyrone had returned to work, she had been reluctant to join him at the morning meal for fear of angering him, yet from what Danika had said in all innocence, those sunrise tête-à-têtes which he shared with Natasha seemed quite jovial. The fact that the cook couldn't understand English had allowed Synnovea to hope that the two were merely talking as friends. Yet at times she was wont to fret. Natasha *was* quite beautiful and still very, very appealing to men, and not so long ago she had lauded Tyrone's praises as if genuinely attracted to him. "You must admire Natasha very much. Even in so short a time, it has become obvious to all the servants that you enjoy her company more than mine."

Tyrone stared at his wife in amazement, thoroughly taken aback by her premise. Then the humor of her accusation struck him, and he began to laugh in hearty amusement. "Good heavens, Synnovea, all we ever talk about is you. Between Natasha and Ali, I've learned more about you than either one of them."

Synnovea lifted her dainty chin in some annoyance. "By now you must understand me quite well, then."

Her husband scoffed at such a farfetched notion. "The workings of your mind, madam, are far too complicated for a mere man to comprehend. But then, perhaps I'm not the only one you're able to confuse. At times I think you completely baffle your closest friends and, if I may be allowed to venture a guess, yourself as well."

His wife was a bit astounded by his conjecture, but then, she had to admit there was some truth in what he had said. She hadn't always been able to clearly discern her own emotions. Not so terribly long ago, she had been certain that she wanted nothing to do with Tyrone Rycroft. His audacity had totally repulsed her, or so she had thought, yet she had been unable to cast him from her mind. Now here she was, yearning for him to be just as bold as he had been in the bathhouse.

The sight of his hardened chest drew her forward as if she had no will of her own. Though wary of provoking his ire again, she lifted a hand and stroked it admiringly over the muscular expanse. She could feel his heart thudding beneath her palm and wondered if she had the ability to spur it to a swifter rhythm. Searching the luminous orbs above her own, she pushed the shirt off his shoulders and dragged it down his arms. She had elicited his wrath much too often for her to feel at ease with her seduction, but this time she found no hint of a frown and was encouraged by his quiescent stillness. She traced her fingers admiringly over his lightly furred chest and followed the ridge of hair that trailed downward to the top of his breeches, making him catch his breath. Lifting smoldering eyes to his, she silently beseeched him as she slipped her hand beneath the breeches and took hold of the rapidly thickening flesh.

Tyrone's heart leapt as if jolted by a lightning bolt. His awakened senses were completely alert to every detail of the feminine form that leaned into him. With some difficulty he released a halting breath as he met her inquiring gaze.

"Is something wrong?" Synnovea queried, feigning a smile. She was on pins and needles, awaiting his reaction.

Tyrone was reluctant to consider the gut-wrenching agony that would be inflicted upon him if he rejected her overtures.

Fires had been lit that could be assuaged only by making love to her. Yet he worried at the control she'd have over him if he submitted to her seduction. In a halfhearted attempt to break the spell which bound him, he murmured huskily, "I think I'd better finish rinsing the horse's tail."

Synnovea's heart nearly crumpled with disappointment, but her pride had been vanquished weeks ago, and she was not above beseeching him. The warm flesh in her grasp encouraged her to be bold. "Please, Ty, don't deny me the pleasure of touching you," she breathed in plaintive appeal. "I couldn't bear it if you did. Am I not your wife? Do I not have the right to make a claim on you? You don't know how many times I've wanted to do this. I'm beset by cravings you have awakened within me. I yearn for your touch . . . for your husbandly affection. How long must I wait? When will you let me touch you without fear of being chided? Or are you intent upon punishing me for the whole of our marriage?"

"Punish you?" Tyrone rasped. His whole body was shaking from the intensity of his needs, and he gave up his futile efforts to keep his resolve. Sweeping an arm around her, he snatched her close in sudden ardor. "Nay, I'm the one who has been punished."

His mouth swooped down upon hers in frenzied greed, snatching her breath with the sweet, brutal intensity of his passion. His face slanted across hers as his tongue plundered the warm, sweet cavity of her mouth. It was a wild, rapacious search, unrivaled by anything that Synnovea had ever experienced before, yet she felt driven to answer him with her own craving hunger. With a softly muted moan, she looped her arms tightly around his neck and molded her womanly form against his steely body, hoping to drive him beyond the point of resistance. She had no need to worry. His fingers were already slipping the ties of her blouse free, and soon he was baring her breasts and pressing her backward over an encompassing arm. His open mouth claimed a pliant peak and nearly devoured her bosom with ravenous hunger, halting her breath at the sheer ecstasy of his stroking tongue and suckling caresses. In the depths of her body there bloomed a heightening craving that yearned to be sated as sparks sizzled upward from her loins in quickly flaring bursts of ecstasy.

Tyrone raised his head, his features sharply chiseled with his lusting need. His gaze plunged into hers, searching out her true intent. If this was another game, he would know it now rather than later. "Is this what you really want?"

"Oh, yes . . . yes," Synnovea whispered, fearing he would leave her bereft of his manly attention. She didn't want to give him time to mull over the matter and remember what she had done to him. Eagerly plucking open his breeches, she clasped the hot flesh once again and began to pleasure him in a more daring manner than she had tentatively done weeks ago.

"What are you doing to me?" he rasped huskily.

"Only what you once instructed me to do," she breathed, drawing him backward toward a darkened corner of the stable and the large mound of fresh hay that she knew was there.

"We'll be discovered," Tyrone cautioned, finding no will to resist. It seemed a recurring dream he was having. She had him by the gutstrings of his being, and he was following much as he had done before, like a bleating lamb to slaughter.

"Natasha is off visiting Prince Adolphe and his daughter and won't be back until late," Synnovea whispered warmly. "Stenka and Jozef have taken Ali to the marketplace to fetch some things for Danika. The door is locked, and we're quite alone, my darling."

The desperate catch in her voice conveyed desires that were no different from his own, Tyrone realized. Upon reaching the haystack, she sank back upon the sweetly scented grass and smiled up at him as she released the tail of her skirt from her waistband and let it fall away from her thighs. As he watched in mounting enthrallment, she doffed her clothes and spread them beneath her before lying back in all of her naked glory. Her smile was inviting as she wrapped her arms beneath her breasts, thrusting their delicately hued peaks upward in an invitation for him to taste and fondle. The lustrous orbs glowed in the dim light, like lush melons just waiting to be devoured. It was an enticement that Tyrone no longer wished to ignore. She was his, and she was offering him what he had been lusting for ever since their first naked embrace.

Slipping off his shoes, he dropped his breeches and kicked them aside. A brief glint of awe flickered in Synnovea's eyes as she eyed the stalwart blade. It seemed immensely bold and threatening, yet this and oh-so-much-more were what she had been yearning for since their wedding day. In welcoming invitation, she smiled and lifted her arms.

Tyrone felt the hot blood coursing through him, and in mounting eagerness, he dropped to his knees and leaned forward between her eagerly parting thighs to hungrily mouth her soft, round breasts, caressing the sensitive peaks and evoking ecstatic gasps from his wife. She arched her back, thrusting the delectable fullness upward to meet the sultry heat of the torch that branded her as his mouth stroked across the pale peaks. His hand moved over her thigh in a sweeping caress, moving along her flank and then inward and upward over her sleek limb. Synnovea caught her breath as he intruded into the dewy freshness, making her writhe at the bliss he created within her womanly softness. She breathed an anxious plea for him to join himself to her. He readily complied, pressing the hardened shaft into the velvety sheath, drawing a muted gasp of awe from her.

"Oh, Ty, it seems so long ago since we came together like this," she whispered near his ear, clutching him to her. "I was afraid you'd deny me forever."

His hands clasped her buttocks, fitting her snugly against the vibrant hardness that filled her as he lifted her up to him. He moved his hips with slow, purposeful strokes eliciting blissful sighs from her lips until she was nigh giddy with the ecstasy washing through her. In rapidly advancing degrees the manly thrusts quickened and became more dedicated until the billowing spasms began to wash over them. Joy filled Synnovea's heart when she heard her husband mutter her name in the throes of his passion, and then, just as quickly, astonished gasps were wrenched from her as she joined him in that lofty climb. Together they soared to heights far beyond the silky white clouds that seemed to shimmer all around them. It was rapture in its most sensual form, the sweetness of marital union, a blissful haven for each to savor and the coming together of two beings beautifully formed for one another.

When at last they grew still within each other's arms, Synnovea crooned near her husband's ear, "That was much nicer than it was before, very, very pleasurable, in fact."

"Aye, madam, we were interrupted before we were able to finish." Tyrone kissed her again, feeling as if a weighty burden had just been lifted from him. "I should have done this sooner."

Synnovea smiled beneath his caressing lips. "I've been wanting you to."

"I never expected it to happen like this," he admitted with a chuckle. "Not with such a sumptuous chamber at our disposal."

She laughed, thoroughly content now. "You were so wary of our chambers, I didn't seem able to approach you with an invitation." Her eyes glimmered brightly in the shadows. "I was beginning to think you hated me."

"I was afraid of the pain your nearness would inflict upon me," he rejoined with candor. "I was too susceptible to even think of trusting myself around you."

"Are you sorry now that you made love to me?" she queried diffidently.

"Nay, only relieved that my foolishness has finally been put to an end."

"We could have dinner sent up to our chambers," Synnovea suggested coyly. "No one but servants will be in the house."

"After we bathe, madam," he assured her. "You caught me when I'm smelly and dirty. Hardly what a bride appreciates when her husband wants to mount her."

"You smell nice and very manly, and you're not dirty," she argued, "but even if you were, I wouldn't be able to deny you after I've waited so long for you to make love to me."

"We'd better finish what we were doing so we can get on with more important things." Tyrone grinned as he pushed himself away and sat back on his heels. "I've been beset long enough by fantasies of making love to you in a bathing pool, and I'm most eager for that event to take place."

Synnovea rolled away and came to her knees, but when her husband clasped the back of her thigh, she looked back at him in curious wonder. Her eyes fairly flamed as he clamped his arm around her waist and lifted her back into his lap. Willingly she nestled against him and leaned her head aside as his lips nibbled at her creamy throat.

"Perhaps we could delay a few moments more," he suggested, cupping a pale breast within his hand. The fact that he was already aroused again didn't surprise him in the least, considering his lengthy abstinence.

"I was rather anticipating making love in the pool," she murmured with a flirtatious smile, moving her buttocks teasingly against him. The delectable delight awakened by her soft flesh stroking across the flinty hard shaft made her shiver with renewed desire. "But what you're doing now is very nice. Shall we dally in the hay some more?"

"The pool awaits, madam."

Slipping a hand beneath her buttock again, he boosted her to her feet and then followed, springing upward with a swift, effortless movement that clearly evidenced his strength and manly grace. After scooping up her kerchief, he dipped it into the watering trough and, beneath her fascinated gaze, began to wash himself. A moment later, he nearly took her breath away by performing the same service for her, being incredibly gentle and deliciously thorough in his bathing techniques.

"We'll never make it to the bathing chamber if you continue," she breathed shakily. "I like what you're doing too much to even think of waiting until we reach the bathing chamber."

Tyrone had become caught up in the stimulating task as well and extended his ministrations far beyond what was required. "Another taste of such blissful fare wouldn't take that long," he rasped softly, making her catch her breath in delight at his bold intrusion. His free hand came around to cup a breast, and as she leaned against him, his thumb stroked across a soft peak. "And right now, I've no heart for tending the stallion. To be sure, my lengthy wait has made me greedy."

"The door is locked, and we have all the time in the world," she crooned invitingly with a sensual smile as her eyes caressed his handsome face.

Half turning, Tyrone tossed the kerchief into the pail and then swept his wife up into his arms. With a playful growl, he made a pretense of devouring her breast, evoking a dreamy mewl as his licking tongue plied its crest. Whirling her about, he drew her breath out in an excited little laugh before he sprawled back upon the mound of hay and pulled her down astride him. A small, ecstatic shiver went through her as he lingered over the delectable merging, pressing the vibrant hardness upward, seemingly into the core of her being. Synnovea's breath quickened as his throbbing heat filled her, and with eyes that had grown dark and sultry, she held his gaze imprisoned as she swept her hands over her own body, encouraging his to follow wherever she led, over the swelling mounds, along her narrow waist, and into the moist crevice. Nearly shuddering with her rapidly intensifying excitement, she slipped her arms beneath the ebon tresses, sweeping them off her neck as she arched her back and stroked against her husband's loins. Her rhythm intensified with her increasing fervor, drawing his breath out in harsh gasps. Though Synnovea hadn't thought it possible for her to transcend the heights to which she had recently climbed, he seemed intent upon eliciting every degree of delight she was capable of experiencing, making her writhe and shudder with the sensations he created within her until she felt as if she were dissolving in a warm, blissful flood.

In the moments following their soaring flight, only the stallion found reason to fret, evoking his owner's sigh. "Alas, the poor steed still awaits our attention."

"I liked what you did when you bathed me," she whispered, cuddling against her husband's chest. Coyly she stroked her bosom against the muscular hardness of his chest, enjoying the thrills which were readily derived from the caress. "Will you do that again?"

"In the bathing chamber, madam," Tyrone promised huskily, nibbling at her ear. "Else we may never leave the carriage house."

"Would you let me wash you, too?" Synnovea asked, unwilling to move on to a different subject.

"As much as you would like, madam . . . but in the bathing chamber."

She pouted prettily. " 'Twas your idea to delay our departure."

"Aye, I know. I'm very susceptible to the sights. Your derriere is too fetching for me to ignore."

"Do you suffer a particular fetish with my backside, sir?" Synnovea teased coquettishly, continuing to massage his male breasts with her tautening nipples.

"I like all of you, from your dainty toes to the top of your head, but there are places in between that I'm especially partial to, such as this area here," he said, catching a hand around her breast and forcing the crest outward to meet his stroking tongue. "These pale orbs are beyond description. Their sweet nectar leaves me fairly besotted." Though his mouth moved upward to caress her throat, his hand slipped down between them and clasped the dark nest. "But nothing is quite as delectable as the ecstasy I find here in this warm, velvet sheathe."

"I have a feeling we're not going to make it to the bathing chamber tonight," she sighed shakily. "I'm quite besotted from what your caresses have awakened within me."

"We could spend the night out here," he suggested with a grin.

"You'll have to keep me warm."

"I do that now, madam, every night in our bed, but I'd really enjoy holding you again in a bathing pool."

"Then shouldn't we hurry and finish our chores?" Synnovea urged. "Otherwise, we'll never get there with all the delays we're wont to indulge in here."

Tyrone was just as anxious to get there, but he was also wont to linger and enjoy the different views he was presented as he collected his clothing. He was most attentive to his wife's efforts to shake the hay out of her clothes. The rounded orbs now bore a rosy blush after his light bearding, but it was the way they bounced every time she snapped her blouse and skirts in the air that fascinated him. "Do you think you're accomplishing anything, my sweet. The hay seems quite tenacious."

Synnovea paused and smiled back at him. "That's very nice what you called me."

"My sweet?"

"I was afraid you wanted to call me worse things."

Tyrone indicated the horse's tail. "We'd better get to our chores, madam, or we'll never get to the pool."

Synnovea pouted prettily as she sauntered toward him in all of her unadorned glory. His breath hissed outward in a pleasurable gasp as she pressed close against him and fondled him in a way that left his knees weak. She seemed eager to continue, but the stallion whinnied, growing weary of being ignored.

"Later, my sweet," Tyrone promised thickly, cupping a round breast in his hand before leaning down and taking the peak into the heat of his mouth. Then, because he found such sights totally distracting, he drew her chemise and petticoats over her head and then lowered the skirt and blouse into place before turning her and thrusting her gently away from him. Giggling, Synnovea stumbled backward and rubbed her derriere against him, causing a quick response. Since she seemed to enjoy dawdling at length over her playful temptations, Tyrone reached down and clamped a hand between her buttocks, evoking a startled gasp from his young wife as he prodded her forward.

Tyrone chuckled as he took note of the darker hue now imbuing his wife's cheeks. "Do you find that offensive, madam?"

" 'Tis a bit shocking," she replied candidly, twitching a bit as she plucked her petticoat free of the cleavage.

He grinned while he donned his breeches and shoes. "Then you'd best be warned, my sweet. Now that you're my wife, every part of you is fair game. Indeed, you may well rue the day you invited my attentions." He jerked his head toward the stallion. "Now let's get back to work."

Obediently Synnovea bent to the task of spreading the horse's tail as Tyrone supplied a fresh flow of water. After rinsing it, he squeezed the liquid from the strands and began to gently comb through the length as Synnovea picked out the snarls. Finally he snuffed the last lantern that hung near the horses' stalls and turned in time to see his wife casting a repugnant glance toward the straw-strewn path that led to the door; it had been enriched with several droppings of manure prior to her entry into the barn. Tyrone took pity on her plight and bade her to tuck her stockings and shoes in her apron pocket and to climb on a low stool, from whence he lifted her onto his back.

"I haven't ridden like this since I was a child," Synnovea informed him happily as her lips hovered near his ear.

Tyrone slanted a grin at her over his shoulder. "I'll have to teach you better ways to ride."

"What other ways are there?" she asked coyly, folding her arms around his neck.

"I'll show you several before the evening is out."

"In the bathing chamber?"

"That will do for starters, but I'll demonstrate others in our bed." He turned his face in profile as she leaned close over his shoulder. "I've been quite hungry for you, madam, and I don't think I'll be sated until the last of my energy wanes, so you'll have to tell me if you get too tender from my attention."

"I will." She sighed blissfully, stroking his breast with wifely familiarity. She sang a child's song in Russian, cooing softly in his ear as she strummed her fingers across a male nipple. Then she paused in the melody to ask, "Is it as much fun for a man to ride a horse astride as I had when I rode you?"

"Nothing equals a good ride between a man and a woman, my sweet," Tyrone assured her, casting a roguish smile back at her.

"Did you enjoy it, too?"

"Immensely."

"I like your body," she whispered, tracing her tongue over his ear. In all honesty she added, "I would have mourned over my loss if I'd been forced to marry Vladimir. You're so much more handsome and exciting to look at. I regret that you were whipped, Ty, but I'm not sorry you were forced to wed me. I enjoy having you as my husband, and I especially relish the moments when you're aroused. You make me tremble with excitement just looking at you."

Not knowing what to answer, Tyrone pinched her buttock, drawing a squeal from the little sprite who rode his back.

"You bruised me," she complained, rubbing her soft breasts against his back. "You'll have to massage me there later."

"I'll massage you, all right, but not in the way you think."

"In what way do you mean, then?" she queried teasingly.

"You'll see soon enough, madam. Never fear. And then your greedy little hands can show me just how much you appreciate my body."

"Promise?"

"You have my pledge on it, my dear."

"I can hardly wait."

Tyrone carried her to their chambers by way of the private stairs, and then, after donning kaftans, they descended to the lower depths of the mansion, where he dismissed the male servant shortly after a bath was prepared in one of the larger tubs. Once the door was securely barred behind the man, Tyrone approached his wife, who was just shrugging out of her robe. His own had been quickly tossed aside, and he grinned as her admiring gaze swept downward. Taking her hand, he led her to the tub, stepped into the warm bath, and then, bidding her to sit facing him within the spread of his thighs, pulled her legs over his and settled her feet behind his buttocks. Leering at her, he began to soap her body while she, in turn, lathered his. They seemed especially wont to linger over the sensually sensitive areas and grew thoroughly stimulated beneath each other's lingering caresses. They rinsed with as much care and then, stepping from the tub, descended the steps of the pool. Gazing down into her warm gaze, Tyrone pulled her close and gave her a long, thoroughly provocative kiss before sweeping her into a very passionate reenactment of several of his fantasies.

16

*A*li was clearly ecstatic over the idea of being able to view a full-dress parade. Heretofore she had only heard rumors about the exhibitions of horsemanship and colorful uniforms worn by the riders. She had been assured that it would be a lavish spectacle, and now that other cavalry units were competing against her master's outfit, it promised to be an exciting event, one that she hoped would solidify Colonel Tyrone Rycroft as the best equestrian instructor in all of Russia.

The maid was by no means the only one desirous of seeing the presentation. Synnovea was elated over the prospect of watching Tyrone and his men perform on the field for the tsar, yet she was a bit anxious about it, too, considering His Majesty would be comparing the skills of her husband's company to others. Now that there were other troops of Hussars eager to win the distinction of being the best and most impressive riders on the field, she was anxious for Tyrone to accomplish a flawless exhibition.

For the occasion, Synnovea had garbed herself in an emerald-green *sarafan* lavishly embroidered with twining vines and small silk clusters of pale blue flowers. It was one that Tyrone especially liked. Not only did the darker hue accentuate the green in her eyes, but the rich color complimented her fair skin. A matching *kokoshniki* had been created with tufted ribbons of light blue interspersed among green silk leaves, which had been adorned with dewdrops of translucent beading. Lastly she draped a fringed shawl of iridescent green silk around her shoulders, hoping the weather would stay pleasant long enough to allow her to escape the need for a cloak, which she had prudently brought along in the carriage.

Natasha had also been caught up in the enthusiasm of her companions and vivaciously waved and called greetings to friends and acquaintances as she followed to the reviewing stand to which Tyrone had verbally directed them before taking his leave earlier that morning. Prince Adolphe hailed Natasha from afar and hastened to catch up as she, in turn, tried to keep pace with Synnovea. Arriving at the pavilion where the wives and families of the officers were gathering, the younger woman paused to catch her breath, much to the relief of the two older women, who had lagged behind in spite of their attempts to keep up. Rosy cheeks on all attested to their rapid flight across the grounds in the crisp morning air.

"You should be grateful that Tyrone wasn't here to witness your arrival, my dear," Natasha exclaimed breathlessly, dabbing a lacy handkerchief to her cheeks where a fine mist of perspiration now glistened. "Otherwise you might have given him cause to think you're anxious to see him all spiffed and polished in his uniform."

Synnovea had taken a measure of delight in withholding news of their new marital relationship from the older woman. Since it was clearly what the elder had been expecting, Synnovea had no doubt that she'd be teased unduly, and was just as certain that she'd never hear the last of Natasha's gleeful hooting if she even hinted of her growing infatuation with Tyrone Rycroft.

Tossing her head, Synnovea sweetly needled, "And I suppose you just came along to pester me and have no real interest yourself in watching the proceedings. If that's all you've come for, perhaps Prince Adolphe can entertain you while Ali and I watch the festivities." She inclined her head to indicate the gray-haired man who was hastening up the steps of the pavilion. "He's here now to save you from the dreadful boredom of this event."

Natasha chuckled at the girl's spirited rejoinder. "You should know by now that a team of Adolphe's finest horses couldn't drag me away from here today."

"Of course," Synnovea answered with a smug smile. "But I just wanted to hear it from your lips."

Both women swept into deep curtsies as Prince Adolphe joined them. The man's dark eyes twinkled admiringly as he complimented Synnovea on her apparel, but when they settled on Natasha, a different light glowed in their depths, one that closely resembled adoration. Even after being gently rejected several times, the widowed prince hadn't yet lost hope that Natasha would someday relent and accept his proposal of marriage.

"Perhaps the two of you should adorn the tsar's pavilion, where your beauty can be better viewed," Adolphe suggested with a chortle, "and where I can also benefit from your radiant glow while adhering to my duties."

The two women laughed at his magnanimous compliment, but Synnovea kindly rejected his gallant invitation. "My husband will be expecting to see me here, Prince Adolphe, and I wouldn't want him to think that I hadn't come. Therefore I must forgo the privilege of joining you. But there's no reason why Natasha cannot."

The prince was eager to convince the older woman. "So many of our friends are already there, Natasha." Puckish humor tugged at the corners of his mustached mouth. "But then, there are several who might not be quite as pleased to have you there as I. Princess Taraslovna has made a point of joining her cousin, perhaps in a quest to get back in good stead with him. That sober little cleric she dotes on is also trying to gain favor with the tsar *and* Patriarch Filaret, but his duplicity seems ill-timed."

The last time Natasha had seen Ivan, he had been trying to rally support for a second advisor to be appointed for the tsar. She wasn't at all surprised by the cleric's cozenage, but she was curious to know why it seemed inappropriate. "How so?"

"From what I understand, the good patriarch got wind of Ivan Voronsky's efforts to see himself appointed as counselor. Right now, the cleric is rather hampered by a swollen jaw and can't offer explanations as skillfully as I'm sure he would like."

"But what happened to his jaw?"

Adolphe chuckled. "Prince Vladimir and his sons got miffed over a remark that Ivan made about a certain colonel's wife. Well, you know their tendency to pick a fight with anyone they find fault with. I'm afraid poor Ivan didn't fare too well in the process."

Natasha cast a quick glance toward Synnovea, whose attention had been snared. The older woman carefully voiced an inquiry. "Was the colonel's wife anyone we know, Adolphe?"

"None other than your beautiful house guest, my dear."

Synnovea could imagine the insults that Ivan was wont to lay upon her and gingerly offered a supposition. "I assume the remark was terribly offensive."

"It was," Adolphe Zherkof admitted, "but after Sergei nearly fractured his jaw, Ivan has been extremely hesitant about repeating the slur lest that brawling brood come after him. At the time, he probably thought Vladimir would agree with him when he said something about you supposedly being caught with the Englishman soon after the document for your betrothal to the old prince was signed, but from what Feodor told me about his brother's attack, Ivan's slander not only incensed their father, it outraged the whole family. 'Twould seem they are still much taken with you, my dear."

"I knew I liked those boyars," Natasha chimed in with amused laughter. "I just never knew how much until now."

Adolphe grinned. "I thought you'd enjoy that bit of news, my dear. In fact, you'll probably hear more delectable tidbits if you'd consent to join me in the tsar's pavilion."

"I'd love to, Adolphe, but you'll be busy introducing diplomats and foreign emissaries to His Majesty, so if you wouldn't mind, I'll come after the parade, when you'll have more time." Lightly resting a hand upon his arm, she asked, "Will you be able to join us this evening for dinner, or must you attend the banquet for the dignitaries?"

"Alas, my services will be needed at the banquet." He peered at her hopefully. "Tomorrow, perhaps?"

Natasha smiled. "Of course, Adolphe, but we can talk about it later."

His dark eyes gleamed back at her. "After the parade," he assured her, lifting her hand to bestow a kiss upon her slender fingers. "I'll return to fetch you."

"I shall be awaiting you," the woman told him with a soft, warm light shining in her own eyes.

Synnovea slanted a curious stare upon her companion after the prince made his departure. "Do you suppose you'll ever marry him?"

A sigh of contentment slipped from Natasha's smiling lips as her gaze followed the man. "Aye," she breathed. "When I no longer have to worry that my late husband will come between us. After enjoying a love that seemed without equal, I fear at times that it might not be the same with Adolphe."

"If I'm any judge of men, Natasha, I rather doubt that

you'd ever be sorry if you married the prince. He loves you very much, and if I may be so bold, I think you're also in love with him, but just too reluctant to let go of your memories."

Natasha's dark eyes danced with humor as she met the other's gaze. "Not so long ago, I was the one giving counsel to you. Now here you are advising me. What a turnabout indeed."

Synnovea laughed. "Aye, and 'tis sweet revenge to be on the giving end," she teased, squeezing the other's fingers fondly. "At times some women are blinded by circumstances when a matter is too close to the heart, but they're able to see things much more clearly from a distance."

"I can hear the gossips now," Natasha replied with a feigned sigh of lament. "That awful Natasha Andreyevna, they'll say. Married again for the fourth time! Disgraceful hussy! And now she's a princess, for heaven's sakes!"

"There's not a woman your age who isn't envious of you," Synnovea reasoned.

" 'Twill certainly give Anna Taraslovna something to talk about," the older woman predicted. "After all these years, she has never forgiven me for being Aleksei's first choice for a wife."

Synnovea was taken aback by surprise. "I didn't know."

Natasha lifted her slender shoulders in a casual shrug. " 'Twas nothing of any import. We met while visiting mutual friends at their home. We were together for several days after a snowstorm hindered us from leaving, and although nothing untoward occurred, Aleksei vowed afterwards to have me as his bride. At the time, I was a bit overwhelmed by his charm and good looks and fervently hoped something more would come of it. Aleksei offered my parents a contract of marriage, but by then they had already promised me to my first husband. Like you, I preferred the younger man, yet my parents were alive and I could neither disobey them nor ignore the contract. It was as simple as that. Nothing more came of it, and a pair of years later, Aleksei and Anna were wed. I was widowed a week later, and when the Taraslovs came to offer their condolences, Aleksei whispered that he should have waited. I'm not sure whether he told Anna about his offer of marriage to me or she found out on her own, but she took it upon herself to draw me aside during that same visit. In short, she warned me to stay away from her husband."

"All this time I couldn't understand why Anna hated you so intensely," Synnovea said in amazement. "But now I understand. She'd begrudge any woman who her husband thinks is attractive."

"Anna must be eaten up with jealousy by now, considering the legions who've been beguiled by him," Natasha observed. "I can count myself fortunate that I never had to worry about a promiscuous husband."

"Perhaps Aleksei would have been of a different bent if he had married you," Synnovea ventured to suggest.

The countess sighed. "Nevertheless, it has seemed my good fortune that I didn't marry him. Who knows? I might have turned out to be as shrewish as Anna."

"Good morn'n'!"

The greeting came from behind them, and though the voice was strangely familiar to both women, neither Synnovea nor Natasha could place it until they each turned to find Aleta Vanderhout moving toward them. The woman's eyes swept over their elegant Russian apparel and chilled perceptibly above a stiff smile. "My, my! Yu two certainly make every effort to claim masculine attention, don't yu?" she simpered in a voice dripping with derision. "Why, it's a vonder the two of yu aren't avaiting the soldiers on the field."

Synnovea's own smile was rather stiff as she rejoined with a fair measure of sarcasm, "We don't need to follow them as some women are wont to do, Aleta." Glancing aside at Natasha, she lifted a hand to indicate the newcomer. "Do you perhaps remember Madame Vanderhout? She came to your house with her husband, General Vanderhout . . . after my wedding."

Natasha could hardly forget the general's shouts filling the manse when he had chided Tyrone, or his angry search for his wife when he had sought to storm out in vexation after being gently reprimanded for his rudeness. "Of course, how could I forget?" she replied, bestowing her attention upon the blonde. "Your husband was quite insistent that I find you and wouldn't allow me to desist until you finally made an appearance. Ever since then, I've been wondering where you had wandered off to. Did you get lost, perchance?"

"Tell me, Synnovea," Aleta urged snidely, ignoring the countess's query. "Have yu come to view your husband at this affair, or does some other man interest yu?"

The flashing green-brown eyes conveyed Synnovea's irritation. "When my husband is the most handsome among the tsar's troops, why in the world would I look elsewhere, Aleta? But I can certainly understand why *your* eyes are inclined to roam."

Though the insult was only vaguely subtle, it took Aleta a full moment before she recognized the slight against her own spouse. For a lengthy moment she stared agog at Synnovea, unable to find an adequate retort. Then her eyes hardened, and her mouth tightened, at least until she glanced beyond them. Then she brightened and hurriedly excused herself before bustling off toward the stairs and taking her leave of the pavilion.

Natasha leaned near her companion. "I sense by your chilly retorts that Aleta has given you ample cause to dislike her."

Synnovea glowered after the departing woman. "That shameless little trollop had the nerve to accost *my* husband right in *our* chambers! That's where she was when you went searching for her."

"The unmitigated gall of that hussy!" Natasha's lips curved

with amusement as she glimpsed an honest display of wifely jealousy on the part of her young friend. "If I may ask, how did Tyrone handle that brazen trollop's overture?"

Synnovea's eyes began to dance with delight as she returned her attention to her friend. "Thankfully, he answered in a manner that any wife can approve of, and since neither was aware of my presence, the rebuff seemed genuine."

"I'm glad Tyrone didn't disappoint you, my dear, but I never thought he would. He's quite enamored with you, you know."

Synnovea sighed wistfully. "The same can be said of me."

Natasha laughed in pleasure and patted her friend's arm. "I'm glad you've finally arrived at that realization, my dear. It took you long enough."

The younger suffered a twinge of surprise. "How long have you known?"

Natasha smiled contentedly. "Since he carried you to my carriage."

The sweeping brows lifted in amazement. "That long ago?"

"Aye," the elder assured her, "but, of course, I wasn't with you before that day, so I really have no real ken how long you've actually been in love with him."

"In love with him?" Synnovea repeated with deepening astonishment. "How can that be? Not so long ago I thought I abhorred him."

Natasha laughed and lifted her slender shoulders in a shrug. "Sometimes love can hide behind different faces, my dear."

Synnovea was still mulling over the wonder of it when she happened to glance toward the direction in which Aleta had gone. It seemed the woman's goal had been to reach a Russian boyar whose head was being turned this way and that by every young and winsome lady who passed in front of him, but when Aleta laid a hand upon the man's sleeve, he turned promptly to face her.

"Aleksei!" Synnovea clutched a trembling hand to her throat as a sudden vision of Tyrone hanging by his wrists loomed before her eyes.

Noticing her sudden pallor, Natasha grew immediately concerned. "Dear child, what has taken hold of you? You look as if you've just walked over your own grave."

Synnovea could no more subdue her violent trembling than she could halt the memories that assailed her. "Aleksei nearly killed Tyrone for what I did, Natasha," she stated in a voice fraught with emotion. "In my selfish quest to gain my freedom from Vladimir and choose my own husband, I nearly saw Tyrone's life forfeited."

"Hush, dear," Natasha gently soothed, slipping a consoling arm around the girl's shoulders. "That's all in the past now. Things have turned out well in spite of everything. 'Twas Aleksei's selfish desires that nearly saw you both undone."

"Aye, but I see no reason for him to be here today except to cause trouble for my husband," Synnovea replied worriedly.

"How can he, my dear? Tsar Mikhail is here to see whatever that crow might try to do. Even Aleksei wouldn't be foolish enough to start something in front of so many important witnesses."

"That may be true, but I still don't trust the man," Synnovea declared emphatically. "He's as wily as a serpent."

"I agree, my dear, but that doesn't mean that I'm going to let that viper steal my joy." Natasha affectionately slid an arm around the younger woman and squeezed the slender waist. "Now, let me see the radiant greeting you'll bestow upon your husband when he rides out."

Synnovea forced a smile and grew amused at the comical look of exasperation the elder bestowed upon her in return. Her qualms swiftly vanished. It wasn't difficult at all to accept Natasha's reasoning. Aleksei was too shrewd and too much of a coward to start trouble in a place where he'd likely suffer defeat. Hadn't he proven himself recreant on the night of Tyrone's flogging, letting Ladislaus or his men confront whatever danger lurked in wait for them before he dared to venture forth?

"You've always been as wise as my own dear mother, Natasha," Synnovea assured her friend. "It's comforting to hear such sage advice."

"Considering the fact that your mother and I were the dearest of friends, I'll accept that as an enormous compliment, my dear," the countess replied with a radiant smile.

"Me lamb, look!" Ali cried from nearby. Nearly jumping up and down in her excitement, the tiny maid pointed toward the mounted troop advancing across the field. At the vanguard rode Tyrone, resplendently bedecked in a short red doublet embellished with braid and looped cords of shining gold and trimmed with midnight green around the cuffs and the banded collar. Matching green breeches were tucked into sleek black boots polished to a glossy sheen. The narrow brim of his silver helmet was worn low over his brow, and a red plume adorned the headgear, signifying him as the commander of the regiment, the smaller unit of which rode behind him now. The feather was readily visible as it dipped and fluttered in the buffeting breezes, allowing Synnovea to locate him easily as he and his men rode across the grounds to pay homage to the tsar. They saluted His Majesty, who acknowledged their presence with a wave of his hand, and in response, the cavalry unit returned to the center of the field and took up their positions.

Synnovea's heart began to beat with swiftly expanding exhilaration as the trumpets sounded a fanfare. In the next moment the horns fell silent, and a low rumble of drums began. The volume grew by ever-strengthening degrees until the drumbeats became pulsing vibrations that matched the smoothly sweeping advance of the mounted Hussars. The men rode as if they were of one body and in complete harmony with their steeds, seeming firmly attached to their saddles, contributing to the graceful smoothness of their ride as they performed a maze of maneuvers that held Synnovea spellbound. In rapt attention she watched the cavalrymen approach. Upon nearing His Majesty's pavilion, they split in twain and circled the grounds in opposite directions. As they did, the two lines separated into smaller units, becoming echelons of riders who crisscrossed the paths of others from the opposing string before merging again in a dazzling, intertwining exhibition of horsemanship. A moment later, they divided once more, this time in squared-off columns. After another circling sweep around the field, they melded like cards being shuffled together. On and on they rode in intricately performed equitation, fascinating the spectators, whose gasps of pleasure and frequent applause attested to their enthusiasm.

The thrills intensified for Synnovea soon after the troop began to execute its maneuvers in front of the pavilion where the wives had gathered. Ali skittered about like an excited hen, pointing at the colonel and boasting to other servants that he was her master. Even a warning twitch or two on her skirts by her mistress wasn't enough to remind the maid to pay attention to proper decorum.

"Magnificent!" Natasha exclaimed.

"Yes, he is, isn't he," Synnovea murmured, completely absorbed in watching her handsome husband. With sudden certainty, she knew that none of the other regiments would be able to thrill the tsar as much as Tyrone's troop now did. If her own reaction was any indication, then His Majesty's heart would be nigh thumping out of his chest.

The corners of Natasha's lips lifted in a sublime smile as she cast a glance askance at her companion. "I was talking about the performance in general, my dear, but of course I agree with you. Your husband has always been quite impressive, even before you realized that fact."

Synnovea's cheeks pinkened lightly as she glanced in some embarrassment at her friend, but Natasha's laughter was warm and inviting, completely infectious. Synnovea's own amusement rallied, and together the two yielded to their bubbling mirth.

Zelda left her own husband to tend to his duties in the tsar's pavilion shortly after Tyrone's unit had ridden off the field, and hurried over to join her friends. "What did I tell you, Synnovea?" she exclaimed enthusiastically. "Isn't your husband magnificent?"

Natasha and Synnovea relented to their merriment again, completely bewildering Zelda until Synnovea laughingly explained that they had just been elaborating on that very fact. Zelda joined them in their amusement, nodding in agreement.

The princess was nearly bubbling with excitement. "Vassili said there are many *boyarinas* and daughters and wives of foreign officers who are of the same mind," she eagerly confided as another troop rode onto the parade grounds. "You'll likely be seeing a fair sampling of the colonel's ardent following when this affair is over, my dear. The women simply adore him and will probably rush upon him to offer their congratulations, so be warned."

Synnovea smiled at the animated ebullience of the princess. "What do you suggest that I do to stake my claim upon him?"

"Didn't your husband tell you?"

"Tell me what?"

"Why, my dear, it has become a private tradition among the wives and fiancées to present their colors to their men." Zelda was surprised that her friend hadn't yet been informed, but then, she could understand a man not wanting his loved one to think that he was demanding such an honor. "By doing so, you'll be able to frustrate the hopes and aspirations of all the women who desire to have your husband as their own. I'm sure there are many who've become cognizant of the fact that in the past, Colonel Rycroft has finished these affairs without a special lady in attendance. Just as many have no ken of his recent marriage and will no doubt try to offer their colors as consolation."

Synnovea's eyes clouded with sudden concern. "But Tyrone didn't tell me. What must I do when I have no colors to give him?"

Thoughtfully Zelda scanned Synnovea's apparel and took note of the scarf that was casually draped over her shoulders. "Your shawl will certainly suffice. It must go around his waist, you know, so it should be about the right size." Glancing toward the older countess, she asked, "Would you deem it suitable, Natasha?"

"Absolutely," that one agreed cheerily. " 'Twill be the most gorgeous of the colors received here today."

The last group of Hussars concluded their performance and vacated the field. Then the commanders led their troops in order of appearance in a final review before the tsar's stand. If the applause was an indication of the one which the spectators thought offered the finest performance, then it was thunderous enough to evoke cringes of pain when Tyrone's unit passed in review.

At the conclusion of the event, the officers dismissed their men and rode back to the pavilion where their families awaited them. As Tyrone swung down from his mount, nearly a score of young women hastened forward in an eager quest to be at the vanguard of those who met him. Vying for attention, they fawned over him, stroking their hands caressingly along his sleeves, patting his back, and complimenting him profusely on his horsemanship. As Zelda had predicted, many clasped scarves in their hands and were desirous of having the distinction of being the one to wrap her color around his lean waist.

Tyrone politely demurred their offers, evoking disappointed sighs, and upon leaving them, briskly mounted the pavilion steps. As he strode toward his wife, his eyes melded in warm communication with hers, and though nothing more than a grin came from his lips, he revealed his pleasure with her appearance in a slowly exacting perusal that swept the length of her. When he halted before her, he leaned down to brush a kiss upon her cheek, daring much by his display of affection. He gathered her slender fingers into his, squeezing them fondly. "This is the first time my heart has soared with so much pride after one of these events," he said in a husky murmur. "I never fully realized until now what I was missing. I wish I could kiss you as I yearn to do."

Her soft lips curved in a radiant smile as her eyes plumbed the depths of those sparkling orbs. "I suppose we shouldn't be so forward while we have such a vast audience of onlookers. You seem to be the darling of the parade, sir. Even so, it would be nice to claim you with a kiss. In lieu of that, I must resort to other methods." Synnovea drew forth the shawl, which she had folded and draped over her arm. "I've been told that it's customary for wives and sweethearts to present their men with tokens of their regard. Would you honor me by accepting my colors, sir?"

"With great delight, madam," Tyrone breathed warmly. Retreating a step, he spread his arms and waited as she wrapped and knotted the scarf around his waist. When she lifted her head and offered him a loving smile, he could resist no longer. Ignoring proper decorum, he placed a soft kiss upon her mouth, which rapidly slackened in surprise. Astonished gasps were wrenched from older matrons, while giggling twitters were elicited from the younger women who had followed him into the pavilion and then had watched from a discreet distance. Tyrone paid neither group heed as he lost himself in the warmly glowing green-brown orbs. "That will have to suffice until we get back to our bedchamber, my sweet."

Synnovea's cheeks brightened with a blush of pleasure. "You make me anxious to return."

Gazing into those luminous depths, Tyrone had to remind himself to breathe. " 'Twas thrilling to have you in attendance as my wife."

"Not as thrilling as it is to have you as my husband," she murmured with adoration shining in her eyes.

Natasha leaned near and whispered a warning, "General Vanderhout seems to be coming this way at a fast pace, Colonel, and if you ask me, he doesn't look at all happy. So be careful. He's almost behind you now."

Releasing an irritated sigh, Tyrone turned to meet his scowling commander. "Good afternoon, General," he greeted stiffly. "Did you enjoy the presentation?"

"Blasted waste of time, if you ask me," Vincent Vanderhout grumbled. "I hope after today you'll lend your attention to more important matters. It's about time you took the men out on maneuvers and trained them in warfare. After all, that's what you came here for, not this flamboyant extravaganza."

"Your pardon, General, but I *have* been training my men in military tactics. I started the day I assumed command."

Vincent scoffed. "I haven't seen much evidence of that lately."

Tyrone offered him a blunt supposition. "Perhaps because you haven't been around to see it."

The general's eyes flared. "Are you suggesting that I've been ignoring my duties as you seem wont to do?"

Tyrone sought to curb his own rising vexation. "I don't know what you've been doing, General, but my men and I haven't seen you in the last week or so." He failed to mention that he had enjoyed the man's absence. "Otherwise, you'd be aware of what we've been doing to prepare ourselves for maneuvers in the field."

General Vanderhout faced Synnovea with a tense smile.

"If you'll excuse us, madam. I'd like a private word with your husband."

"Of course, General." Synnovea glanced worriedly at Tyrone, who squeezed her hand reassuringly before he followed his commander from the pavilion. Anxiously she watched them, wondering what insults the general would heap upon her husband this time, no doubt in a tone that everyone could hear.

Zelda had witnessed the general's approach and the fact that he had claimed Tyrone. Returning to her friend's side, she offered counsel of her own. "Don't fret over anything that man may try to do, my dear. He's like a large bubble ready to pop. If Tsar Mikhail hasn't noticed, those close to him certainly have, including the field marshal."

General Vanderhout stalked around the far end of the pavilion to a place well out of sight of the royal pavilion. By the time he faced his second-in-command, it was obvious he had grown even more irate, for his cheeks now bore a florid, mottled hue. "How dare you suggest that I've been lax in my duties, Colonel!"

"I didn't suggest anything of the kind," Tyrone countered. "I simply said that I didn't know where you had been." Then, because he couldn't resist gently needling the man, he queried, "Were you lax in your duties?"

"Certainly not! I've been indisposed."

"I hope nothing serious," Tyrone quipped.

Vanderhout glared back at him. "Just what do you mean by that?"

The colonel lifted his broad shoulders in a casual shrug. "Only that if you were ailing, I hoped it was nothing more than a passing malady."

"Who said I was sick?"

"Actually, no one," Tyrone replied. "I naturally assumed that was what you meant."

The general blustered. "Well, you were wrong to make

such an assumption. My health is not the problem here. You are. Just because you've entertained the tsar with your horsemanship, you probably think you're now the favored one in his eyes. 'Tis my duty to remind you of your lowly position."

Tyrone canted his head, just now beginning to understand what was driving the man. Vanderhout's jealousy was like deadly worms eating him alive. "The parade is over, General, and very soon I'll be leaving Moscow to search out Ladislaus. In view of that fact, I can see little reason for your reprimand. Can you?"

Vanderhout clenched his teeth to still an acid retort. He had been hoping to see the younger man shaking in his boots, but apparently that wasn't going to happen. "I'll let you off this time, Colonel, but you'd better keep your wits about you or I'll see you sent back to England."

Tyrone's lips drew into a laconic smile. "Thank you for your warning, General."

With that, Tyrone gave him a crisp salute and, pivoting about-face, strode back to the pavilion. Vanderhout glared after him, wishing he could carry through with his threat, but he was painfully aware that his own career would spiral sharply downward once the colonel was gone and he could no longer claim the man's accomplishments as his own. Thus far, he had been lucky in spite of the fact that his rank had been purchased by a wealthy father who had entertained aspirations of his son becoming a great military leader someday. Vanderhout heaved a sigh. Sadly enough, there were times when he felt completely inept at commanding men, and he knew well enough that the resentment he was harboring against the colonel was nothing more than his own envy spurring him on to vindictive accusations.

Synnovea's attention had been drawn away from the two men when Natasha whispered another warning, "I do believe Anna is coming with that goat Ivan. She seems as vexed as the general. Do you suppose she could still be stewing over your marriage to the colonel?"

Synnovea steadfastly faced Anna as that one strode across the pavilion toward her. The woman's thin jaw was rigid, and her eyes could've been likened to two penetrating slivers of gray ice. Obviously she hadn't been able to reclaim the ground she had lost with the tsar, for at the moment, her rage seemed undiminished.

"The minute my back was turned, you started playing your foul little games to embarrass me before my cousin. Had I known what mischief you intended to brew in my absence, I would never have left Moscow."

Recognizing the woman's venom, Zelda interrupted cautiously. "This really doesn't concern me, Synnovea. I must leave anyway and find my husband before he comes searching for me." She pressed a cheek against her friend's and voiced a conjecture in a muted tone. "Anna is merely irate because you escaped her malicious ploy to see you married off to Prince Vladimir."

Stepping back, Zelda almost stumbled over Ivan Voronsky, who had halted close behind her. Perhaps the man's intent had been to overhear what was being said between the two younger women, and though neither Synnovea nor Zelda doubted the capability of the cleric to resort to tactics of that sort, they were both amazed that he wasn't more discreet.

Ivan sneered at Zelda in obvious distaste before she offered a hurried excuse and made her departure. Then he turned and bestowed a snide smirk upon Synnovea as he queried, "Another little witless friend of yours, Countess?"

Synnovea gasped in outrage. "Princess Zelda can hardly be considered witless, sir!" she protested, sharpening the man's glare. "Nor can you accurately judge the *wisdom* of another when you have no idea what that particular word means!"

"Have you room to boast on any account?" Ivan challenged officiously. "I know what you are! I've known it all along! You're naught but a filthy little slut!"

Ivan's thin arm was immediately seized in a steely vise, eliciting a sharp yelp from the man. Looking around in painful surprise, he almost gulped when he met the glaring blue eyes of the Englishman.

"Be careful what you say, little toad," Tyrone rumbled. "Someone may be tempted to do the world a favor and break your scrawny little neck. In other words, if you can't keep a civil tongue in your head when you're talking to my wife, I'll be obliged to do the deed myself." Releasing the wide-eyed man as if he were something tainted, Tyrone gave Ivan a meaningful stare as if to affirm his pledge. "Be warned."

Anna dared to intervene. "If you should attempt such a thing, Colonel, I'm sure every Russian in Moscow will be amused to see your head lifted off your shoulders at the Place of the Brow."

Tyrone scoffed in derision. "What? For killing a rat?"

Ivan blustered in outrage, but Tyrone pulled his wife's arm through his and gave them a curt excuse. "His Majesty has bade me to bring Synnovea to his pavilion ere we involve ourselves in any of the celebrations to be held afterwards. So if you'll excuse us, the tsar is waiting."

"I'll tag along," Natasha announced cheerily. "Adolphe wanted me to join him anyway, and since the air has grown quite offensive here, I'd like to seek a more fragrant site." Taking it upon herself to give Ali leave to stay and talk with the other servants, Natasha waved to the tiny maid and then turned, meeting Anna's glower briefly before she hastened to join the handsome couple, who were already making their way toward the royal pavilion.

Tsar Mikhail was standing with the field marshal when the three arrived, but he readily excused himself from the man and lent his full attention to Tyrone and Synnovea as Adolphe hurried forward to claim Natasha and draw her aside.

Mikhail's dark eyes gleamed with pleasure as he considered the newlyweds. "I'm happy to see you both looking so fit. Obviously marriage agrees with you, Colonel." He bent a smile upon Synnovea. "You also seem quite happy, my dear. Is all well with you?"

Her smile wavered enticingly between timidity and radiance. "Very well indeed, Your Majesty."

Mikhail eyed the man at her side. "I've never seen a better performance from your outfit as I saw today, Colonel Rycroft," he declared with enthusiasm. "In fact, I thought you seemed in remarkably good spirits while you were out on the field." A threatening grin tugged at the corners of his lips. "Though in the past I've been much awed by your presentations, I was curious to know what had motivated you to such perfection today. Then I chanced to witness your haste to reach the other pavilion after the event. Obviously you had your mind affixed on pleasing your wife more than anyone else."

Tyrone's bronzed features took on a ruddy hue. "My most humble apology, Your Majesty, if I seemed distracted. . . ."

Mikhail held up a hand to halt the polite plea. "I welcome whatever it was that encouraged the unparalleled excellence of your performance, Colonel. You delighted me—and my guests—far beyond the measure I was expecting." Thoughtfully he tapped a forefinger against his lips. "It wouldn't grieve me at all if you'd allow that particular inspiration to motivate you in the future. If such exhibitions are enhanced to the degree that I've seen here today, then I can only determine that it's in my best interest to allow you to perform them in the main for your wife."

Though relief flooded through him, Tyrone responded with a crisply executed bow. "I'm grateful for your kind indulgence, Your Majesty."

"Perhaps when it's convenient for you, we should discuss your last petition. I have a feeling that you'll want to consider withdrawing it."

Tyrone's eyes dropped briefly as he suffered through a moment of painful chagrin. He was embarrassed that he had ever let his ire rule his head, but he squared his shoulders. "You see through me quite well, Your Majesty. I'd feel kindly favored if you'd forgive my impertinence and allow me to retract the petition. It has already been nullified."

"I thought as much," Mikhail replied with an amused chortle. "You seemed too happy with your present situation for me to believe otherwise. But then, I was sure in time you'd have a change of heart."

"My heart has always been firmly ensnared, Your Majesty," Tyrone dared to correct. " 'Twas only my head that was led astray by my resentment."

17

*T*yrone was usually very punctual about getting up before dawn, but on this particular Saturday, when he had a day free of duties, he didn't even stir when Synnovea slipped from their chambers and went downstairs for her morning toilet. It was a pair of hours later before he roused from slumber and, upon realizing the place beside him was empty, launched himself from bed before he noticed Synnovea sitting in a chair near the windows. For a moment he savored the stirring vision as he recalled the passion they had enjoyed during the night. At present, she looked sweetly demure in a softly hued dressing gown. She was repairing a snag in a pair of his newer trousers that had been torn by a lance during one of the practice assaults in which he had been training his men. Yet there had been moments in their night-long feast of sensual delights when he had glimpsed again the wily temptress who could make him tremble in lusting fervor. Although newly indoctrinated into the rites of love, Synnovea was warm, responsive, and creative. Indeed, he found himself thoroughly enthralled with his young wife, for he was wont to think that she could portray the bewitching seductress better than the most knowledgeable strumpet.

"Good morning," he murmured, his lips slowly tracing into a grin.

Synnovea's smiling gaze swept his long, naked torso in admiration before she met his warmly inquisitive stare. "Good morning, sir. I trust you slept well."

Tyrone raked his fingers through his hair, somewhat amazed by his tardy rising. "I had no idea I could sleep so late." He cocked a brow at her and teased, "I think you wore me out, madam."

"Strange, I seem to remember a time or two during the night when you woke me up wanting more," Synnovea rejoined with a soft chuckle. Setting aside the mended breeches, she rose and brushed close against him in passing, rousing a whole volley of delectable sensations before she moved on to the anteroom. "I told Ali that I would let her know when you were up so Danika could prepare you victuals. Would you like Ali to bring you up a tray or would you prefer to go downstairs to eat?"

Tyrone let his breath out slowly, somewhat amazed at himself. Even after spending such an adventuresome night in bed, he was still anxious for more. Scrubbing a hand over the stubble bearding his face, he crossed to the dressing room. "If Ali wouldn't mind fetching a tray, I'd rather eat up here."

"Ali lives to please you, Ty," Synnovea assured him, pausing near the door of the anteroom. "Your will is her command."

"What of her mistress?" he queried, leering at her.

Synnovea laughed and shook her head. "If I were to yield that bit of knowledge to you, my dear husband, you'd probably take advantage of me, perhaps even seek retribution for past offenses. I don't think it would be wise to reveal how my heart races at your slightest touch. You see, only a few days ago I was sure you hated me."

"Have I not been a most attentive husband these past two nights?"

"Aye," she agreed with a husky warmth imbuing her tone. "So attentive you make me yearn for more."

"Then you'd better send Ali for a tray, madam. I'll need nourishment if you want me to stay up here and make love to you all day long."

"Your servant, sir." Her laugher flowed behind her as she hastened to the outer door.

Chuckling, Tyrone made his way into the bathing chamber, where he paused to wrap a towel around his hips before beginning his morning routine. When Synnovea leaned in a few minutes later, he was spreading lather over his cheeks.

"I think it's about time I devoted some attention to teaching you Russian," she announced. "Are you agreeable?"

"I was wondering when you'd get around to it."

With an air of playful indifference, Synnovea tossed her loose tresses. "You haven't been home long enough for us to even speak, much less allow me time to instruct you."

"I'm here now, madam, and I can assure you that you have my complete and undivided attention." Stepping near, Tyrone braced a hand against the jamb above her head and leaned down to nuzzle her throat, unintentionally bearding her as he smeared a fair measure of soapy froth over the long, graceful column.

Synnovea squealed in protest and sought to escape, but he clamped an arm around her to hold her secure. One broad hand clasped her buttock, snuggling her up against him, while his other slipped inside her robe to cup an unfettered breast, but she slapped at his wrist playfully. "If by that remark you mean to make love to me again, sir, you'll have to get rid of that awful beard. I swear you've drawn blood."

"My apologies, madam," Tyrone mumbled in chagrin as he stepped back. "I didn't mean to."

Her eyes glowed back at him. "I know that."

He stepped to the washstand again and picked up the razor, but she followed and, taking it from his hand, carefully pronounced, "*YA khaCHU paBRItsa*. I want a shave." She urged him to repeat the syllables as she drew him to a straight chair in the bedchamber and pressed him down upon it. Plying the sharply honed edge slowly along his cheek, she shaved away both the stubble and the lather as he eyed her warily. "*YA khaCHU paBRItsa*. Now repeat it."

"*YA khaCHA paBRItsa*."

"CHU!" She took his chin firmly in hand and, lifting it up, forced him to look into her face. "*YA khaCHU paBRItsa*. Say it right this time."

"*YA khaCHU paBRItsa*."

"Excellent!" Synnovea smiled as their gazes melded. Then she leaned forward and carefully whisked the razor over the rest of his face.

Tyrone raised a dubious brow as she laid aside the razor and picked up a pair of scissors. She brought them threateningly near, prompting him to lean back in sudden distrust of her intentions.

"*YA khaCHU paSTRICHsa*. I want a haircut," she stated, her lips twitching puckishly as she snipped the air in front of his nose.

"How do you say 'I don't want a haircut'?" he inquired dryly.

A giggle punctuated her answer. "*NYE NAda paSTRICHsa*."

"*NYE NAda paSTRICHsa*," he repeated with a grin.

"Coward!" she accused through her laughter as she ruffled his short locks. With another playful roar, he moved forward out of the chair, dipping a shoulder and sweeping her onto it as he surged upward.

Synnovea laughed in glee and braced her hands upon his back as she tried to right herself, but Tyrone whirled her about the room until it seemed to sway and dip around her. Upon halting, he let her body slowly slide down the length of his as his hand slipped the tie on her robe free. With a shrug of her shoulders, Synnovea banished it to the floor and sighed softly in rapturous bliss as his mouth feasted upon her bosom. The towel was tugged free, and with stunning results, her hips came to rest against his loins.

Synnovea stared into her husband's sharply chiseled features, feeling his throbbing excitement. The bed was conveniently near, and Tyrone moved to its edge, where he laid her back upon the mattress. His hands swept down her lithe body in a long caress until they clasped her thighs; then he gently parted them and settled into the welcoming warmth of her. Synnovea caught her breath as his loins began to caress hers, and his mouth covered hers in a heady kiss. She dug her heels into the edge of the mattress as she lifted herself to meet his leisured thrusts, and soon she was gasping and writhing. Their breathing grew harsh and ragged as the rushing spasms washed over them, sweeping them out into a sea of ecstasy where they floated detached from the world of reason and reality.

A light rap sounded on the door, evoking a startled gasp from Synnovea, but Tyrone held her fast in a gentle embrace and, lifting his head, called out to the outer portal. "Who is it?"

" 'Tis Ali, master," the maid announced through the thick wood. "I've brought yer victuals, but there be a messenger awaitin' yer instructions downstairs. He says yer scout returned wit' word that he's found Ladislaus's camp an' wants ta talk wit' ye about it. The messenger wants ta know, sir, if'n ye'd be wantin' Avar to come here or if ye'll be returnin' ta camp any time today."

"Leave the tray beside the door, Ali," Tyrone instructed.

"Then go down and tell the messenger that I'll ride over and speak with the scout."

Leaning down to Synnovea, he grinned and caressed her mouth with a most ardent kiss. "As much as I hate to leave you, my sweet, I must, but at least we've started the morning off in a most eventful way." He slid his hands up to cup her breasts and drew a trembling sigh from his wife as he slowly plied a nipple with a languid caress of his tongue. "I'll return as soon as I can. Will you wait for me?"

"I must," she crooned, threading her slender fingers through the hair on his chest. "You've lit another fire within me, and it must be quenched."

His loins moved against hers again, quickening her blood as well as his own. "This will never do," Tyrone said in some amazement, feeling himself growing hot and hungry again. He kissed her again and reluctantly withdrew, shaking his head at the wonder of it. "I swear you've bewitched me, madam, or at least given me some strange potion to keep me always eager for you."

"Aye, husband o' mine," she warbled through silken laughter. "And I'm the only one who can ease your plight, so be warned. Lifting the skirts of other maids will do you little good."

"You tell me nothing new, sweet spouse. I've known that from the first moment you blinded my eyes to other women."

Synnovea gave him a pert nod. "Good! Then I command you to hurry back to me."

Tyrone kissed her passionately, holding nothing back, and then drew back to whisper, "I will, my sweet, just as soon as I can."

A short time later, Synnovea waved to him from an upper-story window where she solemnly watched his departure. It was not within her capability to describe the anguish that now weighed down her heart. She knew by the message he had just received that he'd soon be leaving her and going out in search of Ladislaus. She could not be sure what might happen or if he would even come back alive. She had no doubt that she'd be in constant fear for his safety until he returned hale and hearty from that quest.

The darkening brumes of gloom descended much sooner than Synnovea had expected. The dreaded harbinger came in the form of Major Nekrasov, who, after passing Tyrone in the square, finally deemed the time was ripe to inform the lady of her husband's plan to leave her. Thus it was that Nikolai presented himself at the Andreyevna manse and politely made a request to speak with the Lady Synnovea in private. He was allowed entrance and then bidden by a servant to wait in the open area of the great hall until the lady could be summoned from his mistress's chambers. A moment later, Synnovea entered the room and came forward, graciously extending her hands to the major, who clasped them and eagerly bestowed a kiss upon her fingertips.

"How good of you to come to see me, Nikolai," she murmured with a smile. Indicating an oriel where they could be observed but not heard, she led the way there. "I trust you've been well."

"Well enough, my lady," Nikolai replied, awed by her beauty. Delicately hued shards of light streamed in through the translucent mica panes, bathing her in a pale pink light. He was certain that no angel from heaven could have looked as radiant, or as appealing. "But I must confess that I've been much distressed by your marriage, so much so I haven't had the heart to seek solace in the company of another woman."

"Oh, but you must try, Nikolai!" Synnovea encouraged. "There can never be anything between us, and it grieves me to see you saddened by my marriage to the colonel."

"How can you be happy with him?"

The question startled Synnovea, and though some instinct deep within her warned her not to ask the major to explain, she stared at him in growing confusion, goading Nikolai to continue.

"Does he treat you as a husband should?"

"Of course," she replied cautiously. "I'm his wife. Why should he not?"

Nikolai rushed on, fearing the Englishman had already yielded to the temptation of her beauty. "I must bare my heart, my lady, as much as it grieves me to do so. Your husband had the effrontery to ask His Imperial Majesty to grant him an annulment from your marriage ere his return to England."

"You must be mistaken . . ." Synnovea began, feeling a coldness seeping into her heart.

"I heard him myself!" Nikolai insisted.

"But how can that be?" she queried, her heart constricted by pain. "We're man and wife."

"Has the marriage gone that far . . . or is it still a sham, Synnovea?" Nikolai probed with care. "Colonel Rycroft said he would hold himself from you until the time came for him to leave. Did he lie?"

Synnovea was suspicious. "Why have you come to tell me this thing now? What is your purpose?"

The major detected a note of irritation in her voice and rushed to allay her distrust. "I came here to pledge my loyalty should such an occurrence happen. If you'd consider accepting my proposal, I'd be honored to exchange the vows with you once your present marriage is dissolved. I'd cherish you as no man could."

Struggling to hold back an eruption of tears, Synnovea stiltedly faced the window. She had no idea what Tyrone meant to do now that their marriage had been solidified by their intimacy. That uncertainty evoked visions of her being left behind on the docks as he boarded a ship bound for England. Would she be carelessly discarded as a wife? Would he, after he reached his homeland, replace her with another light-o'-love and, in time, forget her?

Casting a glance over her shoulder, she questioned in a voice fraught with emotion, "How long does my husband plan to remain here?"

"A little over three years—until his tour of duty is fulfilled."

"Three years?" she repeated in a tiny voice.

"And some months, my lady," Nikolai added.

"So much time betwixt now and then," she murmured reflectively.

"The colonel was adamant that the tsar grant his petition at that time," the major insisted.

"When was this?"

"When you came to see His Majesty shortly after the colonel's whipping, and it was announced that you and the Englishman would be wed."

"Colonel Rycroft was very angry, as I remember," she rejoined in muted tones.

A brief, scoffing laugh evidenced Nikolai's ridicule. "*Enraged* would better describe the colonel's emotional state that day, my lady."

"You're saying that he was deeply outraged by the tsar's decree that we wed?"

"Exactly."

"That was to be expected, considering what I did to him," Synnovea stated quietly. "I used him to escape marriage to Prince Vladimir, and he was brutally whipped for it. Wouldn't you be irate if you were treated in such a fashion?"

Nikolai preferred not to excuse the colonel for his offenses and gave no answer.

Synnovea faced him with sorely strained pride. "Thank you for your warning, Nikolai," she murmured graciously, "but I'm afraid I cannot promise my hand to you when no one can predict what three years and some months may bear.

Perhaps you'll fall in love with another and regret any troth you pledge to me now."

"Never!" the major cried emphatically.

"Nevertheless, 'tis best to bide our time till that day Colonel Rycroft leaves for England. I wouldn't have him think me unfaithful to the vows we exchanged until they are truly severed."

"You'd hold true to such oaths when you know they mean nothing to him?" Nikolai inquired in amazement.

Synnovea met his incredulous stare with all the dignity she could muster. "There is still a lot of time for my husband to change his mind. I wouldn't want to jeopardize that possibility."

"But why?" Nikolai insisted, unable to understand. "Surely any other maid, upon hearing what I've just revealed, would be sorely offended by her husband's plans to annul their marriage."

A restrained shrug preceded Synnovea's rejoinder. "I believe the colonel spoke in the heat of anger when he begged leave to dismiss me from his life. The hurt that I had caused him wounded him more deeply than the whipping he had received." A sad smile curved her lips as she added, "But then, I love him too much to give up the battle ere it has barely begun, Major."

Nikolai's shoulders slumped suddenly in defeat. Unable to find an effective argument against her declaration, he sadly took his leave.

He was in the process of gathering his horse's reins from the iron hitching post when he espied the lady's husband riding down the lane toward the manse. Though he hurried to mount and be on his way before the man reached him, his haste lent incentive to the colonel, who nudged his heels into the flanks of his own steed, sending the animal racing forward.

"Major Nekrasov!" Tyrone nearly gnashed his teeth as he

forced a smile. "What brings you here? Should I assume that you've come on some errand from the tsar, or have you taken leave to visit my wife in my absence? I saw you earlier in the square, and it comes to me now that you did pause and watch me pass. What should I think? Have you come on my heels again to claim a chance to have my wife for yourself?"

Nikolai's face reddened with ill-suppressed ire. After his disappointing meeting with Synnovea, he was in no mood to give banal excuses. "I did indeed come here to see your wife, Colonel, but what does it matter to you? Wouldn't you be relieved to have some other man take her off your hands?"

Tyrone snarled and, jumping off his horse, flung himself toward the other's mount. Catching the major's coat, he dragged him from the saddle and gave him a harsh shake. "If it's your intent to try and take her from me, Major, then we'd better settle it right here and now. I'm tired of you going behind my back in your efforts to steal her from me."

Angrily Nikolai thrust the colonel away from him. "The matter has already been settled," he stated sharply. "The lady obviously wants to believe that you won't leave her behind when you return to England."

Tyrone's brows shot up in surprise. Then he abruptly recalled that the major had been in attendance when he had finagled his foolish commitment from the tsar. He sneered at the man. "Now I understand why you came slinking here behind my back like some defeated cur. You hoped, by telling Synnovea about the commitment that I had gained from the tsar, that you could advance your own cause and console her like some infatuated swain in my absence. You didn't care how you'd hurt her with your revelation. All you wanted was to have her for yourself. Well, Major, let me be the first to tell you that I've already retracted my petition from His Majesty. I've consummated our marriage vows, and the only way you'll ever have her is if I'm struck down and she is widowed. In other words, I don't have any intention of leaving my wife behind for you or any other swain when I return to England. I intend to make love to her every chance I get and keep her belly so fat with growing babes that you'll have no chance to interfere again. Now be gone from here before I thrash you to a bloody pulp."

Nikolai was not one to back down in the face of threats. He retorted with a warning of his own. "If I should hear one whisper of your mistreatment of the lady, Colonel, be assured of one thing. You'll rue the day you ever came to Russia. That much I promise you. Do I make myself clear?"

" 'Twill be a bloody cold day in hell ere you hear such rumors," Tyrone growled.

"Good!" The major nodded crisply. "Then perhaps you'll live long enough to return to England."

Nikolai swung into his saddle and, reining the horse about, sent him down the road in a thunderous departure. Tyrone watched him for barely a moment. Then, with a muttered curse, he whirled and raced into the manse. Finding no evidence of his wife's presence in the lower rooms, he leapt up the stairs to seek her out in their apartment. The door rebounded against the wall in his haste to gain the bedchamber.

Synnovea turned from the windows with a start of surprise and quickly brushed at the tears streaming down her cheeks as he came toward her.

"Major Nekrasov was here." Tyrone spoke the obvious as he searched her face.

"He came to see how I was faring," Synnovea replied stiltedly. Sensing his intention to discuss the details of the man's visit, she moved past him to the open doorway. "Natasha has delayed the meal until your return and is awaiting our presence down below."

Tyrone tried to curb his impatience, knowing the issue would have to be discussed at length in the privacy of their chambers. It couldn't be aired before others. Lifting his arm in invitation, he watched his wife carefully as she, in turn, slipped a hand into the bend of his elbow.

"You look especially beautiful tonight, Synnovea," he murmured in an effort to break her strained silence.

"Do I?"

"Almost as beautiful as the day you came into the palace to speak the vows with me."

"I wasn't aware that you had even noticed me then," she replied distantly. "You seemed quite disturbed by the whole affair, so much so that I was expecting you to call a halt to the ceremony ere it was done."

"I was greatly troubled."

"I suppose any man hates to be coerced into a marriage that he abhors."

"I don't abhor the marriage, only the circumstances that brought it about."

"Did you resent my encouraging your lusts, Colonel? I seem to remember they were already brewing."

"They were," he admitted. "I've desired you from the very beginning, Synnovea—from that first moment I held you naked in my arms. Since then, I could think of no other woman. You've been the only one I've dreamed of having."

"You didn't seem to want me at all after our marriage," she reminded him. "If not for His Majesty, I'm sure you would have left me."

"Aye," he acknowledged thickly. "But I was angry. You had used me, and you didn't seem to care what I might have suffered because of your ploy. I was very nearly gelded because of you."

"I should have married Vladimir," she muttered dismally, struggling to subdue her tears. "It would have been better for us both if I had."

"No, dammit! I want you as my wife!"

Synnovea lifted her gaze to his, her lips drawn into a poignant smile. "Do you, Ty?"

"Aye! You must believe that."

Natasha joined them at the bottom of the stairs, and her vivacious chatter allowed them to endure the meal with only a modicum of responses. She had no idea what was troubling them, only that something seemed to be terribly wrong between them. Synnovea's aloofness toward her husband was unswerving, while Tyrone's gaze hardly strayed from his young wife. Although he sipped from his glass far more often than was his usual habit, the couple barely touched their food. Natasha found her attempts to draw them into discussions of any sort were for naught. Long, awkward silences followed her efforts at conversation. Any questions pertaining to the tsar's enjoyment of the parade were met by Synnovea's forced smiles, and noncommittal shrugs or brief comments from the colonel. Frustrated by their taciturnity, Natasha finally begged escape as she clasped a trembling hand to her brow. It was now throbbing from the ordeal of watching two cherished friends punish themselves and destroy everything they had come to enjoy together.

Though other men might have shown some sign of being affected by the amount of wine he had consumed, Tyrone felt coldly sober when he finally escorted his wife upstairs. Finding Ali awaiting them, he retreated to the dressing room, where he doffed his clothes and donned the kaftan his wife had made for him. When he returned to the larger room, the Irishwoman was just brushing out her mistress's silky tresses. He lounged in a nearby chair, deeply appreciating the opportunity to watch this ritual and the stirringly beautiful vision of his wife clothed in a softly hued dressing gown, but when Synnovea bade Ali to braid her hair, Tyrone knew her hostility hadn't wavered in the least.

"I prefer it loose," he announced brusquely and waved the old woman away.

Reluctantly Synnovea responded with a consenting nod

when Ali turned to her with a questioning glance. Sensing that something was terribly awry, the servant took her leave and quietly closed the outer door behind her.

Having gained the privacy he had been waiting for, Tyrone went to his wife and tried to take her in his arms. "I need to talk to you, Synnovea."

"There's nothing to be said," she answered coldly and slipped free of his grasp with an irritated jerk. Immediately she crossed to a small writing desk that stood near the windows and, after opening and closing all of the drawers, finally selected a leather-bound volume of sonnets from a shelf near the top. She refrained from meeting the eyes that followed her every movement as she came back to her side of the bed. She swept back the covers that Ali had turned down moments earlier, fluffed the pillows, and hurriedly shrugged out of her robe before slipping beneath the covers, giving him no opportunity to peruse her meagerly clad form. Lying back upon the pillows, she opened the book and made an earnest effort to appear interested in the contents.

Tyrone had no idea how to repair the rift between them and feared his explanations would seem trite. Fretting over his difficult dilemma, he glanced at her often but could find no encouragement in her forbidding manner. He finally took up the conversation where he had left off. "Major Nekrasov was here."

"You said that," Synnovea goaded, lifting her slender nose with a lofty air as she kept her gaze fastened on the verses which she was striving hard to read.

"Is it your custom to entertain men while I'm away?" As much as he realized that he was accusing her unfairly of offenses when, in truth, it was he who should have been explaining, he just couldn't seem to help himself. Perhaps the wine had addled him more than he had thought.

"Nikolai and I were never alone," Synnovea informed him

with unswerving chilliness. "We were in sight of everyone who passed the door—"

"Obviously the major fancies himself in love with you," Tyrone interrupted. "Given the opportunity, he'd take you to bed. He seems most willing."

Synnovea plopped the book facedown upon her bosom and, with a coolly disdaining stare, met her husband's brooding gaze. "Major Nekrasov has been a good friend to me in the short span of time I've known him. If not for the fact that he warned His Majesty of Aleksei's intent, you wouldn't be here today, at least not as a whole man."

"He seems most willing," Tyrone reiterated with emphasis as he approached the bed. "Perhaps as much as I was." He laughed sharply. "I was so anxious to have you that you thought nothing of using me for your little gambit. You had no qualms about letting me touch your soft breasts. Would you let him fondle what you now withhold from me?"

"I withhold nothing from you!" Synnovea sneered hotly, her aplomb disrupted by a fury that her husband had never glimpsed before. "You were the one who sought to draw the limits between us when you asked the tsar to grant you an annulment upon your return to England! After setting such boundaries between us, would you *now* have me welcome you with open arms? 'Twas your intent to leave Russia unshackled, so how can you cast the blame on me because I dare withhold myself from you tonight? What more can you expect? You want neither me *nor* the burden of this marriage. Major Nekrasov, however, is interested in having me as his wife. He overheard your gallant request and came here to ask me to marry him after you leave."

"Did he, now?" This time Tyrone displayed a range of temper that Synnovea had never seen before. It distorted his handsome face, and before that towering wrath, she could do naught but shrink back upon her pillow in sudden fear as he leaned near. "Would he also sample your womanly softness ere he speaks the vows with you and cuckold me behind my back?" He growled at the very idea. "Be damned! 'Twill not happen to me again!"

Synnovea gasped in outrage, and her hand came forward with an angry sweep, cracking loudly against his cheek.

Tyrone's head jerked aside with the impact of her blow. Then, with lean nostrils flaring and cheeks flexing tensely, he bent a fiery glare upon her. "Angelina pledged her troth to me in marriage, too, and then behind my back played the harlot with a despicable rake. . . ."

The green-brown eyes widened as Synnovea stared at him in sudden horror. "Are you saying that you're married to someone else?" Before he could answer, she scrambled across the bed and leapt to her feet on the far side. Tyrone swung around the stout post and stalked toward her. As he neared, she stumbled back against the wall and flailed the air with a clenched fist, warning him to keep his distance. A snarl of rage tore free from her throat as she bestowed an accusing glare upon him. "You deceived me! You let me think you were without a wife! And all this time, while you played the injured one, you were the one who had duped me!"

"Dammit, Synnovea, it's not what you think!" Recognizing her panic, Tyrone tried to take her by the arms, but she pulled away and sneered at him in loathing disdain.

"Don't touch me, you *lying lout!*"

"Listen to me, dammit!" he barked. Catching her by the shoulders, he gave her a harsh shake as he commanded her to give heed to his words. "I was married in England several years ago, but my wife died before I came here! You are quite properly the *only* wife I now have!"

The sharp, piercing ache, mingled with a disturbing sense of having been cruelly betrayed, slowly dwindled into a feeling of reprieve as Synnovea gaped up at him. It was as if her life had been given back to her, as if he had been absolutely lost to her for a time, but was safely hers again. Another memory came winging back, impelling her to carefully peruse the handsome visage so close above her own. "You're the man you spoke about weeks ago, the husband whose wife betrayed him with another. . . ."

A pained frown creased Tyrone's brow. "I'm the one." Leaving her, he made his way around the end of the bed and halted before the windows. Clasping his hands behind his back, he stared into the darkness beyond. "Even before suitors were allowed to call upon Angelina, she had men swarming about, waiting in droves to bid for her hand. She was beautiful, of course, but it didn't hurt that her father had made provisions for an enormous dowry. Once she reached a proper age, she spent much time at court and was entertained by some of the most famous of roués. Our parents were neighbors, and I watched all of this from afar while she was growing up, thinking her naught but a child.

"She saw me out hunting one day after I had returned from a campaign. She rode over to talk with me, perhaps to show me that she had grown up since last we met. She was witty, charming, very lovely, everything a man could possibly want in a wife. She told me that even as a child, she had dreamed of becoming my wife and had set her cap to win me. Though I was amused at the time, she seemed dedicated to the idea of wearing down my resistance, until I finally proposed. I married her without considering that she might become bored with my frequent absences from home. After all, she had been fervently courted by a collection of gallant swains. You know the rest. While I was away in the third year of our marriage, she betrayed me with another man who made light of the affair when she told him that she was carrying his babe. He laughed and ridiculed her for having taken him seriously. He boasted to others of his deed and his bastard whelp that she carried within her womb. I came home and found Angelina trying to hide her condition from the world, though by then she was already well along."

"You say nothing of love, and yet I sense that you cared for her."

"Aye, I cared for her in a way any husband might care for his wife," Tyrone conceded, but checked himself before adding, *But I care for you more.*

"I'm your wife," Synnovea reminded him softly. "Does that make a difference?"

"Aye." Tyrone allowed the single word to suffice for an answer, though his heart yearned to say more. If she really knew how he was wont to treasure even her slightest smile, she'd understand how much he regretted ever mentioning the word *annulment*.

"I'm truly tired, Ty," she murmured, feeling thoroughly drained. "If you wouldn't mind, I'd like to go to bed now . . . and sleep."

"Of course," he replied, allowing that she had had a most trying afternoon. "I yield you that request. If it would ease your mind, you need have no fear that I'll force you against your will."

Synnovea dipped her head in a disconcerted nod and, after regaining her place in bed, turned on her side away from him.

Tyrone heaved a sigh, feeling as if the firebird had just escaped from his hands. It seemed that they were back where they had first started in their marriage. Now it seemed that he would have to woo her and wear down her resistance.

18

Tyrone couldn't even begin to think of making preparations to leave the city when he knew that Synnovea was still reeling from Nikolai's revelation. He wouldn't have blamed her at all if she had decided that she wanted nothing to do with him. It was the same way he had felt after she had carelessly used him. Yet he just couldn't go away, letting her believe that he didn't want her as his wife.

The first light of dawn streamed through the windows, bathing the chambers with a soft rosy glow. Tyrone stood beside the bed, watching his sleeping wife, unable to recall an occasion when he had ever accepted her presence casually. There had been times when he had either smoldered with desire or fumed with resentment, but whatever his reaction, his heart had been firmly ensnared and his senses completely alert to her.

He had dreamed of her again during the night and had

been snatched to full awareness by the pressure of her tantalizing curves against his naked back. Snuggling up close to him was her way of seeking warmth, and no amount of reasoning convinced him that she had forgiven him and wanted him to make love to her. As often as he had taken advantage of her proximity recently, he still ached for her. Indeed, he seemed constantly caught in a rutting heat for her, like some slavering beast sniffing the air for one of its own in season.

It came as no surprise that he enjoyed being her husband. That was more than he might have said about Angelina at times. His first wife had been more like a child, ever vying for his affection or needing affirmations of his devotion in overt displays, hanging onto him when he had just wanted to sit quietly for a few moments and converse with her, or visit with his grandmother or his parents without being embarrassed or distracted by her constant attempts to kiss and hug him. Perhaps she had grown up with the idea that she could command love. Having been the only offspring, she had been pampered and overly coddled by her parents. Her incessant demands had come close to disrupting their lives, for whenever she had been forced to share his time or affection, she had later pouted and complained that he didn't actually love her and that he cherished everyone else far more. Once she had even urged him to prove his love by lending his attention solely to her. When he had countered by promising to comply if she, in return, would give up her friends and family for him, she had vehemently refused. Grudgingly she had had to extend to him the same privilege by allowing him to visit those whom he had esteemed as kin or regarded as close companions.

It was bold in Tyrone's mind that Synnovea was very much a woman in every sense of the word and not at all unreasonable about anyone usurping her rights and privileges as his wife. There had been only one real instance wherein her jealousy and disdain had been manifested, and that was when Aleta had sought to seize his attention, along with other things, in the doorway of their chambers. But no one in his right mind could have disputed Synnovea's right to be offended then.

Now here he was, struggling with an overwhelming desire to awaken her and tell her how much he yearned to stay with her. Yet he held himself in check. He was a soldier; he had duties that would take him hither and yon. Perhaps he wouldn't even come back from his planned campaign to take Ladislaus and the leaders of his miscreants prisoner, and she'd be left a widow. If he was killed, then it might be better if she thought the worst of him. Her resentment would carry her through any grief she might feel over his passing, and she'd no doubt find it easier to forget him.

Heaving a weary sigh, Tyrone moved away from the bed and finally went downstairs to bathe. After dressing, he joined Natasha in the dining hall, but by then he was no less disturbed by his inability to hide his anxiety than he had been the night before.

"You seem preoccupied this morning, Colonel," Natasha commented, having affectionately settled on that particular form of address. In her mind, it most aptly suited him, for he was a man well accustomed to authority. Still, she suspected at times that he was totally at a loss as to how to deal with his young bride. "Is something troubling you?"

Releasing a long, pensive breath, Tyrone leaned back in his chair. "As the time for my departure approaches, I find myself reluctant to leave Synnovea. It makes me wonder if it will get any easier."

Natasha studied him carefully. "If I allowed myself to mull over your statement, Colonel, I'd be tempted to think that you've fallen in love with the girl."

Her conjecture failed to surprise Tyrone. "What am I going to do?" He made no attempt to hide his concern as he confessed, "Major Nekrasov came here yesterday to inform

Synnovea that I, in a moment of inanity, had wheedled an agreement from the tsar that would have granted me an annulment upon the fulfillment of my military contract here . . . if I could confirm that I had managed to withhold myself from Synnovea during our marriage."

Natasha's brows lifted in surprise. "Do you have hopes of accomplishing that feat, Colonel?"

He laughed shortly. "Our marriage has already been well consummated, but after Nikolai's visit, Synnovea wants nothing more to do with me."

"I'm sure her bruised feelings will mend in time," the woman encouraged. "A little patience is required to see it through."

"There lies the problem. I don't have much time. I'll be leaving here fairly soon, and I don't know how long I'll be gone. Weeks or mayhap even months. 'Tis difficult to predict."

"Perhaps Synnovea will consider what is wise and let you speak your piece ere you leave. 'Tis true that she can be obstinate at times, but she usually comes around when she can see a matter clearly." Natasha laid her hand consolingly upon his as she offered him the only advice that seemed appropriate. "Go about your business as usual, Colonel, but watch for the opportunity to talk with her. Speak the truth, and don't be reluctant to tell her that you really want her to be your wife, even after you go home to England." The countess relaxed back in her chair and studied his troubled features. "Do you know what you'll be doing once you return to England? Have you been able to settle your differences there?"

Tyrone lent his attention to straightening the napkin on his lap. "I have a house in London. As for the other matter, it hasn't yet been resolved. Though my father hasn't said as much in his letters, I fear the parents of the man I killed haven't yet forgiven me. He was their only son. Still, I'm determined to establish my home there." He glanced up to meet the dark eyes that rested on him. "Do you think Synnovea will be happy there . . . with me?"

A gentle smile touched her lips. "I think Synnovea will be happy anywhere as long as she's with the man she loves. Actually, she has an aunt in London, her mother's sister, who is now her only living kin. 'Twill be good for Vanessa to have the girl close at hand. Of course, I'll miss you both dreadfully once you're gone."

It was Tyrone's turn to lay a comforting hand upon the woman's thin fingers. "You'll be welcomed at our home any time, Natasha. Your visits would allow us the opportunity to return the favor that you've so graciously extended by letting us live here in your beautiful home."

"Oh, posh!" Natasha laughed and dismissed the idea of repayment with an elegant wave of her hand. "I've enjoyed every moment of it and will continue to delight in your presence until you must leave. Without both of you here, I'd be a lonely old woman!"

"What?" Tyrone chuckled, doubting the possibility. "With all your friends? I find that hard to believe, Natasha."

"Synnovea is as near to my heart as any daughter could have been," Natasha avouched, her dark eyes growing misty with tears. "You both are like family, and although I have many good friends, there is that strong tie which binds my heart to Synnovea that none other will ever replace. Her mother was my dearest friend. She was the sister I never had, and so, my dear colonel, you'll need to indulge me during those times I'm wont to show my motherly concern for you both."

Tyrone grinned. "A mother-in-law by design, eh?"

"Colonel! Show some respect for your elders!" Natasha insisted as her laugher merged with his.

When the meal had been concluded, Tyrone heeded Natasha's advice as much as he was able and rode off to work, avoiding the bedchambers where his wife was ensconced. He returned to the business of planning a foray on Ladislaus's camp and talked in depth with Grigori and the scout, Avar, about the difficulties that could arise before finally laying out the strategy they would use. While the three of them worked with maps, drafts, and diagrams of the area where Ladislaus's camp was located, the lower-grade soldiers took an accounting of supplies, weapons, and equipment; either stocked, repaired, or replaced what was needed and discarded what was not.

In anticipation of their departure, Tyrone allowed his men some time to do as they pleased, but with a stern warning that three days hence they would return to duty coldly sober and fully alert. They would be gone at least a fortnight, perhaps much longer, and in consideration of that lengthy separation from his wife, he also took some time off in hopes of repairing the damage that had been done in his marriage. Sensing Synnovea's continuing reserve, he avoided telling her of his upcoming leave and the time of his departure. Of late, it had become her custom to dally overlong in the dressing room until he had drifted off to sleep, negating any likelihood of their talking or doing other things. Thus he had decided to remain reticent until he had the firebird well in hand.

Synnovea had taken care not to awaken her sleeping husband as she settled down beside him that night. She was aware that he had pushed himself throughout the day and had earned the right to rest. Despite her aloofness while he was awake, she enjoyed closely observing him while he slept. By now his hair was much longer than she had ever seen it. Straggly wisps fell onto his brow and temples, and the results left him looking as handsome as some legendary Greek god.

A chill had crept into the room, as it was wont to do late at night. Synnovea felt it seeping in and moved closer to her husband. He was lying on his side facing her, a change that had occurred with the improvement in their marital status, except that now she was bent on presenting him an ignoring back every chance she got, at least until he fell asleep. Then she could admire him to her heart's content.

Carefully Synnovea reached out and tugged the covers up over Tyrone's shoulder. He must have felt her movement, for his eyes opened slowly and for a moment he stared at her with only a vague awareness. Then a faint, lopsided grin traced across his lips, warming her heart more effectively than any clever argument. Some strange, indescribable joy stirred within her, making her almost catch her breath. Sliding as close to him as she dared, she laid her head on the same pillow and, with a soft, adoring gaze, caressed his face. His arm lifted and came around her, pulling her against his long form, and with a contented smile she closed her eyes, gratified to be within his embrace.

Synnovea woke late the next morning and was surprised to find that Tyrone hadn't yet made his departure. He was presently occupied in the dressing room, and while he was ensconced there, she promptly availed herself of the opportunity to don a robe and scurry into the anteroom. After easing open the door, she slipped out and closed it gently behind her. She called for Ali and, urging the maid to hurry, hastened downstairs, fully intending to claim the bathing chamber before her husband decided he wanted a bath.

Several moments later, Synnovea was in the bathtub when she heard the door open and glanced up in some alarm to see Tyrone striding into the bathing chamber. Anxiously she motioned for Ali to fetch her a towel and folded her arms across her naked breasts as she awaited the covering.

"No need to rush, my dear," her husband assured her as he came ambling toward her. As much as she sought to hide the delectable fullness, it overflowed the confines of her restricting embrace, allowing him a most tempting view of her bosom and a delicate pink nipple. "I have the day off and am really in no great hurry."

"I was wondering about that," Synnovea replied, rising behind the large towel that Ali spread in front of the tub. "You're usually well gone by this time of the morning."

"The men needed a couple of days off to relax before we start out after Ladislaus, and I was much in want of a good rest myself."

"You should have told me." After briskly toweling herself off with a smaller towel behind the makeshift screen, Synnovea quickly smoothed a lotion over her skin and then donned a robe. "We could have been better prepared."

Tyrone smiled in satisfaction, having caught her in the kind of disarray he had been expecting. Warning her would have seen her up and garbed ere he had a chance to rise. "I saw no reason to disturb the usual rote of your day, madam. I just thought I'd come down and share your bath."

Tyrone grinned as the tiny servant glanced around in some wonder. "Ali, will you be kind enough to fetch a bucket of hot water to warm your mistress's bath? 'Twill suffice for my needs this morning."

A giggle accompanied her sprite curtsy before she flew across the room to do his bidding, leaving Synnovea to face her husband alone. The silken robe had molded itself to her damp skin and presented such delightful detail that Tyrone felt his wits lagging as he devoured the sights. Ali sharpened them again when she came back and emptied a pail of water into the bathtub.

"I'd best get in while it's hot," Tyrone mused aloud, sweeping the kaftan over his head.

"Ali, leave us!" Synnovea bade instantly, seeing no hesitancy on his part to disrobe in front of the maid. The small woman scurried out as the garment dropped to the floor behind her, and with a grin, Tyrone settled into the warm, scented bath and idly scrubbed his chest, closely observing his wife as she flounced about and angrily berated him.

"Have you grown so accustomed to the mores of this country that you think naught of stripping yourself naked before my maid now? Why, you would have shocked poor Ali to the core! I doubt she's ever seen a nude man!"

"Perhaps it's time for the woman to glean some knowledge of the male form, my dear," he rejoined teasingly. Although his wife's robe basically hid her nakedness, it clung cloyingly to every curve and hollow it covered. The view was most titillating to a man hungering for some serious copulation.

"Ali has come threescore and two years of her life, and you now say she ought to gain some knowledge about men?" Synnovea was incredulous. "What do you think she should do? Go out and snare herself a lover at this late date?"

Tyrone casually shrugged his broad shoulders. "You never know when she might get trapped in a bathhouse with a strange man. Without proper instruction, she could drown from the shock."

"Oh, you!" At his taunting grin, Synnovea looked around for a weapon and, choosing a bucket of icy water, christened him as no kindly priest would ever dream of doing.

Tyrone caught the full contents of the bucket in his face and, with a shocked gasp, came up out of the tub, stark naked and intent upon catching the winsome culprit. He swung one long leg over the rim and, blinking to clear his blurred vision, searched the chamber for his wife.

Synnovea was already running toward the door, having decided that it was time for her to make a hasty departure. Throwing the portal wide, she raced out, well aware of her husband's padding footfalls rapidly following. Casting back an anxious glance, she gasped in alarm as she found him in hot pursuit. Bent on escape, she faced forward again and then came to a tottering halt, nearly colliding with Natasha. Her startled gasp was immediately followed by another as she took several awkward steps backward into the solid bulk of her dripping-wet spouse. Knowing full well that he was as bare as the day he was born, Synnovea made every effort to keep well in front of him as she forced a smile for the countess's benefit. To say that it was pained would have been an understatement.

"I came down to visit with you," the older woman commented with droll humor, cocking her head aslant in an effort to catch a better glimpse of the muscular flanks that Synnovea was trying so hard to hide. "But I see that you already have more than enough company to keep you engrossed for a goodly spell."

Synnovea stepped cautiously in front of the woman's line of vision as she gallantly sought to preserve her husband's modesty, which, at the moment, she was sure he was seriously lacking. Lamely she stated, "You're probably wondering why Tyrone is here."

"Is that who it is?" the countess teased. "It's difficult to recognize him without his uniform." Then she spoke past the girl, directing her comments to the man. "I missed you at breakfast this morning, Colonel, but I can see you had better things to do."

"I have the day off, Natasha, so I thought I'd take your advice. It might be the last chance I have before I leave."

"I wish you good fortune," she bade, and then crinkled her brows in a perplexed frown as she contemplated the way his hair hung wetly over his ears. "Did someone try to drown you, Colonel? You look a bit bedraggled."

While Synnovea closed her eyes in painful chagrin, Tyrone settled his arms akimbo and gave the older woman a brief nod before he bestowed a condemning stare upon the top of his wife's head. "I hope you'll reconsider your departure now, my dear, and return with me so we can finish our discussion in a more civilized manner," he suggested, quite willing to stand there until his wife yielded. There was already a puddle around his feet, but if she didn't soon relent, the possibility of it growing larger did exist, for he wasn't nearly as sensitive about his nakedness as she appeared to be.

Synnovea responded with a stiff nod, refusing to glance around. "If you wish."

"Good!" Tyrone replied and grinned in satisfaction. "I'll be expecting you, so don't delay. I may completely shatter Ali's innocence if I have to come searching for you." With a dip of his head to Natasha, he pivoted on a bare foot and stalked back into the bathing chamber as Synnovea hurriedly retreated in an effort to hide his departing form.

Natasha's brows twitched upward in amusement as she caught a glimpse of Tyrone's bare backside beyond his wife's slender frame. She couldn't resist a museful comment. "You know, Synnovea, the more I see of the colonel, the more he reminds me of my late husband."

Synnovea rolled her eyes heavenward and, with a mortified groan, whirled and fled back through the doorway.

Natasha waved her hand in dismissal, trying to maintain her poise, which seemed punctuated with brief lapses into laugher. "Of course, my dear," she called after the younger woman. "Anytime."

Synnovea slammed the door firmly behind her and stalked after Tyrone, who was sauntering toward the tub. Grinding her teeth, she demanded, "Have you no propriety?"

Settling his hands low on his hips, Tyrone faced her. "I'm not going to wrap myself up in a monk's habit just to suit your delicate nature, madam, if that's what you're prattling about. Nor can you make me believe that after three marriages Natasha hasn't seen her fair share of naked men. As for that, I'm certainly not ashamed of the fact that I am one."

"You strut about like a proud peacock and display your possessions before every woman who happens to be near!"

"What does it matter to you? I could lay my treasures on a block and you wouldn't care! You'd rather keep that soft sheath reserved for some other gallant's blade than give me comfort and solace."

Synnovea gasped, taking exception to his accusation. "That's not true!"

"Oh?" Tyrone waved an arm eloquently in the air as he derided her denial. "Then, if not for me and not for others, madam, pray tell me the name of the one you reserve it for. Yourself? As a trophy of your departed purity?"

"Of course not!" Synnovea flounced past him in a huff and then, whirling, verbally accosted him. "At least I don't flaunt myself around like some knavish hawk, always eager for a peck or two!"

"If I appear *eager,* 'tis only because I'm starved for want of that sweet succor you now barricade behind that fine belt of chastity. Though I waste away for want of you, you'll no doubt keep the key well hidden in the coffer of your mind."

"Would you have me serve you as a common doxy?" Synnovea came toward him, boldly provocative, with a small shrug encouraging the fall of her robe from a smooth shoulder. "That's how you wanted me in the first place, wasn't it? Unwed, but in your bed? Your paramour? My dear colonel, do you still sorely chafe because you were forced to speak the vows with me? I've heard it rumored that in a thrice of years you intend to deny that you ever spoke them and would no doubt name whatever scion you beget to be your bastard whelp."

"I intend no such thing, madam!" Tyrone declared hotly, wrapping a towel around his hips. "If you refuse to take solace in my simple assurance, then I'll lay in your hands documents to guarantee my name to all my heirs. Would such a deed suffice to appease your anger?"

Synnovea pondered his question aloofly. "In part, it might."

"What else would you have from me?"

"No greater promise can bind you more than the vows we spoke. Thus it remains to be seen whether you will hold true to them or not. Only time will see the true depth of your honor."

"Would you go with me before the tsar to hear me plead for a retraction of my request? It has already been done, but if you insist, I'll go before him again."

Synnovea raised her gaze to his in curious question. "Would you be willing to do such a thing?"

"I wouldn't have offered if I hadn't been."

"Seeing is believing." She tossed her head like a child playing at a game. "Perhaps when such an event takes place, I might be reassured."

"Then can we not be at peace until I leave to search out Ladislaus? Perhaps you'll be rid of me ere the month is out, and this argument will be for naught."

Synnovea felt her heart grow cold with dread. Anxiously she searched his face. "I would have you come back unscathed, Colonel Rycroft."

"I'll try my best, madam, but I can make no guarantees." Taking up his robe, he tossed it over his shoulder and looked at her again yearningly. "I'd like to spend some time with you before I must make my departure. After this week, I may not see you again for a month or more."

Choked by her emotions, Synnovea nodded in willing submission, but when he started toward the door, her eyes skimmed his long form worriedly. The towel was hardly sufficient clothing for her peace of mind. "Would you go upstairs like that?"

"Aye!" Tyrone answered bluntly, squelching any idea that she could persuade him otherwise.

Rather than vex him further, Synnovea acceded to his disregard for propriety and moved beside him up the flight of stairs. Upon entering their chambers, he closed the door behind them and then stepped into the dressing room. When he returned, he handed her a pair of scissors.

"YA khaCHU paSTRICHsa." He pronounced the syllables carefully. "MOZHna pakaROche ZAdi."

Pushing the curling tresses back from her cheek, she peered up at him. "Just in back? Don't you need your hair cut on the sides, too?"

"MOZHna pakaROche pa baKAM—paZHAlusta."

"You're progressing very well, Colonel."

"Bal'SHOye spaSEEba."

Synnovea laughed and tightened the belt of her robe. "You're welcome." Pointing with the scissors to a straight chair near the window, she urged, "Sit over there where the light is better."

Tyrone complied and once again took notice of her clinging robe as she came toward him. It was hard to think of sitting still for a haircut when he had such a strong craving to take her in his arms and make love to her.

Synnovea embarked upon her task by running a comb through the tawny thatch. "Your hair is so thick you need a proper shearing."

Tyrone cocked a brow curiously. "Have you ever done this before, madam?"

"Once or twice for my father, but he usually preferred his manservant to trim his hair."

Tyrone looked at her askance, suddenly leery. "Was there a reason for his preference?"

Synnovea's lips twitched as she strove hard to suppress her amusement. "None that he cared to mention, but I rather suspect that it was the loss of an ear or two which might have encouraged him to let another do it."

Teasingly she worked the scissors near his ear, but Tyrone feigned a grimace and ducked his head, evoking her giggles. "Be careful, madam," he urged. "I'll need both ears to hear that scoundrel Ladislaus."

"Of course, sir. Nor do I desire a one-eared man for a husband." Moving between his thighs, she slipped her fingers through his hair, lifted a lock, and clipped it. Though she dropped most of the residue on a nearby towel, a showering of severed hairs fell upon him, urging him to brush them off his naked shoulders.

"I'll need another bath after this."

Synnovea leaned forward and thoughtfully tucked the tip of her tongue between her teeth as she snipped above his brow. When she finally straightened, she brushed the loose wisps from his face and smiled down at him. "That's what you get for intruding into mine."

"Aye, madam, but the bathing chamber is very accommodating for making love, as you well know. Perhaps we should return there after you finish cutting my hair."

She flung up her head, feigning a scoffing laugh. "I don't intend to be caught sporting with you in the bathing chamber this time of day, sir, especially since we've already been there. The servants will likely wonder."

"Will you sport with me here, then?" Tyrone asked, reaching a hand around to clasp her buttock and pull her closer within the spread of his legs.

Synnovea thrust her hip sharply outward to the side, a motion that not only tossed away Tyrone's hand but raised the elevation of his brows by a high degree when her unbound breasts nearly bounced out of her robe, very close in front of his face. "Be warned, sir. You're at my mercy, and I have no qualms about shaving your head to discourage all those other maids whom I espied drooling over you at the parade."

"Can you do that again?" Tyrone coaxed, slipping loose the tie that secured her robe.

"Behave, or you'll regret it," Synnovea warned, slapping his knuckles.

"You're too beautiful for that possibility," he muttered in a low, husky tone. Leaning forward, he brushed aside the garment and sought to take her nipple into his mouth.

"I said, behave!" Synnovea reached down and twisted a

few hairs on his chest, eliciting a wince of pain from him. The last thing she wanted at the moment was to dissolve in bliss and let him see just how slavish she had become to his ardor.

Rubbing his stinging chest, Tyrone complained. "Woman, you have a way of wrenching the heart right out of a man."

An elegant eyebrow rose challengingly as Synnovea clasped her robe together and once more knotted the tie. "And you, sir, have a way of wrenching the heart right out of me. I have no idea how I'm supposed to react to your overtures when our marriage could likely be dissolved at your bidding."

"I've already offered you assurances. What more can I do?" Growing a little vexed at having to explain again, he set her from him and came to his feet. "Although you might not recall it, madam, you were actually there when I bade the tsar to forget the petition."

"Sit down." Synnovea pushed him back into the chair, dissatisfied with his assurances. She wanted to hear something more, something he was obviously reluctant to yield to her. "I'm not through cutting your hair."

"Why don't you just cut it off and be done with it!" Tyrone muttered sourly. This wasn't going at all according to his aspirations.

She looked pointedly toward his lap where the towel had ridden up. Anger did seem to have a way of chilling his desires. "I don't think you'd sit still for that."

"Hell and damnation!" Tyrone retorted, clasping the cloth over his manhood. "Would you sever my cod, too?"

"Don't curse at me," Synnovea scolded, pouting. "I'm your wife, not one of the men in your regiment."

"I don't need to be told that, madam," he retorted. "Not one of them is as fetching—or as reluctant to accept what I say as fact."

"I'm sure they wouldn't dare! You'd scald their ears with your tirade if they didn't heed every little command you uttered, which brings us back to the point that I was trying to make. I'm your wife, and I won't be cursed at."

"If this is the way we're going to spend the day, I'm going back to camp," Tyrone grumbled, rising to his feet again.

Synnovea laid a hand upon his chest and, pressing him back into the chair, moved in closer, giving him no room to stand. She didn't want him to leave, especially when he was angry. Her fingers idly brushed at the hairs on his shoulder as she spoke in a husky murmur. "I said I wasn't finished, Ty. Now please sit still until I am."

Grinding his teeth in vexation, Tyrone forced himself to endure the clipping. His mood had turned cantankerous beneath her chiding and her refusal to listen to reason. Since he would be gone fairly soon, he had held some hope of their being able to pass the day on more congenial terms. Now that seemed unlikely.

Ignoring her husband's lowering scowl, Synnovea worked the scissors around his ear, not caring how her dressing gown fell away from her bosom as she neatened the area. Gradually Tyrone's irritation ebbed as his eyes began to feast on the sights so near at hand. She twisted slightly to judge the results of her work, giving him ample opportunity to view the ripe orbs beneath her robe. Dissatisfied with what she had done thus far, Synnovea straddled his leg and trimmed the hair near his temple. Then she moved behind his back to cut the hair around his nape, working her way around to the front again. Upon facing him again, she stepped astride his other thigh to clip his sideburns.

"There!" she said at last, tucking her robe between her legs and perching on a sturdy limb to consider the finished task. The fact that her bare knee rested lightly against his loins didn't seem to affect her, yet Tyrone was now of a different bent.

Smoothing the shortened hair beneath her hand, Synnovea commended her own efforts. "It looks good!"

"Am I allowed to move now?" Tyrone queried, running a hand caressingly up her thigh.

As if awakening from a daze, Synnovea met his gaze directly and recognized the passion smoldering in those shining depths of deep blue. In quickening response, her own pulse leapt with fire. "If you wish."

Tyrone leaned near and gently plied her lips with warming kisses as he tugged the ties of her robe loose and pulled it down from her shoulders. Then his hands moved in a slowly ascending voyage from her hips, skimming upward over her ribs until they clasped her soft breasts. His mouth lowered, and a warm, licking torch stroked across the pinnacle of a breast, snatching Synnovea's breath and awakening her desires until she closed her eyes with the ecstasy of it, basking in the delights he aroused within her.

Beyond the framework of the windows on the eastern side, the sun hovered behind a thin layer of clouds, and in the muted light, her pale bosom gleamed with a soft, lustrous sheen, contrasting with the bronze visage that pressed into the velvety softness. Synnovea braced her hands upon his wide shoulders, arching her back as his mouth and tongue bestirred her senses, nearly devouring her. When finally he raised his head, she met his searching lips with a fierce passion that matched his own. Her hand swept downward between them, past the lean waist and the flat, hard belly, until she clasped the fullness of his manhood. For a moment Tyrone closed his eyes and yielded himself completely to her will. When he opened them again, his gaze probed hers as his hand moved down to stroke along her thigh. Synnovea made a valiant effort to turn away from the hypnotic power that held her transfixed, half afraid she would lose herself in those pools of blue, but when his open mouth came upon hers, his searing kiss went through her, compelling her to yield to him everything he wanted. She was lifted briefly and then resettled astride his naked loins. Small, scintillating shards of excitement washed through her at the warmth of his intrusion, and for a long moment they savored the coupling, embracing and kissing, touching and being touched, as only lovers in love are wont to do. Then her hips began to answer his, leisurely at first, and then with a strengthening rhythm as the liquid fire surged through them, sweeping them along on a towering wave of molten passion until the brilliance of their passion burst upon them with a stunning radiance.

It was midafternoon when the couple went downstairs to visit with Natasha in the great room. The older woman could hardly mistake their change of attitude. Each of them now seemed reluctant to be apart from the other for even a short distance or a brief space of time. They held hands like lovers entranced and were wont to exchange unswerving looks that warmly communicated things beyond the discernment of others, except that Natasha knew and understood, having once experienced a great love herself. Synnovea's soft gazes clearly revealed her preoccupation with her husband, which reaffirmed Natasha's belief that the girl's devotion ran deeper than mere infatuation. As for Tyrone, he was clearly involved with his young wife. His eyes devoured her every movement, every smile, every questioning glance. He answered her, asked her opinions, listened to her with interest as he entwined his long, lean fingers with her slender ones or laid an arm around her shoulders to bring her close against his side. Neither of them appeared the least bit abashed by their ardent display of affection, but laughed when they found Natasha smiling in teary joy as she observed them together.

When they retired at an early hour that evening, Natasha was far from surprised. She cautioned Ali to stay away from their chambers until she was summoned, and it was not until midmorning of the next day that the servant was bidden to join her mistress downstairs in the bathing chamber. For the first time in her life, Synnovea felt strangely embarrassed by her own nakedness in front of the woman, but when Tyrone entered a few moments later, no protecting towel was called for. Instead, Ali was banished upstairs where she contented herself by laying out her mistress's clothes for the day and humming gleefully.

Natasha declined Tyrone's invitation to join them on an outing, having accepted Adolphe's plea to spend the day with him and his daughter. Finding himself alone with his young wife, Tyrone was hardly disappointed. Still, he brooded over his growing reluctance to leave her. While Stenka took them on a tour of the city, they discussed a variety of matters, at times serious, other times sensually explicit and titillating as Synnovea probed his manly knowledge and experience. Then there were moments when he listened attentively to the story of her childhood or to her suggestions as to what gifts they should buy for Sophia, Ali, and Natasha, just in case he'd be gone for an extended period of time and be unable to share with them the joy of *Svyatki,* the Christmas season.

As the days had sped past, bringing his scheduled depar-ture ever nearer, Tyrone's thoughts had turned increasingly inward, and he found himself mulling over his affairs like a man whose days were severely numbered. In his military ca-reer he had always had to face the possibility that he might not come back from a campaign, but now he felt a desire to make Synnovea understand that if anything happened to him, she would be welcomed by his family if she should have a desire or a need to visit England. Now that there was a chance that he would leave an heir, he didn't think it right that his parents or his grandmother only receive word of his death and never learn of his wife and the child they had made to-gether. While privately ensconced with Synnovea in the coach, he took the opportunity to reassure her that his family would want to know about her should he be killed, but his statement filled her with dread, and for one brief moment she stared at him as if all her joy had been vanquished.

"I couldn't bear your loss, Ty," she croaked against the tears that welled up within her as he enfolded her against his chest. "You must come back to me."

"I'll do my best, madam," Tyrone murmured against her brow. "Now that I have found you, I pray desperately that I may come back."

"Oh, you must! You must!"

"Dry your tears, my love," he coaxed gently. "We'll be leaving the carriage soon, and people will wonder why you've been crying. They'll think I've been mistreating you in some fashion."

Synnovea laughed at the absurdity of such a notion and, sitting up, dabbed at her reddened eyes and blew her nose with a dainty handkerchief. Then she lifted her gaze to her husband's softly querying smile. "Is that better?"

Suddenly struck by the full import of how miserable he would be away from her, Tyrone clasped her to him again and seized her lips in an ardent kiss. "I pray the time may go swiftly," he muttered as his mouth lifted to hover over hers. "I cannot bear to think of leaving you and not being able to see you, touch you, love you."

Clinging to him, Synnovea strove to be brave. "A month or two from now, the anguish will be over and I'll be welcoming you back into my arms. We must take courage now and pray that no harm comes to you."

Tyrone glanced around as Stenka halted the carriage in Red Square. Then he faced his young wife again with a desperate plea. "We've so little time together. Let us not waste it all here, where I cannot hold you or kiss you as I yearn to do. I'd like to return home as soon as possible."

Synnovea slipped a trembling hand into his, blinking away a fresh start of tears. "We'll hurry, my dearest."

Arm in arm, the couple hastened off toward the markets of Kitaigorod, leaving Stenka and Jozef waiting with the coach. After making their selections, they returned with their gifts, a golden necklace for Natasha, a lace-trimmed nightgown and woolen shawl for Ali, a dress for Danika, and a doll and a brightly decorated wooden dollhouse for Sophia.

Tyrone lifted Synnovea into the conveyance and was about to climb in behind her when he noticed his second-in-command waving to him from afar, trying to gain his attention through the milling crowd. Pledging to return in a moment, Tyrone left his wife and hastened through the throng to where Grigori awaited him.

"You seem happier than I've seen you looking for some time, my friend," Grigori remarked with a smile. "Marriage seems to agree with you."

Tyrone's brows gathered in bemusement. He sensed that something dire was troubling the man, but he had no idea what it could be. "What's wrong? Why didn't you come over to the carriage to speak to me there?"

The captain's face clouded. "I didn't think your wife should hear the news I bear, of which you, my friend, need to be made aware. Aleta is pregnant, and General Vanderhout is boiling mad. He swears it's not his."

"How can he be so sure of that unless they haven't been sleeping together?"

"Which seems to be the way of it. I heard it whispered that he's suffering some infectious malady of late that prevents him from indulging his wife's appetites."

"Infectious malady?" Tyrone frowned in confusion. "You mean—"

Grigori held up a hand to halt the flood of questions that seemed to be on the very tip of the colonel's tongue. "Again I've heard it whispered that he's been forced to consider what wench gave it to him, for he hasn't been exactly faithful to Aleta either."

"Two of a kind," Tyrone mused aloud.

"Anyway," Grigori continued, "Aleta is spreading the rumor about the city that you're the cause of her condition."

"The bitch!" Tyrone cried, and then almost groaned as he thought of Synnovea getting wind of the gossip. "It's not true, of course!"

"I know that, but General Vanderhout doesn't. It seems he's looking for you. You'd better hope we leave ere he finds you."

"Aye! But what can I tell Synnovea? She's bound to hear all this filth while I'm gone if I don't tell her now."

"I agree! 'Tis better you tell her yourself rather than allow anyone else to wound her. Will she believe you?"

"She must!"

Seated inside the coach, Synnovea was content to inspect the gifts that they had purchased, but when she became aware of a shadowed form filling the open doorway, she glanced up with a smile, expecting to find Tyrone beside the coach. Her greeting froze on her lips as she met Aleksei's darkly smoldering eyes.

"Synnovea, my beautiful little ice maiden," he greeted huskily. "I didn't think it possible, but you've grown even more lovely since last we met. Can it be that you've become enamored with your husband, and that the radiance of that devotion is what I see? Perhaps you can even be grateful for my lenience in allowing your husband to keep what he no doubt treasures most."

Synnovea's icy gaze conveyed her contempt, nearly chilling him to the bone. "I'm extremely grateful that Ladislaus and His Majesty kept you from doing your foul deed, Aleksei. But tell me, why do you brave my company when my husband is so close at hand?"

Aleksei seemed taken aback by her statement and glanced around nervously. Then he arched a brow, displaying a rampant distrust. "Really, Synnovea, you shouldn't lie like that. What man would foolishly leave his wife alone where dastardly villains could approach her?"

"I'm not alone," Synnovea reminded him, sweeping her

hand around to indicate the location of the driver and the footman. "Stenka and Jozef are here with me, and should I scream, I have every confidence that they'll both be here a mere step or two before my husband arrives."

"Tsk, tsk!" Aleksei admonished. "You ought to know by now that I can have their hands lopped off if they dare touch me."

Synnovea's eyes grew even colder. "Didn't His Majesty warn you about your manners after you took Tyrone and had him whipped? If you were to dare such a thing, I assure you that Tsar Mikhail would hear from me. But tell me, do you intend to remain here until my husband returns? Or will you flee like the coward you are once he arrives?"

"I doubt he's here at all, my girl, so you can cease your feeble ruse, because I'm in no mood to leave just yet." Slipping into the coach, Aleksei settled himself across from her and, for a lengthy moment, considered her heightened beauty. "You know, Synnovea, I might be persuaded to share my attentions with you after all. You're clearly worth the effort it will take to forgive you."

"Please, Aleksei! Forebear the struggle!" Synnovea enjoined sarcastically. "Lend me your hatred instead! I'm better able to cope with your disfavor."

"I've heard rumors that your husband will be leaving the city soon. You'll need a man to comfort you while he's gone."

"Why should I settle for your attentions when I've had the best there is?"

"You're still such an innocent, my dear." The swarthy prince leered at her in unswerving arrogance. "After you've been with me for a while, you'll learn how to recognize a real man."

"A real man!" Synnovea scoffed. "Why, you pompous, braying ass! You haven't the simplest notion what those words mean! Do you honestly think you can judge a man by the number of trollops he has bedded? Why, you're no better than a boorish swine who mounts the closest haunch to serve his rutting instincts."

Aleksei's face hardened with ill-suppressed ire. "I see you haven't yet learned to curb your tongue, Synnovea. If you think I'm unable to wound you, then you're mistaken. I have ways to make you grovel at my feet."

Leaning forward with narrowed eyes and an evil grin, he caught her wrist in a cruel vise. By slow degrees, he increased the pressure upon the finely structured bones and began to smirk as she writhed in pain. "You remember our ride in the hired carriage that night, don't you? Well, I can think of better ways to deal with your husband than by merely having him flogged, my dear, and I needn't take the blame for it at all. You see, there are enough Russians who loathe foreigners who'd be willing to carry out a proper gutting of any foreigner they find. I need only hint at what great service they'd do their country if they'd take the colonel for a little jaunt beyond the city." Aleksei lifted his broad shoulders briefly. "Of course, he'd never return, and you'd be left a widow—"

Aleksei glanced toward the carriage door as he detected a shadow looming beyond the opening. In the next instant he leapt aside with a start of surprise, reminiscent of a dog that had just been scalded.

"You were saying . . ." Tyrone interrupted caustically and drove a fist toward the man. His blow caught the prince on the cheekbone, forcibly propelling that one toward the door on the far side. The back of Aleksei's head hit the inner wall near the window, and frantically he sought to right himself and reach the door, but a warbling cry of fear was wrenched from him as Tyrone leapt upon the step and, seizing the hem of the man's ruby-red kaftan, dragged him back.

Aleksei frantically searched for leverage against his adversary's relentless vise and clasped his arms tightly around Synnovea's legs as he was being hauled past her. He grimaced with the strain of trying to resist the inevitable force that drew him nearer the beast who held him, and he raised his head to glare at her as she tried to shove him away. "Be warned, Synnovea! I'll do more than see your husband gelded this time! I'll set the dogs to eating his foul carcass! Synnoveaaa . . . help meee!!"

Snatching Aleksei up by the scruff of the neck, Tyrone yanked him away from his wife and growled near his ear. "You sniveling coward! Where is your courage now that Ladislaus isn't here at your beck and call?"

The prince's arms and legs thrashed wildly about as he was dragged swiftly through the door and then launched into midair. He came to earth a short distance away and skidded through the muck of slimy vegetables, which a vendor had just tossed from his cart. The prince scrambled to his feet, and without so much as a downward glance at the clinging bits of offal that adorned his gold-trimmed kaftan, he clasped its hem and made his departure with great, leaping strides.

"Colonel Rycroft!" The name was barked from a different vicinity, and as Tyrone spun around, General Vanderhout stalked toward him with irately flushed cheeks. His outrage was obvious. "What is the meaning of this offense? Have you gone mad?"

"The man was assaulting my wife!"

General Vanderhout blustered in vehement rage. "How dare you attack a Russian boyar when it's you who should be horsewhipped! I've a mind to see you court-martialed for your offenses!"

"My offenses?" Tyrone arched a brow in question. "And just what are they, sir?"

"You thrashed that boyar!" Vanderhout shouted, thrusting an arm after the long-departed prince.

"He deserved at least that much and more for hurting my wife! I should have broken his neck!"

"The tsar will hear of this!"

"Aye, you tell His Majesty! And this time perhaps he'll

have the bloody beggar's head lifted off his shoulders! That toad has been warned before by His Majesty. It might not go so well for him again!"

"Nor for you, Colonel, when I tell His Majesty what you've done!" the general warned irately.

"Precisely what have I done, other than to protect my wife?" Tyrone asked crisply.

Vanderhout sneered in disdain. "You know what you've done better than anybody. Frankly, I'd like to see you gelded."

Tyrone snorted. "That has been tried before, by that very same one who just now tried to accost my wife!"

"Obviously he wasn't successful," the older man snapped. "Or did that happen *after* you bedded my wife?"

The bronzed cheeks flexed with ill-suppressed ire. "I've just heard the rumors about Aleta's condition, General. The only thing I can say is that I'm not the one at fault."

"Aleta says you are, and for that affront, Colonel, I'll see you stripped of your rank and sent home in disgrace."

Tyrone muttered a curse as he felt the sting of Aleta's conniving revenge. No doubt she was seeking retribution for his rejection of her, but he was not about to accept her accusations without defending himself. "I suggest, General, that you seek out the truth of this matter ere you proceed with your claims. You'll save both yourself and your wife a great deal of embarrassment."

General Vincent Vanderhout reddened to the neck of his shirt as he struggled to find an appropriate rejoinder to refute the colonel's claim of innocence. With equal fervor he searched for a threat to frighten the man, but when he met the steely stare of those blue eyes, he could do naught but sputter and spew in frustration.

"I must be leaving now, General," Tyrone continued tersely, "but if you wish to address this matter further, be assured that I have witnesses to testify in my behalf, several high-ranking officers who can vouch for the number of times

I've turned aside your wife's invitations. Her indiscretions are none of my affair, but I promise you, I won't let her lies ruin my life." Inclining his head with a crisp nod of farewell, Tyrone ended the conversation abruptly. "Good day, General."

"This is not the end of it, Colonel Rycroft!" Vincent Vanderhout railed. "You'll hear about this again!"

Ignoring the man's threats, Tyrone turned and gestured for Stenka to make ready to depart before he climbed into the coach and took a seat beside his wife. As the conveyance lurched into motion, he muttered through grinding teeth, " 'Twould truly seem that a woman scorned has the sting of a venomous viper."

Synnovea searched her husband's angry visage, wondering what else had occurred to thwart his good humor. "Beyond our confrontation with Aleksei, what has happened to make you say that?"

"Aleta is with child," Tyrone stated with a heavy sigh, "and General Vanderhout claims he's not the father. 'Twould seem that she has taken the initiative to lie by claiming that I am the one at fault, obviously to cause trouble for me." He looked into his wife's worried gaze. "I'm not, Synnovea. I swear to you that I've never touched that woman except to thrust her out of my sight."

Leaning forward, Synnovea pressed her brow gently against the side of his stalwart neck and, in a soft whisper, dissolved most of his anger. "I believe you, Ty."

Slipping a hand beneath her chin, Tyrone drew it up and searched her softly smiling face for a lengthy moment before he lowered a long, tender kiss upon her lips. When he drew back, his eyes delved warmly into hers. "Have I told you yet, madam, that I love you?"

The green-brown eyes grew misty with elated tears as she searched his face. "Do you really mean that, Ty?"

"Aye, madam, very much. Indeed, I cannot remember a time when I haven't loved you. You've been the one for whom my heart has beat ever since we came together in the pool months ago."

"My dearest, dearest colonel," she breathed as his lips lowered to savor hers again.

As the coach rumbled away from the square, they clung together, luxuriating in their marital contentment. It was several moments before Synnovea broke the revelry by telling her husband of the princely boyar's intent.

"Aleksei has heard rumors that you'll be leaving soon. He has also decided that he would like to resume his efforts to have me in his bed."

Tyrone stared at his wife in some surprise and recognized the worry written on her face. Slipping an arm around her shoulders, he snuggled her close against his chest and soothed her fears as much as he was able. "I'll set men around the house to watch over you in my absence. Aleksei isn't brave enough to confront several armed guards alone. He needs a whole regiment behind him to give him courage."

Synnovea smiled into the beautiful blue eyes above her own. "I'll miss you terribly, Colonel Sir."

"I'll be leaving my heart with you," he whispered, caressing her face with his lips. "Guard it well for me."

"I'll never betray you, Ty," she promised softly, bracing herself up higher on his chest. She traced a fingertip over his lips and chin before lifting shining eyes to his. "I think I love you, Colonel Sir."

In the next phase of a heartbeat, their hungering mouths came together in a kiss that sealed their vows of love more thoroughly than any spoken word. A long moment later, they pulled apart, but that same evening they retired earlier than usual to the upper chambers, where they spent many wakeful hours sweetening their passion with mutual demonstrations of their devotion.

19

The sun concluded its languid journey across the welkin blue and, for a lengthy moment, seemed to pause above the distant line that marked the end of its passage, as if delighting in its own magnificence, much like an actor posturing grandly for his audience before making his nightly departure from the stage. Crimson rays flared outward from the western sky, piercing the thin, ragged clouds that mischievously sought to veil the fiery brilliance of that great and notable visage. Replete in its unyielding condescension, the daystar finally bowed its head of its own accord and sank slowly from sight, allowing the heavy curtains of dusk to close behind it. Only a soft, rosy aura remained to evidence its passing until that, too, dwindled beneath the trailing hem of an ebon cloak that scattered a myriad of glittering crystals in its wake.

The night-born darkness was what Tyrone's troop had been waiting for to mask their advance up the hill. Avar, Grigori, and a small vanguard of soldiers had already ascended to the bluff to take captive there a pair of guards living in a hut and to secure the area so the company could move stealthily into place. On his earlier scouting expedition, Avar had clandestinely observed the lookouts long enough to become familiar with their routine. Whether by soft, reassuring whistles, which came at regular intervals, or by sharper signals that alerted the camp of approaching danger, the scout now had the knowledge to enable the detachment to continue a covert surveillance of the canyon over which they'd be keeping watch. Already Avar had employed a birdlike trill to placate the half-dozen or so stalwarts who normally kept vigil in the camp down below. Everything was in readiness for the soldiers' advance.

It was of paramount importance that Tyrone and his company of soldiers gain the hilltop positions undetected. Only when they were well assured that Ladislaus was in the camp would they launch their attack. If an alarm sounded ere the rascal was securely caught in their trap, the chances of capturing him were nil. Tyrone was adamant that nothing go wrong. He had come too far to think of springing his trap before the fox was in the bag.

Thus, in preparation for their ascent, the horses' hooves had been padded, the axles of the supply wagons and the gun carriages heavily greased, and the wooden wheels wrapped with leather strips to muffle every bit of noise possible. No word was to be spoken except in the faintest whisper. Having already stressed the need for caution, Tyrone swung astride the huge black and casually drew the reins through his lean fingers as his men followed his lead and mounted their steeds. He raised an arm and swept it forward, silently motioning for them to move up the incline.

Long before he had actually started planning the foray, Tyrone had determined that their primary goal would have to be the capture of Ladislaus and the more important members of his band. By stripping away their leadership, he hoped to hamper the remnant's ability to regroup. Without Ladislaus, he could foresee the others being dispersed in a state of chaos or perhaps scattered by those prone to struggle for positions of control. If his planned assault proved successful, then the prisoners would be taken back to Moscow, where they'd be subsequently judged for their crimes. Whatever happened beyond that point wasn't within Tyrone's power to dictate. If found guilty, the thieves would either be held for eons behind dungeon walls or be escorted to the spot near the *Lobnoe Mesto,* where the city held public executions.

Many in positions of authority had intentionally been led to believe that Colonel Rycroft's objective was of no great import. To guarantee that such would be the case, Tyrone had deliberately bypassed General Vanderhout and, with Grigori acting as his interpreter to ensure that he'd be clearly understood, had taken his petition directly to the field marshal, who had proven entirely receptive to the idea of ridding the countryside of Ladislaus's army of bandits. Tyrone's appeal for secrecy had influenced the man to keep the matter to himself while allowing contrary rumors to filter down to the other men in the division. Nearly the whole Russian army thought the English colonel was merely leading his men on another practice maneuver in an area far afield from whence they'd actually be going.

When Vincent Vanderhout finally became cognizant of the fact that he hadn't been advised of Colonel Rycroft's plans well in advance of the actual issuance of orders, he had ranted and raved as if his second-in-command had committed a treasonous crime. The general was even more aghast when he had discovered that the colonel had requisitioned a half-dozen small cannons affixed on their own ribauldequins and twice that number of artillerymen to man them. His bushy brows had shot up to lofty heights of unparalleled disbelief at this affront, for he was sure the younger man was now trying to undermine his command or, at the very least, hoping to reap honors rightfully due him. Taking great exception to the clandestine manner in which these supplies had been obtained by his second-in-command, Vanderhout became resolved to teach the Englishman a lesson. Gaining audience with the highest military authority within his immediate reach, he had vehemently demanded that another be chosen to lead the expedition, but he was informed that his request would have to be approved by the field marshal, who at the time was far too busy to see him.

Vanderhout had then sought to ease his growing frustration and vicious spite by harshly berating his wife for bedding down with a fool and by lambasting the tactics that her lover-colonel had devised for the campaign. By the time he had detailed every flaw he had imagined existed in Tyrone's strategy, Aleta knew as much as any officer in the division and took no pains to keep that information to herself, thereby helping to secure the secrecy that Colonel Rycroft had both wanted and needed for the success of the foray.

The general's disappointment had reached its zenith when his attempt to forestall the scheduled departure of Tyrone's troops came up against a solid stone wall in the form of a direct mandate from the field marshal, whose missive had negated the possibility of *anyone* denying the colonel's requests. Alas, the poor general could do little but fume in high-flying indignation as the colonel and a large company of men from his regiment rode out of Moscow in full view.

Having gotten wind of all the scuttlebutt, the townspeople were positive they knew every detail of the Englishman's mission. Word had also trickled beyond the city, appeasing the curiosity of those who made it their business to be kept well apprised of the whereabouts of the tsar's forces.

A day's journey beyond the city, Tyrone had sent Avar to scout out the area ahead of them with a detachment of twelve Hussars commanded by Grigori. Four of these had served as vedettes who rode outpost fore and aft of the remaining eight during the day. In the evening, two of the twelve reported back to Tyrone and were replaced by that same number of men from the main company who then rode forward to join the advance guard. Ordered to capture any spies who would perchance report back to the thieves, Avar and his small body of men had kept a careful surveillance for offshoots of Ladislaus's band in an attempt to avoid the possibility of the miscreants obtaining advance warnings of their approach. Thus the colonel and his troop had managed to arrive at the foot of the hill with no member of the outlaw band the wiser.

Tyrone carefully scanned the area encompassed by a tangle of woods on either side of them as he led his men up the hill by way of a longer trail that allowed the larger conveyances easier access. The moonlight provided enough illumination for their climb, but it also threatened to reveal their presence if some wayward sound attracted the curiosity of the thieves. When a sudden rattle of a falling kettle made a horse rear and whinny in fear, Tyrone was quick to react. Whirling his own steed about, he came alongside the lumbering wagon from whence the offense had occurred and sternly rebuked the young soldier who drove it.

"Dammit, Corporal!" he hissed. "Belay that racket ere you wake the dead! I told you to secure every last pot and kettle aboard this cook wagon. Did you need a nursemaid peering over your shoulder to remind you to get it done?"

"Izvinitye!" The young man jerked his shoulders briefly upward in an anxious shrug as he apologized and then struggled to find the English words that would adequately answer his commander. "I did, sir!"

"Obviously not well enough!"

"Something broke, I think."

Tyrone jerked his thumb over his shoulder. *"Gavaritye!* Get up the hill! You can make your excuses later."

When the last wagon reached the summit without further

incident, only then did Tyrone breathe a sigh of relief. Grigori and Avar were there to assist him in directing the men in setting up the camp. Though the whole company had been cautioned about the need for secrecy, it was once again impressed upon them that all would be lost if the thieves were alerted to their presence while they labored beneath the cover of darkness.

Whispered orders were given as supply wagons were unloaded and then pushed into narrow niches between towering firs whose boughs provided generous concealment. The horses were tied in similar protected sites close behind the encampment. Cannons were hauled into place and stealthily positioned among the firs buttressing the sharp drop-off forming the hillside, their sights directed outward toward their targets. Near the ribauldequins upon which they sat, leaden balls were stacked in generous mounds. The sod-roofed stone hovel that had once served the guards as living quarters would be utilized as a cookhouse during the surveillance. Beyond its stone steps, no campfires would be permitted in any area where a glow could be detected from down below.

His company of men finally settled themselves to get some much-needed rest, allowing Tyrone to inspect the encampment. Accompanied by Grigori and Avar, he apprised himself of the advantages and faults of their hilltop position and discussed options for remedying the latter. Below him, the narrow basin was spotted here and there with campfires that dimly illumined the steep crags and rocky hills encompassing Ladislaus's hideout. Protected by this impenetrable fortress of stone, the bastard prince and his followers had obviously enjoyed autonomy from the rest of the world for a number of years. The only paths by which a man could enter or leave were through the passes at both ends, each of which was well barricaded and continually patrolled by two armed lookouts. A third sentry watched from the bluff above each, a prime spot for viewing anyone traversing those narrow areas.

The guards' lofty positions made it virtually impossible for a foe to escape detection once he entered the gorge.

Tyrone had finalized his strategy with Avar's earlier observations uppermost in his mind. Although the summit upon which they now camped had been reasonably accessible by the trail that he and his men had recently taken, his scout had forewarned him that descent into the ravine would require a perpendicular drop from the cliff, for which his men had routinely practiced by shimmying up and down ropes attached to the Kremlin wall. In preparation for the actual event, the ends of stout ropes would soon be attached to large trees edging the bluff and their coiled lengths left at the bases of the trunks, where they'd be wrapped in small tarps to protect them from the elements. Ropes frozen in unyielding ice would be of little use to them once the order to attack was given. This and other meticulous precautions were taken to expedite the soldiers' advance into Ladislaus's camp, a strategy the thief would hardly be expecting.

"Everything will be just the way you had anticipated, Colonel," Grigori stated with a measure of excitement and pride imbuing his tone. "Once we utilize the cannons, the outlaws will be imprisoned down there. After our men take them captive, another gun blast or two will open the front pass to allow us to depart."

"The plan seems simple enough to forestall the possibility of failure," Tyrone mused aloud but continued in rueful reflection. "Still, I've seen the best of schemes fail for the most asinine reasons. As yet, we don't have any idea if Ladislaus is even down there, or if he'll soon return if he isn't. We can only bide our time until we actually see him. I pray we won't have to wait too long with winter nigh upon us."

"I shall add my prayers to that petition, Colonel," Grigori readily offered. "I have no liking for the frigid winds that will sweep over this hill."

*   *   *

A cold, blustery morning followed the regiment's nocturnal arrival to the summit. Crisp winds blew in plumes of snow that whisked into the cowls of widely flying cloaks and flapping tent doors and puckishly frosted fingers and noses. The ominous portent evidencing the fierceness of the winter ahead might not have been so difficult to bear had they spotted their quarry. Though Tyrone and his men carefully canvassed nearly every crevice and cranny they could view from their lofty perch, no one caught a glimpse of the lordling thief. Not even the powerfully built Petrov or the towering Goliath was sighted, leaving the soldiers little choice but to suffer through the anguish of waiting until the rascals came within their grasp.

A fortnight came and went, and still they saw no glimpse of their prey. Tyrone grew restive. He could only wonder where Ladislaus had taken himself and others of his band and what mischief they were presently brewing, whether they were busy attacking unsuspecting travelers again or perhaps raiding a village in some area far afield of their camp. Unable to endure the wait without gaining some knowledge of what was happening beyond their hilltop perch, Tyrone sent Grigori and Avar out to search for some trace of the brigands. As he awaited their return, he chafed in unbridled restlessness. He would've preferred to ride out and scour the countryside himself, but he knew the folly of being recognized by Ladislaus. Hence Tyrone was forced to abide where he was, though he longed desperately to have this raid behind him so he could return with fervent haste to the one he loved.

20

*T*he lunar sphere cast a silvery essence down upon Moscow as it climbed in a lofty arch across the night sky. Coldly aloof and forbidding in its nocturnal setting, it lent no warmth or cheer to Synnovea's heart as she stared dejectedly into the blustery darkness beyond her bedchamber windows. If someone had ventured to ask, she'd have been wont to declare that her husband had already been gone for a year or more. Since his departure, it seemed as if her life had paused in solitary flight, much like the moon, which now lent an illusion of being momentarily frozen in its heavenly orbit. It was a cold hard fact that through the remnant of this eventide, she could look forward to nothing more exciting than huddling alone beneath the quilt in an effort to warm herself. If she were fortunate, treasured memories would wash over her like softly cresting waves, bringing mental images vividly to life. At times she could almost sense Tyrone's presence, his face looming before her, lending her solace from her abject loneliness and reawakening her to sweet remembrances of when they had made love, of his huskily whispered words brushing her ear and his long, hard body moving upon her own. Such memories provoked longings that were difficult to subdue, and she'd then lie awake, tortured even more by their separation.

Hourly she fretted for her husband's safety, loathing the wars and conflicts that might snatch his life. Though she sought to keep her fingers and mind actively occupied, she found no abatement for her deepening anxieties. The threat of Ladislaus was too real, too well marked in her memory to allow her to dismiss her apprehensions with menial tasks.

Heaving a disconcerted sigh, Synnovea turned from the windows with no heart to face the solitude of her lonely bed. Aimlessly she meandered about the bedchamber, taking no note of its elegant appointments as she thought back on the weeks which had recently plodded past. She now had a clearer sense of how one could suffer a feeling of unbearable isolation even in the midst of caring friends. Though Ali had liberally practiced her Irish wit in hopes of entertaining her, Synnovea could hardly manage a vague smile for her tiny maid. Even Natasha and Zelda's cheery companionship had failed to ease her gloom.

Social outings had not helped in the least. If anything, they had set her more on edge, especially during those two separate occasions when Prince Aleksei and Major Nekrasov had dared to approach her in public. Though the presence of a pair of hefty guards riding atop her coach or following closely behind while she roamed the marketplaces of Kitaigorod had dissuaded her persistent suitors from extending their visits to only a few moments, they had voiced their causes with equal fervor. Concerned that his earlier visit might have caused her dismay, Nikolai had displayed his merit as an honorable gentleman by offering a quietly spoken apology. Aleksei, however, had proven himself as adamant to have her as he had been in the past. If anything, his quest for fleshly appeasement and simple revenge had grown even stronger since she had become the wife of a man whom he now considered an adversary, as if the idea of stealing her away, whether by captivation or forcible capture, had become something of a challenge to him. Though the pair of guards, whom Tyrone had hired to protect her, both hindered and annoyed the prince, Synnovea wasn't entirely certain that they'd be successful in keeping Aleksei from his purpose.

" 'Tis obvious your husband is afraid of being cuckolded during his absence." Aleksei had smirked in haughty arrogance after falling in beside her during a tour through the marketplace. He cast a glance at the two brawny giants following closely upon her heels. "A chastity belt might have been less costly than those clumsy oafs he has employed."

Synnovea had managed a less-than-tolerant smile as she replied with derision, "Why, Aleksei, can it be that you're outraged because my husband has actually dared to thwart your lecherous little ploys by engaging men whose loyalty to him is unswerving? Such fealty to an Englishman must seem strange to you, what with them being Russians. Why, I'd even venture to guess that their allegiance to him is so firmly rooted that you'll find your princely status of no consequence to them, surprising as it may seem. I don't imagine that you've ever experienced such loyalty yourself."

Aleksei's dark eyes had skimmed her with a strange mixture of angry insolence and hungry fervor. "My dearest Synnovea, you remind me of a well-preened swan gliding over the warm waters of a lake, completely oblivious to the dangers of the hungry wolf lurking in the tall reeds near shore."

Synnovea had responded by lifting a lovely brow in chiding condescension. "Be careful, Aleksei. You could get snared wallowing in the treacherous bogs of conceit ere you learn your lesson. His Majesty hasn't yet forgotten your last misera-

ble undertaking to steal me from the colonel. A second attempt just might cost you your head."

Her reminder hadn't been kindly accepted by the prince,
whose eyes had chilled to a piercing darkness that promised
dire consequences. "You should've learned by now just how
adamant I can be when I set my mind to a matter, Synnovea.
I do so hate to repeat a lesson I've already taught, but it's
evident you aren't willing to take me at my word."

With a last smug smirk, Aleksei had stalked away to his
waiting coach without a backward glance. Now, nearly a week
later, Synnovea had cause to hope that he had given up the
idea of seizing her for his own lecherous purposes, for she
hadn't seen him at all, not even with Anna or others with
whom he consorted. She could only pray that he had left Moscow in search of some new conquest.

Synnovea doffed her robe and slipped between the cool
sheets, recalling the many times that Tyrone had been there,
and his arms had reached out to draw her close against his
hard body. Now an empty void greeted her, and darkness was
the only thing that enveloped her after the tapers were
snuffed out. Solemnly she stared across the room at the moon
hovering in a starlit sky beyond the windows, and she wondered how she'd ever be able to get through untold weeks,
perhaps even months of lonely anguish.

Fighting the chill of the lonely bed, Synnovea rubbed her
hands briskly over the sleeves of her nightgown, but her arms
remained cold beneath them. Nothing sufficed in comparison
to her husband's embrace, and her heart pined to have him
with her once again. She drew his pillow to her breast and
hugged it fiercely, just as she yearned to do with him.

Much later, when Tyrone meandered through her drifting
dreams, it seemed as if she floated on a gently wafting breeze,
and for a while she was content . . . at least until she was
rudely snatched to awareness by a broad hand clapped tightly
across her mouth. It masked nearly half her face, effectively

squelching a scream that was born of terror. Against her struggling efforts, a gag was stuffed into her mouth and secured by a narrow strip of cloth wound tightly between her teeth. Her captor leaned over her as he knotted the rag behind her head, and Synnovea's heart nearly leapt from her breast as she recognized the pale, scruffy thatch that covered the man's head.

Ladislaus!

Her mind screamed the name out in dread as she struggled vainly against the overpowering strength of his huge hands. She now knew this would be no simple robbery which would end in a swift departure of the culprit. As his casual disregard of her emerald brooch had once attested, Ladislaus wanted *her*—and everything a woman could yield to a man!

The renegade prince flipped her over onto her stomach and, seizing her wrists, lashed them securely behind her back. He wrapped the bedclothes around her so tightly that her breathing became seriously restricted. In burgeoning panic Synnovea thrashed her head back and forth, desperately seeking some opening from whence she could draw breath. Finally Ladislaus recognized her dilemma, rolled her over, and tucked the quilt beneath her chin.

"Is that better?" he asked, his voice liberally imbued with humor. In the meager light, the pale orbs sparkled with merriment as he leaned close. "I'd be dreadfully put out with myself if you were to pass away from lack of air ere I've made love to you, my beauty."

A thousand insulting epithets came to mind as Synnovea writhed in protest and glared up at him, but Ladislaus only chuckled and swept her up from the mattress. He tossed her casually over a shoulder and made his way around the end of the bed. Upon passing the open door of her dressing room, he paused to reflect upon the insufficiency of the nightgown she wore beneath the quilt. It would hardly keep his men from ogling her, nor would it keep her from freezing during the long ride to his den.

"I suppose you'd prefer to garb yourself rather than wander naked around my house. Though I'd appreciate such a sight, I rather doubt Alyona would."

Entering the narrow room, Ladislaus rummaged through her armoires and chests, stuffed an assortment of womanly accouterments into a large satchel, tossed a heavy winter cloak over his arm, and then crossed to the anteroom. In the hall outside her chambers, he paused to listen until reassured that all was quiet.

In spite of the awkward bundle and her added weight, Ladislaus flitted easily through the shadowed corridor and then hastily descended the stairs. He left the house by way of the garden door and raced around to the front. Awaiting him in the street beyond the ornate gate were a handful of mounted men, at the fore of which sat Petrov astride a tall, muscular steed.

Synnovea raised her head, frantically searching the garden for her guards, and mentally groaned when she saw them struggling against the sturdy cords that bound them to the base of a tree. Their protesting grunts were muted by constricting gags, and though they writhed furiously against their bonds, they were no more able to free themselves than they were to prevent Ladislaus from whisking her through the gate to the street beyond.

" 'Twill be light soon," the renegade prince observed as he lifted his captive into the waiting arms of Petrov, who laid her across the saddle in front of him. "Prince Aleksei will be expecting us any moment now. Once he realizes I've played him false, he'll alert soldiers in an attempt to halt our flight. We'll have to make haste to leave the city ere the sun comes up."

Synnovea silently cursed Aleksei for the snake he was. Now, thanks to him, she had to contend with another who was just as dangerous.

A deep chortle shook Petrov's massive shoulders. "Prince

warn you to bring her straight to him with no tricks, but what you do, my friend, you tweak his nose. You take his gold an' girl, too. Prince not be satisfied till your head be lifted on a pike."

A wide grin attested to Ladislaus's jovial indifference. "That cowardly toad never paid us for accomplishing his last orders, and though he promised to yield us twice that amount when we brought him the girl, he shouldn't have expected us to believe him. 'Twas his folly to seek us out a second time."

"The Englishman be very angry, too, I think, when he learn you take his wife. Never mind what he say before his whipping. Our spies say colonel now dotes upon the girl. He sure to come after you, an' we know he more dangerous than any ten men the prince can send. Maybe colonel catch you this time—maybe even kill you. You bed the wench, you can expect him to do just that."

Synnovea nodded vigorously, having listened in rapt attention to their exchange. When the two men paid her no heed, she squirmed, trying again, but Petrov only shifted her to free the hand that held the reins.

Ladislaus chortled in amusement at his friend's warnings. "Colonel Rycroft will have to find us first, my friend, and that leaves him at a great disadvantage." Catching the dark mane of the stallion that Tyrone had once owned, he leapt astride the animal and, leaning down, patted the steed's neck as he grinned up at the giant. "You'll see, Petrov. I will ride his wench just as I ride his stallion now. He cannot stop me."

Tyrone swung around in surprise as Grigori tossed back the flap of his tent and swept through the opening.

"Colonel!"

"What is it?" The question was filled with dread, for Tyrone knew his second-in-command well enough to grasp the fact that whatever was troubling the younger man was of a serious nature. If his tone wasn't a clear indication of the depth of his alarm, then his worried frown was.

"Ladislaus is coming!"

Tyrone almost relaxed, thinking he had become too easily unnerved with all the waiting. "At last! I had nigh given up hope."

"Colonel! There's more!"

Tyrone halted, again feeling a coldness creeping through his vitals. "More? What do you mean, more? Does he bring the whole Cossack clan back with him?" The sharp scowl that gathered the younger man's brows did not ease, spurring Tyrone's impatience to know the worst of it. "Dammit, Grigori, spit it out! What frets you, man?"

"It's your wife . . . the Lady Synnovea . . ."

In one long stride Tyrone was across the tent, clasping the front of Grigori's cloak as his apprehension deepened to a cold, hellish fear. "What about Synnovea?"

"Ladislaus has taken her captive, Colonel! She's with him now, even as they ride toward the camp!"

"Are you certain?" In agonizing anguish, Tyrone slowly thumped his limp fists against the other's chest as he demanded affirmation. "Are you positive about what you saw?"

"Aye, Colonel. Avar and I both saw her. She's riding behind Petrov, and it appears that there's a long tether binding her to the brigand."

"*Damn!*" The word exploded from Tyrone's lips as he all but hurled himself from the tent. Heedless of the cold, brisk wind that quickly penetrated his woolen tunic, he stalked over to Avar, who stood waiting. "You saw her, too?"

The scout met the probing gaze of the blue eyes unwaveringly. "Aye, Colonel. There iz no question. It iz yur wife. Ve vere vaiting in the coverin' of trees vhen Ladislaus rode past. Ve vere both near enough to see her face clearly. There vas no mistake."

"How can this be?" Tyrone clamped a hand to his brow

as the horror of their announcement crushed down upon him with merciless gravity. Frantically he searched his mind for some strategy that would secure Synnovea's immediate release, but he knew that none would be totally free of danger. Whirling, he faced his second-in-command as that one joined them. "I've got to free her, Grigori! I've got to go down there and meet Ladislaus face-to-face!"

"Colonel, I need not tell you how dangerous a deed it would be for you to do that," Grigori cautioned, understanding the depth of his friend's distress. "He'll likely kill you without pausing to ask questions. And if you try to take a force of men with you to guarantee his good comportment, he'll likely escape and take your wife with them."

"I know all of that, but that doesn't change anything. If it's Synnovea . . ." Tyrone was set to argue with all of his heart.

"Then you must be exceedingly cautious about what you do. If they slip out of our trap with so precious a prize in their grasp, we may never get her back. You must think this through carefully. We've no other choice but to bide our time until we close the trap around them. Only when the passes are closed will we prevent their escape."

"I've got to go down there alone before the trap is sprung and get Synnovea out of there!" Tyrone barked impatiently. "If I don't, they'll try to use her as a hostage against us."

"If your mind is set, Colonel, please consider the possibility that you'll be giving them a second hostage," Grigori advised, "one they'll likely kill! Ladislaus may have you cut down just out of spite."

Tyrone raked his fingers through his wind-tossed hair as he fretted over the dilemma that now faced him and debated his choices, but only briefly. Arriving at a decision, he spoke brusquely. "Even thieves should know what a white flag is for. I'm going down to talk with Ladislaus, and I intend to make him understand how perilous his position is. If he kills Synnovea or me, then he'll have to answer to the cannons. I must convince him that there'll be no escape for any of them once the passes into his camp are closed. When he's faced with that threat, I rather doubt that even Ladislaus will prove unreasonable."

Moving away from the two officers, Avar crept into the trees buttressing the edge of the gorge and, from there, observed the arrival of Ladislaus and his men as they came through the pass. He silently beckoned the officers near, and when the two joined him there, they watched for several moments while Ladislaus and most of his men dismounted. Then they saw the lordling thief approach Petrov's mount and whisk the feminine form to the ground.

"Colonel, I agree vith yu. Yu shouldn't give Ladislaus time to relax an' settle his mind on yur wife. My sister iz down there somevhere. I haven't seen her since she vas taken a year ago, but I've no doubt she has been sullied by the man. Like yur vife, she iz too pretty for Ladislaus to ignore. My earnest quest iz to find my sister an' take her back home vith me."

Tyrone laid a hand upon the scout's shoulder and then returned to his tent, giving orders as he went for his mount to be saddled and a white cloth to be tied to a standard. Then he donned a weightier leather doublet to better guard against the thieves' weapons. Hopefully it would also lend him some bit of protection from the cold that had settled its frigid breath upon their camp.

Grigori came to inform his commander that everything was in readiness, but the Russian brooded over the perils his friend would be facing without a weapon to defend himself. "You know my concerns, Colonel. I pray that you also give heed to your own welfare in this matter."

Tyrone made every effort to reassure him. "By God's mercy, Grigori, I'll come out of this alive with my wife at my side. I tell you now that I have every reason to live, but she's down there in my enemy's hands. Without her, I think my very breath would cease of its own accord."

Releasing a pensive sigh, Grigori squared his shoulders and met his commander's searching gaze with a rueful smile. "My mother always claimed that I worried too much, Colonel. Perhaps she was right."

Tyrone managed an indistinct smile. "Every man has a tendency to do that at times, my friend. Right now, I'm concerned because my wife is down there at the mercy of my enemy. You know what the plans have been and understand what needs to be done in my absence. When I give the signal to fire the cannons, close their back door promptly. As for the rest, I'll leave that to your own discretion as you observe the sequence of events, since you'll be in command while I'm gone. Above all, we must convince that braggart thief we are deadly serious."

"Don't worry, Colonel. I'll make Ladislaus consider his vulnerability as he has never done before."

"Good! That may be the only way he'll prove tractable. If I find no other means of escape, I'll climb up here by way of a rope with Synnovea on my back. Keep your eyes sharp and be ready to drop one down should I come running."

"Believe me, Colonel, we'll be watching your every movement," Grigori assured him.

Leaving his tent, Tyrone swung astride his horse, gathered the reins, and accepted the flag of truce. After returning a crisp salute to Grigori, he reined the stallion toward the trail that offered him the fastest descent.

In nothing less than pure exhaustion, Synnovea leaned against Petrov's horse as Ladislaus cut the leather cord that had bound her to the brawny giant throughout the major portion of their journey from Moscow. His men were already dispersing to other areas of their small village, gladly leaving the two men to handle their captive.

Ladislaus was feeling in fine spirits after the successful abduction and bestowed a wide grin upon Petrov. "You see, my friend, it's just as I told you it would be. The wench has become quite tame in recent days. Mayhap she's looking forward to sharing my bed."

Petrov grunted in unfaltering skepticism. "Wait till she get her wind back, then you see. Maybe she even come after Ladislaus again to kill him."

"You just don't understand my way with women," Ladislaus argued in good humor. "I'll let this one have a bath and some sleep. She'll be a different woman once she has rested. I tell you, Petrov, she'll be grateful enough to love me when she wakes!"

"Hmph!"

Turning to face the source of the contemptuous snort, Ladislaus bent his attention upon the girl, who glared up at him with eyes smoldering with unrestrained fury. Within the drooping cowl of her cloak he could find little evidence of that richly attired countess he had once seen courageously alight from her coach. He beheld instead the face of a small, grubby sprite who had taken enormous delight in antagonizing each and every one of them. At the very least, a score of his cohorts had felt the sharp sting of her wit as well as the pangs of her kicks, scratches, blows, or bites whenever they had made the mistake of venturing too close. Only Petrov had been exempt from her abuse, no doubt because he had become her protector of sorts, for it was that good fellow who had stepped repeatedly between her and those who had sought instant retribution for the injuries she had liberally dispensed. Though her smugly challenging smile had further provoked those whom she had assailed, none had dared test her benefactor's brawn in their quest for appeasement.

Making no effort to brush back the snarled tresses that formed a tangled, weblike veil across her face, the recalcitrant countess peered up at him jeeringly. Her lean jaw was smudged with a streak of black, and a heavy grime now covered her entire face, a result of their rapid flight across a dusty field. For all of her smirking derision, she seemed much too exhausted to lift herself from her slouched stance, which in the main was supported by the horse's rump.

"You see!" Petrov jerked his thumb toward her. "She kill you quick if you crazy enough to trust her! Just like the other night, when she escape and take my knife."

Ladislaus rubbed the healing wound across his palm as he recalled his foolish endeavor to take advantage of the girl's attempted flight. From beneath drooping eyelids, he had watched her lean stealthily across the loudly snoring Petrov and slip the man's knife from its sheath. Covertly she had slashed the cords that had fastened her to the sleeping giant and then had rolled away from his side.

Though Ladislaus had fancied the idea of creeping into the shadows after her and taking his pleasure while the rest of his men slumbered on, he hadn't been prepared for her vicious assault when he neared the place where she had been hiding. He had barely jumped back in time to avoid the death-threatening slash of her knife. Thinking he could easily disarm her, he had grabbed for the weapon, but, in the next instant, had felt the tip of the blade open a gash across his palm. If not for the fact that several of his men had been awakened by his deafening curse, the little chit might have escaped. As it was, she had been dragged back kicking and screaming while she laid every insult she could think of upon their scruffy hides.

Ladislaus faced his cabin and bellowed at the top of his lungs. "Alyona!"

In the next instant the front door was thrown open with sudden force. It rebounded with a loud crack, and in the deafening silence that ensued, a young, dark-haired woman, ponderously close to delivering a child, emerged from the doorway with dark eyes fairly snapping with ire. Halting at the edge of the porch, she glowered at the dumbstruck Ladislaus for a long moment before her gaze flicked mutinously toward Synnovea, bringing that one to alert attention. Then her gaze returned to the lordling thief, where it settled in cold contempt. "So, Ladislaus! At last yu've brought a woman home to share yur bed, as if I haven't served yur lustin' needs all these many months. Vhat do yu intend for me? Vill yu throw me aside now that I'm fat-bellied with yur bastard vhelp?"

Ladislaus tried to shush her angry questions with a quieting gesture of his hands. "Now, Alyona, you know I've never made any promises that you'd always be the only one. A man like me enjoys a little variety now and then."

"A man like yu, ha!" Alyona tossed her head in disgust. "Yu mewl so sweetly in our bed an' tell me that yu love me vhen yu want my favors. Then, vhen I'm so swollen with child that I can hardly move, yu bring this . . . this . . ."

"Lady Synnovea Rycroft." Synnovea quickly supplied the information, gleaning some reason to hope that she could escape ravishment through the presence of this small, tenacious woman. "Wife of Colonel Sir Tyrone Rycroft, English Commander of His Majesty's Imperial Hussars." Turning sharply to bestow a blazing glower upon her abductor, she ended in a rush of words that completely exhausted her breath. "Who-will-surely-kill-this-bumbling-oaf-if-he-so-much-as-lays-a-wayward-hand-upon-me!"

Sensing an immediate accord with Her Ladyship, Alyona offered Synnovea a smile and swept a hand invitingly toward the front door. At least Ladislaus hadn't yet bedded the woman. Perhaps she had time to persuade him from the idea of serving his selfish lusts and wounding her in the process. "Come inside, my lady. No doubt ye're veary from yur ordeal an' vould like a bath. . . ."

Ladislaus grinned broadly, perceiving Alyona's congeniality as a willingness to yield to his authority. He was now of a mind to think that he'd be able to manage very nicely with two women living in the same house. Having every intention of partaking of the hospitality that Alyona had extended to the countess, he mounted the steps behind his latest captive. Immediately upon gaining the porch, he was abruptly halted by a small hand that had been flung up in unfaltering defiance.

"*Nyet!* Yu go to stable to vash and bed down! This house vill be ours alone!"

"Come, now, Alyona," Ladislaus cajoled and then bristled in discomfiture as Petrov made no effort to curb the chuckles erupting from him. "You can't do this to me! Not even my own men would dare such a thing!"

"Yu stay away!" Alyona railed, stamping a dainty foot in outrage. "I forbid yu to come inside!"

Ignoring the command, Ladislaus spread his arms wide to encompass his mistress in a great bear hug, hoping to placate her, but Alyona snatched away in angry resentment and glared up at him.

"Yu leave here this instant, Ladislaus, or I vill! I von't stay in yur camp an' give birth to yur child vhile yu make another bastard vith the colonel's wife. Do yu hear?"

"Damnation, woman! I can't let you order me about as if I were some young whelp! What will my men think?"

Alyona rose on tiptoes to sneer in his face. "An' vhat vill *yu* think, Ladislaus, if I leave now? Do yu vant me to go? Does beddin' down vith the colonel's vife mean so much to yu that yu do not care if I go or stay?"

"Alyona, you know I'm very fond of you. . . ."

In unabated pertinacity, Alyona stood erect with small fists clenched tightly at her sides. Despite the initial terror she had suffered when Ladislaus had first snatched her from her parents' home more than a year ago, she had come to love him dearly, but she wanted more from him than just a casual dalliance. His child would soon be born, and she wanted him to treat her with the same regard a man would extend to a cherished wife. "Ladislaus, yu make choice now! The colonel's vife or me!"

The lord-of-thieves raised his hands lamely in mute appeal. As much as he wanted to pleasure himself with the beautiful countess, down deep inside he knew he couldn't abide the idea of Alyona leaving him. From the first, she had been like a fresh, sweet breath of wind coming into his stale life. While holding herself from him in staid reserve, she had played the offended maiden to the hilt until gradually it was his heart that had melted. To his amazement he had found himself caring for her in a gentler way, courting her with wildflowers, long walks in the woods, and sonnets of love from a book he had once found in a trunk purloined from a wealthy rake. He had even taught her to read, and she had in turn placated him by sweetly reciting the verses. How could he bear to let her go when he had no doubt that she'd be leaving him bereft of every treasure he held dear?

A gunshot snatched Ladislaus's mind abruptly from the matter of choices to the immediate needs of the moment. Of primary concern was the safety of his camp and everyone within it. He whirled away from the two women as Petrov spun his horse around to face the barricaded entrance to the pass. Above it, a guard was now shouting and waving his arms in an attempt to gain their attention. Petrov raised a hand and held it to an ear to listen, then promptly conveyed the information to Ladislaus.

"One man ride toward camp with white flag. The guard want to know, should he let the stranger in?"

Ladislaus leapt off the porch and, settling his powerful arms akimbo, frowned toward the pass for a long moment before squinting up at Petrov. "Can they tell who the man is?"

The single braid of flaxen hair fell over a massive shoulder as Petrov leaned his head far back and cupped a hand to his mouth to project his shout. "Who comes? Do you know?"

Again Petrov returned a broad hand to an ear to catch

the other's answer. Then he gaped down at his lordling chief, completely astounded by what he had just heard. "They say English colonel come here! He ride your horse!"

"What?" Synnovea gasped, flinging herself to the porch railing. Trembling now, she shaded her eyes from the glare of the sun reflecting off a patch of snow as she stared toward the entrance. As yet, she could see nothing of her husband, but that didn't ease the sudden quaking of her heart.

Ladislaus was of a different bent entirely. Hooting in glee at the idea that his adversary would be coming into their camp, he roared his answer. "Let the rascal enter, if indeed he comes alone!"

Petrified by a sudden concern for her husband, Synnovea waited an eternity before she saw a lone rider emerging from the narrow pass. At the newcomer's inquiring glance toward the one who stood on the knoll above him, the guard pointed in the direction of the house, prompting the newcomer to urge the stallion forward. Synnovea had no need to see his face or the tawny hair now covered by a helm to know that it was indeed her own dear husband who approached, for none rode with the confident grace he exhibited. The stallion carried him forward at a leisurely canter until he reined the steed to a halt before the lord-of-thieves.

Synnovea would have scrambled down the steps and raced toward Tyrone, but Ladislaus flung up a hand to halt her in mid-stride and promptly barked an order for her to hold fast lest she cause some harm to come to her husband. She acquiesced forthwith, but in the silence that ensued, her eyes melded with the blue ones that anxiously searched her face. At the unspoken question burning within those translucent orbs, she managed a reassuring smile to convey the fact that, as yet, she had not been harmed.

Thoughtfully Ladislaus considered the pair who exchanged unspoken assurances of adoration with nothing more than their eyes. Then he turned his perusal solely upon his rival, espying no scabbard or pistol, only an empty sheath where a knife should have been. "Are you a witless fool, Colonel, to enter my camp with naught to protect you but a white flag and your own arrogance? Do you not ken that my men can drag you from my horse and strip the flesh from your bones, just as they did when we last met? Have you no scars to remind you of that event?"

"I've come for my wife," Tyrone stated unflinchingly, leveling his gaze upon the renegade. "I won't leave without her."

Ladislaus laughed with boisterous mirth and spread his arms wide in exaggerated amazement as he mockingly reminded his foe, "But you said that I could have her, my friend. Don't you remember? Now pray tell us, Colonel, have you changed your mind?"

"If it's a fight you want, Ladislaus, I'll give it to you," Tyrone avouched in a low, rumbling tone. "But I'm not leaving here without my wife."

"What? And cheat my compatriots of the sport of tying you between two horses and wagering which steed will get the better of you in the end? Come, now, Colonel, I'm not as selfish as all that."

Tyrone lifted a hand and, glancing briefly toward Synnovea, beckoned her to draw near. She obeyed instantly, evoking a growl from Ladislaus, who leapt forward to catch her, but the thief was brought up short by the bulk of the black stallion as Tyrone nudged the animal into his path. Grinding his teeth in rage, Ladislaus sprang upward to seize his adversary from the saddle, but with a flick of his wrist, Tyrone reined the animal sharply about again, deftly jarring the brigand's senses when that one met the whirling steed head to head, the hard way. An audible thunk was followed by an even louder yowl of pain before Ladislaus stumbled back in a dazed stupor, clasping a hand to his face. A quick swipe of a finger beneath his nose assured him that he was bleeding profusely from his left nostril.

Petrov coughed abruptly to curb another threatening burst of laughter. Then, with hard-won composure, he straightened his demeanor and, assuming his best doleful expression, swung down from his steed. Solicitously he helped Ladislaus to the steps of the porch, where he urged their leader to sit still until he recovered his wits. Alyona flew inside and, reappearing a brief moment later with a wet cloth, gently dabbed at the blood oozing from Ladislaus's nose.

While the rogues' attention was diverted, Tyrone reached down and, grasping Synnovea's arm, swung her up behind him. Petrov's flintlock made a swift and ominous appearance. Its cyclopean bore was leveled convincingly toward the middle of the leather doublet as the huge man rumbled out a warning. "Keep still, Colonel, or you will die now!"

Though Synnovea clasped her arms tightly around her husband's waist and pressed close against his back in anxious fear, Tyrone countered the giant's threat almost casually. "If you kill me, Petrov, these hills will crumble down upon your shining pate. I swear they will."

Petrov hooted loudly in amusement before he jeered at the colonel. "Are you God to call down mountain upon us, Englishman?"

"Heed my warning carefully with an attentive ear, Petrov," Tyrone urged. "If you need proof of my power, I shall give you a small sampling, but I must first kindly insist that you divert your aim for the moment to negate the possibility of your weapon discharging accidentally once you realize I have such power."

Petrov's eyes flicked quickly toward the rugged, tree-lined hilltops as he wondered what to make of the man's proposal. He was curious enough to want to see what would follow. Although he turned the bore away from their foe, he held the pistol positioned where he could swing it around upon the man in the flick of an eye. As he cocked a brow and closely observed the colonel, that one raised the white flag and then brought it down sharply in a fluttering descent.

Instantly a thundering explosion rent the silence, followed in quick, ear-numbing succession by several more blasts, each of which caused both Petrov and Ladislaus to start in sudden shock. They gaped in utter amazement as the cannonballs repeatedly pummeled the hills around the second entrance, loosening large boulders and rocks that subsequently began to tumble into the canyon. The falling debris gave momentum to the guards who had been on duty there. Spurred on by churning fear, they raced away as if the demons of hell were nipping at their heels, all the while casting anxious glances over their shoulders as they sought to outrun the falling fragments.

Hardly anyone noticed Tyrone whirling the steed about and racing off toward the far side of the canyon until Ladislaus scrambled to his feet and thrust a massive arm out to point toward the departing colonel, bringing Petrov's attention to bear upon the two who were obviously attempting to escape in spite of the questionable direction in which they were riding.

"Shoot the horse, dammit! Shoot the horse! If our captives escape, we'll likely lose our heads!" Ladislaus barked, nearly jumping up and down with impatience as Petrov leveled his flintlock and held it steady on his target. Slowly the giant squeezed the trigger, hating to see such a fine animal put down, but cherishing his own head a lot more. The discharge was followed by a mere pause of a heartbeat. Then the horse collapsed in a cartwheeling roll that sent its riders flying helter-skelter.

Tyrone swore as he rolled and tumbled to a halt in a large patch of snow. Gnashing his teeth in fierce determination, he leapt to his feet and raced back to where his wife lay motionless upon the ground. She stared at the sky above her as if utterly frozen, but he had no time to shake her from her stupor. Swooping up her limp form within his arms, he started running desperately toward the hill, from the top of which his men waved frantically and shouted encouragements as they tossed down ropes.

Thundering hoofbeats of at least a dozen horses quickly overtook Tyrone, forestalling his flight to safety as the high-waymen passed him and then drew their steeds to a skidding halt in front of him. Briefly facing the leering men as they brandished their swords in the air, he retreated cautiously, sweeping his eyes about in search of another path to safety. In turn, the men nudged their mounts toward him, grinning like fools lusting for revenge. Tyrone gnashed his teeth in unrelenting fortitude and chose to test them, first dashing to the left and then skidding to a halt on the right, running backward, then forward, all the while dodging, twisting, circling around. Everywhere he turned, the rogues closed ranks, forbidding his penetration of the living wall they had erected. Finally he was brought up short as they tightened the snare around him until it was made secure. He had no choice but to accept his entrapment and perhaps his imminent death, for they allowed him no place to run.

Slowly Tyrone collapsed to his knees and, gasping air into his lungs, bent over his wife, intending to bestow a kiss of farewell upon her parted lips. Then he realized her eyes were closed with a stillness that made his heart lurch in fear. While he rasped in air, he could detect no slightest sign of life, not even a flutter of breath from her lips. He felt an impending shout of remorse building within him, and he let her sag in his arms as he tilted his head far back upon his shoulders and shrieked at the top of his lungs toward the hill.

"Grigori! Avenge us!"

21

The hill above Tyrone seemed to explode as another volley was launched from the cannons, this time in an entirely different direction. The men who had prodded their steeds close around him now scattered like a flock of frightened, squawking geese as the leaden balls began to pelt the opposite end of the valley. Only one of their number kept his wits and demanded aid from another two who were ready to fly with the rest. Commanding their unswerving attention, the brigand held them fast at sword point.

"Ladislaus wants these here two back!" the thief shouted as the cannons ceased firing. "Now get down here, yu yellow-livered rats, an' bind them to yur horses—or, by heavens, I'll run yu both through from gullet to groin!"

The threat failed to hold the two, for in the next instant they glanced around toward the crest of the hill and saw countless soldiers swarming over it and swinging outward on ropes as they thrust themselves away from the precipice and began to descend the hillside with great, bounding leaps. Faced by this new threat, the three thieves were swiftly unified in the strengthening premise that retreat was far better than certain death. Lifting their heels high, they brought them down hard into the flanks of their mounts, catapulting the animals forward in an all-out, breakneck race toward the entrance of the canyon, where an open space still remained in the pass. As they neared the opening, the three hauled their nags to a jolting halt and, almost as abruptly, whirled them in an about-face to send them flying in the opposite direction as Grigori raced into their lair with a company of mounted Hussars riding closely behind him with gleaming swords waving high.

Tyrone gathered his wife's limp form up close within his arms and held her for a long, despairing moment, feeling such terrible remorse that he wanted to die. A building sob was wrenched from him as he buried his face against the side of her throat and began to weep. Then, like the delicate flick of a butterfly's wings, he felt it . . . the unmistakable beat of a pulse. He jerked upright and stared in jubilation as the long, dark lashes fluttered against her grimy cheeks.

Slowly Synnovea roused to awareness with a muffled groan and then stared up at him, seeming momentarily confused. When she made a valiant attempt to smile, Tyrone choked on a grateful sob.

"Synnovea, my dearest heart! I thought you were dead!"

"Wasn't I?" She grimaced as she struggled bravely to move her aching body. Then she quipped dryly, "If this is what happens when you take a lady out for a ride, Sir Knight, may I never be foolish enough to accept your invitation again."

"Are you all right?" Tyrone questioned with anxious concern.

"Nooo!" she moaned. "At least I don't feel all right! The way I hurt, I'm wont to think that I've died and gone to hell, cruel place though it be, for this is definitely not heaven! Indeed, sir! I've never suffered so much abuse in all my life! I fear every bone in my body has been broken—or, at the very least, bruised!"

"This is no hellish prank, madam!" Tyrone assured her with an amused grin. "You're alive! And I most fervently thank heaven because you are!"

"Can we go home now?" Synnovea queried hopefully. "I'd very much like to crawl into our bed and rest my wearied frame for a week or two in your arms."

"I'll take you there, my love, just as soon as my men finish rounding up the thieves." Tyrone glanced around him and was assured that the tide of conflict had been quickly turned to their benefit. Many of the rogues had been caught by surprise and were unarmed, while others, perceiving their impending capture, had given up without a fight. It would all be over in a matter of moments.

Lifting his wife with him, Tyrone rose to his feet again and smiled down into the green-brown eyes as his own glistened with warm tears. "My dearest Synnovea, you are the most delightful joy of my life," he softly avowed. "And I love you more than simple words can attest."

"I love you, Sir Knight, more than I ever thought possible!" Synnovea replied, her voice choked with emotion. Wrapping her arms tightly around his neck, she pressed her brow against his cheek as she murmured in gentle reflection, "I think, Colonel Sir Tyrone Rycroft, that I have loved you since that first moment I saw you, when you came charging through the thieves in your quest to save me. To me, my lord husband, you looked as resplendent as a gallant knight in shining armor."

Content to be safe within his arms, Synnovea snuggled her head upon his shoulder as he carried her back to Ladislaus's house, around which the soldiers were now herding the thieves. Ladislaus and Petrov were sitting on the steps, under the watchful eye of a single lieutenant who had bound his prisoners to a post with a heavy length of chain. Alyona was kneeling beside Ladislaus, dabbing at the trickle of blood still in evidence beneath his nose. His eyes were only for her, as if in the last few moments he had realized that there wasn't much time left for them.

Suddenly Alyona gasped and rose to her feet as she stared toward the narrow entrance where a single mounted rider was leisurely reining his steed through the rock and rubble that had fallen there. As he came near and dismounted in front of the house, Alyona hastened down the steps and threw her arms wide with a cry of gladness before hurling herself into the welcoming embrace of her brother.

"Avar! Avar! Oh, how I've missed yu, dear brother!"

The scout drew back with a querying perusal and laid a gentle hand upon her belly as he softly questioned, "Do yu vant me to avenge yu, Alyona?"

"*Nyet! Nyet!*" She shook her head passionately in a fierce denial and hurried to state her mind. "Avar, if I could, I vould have Ladislaus as my husband, but they say he must go to Moscow now, maybe to be hanged."

"From all accounts ve've been hearing, it iz the justice Ladislaus rightly deserves, Alyona. I cannot stop it."

"Maybe there iz no help for him, Avar, but I still yearn to take him as husband an' give our child a name."

Avar pressed his lips briefly to her brow. "I'm sorry, Alyona."

With an imperceptible nod, the young woman stepped away and, mounting the stairs again, went inside the house. The door closed slowly behind her, and in the silence that followed, they could hear her mournful weeping.

Avar approached his commander, who was applying a cold compress to Synnovea's bruised brow. "Colonel, I've just now seen a curious thing, an' I'd like permission to ride out vith a pair of men to see vhat might be happenin'."

Tyrone peered at him askance as he continued his tender ministering. "What do you think it is?"

Avar glanced around and took a casual count of their soldiers. Then he stroked his chin thoughtfully as he lifted his gaze to meet the curious blue eyes. "I think, Colonel, it may be a full regiment of soldiers passin' near here. Though each vears the garb of a peasant, they ride in line like an organized troop. Only the leader is vearing a cloak that looks familiar. Another is garbed richly in the clothes of a boyar." Avar lifted his shoulders in a shrug. "If I vere to venture a guess, Colonel, I'd say they're Polish soldiers on the move."

"This far inland?" Tyrone stepped back from his wife and stared at the scout in amazement. "Where do you think they're headed?"

"They now ride fast after hearin' cannon, Colonel. Toward Moscow, maybe, or in that same general direction."

"We must stop them!"

"We should, Colonel, but how? They outnumber us two, maybe three to one. Besides that, they have two batteries o' cannons."

Tyrone beckoned a young corporal forward and pointed toward the horse that Ladislaus had ridden in on, the same which the thief had once stolen from him. "Strip that stallion, Corporal, and put my saddle on his back. And be quick about it! I've got to ride out with Avar and have a look around."

Stepping back to Synnovea, he lifted her carefully and carried her into the house, drawing a teary-eyed gaze from Alyona, who had curled up on a corner of the bed to cry. In some embarrassment, the small woman rose to her feet and, sweeping her hand toward the place she had just vacated, encouraged him to lay Synnovea there.

"I vill take care of yur wife, Colonel. No need to fear."

Tyrone lowered Synnovea upon the mound of wolf pelts covering the bed and leaned down to brush a snarled tress from her brow. "I have to ride out with Avar, my sweet. I may be gone for a while. If you're able to rest, do so. I'll return as soon as I can."

Synnovea and Alyona watched in silence as he crossed to the door. At the portal, he cast a backward glance at his wife before making his departure. In a few moments the women heard the rattle of hooves as the two men rode out together.

"I'm too filthy to rest," Synnovea complained, wincing as she braced herself up on an elbow. "I'd like to wash, if I may."

Alyona indicated a large kettle of simmering water hanging from a hook in the hearth. "I was goin' to vash clothes today, but if yu'd like, I'll fill a tub for a bath. Maybe yu'll feel better after a good, varm soak."

"I don't think I've ever heard a sweeter proposal in all my life." Synnovea slowly pushed herself to her feet, grimacing sharply as she did so. All she could remember from the fall was hitting the ground and feeling as if every bone in her body had been broken or at least jolted unmercifully by the impact. Beyond that moment, it seemed as if she had stared at the world through a stunned stupor, her breath frozen in her lungs. Moments after Tyrone had lifted her, she had lost consciousness and known nothing more until she had heard his muffled weeping.

With considerable care, Synnovea stood upright and was of a mind to think that she had accomplished a great feat. Before long she was soaking in a warm bath that the two of them had prepared. Some of the tightness began to leave her muscles, and she became a little more hopeful that she'd survive. She washed her hair, found appropriate clothing to wear from the large satchel which Ladislaus had hurriedly packed for her, and was in the process of helping Alyona empty the tub when the woman gasped suddenly and clutched a hand to her belly.

"It's time," Alyona announced in a tight voice when the pain began to subside. "The baby is comin'." She looked up at her guest and saw the sharp concern in her widened eyes. "Do yu know vhat to do, my lady?"

Synnovea nearly panicked. "Not even a notion!"

"There iz an old woman who lives in a small house down by the creek. She knows vhat to do. If yu vould go and fetch her, I vill lay out vhat she vill need."

"Of course!" Despite the pain that her movements caused, Synnovea was already flying toward the door.

It was nearly an hour later when Tyrone returned with Avar and found Ladislaus pacing restlessly about within the small area allowable by his heavy shackles. Tyrone hardly had time to consider the reason for the man's plight, but when he strode toward the door, the lieutenant informed him of the camp's current events.

"I'm sorry, Colonel. Ladislaus's woman is inside having her baby. Your wife told us all to stay outside. I would presume, sir, that her order also includes you." The young man's forehead crinkled in sudden concern. "Of course, sir, if it's a matter of choices, I must respect any command you give me."

"Rest easy, Lieutenant. I'll not countermand my wife's authority in this instance."

A sigh of relief slipped from the officer's smiling lips. "I'm glad to hear that, sir, because I would hate to disappoint Her Ladyship, since I assured her that I'd keep everyone who wasn't needed out of the house."

"Carry on, Lieutenant."

"Yes, sir."

Glancing back at Ladislaus, Tyrone soon became convinced that the brigand was genuinely distraught over what was presently occurring in his house. To see the unruly rogue deeply concerned about the girl caused him to wonder if he was now viewing a side of the man's character that had never been glimpsed before by anyone.

"Watch him carefully," Tyrone bade the lieutenant, taking

no chances. "Ladislaus has the strength to break any post you chain him to, so be warned."

"You can count on me, sir!"

Grigori came across the yard and braced a foot on the bottom step as his commander turned to face him. "What did you and Avar find?"

"At least a full regiment of spies or Polish-trained mercenaries," Tyrone answered bluntly, descending a pair of steps to speak with him. "There's a strong possibility that they're Polish soldiers masquerading as peasants."

"What are we to do when we have less than a third that number of men here?" Grigori asked in sudden worry.

"We cannot hope to reach Moscow and regroup with the rest of the regiment in time to return and attack them in the field. Besides, before our departure, the good general was demanding that he be given command of my other men during my absence. We both know he has some wild notions, so he has probably dispatched them on some urgent mission of his. I regret now that I didn't have the foresight to bring the whole regiment when we came."

"Your plan was to avoid discovery before we took up our position on the hill, colonel," Grigori reasoned. "We did just that, and your goal to capture Ladislaus and his bandits has been concluded successfully. Not one of us expected this foreign intrusion into our land. Still, I find it hard to imagine that these mercenaries intend to attack Moscow with less than a full army."

"I'm sure you're cognizant of the last two attempts of the Poles to put their own men on the throne. Perhaps the mercenaries are hoping to catch Moscow by surprise again and kill the tsar, which they may well do if General Vanderhout has been foolish enough to strip away a portion of the city's strength and defense."

Ladislaus had paused in his restless pacing when he overheard the men talking, and now hunkered down on his haunches near the edge of the porch as he continued to listen. Peering at them thoughtfully, he finally gained their attention and gave the colonel a grin that was no less than cocky. "You need more men, eh, Englishman?"

Arching a brow, Tyrone fixed the man with an impassive stare. "If you intend to gloat, Ladislaus, be warned. I'm in no mood to accept it graciously."

"I wouldn't dare gloat, Colonel, not when I'll likely be executed soon after I'm taken to Moscow." Ladislaus shrugged his broad shoulders. "With a babe of mine ready to be born, I can't help but wish things had been different, that I might've done something better with my life."

"It's a bit late for remorse now, don't you think, Ladislaus?" Tyrone asked with rampant sarcasm. "You must be as old as I am, give or take a few years, yet I bet you've never considered doing an honest day's labor in your whole life. So you say now that you're feeling put out by it all, no doubt because you've been caught. Well, go weep on someone else's shoulder, my lawless friend. I don't have time to listen to your laments."

"I only beg a moment of your time, Colonel. That is all I ask," Ladislaus bargained. "You just might be interested in what I have to say."

"I'm running short on patience," Tyrone retorted tersely.

"What do you think those mercenaries are up to anyway?" Ladislaus pressed, deliberately ignoring the other's lack of enthusiasm.

"No good! Just like you!"

"Now, Colonel," the leader-thief smilingly cajoled. "Didn't I promise you that you'd be interested in my proposition? But if you're so damned certain that you and your men can force a whole regiment of foreigners to retreat, then perhaps I'm wasting my breath."

A weary sigh clearly expressed Tyrone's growing irritation. "What do you have to say, Ladislaus? I'm listening."

The rogue leader was most eager to voice his suggestion. "Suppose, Colonel, that my men and I joined forces with you and yours to turn back the foreigners . . ." He glanced at the Englishman and then grinned in growing enthusiasm when he realized that he had managed to gain his full attention. "If they're up to no good in Moscow, and my band and I help to send them back to wherever they came from, perhaps the tsar would consider giving me and my fellows a pardon . . . if we make solemn pledges that in the future we'll apply ourselves diligently to honest labors."

Tyrone stared at Ladislaus in disbelief, unable to consider the plausibility of such an offer. It seemed rather doubtful the man could alter his whole way of life at this late date. Indeed, trusting him could prove as disastrous as believing a leopard could amend its natural inclination for devouring its prey.

"What would you do?" Tyrone scoffed. "Milk a herd of goats? I'm sure you can understand why I have difficulty imagining you working at some menial trade. You've become too well acquainted with giving commands and having them promptly obeyed."

"The same as you, Colonel," Ladislaus countered and lifted his broad shoulders in a casual shrug. "Perhaps I could be a soldier like you. If His Majesty can hire foreigners to teach his soldiers to fight, why can't he recruit Russians who can fight already? We don't expect to be outfitted in grand uniforms like the rich boyars I've seen, but we could still fight in the tsar's service and keep the Russian borders secure from invaders."

Tyrone cocked an incredulous brow at the thief. "And once you have your freedom, you would not use it to loot and murder again?"

Ladislaus spread his hands, appealing to the Englishman's sense of justice. "I've been a warrior a good many years, Colonel. Men have attacked me, and I've defended myself as best

I can, but a murderer I'm not! I've never killed anyone who hasn't first tried to take my life."

Tyrone fixed him with a narrowed gaze. "And should I believe you've never lashed a man between two horses?"

"I did but jest, Colonel!" Ladislaus protested with a chuckle. "At times I must intimidate my foes into believing that they'll be as good as dead if they fool with me. I see no harm in that. Such vivid threats have been known to deter men from violence. Besides, you owe me a favor for saving you from that scoundrel Aleksei. 'Twas his most earnest intent to see you gelded." He tossed a grinning glance toward the interior of the house, and then stroked his chin musefully as he reasoned further with his captor. "I think, Colonel, you have much to be grateful for. Your wife seems most appreciative of the fact that you're her husband. She wouldn't let me touch her and swore with great tenacity that she'd kill herself before allowing me to take her. If you consider the whole of it, Colonel, she was probably better off with me than that rat Aleksei. The good prince hired me to kidnap her, but bade me to deliver her straight to him. Consider further, Colonel. Had I ignored his summons, he'd have found someone else, perhaps one of low esteem, to steal her away. That one probably would've served the prince's intentions far better than I."

Grigori laid a hand upon his commander's arm, drawing his attention. Together the two men walked away to where they could talk privately. Ladislaus eyed the pair closely, hoping fervently that they'd allow him the opportunity he had asked for.

"What are you thinking, Colonel?" Grigori asked. "Do you really believe Ladislaus can be trusted?"

"I may never know that, but under the circumstances, I'm willing to take the chance."

"What if he joins with the other regiment against us?"

Tyrone frowned sharply. "Then we'll likely be killed, but I'll make him rue this day for the rest of his brief life. That much I can promise."

Grigori accepted his superior's decision with a nod and then followed behind as that one strode back to the porch.

"I have no idea why I should consider giving you a chance, Ladislaus, in light of all the trouble you've personally caused me," Tyrone stated curtly. "Aleksei can certainly attest to the fact that you cannot be trusted, but his experience with you only whets my willingness to grant you a few concessions . . . *if* you prove yourself worthy of them. Let this be known beforehand. Whatever the outcome today, you'll return to Moscow with me and allow Tsar Mikhail to decide whether to grant you and your men a reprieve. If you clearly demonstrate your sincerity in helping us turn back the enemy forces, I'll personally address my plea to His Majesty for your immediate release, but be warned, I'm in no mood to be tricked. If you make me regret giving you this opportunity, you'll be the first among your followers I will shoot. Do you understand?"

"Quite clearly, Colonel."

"Now, are you absolutely sure your men will follow you in this endeavor?" Tyrone queried as a last consideration toward caution.

Ladislaus chuckled briefly in amusement. "Since they have a fervent desire to live out the hour, I'll venture to say, positively!"

Tyrone accepted the rogue's word and bade the lieutenant to free the prisoners. As Ladislaus and Petrov rose to their feet and stretched, the colonel urged them to hurry. "Get to your mounts and gather yourselves and your men together in front of the house here. We'll have to race ahead of the mercenaries in order to position our cannon and spread our forces on the hills in front of them, so we need to leave here at once."

Ladislaus hesitated as he glanced toward the door and dared to ask the Englishman for another request. "Colonel, I'd like to speak to Alyona for a moment. If I don't come back, I want her to know that I'm at least trying to make a better way for the two of us and our child."

Tyrone approached the portal and, opening it, beckoned for Synnovea and the midwife to come out on the porch for a few moments. Ladislaus dipped his head in a nod of appreciation before slipping inside. Tyrone closed the door behind him and extended a hand toward Synnovea. She smiled in response and, laying her own within his, allowed him to draw her to the far end of the porch. Unable to find the words to tell her that he'd be leaving again and might not be coming back alive, Tyrone gathered her close against him and held her with a growing sense of gloom that immediately conveyed itself to her. She had only to glance around at the soldiers readying their gear to know what was coming.

"You're riding out again?" she queried worriedly, leaning back in his arms to search his face. When she looked past his arm, she realized that weapons were being given to the highwaymen. "What terrible thing has happened to set you in league with thieves?"

"We've sighted a renegade regiment nearby. They seem to be riding hard toward Moscow, for what end I'm not as yet certain, but 'tis my earnest belief that they plan to enter by stealth into the Kremlin and either kill the tsar or take him hostage. It isn't the first time they've tried to seize control of the country by such a plan."

"But how can such a feat be accomplished?" she questioned in amazement.

"By subterfuge—and more than a goodly share of boldness. If they've positioned spies or accomplices inside the Kremlin, then they'll likely be able to enter secretly with none the wiser."

"Be careful," Synnovea pleaded desperately, letting him gather her close against him again. "You haven't yet given me a child, and if it's ever meant that we should be parted by death, I'd like some part of you to remain with me."

Tyrone plied her soft lips with a gentle kiss and then, drawing back, smiled down into eyes brimming with tears. "We've had so little time together, my love, I hope we'll be allowed several decades to spawn many admirable confirmations of our devotion."

Ladislaus strode from the house, prompting Tyrone to crush a fervent kiss upon his wife's lips before he, too, crossed the porch and descended the steps. It caused some confusion for both men when they realized they had halted beside the same horse.

"This is my stallion!" Tyrone declared emphatically, gathering the reins. "Your horse was shot, remember?"

"But we made a trade," Ladislaus tried to argue. "Mine for yours, yours for mine."

"Yours is dead!" Tyrone stepped between him and the horse and swung up into the saddle, from whence he grinned down upon the man as that one growled in protest. "From now on, Ladislaus, you're going to have to limit yourself to your own possessions. I have a serious aversion to sharing my treasures, especially with the likes of you."

Tyrone reined the high-stepping mount about, close enough to allow the animal to flick its tail across the brigand's face, evoking a loud snort of displeasure from the giant. Accepting his helmet from the grinning Grigori, who urged his own horse alongside, Tyrone settled it on his head. Then he lifted his arm and swept it forward in a command for all to follow. It was the chortling Petrov who led a rather shaggy-looking horse to Ladislaus as his leader muttered sourly after the colonel.

"You forgot, maybe, it was your horse you tell me shoot." Petrov inclined his shining head toward the animal he had brought near and grinned. "Maybe this beast not so fine as his or the one I shot, but better than walking, I think."

*   *   *

The foreign regiment rode over the hill and was halfway across the valley before a sudden warning shout rent the silence. The men gaped in sharp surprise as a solid line of mounted, uniformed Hussars, appearing as if from out of nowhere, halted their steeds on the next rise ahead of them. As they watched in paralyzed awe, cannons were hastily rolled to positions on the brow of the hill, interspersing the cavalry unit, while the officer in command slowly raised his sword.

Shouted orders sent a swelling tide of confusion rippling through the foreign ranks, turning their haste into a mad scrambling dash as they sought to bring up the artillery and spread it out in a more impressive line than the one they now faced. Clearly having the larger force, they hoped to counter the threatening attack and roll the foolish ones back upon their heels. Several musket shots rang out from their ranks, and a pair of Hussars toppled to the ground, but in the next instant the Russian cannons began to bark with deafening intensity. Recoiling in large plumes of smoke, they sent leaden balls hurtling through the air to bombard the intruders. The shots landed, eliciting startled shrieks from both man and beast as large geysers of dirt were spewed upward in front of them. When a second barrage was unleashed, it punished them severely for the dead Hussars. A wealthily garbed nobleman shouted at the commander, who, in frustrated rage, snarled out orders in rapid succession to his men. Obeying, those hearties bared their swords and spurred their steeds forward in pursuit of vengeance, just as a cannon lobbed a leaden ball down upon the princely one.

The Hussars seemed to wait on the hill with unswerving patience as their opponents charged toward them. The rival force of mercenaries quickly gained the first upward slope of the knoll, but just as they did, out of the corners of their eyes they caught movements to their left and right. In sudden alarm they glanced askance betwixt the two, and their hearts filled them with fear as they saw other men, dressed in all manner of array, swarming down upon them. The Hussars seemed to come alive as their commander swept his sword forward in a signal to charge. He led his men at a thundering pace, lifting his saber high and rending the air with a warbling wail that raised the hackles of friend and foe alike. The intruders considered their plight forthwith and came swiftly to the determination that it was foolish to stand and fight against such odds. Expeditiously they wheeled their steeds about, intending to flee, but they soon found themselves caught in a box from which they would find no successful escape, for another surge of outlandishly garbed fiends was charging up from the rear.

A pair of darkly cloaked figures crept stealthily through the trees near the Kremlin wall until they saw a wagon carrying fodder for horses moving briskly toward the tower known as the *Borovitskaia*. The two hastened to reach the path as the cart rumbled past and flitted alongside it until the farmer halted the conveyance at the gate, where he greeted the sentry with the warm cheer of a close friend and laughingly conversed with him, allowing the wraiths to slip inside unseen.

The two continued on, one leading the other as if by rote through the trees. They came to a spot near the edge of the Kremlin hill where they had been told to wait until a quarter stroke of the hour. At that appointed time another cloaked shade, this one noticeably smaller than the two, moved away from the *Blagoveshchenskii Sobor* and cautiously approached them.

"What are you two about this eventide?" a subdued voice asked from the deep cowl as the slight one neared the two.

A gruff voice issued an answer. "We've come a-gaming for that fanciful dish tsars are wont to seek."

The shorter one dipped his head in acknowledgment and made the expected reply. "And what is that but a royal seat upon the throne?" The three came together, and the smaller one promptly lowered his tone to a whisper. "Your men have been given their instructions?"

The one with the harsh voice gave the information while his companion stood stoically mute. "At the appointed hour, they will create a diversion for us and start fires throughout Moscow, to which the tsar's soldiers will be dispatched. By then Tsar Mikhail and Patriarch Filaret will have gone into the *Blagoveshchenskii Sobor* to pray. We're to join ourselves with the rest of our men and kill the castle guards who have come to stand watch. We will then slay the patriarch and the tsar in the chapel and hold the Kremlin until the rightful tsar takes the throne and kills the boyars who are wont to reject him."

"Good! I assume your men are waiting inside the Kremlin to help you in this endeavor."

"All is in readiness, my lord."

"The other matter is arranged also?"

"What matter is that?"

"Surely you've addressed yourselves to the safety of the new tsar and have found a place here in the Kremlin where he can hide until he's ready to make an appearance, have you not?" The pointed question was met with a tense silence that demonstrated the perplexity of the two. The small man became incensed. Completely infuriated at the dim-witted simplicity of the dullards, he threw back his hood in a vivid display of rage and advanced upon the pair with a snarl contorting his pockmarked face. The back of his short-fingered hand swiped forcefully across the wide chest of the taller one, who stood the closest to him. "You fools! He's the most integral part of this whole plot! Where is he?"

"Where any rightful pretender should be, Ivan Voronsky," the taller one finally answered.

Ivan's mind halted in sudden shock. Though the man had spoken Russian, the words had been accentuated with an English accent, allowing a sharply goading fear to seize the cleric's mind. He remembered precisely where and when he had last heard it, and that had been weeks ago at the military parade held in the Kremlin.

"Rycroft!"

The tall man approached him, sweeping back the hood of his own cloak. "Aye, Ivan Voronsky, 'tis Colonel Sir Rycroft, at your service." Tyrone swept a hand toward his companion as he casually introduced him. "And my good man, Captain Grigori Tverskoy, to aid you in all your endeavors. Your Polish friends were found out ere they reached Moscow, and I fear your intended tsar was blown to bits by the careless aim of our artillerymen. A tragedy, to be sure. I'm sure Tsar Mikhail would have preferred to see him beheaded alongside you."

Ivan snatched forth a dagger and raised it high, intending to sink it into the chest of that stalwart one who addressed him with scorn, but his wrist was seized in a steely grasp and wrenched around to a painful height behind his back, startling a cry from him as an agonizing jolt of pain wended its way from wrist to shoulder. Almost casually, Tyrone plucked the knife from Ivan's hand, eliciting another highly indignant screech from the grimacing lips. At the sound, there quickly arose from the area of the Palace of Facets a confused burble of voices which soon was overridden by shouted commands that compelled the guards to seek the source of the noise.

Ivan's heart began to hammer as he realized he wasn't going to escape from the trap the two had laid for him. All the money the invaders had put aside for him suddenly seemed a paltry sum in view of the price that would be exacted from him for treason against the tsar.

"I've got gold! I'll give you all of it if you'll just let me go!" Ivan pleaded frantically over his shoulder. He had to be gone before the palace guards reached them or it would be too late to make good his escape! "It's more than both of you will ever make in your lifetime! Please! You must let me go!"

"What portion does Princess Anna receive from what you promise to us? She is your accomplice, is she not?" Tyrone queried as he leaned over the cleric's shoulder.

"Princess Anna? Why, she was merely a pawn I used in my attempt to enlist the aid of wealthy boyars to the cause."

Grigori clasped his fingers in the cleric's lank hair and lifted that one's head to peer leeringly into his sharply honed features. "Have Russian boyars also promised you gold to make it worth your while?"

"No! No! But I tell you there is enough already to fill your coffers to the brim! Those fools wouldn't hear of a Pole claiming the throne. Indeed, they seemed content to let a simple puppet rule the land."

"What fool would seriously consider being subjugated beneath the rule of a Polish tsar?" Tyrone chided. "As for the gold, I think I can speak for both of us. You see, we're quite content with what we already have and are grateful that our heads will remain firmly attached to our shoulders while yours will not."

Ivan Voronsky's demeanor crumpled, and he began to sob bitterly, as if all the woes of the world were crushing down upon him. His loud weeping turned to wails of anguish and frustration, until it seemed as if he had no more strength to stand. Weakly he collapsed against the man who held him in an unrelenting vise. Above his muffled crying, running footfalls could be heard rapidly approaching.

"What goes on here?" an officer demanded, unsheathing his sword as he raced through the shadows toward the three. Over his shoulder, he called for reinforcements before slowing his pace to make a more cautious approach. Closely perusing the cloaked figures, he came to a halt and questioned sharply, "What are you doing here?"

"Waiting for you, 'twould seem," Tyrone replied solemnly, lifting his head to meet Major Nekrasov's startled stare.

"Colonel Rycroft! I thought you were gone!"

"I was," Tyrone answered simply. Then he dipped his head to indicate the grieving cleric, whom he held firmly ensnared by one hand. "We came across a force of Polish mercenaries who had been hired to help this man assassinate the tsar and the patriarch. We camped on the outskirts of the city so none would know of our presence, just in case there were more spies afoot than we had been led to believe. We came here searching for the one whom the mercenaries said they were to meet. The Poles couldn't lay a name to the traitor, so we had to find him ourselves. I believe you've met the man when you escorted the Lady Synnovea to Moscow. He is your prisoner now."

Nikolai peered down at the glowering cleric, who bared his teeth and hissed like a small, poisonous viper caught by the tail. Breathing in some of the foul stench emitted by his harsh breathing, the major became convinced anon that the man's present behavior was a truer manifestation of his character than he had thus far exhibited.

Nikolai gestured for the men who had answered his summons to come forth and take the prisoner away to the tower known as *Konstantin Yelena*. With stoic reserve, the major watched as they grappled with the snarling, struggling man who had taken on the ferocity of a rabid wolf. Finally they managed to subdue him with two lengths of chain and hauled the maddened beast away at the end of his fetters.

After observing their departure until they were out of sight, Nikolai turned almost reluctantly to face his rival. "Colonel, there is a matter of grave concern of which you need to be made aware. Shortly after you left the city, the Lady Synnovea was kidnapped by a band of men who closely matched the descriptions of Ladislaus and his cohorts. Countess Andreyevna said your wife's disappearance wasn't discovered until the next morning, after the guards you had hired to watch her were found gagged and bound in the garden. By then it was too late to scour the countryside with any hope of halting their flight. I'm sorry."

"Ease your mind, Major," Tyrone replied. "At present, my wife is safely ensconced in my camp outside the city."

Nikolai was momentarily taken aback by surprise. "Considering how adamant Ladislaus has been to have Her Ladyship for himself, I was sure no one would ever see her again. How did you manage to get her back?"

" 'Twas my extreme good fortune to be in the right area at the right time." A slight smile etched Tyrone's lips. "You may be relieved to hear that Ladislaus has decided to repent of his lawless ways and has come to ask full pardon from the tsar. At present, he's also in my camp, sporting a wound that's more impressive than serious. Nevertheless, he's happy showing off his new son. Without the help that he and his men gave us, we'd never have been able to capture the mercenaries."

"Ladislaus here? In your camp? Can that really be true?"

A lopsided grin made an appearance as Tyrone gazed back at him. The major only reflected his own disbelief when the thief had made his proposal. "I know it sounds farfetched, Major, but Grigori can confirm what I say."

"I was reluctant to believe it myself," the captain offered, "but it seems that Ladislaus dotes upon the sister of our scout. Now that he's a father, he feels he must make a better way for his offspring than he had growing up. Ladislaus was tutored by some of the best, but his father—a Polish prince—refused to lawfully claim him as his son. Ladislaus has asked the girl to marry him, and if he's pardoned, he'll then avail himself of the opportunity to seek an honest profession."

Major Nekrasov chortled at the wonder of such miracles. Then he cleared his throat behind a hand as he prepared to speak of an entirely different matter. "Colonel Rycroft, I'm not sure if you know that General Vanderhout insisted upon taking the rest of your regiment out, along with troops from other regiments, on the premise of evaluating their performance. . . ."

Tyrone braced himself as he and Grigori exchanged worried glances. "What is it, Major?"

"Well, as far as I've been able to ascertain, General Vanderhout had no idea how fierce Cossacks can be when they're set awry . . ."

"Go on, Major," Tyrone prodded impatiently as that one paused to look at him. "What has happened?"

"There was a complete rout, Colonel. Your men wanted to stay and fight, but General Vanderhout didn't want to take the chance that they'd anger the Cossacks more than they had been already. He ordered your men back to Moscow and followed swiftly with the others, making a valiant attempt to outrun the Cossacks, who had threatened to set fire to his heels if he dallied overlong in their territory. Once the general passed through the outer gates of Moscow, the Cossacks entertained themselves with the debris your commander had left behind in his haste, not only muskets but several cannons which had been requested by him. The Cossacks built large campfires, hooted and cavorted while they harassed Muscovites morning and night with their newfound artillery. No real damage was done, at least none that I'm aware, but 'twas nearly three days before the Cossacks finally ceased their chicanery and took themselves off to seek other diversions. Since then, the general has been in hiding. I believe he's ashamed—and possibly afraid—to show his face."

Grigori burst into laughter and made no effort to curb his amusement as Major Nekrasov glanced at him obliquely. It was a full moment before Tyrone was able to speak without following his second-in-command's example.

"All appears to have gone well in our absence," he commented drolly.

Thoroughly bemused, Nikolai contemplated the Englishman, who seemed to have trouble hiding a smile. "You appear to be taking the news exceptionally well, Colonel. I rather assumed that you and the general were good friends, what with Vanderhout being a foreigner and your commander and all. . . ."

"I needn't look to foreigners or those of my own circumstance for friendship, Major." Tyrone laid an arm around Grigori's shoulder and pulled him close against his side. "Here is a true friend, Major. He is one who seeks my good. As for General Vanderhout . . . well, I value him considerably less than my most casual acquaintances."

Tyrone swept a hand to his brow in a casual salute of farewell. Even as the pair made their departure, occasional spurts of laughter drifted back. With something akin to a perplexed smile flitting across his face, Major Nekrasov turned and made his way toward the Palace of Facets, where he would tell the tsar everything that Colonel Rycroft had related to him. Then he would escort His Majesty to the *Blagoveshchenskii Sobor,* where Tsar Mikhail would meet with the patriarch and priest for an hour of private worship. Father and son would no doubt want to offer a special prayer of thanksgiving because the culprits had been caught before completing their mission.

The citizens of Moscow stood back as the dusty soldiers rode across the area of Red Square, escorting another collection of wildly outfitted warriors between their ranks. A pair of women, one bearing a wee babe wrapped in a swaddling blanket and the second garbed in an encompassing cloak, rode in a small cart filled with hay, a preference each had insisted upon for at least two diverse reasons. A battery of cannon followed. At the rear of the procession came the wagons, a pair of which were filled with the wounded.

It was this sight that greeted Aleksei as he stepped from his sledge. He was still gaping when he took note of the dark-haired woman in the cart, that very one he had ordered Ladislaus to kidnap from Natasha's manse. And if that wasn't enough, her abductor now rode at the fore of his cohorts, like some valiant soul on his way to receive a medal.

Aleksei felt his chest instantly gripped by a coldness that

nearly halted his breathing. Only that morning he had been in his chambers and had heard Anna wailing in fear because she was being summoned to the tsar's palace to discuss what she knew about the matter of Ivan Voronsky's treasonous attempt. She was convinced that within a matter of days she would be escorted to the Place of the Brow, the *Lobnoe Mesto,* where she would pay for the crime of befriending a traitor, except that she fervently contended that she had lacked any knowledge of the man's real intentions.

Now here he was, Aleksei brooded, seeing his own life pass before him as the death knell tolled out the hour of his impending doom. Tsar Mikhail had warned him, but he had foolishly given little heed. Instead, he had taken great delight in arranging Synnovea's abduction, like some lecherous fool intent upon getting his head separated from his body. It was unmitigated fear that now restricted his breathing and made his heart quail within his breast.

A crowd had quickly gathered in the square, having heard of the success of the company of soldiers that they were now viewing. Purportedly, Major Nekrasov had first reported the incident to the tsar, who then had called the matter to the attention of the Russian delegates, the *zemskiy sobor.* From the boyars, the story had spread to every area of the city until the loyal citizenry were in awe of the miracle of it. To totally immobilize an invading force, rumored to be at least five times larger, and then to subsequently halt the assassination of not only the good patriarch but the tsar himself . . . why, it was a feat worthy of eminent recognition!

Aleksei ground his teeth in vexation, abhorring the assembling throng of humanity crowding in around him. To be completely surrounded by those intent upon hailing the English colonel and that barbaric Ladislaus as champions of the day was the most outrageous affront he had ever had to endure. He yearned to see both men fed piece by bloody piece to the ravens, for each had stolen that very treasure he had endangered his life to possess.

"Excuse me! Excuse me!"

Aleksei glanced around with a start as a foreign officer jostled him in his haste to press past him. The man gave every indication that all the demonic guardians of the netherworld were after him as he tossed a frantic look over his shoulder.

"Excuse me!" he asserted again and was about to forge resolutely past the prince when a feminine voice called to him from the midst of the crowd.

"Yoo-hoo, Edvard! I must speak vith yu! Vait!"

Almost frantically, the one called Edward pressed forward, nearly shoving Aleksei aside as he sought to wedge his way through the ever-increasing mass of people, as if by some small miracle he hadn't heard the woman. Muttering to himself, Edward berated his own wisdom for having gotten involved. "Fool! Fool! Weren't you warned? But no, you dullard! You just had to bed down with the general's wife! What a fine kettle of fish you've gotten yourself into! Your whole career will be ruined!"

The one who had hailed him from afar became more insistent. "Edvard Valsvorth! Yu vill not escape for long if I sic the general on yu!"

Edward growled a curse, motivating Aleksei to lift a brow sharply, for the expletive was issued very near his ear. Nevertheless, the younger man seemed immediately convinced of the importance of conversing with the woman. Pivoting on his heels, he did an abrupt about-face and, spreading his arms wide, approached the woman with a great show of enthusiasm, as if actually delighted to see her. "Aleta! How beautiful you look, my darling little flower!"

Aleksei's brows lifted to a greater altitude as he tossed an oblique glance toward the couple in an effort to catch a glimpse of the source of the officer's dismay. Except for her wide skirts, the woman remained hidden behind the tall man whom she had accosted, but her chiding voice was hardly subdued, allowing the prince to hear everything she said. He supposed they thought since they spoke in English that none of the Russians who stood within hearing distance could understand, but what now filled Aleksei with a strange uneasiness was a growing suspicion that he knew that voice.

"Yu naughty man, yu! If I didn't know better, I'd think yu vere tryin' to avoid me. I should tell Vincent it vas yu he should be searching for instead of Colonel Rycroft! If yu think I'm goin' to remain silent about all of this vhen yu've made no further attempt to see me, I vill call down the hounds of hell to seek yu out and name yu the father of my babe! It's all yur damn fault anyvay. I told yu to be careful, but no! Yu had to be as inept as a little schoolboy tumblin' his first chit! Vell, I vant something done about it, do yu hear?"

Lieutenant Colonel Edward Walsworth shrugged his shoulders lamely as he cajoled, "Now, Aleta, how can you be so sure that I was the one responsible? You were seeing some Russian at the time, weren't you? I vividly recall having heard you say that you had played a prank on a prince by telling him that you were the general's daughter and an innocent little virgin. You mean, with all your subtle enticements, the two of you never went to bed together?" Edward's tone sounded more than a bit satirical. "If the Russian isn't at fault, then perhaps your husband is. Surely you haven't tossed him out of your bed yet."

"Yu oaf! Yu von't get out of this by blaming someone else! Vincent has become painfully impaired with a malady vhich has stricken him to the heart and prevents him from carrying out his husbandly duties. No doubt he caught it from one of those little doxies he likes to cuddle, though he had the audacity to try and put the blame on me!"

Surprised gasps were simultaneously rasped inwardly as both Aleksei and Edward caught the full import of her statement. Aleksei glanced wildly about, seized by a dreadful panic, while Edward demanded harshly, "Be damned, woman! That takes a lot of spite to entice a man into your bed when there's a chance you've been befouled!"

Aleta screeched in rage. "Vhat?! Do yu think I've been besmirched, too? Vhy, I haven't been so insulted—"

Seething, Edward leaned toward the woman with a snarl contorting his face. "The way you hunt for lovers, Aleta, there's no telling how many men you've thus far caught in your trap!"

Aleksei choked in revulsion as he felt his gorge rise higher in his throat, and like a man who had imbibed far too much, he reeled in a daze until he reached the outer limits of the crowd. From there, he staggered through the snow to his sledge. His face was ashen and drawn as he threw himself into the seat. He had already forgotten the pair who were still viciously arguing the point; he only realized his folly in believing the woman's ploy.

Somehow Aleksei managed to get home. Stumbling into the house, he called for vodka and scalding hot water to be brought up to his chambers. Servants scurried to obey, and soon a steaming bath was prepared, closely conforming to his instructions. Glaring at the valet who waited to attend him, Aleksei sent him out with a snarled command and undressed himself.

He sucked in his breath as he settled himself into the steaming bath. Undaunted, he scrubbed himself vigorously until he was nigh bleeding from the abuse. Then he leaned back in the tub and quaffed nearly a third of the decanter of the wickedly intoxicating brew. When he finally stumbled to his feet, he was feeling sufficiently blistered inside and out. He was extremely hot, weak, and totally inebriated. Seeking some relief from the agony of his emotions, he flung the bottle away and staggered unsteadily to the bed, where he collapsed facedown upon it. In a dazed stupor he stared across the room and began to mumble incoherently about the awful gore he remembered seeing as a child when his father had taken a knife and ended his own life.

Anna didn't return home that night, nor did the servants dare to venture up to the master's chambers. By late the next day they were almost relieved to hear riders halting before the manse and, a moment later, an insistent pounding of a heavy fist upon the front portal. Boris hurried to open the door, and then stumbled back in some awe as the English colonel and three of his officers barged into the hall without so much as an apology. This time the Englishman spoke in Russian and demanded to see the master of the house forthwith.

"Prince Aleksei is upstairs." The servant's voice quavered as he gestured tremblingly toward the higher level where the man had ensconced himself. "He hasn't been down since yesterday, when he ordered us to prepare him a bath. He was in a foul mood, sir, and we were afraid to disturb him."

"I'll disturb him!" Tyrone growled, leaping up the stairs with his men following closely behind.

Boris trailed them, struggling to keep up as he pleaded with the officers to take care lest they endanger their lives. "Prince Aleksei may be indisposed . . . with a woman . . . and will resent being intruded upon. It's not the first time he has locked us out, but usually he bids us to bring up food for him and his companions to feast upon."

Tyrone's lip curled in a snarl as he tossed a dark glower over his shoulder. " 'Twould seem you've coddled that bastard far too long, my friend. Today he'll reap another kind of reward, his just due! The tsar has granted me and my officers the special duty of escorting your master to prison, and I've come to do so with relish."

The colonel paused briefly before the portal which the servant indicated. When he grasped the knob, Tyrone found the door locked, but with a thrust of his shoulder, he flung the heavy plank wide. High-flying rage propelled him inward, and he was nearly halfway across the room before he came to an abrupt halt and stared for a moment in rampant revulsion at the sight sprawled upon the bed. He had been a fighting man for a good many years, but in all of that time he had never seen the likes of that which now wrenched his stomach. It was a terrible thing when a man became so demented that he had to cruelly lacerate his own body before gaining enough courage to end his own life.

Tyrone turned on his heel and stalked back toward the door, where his men had halted. Grigori searched his face, causing him to shake his head. The distasteful grimace twisting his lips gave mute testimony to the horror he had just seen. Boris would have stumbled past to see what the colonel had viewed, but Tyrone held up an arm to bar the servant's entrance into the room.

"My men and I will wrap the prince up in the bedclothes and take him downstairs for you. He should be kept where it's cold, at least until he's buried."

Synnovea stood at the front windows of the Andreyevna manse, anxiously awaiting her husband's return. Grigori and two other officers of the regiment had arrived an hour earlier to inform Tyrone that the tsar had given him the special duty of arresting Prince Aleksei and that they had come to accompany him in that endeavor. Naturally Tyrone accepted the task as a privilege, one he would no doubt enjoy immensely, but Synnovea had become immediately fearful of what lengths Aleksei would go to keep Tyrone from that purpose. She could hardly forget the threats he had made against her husband shortly before Tyrone had left on his quest to find Ladislaus. Aleksei would not be above rallying the ire of fanatics against the one foreigner he longed to see mutilated and killed. Nor did she doubt the prince's ability to disappear once he had finished off his enemy. He was like a snake in the grass, striking with venomous poison and then slithering off to lurk in wait for another victim.

A lone figure of a man riding a glistening horse down the lane toward the house made Synnovea catch her breath in sudden joy. She could not mistake that proud, easy way her husband rode or the dark chestnut stallion he had reclaimed from Ladislaus. Standing with trembling fingers pressed to smiling lips, she observed his approach through a wealth of thankful tears, detecting no smallest hint of a wound on that fine, dapperly uniformed frame.

The realization dawned on her as he neared that his expression seemed strangely serious, as if something dreadfully wrong had happened at the Taraslovs'. Then it came to her: he was returning much sooner than she had expected, even for all of her fretting over the length of his absence. Had he been successful in arresting Aleksei, Tyrone would've then been required to deliver him to the Kremlin, the completion of which would have taken a good deal longer than his expeditious return seemed to affirm.

Of a sudden doubt and uncertainty assailed her. The possibility that Aleksei had made good his escape left her feeling stricken, as if she had just awakened from a horrible nightmare and hadn't yet been reassured that her dreams weren't real and couldn't harm her. She hoped fervently that she wouldn't be thrown back into that dark, cavernous pit of hellish horror by the realization that Aleksei was free to persecute them from some other safe abode.

"He's far away by now," Synnovea whispered to herself in an effort to ease her qualms. "He wouldn't dare come back. Why, he's probably trying to find a place right now to hide from the tsar and all of his men."

Synnovea heaved a sigh to quiet her rambling thoughts as Tyrone turned his horse into the narrow lane leading to the stables. It was foolish to get herself in such a state of panic when she had absolutely no idea what had really happened.

She was immensely happy to be home, and that was a fact Aleksei could never take away from her. After a whole blissful night spent in lustful pursuits with her husband, it had seemed as if she had been lifted on a cloud somewhere in the firmament. Now, thwarted by trepidations, she felt as if she had descended into the darkest hell.

Synnovea frowned and canted her head worriedly as she wondered what was keeping Tyrone. At this time of the day, he would normally have left his mount in the care of one of the grooms in the stable. Yet she could hear no one moving about the house, which at the moment seemed as quiet as a tomb. Natasha had escorted Ali, Danika, and Sophia to a fair, leaving the house virtually empty, no doubt intentionally for the couple's leisured pleasure. Even the servants, who had been instructed by Natasha to appease their every wish, refrained from being seen unless bidden.

"Synnovea . . . ?"

The masculine voice seemed to drift up from the depths of the house, as if from the distant end of a long tunnel far, far away.

Lifting her head, she answered. "Yes . . . ?"

"Come, my love, I have need of you."

"Tyrone? Is that you?" she queried as her feet carried her from the front room to the stairs that led downward into the bowels of the house. The summons had been spoken in English, but the voice had been strangely muffled and subdued.

"Are you coming, my love?"

"Yes, yes, I'm coming! Where are you? I can barely hear you. Please tell me, is anything wrong? You sound so strange."

"Hurry!"

Her heart leapt in heightening fear. Something was wrong! Something had happened! But where was he? "I'm hurrying, my darling! Wait for me!"

"I am, but you must hurry. . . ."

Her feet were flying now, merely a vague blur on the

stairs, going deeper, deeper into the manse. Finally she burst through a portal, her breath snared in her throat. She had no idea what she might find. Then she came to a stumbling halt—and stared agape.

From the middle of the pool Tyrone grinned back at her. Throwing aside a long, flared instrument that Natasha sometimes used in calling her servants from afar, he lifted a hand to beckon her forward. "Come join me, madam. I'm feeling in rare good form tonight and think we ought to consider appeasing your petition."

"What petition is that, Sir Knight?" Synnovea questioned, stripping away the veil that covered her hair and hurriedly loosening the silken closures of the *sarafan* she wore.

"I've decided, madam, that we should seriously consider the possibility of further involvement. . . ."

"Indeed, sir?" The corner of her lips lifted in a tantalizing smile as she shrugged the silken *sarafan* from her shoulders and wiggled out of it, aiding its descent to the floor. She made haste to doff the light gown she wore beneath before asking in guileful innocence, "How can we be more involved than we are already?"

Tyrone debated her question only briefly. "I was struck by Ladislaus's infatuation with his son and was of the mind to think that we should prove our love by a similar offering to the world."

"I barely know you, sir," Synnovea teased, loosening the heavy braids that held her hair confined.

"Then come, madam, and I will make you acquainted with what I have in mind. You see, I'm most eager to share the bliss of our connubial bond with you."

Synnovea chuckled softly. "That sounds strangely like a lecherous invitation to me, Sir Knight."

" 'Tis a most honest invitation, madam, I assure you. Indeed, I've never been more earnest in my entire life."

"Earnest about instructing me? Or earnest about making a baby together?"

"Both, madam, both! Just come into my arms and let me show you how sincere I am."

Draping her stockings over a bench, Synnovea descended the steps of the pool totally bereft of clothing. She felt her husband's gaze devouring all the sights and, with a smile, swam across to where he awaited her with open arms. Lifting her up against him, Tyrone enfolded her within his embrace and met her loving gaze with warmly glowing blue eyes.

"Now I no longer have to be concerned about some infatuated brigand or lecher trying to steal you away from me, madam. My fears have been completely set aside by the prudence of one to change his life and by another's decision to end his." Tyrone took advantage of the startled gasp that parted her lips by hungrily covering them with his mouth. After a long, thoroughly provocative kiss, he readjusted her slippery wet body to fit more intimately with his unyielding flesh and continued in a softly hushed voice, thoroughly stimulated by the sensuality of their embrace. "Aye, madam, we need not fear Aleksei ever again or be afraid that Ladislaus will lose sight of his love for Alyona and his son. Now that he has been granted a pardon and the promise of a yearly stipend from the tsar to patrol our borders and keep them safe, 'tis doubtful that we'll ever see him again. Even Anna has been stripped of the possessions and esteem from which, as the tsar's cousin, she might have once profited. She has been ordered to return to the house of her parents, where she will be placed under their authority and supervision. What becomes of her will be left entirely to their discretion. Any disturbance she might cause in their house will be subject to review by the tsar, who might then be tempted to seek recourse. 'Tis her punishment for not having had the wisdom to discern what Ivan was about, since so many boyars have said that it should have been obvious to the princess more than anybody, considering how devoted she was to the man."

"Amazing how things have worked out," Synnovea breathed beneath her husband's warmly caressing lips. "It seems now that the only uncertainty we'll have to contend with is whether Ladislaus will remain true to his word or not. I hate to think of you going out after him again. Indeed, husband, I am loath to think of you leaving me at all."

"There may be less chance of that from now on, madam. The tsar has requested the immediate departure of General Vanderhout and his wife from Russian soil and has asked me to be the commander of the foreign-led division in Vanderhout's stead, which means, my love, a promotion to brigadier general."

Synnovea gave a gleeful cry and tightened her arms around his neck. Holding her close, Tyrone laughed, immeasurably pleased that she was his and that he wouldn't have to leave her but on rare occasions. Then he heaved a sigh, already regretting the fact that in years to come they wouldn't be able to enjoy the luxury of such baths in England. But then, he could be quite determined in seeking what he wanted. Once he returned home, he'd just have to rectify that matter.

Epilogue

The ship furled the last of its sails as it nudged against the London quay. As it did, an older man alighted from a large coach, which had been waiting alongside the cobbled wharf, and turned to lend assistance to a tall, slender woman several years younger than he. Her artfully arranged tresses, once a tawny hue, had paled with the passage of years and now shone with a luster of creamy satin. Another stately garbed woman, at least a score or so years older, was also handed down. As the gangplank was lowered to the dock and passengers began to descend, the three moved forward eagerly, searching for a face they had not seen in several years.

Aboard ship, passengers were still emerging from the companionway. A tall man carrying a towheaded youngster of an age about two years stepped into the mists that swept over the ship's decking and the River Thames. Standing aside, he held the door open for a slender, dark-haired woman, who paused for a moment to fold a blanket over the face of a small infant nestled within the crook of her arm before accepting her escort's proffered assistance. Behind her came a tiny, black-garbed, bonneted maidservant who toted a sizable valise filled with blankets and clothes for the children. The younger of the two women turned to the tawny-haired man with a worried question, and in quick response he smiled and slipped an arm about her shoulders.

"Don't fret, madam. My family will love you almost as much as I do. How can they not when you've gifted them with two wonderful grandchildren?"

His hand descended to the small of her back and rested there as he escorted her toward the gangplank. As they waited for others to descend, he drew her to the rail, where he searched the wharf for a familiar face.

"Tyre! Tyre!" the elderly woman cried through tears of joy as she hurried forward and lifted an arm to gain his attention.

Eagerly waving back, Tyrone called down to her. "*Grand-mère!* I see you got my letter. I wasn't sure you would and wondered if anyone would be here to greet us."

"We wouldn't have missed this for the world, my son," the older man called back as he joined the elder. "We've been counting the days and watching every ship that passed until we finally espied one bearing a Russian flag. Hurry down! We want to meet our grandchildren."

Tyrone leaned his head near the boy's as he pointed toward the one who had just spoken. "Look, Alexander. That's your Grandfather Trevor."

The youngster's blue eyes moved curiously from his father to the three who vied for his attention on the dock. "'Gran'pa?"

"Alexander . . . Alexander, look this way, darling," the pale-haired woman coaxed excitedly.

Tyrone waved to the woman and then informed his son, "That's your Grandmother."

Sticking the tip of his finger into his mouth, the little boy peered up at his father again. "Gran'ma?"

Tyrone laughed, sure the little tike was already becoming confused by this small assortment of strangers. "That's right, Grandmother Elianna."

With the small, but now wet digit, the youngster pointed toward the baby his mother carried and proudly announced to his grandmother, "Tat's my baby sistah."

The boy's pronunciations drew another amused chuckle from his father. "Can you tell your grandparents your sister's name?"

"Catha," Alexander announced proudly to the three and wrinkled his nose as he giggled.

"Catha?" his grandmother queried in a sudden quandary. Word of the baby's birth hadn't reached them, only the fact that Synnovea would probably be delivering before they left Russia. "What kind of name is that?"

"Catharina Natasha," Tyrone corrected with a chuckle. "Alex is still a bit stymied by the pronunciations."

"Oh, that's much prettier," Elianna Rycroft declared, laughing in relief. "Do hurry, Ty, and bring your family down for us all to meet, dear."

"I will, Mother, just as soon as we can make our way to the gangplank," Tyrone assured her. Bending near Synnovea, he drew away a corner of the blanket to lovingly peruse the tiny, angelic face cuddled against his wife's breast. "She's not going to like being awakened by all her adoring grandparents."

"Maybe not, but ye can expect the li'l darlin' will be wantin' ta be fed as soon as she can," Ali chimed in from close behind them. "It's gettin' time."

Synnovea smoothed the fine, dark hair of the newborn, whose eyelids flicked briefly at her touch. "She appears quite content right now, Ali. Perhaps she'll sleep long enough for us to get through the introductions and reach a private spot."

"She's a good li'l girl, just like ye were," Ali eagerly lauded.

"Come, my love," Tyrone urged his wife, seeing the path opening up ahead of them. "My family is anxious to meet you and our children. I'm sure you can nurse Catharina in one of my parent's bedrooms while we visit with them for a few hours. Then I'll take you to our home where we can get the children settled."

As his arm gathered her close, Synnovea dropped her head lovingly upon his shoulder, telling herself that she had no reason to be nervous about the forthcoming meeting with his parents. Her husband's lips brushed a kiss upon her brow, and the softly murmured words "I love you" banished her trepidations and filled her heart with joy. Upon straightening, Tyrone escorted his family with great pride and care down the plank.

Elianna hurried toward them with arms held wide as they stepped from the planking. "My son! My son! It's so good to have you back! We've missed you so much!"

The Rycrofts clasped their arms around each other with great displays of affection before Tyrone stepped back and eagerly made the introductions. Bringing Synnovea close to his side, he gave them an ebullient smile. "Father, Mother, Grandmère Meghan, I'd like you to meet my wife, Synnovea. This is our maid, Ali McCabe, and our two children, Alexander and baby Catharina. They're named after Synnovea's father and our close friend, Princess Natasha Catharina Zherkovna, who'll be visiting us this summer with her husband and another close friend of mine, Major Grigori Tverskoy, and his bride, Tania."

Meghan drew the youngster from his father's arms and whispered a secret in his ear, drawing a giggle from the boy, who then pointed at his father.

"Horse! Papa!"

Tyrone grinned down at his grandmother. "Aye, I've already taught him to sit a horse in front of me, so perhaps your desire to see him ride with the best will eventually come to fruition."

Through grateful tears and a smile brimming with joy, Elianna embraced Synnovea and welcomed her into the family. "Thank you, my dear, for making my son so happy and for giving us these small treasures of delight upon whom we can lavish our love. I had begun to fear that I would never see an end to the years that kept us apart. Now that the king has given Tyrone the task of establishing the techniques for drilling cavalry units, we can feel confident that he won't have to leave England to fight in some foreign campaign ever again. Perhaps his father can eventually entice him into learning the business of building ships."

Tyrone dared to broach the subject which had caused him to leave England more than a thrice of years ago. "What has happened in my absence?"

"Everything has been settled, my son," Trevor Rycroft assured his son, settling a hand upon his shoulder. "In fact, when Lord Garner heard that you'd be returning, he came to offer apologies for what his son had done to Angelina and for what they had tried to do to you after the duel. He said a man has every right to defend his wife's honor and good name from anyone who would besmirch them. He regrets that his arrogance and rage forced you to flee to Russia."

"As you can see for yourself, Father," Tyrone replied, "it was good that I went away, for I found there a far richer treasure than I ever had here."

"I must say, my son," Elianna replied, marveling at his undiminished good looks, "you've come back obviously much happier than when you left . . . and richer by far with your family and friends."

"Aye, Mother," Tyrone agreed, glancing aside at his adoring wife. "I am indeed a very rich man."